FALLEN KING

Written by
Eric Lorenzen

Book 1
Cirian War Saga

Reader Hill

Published by
Reader Hill
PO Box 490
Yucaipa, CA 92399-0490
http://readerhill.com

Reader Hill logo and colophon are trademarks of Reader Hill.

Dedication

To my beloved Amy. Thank you for believing in me and taking the journey of life with me. I will love you always.

To my parents, Gunther and Anna. Three decades ago, you let me spend a year of my life writing a book and now, in a roundabout way, it has finally come into existence. Thank you for that time and thank you for your love.

Acknowledgments

I want to share my appreciation for the many people who helped to make this book a reality, including Amy Lorenzen, Irene Robinson, Traute Tate, and Amanda Garcia. I am also thankful for the Writers' Gallery, who have always given their honest critique to every bit of writing that I have presented. Thank you, everyone, for your words of wisdom.

Na Ciria

Empty Isles

Eversnow Mtns.

Dark Mtns.

High Wall

Josgun Peninsula

Cirian Bay

Horsehead Point

Newtown

Pinnacles

Wind Plains

Warhaven

Darsheol

White Mtns.

Freetown

Sunset Ocean

Singgorn Plains

Rhendora

Border Mtns.

Windswept Isles

Tor Randis

Grandgorn

Regalis

Grizzly Mtns.

Tlocania

Lakelands

Yucai Wilderness

Waybridge

Deep Crossing

Cleargorn

High Wall

Jagged Coast

Wind Plains

Waterflow Mtns.

Copyright 2011 by Eric Lorenzen

Midcirian Plains

Port Bounty

Sunset Mtns.

Windtrill

Osburn

Westbend

Sala Moyia

Ambeth Deep Port

Grandgorn

Bardon

Summerhill

Grandgorn Delta

Fairgreen Mtns.

iv

CHAPTER ONE

Borderheart Retreat

WINTRON

The prince's cheek bled, dripping into his full beard, as he rode his horse through the now-deserted streets of Glenford. Wintron Dabe usually liked peaceful early mornings, but not when the quiet was so unnatural. Most of the residents had fled northward to escape the invaders, leaving the city abandoned. The crown prince had done what he could to slow the attackers and give those fleeing more time, but the army was already too worn out. The enemy would soon be storming these very streets.

With the prince rode his personal guard of thirty. They pressed close in these narrow ways, but his proud stallion was too tired to protest the nearness of lesser mounts. The soldiers talked very little, weary from battles and hard riding. These thirty were some of the best in the army but even they could not fight forever.

Wintron felt the need to be confident and strong for them. The years had already added some snow to his dark hair, as well as touching his full beard, yet his stamina compared to that of a much younger man. He was thankful for that, because he had gone two days now without sleep. His fine clothes showed the wear of ceaseless fighting, but at least he still lived while so many others were now dead. Wintron was the only leader left on this sudden war front, so he had to remain strong for the men, to give them heart as they tried to slow the invaders from the south.

Overhead, brooding clouds filled the sky, barely clearing the city's highest spires. In lands further south, they named this cloud cover the Dragon Shadow. Somehow, the enemy brewed these rainless clouds and directed their movement, for the unnatural darkness preceded the invading Tlocanian Empire. It was a weapon for them, for red lightning crackled among those clouds. Some of their leaders and priests could call down the lightning, with devastating results.

Although the Borderfolk had heard about the Dragon Shadow for a few years now, it had seemed an evil confined to the lowlands. Who would have thought that Tlocania could push it up into these high mountains? It had certainly not been expected by his father, the king, or by any of the Border Realm's generals. And yet, the Dragon Shadow now loomed over the city of Glenford, hiding the high peaks that towered over the deep valley.

Just then, another lightning bolt slammed into the city's south wall. Wintron paused to look back. Even though he and his guards were two blocks away, small chunks of rock still pelted them, causing his men to duck and their horses to dance. He ignored the commotion as he watched another large section of the wall collapse, some of it falling on buildings inside the city and some dropping into the river beyond. Well, at least none of his men had died in that, for they had already given up the ramparts and started the final evacuation of the city.

Wintron had tried to stop the Tlocanian army here, for Glenford seemed the ideal place to make a stand. The city nestled inside a bend of the river, at a spot where the Cleargorn had carved a cliff into the Borderheart Valley's eastern wall. Land was precious in that narrow bend, making this a city of tall buildings and narrow streets. There was no other way up the valley, except over the South Bridge, through the city, and then over the North Bridge. Before any other army, the city could have held out for months, but it had taken the Tlocanians only a few hours to turn the place into ruins. No army can prevail against such an overwhelming force, especially not when the enemy has magic as a weapon.

"My prince, we must keep moving," suggested Bilshor, the head of his personal guard. In seeming emphasis to his point, a red bolt seared out of the Dragon Shadow. The lightning slammed into a row of buildings on a connecting street, sending burning rubble down on the cobblestones. So much of Glenford burned unchecked now.

Wintron gave a reluctant nod, realizing that he had come to a stop, as had all the horsemen with him. He motioned them to ride on, setting the example. As he rode, he wiped at tear-filled eyes with the back of his hand, tears caused by the burning smoke and his own raging helplessness. He could do nothing to save the city.

They had gone only two more blocks when Bilshor suddenly yelled out. "Flee to the right!" He pointed to an alley. Wintron's attention caught on Bilshor's head, where the short, fine hair now stood on end. Lightning was in the air.

Men yelled orders at their mounts as they all rushed to obey their captain. Horses and men jostled, trying to get into the narrow opening. All thirty aimed their horses into the alley, but not all made it. Wintron and Bilshor charged at the head of the group, dashing for shelter. For a moment, everything turned red and then a roar filled their ears as lightning hit the building next to them. Though Wintron heard screams of agony behind him, he dared not stop in the narrow alley. If he stopped, all the others would be caught behind him. Bricks and burning wood were already raining down. He kicked his horse onward, in a mad race for safety.

They came out on another street, where it seemed calm. Captain Bilshor quickly assessed their ranks and found ten missing. He sent two men back into the alley to see if any of the others could be rescued. It did not look good, but neither prince nor captain wanted to leave behind any wounded.

As he waited, Wintron looked around and saw a portly craftsman still loading an already overburdened wagon full of fine furniture and woodworking tools. Two apprentices dripped sweat as they heaved up another richly carved chest to add to the load. A rage came on the prince and he rode over to confront the woodworker.

"What are you still doing in Glenford? Everyone was ordered to flee by dawn."

The craftsman glared back. "It is none of your concern, soldier, for I am not blocking the road. I will leave as soon as I am ready."

Bilshor came up beside his liege. He answered in a calm yet dangerous tone. "You address your prince and not some mere soldier."

The heavyset man gave Wintron another glance but showed no fear. "As I said, I will go when I am ready."

Wintron swallowed a retort, for he did not have time to argue with a fool. Instead, he looked at the two young men helping the craftsman. "I offer the two of you rides to safety. Choose now. You can stay and die with your fat fool of a master or you can live. What will it be?"

The two young men exchanged a look, then one let go of his corner of the chest and came over. The other one had to let go too, to avoid the falling trunk, but he made no effort to leave the woodworker.

The craftsman cursed the fleeing apprentice; at least he did until

Bilshor touched a sword tip to his neck. He then fell into a sullen silence. When the captain removed his blade, the man returned to his threats. "I will keep your season's wages to pay for that damage, Kol, and I will see to it that you never get another apprenticeship. You have just condemned yourself to a pauper's life."

His anger increased. "Bilshor, take that fool's purse. I do not want to leave his money for our enemies."

"Gladly," replied the captain. With a swift maneuver, he slashed the leather straps that secured an exposed money bag to the woodworker's belt. The heavy purse fell to the cobblestones with a solid thud.

"Take the coins, Kol," ordered Wintron.

The fellow obeyed, though with obvious fear.

Bilshor kept the craftsman back with his sword, so the master struck with his tongue. "You rob me! What kind of a prince are you?"

He considered the plumpness of the purse that Kol now grasped. It obviously contained far more than an apprentice's salary. "You can have the excess back if you ever reach Regalis. I will let the king decide what will be Kol's fair share, so make your appeal at the Keep. Until then, I will leave the money in Kol's care."

"He will turn all my golds into coppers!"

Wintron motioned the apprentice closer, looked into the purse, and then gave the money back to Kol. "I see far more silver than gold. If a question about the contents arises, then my father can call on me. However, I think you will be dead before the day is over, so you will never have the chance to reclaim it. If you do not make it to Regalis within three days, then the money belongs to Kol."

The prince turned his horse away, convinced that his father, the king, would never have to rule on any of this. The craftsman's greed would be his death. As he turned away, he was confronted by the two soldiers who had gone back down that alley. A sad shake of the head confirmed that no others had survived. Ten good men, lost to the rubble of a falling building.

The men did retrieve one stray mount. The prince offered it to the apprentice, but the young man reluctantly admitted he had never ridden before. Seeing no other option, he set the apprentice behind one of the soldiers instead. Stray horse in tow, they set off again, fleeing the soon-to-be overrun city.

* * *

The crown prince and his guards finally came to Glenford's

northern wall. Even this far from the front, a building burned, the smoke mixing with swirls of fog. This was probably the work of the Red Dragon. The Border army might have held out longer, if not for that flying beast. The dragon had swept out of the clouds to flame the city, burning both buildings and people. The beast's roars had caused soldiers to cower, fearing not just the flames but also the wrath of a dragon-god. Looking at burning Glenford, he wondered where the dragon hid now. It had only taken four passes on the city, but that had been enough to speed their defeat. Having no spare men, they could only watch as the flames spread to engulf whole neighborhoods.

Wintron and his escort rode into a large square and came into sight of the North Gate. They slowed as they came upon the infantry trudging across the plaza. They slipped between two companies and passed out the gate and across the North Bridge.

It felt like he was abandoning someone in distress, but Wintron knew he had no other option.

A group of five elderly men waited beyond the bridge. They sat on horses on a hillock, watching the Border army march out of the city. When they saw the prince, they headed his way. Wintron recognized the councilmen of Glenford, for he had worked with them much during the city's final hours. The five had stepped in to rule after the duke was murdered two days ago, for the duke's sons were still too young. They had stayed long, knocking on doors and checking for any forgotten folks. Even as they grieved for their city, they had done their duty as leaders. Now they rode over to him with grim countenances.

He turned off the road to meet them, catching them halfway up the hill's slope. "We tried our best to hold Glenford, gentlemen, but the enemy is too powerful. You have my condolences."

Their hard faces stayed that way. Only Councilman Choren responded. "You did indeed try, my lord. If we set blame at anyone's feet, it will be in front of the Halen-Dabes. We heard how your cousin betrayed our land, opening the gates to Lower Fort."

Wintron grimaced. The opening of Lower Fort was not even the worst of Drass Halen-Dabe's offenses. His cousin had also ordered the poisoning of General Erileon, the man who led the realm's southern defense. Only by happenstance had Wintron not joined the general for that deadly meal. He suspected that Drass had intended to kill him too.

"I have sent my father word about the betrayal. He will investigate to see if any others aided Drass." That is, if there was time to do such an inquiry. He doubted Regalis could stand, when Glenford fell so quickly. They would all have to retreat to Tor Randis, the high mountain keep, and that raised other concerns. The ancient redoubt sat in the palm of Drass's father, Wintron's uncle, Duke Fors Halen-Dabe. To whom would Fors be loyal? To his brother, the king, or to his second son?

Wintron dared not state his concerns aloud though, for too many already felt hopeless. Instead, he redirected the conversation. "Is the city cleared out now?"

Choren spoke again. "All who will leave have done so. Some still refuse to abandon shop or house. A few others prowl about, trying to loot what they can before either fire or the Tlocanians take it all."

One of the other four finally spoke. "If only we had some of our City Watch back," mumbled Councilman Hovardis. "We would see to the proper punishment of those who disobey." Two others nodded their agreement.

Wintron shook his head at the futility of such an idea. He had already absorbed the City Watch into the army and was not about to give them back. "The looters have already sentenced themselves to death. Soon we will destroy the North Bridge, and then where shall they flee? However, you remind me of another task for our soldiers."

He motioned a passing cavalryman closer. "Sergeant Yosif, take your squad back to the North Bridge. You will not allow any more to leave the city without being stripped of all valuables. Seize any wagons or mounts. Take any packs or satchels. Empty their pockets and search for any money purses. Leave them only the clothes on their back and any foodstuff they can carry. Bring back any jewels or coin, but throw the rest into the river. Tell them that you follow my orders, for I declare them thieves. Some may be just sluggards late at leaving, but even those deserve penalty for their folly. If anyone refuses to turn over his ill-gotten gain, send him back into the pyre of Glenford. Do you understand your orders, sergeant?"

"I understand, Prince Wintron, and it shall be done." The man called out his squad and they galloped to their new duty.

Wintron turned back to the lingering councilmen. He did not want them to get underfoot, for this was no place for civilians. "Gentlemen, I suggest you get on your way. Perhaps the people of Glenford will be encouraged seeing their city leaders riding alongside. Do what you can to urge them to move quickly and to abandon any burdensome loads. The army will not help carry grandmother's china cabinet or lug some prized bed frame. Nor will we defend those slowed down by such foolish weight."

He sensed that at least two of the men wanted to remain, maybe out of some macabre desire to witness their city's death throes. However, since the others moved to leave, those two did as well. They all wished him well and then rode away.

Wintron decided to remain on that hillock to watch the abandonment of a once-fair city.

Over the next hour, he saw Yosif confront over a dozen fleeing the city, though the woodworker never appeared. Some obeyed his orders quickly, some seemed to argue, and two refused, turning back.

As Wintron and his guards waited on the knoll, the lightning began to strike the northern section of the city. A few bolts even landed beyond the city walls, but he realized they were still just random blows so he did not abandon his location. This red lightning did not act like normal strikes, for it snaked towards humans instead of hitting the highest ground. However, it seemed to be most accurate when the Tlocanians could see their targets and they were not that close yet. He saw no advantage in trying to shelter from it out in this open country of farmlands. However, he did order his guard to spread out more. If one of those bolts hit here, he did not want it to take out more than a handful.

He watched until evening, as the last of the Border army marched out of the city. Finally, Captain Jandon and his company charged their horses over the North Bridge, yelling for the sappers to get at their work. Only a few minutes later, the North Bridge shook and then collapsed into the Cleargorn's cold waters. Wintron nodded in satisfaction, though his gray eyes shone coldly with suppressed rage. Glenford had been such a lovely place before this savaging by the Tlocanians. He gave orders and his guard joined Jandon's squads.

As night approached, the Dragon Shadow seemed to settle on the land, like a wispy shroud of death. The only light came from the still-burning city and the regular flashes of red lightning, light that had no comfort for the prince.

GALDON

Captain Galdon of the Tlocanian army rode over the just-built bridge into burning Glenford. He led the twenty-man escort for Lord-General Hraf Kelordok, his commander. The soldiers all wore deep red cloaks. Galdon and the general also wore dragon helms, required dress for all officers. Next to Galdon rode the general's banner man, holding high the black flag with its red dragon in flight. The bridge swayed under their weight, but held. Nonetheless, he was glad to be off it and inside the night-shrouded city. Smoke and fog swirled through the narrow streets. Only hungry flames moved in the city and they offered little light to the now-dead city.

Focused on protecting the general, he ordered his men to watch the dark windows to either side. He may not personally like his commander, but he respected Lord Hraf's military acumen. In addition, Galdon never shirked his duty.

This was one of those times when the captain wished he could pull off his helm, for it limited his vision. He wanted to keep an eye on all the many buildings they rode past, for he worried that an assassin might be near. However, he resisted the temptation to go bareheaded, for the general might kill him for such insubordination. All officers were required to wear a dragon helm whenever on duty. He knew it was a way to protect the eyes of those officers who were Embraced, those indwelled by a demon. It seemed that demon possession made a man sensitive to light. No matter that Embracing gave a man great strength and strange powers, he was glad not to be one of them.

Leading the general's personal guard was a new role for Galdon, for his predecessor had died under a downpour of arrows at midday. Galdon's squads had been on the flank of the general's, so he had been near enough to see it happen. The corpse had fascinated him, for the man had been an Embraced One and such men were notoriously hard to kill. It was good to know that even the demon-possessed could die. While he was looking down at the corpse, Lord Hraf suddenly named him the dead man's replacement. The general probably chose him because he was the nearest officer, but no matter the reason, he was now the temporary head of the lord's personal guard. It was not a position he wanted to retain, for he cherished his life too much. If he caught Lord Hraf's notice too much, the general might want to turn him into one of the demon-men. The thought gave him gooseflesh.

Galdon suddenly caught himself, giving a furtive glance toward the general. He had let his thoughts wander, a dangerous thing to do near an Embraced One. He knew that they had some skill at hearing others' thoughts, especially intense feelings, and he had no desire to be accused of traitorous ideas, for he was loyal to the Tlocanian army. He turned his attention to his duty and to the possible pickings that might go into his pocket from Glenford's sacking. Galdon had learned such thoughts protected him, for Embraced Ones expected soldiers to think of money, fighting, and women. Any other thoughts could cost him his head or even his soul.

* * *

They came to the city's heart, a paved square with a large fountain gurgling at its center. They stopped before the duke's hall, a towering building that showed no damage from either lightning or dragon fire. Other men under Galdon's command were already here, having secured the building for the general's use. The whole party dismounted and went inside with their leader; the horses left for other soldiers to secure.

Galdon kept to the fore with four others, leading the general to the audience hall. The rest of the twenty kept to the sides and back. Whatever lighting had been in the hall, it was now gone. In its place hung the red-shaded lanterns preferred by the Embraced, giving a weak crimson glow to everything. He walked up the center of the marble floor with his four men, their boots loud on the marble flooring. The general strode right behind him. The rest of the guard spread out around the large room, joining those already at their stations.

Galdon took note of who waited for Lord Hraf. Three dragon priests in their black robes stood to one side, their faces hid in deep cowls. In addition, four army officers also waited on the general, standing at attention to the other side.

A row of large, ornately carved chairs sat at the head of the hall, none occupied. Galdon assumed the city leaders must have ruled from those seats. There was no larger throne for the city's duke, so either the duke had been a humble man who sat among his councilmen or he had never bothered to rule on daily things. He thought the later more likely.

Upon reaching the chairs, he turned to the general. Lord Hraf walked up to the center chair and threw its thick cushion to the side, then sat down. He motioned for Galdon to remove the other chairs, which he quickly had his men do, carrying the seats to line the back wall. That done, Galdon took his place behind the general. He gave a whispered order for his last four men to line up at his back. They fell silent, yet remained alert.

Lord-General Hraf Kelordok motioned to the priests. Their spokesman stepped forward.

The general spoke before the priest could utter a word. "I sense failure, Brother Prekor. What disappointing news do you have for me?"

The thin priest gave the general a bow. "We remain isolated from

Tlocania, my lord. The city fires caught the Five Dragons Temple, burning it to the ground."

The high-backed chair blocked Galdon's view of the general, but he could tell from the priest's rigid stance that Lord Hraf was irate. Yet when the general spoke, his voice still sounded calm. "There is more, is there not?"

Brother Prekor gave a slight nod. Galdon could see nothing of the man's face, hidden as it was under the hood of his robe, but the priest seemed cautious. "Brother Zaphrion reports that the Border army maintains its order as it falls back towards Regalis. It seems the betrayer failed to kill one of their officers. Some nobleman."

"Tell Zaphrion to send his hounds after him," replied Lord Hraf, "even if it costs half his pack to bring this one down, it is worth the price. We want these soldiers without a leader."

Prekor gave a bow of understanding. "I hear and obey."

The priest would have stepped back, but Lord Hraf raised a hand to delay him. "Have you heard anything from Brothers Cavish or Verdrof?"

"No, my lord. They escaped Glenford after killing the duke and are still in the woods between here and Regalis. They know their duty; they will make sure no messengers travel between Regalis and the Border army."

"I hope not. I do not want them to learn about the second betrayer until it is too late. Right now, the Border army retreats slowly, trying to shelter the refugees. I do not want them rushing home before our ally can secure the heart of Regalis."

Prekor gave another nod of understanding.

"Is there anyone from the Strikers among your brothers?" asked Lord Hraf.

"No, my lord. Those brothers all rest at an inn we have confiscated. They are all worn from their work."

"As to be expected," replied the general. "Leave orders that when they recover, I want only scattered lightning strikes. The enemy should be uneasy, but not unnerved."

"Yes, my lord."

"As for you and your fellow Houndmasters, I want you to send your packs through the city and sniff out any locals still lingering. I am sure the dogs will find enough to sate their hunger." The general motioned dismissal of the priest.

Prekor bowed again. "We hear and obey." He stepped back to his fellow priests and then all three gave another bow. They withdrew from the hall, leaving only the military.

Lord-General Hraf Kelordok turned his attention to his assembled officers. "Colonel Ulen, what is the city's status?"

The colonel stepped forward. Galdon knew the sinewy man to be a harsh but wily officer. He respected Ulen for his military skills, though Ulen was also one of the Embraced. The colonel offered a sharp salute and then gave his report in a crisp tone. "Glenford is ours. There is no organized resistance left. They pulled down the bridge out of the city, but we will have it replaced by dawn. There are many fires in the city still, but we can have them extinguished by midday tomorrow."

"Let it burn," replied Lord Hraf. "This city is of no value to us. I doubt the troops will find much loot here. We only sweep through this backwoods kingdom so that they will not harass our supply lines. We will want Regalis standing but all the rest is mere kindling to the Dragon Lord, our beloved emperor."

Galdon gave a slight nod to what the general said. This land *was* a backwood, unworthy of much effort. That the army was taking the time to sweep up this mountain valley told Galdon that the war against Rhendora would be starting again soon. By securing the city of Lepis Fra earlier and now clearing these mountains of opposition, Tlocania would have no worries in using the Upper Road through the Yucai Wilderness. Galdon had sat on that stalled front in Rhendora for six months, wondering why they did not advance. It gladdened him to be back at war, since it was his greatest skill, even though his opponents were a bunch of mountain rustics. It felt good knowing that he was doing his part to help his brother soldiers further to the east.

Galdon reined in his wandering thoughts as the general continued to question the colonel.

"Where is the traitor?" asked Lord Hraf.

"Drass Halen-Dabe and his men ride watch over our supply wagons. He still grumbles because I have not allowed him to come forward and ride at your side."

"If he grumbles too loud, take his tongue," replied Lord Hraf. "Our aim is to woo him into an Embracing and not to please him. Let him stew a bit. Let envy grow. I want him to desire more power." The general leaned forward. "In addition, I do not want his presence to incite our foes. They flee in fear of our army, but sight of Drass or his men would turn our foes' fear to rage and might give them a backbone. No, keep Drass well back. He can play at command once we unite him with his brother, the king slayer, in a docile Regalis." The general waved for the colonel to withdraw.

The colonel saluted. "I hear and obey." He turned sharply on his heels and marched from the hall.

"Major Kushren, what news do you have for me?"

The indicated officer stepped forward. He was unknown to Galdon, who knew all of the high officers serving under Lord-General Hraf after five years of almost constant campaigning with him. He had heard of Kushren's arrival, but not the reason. He did not know if this man hosted a demon or not. Was this Kushren newly promoted or some messenger?

The major saluted. "I bring word from the emperor, Dragon Lord Silossiak."

"Horses are slower than dragons," replied Lord Hraf. "The emperor himself was just here, blessing us with his aid in taking the city. He told me a messenger would be here shortly." Galdon knew it was unusual to use a courier for a message. Normally, word came directly from the Speakers Tower in Tlocania to the nearest Five Dragons Temple by some magic of the demons, then a local priest carried the message to its intended recipient. To use a human courier over such a long distance implied that the emperor wanted to keep the priests ignorant of its contents. Galdon found that intriguing.

Lord Hraf held out his hand for the sealed scroll that Kushren held. The major stepped forward, surrendered it, and then stepped back. The general made no effort to open it. "How was the ride up here, major?"

"The roads remain free of bandits and foes," the major replied.

Galdon almost laughed, though he was too much of a Tlocanian to do that. He had heard that Major Kushren came in with fifty men. What bandits would dare attack that many soldiers? Once again, he wondered what kind of secret deserved so many guards.

"I should think the roads would be clear of such riffraff," said Lord-General Hraf. "I made sure that Lepis Fra was well and truly in our hands. I am glad to hear that nothing has changed for the worse." He paused for a moment to look at the major. Galdon had the impression that the general had no difficulty seeing inside that great helm and catching the major's eyes. Whatever he saw brought a slight nod. "Thank you for your efforts, major. Go and find rest somewhere in this city. I will see you at midnight for my response. The emperor may be back in the morning, but he will most likely not be landing in

Glenford. That means you will have another long ride, back to Tlocania, to deliver my reply. Such is the cost of duty."

"As always, I hear and obey." The major saluted and then took his leave.

Galdon grimaced as he realized the general intended to work late tonight. That was typical for an Embraced One, for they did not seem to need much sleep and they favored the nighttime. However, he had been hoping for some relief tonight after fighting since before dawn.

Lord Hraf had just called for more of his military advisors when a disturbance happened at the door. Suddenly, Lord Drass Halen-Dabe stepped inside, shaking off the restraining hand of an army aide. Two guards were about to show greater force. Galdon stepped forward to see what the general would want. Hraf gave a slight nod, seeming to be more amused than upset. Galdon motioned for the door guards to let the Borderman approach. He did not step back behind the general, for this man might be an actual threat. Somehow, the noble had avoided Colonel Ulen and made his way in here. That showed resourcefulness and a certain sly cunning.

Lord Drass strode quickly up the hall, his rich otter-lined cape billowing behind him. He did not stop at a humble distance; he approached right up to the seated general. Galdon set a hand on his sword, but Drass ignored him. Instead, the Borderman had intense eyes only for the general in his red-plumed dragon helm. Drass gave a deep bow of respect, though, and his words came out with restraint. "Thank you for seeing me, Lord-General Hraf. I have a concern to bring to your attention, if you would be so kind as to hear me."

"I am always willing to hear the counsel of our allies, Prince Drass," replied Lord Hraf. "Please share with us your concern."

Drass straightened. Galdon could tell that the noble was aware of the others around him but Drass kept his eyes on Hraf. "My brother is in a precarious position. His forces in Regalis are not so great and we push a large army his way. I ask your permission to lead reinforcements to his aid. I will take them up the far bank of the river, where we will not be harried. We will have to leave our mounts on the far bank, but the men can cross on the tethered boats that run across to the city's river gates. It will get us to Mordel's side before the bulk of the enemy can fall on him."

Hraf sat back. "Your plan has merit, Prince Drass, but I do not think you are the right man to lead such an expedition." He raised a hand to forestall any objection. "Please understand, I have no doubt of your cunning or your skill at arms. You proved both at the taking of the boundary forts. No, the reason I say this is because there is a more vital mission for you."

"I beg to differ, my lord, but what could be more important than the taking of the realm's capitol?"

Hraf actually laughed. "Prince Drass, your words are civil, but your thoughts seethe with anger. Never forget that we Embraced Ones can hear thoughts almost as clearly as you can hear words."

Drass stepped back as if slapped, suddenly less sure. "My lord-general, I meant no offense by my unruly emotions. Certainly you must understand my concern for my brother..."

"Leave off the honeyed words, Drass," interrupted Hraf with a sharp tone. "Yes, I can hear some concern for Mordel, but also there is greater hunger for your own fame, for glory. Do not try to deceive me. More important still, do not deceive yourself. Acknowledge your pride, your envy, your anger, for they are as much a part of you as is your fear for Mordel's safety."

Hraf paused to look at Galdon, making a slight motion for him to step back. He immediately obeyed, noting that Hraf orchestrated this confrontation like some great play. He threatened the local noble and then withdrew some of the threat.

Hraf's next words confirmed Galdon's perception. "Allow me to relieve at least that one fear: your brother has powerful men at his side who will keep him safe, men of my own choosing. He will easily secure the King's Keep and should be safe behind those stone ramparts." Hraf settled back into his seat, appearing very relaxed. "Now, do you want to hear about this other mission?"

Drass took a deep breath, probably trying to restrain his emotions, thought Galdon. The noble gave a slight nod. "I am willing to hear your advice."

"That is good, for this mission will bring you more glory than simply leading some reinforcements. Leave that task to lesser men. I want to send you to the Highlands to secure the lands beyond Tor Randis. You will be able to conquer those lands and then cut off that great fort from behind. Would you like to be the Conqueror of the Highlands?" Hraf paused again to let the fragrance of the words penetrate.

Galdon saw Drass give the slightest of nods, something the lord was probably not even aware he did.

The general continued. "You will even be able to seize your

family's estate. What is it called again? Halentown…Halenville?"

"Halenvale," replied Drass, caught up in the thought.

"Halenvale," repeated the general. "You will take away your father's lands and you will force him to retreat to Tor Randis. *You* will do all of that, Drass, and not your brother Mordel."

Drass gave another nod, but his face still showed doubt. "How is it that you expect me to reach the Highlands? It would take months to ride all the way around the Border Mountains to climb the White Owl Pass. The only other entrance is through the fortress Tor Randis, and that place will not fall like some overripe fruit. Surely, you do not expect me to scale cliffs with fully-armed soldiers."

"Drass, you underestimate the resourcefulness of Tlocania. We have another way to reach your isolated Highlands. You might say that we have built our own stairway." Hraf motioned one of the nearby officers over. "This is Major Horvin. He will lead you to the great lifts that we have built to scale your soaring cliffs. You and your men will be carried up to the Highlands without having to do anything more than stand in a wood-and-wicker basket. I think you will find that ride very invigorating."

Hraf paused a moment to let Drass consider, but the general did not wait for a verbal response. "I can tell the possibilities are starting to fill your mind, which is good. Now go gather your men, Prince Drass. You have new glory to attain, Conqueror of the Highlands."

The prince smiled and gave another deep bow, having reached a quick decision. "I will take your offered challenge, with thanks. Will any Tlocanian soldiers be joining me?"

"But of course," replied Lord Hraf. "Tlocania always supports its allies."

Eric Lorenzen

CHAPTER TWO

Mountain Run

AFRAL

As his final prayer ended, fifteen year-old Afral lowered his arms. He opened his eyes and realized that dawn had arrived. The boulder on which he knelt had soaked up the night's cold, chilling through his pants, but he ignored the discomfort. For just a moment, he lingered in the peace that comes from communing with El. He had spent the whole night up on this mountain ridge, devoting the hours to contemplation as practiced by the Modest School of Prayer. His parents insisted that he learn the basics of each of the seven schools and, although he doubted he would ever need so much knowledge, he found the various practices to be intriguing. He had not realized that there were so many ways to pray.

His thoughts wandered from his god to the people who served El. He and his family were of the Attuls, those called Prayer Warriors in many legends. He knew that not all Attuls reached the status of warrior, but that was the hope his parents had for him. They wanted their only son to return to their homeland and join the other students at Lorekeep. They wanted him to become a Prayer Warrior, but it was a dream that Afral found daunting.

Although his ancestry was Attul, he felt a greater kinship with the Borderfolk, the people who were his neighbors and friends. Afral had never seen Warhaven, the hidden redoubt of his people, but every day he saw the storekeepers and workers of the Border Realm. He understood their humor and appreciated their friendship. He had no desire to leave these mountains for some land of strangers. Here lay his home.

Afral rose to his feet and then bent over to retrieve the sword still resting on the boulder in front of him. As soon as his hand closed on the sword's grip, the blade began to shine softly with a white light. The glow was faint, but a true light nonetheless. It stopped as soon as he sheathed the sword in the scabbard that hung at his side.

As he secured his blade, he thought ahead; if he hurried home, he might get in a few practice rounds with his father. He needed to work on his sword skills if he ever wanted to be a member of the King's Men, and sparring with his friends barely challenged him these days. Sergeant Finser once told him he was already good enough to be a regular trooper, though Afral doubted that. Besides, he wanted to earn a place as one of the king's protectors, which demanded far greater skill than that owned by a typical soldier. He did not think a glowing sword would impress the King's Men, for they wanted only expert swordsmen among their ranks. No, he needed far more blade practice.

He jumped off the rock and strode over to where his night's fire lay, now just faint embers as the sun lightly brushed the sky overhead. With his well-worn boots, he kicked dirt over the charred wood, making certain to extinguish the fire thoroughly. It had served its purpose, for even though no snow lay on the ground here, it still covered the inaccessible reaches above him. Many times last night, he had stopped his prayers to feed the flames and even so, he had shivered much.

Satisfied that the fire was now out, Afral almost left, but then remembered he had one final prayer to say. He needed to thank El for his creation, so he climbed back up onto that boulder and looked out at the valley beneath him. The deep vale still held the night's darkness. In the sleepy shadow lay his hometown of Regalis, the capitol of the Border Realm. He lifted his gaze to the peaks across the deep valley from him, where the sun's first glow made the snow shine. Those snows would linger until high summer, as they did every year. Closer by, an evergreen forest covered the mountainside around him. The woods sighed and the highest tips waved as a breeze arose. He pulled his cloak tighter. His brown hair moved in the new wind, but he did not care if it became disheveled. All seemed peaceful and right in the Border Realm. Afral quietly spoke to his god, sharing his appreciation for the beauty of this land.

Once done, he still lingered. He let his eyes follow the long valley southward, towards the distant city of Glenford, and caught on something odd. Far to the south, a murkiness seemed to hang over the mouth of the Borderheart Valley, a shadow that had nothing to do with the early hour. When he had arrived at this perch yesterday evening, he had not bothered to look so far away, but now he wished he had. He wished that he knew if the dark clouds had been brooding there last night also.

"Dragon Shadow," he whispered, his plans for sword practice now forgotten. He continued to stare southward and began to worry. No one ever spoke about the fall of Lepis Fra in public, but everyone in the mountains knew that ominous clouds came with the invading Tlocanians, a shadow full of red lightning and other terrors. The lowland city had fallen in a day.

Afral felt a chill that had nothing to do with the cold morning, but he shook it off. "You are being foolish," he told himself. The Dragon Shadow might loom over the Forest Hills and the Cleargorn Valley, but the Border Mountains stood high above its reach. And yet, he could not look away.

Suddenly, a red flash tinted some of the cloud cover. A brief flash, but an unnatural one. Afral's breath caught. Hoping that maybe he had just imagined it, he kept staring. Two more flashes of red lightning briefly lit the dark clouds, too distant for him to hear the accompanying thunder. His thoughts became dazed by fear. He did not know what to do, so he just stood there, watching.

He saw something fly out of that red-lit darkness. At first, Afral thought maybe a hawk or eagle rode the air currents nearby, until he realized this was something further away and far larger. It approached at a startling speed. The beast kept low enough to avoid the morning light as it raced up the Borderheart Valley, becoming more distinct as it approached. Only once did the morning light touch it and that sunlight revealed a metallic red sheen to the great wings. The Red Dragon flew through the valley. That was another thing people said, though they shared it carefully so as not to offend any of the dragonsworn. One of the five dragon gods now served the Tlocanian Empire. He watched the great animal-god race up the valley.

His perch on the mountain ridge was nearly as high as the beast's route, so that he could stare straight out as the dragon soared by. He distinctly saw the rider on the great animal's back, a tall man in a dragon helm, and he could guess who sat on the beast. The emperor of Tlocania, the Dragon Lord everyone whispered fearfully about, now flew over the Border Realm. He felt dread at the thought. Neither the dragon nor its rider noticed the youth watching from a far-off ridge, but he could not take his eyes off the beast. It circled over the city: once, twice. Then the dragon turned back, quickly passing the ridge where Afral stood, and heading back towards the clouds.

Afral realized that he had not been in error; the Tlocanians must be invading. With a start, the young man understood that terrible events were happening as he lingered there on that mountainside boulder. Finally, he came to his senses and ran. He did not run away, but charged down the mountainside to bring warning. At times, he slid on the steep path, clutching rough pine branches to keep aright, but he gave no thought to his own safety.

His eyes focused on the path while his thoughts kept going to the people below. He raced down the mountainside, occasionally seeing the city through the trees. At one of those breaks in the trees he stopped, horrified. Looking down on his beloved home city, he saw smoke. Not the lingering wisps of morning cook fires, but the black ugliness of burning buildings. He had a sudden fear that he was too late, that the city had been invaded, but then he convinced himself that it could not be the Tlocanians. The Dragon Shadow had not yet arrived. He studied the smoke and realized that it rose from the heart of the city and not at the outer walls. Smoke rose from the temple district, the central market, and possible from somewhere closer to the King's Keep, though he could not be sure of that since the keep was now obscured by the nearer smoke. Trouble, yes, but he doubted any enemy would have gotten past the city's encircling palisade that easily. Whatever its cause, the smoke gave an increased urgency to his descent and he ran that much faster. He plunged down the narrow trail recklessly.

In spite of his speed, the sun arrived before him, bringing dawn to the whole valley. He finally made it down the ridge, following the path into a just-blooming meadow. He stopped there in the sunshine to catch his breath, holding his sides. He looked southward, but saw nothing of the Dragon Shadow. Looking towards the now-hidden city, he did not even see any of the smoke. From down here, it seemed just another beautiful morning: tall evergreens pointing toward the deep blue sky, high mountains lining the valley, birds singing, and flowers lifting their heads toward the just-appearing sun. Afral took another deep breath and then ran on, for he knew what lay over the horizon.

Finally, he came to the tall wooden palisade that ran the edges of Regalis. The Border Realm had not seen war for generations, so the walls served more for keeping out wild animals than to keep invaders at bay. There was no walk on the wall, only a series of watchtowers. Six gates allowed entrance. Two gates opened westward onto river piers where fishermen cast their nets and the two shallow-keeled ferries followed guide ropes across the swift current to the farms on the far bank. Two more gates opened to the east, allowing farmers easy access to the fields that spread out there. The north and the south walls each held only one great gate, letting the Valley Road enter and exit the capitol. He ran up to the south gate, breathing hard. The gate was still shut, though they always opened it with dawn's arrival.

As he neared, he looked up at the gate tower, waving for the guard's attention, and almost died for his effort.

An arrow came flying. The deadly shaft whistled past him, bringing Afral to a startled stop.

"Leave off! Can you not see that he is one of our youngsters?"

Afral now saw that the tower was crowded with men, all with bows aimed his direction. He heard someone cursing and saw a burly man knocking the bows away.

Once the sergeant had his charges under control, he leaned out of the tower and shouted to Afral. "Come closer, youngster, so we can be sure you are alone. Pardon the arrow, but today's trouble makes everyone a bit jumpy."

Afral approached with caution, craning his neck to look up at the six men filling the tower.

"That is Councilor Rolen's son," advised one of the gray-uniformed men. "We saw him go out late yesterday for a hike up the mountainside."

Their sergeant leaned out of the tower to look down on him. "Afral, is it not?" He did not wait for a reply, but shouted over his shoulder. "Open the gate to let him in, but close it fast enough to catch his cloak!" He then turned to the others sharing his perch. "Men, aim your bows at the forest beyond him and make sure nothing tries to follow him in."

As men worked to open the gate, he looked back down at Afral. "Are you hurt, boy? Is anyone chasing you?"

Afral, still breathless from his run and a bit shocked by the near mishap, could only get out a single word. "No."

Once he was inside the city walls, a heavily breathing Afral faced the sergeant.

"What bad news do you have to add to our day?"

Afral held his sides again, eyes closed, as he tried to regain his breath. "The Tlocanians are coming! The Red Dragon flies our way... I saw the Dragon Shadow... red lightning flashes in the lower valley... We are under attack..."

"Slower, young man," urged the sergeant, offering a waterskin. "Drink this and begin again."

He took a swallow and then started over, but this time the sergeant interrupted his rushed words often enough with questions to get a coherent story.

"Your tale explains what happened earlier," said the sergeant, frowning. "Nearly a dozen black dogs charged the gate just after we opened it this morning. They were huge beasts, though lanky. One of my men tried to stop them and lost his life." The man gave a quick glance to one side at a spot still wet from washing away the blood. "We have heard about such monsters in the lowlands, black dogs with a love for human flesh, but I never expected them to range this high into the mountains. However, now those beasts are loose in the city, maybe as forerunners of an invasion." He shook his head in disbelief at his own words. "I have sent a messenger to King's Keep, but have heard nothing back yet. Can you pass our news on to your father as well? I know he has King Varen's ear."

Afral assured the squad leader that he would. "What else is happening in Regalis? I saw smoke..."

The sergeant grimaced and shook his head. "I wish I knew. We received a drum message to close the gates and hold our positions. It said the fire was under control." He spat to one side. "Our message drums are too limiting at times, but I am not about to disobey orders sent down the wall."

Afral nodded understanding, though he looked towards the billowing smoke rising from the heart of the city. It did not look under control. "I will tell my father about that as well."

He then made to pass on. However, the sergeant put out a restraining hand.

"Will you wait until the next city patrol passes? I would feel better seeing you go on with an escort."

He shook his head. "I need to reach my father before he leaves for the day's court. I will be careful, sir." He patted his sword to indicate that he was well armed.

The sergeant frowned yet nodded, removing his hand. "I relent only because a patrol squad just swept the area. Nonetheless, be a careful lad. Let your father know that we will keep the gates closed, as ordered. Be wary, for this day calls for extra caution." The sergeant added one more bit of information. "Tell him also that I ordered the last patrol to head towards the fires to learn more, just as a precaution. Most likely, some fool let her kitchen fire get out of hand and caught a row of cottages ablaze. You know how some of them ladies get distracted with youngsters underfoot..." He stopped, as if he remembered that he was talking to a youth. "Well, you just tell him about the smoke too. Understand?"

Afral agreed to do so and the sergeant let him leave. As Afral walked on, he heard the huge crossbars thud into place across the gates. The sound gave no comfort, not with a pack of vicious dogs also inside the city. His stride quickened to a run.

The south end of Regalis was lightly populated. Unlike the city's center, the streets here were still dirt and gravel except for the main Valley Road. Each house had its own garden plot and many trees grew here. From what he understood, his mother had insisted on a home in this district when his parents first came to Regalis. His mother felt more comfortable among greenery. His father agreed to her wishes, though it meant a long walk each day to the king's hold where he worked.

Afral had once asked his father why they did not have a horse to speed up his daily trek. His father had just smiled and declared horses too costly and time-consuming. His mother had seen through Afral's ploy and declared that they were not getting a horse just to fulfill his own riding desires. Abashed, he did not ask for a horse again, though he did regularly beseech his father for chances to ride along on trips around the realm. His father permitted it enough that he could sit a horse, though he was by no means an expert rider.

An exhausted Afral wished he had a horse now. He turned down a side road, heading towards home. He looked to his right when he heard his name shouted. A friend beckoned him towards a garden gate.

"I have no time, Landis," he yelled back. "Beware. There are wild dogs loose in the city and they have already killed one guard." He chose not to say anything about invaders or fires, for the younger boy might become overly frightened.

Landis looked around quickly, as if the dogs lurked at Afral's heels. When he saw none, he demanded that his friend stop long enough to share the news in full. Afral simply ignored the order, having no more breath to argue.

Instead, he hurried on towards home.

He had slowed to a walk again, when he finally saw the house. The sight inspired him back to a run. The comfortable place beckoned him, sitting between a sycamore and an old oak tree, with fruit trees in back and a just-sprouting vegetable plot on the sunny side of the house. He felt relief when his hand finally touched the rough wood of the small front gate.

When Afral entered the house, he found his father already gone. His mother, Tolara Quickblade, stood at the washbasin rinsing pots. She had paused at Afral's abrupt entrance, the washcloth still pressed against the side of a wet pan.

"We are under attack!" Afral exclaimed breathlessly. "Where is Father? I must let him know."

His mother left off her washing, drying her hands on her apron. Beneath her apron she wore pants like a country woman, for his mother was a practical person. "Your father left early for the king's court. Now explain what you mean."

"I saw the Dragon Shadow... the clouds fill the lower valley... a pack of killer dogs stormed the gate and are loose in the city... we need to get to the king..."

"Slow down, beloved," urged Tolara, coming over and laying a comforting hand on his shoulder. "Tell me this tale from the beginning. Were you not up on the mountain to pray?"

Afral nodded, quickly collecting his thoughts. This time his telling was clearer and very disturbing. He told of what he saw up on the mountain and of his run down. He also shared the sergeant's report.

Tolara frowned. "I wish your father could have heard all of this, but he left as soon as he noticed the fires." She took off her apron and went to retrieve her sword from the bedroom. As she buckled on the sword belt around her waist, she gave her son hasty orders. "Eat some of the food I saved for you and drink, for you will need your strength. I am afraid your running is not yet done for the day."

Afral gave her a puzzled look.

"You and I must get to the King's Keep quickly, for Varen needs to hear all of this. Eat, while I go out and feed the hens." She poked inside the stove and banked its fire. "I have a feeling this will be a long day for us."

* * *

Afral ran again, this time chasing his mother through the streets of Regalis. She led him to the Valley Road and followed its cobbled route towards the heart of the city. He kept his eyes on her back; her long ponytail of brown hair seemed to be whipping her to run ever faster and he struggled to keep up. The streets were nearly deserted, causing Afral to wonder if the people had already realized that something was amiss.

They came to the heart of Regalis, where buildings stood shoulder-to-shoulder and trees were rare. Many of the buildings rose two stories, for proprietors often lived above their shops. Even the side roads became paved ways here, with proper curbs and gutters. Afral kept running after his mother, their boots the only sound in the early morning as they approached the intersection where the Valley Road met the King's Way. They passed a market where some of the empty booths burned. A handful of people were trying to stop its spread, but their bucket line was too stretched. The flames were quick to recover from each soaking. Mother and son slowed as they entered the area heavy with smoke.

Afral saw his first corpses there, a few bloody bodies abandoned on the cobblestones.

He stopped in shock, pointing at the bodies. "Should we offer our help?"

"Those poor people are beyond our help, Afral. It looks like those killer dogs came through here. We must seek King Varen first," replied his mother, "and then he can send help."

"Why has none been sent yet?"

"That I do not know and it worries me."

She started to run again, forcing Afral to do the same.

.They entered the temple district, which lay just past the market. The smoke thickened again, causing Afral to cough. Looking down a side street, he saw a building burning, a place that he knew well from attending weekly worship. The Elhall. He gasped. "Mother, the hall burns."

She stopped to look, her face showing her sadness. "By the end of these troubles, much more will be in ashes." Her green eyes caught her son's stare. "Remember your calling, Afral, and pray as we run. There is much to beseech El for today, including the safety of pagans and Elsworn alike. An assembly hall can be rebuilt, but lives are precious."

He nodded understanding, though his eyes drifted back towards the burning building. His mother started moving again, now at a fast walk. They followed the road past the temples dedicated to the mountain gods.

As they passed the House of Avoli, the winter goddess, an old woman stepped out of the shadows. "You have brought the wrath of the gods upon us!" Afral recognized her, a hag in mismatched rags. He had seen her often enough, a harmless rambler at the market, but now she seemed ominous. "You El servants are the cause of this. Too many have abandoned our gods to follow your lies, and now vengeance is upon us."

His mother ignored her and kept walking.

"I curse you, Tolara, for misleading the Borderfolk. The goddess Kila will withhold her light from you and curse you with a life of weeping for all the sorrow you have brought us. The god Cha will send his holy flame to burn your false god's house for how you have caused our altar fires to grow cold. The goddess Avoli will rob you of your son..."

"Enough, Hilda!" rebuked Tolara, finally reacting. She turned and approached the broad steps of that temple. The old woman cowered back into the shadows, but Afral's mother pursued her and pulled her out into the light. Tolara held firmly onto the hag's robe with one hand while the other unsheathed a blazing sword. For a moment, Afral thought she meant to behead the prophetess, but his mother just stared at the woman and then spoke, "Your curses are empty words, but they do trouble others. Now is not the time to bring strife; it is time for the Borderfolk to come together and defend this fair city against invaders. May my god El silence your tongue until you learn to speak well and not ill of your fellow humans." The sword blazed even brighter, making the old women cover her eyes. His mother touched the flat of the blade to the hag's forehead, causing her to scream. When Tolara let her go, she crumbled to the ground.

Tolara turned her back on the hag, but Afral kept watching and saw Hilda try to speak. Her eyes widened in horror as she realized that her voice was gone. Afral gazed then at his mother in utter surprise, but Tolara ignored the woman now. Instead, she beckoned Afral to follow. "Come along, my son. We still need to reach the king."

His mother did not put away her sword, but carried it like a beacon. He decided to keep his own sheathed, for he was no Prayer Warrior yet and his spirit sword was still faint compared to hers.

They had just moved past the last of the temples when they both saw the huge black dog. It stood in the middle of the King's Way, feeding on its prey. Afral nearly retched when he realized that the victim had been a person. The beast lifted its black maw, fresh blood splattering with the sudden movement. Red-glowing eyes seemed to lock onto his mother's shining sword and the dreadhound let out a howl. Others answered, from every direction.

Eric Lorenzen

CHAPTER THREE

King's Keep

AFRAL

When Afral saw the black dreadhound, he reached for his sword. However, when he raised his weapon, it only glowed fitfully. His fear surged.

The dog bayed loudly and other hounds answered.

Afral's mother grabbed his sleeve. "Beware, Afral. It calls for the rest of its pack. I want you to run into that alleyway. If we stay on this wide road, they will surround us. Go, now!"

He ran through an opening between two shops, his mother right behind him. The dreadhound barked its anger and came charging after them. His mother turned to face the beast just beyond a bend in the alley, telling Afral to remain behind her. She positioned herself, taking the Crouching Lynx stance and whispering prayers to El. Afral tried to emulate her, but his positioning was awkward and his heart beat so loud that he wondered if El could even hear his fumbled prayers.

Suddenly, the dreadhound was there, springing at his mother. Tolara stepped aside and struck with her sword, giving it a glancing a blow. Afral nearly panicked when the beast landed near him. He swung his blade wildly, trying to keep the animal away, and backed up against a stone wall. It would have jumped on him if his mother had not stabbed it from behind. With rapid succession, her blows rained down on the black beast, until it stopped moving.

Tolara wiped her blade on the animal's black coat and then looked toward her son. Mercifully, she said nothing about his obvious fear. Instead, she held a hand out for Afral, urging him to jump past the carcass. "We must run, for the rest of the pack is still coming."

They ran down the alley until his mother spotted a ladder leaning against a shop. They climbed up and then Afral pulled the ladder up behind them. They scrambled across the roof tiles, carrying the awkward thing, and then lowered it down the front of the shop, onto a different street. Quickly, they climbed down and then ran up another alleyway, hoping the break would throw the dogs off their scent.

They dashed down lanes and across avenues, making their way to the huge keep where it sat on the banks of the river Cleargorn. The dogs still barked and bayed, yet they were still a few blocks away. Finally, they came within sight of the King's Keep. Afral would have hurried on, if his mother had not put a restraining hand on his shoulder.

"Why are the front gates closed?" she asked.

Afral paused, realizing that it was true. "Do they fear the dreadhounds?"

"I do not think so." His mother pointed up at the ramparts. "Those uniforms are wrong. They are Halen-Dabe colors. I remember your father saying that the king's nephew had come for a visit…" She looked to him to confirm her memory.

Afral nodded. He spent more time at King's Keep than his mother did. "Lord Mordel brought guards from his father's house. Maybe they are helping the king to hold the walls."

"Against what?" asked his mother. She pulled him back into the shadows. "Your father mentioned nothing of such an arrangement, and he would have known. The keep is in no danger from mere dogs. I do not like this." She considered for a moment. "Let us see if any of the other gates are open."

They slipped down another alleyway, heading towards the back of the fortress. When their route came out on a smaller street, Afral looked towards the ramparts and saw smoke rising from behind the keep's walls. He worriedly pointed it out to his mother.

She frowned. "There are troubles here that are far worse than killer dogs. Do you notice how empty the streets are this close to the keep? How windows are still shuttered and doors seem locked? The people already sense that something is amiss."

They hurried on, following a lane lined with small shops. Afral heard the dreadhounds still, but they were not yet close. The road took them nearer the high walls and, at many spots, the fortress could be seen over the rooftops. Afral looked that way often, but the wall walk seemed deserted of guards. Finally, they came in sight of the Trader's Gate and found it still open.

"What now?" he asked of his mother as they peeked around the corner.

She sheathed her sword and motioned for him to do likewise. "Let us not announce who we are. However, be ready to draw quickly if we are endangered. We will enter at a walk, but be prepared to run at my order. The gate tower seems empty, but someone may be lurking in the shadows up there.

"I fear there is rebellion inside the keep, or at least turmoil. Remember, we are looking for two people: the king and your father. We cannot allow any fighting to distract us from our goals, so resist the temptation to flash your sword or chase after some perceived adversary. We do not know who is fighting whom, nor do we know who supports the king."

Afral felt sudden fear. "Do you really think it is that bad inside?"

Tolara avoided his question. "Keep behind me and please stay close."

They cautiously approached the gate. Afral kept looking to the gatehouse overhead, but no one stirred. They encountered the guards once they were in the shadow of the gate. Dead guards. All four gray-uniformed corpses had obviously been killed by swords.

Afral felt queasy at the sight. "Who would do this?"

"Someone allied with the invaders," answered his mother tersely. She took a quick look inside the gatehouse and then urged Afral to follow her past the killed soldiers.

He came, but could not keep from looking back at the bodies. He had never seen such cruel deaths and it frightened him.

They went through the gateway and entered the outer grounds, but then his mother hesitated, seemingly uncertain which direction to take. To the left stood the main keep, a four-story stone building topped by four corner spires and the massive Farwatch Tower that loomed over all the other buildings within the outer wall. Ahead of them, lay the two-story wing that housed servants and court officials. Through an archway lay the King's Men courtyard. The fire came from that direction. Still, his mother paused.

"Where are we going?" he asked.

"The assembly hall, for we are most likely to find the king there. I just pray that your father is in attendance as well. However, I do not want to approach by the front entrance. What other route can we take?"

He considered. "We can enter through the kitchen and then follow the servant's passages to the dining room. It will get us close to the assembly hall."

He then considered how to get to the kitchen and it worried him more. "The quickest route to the kitchen is that way." He pointed towards the billowing smoke.

"So be it," replied his mother and she ran towards the archway directly ahead. Afral hurried to follow.

They came out on the practice yard for the King's Men. Whenever he was at the keep, Afral would often linger here to watch the men at swordplay. It was one of his favorite places. However, when he came out onto the practice yard this time, he could only gasp. Fire seemed everywhere. Horrible fire. The barracks was a giant pyre, all flame and smoke.

A dozen servants were busy tossing water on the neighboring roofs, trying to prevent the inferno from spreading. Four other soot-covered servants stood over the half-dozen recovered bodies they had just finished pulling from the fire. Shocked, Afral and his mother came near and looked down at the corpses, most too burnt to be recognizable though bits of their uniforms identified them as King's Men. The sight and smell caused Afral to retch on the cobblestones, splattering his boots and trousers.

One of the four recognized Afral's mother. "Lady Tolara, you must tell the king about this. We have already sent one man running, but Varen may more quickly believe you."

"What happened?" she asked, her countenance bleak.

Part of the barracks collapsed in a thundering roar of flame, causing all of them to flinch.

"The King's Men were murdered, burnt inside their own barracks."

Tolara shook her head at the claim, showing her doubt. "Their death by fire is obvious, but why do you call it murder by fire? Was the door barred from outside? The windows boarded shut? Or do you mean that they were first slain and then their barracks were set ablaze?"

The servant stepped closer, his frustration obvious. "I meant what I said, my lady. I pulled out three of the bodies myself. They were already burnt *before* the fire could have reached them." The servant turned his glare toward the barracks. "Someone killed them with fire and then set the place to burn afterward."

Afral startled at the accusation, wondering who was capable of killing with flames like that.

"Where are the survivors?" asked his mother. "What do the other King's Men say was the cause?"

"None still live," replied the servant, "that is, unless they were away from here, at the king's side. We retrieved only a few of the bodies that we saw inside, for the smoke and fire sped through the place, but many more died in there. At least twenty fell and maybe more. Can you please speak to the king? He must hear of this."

"I will tell him," declared Tolara.

Afral's thoughts were in turmoil. Only fifty men earned the rank of King's Man, for they were the best warriors in the realm, but the servant claimed that almost half of them had just died. He imagined Good King Varen's devastation when he heard of this killing, for the king held his Men dear. The old man's heart might burst with either anger or sorrow. Afral found it hard to grasp that so many had been killed so quickly.

"Who is fighting in the keep?" his mother asked of the gathered servants.

No one could tell her, for they had been too busy dealing with the fire to notice anything else amiss.

"Do you know who killed them?"

Still no answers. Afral could see that his mother was frustrated.

She promised them again that the king would learn of this, and then she and Afral set off again. They skirted the flames and kept going. As they ran on, Afral had to ask her about what he had just seen. "Mother, why would someone kill those good men? Why?"

"I do not know that answer. Men can do terrible, unexplainable things."

"Why would allow El allow it?"

"Do you think El has no grief for them? He surely does. However, El has given us humans a great and fearful power. He has given us all the power to choose. Sadly, some use their power to choose evil."

The answer did not comfort Afral. He wished the world were not so cruel.

They ran on in silence until they came to another archway. They stopped just before entering the kitchen courtyard, pressing against the cold stone wall to observe what lay beyond. Afral saw two handcarts full of spring produce, only half unloaded. The only sound he could here was cooing in the dove coot and cackling from the hen house. There were no kitchen staff in sight.

His mother frowned. "Where is everyone?"

"Who are you looking for? The killers?" Afral looked over his shoulder towards the fire.

"No, for they would not linger here," she said. "Something has distracted the servants from their duties. There is trouble inside the keep too." She pulled free her sword, apparently deciding she needed the weapon more than she desired stealth. The blade shone brightly in the shadowy archway. Afral pulled out his sword too, though its light was far fainter and less sure. To Afral's relief, his mother made no comment about its questionable light.

"Let us get inside and see if we can find anyone to question. I would like to know what is happening."

"Do you truly think someone is trying to usurp the king?" asked Afral.

She again avoided his question. "We need to hurry to King Varen's side. Let us hope your father is there also."

Just as they were running across the yard, heading for the kitchen doors, an arrow hissed past them and skittering across the cobblestones. They kept going, looking around for their attacker.

"On the keep's walk!" yelled Afral, pointing with his own bare sword. Another arrow came in answer, but it flew wide. Afral could not make out the archer's uniform, for the man stood behind a crenel of the battlement, but someone took them as a foe. He kept running, head down.

They made it across the courtyard and pressed against the cold stone wall next to the weathered doors, making sure they were sheltered from anyone overhead.

"Afral, can you pull open the near door? I will jump through and then you follow."

The youth nodded. At a signal from his mother, he threw open the door and she rushed through into a dim kitchen, looking everywhere for a foe. Afral ran after her, uncertain what he would find. He found chaos. A dozen maids huddled in one corner, one of them wailing. A pair of cooks, meaning to defend them, advanced on Tolara with raised cleavers. She fended them off, yelling her loyalty to the king in hopes that they would come to their senses. Finally, they recognized her and stepped back.

Once they were calmed some, his mother began her questioning. "What is happening inside the keep?" Afral could tell that she tried to speak gently, but it still came out as a demand.

"The girls claim there are bodies everywhere," one cook said, sounding scared but still a bit doubtful. "We did hear some fighting echo down the hall, but nothing has yet come this way."

Tolara looked around the kitchen and saw the neglected tasks. "Where are Master Cook and the rest of the staff?"

"They took up knives and set off to find the king," answered the other cook. "We stayed here to protect the women."

Just then, they heard the clash of metal and men yelling from somewhere deeper inside the keep.

"I do not think this will be the safest place to linger," noted Afral, frowning. He and his mother needed to go, but while he could not offer these people any protection, he did not want to leave them vulnerable. "Maybe you should flee the keep."

His mother nodded agreement. "Yes, please flee the keep until the king can restore order. The Trader's Gate lays open, so that is your best route. Keep close to the walls until you are safely away, for arrows are flying out there." She pulled one of the cooks closer and lowered her voice, though Afral still heard. "There are dead soldiers in the King's Men courtyard and also near the gate. Try to shelter the women from the sight, if you can."

The man's eyes shifted between Tolara's face and the shining sword, answering with an emphatic nod. She let him go and gave the older man an encouraging smile.

They did not wait to see if the servants obeyed, for the sounds of battle became louder. Sharing a nod, mother and son ran out a far door, following a servant's passageway deeper into the King's Keep. Afral took the lead, since he knew the keep better.

The bare corridor echoed with yells and screams from deeper inside the keep. Afral sprinted, hoping to find a way to the assembly hall before any skirmish caught them. This route offered no side doors but it would bring them nearly halfway to their destination, ending at the grand dining hall. Unfortunately, the sound of battle grew ever louder. They were heading into the middle of some fight. He was about to suggest to his mother that they go back and try another doorway out of the kitchen, when the fighters spilled into the far end of the passage. Men in gray uniforms and one civilian with a shining sword. Afral's father.

Rolen Strongarm stood his ground at the entrance to the hallway, letting soldiers flee past him. Where Afral's spirit sword glowed with a soft light, his father's blazed brightly. He held up the sword with both hands. Afral wondered that none of the soldiers lingered to fight at his side. Some of the soldiers did pause once they were inside the corridor, but then a sergeant ordered them to keep going, heading straight at Afral and Tolara. The two pressed against the cold stone wall to let them pass.

"Afral, maybe you should flee with them," suggested Tolara.

He did not respond, for just then an angry ball of fire roared toward his father. With incredible skill, Rolen danced with the flames, his sword leaving a trail of white light as it met the fireball in midair and somehow deflected it to the right. There was an explosion, followed by thick smoke. Afral guessed that some wall hanging in the dining hall now burned. Two more fireballs followed, both were met and deflected. His father stepped back, though, under the intensity of the assault.

The last of the soldiers came up to them, a sergeant who stopped to confront them. "Come on, you two, you must flee. Lord Rolen cannot hold them off for much longer and he will need a clear way so that he can flee."

Tolara resisted. "But, he is my husband…"

"I know, Lady Tolara, but do you really think there is room in this narrow hall for more than one of your bright swords? You must flee. You do not want Lord Rolen to worry about your safety too. He is already near his limit with two magical foes. Move it!" The sergeant gave Afral a hard shove to get him going, ignoring the youth's shining sword. With Tolara, he was more polite but just as insistent.

They obeyed, reluctantly, and left Rolen behind.

CHAPTER FOUR
Rider Meet

MYLANA

In southern Na Ciria, a peaceful morning dawned. Mylana Farsight rode watch over her father's herd of horses under clear skies. Her eyes were not on the animals though. Instead, the seventeen-year-old watched a group of men and women meeting under a lone oak tree. They had started arriving during the night, riding alone or in pairs. Nearly two dozen now mingled in the dell around the tree, warming at a small fire or conversing, as they waited for the Meet to start. The family's covered wagon sat nearby, its canvas ends tied open to catch the coming day's breeze. A table sat next to the wagon, laden with food for their guests, though few wandered over there. At this distance, she could not hear their conversations but, as the day brightened, she noted that no one laughed or smiled.

She fingered the spirit sword at her side, frustrated at being excluded. This was a Watch Meet of the Guardians, the leaders of Attul Watch Riders, so she would normally not be so upset at being left out. However, her older brother Mandor stood in that morning shade, sharing about his latest circuit ride down to Westbend. She had been on that ride as well, so why was she not allowed to report? Mylana knew she was being childish, that Mandor would be able to tell the facts as well as she, but it still galled. For all her life, she had ridden in Mandor's shadow. Today, when her father ordered Mylana and her younger brother Migesh to keep watch over the horses, she had come close to arguing. When he had added they would also be serving as the Watch Meet's sentries to prevent anyone sneaking up on them, it did not fully sooth her ruffled feathers.

Mylana frowned. Would her father ever see her as a full Attul? It had been almost a month since her Proving Day, and yet nothing seemed to have changed beyond adding her Gifting Name of Farsight. It was not that she so hungered to listen in on the Guardians; she merely wanted to be recognized for the Rider rank she had attained.

She forced her eyes away from the group. Out of habit, she picked out Whitefoot, the herd's stallion, to make certain he was behaving. At the moment, the proud stallion quietly grazed among his mares.

"Mylana! Mylana! Others approach."

She looked over at her younger brother, Migesh, who excitedly pointed off in the distance. She gazed in that direction, and saw another three people riding up the faint trail from Gala Vale. Their father had told them to watch for any hunters, be they human or beast, yet she doubted anyone would try sneaking up across the rolling grasslands. More Guardians arriving late, she thought, but it was best to be cautious.

She looked back at Migesh and saw his tenseness. Her little brother seemed ready to draw his weapon, but even in daylight a spirit sword's light could be noticed over a great distance. Having just started his training, Migesh now had a sword and was eager to show it. "Hands off that sword, Migesh! No need to announce who we are."

Her younger brother glared at her, but he did stop fondling his sword's hilt. Mylana nodded her approval, and then rode to a small rise to await the newcomers. Migesh came over as well.

As the three came nearer, she recognized Coursen, her older brother's best friend. His presence eased her concern, for Coursen was trustworthy. The other two were a gray-haired couple who still rode well. All three had swords at their sides, but she expected that. The couple had to be two more Guardians answering the summons from Mylana's father. She pointed out Coursen's presence to Migesh. "Coursen rides in, so you needn't be frightened, Migesh. They are friendly."

Her younger brother gave her a scowl, acting as if he had never been afraid at all. She ignored him.

When the three came close enough to hail, she gave them greeting. "El's blessing on you, Guardians. I am Mylana Farsight, daughter of Harwin Trueaim. This is my brother Migesh. El's blessing also on you, Coursen Highjumper."

The elderly couple introduced themselves as Wert Longstride and

Polaida Hopeholder. Coursen spoke up, cutting the greetings short. "Please excuse us, Mylana and Migesh, but the Guardians are already late and are expected at the Watch Meet."

She assured them that she understood. As the three rode on, Migesh shook his head. "Mylana, if they let Coursen stay at the Watch Meet then I will sneak closer. It would not be fair if they let him in. He certainly is no Guardian; he is only ten years older than me!"

She frowned at him, but chose not to dignify his sulk with an answer. She also was not about to admit that she had thought of doing the same thing.

However, Coursen was not allowed to stay. In addition, when he rode away from the gathering, Mandor rode with him. The two chose to head off in another direction. She chose not to pursue them, for she had her dignity. Migesh at first aimed his horse towards them, then reconsidered and instead rode off in a third direction. They kept apart, but all remained within hailing distance of the lone oak tree. Mylana did her duty, keeping a careful watch over the area, though she occasionally let Sundancer drop her head to graze on a particular flower that was the horse's favorite.

* * *

The Watch Meet went for the rest of the day. When they finally concluded, the western sky glowed orange, fading to purple. To the east, stars already sparkled. The herd had settled for the night. Mylana looked to the tree when she heard their father's wooden whistle. The high-pitched series of notes signaled 'report'. She rode over and, as she drew closer, noticed the others doing likewise. They converged on Harwin, dismounting and tying their horses to the nearest horse line.

"Children, please help me play host," he said. He included Coursen in his request, for the young man was like a third son. The four hastened to obey, preparing food for the visitors. They handed out wooden plates filled with dried fruit, bread, cheese, nuts, and cold turkey rolls. The elders already had beverages of water or juice, but Migesh refreshed their mugs. Harwin lit a lantern and set it on the table, though he set its blinders so that the light only shone downward. He did not want any beacon shining out over the grasslands.

As Mylana served the Guardians, she noted their somber mood. When she had been a child, her father had hosted numerous joyous get-togethers for visiting Attul leaders. Of late, though, all meetings seemed troubled and tense. The Watch Meets were becoming rarer as well, for the times called for much more caution. Not that many years ago, when her family still had their estate on the outskirts of Westbend, riders would come and go regularly, and not just those of the circuit where her father led as Guardian. Riders came from all over Na Ciria, passing along reports from one circuit Guardian to another. Many nights, they had listened to the tales and songs of those visitors and most of those stories were lighthearted. However, ever since they had fled the conquering of Westbend, it seemed that all the stories and songs had turned dark.

Those gathered under that isolated oak included all the Guardians left in southern Na Ciria. Mylana knew a few of them well, but many were strangers. Even though she did not know everyone in their ranks, she was that many were missing tonight. Whether dead or just unable to make it here, it showed that the Watch Riders were endangered. She wondered how many circuits were no longer ridden, how many areas were no longer watched. Now that the enemy was here, it became too dangerous to ride in ever more areas. When would the Prayer Warriors get here? Why have the Watch Riders scouted for so many generations, if the army refused to march when the enemy was located? Over the last few years, she had heard numerous Riders ask similar questions of her father, and all that he could do was remind them to see to their duty and trust El that the Prayer Warriors would do theirs.

She paused as she realized that was probably the reason for today's Watch Meet. The gathering was not just to hear about the terrible events in Westbend, that much she knew. Messages could have been sent with that awful report. No, her father had called the Watch Meet because of some other news. Whatever the reason, she expected that they would be moving the herds again, and not just to seek new pastures.

The Guardians did not linger long over the refreshments. They left in small groups, heading off in all directions across the dark grasslands. Soon there was only Harwin, his three children, and young Coursen. None of them asked what the Meet was about. They just went about their responsibilities as they waited for Harwin to decide what he could share. Mandor returned to his horse and rode out to keep watch on the herd, while the others put away the food and then bedded down for the night under the tree.

* * *

The sun rose in a partially cloudy sky, as Mylana watched over the horses. She had relieved Mandor at midnight. Mylana stifled a yawn; she always found the second night watch the hardest. At least there had been no wolves or coyotes tonight. She sat among the grasses on a rise to the east of the oak tree. To keep awake, she brushed her long brown hair, working out the tangles. The air sat calm and still, but she still worked a good pace. She knew that a breeze would soon stir the air back into motion, for the Midcirian Plains seemed the wind's favorite playground. She finished combing her hair and then tied it back with a black ribbon.

She looked about at the horses. So far, Whitefoot was behaving, content to nibble the spring grass and not rile up the herd. Of all of her father's herds, the one Whitefoot ruled was the most prone to try fleeing. Her uncle and his grown children were out with the rest of the horses. They ran in four distinct herds, spread out to get the most of the grazing and to keep the dominant stallions from challenging each other.

Suddenly, Mylana noticed that someone rode out to her. She recognized Migesh's usual mount and was surprised that he did not still sleep. She continued her brushing while she awaited his arrival. When he drew near, she stood up and walked over to her waiting horse. She put away the brush in Sundancer's saddlebag just as Migesh reined in beside her.

"Father wants to talk with you," he said quietly. He seemed upset.

"For what reason?" she asked, climbing up onto her horse.

Migesh grimaced. "Father will have to explain. He wants to talk with the three of you."

Mylana could easily guess who the other two were, but realized that Migesh was determined to say no more, so she headed off for the camp. They waited for her, seated at the trestle table. Her father even had a meal ready. She tied off Sundancer and walked over, sitting down between Mandor and Coursen. Her father motioned for her to eat, so she took a mouthful of oatmeal even though she did not feel hungry at the moment. All of them remained silent until Mylana had swallowed three more spoonfuls. Only then did her father clear his throat.

"Great changes are coming," he said roughly, "and I do not just mean the evil that lurks to our south. The events in Westbend are just a fly's bite to what comes." His big, calloused hand swept the horizon as if he could sweep the Dragon Shadow away.

He paused to stare into each face. Whatever he saw, it seemed enough for him to continue. "I do not like the task I must give you, but the Watch Meet has ruled and so I must obey." He sighed and ran a hand through his graying hair. "By El, I do not even like the task they have given me, but it is necessary." Again he paused, and Mylana wondered at his hesitancy. Most called her father direct in his speech, if not rude in his frankness. What could be worse than the fall of Westbend to demon-possessed soldiers?

"The Watch Meet has decided that the Attul army is not coming," he said in a rush. "Furthermore, the Attul Watch Riders will be going to war without the Attul Prayer Warriors. They have decided that we cannot delay any longer; we are Na Ciria's last hope. I will be rounding up our herds and taking them to the Waterflow Mountains, where I shall begin training a cavalry. Your uncle Bergen, your cousins, and Migesh will be going with me."

"What is to become of us?" asked Mandor. Mylana doubted her voice would have been so calm. Scouts do not form an army; they spy out the land and report back to the main force in Warhaven. All Attul Watch Riders learned this by early childhood. She doubted anyone among the Riders knew the first thing about battle tactics.

Harwin stood up and began pacing, his irritation obvious. "The three of you will take one final message to Warhaven. You will take it all the way there."

It took a moment for those words to sink into her. All the way? Were they not just riding to the next circuit or post? The whole route would be revealed to them. Why would the Guardians take such a great risk? This was unprecedented: no rider was ever told the complete route to Warhaven. Careful rumor said that only a handful of Guardians in the south even knew the message routes beyond the Midcirian Plains. The Riders guarded the secret of Warhaven tightly, even from their own, so that no one could reveal too much.

Harwin stopped his pacing and faced them. "I do not like giving you these orders, but the Watch Meet has decided. Know this; it will be a difficult and dangerous ride. We do not know for certain, but we believe every route has been compromised. Every Rider circuit. We do not know when the last message from the southern circuits made it through, but I would assume it has been at least a year. You will be unable to trust any circuit or post beyond the Midcirian Plains. I would go so far as to encourage you to avoid all Watch Rider posts unless the situation is dire."

"How far will we be traveling?" asked Mandor.

"Where is Warhaven?" asked Coursen.

Harwin held up his hand to stop the questions. "The Guardians have still insisted on some protections. We are revealing secrets that are not really ours to tell. However, desperate times force our hand. Out of respect of the Guardians who might still survive in the north, none of you shall learn the whole route to Warhaven. I will just say to all of you that Warhaven stands guard in northern Na Ciria. For the rest, we will talk separately."

He turned to Mandor. "I will start with you, my son. You shall learn your leg of the ride." Harwin looked to the others. "Could you two please wait upon the rise until it is your turn?"

Mylana and Coursen obeyed, striding up the long slope and well out of hearing range. They stood there some time, waiting.

Impatient, Coursen began to pace. "Which one of us do you think will learn the last leg?"

Mylana knelt, picking wildflowers. She looked up at him. "I do not know. It may be that Father is telling that leg to Mandor right now..."

"Do you think so?" Coursen stared at the two sitting under the tree. He took three steps in their direction, and then stopped. "I have always wanted to know where Warhaven hides. Have you never wondered why its locale is a secret? Why conceal the mighty Attul army?" He still stared.

She stood up, dropping the flowers and brushing off her hands on her breeches. "Belere Anonral's army was great, but the victory cost so much. You know as well as I that we lost eight out of ten by war's end." Her voice was still soft but her tone reflected her disapproval.

Coursen turned away from the tree to face her. "That was two centuries ago. Surely, the Prayer Warriors are back to full strength now. Why do they still hide like marmots among the rocks, fearing the hawk?"

"The Prayer Warriors have their duty and we Watch Riders have ours," replied Mylana. "They are not accountable to us, Coursen. They are answerable to El. However, I believe that when we do reach Warhaven their reasons for secrecy will become clear to us."

Coursen's demeanor changed; he gave her a sheepish grin, then a roguish bow. "Pardon my carping, fair lady. My impatience makes me as surly as a Westbend lord awaiting the birth of his heir."

She could not resist smiling back at him.

After another hour, Mandor rode up the slope. He raised his hand to forestall any questions. "Father asked to talk with Coursen next."

The young man nodded and set off at a fast clip, almost running in his eagerness for information.

"I am going out to help Migesh with the herd, for I doubt that

Father would appreciate me just standing around," stated Mandor. "Once Father is done with you, please ride out and get me. We still have much to prepare for our long ride."

Mylana nodded her agreement, wondering at her brother's terseness.

Mandor mistook her silence as worry. "Cheer up little sister. Coursen and I will make sure no harm comes to you on our ride to Warhaven."

She smiled up at him as he sat up straight on his favorite mount. "I would never question your bravery, big brother. Go soothe Migesh, for I think he is very disappointed at being left behind. I will gather up you and Coursen when it is time."

* * *

By the time Coursen came riding out, it was late afternoon. He waved at her but rode off towards the distant herd. She was happy he did so, for she felt too nervous for any small talk. It was hard enough not to run down the slope in her eagerness to get this over. Her father walked out to meet her, giving her a bear hug and then laying an arm over her shoulders as they strode to the table.

"Well, my little wildflower, it is your turn. I must admit that sending you is the hardest part in all of this. The other Guardians kept reminding me that you were now a Watch Rider, but it is hard not to see my little girl when I look at you."

"Father, I have my Gift Name now," gently argued Mylana.

He nodded, but still offered his hand to help her sit. She politely took his offered help, though she did not need it. Harwin sat down across from her.

"I have saved the last leg of the journey for you, Mylana. Mandor and Coursen will have to guide you through some dangerous lands first, but I leave it to you to faithfully complete this Ride and deliver a message from the southern Guardians to the Attuls in Warhaven. The other two know of this and swear they will protect you from harm; they will need to if they want to succeed with this mission. You must keep the knowledge of Warhaven to yourself though, no matter how much the other two try to argue it out of you. As your ride brings you closer, they will begin to guess your final destination, but still keep it to yourself. Do you swear to keep in confidence what I am about to share with you?"

His daughter answered, "Yes Father, I swear before El that I shall guard the secret of Warhaven with my life. I will see to it that we get our message through to the Prayer Warriors."

Harwin nodded at her word. "So be it. To be brief, Warhaven is in far northern Na Ciria, in the Pinnacles overlooking Cirian Bay and the ruins of Darsheol."

"So far away," whispered Mylana, but realized that the location made sense. Darsheol was where the demons had made their last stand in the Great War. If any place in Na Ciria could be considered evil, that would be it. "If we are to avoid the Rider routes, then how are we to find our way? We will need to know landmarks."

Her father reached across the table and touched a finger to her nose. "My little Mylana, always looking to the horizon. You are rightly named Farsight." He pulled back his hand, resting it on top of the other. His faint smile faded as he focused again on the mission. "I judge that the greatest danger will be in the lands this side of the Border Mountains. You will need to trust Mandor and Coursen with that part of the ride; they have been instructed on landmarks as well as Rider routes and posts. I add this warning: You will likely be riding into a war, for there are dragonsworn to the north marching under the Red Dragon's Shadow. You will see more of what you saw in Westbend and probably far worse. Are you ready to endure such?"

"I will do my duty," she responded.

He stood up, and began pacing before her. He was plainly agitated, but hesitant about something. Mylana wondered if he was having second thoughts about sending her. She silently prayed to El that her father would not change his mind, for she wanted to make this ride. Her father paced back and forth four more times, then came around the table and pulled her to her feet for a hug. When he stepped back, tears shone in his eyes, which truly worried the young woman. Her father was not one for emotion.

"What is the matter Father?"

"You have your mother's blue eyes," he observed, avoiding her question.

She waited, her concern rising; he was going to remove her from the ride. Her mind swirled with arguments, ready to defend her value, but still her father said nothing. He just stared into her eyes, his face sad and tears now wetting his cheeks. He took her hands within his own and held them tight. "I fear that this ride is even more dangerous, my beloved daughter. One of our own has betrayed the Riders, and we do not know who the traitor is. The Watch Meet insisted that you should hold the secret of Warhaven, for all others are suspect."

"You cannot think that of Mandor. He is so concerned with fairness and duty," protested Mylana.

Her father grimaced. "No, I cannot believe it of my own son. Nor of Coursen. However, the Rider Meet has ruled and you will respect that decision. All riders are declared suspect, which includes both Mandor and Coursen. I do not think either of them is involved in betrayal, however you must follow these instructions: keep Warhaven's secret from every Rider you encounter. Do not speak of it even to a Guardian.

"I am sorry to ask you to ride two galloping horses. On one hand, I tell you that you must trust Mandor and Coursen to win you through dangerous lands, yet on the other hand, I must order you to beware everyone, even them. May El grant you great wisdom on this wild ride, Mylana." He gave her another hug. "Are you ready for your formal instructions?"

She nodded. "Yes Father. I am ready to ride, awaiting the message I am to carry."

Harwin nodded at Mylana's formal tone. He handed her the actual message that all the southern Guardians had signed, a message that was sealed with wax, wrapped in a waterproofed pouch, and placed within a small leather messenger's satchel. "Carry this close to you at all times, Mylana Farsight. This is our final scouting report to Warhaven."

She accepted the satchel and hung it around her neck, placing it beneath her shirt. "I will guard it with my life, remembering always my duty before El."

Harwin paused to stare again at his daughter.

He had been a Guardian for over twenty years and had done this ritual with dozens of other Riders. Mylana had witnessed it often enough, but it seemed so different now that it was between her and her father. He looked almost old as he handed her the message. He sighed, moving around the table to sit down again.

Harwin continued with the formal instructions. "Now attend my words, Attul Watch Rider, for you have a message to deliver." With those ritual words, he began.

* * *

That evening, as the sun dropped towards the horizon, the three young Attuls discussed what they needed to bring on their long journey. Mylana found it awkward guarding her words around them. They spoke of the ride, but could not mention anything about direction or distance, especially not in front of Migesh. She felt even more isolated due to her father's cautions about a traitor.

Coursen teased her for being so quiet.

Mandor expressed concern that this ride might be too much for her.

Her little brother, Migesh, just called her conceited and stomped off to help their father pack the wagon.

Trying to act as if it were just another evening on the grasslands was just too much for her. Tomorrow morning they would be leaving and probably would never return. It had been hard when they had fled their estate in Westbend, but these grasslands had become a second home to her. Now, Mylana was leaving this home too. She looked over at the covered wagon that Migesh and her father were loading. That had been her home for six seasons.

* * *

Mandor led his sister and his friend northward, for he was the guide for the first leg of their journey. He led them confidently, for the grasslands held little threat to them. He followed their father's directions, crossing the rolling grasslands in a way that avoided the few farms. He kept them out of the Cleargorn's valley, for that was the most settled area of the Midcirian Plains. However, they traveled parallel to its route and sometimes came within sight of the ribbon of blue.

Each day, Coursen took charge of the two spare mares that they had been given: Fleet and Surefoot. The packhorses were loaded with food and feed, since they would not have the opportunity to resupply at any Rider Posts.

The two young men always kept near to Mylana, taking their assignment as her protectors seriously. All three knew that the success of this mission depended on her surviving. The responsibility weighed on her, for she did not want to fail at this, her first and, most likely, longest ride.

After a week of uneventful traveling, they came to the northern reaches of the grasslands. At midday, they topped a long rise and saw a bank of gray clouds on the horizon.

"Is it weather or Dragon Shadow?" asked Mandor.

Just then, they saw a red flash among the clouds

"There is your answer," observed Coursen. "We have found more of the Dragon Shadow. It has come further south from when I last traveled this way on a Ride." He paused a moment as they all watched more lightning flashes in the clouds. "It is time for our first choice."

"I agree," said Mylana. "We must make our first decision. Do we pass around the Border Mountains to the west or to the east? I say we go eastward."

"But we already know an army sits in the Grandgorn Valley," argued Coursen. "I say we go westward."

Mandor frowned. "You are both being impetuous. Have either of you heard from El?"

Mylana shook her head. "I have not," she admitted.

Coursen said nothing, which was answer enough.

"So our path is still not clear," observed Mandor. "I think we should go into our enemy's nearest town and see what we can learn. We are Riders; we know how to reconnoiter."

The others agreed, so they kept northward until the clouds swallowed the sun. Once under that permanent darkness, they turned towards the Cleargorn Valley. They thought to avoid notice by crossing the border where no humans dwelt.

* * *

Their first night under the Shadow, they hunkered near a pitiful fire. Mylana kept her cloak wrapped tight, for it was winter-cold. The dried brush did burn hot, but much too fast, requiring them to keep adding more.

She stared into the flames and wondered what they had gotten into. She had her doubts about whether they make it to Warhaven, when so many others had already been lost. Even if they won through, there was no assurance that the Attul army be able to march south. They might already be engaged in war.

The young woman sighed, realizing that it was not the road ahead worrying her this night. She worried about her father and little brother. She even felt concern for Uncle Bergen and her snot-nosed cousins. Would they make it safely to the Waterflow Mountains? Stealth would be hard when driving hundreds of horses. Even if they avoided the Blacks of Ambeth and the Grays of Osburg, there were still bandits and horse thieves.

"What troubles you, little sister?" asked Mandor, his chiseled face looking almost harsh in the flickering light.

"I worry for Father and Migesh," she admitted.

He nodded. "It will be difficult to drive the horses that far, and I do not think the mountains will provide much pasture. I have never been up there, but I hear they are steep and thick with trees."

"That is truth," said Coursen. "I once carried a message to a circuit in the Southrun Pass. Those mountains towered over me like a wall stretching to the sky. The Guardian of that circuit told me the Waterflows rise so high they rip the clouds open, bringing almost non-stop rain on the western flanks. I cannot imagine it is much better on the eastern flank. It is a vast wilderness; I do not know how we will find any of those three villages that Guardian Harwin mentioned."

"We will cross that stream when we get to it," stated Mandor, feeding more twigs into the fire. "I think we will find that search to be simple after completing our present ride. Let us worry instead about the path to Warhaven."

They fell silent, with only the crackling fire and a cold night's breeze making any noise. Suddenly, in the distance, they heard a dog howl and then an answering bark. They assumed it was a pack of wild dogs, for they thought no dreadhounds could be found this far north.

Eric Lorenzen

CHAPTER FIVE

Regicide

AFRAL

Afral and his mother ran from the hallway, the sergeant right behind them. When they came to the kitchen, Tolara and the sergeant stayed at the door, turning to watch for Rolen. Uncertain what to do, Afral stopped in the middle of the kitchen and looked around. The soldiers seemed to know their duty without anyone telling them, for they spread out to guard the other doors of the kitchen.

Afral watched them and wished he knew his duty. He wanted to help, but could not think clearly. Instead, he just stood there, glowing sword in hand, worrying about his father. He looked over at his mother and the sergeant. They stared intently back down the corridor. He heard more explosions. Finally, he came up behind his mother and peeked over her shoulder to see what was happening.

His father was backing down the hall, glowing spirit sword held high. When a black-robed man appeared at the far entrance, Rolen thrust his sword in that direction. The shining blade sent off a blaze of white light, sizzling toward the priest, who quickly sprang out of the way. Rolen turned and ran for safety, but only made it halfway before another robed man appeared. Afral's mother yelled out a warning as a red fireball roared at him. Afral saw his father dive to the ground and the energy passed over him, heading at those watching. They sprang back from the doorway as the fireball flew past, exploding on the far wall of the kitchen and splattering flames everywhere. Afral was barely aware of the soldiers trying to quench the blaze.

His mother stepped back into the doorway and yelled for Rolen to hurry. By the time Afral looked, his father was almost there. Only a few feet away, he had to turn and fight again. A burst of white power collided with a red fireball in a massive explosion. The whole keep seemed to shake, as the hallway collapsed. The impact's force tossed his father and he landed heavily on the kitchen tiles. The explosion also flung Afral backwards, banging him into a wall. Dust and smoke now filled the room.

He hurried to his father's side, joining his mother and the sergeant as they sought to wake him. Afral was thankful to see him still breathing, but Rolen was slow to open his eyes and moaned when they helped him to his feet.

"We need to get out of here," stated the sergeant. "Those priests might not be able to follow us down that crumbled passage, but there are other ways to get here." He looked around at the disaster of a kitchen. "Besides, there will not be much left of this place soon, with it burning like this."

"Agreed," said Tolara. "Afral, sheathe your sword and help him carry your father. I will go ahead of us and make sure the courtyard is clear."

On terse orders from their leader, the soldiers formed up around them. The sergeant helped Afral lead his father outside. Once they were in clear air, though, Rolen recovered enough to stand on his own.

He hugged his family. "I thank El that you are both alive." His voice cracked with emotion.

They hugged back.

While the three of them were in that hug, Afral heard his mother whisper. "Beloved, you will have to teach me that trick with throwing the sword's power. That is not something we learned in Warhaven."

His father kissed the top of her head with obvious affection. "I will teach you as soon as I understand it myself. I was just desperate to fight them off and it suddenly happened. El can use even the ignorant, as long as we are willing."

His parents shared knowing smiles that Afral did not fully understand.

The sergeant cleared his throat. "We need to keep moving, my lord."

Afral suddenly remembered his other duty. "Father, we cannot flee until we reach King Varen. I must tell him about what I saw to the south…"

Rolen touched his son's lips with a finger to silence him and then put a restraining hand on Afral's arm. He gave him a sad look. "You will not be telling Varen anything, my son. The king is dead, murdered by Mordel."

"Dead? No. How can that be?" Afral tried pulling away from his father. "You must be mistaken. Let us go find him now and make sure he is safe."

Rolen kept a strong grip on him. "It is no mistake, Afral. I saw his body. The king has fallen, killed by his own nephew, and now King's Keep is falling too. We must flee this place while we can." He motioned for the sergeant. "Send men to the stables to see if they are guarded. I would like to deprive Mordel of the horses if we can."

Four men ran off in that direction, through an archway towards another courtyard.

"The Trader's Gate sits open and unguarded," volunteered Tolara. "The King's Men courtyard burns, but we should still be able to pass through it. Someone slaughtered the king's guards within their own barracks."

The news did not seem to surprise Rolen that much. "I wondered why the rest of the King's Men never came to their king's aid. By the time I reached the assembly hall, King Varen and his four guards were dead, as were Steward Floren, Lord Jost, and Lord Tullis. Two dragon priests that are strangers to the realm were with Mordel. Those were the two who attacked me with magic, and forced me to flee." He shook his head at the memory, and then he seemed to get new resolve. He turned to the sergeant. "Do you think we can secure the gate? I want to make sure we have a way to get out of here."

"We will try, my lord. It depends if they have manned the gate tower." The squad leader sent another four men running that direction, which left him with just six. "Should we not move away from the kitchen, my lord? The dragon priests…"

Afral wondered what the man had left unsaid. Had those fireballs been from dragon priests? He had never heard of them doing magic, but someone had tossed the fireballs. The kitchen was now fully on fire, smoke pouring out the doors and windows. He wondered if the priests could pass through that inferno unscathed.

Rolen agreed with the sergeant, so the last of their party sprinted across the courtyard and into the relative shelter of an archway. They lingered there, hoping to hear from the two parties sent out.

"Father, why would anyone kill Good King Varen?"

"I do not know Mordel's mind, but men often justify their evil deeds with twisted logic. Maybe he thinks he can rule better or that he deserves the throne. Maybe he had some grudge against the king. Frankly, I care not what his reasons, for they are lies meant to cover up his lust for power. He and his henchmen killed the king and for that they will face judgment."

His father looked over at the sergeant to include him in what he said next. "We will regroup somewhere in the city and send word to the crown prince. When the king's heir arrives, we will drive them from the keep and see Mordel executed for his crime along with his allies, especially those who attack the innocent with magic."

"You may not have time," said Tolara softly. "The reason Afral and I came here was to report what he saw while up on the mountainside. The Dragon Shadow has risen from the lowlands. The Tlocanians are invading."

For a moment, Rolen just stared at her.

"El help us all," he finally whispered.

GALDON

Captain Galdon escorted the two dragon priests in to see Lord Hraf in his temporary abode, a rich man's house that included numerous gardens within its high walls. The two priests wore black robes with deep hoods that hid their features even in the glare of lanterns. Their ebony-colored robes were interwoven with shimmering accent threads of red and gold, far richer than the robes worn by most of the priests. He estimated that he could get five golds for the garments, maybe six considering the extra cloth used on the fat priest.

Galdon considered his own clothing in comparison to theirs. His uniform was well tailored to show off his physique. His red army cloak had elegant stitching, even on the hood, and fur lining. Since he had neither family to spend his officer salary on nor any lovers to waste his war booty, he splurged on himself. Spending money on trinkets would only weigh down his saddlebags, so investing in clothing made sense. In this, he had something in common with the dragon priests he escorted: an appreciation for quality garments.

Galdon marched them through the hastily straightened room where others busily worked reviewing dispatches and organizing billets for the Tlocanians, for this mansion now served as Lord-General Hraf Kelordok's headquarters. He led the priests past the workers and down a hallway where rich tapestries covered the walls. The place still held many such treasures, but now that it belonged to the army, Galdon would not even consider taking a moldy scrap. That would be stealing.

"This way, holy brothers," he said with apparent respect, even while surreptitiously eying the thick rings on the one's pudgy fingers. He opened a door to an inner courtyard, lighting a makeshift torch to guide their steps along the uneven paving stones. The general preferred to have his visitors approach through this garden. In other circumstances, the shadowy place would be a good place to waylay a pair of wealthy temple servants...

"Mind your thoughts, captain," warned the fat priest. It may have been some trick, but his eyes seemed to glow red from within the shadowy hood.

Galdon caught his breath, realizing his error. He had sought to hide his thoughts beneath avarice, but his lust for money had mixed with his distaste for the priests. "My apologies, most holy brothers. Months in the field have made me uncouth." He bowed low, though he did not fall to the ground. They might still kill him for impertinence, but he dared not grovel in uniform. He would never bring dishonor to the army, for it was his all.

"Guide us captain, instead of staring at the pebbles," ordered the thinner one.

"You will live for now," added the fat priest. Galdon sensed a calculating smile even though the hood's darkness hid all. "Just remember to live for your emperor and not your greed. The next time I find your thoughts straying towards my rings, I may just turn you into a toad."

Galdon sincerely hoped he would never again see these magician priests, but then clamped down on the thought. He focused on the path and getting them to Lord-General Hraf Kelordok as quickly as possible. Behind him one of the priests chuckled, though he was not certain which one.

AFRAL

They still waited in the archway just off the kitchen courtyard, waiting to hear from the soldiers that had been sent out. His mother, who was gifted in healing, was examining the wounds of the soldiers. Apparently, she found none too serious, for she did not draw her sword to invoke an El-healing.

Afral looked back at the kitchen and saw that it was fully engulfed in fire. No one tried to extinguish it. He wondered if the fire would threaten all of the keep. He also wondered about the fire magic the dragon priests had exhibited.

"Father, do all dragon priests have such magic? I have never heard of them throwing fire."

Rolen, who had been quietly consulting with the sergeant, turned to his son. "Do not paint their crimes on all of the servants of the Five Dragons Temple. I have known many of the local priests and they all seemed to be fine men, dedicated to their gods. However, those two priests came up from Tlocania. King Varen had received troubling reports about a twisting of the dragon faith in the lowlands." He turned back to the sergeant. "Are any of your men dragonsworn?"

"Three, but they are good Bordermen. I think they proved that this day."

Rolen nodded. "That is not what I meant to imply. I only worry that the other men may become suspicious towards them. Let your men know that the king had heard rumors about priests with unnatural powers for a few years now. We just never thought such things would come to our idyll kingdom. The local High Brother even swore fealty to Varen to appease just such concerns. To our rue, we thought we were too insignificant to the empire, too isolated. It looks like the Tlocanian Empire had plans to meddle in our affairs after all. This was not some plot by any local dragonsworn. Make sure your men know that. The Tlocanians control the two priests that helped Mordel usurp poor Varen."

"I will tell them," said the sergeant, "once we reach a safer place."

Afral still did not understand today's violence. "Why would Tlocania hate our king?"

"I think they helped Mordel not out of anger but for selfish gain. Now enough of this chatter. We need to keep moving." Rolen looked over at the sergeant again. "Any word from those you sent out?"

"Something stirs in the courtyard beyond this one, at the stables. I do not know yet if that is a good sign or not. As for the four who went to the gate, one returns right now."

The soldier reported the gate still open and the outer wall deserted. At Rolen's nod, the sergeant ordered everyone to sprint for the gate. They could no longer wait for those sent after the horses.

As they hurried across the King's Men courtyard, Afral saw that the quarters were just a smoldering mess. Two adjoining buildings now burned but the servants who had been fighting the fire were gone. He hoped that no harm had come to them, for they had been respectful towards the fallen guards.

Afral saw that the dead still lay in the yard, but had been placed well away from the flames in an orderly row, the bodies modestly covered by an old tapestry and an assortment of rugs. He wondered if any of the King's Men had survived this day, but there was no one to ask about them. His dream of someday joining their ranks turned to ash, for there seemed to be none left from the elite guard.

He ran past the debris, with his parents and eight soldiers.

When they came within sight of the gate, they saw one soldier guarding the road. Afral wondered where the other two were, but then spied one of them up in the gate tower. Here, too, the slain had been treated respectfully. The soldiers had placed their comrades to the side, covering them with blankets. Afral and the others had just stopped in the shadow of the wall, when the sergeant yelled out warning. Quickly, everyone squeezed into the tower's doorway, for they now heard horses galloping in pursuit.

Afral did not see much of what happened next, for he was pressed tight between men smelling of sweat and smoke, unable to see out the doorway. They were less than a dozen in here, but the narrow room was already crowded with cots, a stove, and cupboards. He heard horses thunder through the gate and men shouting. He was surprised that the riders did not stop and throw fire into the guardhouse, for it would have made for a sturdy oven. He was even more surprised that the sergeant yelled after the horsemen.

When Afral finally was able to squeeze out of the guardroom, he realized that the horsemen outside were friends and not foes. The four soldiers, along with the Stable Master and the stablehands, had freed all the mounts and driven them out of the keep. Most were still running, chased by the stable staff down the city streets, but the four soldiers had stopped and were surrendering their horses to their sergeant.

* * *

Afral's father and the sergeant had already decided on where to gather those still loyal to now-dead King Varen. One soldier galloped off towards the city's closest gate to forewarn the guards and to send out a drum message calling all troops to gather there. The remaining three horses were given to the councilor's family.

Afral felt awkward taking the steed, for he thought any of the soldiers would be more worthy, but he still took it upon his father's request.

The sergeant gathered what was left of his squad, while Afral and his parents mounted up.

"You and your men have fought well," his father said. "You fought valiantly, but the enemy had surprise and cruel magic on their side. It is no dishonor to retreat from the keep, for the place has already fallen. We retreat, but only for a time. The Border army will return with justice for the wronged and vengeance for the wrongdoers." Rolen paused, as if uncertain what else to say, and then settled on some simple instructions. "Make straight for the Upper East Gate. We will regroup there."

"Be careful marching across the city," added his mother, "for those black dogs are still out there."

* * *

Most of the smoky city passed unnoticed by Afral, for he suddenly felt very overwhelmed by loss. Even though his parents lived, almost everything else had died, especially his dream of one day being a protector of Good King Varen. There was no king to protect anymore and Afral mourned for him.

He followed his parents through Regalis. They avoided the main roads, in case the usurpers sent out a patrol, but eventually they came to the Valley Road. They followed that road for a ways and then turned down the road to the Upper East Gate. Afral did not see any of the dreadhounds, although he did hear some barking at a distance. Eventually they came to the now-closed gate where three dozen soldiers awaited them. As they brought their horses to a halt, a captain came over to greet them. The officer was middle-aged, with gray at his temples.

"Lord Rolen, I am Captain Gish. Your messenger told me of the horrors at the keep. What is your command, sir?"

"I am not your commander, captain," stated Afral's father as he dismounted.

"You were one of the king's councilors. In the absence of any high officers, I feel you should be the one to direct us. At least you can until we find Crown Prince Wintron." The captain crossed his arms with finality, looking ready to argue the point. He reminded Afral of an old oak to the south of the city: weathered yet strong. Not easily bent or uprooted.

Rolen frowned, but gave a reluctant nod. "So be it. Are these all of the men we have left?"

"From what has been reported, there are many more in transit.

Our drum language is too limited to give us exact counts, but I expect a few hundred. All of the towers have reported in, so we hold the whole palisade as well as the city gates."

"At least we have the city walls," agreed Rolen.

"What are your orders?" asked the captain again.

"First, organize these men into new squads. If there are not enough squad leaders, promote some of the more experienced soldiers to corporals. Second, send a messenger to the constable's compound. I want the city watch to join us as well. We will need their numbers. Third, send out a mounted squad to watch the keep. We need to know if Mordel sends out any patrols. If you do not have enough horses for the men, then you can take ours." He motioned to include the three horses his family had ridden.

"We have enough mounts," replied Gish, "though I do not know if we have enough experienced riders. These are common soldiers, my lord, and not any elite guard. As youths, they may have walked behind a plow horse, but most have never sat in a saddle. I may only have enough to send out a half-squad. Let me see." He gave a sharp salute and then walked off to follow Rolen's orders.

As the captain strode off, a group of riders came into view, riding down the Wall Road from the North Gate. Six of them wore the gray uniforms of the Border army, while the elderly man at the fore was in civilian garb. As they came closer, Afral recognized Lord Gordrew, another of the king's councilors. The group stopped in front of Afral's father.

"I see you, Rolen."

"And I see you, Gordrew. Please tell me where you stand, old friend. Are you loyal to Mordel or to Crown Prince Wintron?"

"I am no follower of Mordel, the king slayer. How could anyone trust that man?" Gordrew shook his head at the idea. "I was at the North Gate, ready to ride for Tor Randis, when your drum message arrived. I thought it best to come here first and see what you are planning. Where are your loyalties, Rolen? You seem to have taken command of the army..."

"I only do what I must, trying to hold at least part of the city, until Prince Wintron can get here. You can join me in commanding the men, unless you have brought a high officer with you."

Gordrew raised one shaggy, gray eyebrow in slight amusement. "I know nothing of military maneuvers and my sword skills have always been mediocre, so I will leave the troops to you. As for officers, I saw nothing higher than a handful of sergeants as we rode along the wall. There are a few dozen more troops coming up behind us, but they are all on foot and follow squad leaders." He paused a moment in thought. "Do you think Mordel was so devious that he had all the officers killed?"

"I doubt that. More likely, there was none along the city walls. Sometimes officers avoid the more boring assignments. I have one captain so far and we will gain more officers when the constable joins our ranks."

"Well, do not give command to old Boar Face Balto. The constable may know how to suppress a tavern brawl, but when did he ever face an armed force like Mordel's? Have you sent messengers to Tor Randis and Glenford for reinforcements?"

Rolen shook his head. "I do not have enough men to send any on a long journey. Hopefully, by this evening we will have enough of a force to send out the riders. I just hope they will be welcomed at Tor Randis."

Afral startled at his father's implication. Duke Fors Halen-Dabe, brother of the king, was one of the realm's generals. He commanded at the great fortress of Tor Randis, which protected the Border Highlands.

Gordrew's gray eyes widened a bit. "Do you suspect that the Old Fox might be in league with his eldest son?"

"I pray not, for if Tor Randis is closed to us then we are surely lost."

Afral's mother interrupted them. "Tell me, Lord Gordrew, how did you manage to escape the slaughter at the keep?"

He gave her a wintery smile. "I have spent more time at the King's Keep than I have at my own estates for many years now, Lady Tolara. I know how to sneak about the place. Most of Mordel's soldiers are either Highlanders or mercenaries from the lowlands, so I easily eluded them. I slipped out the River Gate before Mordel's men could secure it." He turned his attention to Afral's father. "Why were you not able to stop them with your magical sword, Rolen?"

"Two dragon priests helped Mordel, priests who throw fireballs as easily as a blacksmith tosses horseshoes."

"So the rumors reported to Varen were true, the Tlocanians endow their priests with magical powers. Unfortunately, I do not think we have any way to prove their involvement in all of this. Maybe, Wintron will send the Tlocanian Empire a stern message after his coronation."

"Oh, there is proof enough of their involvement," argued Tolara. "They have invaded the realm."

Gordrew gave a puzzled look.

"It is true," said Rolen. "My son was up on a mountain ridge and saw the Dragon Shadow coming up the Borderheart Valley."

Gordrew suddenly looked at Afral, his shaggy eyebrows lowering in a scowl. "What is this? Are you certain? Might the boy be imagining things, trying to play the role of an imaginary hero?"

"I know what I saw, Lord Gordrew," replied Afral, polite yet firm in tone. "I saw the Dragon Shadow with its red lightning. I also saw the Red Dragon circle over Regalis twice and then head southward again." When Afral saw one of the councilor's gray eyebrows arch up with doubt, he felt angry. "I do not lie, sir. I saw both harbingers and they say both come with the Tlocanian army."

"No offense, child, but I will wait for proof that an actual army is invading. Clouds and flying beasts are not soldiers. Maybe they have sent their clouds and dragon to intimidate us. They are already heavily committed on their front with Rhendora, from all that we have heard. Why bother with our little realm?" The pale lord turned back to Afral's father. "Have any messengers come in from Glenford or the boundary forts? Any eyewitnesses of an actual invasion?"

Tolara spoke up. "Well, have your doubts if you must, but we do have war right here in Regalis and it is not nearly over. I think I will set up a hospital while we have a lull." She pointed to a long line of houses up the street. "There is an inn just beyond that row of cottages. That shall be our hospital. I will let the innkeeper know my intentions, for I recall her to be a friend of King Varen." She turned her horse in that direction and set off, though she still talked to them over her shoulder. "See what you two councilors can do with providing some coins to compensate her, for I think I will have all of her beds filled with wounded soon enough. Come along, Afral. You can help me gather supplies."

Eric Lorenzen

CHAPTER SIX
Dreadhound Attack

WINTRON

The crown prince looked down at the corpse and shook his head. This was the sixth dead soldier they had found along the Valley Road, all of them mauled by animals. The beasts had also slaughtered the scouts' horses but had left them uneaten. Apparently, the animals preferred human flesh. This corpse was no different. It appeared to be nearly half-consumed. "Was he sent from us?"

"Not this one," replied Sergeant Yosif. "This one came from Regalis according to Harl, one of our own scouts."

Wintron accepted his word, though he wondered how the sergeant could identify the remains so certainly. "Do you think any of our messengers have made it through?"

The sergeant shook his head. "It is the work of those black dogs that we saw during the battle at the boundary forts. Some of their packs must have slipped past during our stand at Glenford to get ahead of us."

"Have you checked him for any written message?" He saw no messenger satchel, but maybe it lay under the dead horse.

"Nothing, my prince. I would say he was searched."

"Surely not by some refugee," protested Wintron. He could not imagine any of the Borderfolk stooping to rob a chewed corpse.

"Scout Harl says it was done by whoever is running the hounds. The dogs were not just set loose to harass us, for their attacks are too strategic. Someone is guiding the beasts."

Wintron turned away from the carnage, his stomach unsettled.

"We have no time to bury the poor fellow, but at least build a small cairn over him. He died serving his king."

He left the sergeant and his squad to take care of the body and returned to his personal guards waiting nearby. As he mounted, he gave a nod to Captain Bilshor, signaling that he was ready to move on.

The retreat up the Borderheart Valley was not going as well as he had hoped. Too many of the refugees clogged the road, forcing the cavalry to string out as they wove their way through the crowds. It was even worse for the infantry, trying to maintain its ranks on a road congested with wagons, livestock, and pushcarts.

Every few miles, they had passed abandoned items that their owners had finally decided were too heavy to carry, from bed frames to chests to a barrel of pickled fish. The people they passed were weary. Wintron found it all frustrating and also heart-rending. These Borderfolk should not have to flee like this, abandoning their homes and shops. The realm had done nothing to provoke an invasion.

Wintron and his guards returned to the main road, finding it empty of refugees at the moment. He wanted to be alone, so he motioned for Bilshor to give him some room. The captain frowned but obeyed, spreading the guards out more. Bilshor knew the prince too well to argue, though he did not let him ride off on his own. Soldiers rode before and behind him, keeping ever vigilant for any dangers.

Wintron accepted the compromise and rode in silence for a while. He brooded on the realm's predicament, wondering how they could ever turn this rout. Regalis would fare no better than Glenford, so that would mean a retreat all the way up to Tor Randis. He did not look forward to facing his uncle, Duke Fors Halen-Dabe, with the news that his second son had betrayed them. Thankfully, it would be the king and General Tesh who would have to deal with the duke the most.

The way became shadowy, made even more so by the overcast of the Dragon Shadow. Wintron had already ridden under the first boughs when black dogs suddenly arose among the bushes to either side. They made no sound, so that Wintron at first did not even notice them among the shadows. Only when they began charging at him, did he see the danger. The hounds did not bother with his guards; instead, they ran directly at him. They came out on the road both in front of him and behind him. He pulled out his sword and yanked at his horse's reins to bring the stallion around, toward the nearest pair. As the dogs swarmed his mount, he slashed at them desperately. He could hear his guards shouting as they rushed to help, but they were spread-out at his own request.

He fought hard even as he tried to urge his horse to gallop off, but it was too late. A hound bit into Wintron's left leg, though his high boot kept it from being a mortal wound. He slashed the beast off. Another hound scampered over the pack and then leaped at him. He deflected it at the last moment, but the dog's weight almost pushed him from the saddle. He was leaning to the side when another dog almost bit his dangling arm, catching and tearing the sleeve instead when Wintron pulled away quickly. He struggled to right himself, but just as he did, another dog sank its teeth into the horse's neck. The mount screamed and kicked. Blood flew everywhere when the horse tossed its head, eyes wild with agony. As he felt his horse faltering, Wintron pulled his boots free of the stirrups and prepared to jump. The horse collapsed, falling on the lead hound. The dog did not scamper away quick enough and was caught under the dead weight.

Wintron landed clear of the dying horse, but then had to fight ferociously as the remaining dreadhounds pressed in. He would have been lost then were it not for his guards. The men drove their horses between their prince and the dogs, swinging at the beasts. In spite of their efforts, Wintron thought he would surely become dog food. However, four of the dogs died in quick succession, one of them by the prince's hand. The last of the hounds suddenly lost their passion, turned tail and ran off into the woods. For a moment, he just stood there breathing hard. Finally, he recovered enough to see the hand being offered to him. He took hold and climbed on behind Captain Bilshor.

* * *

By the time they reached the cavalry's camp, Wintron's leg was throbbing horribly. Bilshor took him straight to the medics' tent and then helped him to the nearest empty cot. A medic removed his boot and rolled up his pants, revealing a wound that was already ugly and darkening with infection. Wintron grimaced at the sight, but he did his best to hold still as the fellow examined the bite and then started cleaning the wound.

Feeling helpless, he decided to focus on other things. He demanded that Bilshor send for the cavalry's captain, for he wanted a report of how the retreat was fairing. What he heard just aggravating him more. He had ordered the rear guard to destroy every bridge they crossed, but lagging civilians slowed them down. Frustrated, Wintron gave the order to stop such dangerous courtesies. They were to give a brief warning to any they passed and tell the stragglers to abandon their loads and run if they wanted to get across. Now was not the time for foolish mercy, not when it brought risk to the whole army.

He dismissed the captain as he noticed three field medics coming over to examine his darkened leg. Wintron found no comfort in the intense stares. Although he still felt hale, except for the throbbing wound, he now feared that death might come before he could reach his father. "Tell me true. How bad is it?"

The senior-most medic gave him a sad look. "We fear the worst, my prince. We have seen many others bitten by these awful black dogs in the last few days. Always it brings a raging infection that has killed most. We can sacrifice the leg to try to save the rest of you…"

"I think not," replied Wintron, knowing that such butchery would be almost as dangerous. "Do what you can to clean it and then bandage it up."

The medic nodded, having expected the prince's refusal. "Then our only hope is to get you to Regalis and the Cha temple healers."

Wintron nodded agreement, though he wanted someone else to see to his healing. Councilor Rolen's wife had unique skills in healing infections and unnatural wounds. He had seen her work with that glowing sword a few times, always with great success against some pestilence. That was the one he would seek out.

The medics bandaged his wounds and helped get his boot back on, for Wintron was now growing impatient. The prince had made a quick decision, appointing three captains to oversee the retreat and then calling for a new horse.

"Bilshor, we will ride for Regalis. Will you promise to get me to Lady Tolara Quickblade?"

The captain of his guard nodded solemnly. "I promise, old friend. I will get you through to your father and see that Lady Tolara sets her blazing sword to your wound." He offered the prince a shoulder to lean on as led him toward a replacement mount.

DRASS

Drass Halen-Dabe had ridden with his men north from Glenford, though his Tlocanian guides kept him well away from the retreating Border army. Counting all of his men, soldiers and workers, his force numbered over one hundred. It gave him pride to ride at its head.

With him rode a Tlocanian sergeant and his squad of twenty. Drass found the fellow bearable, if a bit too talkative. They turned up one of the many narrow box canyons that fed into the Borderheart Valley and followed a winding trail up among the boulders and pines. It did not seem a promising path up to the Border Highlands, but he held his tongue for the moment. After nearly a half-hour, he began to wonder if this was just a hoax to get him out of the way. Still he held his tongue. Finally, they rounded another bend and he saw the Tlocanian contraption.

A large wooden platform stood at the foot of a sheer cliff, with a stairway leading up to it. Upon that platform sat a large wood-and-wicker basket with ropes extending straight up the cliff. Drass looked up to see where it was tied, but the ropes' ends were lost in the fog. Tlocanian soldiers busily loaded supplies into the basket, carrying items from stacks that waited off to one side.

As Drass came closer, he saw another basket come into view, lowering out of the clouds like some hay bale on a farmer's barn pulley. It spun and bounced as it dropped, empty of any load. The sight mesmerized him so much that he did not pay much attention to the picket lines they passed, leaving it to Sergeant Biverd to gain them entrance.

They rode up to a rock-strewn clearing surrounded by a split-rail fence. They left their horses in a makeshift corral, leaving the tack in an open shed. During the time it took to unsaddle the mounts, the first basket had disappeared up the cliff and the second basket was now being loaded with supplies as well. Drass could not help but be impressed at the ingenuity of the contraption and the efficiency of the loading crew.

As he walked the rest of the way to the platform, Drass saw the second basket lift off, rising steadily into the air until it disappeared into the clouds. The talkative sergeant kept to his side while their men followed.

Biverd spoke again as he and Drass climbed the wooden steps up to the platform. "We cannot lift horses, for they would become too frightened. Could you imagine one of them kicking out the side of a basket and then plunging to its death? A waste of horseflesh. We will have new mounts up on top."

"You have been up this contraption already?" asked Drass, craning his neck to look up the mountainside, wondering about the height of the cliff at this particular spot.

"Oh yes, I have taken the trip twice already, for I was part of the work crew that assembled the platform." Biverd gave the railing a solid whack. "We built it to last, we did. That is the Tlocanian way."

Drass became curious about how the work crew was able to get up here without the Border army noticing and he said as much to Biverd.

The young sergeant laughed. "We infiltrated your little kingdom months ago. My squad came dressed as fur trappers, with our work tools and weapons hidden under the pelts. We were up here sawing and hammering for weeks without anyone's notice."

Drass was no Border loyalist, obviously, but he still wanted to strike the smirk off the sergeant's mouth. Once this little war ended, Drass would have to talk with his brother Mordel about tightening the realm's borders. He did not trust the Tlocanians to cease their spying just because they now had a more amiable ruler.

They were climbing the last flight of stairs just as the first basket reappeared, descending swiftly. Drass paused to watch it drop out of the fog. A crew of six on the platform caught its lead lines and directed the last of its descent. He expected to hear a loud thunk when the lift collided with the wooden deck, but it slowed at the last moment and then came to a rest almost gently. He looked back at his men below him. The last were still releasing their horses in the corral and hefting their saddlebags and gear, but most many had already started climbing after him. "How long will it take to bring up all of my men?"

Biverd shrugged. "If the weather cooperates, by the end of this day. However, some afternoons vicious winds swirl in this narrow canyon and will toss the baskets fiercely. The priests will not risk the baskets to such a beating, so if the winds come then it could take two days to lift your hundred.

* * *

Drass stood in a huge basket, holding tightly to its woven side. With him rode four of his soldiers. Thank the gods, Sergeant Biverd stayed behind. Drass looked out as the basket continued to sway in its jerky ride up the cliff's face. Far below, he could no longer see the rest of his soldiers patiently waiting their turn, for the Dragon Shadow had crept into this narrow canyon too. The entered a misty darkness as they were yanked up through the clouds, losing sight of everything except the basket and sometimes the cliff's face. He startled when suddenly the other basket passed their, empty and descending rapidly. Finally, the clouds thinned and they broke through to the sunshine. He looked up and saw the mighty wooden arms that supported the lift's ropes, but the sight made him queasy, so he looked away.

Fallen King

He gazed at the other side of the ravine, spotting a falcon's nest among the crags, gray with age and unoccupied. The steep canyon rose high above the Borderheart Valley so Drass could see a small sliver of that far-broader valley towards the right whenever the basket swayed outward. From this altitude, he could now see over the top of the Dragon Shadow, a gray river filling the Borderheart from mountainside to mountainside. He found the ride exhilarating, though he noticed that the soldiers going up with him did not seem so enthusiastic. They preferred to hunker down, not wanting to see all the air beneath them.

Finally, the basket slowed as it approached the end of its ride. Drass looked up again at the huge wooden arm of the hoist, feeling a sense of awe that the Tlocanian army had designed these machines. How had they built this without anyone noticing it? He smiled, finding it amusing that the Tlocanians had outwitted his father, the pompous fool. General Fors was supposed to be overseeing all of the Highlands as Duke of Halenvale and Commander of Tor Randis, but he had certainly missed all of this. He chuckled a little as he thought of them shipping parts through Tor Randis itself, without Fors noticing.

As the basket stopped its ascent and swung over the cliff's lip, Drass spotted four of the dragon priests who supervised the two hoists. Being leaders, the priests held themselves above any actual labor, of course. They sent gray-robed temple servants rushing about with their orders. Locals led the six-horse teams that did the actual pulling of the thick ropes, plodding back and forth across a churned meadow. The team pulling his basket now rested at the far end, finished with their task, while men wrestled the basket in place. He had to hold tight to the side as the basket rocked over a wooden platform. The workers signaled for the horse team to slacken the line and the basket thumped down solidly. Drass did not wait for them to open the basket's door. Instead, he clambered over the high side and dropped down on the planking. A temple guard officer stood close by and, as soon as the lift's door opened, yelled orders for the men to march to the meadow's western edge to get them out of the way.

Drass motioned for his men to obey.

He walked over to where the priests stood on another platform between the two hoists. One of them acknowledged him with the merest of nods, but they kept their focus on overseeing the lifting of one hundred soldiers. He took no offense at being ignored, for he saw that they were busy. He only came here because this is where his troops would expect to see him. Therefore, he stood on the platform with the priests for most of the day, as his men were brought up to the Border Highlands.

As soon as the last man stepped off the platform, Drass ordered the troops to march, in spite of the day being nearly over. He was offered a mountain garron as a mount, as were his scouts. He accepted them gracefully, but only to avoid offending the officer of the temple guard. Most of his men would be walking the rest of the way.

Drass mounted one of the shaggy horses, finding the short thing barely acceptable. He had disliked riding them as a youth in Halenvale and he still saw them as little more than a child's plaything. He knew the mountain garron could handle this wild country better, but he still regretted leaving his fine steed far below. Drass ignored the priests, as they had him, but he gave his thanks to the supervisor of each horse team before setting his new mount trotting after his already-moving soldiers. He was eager to reach Halenvale and to seize the family estate as his own.

WINTRON

Prince Wintron grasped the pommel of his saddle as he swayed on his horse. Sweat dripped down his face and soaked his back even though it was a chilly day under the Dragon Shadow. He tried to focus on his surroundings, but could not recall ever having passed these farms before. He hoped that Regalis was near, because he doubted he could keep up this pace much longer. His leg throbbed horribly. He began to lose all awareness of his surroundings, dozing in a fevered sleep as his escort tried to rush him to help.

Sometime later he became aware that Captain Bilshor was speaking to him, but he could not understand. Focusing harder, he finally heard. "…the village elders ask what they are to do."

"What elders?" asked Wintron, confused.

Captain Bilshor's face showed his relief that the prince had finally responded. "This village was attacked by some of the black dogs. Many people are either dead or wounded. The elders ask what they are to do now. I think they hope that we will sweep the woods and root out the dogs."

Wintron finally realized that they no longer moved. He looked around and saw that they were in the middle of a small hamlet. A collection of a dozen cottages, a handful of shops, and one humble inn. He vaguely recognized the place, though its name eluded him in his fevered state. The village residents were gathered in front of the inn, looking at him with a mix of hope and concern. He still sat on his horse, but Bilshor stood at its side, his comforting hand on the prince's good leg. It took a moment for Wintron to find his voice. "I... I have no strength to parlay with them, so you will need to be my voice." He paused to swallow, his throat too dry. He fumbled for his waterskin, humbly accepting Bilhor's help. He took a swig, some of it running down his beard. He did not have the strength to wipe the dribble. "Tell them that war is coming by tomorrow. They must flee quickly for Regalis, keeping together to discourage any more hound attacks. It is the best advice I can give."

Captain Bilshor nodded, and then motioned for the others to keep going while he explained to the village elders. Wintron's horse began to move and he realized that another soldier led the beast. He was too weak to protest, though, and was soon lost in a fevered haze.

Eric Lorenzen

CHAPTER SEVEN
Surrender of Regalis

AFRAL

Two days had passed in Regalis, with many small battles and skirmishes between the loyalists and the rebels. So far, they had kept Mordel and his men confined to the keep, but the city still suffered. Whole blocks had burned. Citizens were cut down by Mordel's mercenaries or mauled by dreadhounds.

Messengers rode north to Tor Randis and south to Glenford, but no one had yet to return. Afral's father still served as commander, with Constable Balto as his second.

In the midst of all of this, Afral helped his mother set up the makeshift hospital. Soon they had a flood of patients, both soldiers and city folk. Thankfully, some of the herb women came to help.

Night came early on that second day, for the Dragon Shadow finally arrived, smothering the last of the sunlight in a blanket of darkness. Red flashes chased between the clouds but, so far, there had been no lightning strikes. There had also been no other proof of an invasion. Nothing.

As night deepened, Afral fought to stay awake inside the inn that served as a hospital. He wanted to be of help to his mother, but he was exhausted. The common room of the Carved Pine Inn overflowed with wounded, lying on the tables and on the hastily swept floor. They were the victims of battle, fire, and beast, brought in from all over Regalis. Many of them moaned in agony even now, for his mother had to restrict her prayer-healing skills to those most in need. She and another woman went from person to person, setting bones and applying bandages as needed. Afral had done what he could, from fetching water and blankets to holding patients while the women set a bone. It was tiring work after everything else. He wondered if this day would ever end.

He stopped at one of the inn's unshuttered windows, looking out into the lightning-traced night. The nearest houses and shops were dark, possibly abandoned. His father was still out there, riding with the soldier patrols, trying to secure the city. From the inn's window, he could see that some parts of the city still burned, an orangish glow in the direction of the nearby temple district.

Afral turned from the window, suppressing a yawn. A second yawn came and he surrendered to it. His eyes drooped some. The hardwood floor looked almost as inviting as a soft bed. He considered asking his mother if he could rest just for a little while, but then the front door banged open and a Border officer strode in, followed by soldiers carrying another victim.

"We look for Lady Tolara Quickblade!" the captain shouted, looking around the common room. His tone colored by both anger and fear. "Lady Tolara?"

"I am here," she replied, straightening up from the person she was helping. "Keep your voice down. The wounded are trying to sleep."

"Please, my lady, the prince needs your aid, for he is near death," the captain implored. He motioned for the soldiers to set their burden on an empty table. They placed him there carefully and then stepped back, though they kept their eyes on their sick leader.

Afral came fully awake. He now recognized the prince, his grizzled hair wet and disheveled by fever, his clothes soaked, despite the cold night. Afral's breath caught, for the man he had called "Uncle Wintron" as a small child looked nearly dead. There was no response from the necessarily rough handling, not even a feeble moan. Afral's mother rushed to the crown prince's side, calling out for cold water and washcloths. Afral just stood there staring, until his mother repeated her order. Abashed, he hurried off to obey.

His mother ripped Wintron's pants apart to expose the festering leg wound. A stench rose from the black bite. Afral gagged at the smell while two of the soldiers stepped back involuntarily. It did not seem to affect Tolara though, as she bent closer to examine how the infection was spreading. She pulled free her sword and used its white light to better inspect her newest patient.

"El, I need your strength most desperately for this one," she whispered. "Do not take him from this world, for he is needed by this poor realm."

She began an Attul healing. With fervent prayers, she set her healing blade against the ugly wound repeatedly. Attul healing was done with a spirit sword, by laying the flat of the blade on an infection or wound while praying to El. Afral understood that all Attuls were trained in this skill as part of their Prayer Warrior training, but only a few had a talent for it. His mother was one of the gifted.

Once, when Afral had asked why healing drained the healer as well as taking some strength from the patient, his mother compared it to sword work. He did not quite grasp the reference, but he certainly saw how his mother labored over the prince, sweating more than he had ever seen her do while practicing with swords.

Over the next two hours, his mother fought to keep the prince alive. Slowly, the prince drew back from death's gate. Afral watched, fearing for both the prince and his mother, as he soaked the prince's body in cold water, not even waiting to remove the rest of the man's clothing. The other healer woman also worked to draw down Wintron's fever, wiping his forehead with a cold cloth and dribbling a few drops at a time into the prince's mouth. The soldiers watched helplessly, until Tolara ordered them to care for the other wounded as best they could, for she did not want them neglected.

Finally, his mother finished her ministrations. The wound no longer looked deadly with infection, but it still looked horrible. Tolara had to hold the table's edge to maintain her balance.

"Will he live?" asked the captain.

As if in response to the captain's voice, the prince stirred and moaned but he did not open his eyes.

She nodded, her exhaustion obvious. "He will live, at least for the night. He is still grave, but I have done all that can be done to help. It is up to Prince Wintron now, and he is a fighter. Take heart, soldiers. You did well in bringing him here so swiftly. Now, help to carry him upstairs to one of the inn's rooms."

They quickly obliged, carrying the prince up the wooden stairway. The man moaned more and even seemed to protest once over their rough handling. Afral took this as a good sign. The innkeeper hurried ahead of them to open the door to one of her few empty rooms. Afral followed behind them, watching through the doorway as they settled the prince into bed. The prince muttered some more but then seemed to settle into a more-normal sleep.

He stepped back when the soldiers and innkeeper exited. The innkeeper went downstairs, while the soldiers milled in the hallway until their captain came out with Afral's mother, in the middle of a discussion.

"...if you leave one in the room, that will be helpful," his mother was saying. "Just be certain that he does not disturb the prince's sleep, Captain Bilshor. I will come by regularly. If he awakes, you may offer him water but no food yet."

The captain nodded, and then turned to the nearest soldier. Tolara walked over to where her son leaned against the wall. Afral tried to suppress a yawn, but she still saw it. "It is late. Go to the room the innkeeper has provided us and get some sleep."

"What about you and Father?"

"I will go to bed as soon as I am finished. I want to look at the soldiers that came in with Prince Wintron, for some of them are also wounded. As for your father, I do not know when he will return." She gave him a quick hug and then a little shove in the right direction. Too tired to resist any further, Afral obeyed.

Later that night, he awoke to a great commotion. Rubbing the sleep from his eyes, Afral looked around the darkened room and noticed that his parents still had not come to bed. He heard yelling and sobbing from outside his room. Curious and a bit worried, Afral opened the door to look. Farther down the hall, soldiers still stood outside Prince Wintron's room. The men seemed frustrated and concerned. The wailing began again and Afral realized it was from the prince on his sick bed, a fierce sobbing that was interrupted by bouts of coughing and then some hoarse and angry yelling. Afral frowned, guessing rightly that the prince had just learned of his father's murder. Whenever the prince's weakness forced him to quiet down, Afral could hear the calmer voices of both of his parents trying to comfort the grieving man.

He considered going in there too, but he had no idea what he could say that might help. Just thinking of the loss of King Varen brought a tear to Afral's own eye. If he saw the distraught prince, he would surely start wailing himself. Sniffing back the moisture, Afral grimaced and went back inside, trying to get back to sleep. The noise did not last long, for Wintron was still very weak, but the return of silence did not mean a return of slumber for Afral. Instead, he tossed and turned on the hard bed, memories of Good King Varen haunting him.

Fallen King

* * *

Morning brought a dim light to the room, muted by the continuing overcast outside, but it was enough brightness to awaken Afral. He stirred and then sat up. He looked over at the second bed in the room and saw that it had been slept in, though he had never heard either of his parents arrive or leave. He had slept in his clothes, for it was a chilly night, so he only needed to pull on his boots, buckle on his sword belt, and drape his thick cloak over his shoulders. He looked out the window before leaving the bedroom and saw that it was now foggy, as if the Dragon Shadow was resting its belly on the city. The thought troubled him.

He stepped out and headed towards the stairs, but found a dozen soldiers outside the prince's room congesting the hallway. He slowed his stride and began to thread through the group. As he neared the door, it opened as an inn's servant stepped out with an empty food tray. From within he heard chanting. Curious, Afral peeked in. None of the waiting soldiers bothered to stop him, for they knew he was the healer's son.

Prince Wintron still lay in bed, but he was awake and aware. The prince watched the High Priest of Cha as he sang his healing chants. Afral recognized the white-haired man, for the temple leaders sometimes visited with his parents, but he could not recall his name. The gray robed priest waved a burning incense stick in his left hand while laying his right hand carefully on the prince's leg. He sang his prayers to the Protector God with fervor.

Afral waited in the doorway, out of respect, though he really wanted to hurry into the room since he saw both of his parents inside. The priest's song rose in volume and ended on a high note with an accompanying flourish of waved incense.

Wintron reached up and gave the priest's hand a firm squeeze. He spoke in a strong whisper that Afral heard clearly from the doorway. "Thank you, Father Bilchaso, for your blessing from Holy Cha."

The elderly man gave a warm smile in return. "You are most certainly welcome, Crown Prince Wintron." He handed his incense stick to an acolyte, and then stepped back. "I think we should all probably withdraw now, for you need peace to recover." He looked to the other religious leaders and motioned them to follow him. Afral stepped back from the doorway and let the group leave: the priestess of Kila (the Provider Goddess) and the priest of Winiem (the God of Change) followed Father Bilchaso, along with their assistants. Afral noted that the fourth Mountain God had no representative in the group, but Avoli was the Death Goddess so her priestesses would not be welcome at a wounded man's bed.

As soon as the room cleared of clergy, the youth hurried in. He could not help staring at the prince, wondering if he would live.

When Wintron gave him a slight nod of recognition, Afral's fears lessened considerably. The prince even greeted him with an old nickname. "Hello, Brave Cricket."

"Hello, Crown Prince Wintron."

"What? So formal? The last time I saw you, you still called me Uncle Win."

Afral gave a quick glance toward his parents, embarrassed. "I want to be respectful…"

Wintron chuckled, but then his laugh turned into coughs that brought a pained flinch. Afral felt doubly embarrassed now, for he had distressed the wounded man. The prince recovered and gave him a weak smile. "Do not look so down, Afral. None of this is your doing. In truth, you have been something of a hero. I have already heard about your run down the mountain to give the city its first warning. Thank you."

Afral wanted to argue that he was no hero, for he had arrived too late to save King Varen.

The prince seemed unaware of Afral's hesitancy. He scooted up in bed so that he could better see the others in the room. The movement caused a grimace, but he fought off the pain. He looked over at Afral's mother. "And I must thank you Lady Tolara, for it must have been you who healed me. I appreciate the added prayers from the others, but I know you are the reason I am still alive."

"The thanks belong to El," she replied softly.

"Thanks to El for using you, then."

"We should leave you alone to rest," stated Tolara, motioning for the others to head for the door.

"Wait a moment," protested the prince in his weakened voice. "There is no time for resting, from what I remember. Do you think I have forgotten what I overheard last night? You were all loose enough with your tongues when you thought I was senseless in my pain. Much is a fog, but I remember enough to know that my father has been murdered." His countenance became cold, hard. "I know who killed him and I will avenge the foul deed."

He looked at Afral's father. "Councilor Rolen, what news of king slayer Mordel? Is he still at the King's Keep or has he scurried off?"

"He still hides in the keep," replied Rolen. "We have the place surrounded, though we do not have enough soldiers to attack it yet. Councilor Gordrew has gone to the barricades. He will be able to update you when he returns."

"Many more soldiers will be here soon," said the prince, though he did not look encouraged by that fact. "If only we could retake the keep and capture Mordel. He needs to hang. However, the Tlocanians chase us. They are right on our heels..." He dropped back onto his pillow and closed his eyes, looking exhausted.

When no one assured the prince that they could conquer the keep, Afral looked at his father and saw the doubt there. Afral spoke up in his place. "We will flush them out, for we have righteousness on our side."

Wintron opened his eyes and looked at him. "I appreciate your courage, young Afral. The gods willing we will retake it, though even they can be fickle." He turned his head towards Afral's father. "Lord Rolen, talk to Captain Bilshor. He will update you on what we have already endured these last few days. You, Bilshor, and Gordrew are my new war council."

"We need to let the prince rest," said Tolara, putting a light hand on her son's shoulder. "Get some sleep Wintron or I will not let you meet with your council later."

He shook his head at her warning, yet his eyelids drooped shut.

Afral and his parents quietly withdrew, leaving only two guards. Tolara pulled the door shut behind them and then the three of them strode down to the common room. While his mother visited with her many patients, he and his father went to the kitchen for a quick breakfast of bread, sausage, and cheese. The innkeeper provided a meal for Tolara too, wrapped in a towel to keep warm.

Rolen turned to his son as they waited for Tolara to finish her quick inspection of the wounded. "Afral, we will be leaving for home now. It may be our last time there."

He gave his father a puzzled look. "We will be staying at this inn?"

"No, we will be leaving Regalis. The prince will realize that we cannot retake the keep. There is no time for that nor could it be held against what is coming at us. The Tlocanians are just too strong. The whole army will have to retreat up to Tor Randis for its last stand."

"But why? We cannot abandon Regalis. This is the capitol. Once Uncle Win is stronger he will command us to fight..."

"No, Afral. It is the prince who ordered everyone to withdraw. He spoke only wistfully about retaking the keep. There is no way to hold the city, even if we held the King's Keep. Not even the far stouter boundary forts could withstand this invasion."

"They did not have Attul Prayer Warriors there. Surely, you and mother will make the difference. El would not allow such evil men to win…"

"It is not that simple, son. El grants us all free will." Rolen paused as Tolara approached. "Are you ready to leave?" he asked her. She nodded.

His father turned back to him. "Afral, we can talk more as we ride home. I am sorry, but we must do this."

The three of them retrieved their horses and set off. Afral did not feel like talking, so he let his horse lag behind his parents' mounts. His father allowed him the time to think, while his mother ate her breakfast as she rode.

They followed the Valley Road southward. To him, the city seemed muted by more than just the fog. He saw people about, but they were heading northward with grim faces, guiding stuffed wagons or pulling carts full of belongings. He did not recognize any of these travelers and he suspected that many were not even residents of Regalis. He saw others, people who did live in the city, carrying things out of their homes and shops and loading their possessions onto wagons, carts, horses, or mules. He heard no children running in the streets at play, for today their parents ordered them to stay close and help pack. He saw neither street vendors nor delivery wagons.

Afral found the whole city oddly subdued. Whenever the red lightning flashed somewhere in the fog, people would startle or duck, but then return to their labors with more fervor. Seeing so many packing, he realized this was no dream or jest. They were really going to flee the city.

* * *

Afral finally arrived home with his parents. Though morning, his father lit all of the lamps to brighten their rooms. His mother began to sort out what they would take. Afral just stood there, uncertain, not truly grasping that this would be their last time here; that they were abandoning the only home he had ever lived in.

"Afral, my dear, could you gather up your clothes and your thickest blanket?" asked Tolara, sensitive to her son.

Her tone caused him to watch what she was doing. She placed a carefully folded banner into her own saddlebag. He knew it be an heirloom flag from a grandfather he had never met, a banner that Afral had never seen unfurled. She also packed a tightly wrapped sword, the blade intended for the second child his parents never had. When his parents had left Warhaven twenty years ago, they had been given a prophecy about two sons, so they had taken along two extra swords. Afral now carried one of those swords, but this one was still without a bearer.

She noted his attention and gently reiterated her request. "Please see to your clothes and blanket."

Afral did as she asked, going into his bedroom and folding the clothes compactly and then squeezing them into a saddlebag. His father gave him some twine and instructed Afral to roll up his blanket tightly. His mother gave him a package of food to pack and then told him to pick out three toys or trinkets to keep. Afral stared at the shelf over his bed and suddenly most of the toys seemed too childish. He could not imagine himself ever again playing Tiddle Sticks or Ball-and-Thorns. His collections of large pinecones and polished river stones seemed somehow foreign. He decided to leave it all behind. Absently, he took his pet frog, went to the back door, and let it go free. His vision blurred.

"Afral, help me pack the horses," said Rolen softly.

He followed his father out, with his blanket in one hand and the saddlebags in the other. He set them on his new horse and then stared off into the foggy day. Across the way, he could see their neighbors also packing. He wondered if anyone would be left in the neighborhood by morning.

"Could you please stay out here and guard the horses?" asked his father.

He muttered an affirmative, but his eyes caught on his tree swing where it hung in the pooled shadow of the old oak. He still stood there when his parents came out with their loads. He looked at their few things and suddenly realized that they intended to leave everything else behind. He protested.

Tolara came over and hugged her son again. Rolen strode over, put his arms around both of them, and said, "Afral, I am taking my most important valuables with me: my family. We can replace pots and tools, bedding and furniture. Our loved ones are uniquely precious, however. It would be foolish to overburden our horses, for then we would lag behind and maybe even fall prey to the army advancing on the city. No possessions are worth that risk, would you not agree?"

Afral nodded, though tears still stained his face.

After a moment of silence, Rolen tightened his hug and then let go. "We must get going. We still have a duty here and time is pressing. Prince Wintron needs us at his side."

Their ride back to the inn was even more silent, each one absorbed in memories of their life here. They arrived just as Councilor Gordrew came out of the inn's stable. He waited for them and then they all went to see the prince together. Afral was glad to join them. They walked into the inn, carrying their scant possessions, entering a common room still full of injured people. They were about to go upstairs, when the woman who oversaw the care of the hurt intercepted them and quietly informed them that the prince was downstairs, in the inn's private dining room. They thanked her and changed direction. Passing down a short hallway, Afral passed vigilant guards, and followed the others into a small room where four officers sat at a table with Wintron. The prince was dressed and did look much better, though still weak. He also looked angry.

"Rolen! Gordrew! I have need for both of you." Wintron waved them to the two remaining chairs at the table. "Lady Tolara, if you and Afral would care to linger, I would appreciate your wisdom too."

The last of the old king's councilors took their seats. Tolara agreed to stay, sitting on one of the straight-back chairs that lined the far wall. Afral sat next to her. He was surprised at the invitation to stay and eager to listen. It was enough to shake his melancholy over leaving home.

"Captain Gish, update the councilors on what you reported, though make it brief."

Gish nodded, and turned his attention to Gordrew and Rolen. "I have informed the prince that all the city gates are now secure. At the south gate, we are starting to let in refugees, but it is only a relative trickle so far. The cavalry has arrived and joined those men keeping watch on the King's Keep. We expect the rest of the army to start marching in by late afternoon."

"Thank you," replied Wintron. "Scout Harl, share again about our enemy's advance."

The scout, who had been standing against a wall, stepped forward and reported. "The Tlocanians are through Glenford. When I last saw them, they were stalled at Moonspring Creek, cutting logs to replace the bridge we tore down. They felled one tree right across the water to serve as the bridge's spine. We would have lingered longer, but as soon as the tree came down, a pack of black dogs scampered across and sniffed us out. Me and Gaddy had to ride like the wind to keep ahead of them. When we came to the Spinning Leaf Creek, we told the sappers to take it down without delay, before those beasts could fall upon us. I left Gaddy to watch there. He will ride in once the Tlocanians get that far."

"Thank Winiem for the spring melt," replied Gordrew. "The Spring God shelters us behind full streams."

"Let us hope Winiem keeps his ploys aimed at the Tlocanians," said Wintron with fervor. The Spring God was also known as the Trickster, fickle as spring weather. "Have you anything to add from the King's Keep, Gordrew?"

The elderly man nodded, though he frowned. He stood up and leaned over the table towards the prince, handing him a folded and sealed letter. He passed it with the seal up so all recognized the Halen-Dabe crest of a pinecone beneath crossed swords. "This came from the Keep for you, my prince."

Wintron took it, but the distaste showed on his face. "It seems my craven cousin has not yet found the royal seal," he observed. "May we unseat him before he does."

The crown prince broke the seal and unfolded the message. He silently read and then cursed, throwing the offensive thing on the table. The others waited until he calmed enough to explain. "Mordel offers a deal. If we retreat from the city without burning or pillaging it, then he will provide his protection to the citizens who remain, including any sick, injured, young, or elderly."

Those at the table broke out in loud protests. Captain Gish declared that the keep could be overrun within two days, once the army's bulk arrived. Councilor Gordrew begged the prince not to trust the king slayer to hold to any promises. Afral's father was not as loud, but his words caused the others to fall silent.

"What other option have we?" asked Rolen. "We do not have the time to take the King's Keep. Try it and we will feel the Tlocanians' breath on our back just before they cut us down."

"Rolen has the truth of it," spat Wintron, obviously angry. "Most of you have heard Scout Harl's report twice now. The Tlocanians are barely slowed by our sabotage, curse their ingenious engineers. They will be on us in three days and then there will be no retreat. As much as it grieves me, we must surrender Regalis to this horde and to the rats hiding behind the keep's high walls."

"What of justice for Varen?" asked Gordrew.

"I swear that I will see to it," vowed Wintron fervently. "Mordel, Drass, and any others who have helped in this foul usurping will die." Those in the room fell silent before his passion-filled words. "I swear I will execute them all!" He stopped, realizing that he was half out of his seat. He sat back down with force. "And yet, it will not happen this week. Duty to the Border Realm outweighs the personal duty of a son to avenge his father, even if that sire is the king. I cannot allow the Border army to be surrounded just because I am anxious to see Mordel's head on a spike. No, I must take Mordel up on his offer, though trusting a king slayer seems utter folly. We will retreat to Tor Randis for a time, but I swear that we will return. I will have all of the Borderheart Valley free and these traitors punished."

GALDON

Galdon detested dreadhounds. He watched carefully as the dogs trotted in at the heels of the dragon priests who served as their Houndmasters. The presence of dreadhounds also told him that the priests were Embraced Ones. Only the demon-possessed had the ability to control the vicious beasts. Galdon's main reason for hating the animals was their tendency to attack Tlocanian soldiers when there was no other human flesh nearby. Their claws on the marble flooring made a very distinct sound, as the dogs followed the priests up the grand hall to stand before Lord-General Hraf Kelordok.

"What have you to report, Brother Prekor?" asked the general.

The called-out priest gave a brief bow. "We have five things to report, my lord." Galdon sensed a cockiness in the thin man and guessed he must have something important to reveal.

Lord Hraf motioned for the priest to continue, showing just a little bit of impatience with the grandstanding. It was enough to scare the priest into hastily continuing.

"First, Glenford has been cleared, with all humans imprisoned or killed. Second, the road to Regalis is crowded with refugees and frightened soldiers fleeing our great army. Third, Regalis is aflame with rebellion. Fourth, the crown prince of this land has been wounded by a dreadhound. He suffers and may even be dead by now. Finally, we have found an Attul in the Border Realm capitol."

Galdon noted that the general leaned forward with interest. When

Lord Hraf spoke, though, he still sounded slightly bored. "An Attul?"

"Yes my lord. Brother Zaphrion confirms it. There may have been more, for he thought he caught a glimpse of a second white light. However, his hound died before he could direct its gaze that way." Prekor licked his lips in nervousness at the other priest's failure.

"Is this Attul another of those Watch Riders, or have we finally found their main force?" The general's tone implied that he doubted that.

"That I do not know, my lord. Alas, Brother Zaphrion strained himself too greatly in his rush to bring us this news. He was unable to use the road, so he had a hard ride back. His horse died before it ever reached Glenford, so Zaphrion ran the rest of the way as a were-dog. He fell unconscious as soon as he completed his report." Prekor gave an apologetic shrug. "I will personally bring him to you as soon as he can be revived."

"See that you do, Prekor-Swerkrad." Hraf spoke with a chill to his voice. Galdon's eyebrow rose upon hearing the double name used for the priest. He had been around these Embraced Ones long enough to know that the second name was that of the demon inside the man. However, the demon-possessed rarely spoke those names in front of mere humans. Only the emperor used his demonic name openly, and he only used his demonic name: Silossiak. That Lord Hraf had spoken so openly implied a great anger.

Brother Prekor dropped suddenly to the ground in full obeisance. The priests with him did so as well. Behind them, the dogs whined as they sensed their masters' distress. With his face pressed against the cold marble floor, Prekor replied in obvious fear. "I hear and obey."

Lord-General Hraf Kelordok ignored him. Instead, the general looked over his shoulder to where Galdon stood at watch. "It is time to send you back out, Captain Galdon. Gather just two of your squads to leave in the morning. More than that and you will have a hard time slipping past Regalis to set your traps. You will escort Brothers Prekor and Zaphrion back towards Regalis. I give you three duties: kill the crown prince, capture an Attul, and harass those fleeing the city. If you and the priests cannot ensnare the Attul, then at least mark him out so that we can send a great enough force after him."

Galdon gave a sharp salute, as proper to a military superior. He did not like the idea of leaving half of his troop behind, but he had been a soldier too long to question such a thing aloud. "I hear and obey, my lord."

Eric Lorenzen

CHAPTER EIGHT
Cleargorn Valley

MYLANA

The three Watch Riders approached the small city of Trela Kolono, which sat on the eastern bank of the wide Cleargorn. They were now on a road known as the Middle Run, one of Na Ciria's great trade routes. Merchants traveling between southern and northern Na Ciria followed one of three main routes. The seacoast route required traders to weigh the risk of Jagged Coast pirates against the benefit of quick sea passage. The Eastern Run came up the Grandgorn Valley from Westbend through what had been the Riverrealm and continued on to Rhendora. The Middle Run followed the Cleargorn Valley and passed through this town of Trela Kolono on its way to the Seven Kingdoms of Cleargorn, which was now the heart of the Tlocanian Empire.

Mandor, though he had never been to this town, knew of its recent history from their father. He shared the story with Mylana as they approached. Coursen seemed only to partially listen, for he had ridden through here twice before, even though it had been before the Dragon Shadow had spread this far south from Tlocania. He did remark that the area looked to be thriving still, in spite of its gloomy overcast.

The town elders had surrendered to the Tlocanian army without a fight almost a year ago, according to what the Guardians had learned. The army had marched through without doing much damage compared to what happened in Westbend. The largest manor in town, which had belonged to one of the wealthiest merchant families, was seized. The Tlocanians razed the mansion and declared the land holy, handing it over to the dragon priests. Construction of the Five Dragons Temple began on that site. Soon after its foundation was laid, the priests began doing animal sacrifices to the dragon gods and offering up prayer incense. The citizens quickly joined in, for no one wanted to anger their new masters, especially after seeing how they treated those who rebelled. They did their prayers three times a day and neglected their ancestral gods. At least they did so in public.

Mandor's knowledge ended before the temple's completion, for the Watch Rider post in this town had been destroyed six months ago. Four Attul families had lived here, but only two people escaped to bring word of the post's razing. The area's Guardian was among those who had perished.

Coursen spoke up. "I remember Guardian Peler. When I came through here, months before Tlocania invaded, he was already worried. His riders were spying on the Five Dragons Temple in Waybridge, risking much as they tried to track the dragon priests' schemes. Maybe it was his aggressive tactics that exposed the post."

"I think we had better be cautious," said Mandor, "for there will be some in this area familiar with a spirit sword's glow. Keep your blade sheathed, Mylana."

She felt agitated by his warning. "I will not be swinging my blade over my head like our little brother Migesh. Do you forget that I am also a Watch Rider, brother?"

Mandor lifted a hand in mock defense. "No need to assault me, little sister. I am merely offering a word of caution, for you are still so new to our ranks. Would you be so quick to take offense with any other veteran rider, or is it just because I am your older brother?"

Coursen laughed at the sibling squawking.

Mylana suddenly felt embarrassed. "I am sorry, Mandor. You are right. We must be careful. Indeed, I am glad that the Guardians gave us such detailed directions for this ride."

As they rode onward, silence settled in. Mylana was too embarrassed by her outburst to say anything more, while the two young men seemed distracted by other thoughts or memories.

* * *

It was almost midday when they drew near to the small city, so they had to delay their plan. They dared not enter at noon, for that was when everyone had to pray to the five dragon-gods. Harwin had told them that the Reds required worship thrice a day, just like the Grays and Blacks in the south. Mylana knew that when the temple bells rang, everyone was required to fall to the ground, facing towards the sound. You prayed aloud until the bells sounded again. Anyone who did not kneel or pray would be arrested and beaten. That was a problem for anyone sworn to worship only El but had to spy on cities where people had to worship other gods at sunrise, noon, and sunset. Watch Riders had learned to time their journeys to avoid public places during those worship times.

So, realizing the time of day, the threesome turned off the road and hid under a stand of aspens. Outside the city, people were not as diligent to obey but farmers would still pause at the plowing and look around for any eyewitnesses. It would not be good for the three to be seen disobeying the law so blatantly.

The bells sounded while they hid, echoing over the countryside. They waited, quietly nibbling some cheese and bread while remaining in their saddles. It was quiet out here, the only sound coming from a wind stirring the trees overhead. Finally, the bells sounded again, calling an end to the worship time. Mandor had them wait a little while longer and then they continued.

They followed the Middle Run into town, so they attracted no undue attention. A high palisade surrounded the small city, but its gates stood open and the guards did not stir from their resting places, sheltered from the chill breeze. Mylana noticed that the city's walls were made of wood, even though it sat on the edge of the Midcirian Plains, where stout trees rarely grew. She guessed the city leaders had traded for the wood with those further north. Within the walls, many buildings looked like typical buildings from the plains, made of mud and topped with sod roofs. However, the larger, more prosperous buildings were out of wood or stone, with tile roofs. Most stood no higher than two-stories; however, the Dragon Temple's unfinished spires soared five stories in height.

The townsfolk were done with their prayers and back to their business. It was not so crowded that the Attul Riders had to worry over cutpurses, but there were enough people about that they had to slow their horses to a measured gait. They had agreed beforehand to search out an inn where traders gathered, for they wanted to hear any gossip of what lay further north.

Tradition in central Na Ciria was to hang a green lantern above an inn's door, to make it easier for travelers to locate it in foul weather or after dark. With the gloom caused by the Dragon Shadow, the town's inns all had their lanterns lit even during the day. Mandor chose a likely place, where the Middle Run intercepted another wide road that ran down to the river docks.

They rode into the inn's large yard, handing over their mounts to a stablehand. Even though they planned to be in the town for a few hours, Mandor instructed the lad to leave the horses saddled and loaded. They paid a bit extra to assure that their things would be well watched, even though there was not much to pilfer among the food and supplies. The inn, made of timber and stone, was one of the few three-storied buildings and it loomed around the stable yard on three sides. Mylana craned her neck to look up at the dark windows, but could not tell if anyone looked out.

The three walked into a gloomy common room, its only lighting a fire and a scattering of hanging lamps. Coursen strode ahead, to a table in the center of it all. The siblings followed. They had barely sat down when a serving maid came to take their orders. They decided to order a light fare, for what they had eaten earlier had not been enough to sate their day's hunger.

When their food arrived, they bowed their heads and gave silent thanks to El for his provision. If the other patrons mistook them for pious dragonsworn, so be it. They ate quietly, trying to overhear what others discussed. At the nearest table sat a trio of merchants, middle-aged and well dressed.

"But when will you leave, Grethorn? If you wait another three days, I will have a shipment to fill that gap on your fourth barge."

"I might be able to wait that long, for the right commission."

The third merchant laughed, slapping the first man on the back. "Lashek, you should know by now that Grethorn is always willing to do a favor, but only if it will drop extra coins in his pocket. You two and your river rafts. I think its too much bother to build a new float every time you want to send something down the Cleargorn. At least with my mule trains, I have transit in both directions. You might save time, but these days I enjoy the extra week in the sunshine. The only other time I get out from under the Shadow is when I take a run to the Lakelands."

Grethorn chuckled back. "Are you still leading your mule teams, Bogir? Can't you trust that son of yours yet?"

"Oh, I trust Larth; I only take every other trip." Bogir stretched his feet under the table and put his hands behind his head. "But I think the head of a merchant family should stay active in the business and not just sit in his strongroom counting his money. Besides, I do not want to get as pale as the two of you; this Dragon Shadow turns everyone a sickly pallor."

Grethorn smirked. "Let us see how much you boast when the priests come in for their afternoon drink. Try using your pale skin jest on them."

Bogir sat up straight, raising his hands in supplication. "Oh no, I will try no humor on those shrouded ghouls. That is another reason to lead my mule trains; at least my beasts will bray at my jokes."

The other two laughed, and then Grethorn rose to his feet. "Well, Lashek, do you want to come down to the docks and see if my space will be adequate for you? We can talk passage fees as we walk."

Lashek also stood. "Let us do that. Maybe if we cannot reach a decent price, I can ask Bogir for room on one of his laughing mules." They both chuckled again and then said their good byes to Bogir and to the innkeeper. Bogir remained seated, nursing his ale.

The Attuls continued to eat slowly and silently, catching other conversations but hearing nothing worthwhile.

Coursen apparently decided to be more direct, so he scooted his chair back and turned to the merchant. "Excuse me, sir, but can I buy you a drink?"

Bogir chuckled and signaled the serving girl. "Certainly, but I forewarn you that I am not looking for any more caravan guards."

Coursen smiled. "That is fine, for we are not looking to hire on anywhere. However, your candor deserves fair return. We are looking for information."

Bogir ordered a refill, and then came to sit with the Riders. "What sort of information, young man?"

Coursen caught the serving girl's sleeve and added drinks for himself and his companions.

Mandor spoke up. "My sister, my friend, and I are traveling northward and are wondering about the roads ahead."

Bogir ignored the question for a moment. "Sister, eh? I see the similarity. My name is Bogir, of Moralin Trading House, merchant of Trela Kolono. What are yours?"

The servant girl returned quickly and set mugs down on the table. Coursen and Bogir each took a quick swallow.

"I am Mandor Trueword. My sister is called Mylana Farsight. And our friend behind the mug is Coursen Highjumper."

One bushy eyebrow rose. "Interesting surnames. Different fathers? Oh, ignore that question. Bluntness is my greatest fault, I think, though my wife claims it really is my stubbornness. So, you are wondering about traveling conditions. Well, the road to the Seven Kingdoms is clear, but you need to be wary of bandits. The Tlocanians are quick to stamp out any rebellion, but they are sloppy with robbers and minor criminals. Rumors say that there is war further up the Cleargorn, where the Tlocanians have taken Lepis Fra and maybe more, but I do not trade that far north. My son just came back from the Lakelands, so I can say that road is fine all the way through the Lonpin Deep Gap. If you are planning to travel into the Forest Hills, look elsewhere for information; not much trade to be found in those wild lands since the fall of Halfhill."

"What do you hear about the Grandgorn Valley?" asked Mandor.

Bogir laughed heartily. "Son, you should have taken the Eastern Run if you wanted to go anywhere over there. It is far easier to cut across on the grasses than the rugged country that lies east of here."

"Sir, how did you know that we are from the south?" Mylana asked, unable to hide her surprise.

Bogir took another swig from his mug, while lifting his other hand to show three fingers. After swallowing, he counted off his reasons. "One, your clothes are southern; you will not see such pretty lining on cloaks up here. Two, your speech proclaims you as southerners; those from below the plains have a crispness about their words. Third, your very question marks 'paid' to that fact; people up here do not consider this the north. To us, the north is the wilderness beyond the Border Mountains."

Mandor looked chagrined at the error.

Mylana smiled. "Yes, we are from the south, from the area of Westbend."

Bogir nodded. "The Grays of Osburg hold that land now, I hear. I also heard that it was a…. difficult… transition. Well, I will not ask what brings you up the Cleargorn, for sometimes it is best to be ignorant. I will tell you this: if you are planning to settle anywhere up here, you need to realize that the Shadow makes farming hard and that city life demands daily kneeling to the dragon gods. Stand stiff too many times and the priests will point you out to the soldiers for persuading." His grimace gave silent testimony of what he thought of such coercion.

"What areas are not under the Shadow?" she asked softly.

Bogir waved off the serving girl, to keep her from overhearing. Mylana guessed that that he considered breaking off the conversation, but he did not. "The Shadow has spread from the Seven Kingdoms, to cover everything from the Grizzlies to the High Wall. If you are looking for sunshine, head back to the plains or take the road to the Lakelands. The lands around Monarch Lake have their share of overcast and fog, but it is a natural thing. I suppose the far north is still clear, since there is nothing worth conquering up there."

"Is the Tlocanian army on the move also?" asked Mandor. "In the south, the Blacks are moving up the coast and the Grays are taking ship up the Grandgorn."

"The Grandgorn is practically conquered already, with the Tlocanian army holding most of it in central Na Ciria," stated Bogir, dismissing the news. "Whatever is left between Riverrealm and Westbend will not be much of a challenge for the Osburgens. I hear they have also sent a force into the lands further south, looking to capture the gold mines of distant Summerhill. Rumors say the dragon force may even look beyond Na Ciria." He leaned forward and lowered his voice. "I do not want to know if you are rebels or just refugees, but realize the dragonsworn are the same whether they serve the Black, the Gray, or the Red. Be very careful around them; I would not want harm to come to the three of you, especially to you, pretty lady." Bogir stood up, swallowed the last of his ale, and gave them a smile. "Thank you again for the drink."

Bogir paused as he set down his mug and then leaned over the table again. "Here is another tidbit for you: be very cautious when you reach the city of Waybridge, for it is a rough place. There are good reasons why many of us local merchants choose this town for our homes, in spite of the trade rushing through that city. My eldest son, who has no family yet, keeps watch on House Moralin there. Should you need an odd job, go by to see Larth and tell him that I sent you. The job will not be much, but enough to keep you out of the poor kitchens." Bogir straightened up, not giving them time to reply. With a grunt, he turned away.

They watched as the merchant walked out. As he opened the door, someone about to enter surprised him. Bogir stepped back, while still holding the door, and gave a polite bow. Two black robed priests strode in, giving the trader only a cursory nod. After they passed, Bogir quickly exited without looking back. A serving girl was cleaning off the table where the merchants had met and her activity attracted the priests. They sat down, placing their drink orders as they did.

Mylana tensed, wondering if these priests were demon-possessed or not. She would have quickly left, but the boys showed no eagerness to leave. The Attuls lingered for a little time, but the priests were a quiet pair, absorbed in their own thoughts. It was obvious that the two would not be glibly revealing secrets in front of strangers. Mandor and Coursen exchanged slight nods and Mylana realized that they had decided it was best to leave. She envied them their years of working together, able to communicate without even a whisper. Some day, she hoped to be a seasoned Watch Rider too.

They left their horses at the stable, choosing to walk around the town. After a few more hours of visiting a market, a tavern, and another inn, they gave up without any more news. Though the perennial gloom of the Dragon Shadow made the time of day harder to know, it was obvious that sunset approached along with the next call to worship. They hurried back to the first inn and retrieved their horses, making quick time for the city's north gates.

They had not gone far when they heard the temple bells ring out. Mylana looked around, but the only sign of humans she saw was the faint light from a farmhouse across a large field. The boys decided that they should keep moving, for the risk was minimal and they needed to find a decent campsite.

Darkness descended quickly under the dark clouds, but they rode well into the night, still looking for a place to shelter. It was an open countryside, full of farms and fenced meadows. Frustrated, Mandor led them off the main road, still searching. None of them wanted to sleep out in the open. It took some time before they found a promising place to camp, among some bushes that lined a small stream. The plants were tall enough to hide the horses. They flattened an area among the high grasses and bedded down on the damp ground, choosing to go fireless this night because of the wind.

BRODAGAR

Dragon Priest Brodagar did not enjoy nights like this, prowling the cold roads of the countryside, but he did his duty as required. With him rode a dozen temple guards, all proven veterans who knew how to defend their superior. He thought it a waste of their talent and his own to be used as mere patrollers, but he was not about to voice such thoughts. To be Tlocanian meant to obey. To be an Embraced One meant to obey immediately. Brodagar and his men looked for three young people who had ridden out of Trela Kolono just before the evening prayer, but they had failed to find them. Tracking by flickering, harsh torchlight hurt his eyes, so he did not bother looking for their trail. Being houndless, he had no way to sniff out their path, so he could only assume they followed the road. He pushed his men hard, even sending two out at a full gallop, but they had not even seen the strangers.

He wished he had those dreadhounds, but there was only one pack in this town and Brother Juress had them tonight, out on the grasslands further east. Lord-Governor Krev Zendron did not explain his orders, yet it seemed he was casting a wide net to catch someone.

"I dislike depending on the governor for directions, Sahak," muttered Brodagar to his Other half. He sometimes slipped into actually talking aloud when addressing the demon inside of him. "How will I ever gain greater power serving in this half-forgotten place?"

Patience. We must prove ourselves dutiful. Only then will we get the opportunity to rule more. Zendron-Swerkrad will see our worth and will soon call us to serve in Waybridge beside him. Just have patience, human.

"He sends us to this dirt-clod of a town for a month, with vague orders to search out Attuls. But he forbids us to kill or capture any. Where am I to find legendary Attuls? I thought them a fable until you taught me otherwise Sahak, but I still have no idea what one looks like…"

The glowing sword.

"It will be too late if he already has a sword drawn," complained the priest to his demon, "That will only end in either our death or his."

Frustrated, he signaled for his men to halt. This chase seemed foolish. If these three were from the group of Attuls that Juress was sent out to track, then they would soon be under Juress' careful eyes. Brodagar motioned for the troops to turn back. The men obeyed quickly.

The priest set a swift pace now, having given up on the search. He had to use his free hand to keep his hood in place. It was not that the torches would blind his light-sensitive eyes, but he had no desire for the discomfort the glare would cause.

If the gate guards had been quicker in reporting to the temple, he might have caught the three, but the locals never felt any urgency. He would have to punish someone for that failure. Whoever the three were, they had slipped away in the night.

* * *

Near midnight, Brodagar rode into the courtyard of the Five

Dragons Temple. In larger cities, such temples filled with patrons both day and night, but he found the courtyard deserted. The good folks of Trela Kolono were snuggled in their beds. He and the temple guards rode around the side of the main building to reach the stables. The priest dismounted and gave the reins to one of the grooms. A servant waited for him.

The gray robed elderly man gave an appropriate bow. "You have a visitor, Brother Brodagar. It is Captain Nesron."

He repressed a sigh. He had no desire to confront the Tlocanian officer this night, but he could not just ignore the man. "Where is he?"

"He awaits you in the worship hall, holy brother."

Brodagar gave a slight nod to indicate that he had heard and then strode away from the stables and back around to the front courtyard. He walked boldly towards the lighted worship hall, where he could hear the sound of the worship gong. The smell of incense tickled his nose as he passed a lone worshiper exiting.

As he neared the open doors, another priest stepped outside. It was Brother Hoslar; the one assigned to the Listening Room. He found the tall, lanky man rather odd. He planned to walk right past the Listener with just the merest of nods, but Hoslar held up a hand to delay him.

"I received a message for you, Brother Brodagar. It is from Zendron in Waybridge."

Brodagar stopped and gave his full attention to Hoslar. "I am ready to hear," he replied formally.

Hoslar looked about to make sure no one could overhear and then spoke. "Lord-Governor Krev Zendron sends orders for Brother Brodagar and Captain Nesron. You are to follow a trio of Attuls that have just entered our lands from the south. You are not to capture or kill these three. You are only to follow them and make sure they come to Waybridge."

The number to watch for could not be a coincidence. He had been already following the three earlier, and had lost their trail for lack of dreadhounds. He waited for more, but that was it. Typical of Zendron. He offered no more information on these three, even though he apparently knew where they were. "Have you already told Captain Nesron? He is inside the worship hall right now."

Hoslar shook his head. "How would I know this to be your Nesron? Tlocanian officers all look alike to me. They all flaunt their helm, sword, and angry stride."

Fallen King

Brodagar smirked. There was only one Tlocanian officer in Trela Kolono. Who else would be in a dragon helm? All the other officers were local militia in their mud-colored uniforms. He wondered if Hoslar's ignorance was a purposeful choice or just naivety. It seemed that too much time working a Listening Room could rattle the best of minds, and Listener Hoslar had probably not started out that strong. Brodagar chose to give him a short answer. "I will carry the message to Captain Nesron."

Hoslar nodded and wandered off into the night. Brodagar hoped he did not stray out of the temple complex, for he might not find his way back. The locals could do Hoslar no harm, not with a demon indwelling the man, but he still might get lost or go on a sudden killing spree. Brodagar wanted neither of those headaches. He would have to warn the temple's High Brother to keep the Listener under better watch.

Brodagar took a moment to compose himself and then went in to find the army captain. Inside, he paused, looking through the cloud of incense for the Tlocanian officer. He spotted him in the shadows, watching the attendant priest avidly. Brodagar remained at the rear of the hall and just watched Nesron staring at the hour's sacrifice.

The priest, an unEmbraced simpleton, stood before the altar, holding a pigeon in his hands. Only three others were in the large hall besides the officer: two petitioners kneeling at the front and a temple attendant standing next to the gong. The heavy-set priest in black robes lifted the struggling bird over his head, muttering prayers, and then set it on the stone altar. With one hand, he held it in place; with the other, he grabbed a large knife. Nesron watched avidly, but Brodagar knew it was not out of devotion to those stupid dragons. The officer focused on the struggling bird and when the blade fell, Nesron licked his lips as he watched the blood splatter on the stained altar. The soldier gave a little sigh as the ritual finished and the gong sounded.

He hungers for a personal sacrifice, noted Brodagar's Other. *We can use that to our advantage. We should meet him among the pens.*

He nodded his agreement and quietly left before Nesron saw him. In the hallway, he caught a servant and gave the order for Nesron to be escorted out to the cages behind the stables. There was no time for Brodagar to stop by his cell to change, so he had to do with robes smelling of horse and leather. He did stop long enough to splash his face with water from a basin and to pick up a mint leaf to chew, for the pens were notoriously smelly.

The cages behind the stables held humans and dreadhounds. Brodagar could stand the dogs, but the human prisoners made no effort at cleanliness. They knew that their fate was to be sacrificed for their power, and so most no longer cared. Their only baths came when it rained. Brodagar always made sure any of his personal sacrifices were washed off before being brought into his presence, though not all Embraced Ones were so fastidious. Usually, he avoided this area, but he knew that the humans would be more tempting to Nesron.

He chose to wait next to a full pen, making sure the wind blew the stench away from him. The prisoners knew better than to plea for help. Instead, they shuffled to far side of their cage, as if that small distance gave them some protection. Brodagar ignored the chattel and watched for the Tlocanian captain. Finally, Nesron approached, striding purposely towards the priest. They exchanged no handshakes or bows, for they were comrades but not friends. Brodagar gave a little nod, and then pointed towards the cell. "Do you want an appetizer before we chat?"

"Leave off trying to tempt me, priest," the captain replied firmly, though his eyes lingered on the humans. "We must talk. I understand that you hunt Attuls."

Brodagar gave another nod, surprised that the other had heard. The orders from Zendron had come just a month ago and only for Brodagar and Juress. Someone at the temple had a loose tongue. He doubted that it was one of the other Embraced Ones, for they all understood and accepted his leadership. Even the temple's High Brother was respectful of him. Most likely, some temple servant or guard had been compromised. This was a small matter, but still troubling nonetheless. That Nesron flaunted his inside source said that he did not care if the person was found out. That also troubled the priest. Did the officer find it that easy to recruit spies at the temples?

Brodagar realized the game of temptation would not work this night. He decided to continue their conversation inside, where others could not overhear, so he motioned for Nesron to follow him. He led the man through the maze of pens, past the nicer cages where the dreadhounds usually lounged. Those stood empty, since Brother Juress was not back yet. He paused at a door back into the temple, taking the time to wipe his boots on the mats set out there, and then led Nesron inside. They went to the modest quarters allocated to him as a visiting priest. Brodagar made no effort to light a lamp, for they were both Embraced and saw the dark room as if it were in full daylight. The priest went to the basin and poured water from the pitcher over his hands. After assiduously washing, he offered the remaining water to Nesron. The other gave a slight shake of his head and sat down on the room's only chair.

Brodagar chose to perch on the edge of his cot, careful not to mess up his own bedding. It was time to tease the captain and see how much he knew. "You noticed that the whole pack is out?"

Nesron gave a slight nod, but said nothing.

Brodagar gave him another tidbit. "Do you know what the hounds are sniffing for?"

The officer raised an eyebrow at the choice of topics. "I do not, though I can guess."

"They went to smell out Attuls. Apparently, three of the Enemy's lackeys have slipped into the empire."

"Why was I not informed about this intrusion? My men are merely human, but they are hardened warriors nonetheless."

The priest shrugged. "I do not know Zendron's motives. I can only hear and obey. However, his orders have changed and they now include you."

Nesron nodded, apparently having expected as much. "Three strangers spied out the town earlier today. The local sword-hackers told me that much when we rode in this evening. They also mentioned you going off in pursuit. Might the strangers be your Attuls?"

Brodagar touched his lips with his right index finger. He ignored the question. "You were patrolling to the south, as I recall, and on Zendron's orders. Did he command you to look for Attuls too?"

The captain grimaced, obviously perturbed. "You know all of my orders as well as I do, since they are coming through the temple's Listening Room. I heard nothing about Attuls. It was just a routine patrol."

Brodagar sensed no lying from Nesron, though it was not always easy to read a fellow Embraced One. Yet Nesron's ignorance seemed genuine. Although the governor could have sent a messenger from nearby Waybridge, Brodagar doubted that Lord Krev did. "Well, Zendron-Swerkrad has issued new orders for both of us. We are to follow these Attuls closely and make sure they go to Waybridge. If they try to veer off that path, we are to harass and frighten, but not to kill or even capture them. We leave tonight."

Nesron stood up. "I will need a few hours to gather my men and make sure they are provisioned."

The priest offered a wintery smile. "That is acceptable. Brother Juress should be back shortly, but the hounds will need to be fed before we take them out again." He also stood, straightening his black robes as he did. "I will bring the pack and all of the Embraced, except for the High Brother and the Listener. I do not think we will be returning to this town any time soon."

"I am glad of that. I tire of this backwater. Shall we meet at the north gate?" The captain had suddenly become almost bearable now that he had a new mission. Maybe his surliness came from boredom.

Brodagar pulled on a bell rope and it rang somewhere in the servants' section of the temple, calling for aid. "You should take a pair of sacrifices before you go, to strengthen yourself for the road."

There were no prisoners at the army barracks and the both knew it, so Nesron accepted. "Two will be fine."

"A servant will be here to help you select your victims." Brodagar moved to the door and held it open. "Oh, and the north gate will be fine. Let us meet there four hours from now."

Nesron said no more; he just gave a slight nod and walked out, the red bristles of his dragon helm brushing the top of the door's frame. The servant had just appeared, so the officer ordered him out to the pens. Only when Nesron turned a corner and was out of sight, did Brodagar close his door and return to his cot. Sitting down, he mulled over what to do now.

CHAPTER NINE
Chased through Fog

AFRAL

Afral rode through a grayness that clung to everything. Occasionally, a red glimmer came to the fog and distant thunder sounded. It was cold and damp, moisture beading on his thick cloak and dampening the horse's mane. The Dragon Shadow had washed over Regalis during the night and then had continued on, up the valley. Due to the elevation, the clouds came as a dark fog. Now the Border army retreated through this unnatural fog, with Afral and his parents joining them. He tried to recognize his surroundings, but failed. He knew they headed up the Valley Road towards Tor Randis, but everything seemed different in the mist. He pulled his cloak tighter against the chill, the last rider in amongst the cavalry.

His parents rode up ahead, with Uncle Win... He corrected his thought to prince, not uncle. The soldiers always called him "my prince", so Afral determined to do the same. The prince was not really his uncle anyway, just a good family friend. Ahead of his parents and the prince rode two banner men, one carrying the cavalry's flag and the other carrying the prince's personal banner. Behind Afral marched the standard-bearer for the infantry and the ranks of foot soldiers. The captain of the infantry had ridden his horse towards the rear and was now out of sight. The soldiers gave an occasional muffled comment, but no one spoke louder than a strong whisper.

Suddenly everything became darker up ahead. Afral realized that they had reached the edge of a forest, the dark trunks barely visible to either side. They kept going and soon were in the thick of the woods,

101

the trees pressing the soldiers into a tighter formation. The fog did not leave under the trees. Instead, it swirled and eddied through the branches.

A white light appeared up ahead, so one of his parents must have lifted a spirit sword as a guiding light. The fog seemed to pull away from the blade, enough so that he saw his father with arm raised. The light was comforting. Behind him, Afral heard one soldier complain about magic, while another claimed it was a miracle from the god Cha. He wanted to correct them both, to explain it was the power of El, but he did not feel it was his place to speak up. He was a mere boy pretending at soldiering, but he was well aware that those men were the true warriors.

At that moment, the forest filled with the deep-throated barks. Afral's horse reared as two dogs sprang onto the road in front of its hooves: two ink-black shadows moving swiftly. The dogs ignored his panicked horse and instead leaped up the road after the prince and his parents. Afral let out a shout of warning, trying to bring his horse under control and unsheathe his sword at the same time. The horse got its bit, however, and ran.

Afral stopped trying to draw his sword and instead pulled desperately at the reins with both hands.

The horse ran into the woods, and now tree branches painfully slapped him. He held on, even while his cloak snagged a branch and ripped off him. He barely kept mounted during the mad ride through the forest. Briefly, he saw other soldiers lurking among the trees, but they soon vanished in the darkness and fog.

He fought to regain control, as his horse broke free of the forest. It ran across a fallow field, finally slowing as it came upon a stream at the field's edge. The mare let go of the bit as it slowed, so Afral reined it in. He suddenly felt very alone in that blanket of unnatural fog. He listened for his companions, but heard only the gurgling stream. He looked every direction, uncertain where the road lay. He saw nothing but the gray fog on all sides.

Afral let his horse drink from the stream as he tried to decide what to do next. Where were his parents? He was not even sure which direction his horse had run. Uncertain, he just sat there on his mount. With his left hand, he wiped cheeks that were wet with more than dew. He considered pulling free his sword, but worried that the light might attract those horrible dogs. He felt so alone. Even El seemed far off.

Just then, a dog's howl broke the silence, sounding far too close.

He almost kicked his horse to a run, but restrained his hysteria. Charging blindly into the fog would do nothing except maybe send them tumbling into a ditch.

He finally decided to follow the stream's flow, hoping it would cross the Valley Road somewhere downstream. He forced himself to set a steady pace, though he wanted to gallop.

The dog had not been that close.

As he rode, he passed shadowy trees and mist-covered fields. One farmhouse appeared out of the fog, a black shadow in a gray world, but he did not stop. Maybe the holders worked at the far end of the fields, hidden in the fog, but the place seemed deserted. No lights glowed in the windows, no chickens scratched in the yard.

He suddenly wished he still had his cloak to keep the dampness off him, for it felt so cold and wet. So alone.

He patted his horse's neck and urged it on. Afral rode by an apple orchard, most of its flowers fallen to the ground in a snow of petals. Did the biting fog cause that? Beyond the open rows of the orchard, the stream entered a stand of trees. The woods looked foreboding, causing him to pull the horse to a stop. Should he try riding around the woods and risk losing the stream? It would be easier travel going across the adjoining field, though the farmer might not appreciate his churning up the freshly planted rows. But his greater fear was that if he left the stream's side he might never find it again and it was his only reference point.

He had just decided that he would have to go through the woods, when a loud howl came from nearby. He startled at the sound. The call came from somewhere beyond the farmhouse he had just passed. Afraid but trying not to panic, he urged his horse onward, into the dark woods.

A faint path appeared next to the stream, winding its way into the forest. Afral followed it, keeping his horse to a steady pace as he kept careful watch that he did not lose either path or nearby stream. It was a gloomy forest of aspen, sycamore, and cedar, the spreading branches overhead robbing what light there was in the dim day. The path was rough, for shallow roots dug under the dirt reaching for the water. There were still no sounds beyond the horse's passing. No bird call, no squirrel chatter. Afral kept looking over his shoulder, worried about the black dog out there in the fog.

He wondered how close it was, and then heard more baying that seemed much closer. Should he ride hard or find a favorable place to make a stand? What would his father or mother do if they were here? Of one thing he was certain, he would not be caught with his sword sheathed again. Afral pulled it free, the weapon's blade glowing brightly as he held it up in salute position. He knew he should be praying now and setting himself in one of the twelve opening positions for horsemen, but he could not get his fleeting thoughts under control. He tried focusing on beseeching El, but his mind kept dancing away.

The young Attul looked over his shoulder after more baying, but saw only trees and fog. He looked forward again, frightened and hoping this forest would soon thin. His horse became greatly agitated, sensing danger close by, and began to pick up the pace. He began to wonder if it was something closer that disturbed the horse. He gazed into the shadows to either side, but saw nothing. He was just beginning to look back again, when a sound jolted him.

The bushes on the right shook violently and suddenly a huge black dog sprang out, directly at him. The horse screamed and leaped sideways. He tried to bring his sword down on that side even while the horse's sudden movement nearly caused him to fall off in the other direction.

The dreadhound leaped so fast that Afral saw only a black blur coming at him. His being unbalanced saved him though, for he was leaning far to the left. The hound missed him, sinking his teeth into the horse's neck instead. The dog's massive shoulder did strike Afral's leg. The impact hurt, but nothing broke. Before he could think of anything else to do, he lost his mount. Afral quickly pulled his feet free of the stirrups as he felt his horse falter. The blood soaked horse collapsed, throwing Afral into the brush and sending the dog scurrying to get out of its way.

"El! Oh, my El! Help me!" shouted Afral in terror as he scrambled among the branches. He kept his sword pointed at the dog, though it was hard to see it in the shadowy gloom. The thrashing horse kicked against the dog, forcing it to leap aside instead of at the youth.

Choking back a sob, Afral rose to his feet just as the dog came at him again. Desperate, he swung wildly at the beast and it pulled back. The sword's glow flickered some as his faith faltered. His fear doubled at the thought of the sword extinguishing and he began praying more fervently under his breath.

Hound and youth stared at each other, while the horse went through its death throes. The dog's red eyes glowed, as it seemed to evaluate Afral. It especially seemed to focus on his spirit sword, but did not shrink from it. He also noticed that it had no desire to eat the readily available horseflesh. Yet the dog hesitated to attack him.

Afral forced his breathing to a calmer rate. He stepped free of the brush and took a proper stance, assuming the Spring Reed position, flexible and fluid. Maybe this beast would give up on him now that it saw his blade. Surely, El's power that shimmered through the metal would frighten off this evil beast. His heartbeat calmed as the dog continued to hold back. He began to hope that he would survive, that maybe this evil hound would rather flee than face a spirit sword.

That hope quickly shattered, though, as the dog sprang at him again. With a fury bordering close to hysteria, Afral defended himself. His blade hit home and the dog howled in pain and rage, the smell of charred fur filling the air. His sword had sliced a forepaw, making the dog favor the leg. Yet the hound did not give up. Repeatedly it came at him, pressing him hard in spite of its injury, but never closing for the kill. He felt like a mouse caught by a house cat, and wondered when the dreadhound would tire of this game and pounce on him. Then he heard the other hound, now much closer.

He realized he could no longer just defend himself; if he did not press the attack now, he would soon be facing two of the beasts. So he changed tactics, shifting stances from the Boulder against Storm to the aggressive stance called Angered Ram and attacked, pressing in on the dog. His sword left a trail of light as he swung repeatedly at the animal. When the hound attacked back, he wove the defensive attack known as the Tapestry of Thorns, which kept the dog's teeth and claws away while forcing it to pull back. Finally, his blade hit home; he struck the dog's side. It howled again in agony and tried to flee, but he kept after it. He struck the beast repeatedly to make sure it was dead. He then wiped his blade on the black fur, wiped tears from his face, and made ready to face the second dog that had to be very near.

Afral took a stand with a large sycamore at his back. He listened for the prowling hound, but heard only his own hard breathing. Straining, he listened harder and then made out the approach of a fast-ridden horse. He stood ready. The galloping drew nearer, but he could see nothing through the mist. Was the other dog coming with that rider or was it stalking him from another direction? He was careful to keep looking in all around.

Suddenly, a brown horse with a rider came into view: a Border soldier in gray uniform. Afral felt a surge of relief, but then it fell. Was he one of Uncle Win's men or one of the traitors in a standard uniform? Realizing that he could not know for certain, Afral prepared to defend himself. His eyes were on the approaching soldier while his lips called on El.

"Young Afral? Is that you?" asked the soldier.

"How do you know me?" he asked, his hope rising again.

"I am one of Prince Wintron's scouts. My name is Orgel." The man quickly took in the dead horse and dog. "Hurry, we do not have much time. Gather your things and climb on behind me. Those dogs usually run in packs."

Afral hesitated a moment longer, but then decided to trust the man. He sheathed his blade and obeyed the man's orders. He went over to his fallen steed, the smell of blood and guts filling his nose. He removed his blanket roll but could not get his saddlebags pulled out from under the carcass. Orgel had to dismount and do it for him.

"Leave the saddle and tack," ordered Orgel as he remounted. "That would be too much for us to carry."

Afral just stood there, dazed as he looked up at the scout on his horse. The soldier held out a hand, which he finally took. Orgel pulled the youth up behind him and then set off again, but at a slower pace now. Afral laid saddlebags and blanket between them, and then held tightly to both rider and his last belongings.

A horse carrying two men cannot go far nor fast, even when one rider is a youth not yet into his full stature. The scout of course knew this, and so looked for a way to out-trick any pursuers instead of trying to outrun them. Afral saw the wisdom of this and wished he had done so himself. Maybe then his horse would still be alive. He was not sure that human pursuers were near, but Orgel's caution told him that it was a possibility.

Orgel turned off the path, riding down the center of the stream in order to hide their scent. Once the gloomy woods surrounded them, Orgel sent his horse up the opposite bank and weaving through the trees. Darkness seemed to pool here, but Afral doubted it would fully conceal their passing, not with those huge dogs about. He only expected that it would delay them, but hopefully that would be enough. Afral just wanted to get back to safety.

He silently thanked El for Orgel. The danger was not over, but he could now hope to see his parents again. Afral did not look forward to confessing to his parents how he had failed to control his horse, but it would still be good to feel his mother's hug. He felt shame over his many errors today. How could he have ever thought himself a possible candidate for the King Varen's personal guard? A King's Man would never make such mistakes, let alone an Attul Prayer Warrior. His swordsmanship had been lacking and his prayers weak. He wondered if he would ever measure up, if he would ever master the skill of interweaving prayer and warfare.

Two hours later, they rode into a small hamlet. Orgel told Afral that he had once delivered a message to its mayor. "I do not remember the name of this place or the name of its balding, chubby leader, but at least I recognize it. That is something, young Afral. From here, it is not too far to the Valley Road. Let us just hope we can catch up with the army soon."

The village appeared empty, though everything seemed to be in order and properly latched. The community had been stripped of goods and locked up. Even Afral could see that. "Where is everyone?"

"Running for the peaks, I suspect. Prince Wintron sent messengers up the valley last night, telling all to flee. This village seems to be one of the sensible ones and actually listened."

Orgel let his horse slow to a walk, for the constant drizzle had turned the road muddy and of questionable footing. He pointed at an empty corral up ahead and the large building next to it. "On the far side of that inn is a way heading back towards the Valley Road. We will turn up that way and find our way back, however I do not know if we are still ahead of our army or fallen behind." After a pause, Orgel added, "I just hope we are still ahead of the Tlocanians."

* * *

Returning to the Valley Road was not as swift a journey as Afral expected. Soon it became apparent that Orgel's horse was tiring, so they both dismounted and walked for a time. They talked little, for the fog seemed to dampen all sounds. Instead, Afral strained to hear any noise of dogs or soldiers. The road ran between a bare orchard on the right and a recently tilled field on their left. He watched the furrow rows fade into the gray and wondered what lay hidden at the other end of the field.

He felt vulnerable.

They had been walking for almost an hour when a noise caused them to stop mid-stride. Both of them froze as they heard dogs barking just ahead of them. The horse almost yanked free of Orgel's hand as it pulled back. Afral saw nothing, but the dogs were not far away. They seemed to be fighting over something. Hurriedly, Orgel mounted the skittish horse, fighting it for control.

"Easy, Brownie." He patted his mount until it calmed, and then pulled Afral up behind him.

"Where to?" asked Afral in a whisper, as they heard the dogs growling and yipping, as if over their meal.

"Anywhere that they are not," answered Orgel, turning the horse to the right, away from the snarling beasts and avoiding the loose earth of the plowed field. He sent the horse through the orchard, heading south between rows of still-bare fruit trees.

Orgel did not stop or turn when the orchard ended at an overgrown wood. He sent the horse straight in, under the dripping trees.

GALDON

The captain did nothing to stop the young rider who rushed past. The youth could not have been important. Probably just some lordling's son, too haughty to march among the infantry. Instead, Galdon concentrated on the two priests who were but darker shadows next to him. He knew their names of course: the fat one was Brother Zaphrion and the thinner one was Brother Prekor. He knew their names and he knew their kind: pompous and cruel. The priests were linked to the dreadhounds, for they were Houndmasters. It seemed to be a particular ability of the priestly Embraced Ones.

Because the hounds distracted the two, Galdon allowed his feelings towards them to surface, giving the thoughts some time to wander through his mind. He never liked being around an Embraced One, since they often could overhear a man's thoughts, but at least the military Embraced were part of what he considered his extended family. Like the lord-general, he often respected their military prowess while fearing their demonic possession. Galdon had to admit to himself that it was fear.

The lord-general had sent them on this mission, allowing Galdon only two of his squads. He thought it a stifling limitation, but understood the need for stealth. They had ridden hard to get north of Regalis to await the Border army's retreat. The men had been given ordinary garb so that they could blend with any refugees if needed. However, there was a limit to the lord-general's wish for disguise. Galdon remained conspicuous in his dragon helm and the priests still flaunted their black robes, for the empire would never allow its leaders to hide their rank.

He had taken his best archers along and, once they had slipped past Regalis, he had sent them ahead in pairs to do what they could to harass those fleeing northward. That was the easiest of the three duties the general had given him.

Galdon had also brought along the scouts from all three squads, for he knew he would need them even with a full pack of dreadhounds. It was the scouts who found this excellent place to ambush the leaders. And yet, Galdon had to let the priests direct the actual ambush. It promised to be an excellent location for the lithe dogs.

He kept his men at the ready, waiting for the priests to finish their business. It was what the priests had ordered, for they wanted their dogs to get the glory of bringing down the prince and flushing out the Attuls. He obeyed their order not to interfere, but he expected that he and his men would have to assist soon enough.

"They protect the prince," complained the fat priest, breaking his link with the beasts. He sidled his horse closer to Galdon. "There are two Attuls on the road and they have killed four dogs already."

"Well, can you use your magic to do something?" His impatience showed, though he always tried to hide such feelings near a dragon priest. "We must complete our task, holy brother."

In the darkness, the priest's eyes shown red again, just like one of the possessed dogs. The similarity gave Galdon pause, realizing he was baiting a powerful man. He carefully spoke on. "What can I do to help? Do you want the men to attack now?"

"We will withdraw for now," replied the priest. "There is still one more Attul out there somewhere. We sensed him briefly, but he seems to have fled."

"Withdraw? What will I report to my lord? Failure will mean my death, holy brother. The general bides no failures and I will not disappoint him."

"Calm yourself, soldier," rebuked Brother Zaphrion. "We only regroup. The run was even harder on the dogs than it was on the horses, making them too exhausted to stand against such power. Know this, officer: I am determined to see an Attul captured. The orders come from someone far higher than the lord-general. The Dragon Lord, the Emperor Silossiak, demands it."

"The emperor is more concerned about these walking legends than he is about the heir to this realm?" asked Galdon, surprised at the other's openness.

"Our Great Master does not deem the heir of this mountaintop hovel worthy of his thoughts. The Border Realm already rests in our hands courtesy of the princeling's cousins. No, his thoughts are on the Attuls and the false stories that swirl around these people."

He fleetingly wondered if the stories might instead contain a nugget of truth about powers as great as any dragon priest, but then he carefully refocused his thoughts on safer topics. He wondered where the third Attul might be and how to capture one of these enemy warriors alive. "So we are to withdraw for now?" asked Galdon, verifying the other's order.

The fat priest just nodded, his thoughts returning to the dreadhounds.

Galdon obeyed, ordering his group away from the Border troops, making certain to avoid the larger Border army and its outriders. The two priests rode nearby. Each had a soldier as escort to lead his mount, for when they linked to the dreadhounds they became oblivious towards their surroundings. The pack must have been close, for several of the mounts became skittish. He turned to the thinner priest, tired of the other's condescension. "Could you send the hounds ahead of us, holy brother? I do not want any horse bolting." He had to repeat the question three times before the other heard.

The hooded man's nod was barely noticeable in the forest's murk. After a moment of silence, he responded. "I have sent them off to hunt, since they did not have a chance to feast on the soldiers they killed."

"Thank you, holy brother. It will mean fewer peasants for us to worry about." Dreadhounds preferred eating human flesh.

The captain led his forty-man party away from the main road, towards the wide valley's wall. He called a stop at an isolated farm that his scouts had found to be deserted. The two priests still lingered in their trances, so he had his men help them from the saddle and into the house, settling them in stuffed chairs. He ordered the men to water the horses and see to their own needs while he went inside to wait on the demon lovers to finish their communing with dogs.

* * *

It had been a few hours of just staring out the open door at fog-shrouded fields when Galdon finally heard from the dragon priests again.

"We have found the other Attul."

The words from the fat priest brought Galdon out of his personal musings. "Where?"

"Two dogs track him on a path, north of us. We will keep the hounds from killing him, though they hunger for his flesh. Take us there."

The captain frowned. That would take him away from the prince he was to kill. "But we have two of them much closer. Why cannot the two of you take one of them while I kill the Border prince? That way, we can both accomplish our tasks."

"We go after the lone Attul," stated the thinner priest, also returning from his mind link to the dogs. "He is isolated and young, so we should be able to capture him alive."

Galdon became truly worried. He had been ordered to kill the prince in addition to capturing an Attul. A half-finished mission was still a failure. "But you have your power and the dreadhounds. Surely you can also corner one of those with the prince, and then I will be able to..."

"Enough!" The fat priest's voice came out in a far deeper tone. The demon in him was talking. He held up his right hand and red flames danced there. "Obey, soldier, or someone else will command these men."

Galdon swallowed, realizing that the demon now dominated. He knew enough about Embraced Ones to avoid angering them when their other side was in control.

"I hear and obey," he said with fervency. He would have groveled on the ground, but that was not permitted of the military. He did give a deep bow. An angered Embraced One often killed merely out of spite. Still bowed, he quickly replied, "We will head after this lone Attul immediately."

His life was spared.

Galdon gave the orders for his men to reassemble and mount up. He had no choice now. He had to send whole troop after this isolated Attul. He sent four scouts off at a gallop, with orders to track but not kill. He then assigned two men to guide the priests' mounts, since they were again falling into a Houndmaster's trance. That done, he set the whole troop on a fast gait after this lone rider. He was determined to have at least one success. He would capture an Attul for his lord.

* * *

Galdon and the men under his command made good time, staying ahead of the Border soldiers. He led his troops back to the main road, trusting that the priests would let him know when to turn off, for these Embraced Ones had a keen sense of direction. They cantered past

Eric Lorenzen

refugees with wagons and handcarts and pack mules. Most of the locals scattered off the road when they heard the approaching horses, but some just kept trudging along, heads down, unaware of their danger. More than once, his men were forced to kick some fool to prevent a trampling or stab some mule before it collided with his troops. It frustrated him, but this was still the quickest route to their goal. The Border army would soon know that Tlocanians were somewhere ahead of them, with so many witnesses of their passing. Galdon wondered if his hunters would now become the hunted.

The two priests were united in thought with the dreadhounds, keeping a watch on the lone Attul. At one time Brother Prekor yanked his head back with a curse. Apparently, his hound he had just been killed. However, soon he fell into a trance again, linking with some other dog in the pack. From experience, Galdon knew that this was one of his few safe moments, when he could let his thoughts be free. The priests and their demon partners were distracted, so they would not be able to catch any snatches of his ideas or emotions. He detested how they could grab his thoughts, but he had learned to discipline his mind and keep focused on safe ideas and emotions. That thought brought on more memories.

For twenty years, Galdon had served in Tlocania's army. It was his only family, for his parents had died when he was just fifteen. He had been homeless, hungry, and alone. In desperation, he had joined the army to keep from starving. The army had taken in the youth, fed him, and taught him his trade: soldiering. He served Tlocania, proud to wear its uniform. He rose to the rank of sergeant, and enjoyed his simple life. But then the Dragon Lord swept in.

At first, all had celebrated the victories of the newcomer, who served Tlocania's king so successfully. However, even then the man had been mysterious, titling himself General Dragon. Most others were quite comfortable with the stranger because he brought glory to Tlocania and that was all the mattered to them. Maybe the king was himself giddy with the victories, for he certainly did nothing to rein in General Dragon's power.

Galdon's homeland had always been strong among the Seven Kingdoms of Cleargorn, but never before had it possessed more than one other land. Then General Dragon conquered three of the seven. The captain remembered the many campaigns, the booty, and the celebrations when his battalion returned home. He also remembered his first encounters with Embraced Ones, their cruelty and might.

112

Quickly, he learned to avoid those priests and officers who were demon possessed. They saw too much; they somehow could catch glimpses of a person's feelings and plans. These people also had strange powers, gaining magic from their demons.

Galdon continued serving faithfully, though he guarded his thoughts around some of those in his army family. When General Dragon returned from that third conquering, however, the man turned on the king. Galdon had still been in the field, along with most of those not in the demon-led squads. He learned of the betrayal when it was already history, and never had the opportunity to stand up for his king. Being practical, he accepted this new reality, as General Dragon now became the Dragon Lord and then Emperor. Galdon learned how to control his thoughts in a way that would help his career yet would keep him from becoming a candidate for possession. He kept his thoughts on his love of the army and on his greed. As needed, he overemphasized the later, gaining a reputation as being loyal but avarice-filled. His scheme worked, gaining him minor promotions while remaining free of demon control.

For the last five years, Galdon had been in the field constantly. The army conquered the remaining Seven Kingdoms and then marched on. They took the Forest Hills, destroying the Ejoti stronghold at Halfhill. Galdon also joined the army's march up the Grandgorn Valley, taking the Riverrealm and then all of its towns and villages until they came upon Rhendora. There the generals called them to a halt, deciding for some reason not to crush that land yet. He spent two seasons on that stalled front until his battalion, under Lord-General Hraf, came west to start this new campaign.

Galdon remained loyal to the army, though it was a loyalty to Tlocania and not to Emperor Silossiak. He obeyed orders, led his men well, and gathered enough loot to maintain his reputation. However, he also remembered what it had been like before the coming of the Embraced Ones. When he had moments like these, when the often-present demons could not listen in, he recalled his younger years. He longed for a return of the olden days, when a simple man ruled as his king and Tlocania was a strong yet fair land. When the sun sparkled on Lake Tlocan and beautiful sunsets painted the skies over the Forest Hills. He longed for the days before demons and endless overcast.

Galdon had considered deserting and fleeing to some distant place beyond the reach of the depressing Dragon Shadow. Yet he doubted any part of Na Ciria would be clear in five years. He had heard rumors of an even bigger cloud forming in the far south. Were there other leaders like the Emperor Silossiak and his demon lords or was his reach even longer than Galdon knew? Whichever the answer, he once again decided that this was not something he could outrun.

So Galdon again decided to keep his career as a loyal Tlocanian soldier, doing his best for his men, for his country, and for himself. Today that meant leading forty men behind enemy lines while accompanying two dragon priests and their dreadhounds. He had succeeded in getting them past Regalis without notice and had then sent a third of his men, all decent archers, to scatter and do their best to disrupt the pending Border retreat. Lord Hraf had ordered him to do so and Galdon obeyed, though he disliked dividing his troop. At least that part of the general's orders would be accomplished.

He looked over at the two priests and felt anger. These two Embraced Ones grated on him. He understood some of the attraction of being demon-possessed: the strength, the hidden knowledge, the magical power. Nevertheless, such things were unnatural.

The captain had once considered fighting against the corruption that had polluted his beloved army, but no mere man could stand against a horde of demons. If there had been a true resistance to join... but there was none. And yet... Galdon was very curious about the demons' obsession with Attuls. Could there be a resistance after all? He grimaced and shoved those musings away. Even idle thoughts were too dangerous with Embraced Ones nearby, no matter that these two seemed focused on their distant dogs. Instead, Galdon forced his thoughts on the looting of Regalis and what kinds of rustic treasures might be had.

Within minutes, his caution proved him wise, for the fat priest suddenly spoke up. "Take the next side road."

Galdon left his musings of gold, and focused on the dragon priest. "Is he near?"

"We should have our Attul prisoner very soon." Brother Zaphrion's red eyes faded into the shadow of his robe's deep hood as his link to the dreadhound severed. "Once we have the Attul captured, we can pursue that petty prince..."

The thin priest, Prekor, interrupted. "Zaphrion, reunite with your beast quickly! The dogs smell fresh human blood and I am cannot control all three."

Galdon watched the priests struggle to regain control. He could tell it was not going well, for they muttered and cursed. Apparently, one of

Galdon's own men had fouled their plans inadvertently. He had sent out the archers to harass the retreating Borderfolk, and now one of their victims lay on the same road that this Attul was on, sending the dreadhounds into a blood lust.

With a curse, Galdon set his squad to a trot. Their net was unraveling quickly and he did not want to lose this Attul. He made sure two soldiers led the priests' mounts, for their thoughts were off with the dreadhounds. The road they followed was a smaller one that wandered beside fields and orchards. They came across refugees, all heading towards the main road. The people scattered in fear when they saw the strangers, but Galdon had no time to bother with these civilians.

Up ahead, he saw two other corpses, the black-fletched arrows still protruding from them, but they were not the ones the dogs were fighting over. The road seemed to never end, as Galdon tried to catch up with the dreadhounds and their common prey.

Finally, they came upon a shredded corpse where two dogs still feasted. A third hound stood to one side watching the other two with red-glowing eyes. The beast's blood-smeared muzzle gave testimony that it too had eaten before one of the priests restrained it.

The captain turned on the dragon priests. "Is that all that remains of the Attul? Have your hounds devoured him?"

Prekor turned his head toward him. His response was cold. "That is not the Attul. He has fled off the road with his soldier escort. They are riding double, though, so we may still be able to overtake them."

Galdon restrained another curse, but his anger showed. He ordered his men to ride past the chewed corpse and sent them to look for the Attul's trail. Soon they found where a horse had left the road. He led his men through an orchard and to the edge of a dark wood. With a shake of his head, he realized they would have a hard time following the Attul and his companion through the murk. Galdon signaled for two scouts to start the hard work of tracing their route. Now would be a good time for a dreadhound's keen sense of smell. He looked to the priests, but they were of no help. The two still wrestled with the minds of the dreadhounds.

AFRAL

Orgel led them over a stream and up to a low ridgeline. In the fog, Afral could not see any landmarks, but at least the undergrowth was less up here. They followed the ridge eastward, until they found an overgrown path crossing their way.

Afral looked over the lanky scout's shoulder. "Which way do we take, sir? I am all turned around and have no idea of our direction."

"North is that way," said Orgel without hesitation, pointing to the left. "If the way does not twist too much, it should take us back to the road we fled. I can only hope that it will intersect far from where we turned off. Better still, if it turns eastward it may take us directly to the Valley Road. To our right there may be another crossroad, or it might end at some woodsmen camp or hermit shack. We cannot risk a dead end, so it is to the left we go."

They rode onward, Orgel deciding that speed was more important than sparing his mount, for they began to hear the hounds braying again, somewhere off in the woods below them. The faint route meandered quite a bit and then turned eastward, just as Orgel had hoped. Soon thereafter, they came out on the Valley Road. The way had been heavily traveled recently, with so many refugees fleeing towards Tor Randis, but the scout found no sign that the army had already passed. Orgel turned south, telling Afral that he hoped to find the army's outriders soon.

His wish was fulfilled. Within two hours, they were escorted into the prince's presence. Afral's mother enthusiastically welcomed him back, practically pulling him off Orgel's horse so that she could embrace him. For once, he had no qualms about his mother's hugs. His father was also there, slapping him on the back enthusiastically. Afral cared nothing about how it appeared to the soldiers. He cried in relief.

CHAPTER TEN
Mountain Climb

AFRAL

"He has cost us a horse and wasted hours," stated Gordrew. "We cannot spare another mount and we certainly cannot have him clinging behind either of you. It would be too much of an encumbrance."

Afral felt too embarrassed to protest, but he hoped his parents would speak up for him. He stayed at the edge of the firelight, wanting to stay near his family and yet knowing that he did not belong among the leaders who encircled the crackling wood. As usual, he did not quite fit in. It made him feel even more alone.

He saw his father touch his mother's elbow to forestall her rebuttal, and maybe that was best since his mother could overwhelm with her intensity. His father spoke calmly, "You are right, councilor. My son will have to walk in the infantry ranks."

Afral looked at his father with sadness, realizing the rightness of his decision. He was not about to argue, for he knew he deserved nothing better.

His father turned to the crown prince. He spoke to him formally, well aware that others listened. "Prince Wintron, may my son join the front ranks? I know he does not have the right, but it would relieve his mother's fears to have him within sight."

Wintron raised an eyebrow, but did not question Rolen's reasoning. "Of course, for the sake of a mother's worry. Captain Gish, have the boy march next to the standard bearer when we set out in the morning." Gish led the infantry, for there was no higher officer left.

Afral decided that he had better not linger, not where he was unwanted. With a fallen countenance, he made his way to the family tent and climbed under his cold blanket in a cold tent.

* * *

That was how Afral ended up on foot, walking next to the standard-bearer who carried a limp flag. He kept his now-returned cloak pulled tight against the chill, thankful for its return but embarrassed that he lost it in the first place. His mother had already mended the tear where the tree limb had snagged it off his shoulders. His father took his saddlebags and blanket, relieving him of that burden, though his heart was still heavy.

The retreating army finally came to the Valley Road's end, where the Borderheart Valley split at the foot of a huge stone monolith. Afral had seen Old Man's Face on sunnier days, but now it lay hidden above the fog. The granite face had seemed eerie back then, but now he would be happy to see it again. The Cleargorn began at the foot of the huge rock face, where two flows converged: the Clear River and the Running River.

A small army post sat near the confluence. It served as a place for messengers to switch mounts before taking the steep road up to the Highlands. He saw Councilor Gordrew, the cavalry captain, and scout Harl go into the building.

"I would guess that they are ordering the post abandoned," said Paon, the infantry's standard-bearer. The man had occasionally shared his observations with him while they marched. Afral felt grateful that the soldier did not disdain him for his bumbling. "I also think Harl is getting a new mount so that he can charge ahead. They have to find out if old General Fors is still on our side. I do not envy Harl his ride. What is he to do? Knock on the gates and ask the general if he is a traitor like his sons?"

Afral did not know what to say, so he just nodded.

Beyond the rider post, a new road began the climb up to the Highlands. It followed the canyon to the right of Old Man's Face, the same canyon that the Clear River came roaring down. The retreating Border army started the steep climb on a road the kept well above the churning waters to avoid the boulder-strewn riverbed.

Harl went galloping past. Following him, extra scouts were sent out, for the rugged terrain offered many places for ambush.

* * *

After hours of climbing the road with its endless number of switchbacks, all of them felt fatigue. Afral realized this, even while he wished they would show him some mercy. Many of the soldiers around him had been on the move for almost a week now, having fled the boundary forts, Glenford, Regalis, and now retreating again. He knew this, but still longed to take a break, feeling that they were demanding too much of him. His feet and calves hurt, for the road was steep.

He took a moment to look back down the canyon and saw a mounted Councilor Gordrew making his way past the foot soldiers further down the canyon. Afral stumbled on some rock and quickly brought his eyes back on the road in front of him. Once more, he rued how his stupidity and awkward swordsmanship had cost him a good horse.

The youth kept his eyes on the rough road, determined not to be embarrassed more by tripping or worse. The dirt way had many loose rocks that seemed to cluster directly in his path. To either side of the road stood tall pines and numerous boulders. The steep slope on the left dropped off into the fog, and occasionally he heard the roaring river below. He stepped to one side to avoid horse droppings, another hazard of a foot soldier, and then quickly stepped back into line.

He noticed that Paon no longer bantered. It comforted Afral a little to know that others also suffered, but then he felt chagrin at his mean thoughts. Attempting to make amends, he offered to carry the infantry banner for him. "Sergeant Paon, do you want me to carry the standard for a while?"

The other gave Afral a startled look, and then smiled. "Thanks for the offer, but no. I have a few hundred behind me who are itching for the honor, should I fail at my role. A standard-bearer must always be up to the task, for the battalion's honor is in his hands. I can show no weakness, for the men look to the flag for direction. I need it in hand, ready to signal charge or retreat, as the captain orders. Thank you again for thinking of me, but do you understand why I must refuse?"

Afral nodded, though embarrassed at his own ignorance. He was learning that there was much more to soldiering than just swinging a sword.

A short time later, he heard Councilor Gordrew behind him, calling out "make way" so that he could pass up the road. Afral and Paon stepped aside to let the advisor ride by. As Gordrew passed, Afral looked back down the line, seeing soldiers return to formation. Captain Gish, who rode right behind Paon, had pulled his horse to the edge of the way. He nodded for Paon to return to their previous pace, so the standard-bearer stepped back onto the middle of the road and held the banner high. The infantry kept to its disciplined march. The captain brought his horse in right behind Paon and Afral, just ahead of the first rank of the infantry.

They had continued their climb for a few more switchbacks, when Paon spoke up. "The fog thins."

He gave Paon a quizzical look, but then noticed that he could indeed see further. The road climbed up a ridge and then started another round of switchbacks, crossing the same slope again and again. Afral looked up and spotted his parents and the prince on the roadway above. He also saw that Lord Gordrew was about halfway through the cavalry's ranks as he made his way back to the prince.

The sight of his parents gave him a moment of comfort, but then the standard-bearer of the cavalry fell from his mount, his banner rescued by a quick-thinking horseman. The mounts milled about as men shouted, some pointing further up the slope.

"What is happening?" asked Afral.

"We are under attack," responded Paon, looking to his captain for direction.

"Keep the men on an orderly march, Paon," he ordered. "They need to keep moving, but I do not want them choking the road up ahead. I will take a small force forward." He turned in the saddle and motioned to the nearest squad leader. "Sergeant Fioler, set your men to a force run and follow me!"

The captain trotted his horse past, with a squad of foot soldiers running behind him.

By the time Afral and Paon came upon the site of the attack, things were calm. Afral was near enough to hear the report the captain received.

"...two archers, but they slipped away. The prince expects more attacks before we reach the shelter of Tor Randis. All are to be extra attentive now that we are above the fog and more exposed. Prince Wintron asks for a man to stand watch over the fallen bearer. He is to be placed in the last wagon."

The captain thanked the messenger, who rode back up. The captain then ordered Sergeant Fioler to pick one soldier for the death duty, adding that the soldier should stay back with the wagons for the remainder of this trip.

The army marched onward. Afral could not help but stare at the fallen standard-bearer, lying at the side of the road and covered by his cloak. The soldier picked by Sergeant Fioler stood in stiff respect next to the corpse, making sure no one accidentally disturbed the dead.

* * *

Soon all of the Border army was above the fog, finding it to be a beautiful, clear evening. The sun had sunk low enough that the canyon already lay in the shadows of the high mountains around it. The peaks still shone in the sunlight, though, and beyond them a deep blue sky spanned the horizon.

As he climbed the road, Afral kept scanning the slopes around them. He saw no movement, except for a herd of mountain sheep leaping from rock to rock. Though he saw no threat, he still worried, for there were so many places where the enemy could be hiding. This steep canyon was a jumble of boulders, trees, crevices, and shadows.

As Afral stared up the slope again, he heard a faint horn echo off the rocks. The sound seemed to have originated from below them, but he was not certain due to the echoes. He was surprised when Paon unfastened a horn from his belt and gave a quick return call.

"What do they say?" he asked, unable to restrain his curiosity.

Paon ignored him, his focus completely on the captain.

"Sound warning to the cavalry ahead of us," ordered Captain Gish, "and then jump onto the rear of my horse, Paon. I need you at my side and I cannot wait for you to run after me. It seems that the Tlocanians have caught up with us." Gish spared a moment for Afral. "Stay up here, youngster. You can join Sergeant Fioler's ranks."

GALDON

Galdon ran his blade through another Border soldier, frustrated that neither the prince nor the Attuls had come back to defend their rear. Doing his job, he caused as much grief for the enemy as possible, but he knew his mission was a failure. He had too few men to take on a full battalion, even one so worn and battered, so there was no way that he could fight his way through to reach either the prince or the Attuls.

Galdon had never failed Lord Kelordok like this and he expected it would lead to his demotion or maybe even execution. The general did not tolerate incompetence.

Leaving off the slaughter, Galdon rode back down to where the two priests huddled in the shadows, where the fog still whirled. Over the years, he had seen this habit from most Embraced Ones, a preference for darkness. "What of the dogs, holy brothers?"

The fatter one responded. "It grows more difficult in this narrow canyon. We have already lost one to the bloodlust. It killed five men, only to be quickly slaughtered."

Galdon shook his head. "Have you any other plan?"

Brother Prekor raised his arms and pulled back his sleeves to reveal a thick black bracelet on each wrist. "Do you know what these signify?"

He dropped his caution and admitted his knowledge with a nod. The priests were shape shifters, were-dogs. "But two more hounds will not help here. The prince and his Attul bodyguards are effectively beyond our reach, unless we can butcher our way through their army and I have not the manpower to accomplish that."

"The Attuls must be taken, so we will have to find another way," said the thin priest as he dropped off his horse. The fat Zaphrion also dismounted.

"What are your plans, holy brothers?"

"There are other ways up to the Border Highlands, paths too steep for an army but manageable for us. We will take the pack beyond this fortress and lure the enemy into our hands," stated the thin Prekor. "Now take these reins, captain. You know how skittish horses are around dreadhounds."

"And turn the other way," ordered Zaphrion. "The holy transformation is not for your callous eyes."

Galdon may have felt daring in the face of his sure death, but he would rather be executed tomorrow by Lord Kelordok than by dragon priests today, so he heeded their demands. He rode his horse away from the priests, leading the other two mounts. Galdon felt a sudden chill over his back and all three horses whinnied concern. Turning back, he briefly saw two huge dreadhounds slinking off through the forest. Soon he heard the whole pack baying as it headed back down the canyon to the safety of the Dragon Shadow.

Out of habit, he went back to retrieve the priests' robes, deciding that the cloth might not bring as much as he had first thought since both looked rather soiled. He stuffed the robes into his saddlebags nonetheless. The priests were not part of his army family, so he had no qualms in turning a profit from their leavings. He found no coins or jewelry among their abandoned clothes or in their saddlebags, but then he knew that a were-dog usually wore a black collar with a pouch attached. He did find religious instruments, which he tossed down the hillside. Such items brought no buyer, not when the people feared the dragon priests so much. He did find a few trinkets that might bring him extra coin and added those items to his own belongings. It was a shame that the horses were army-issued, for they would have brought good money.

Galdon rode up the trail to where his remaining troopers waited. He handed the extra reins to a soldier, not bothering to explain where the priests had gone. If the men thought he had killed the two, so much the better for his reputation.

"We are done here. We ride back to Regalis. One other thing men, no more killing of the civilians that we will be passing. Before, their death was for our use, disheartening the enemy and slowing their progress, but now I want as many refugees as possible to flee up there. Let them drain their resources trying to feed these lemmings."

He led the way back, expecting this to be his last command, if not his last ride. Lord Hraf Kelordok demanded success from his officers. Galdon respected that, though it would mean his commission for this utter failure.

Eric Lorenzen

CHAPTER ELEVEN
Tor Randis

WINTRON

Just as he heard the horn cry announcing an attack at the rear, Wintron felt an arrow whistle past. Yanking furiously at his reins, he shouted warning. Another arrow flew by, and then Rolen was between him and the attackers, his shining sword tracing a defensive pattern in the air that left a light trail. Wintron doubted that any blade could stop an arrow, but he said nothing.

The front ranks of the cavalry charged up the road, looking for the archers, while Wintron's personal guards escorted him to the shelter of a thick stand of young pines. Captain Bilshor was like that. He would not let the prince do anything stupidly heroic like charge after the attackers himself. The prince allowed the mothering, for he understood Bilshor's reasoning.

Two cavalrymen died in their rush up the road, but the rest succeeded in killing one of the archers in return. The dead man wore only simple clothes, with nothing to identify his allegiance. He may have been a Tlocanian or one of Mordel's mercenaries and that would be bad enough. However, he might as easily have come down from Tor Randis. Wintron still worried that his uncle might be an ally of his two murderous sons. He worried, but did not say anything, for he was determined to give the men hope that a secure refuge awaited them at the top of this long climb. If Tor Randis' doors stayed shut to them, then they would be slaughtered in this canyon, pressed against its walls by the following Tlocanians. Yet Tor Randis remained Wintron's only hope. He just prayed to all the gods he knew that Duke Fors would have more loyalty toward his dead brother, King Varen, than to his eldest sons, Mordel and Drass.

Finally, Bilshor let the prince leave his pine shelter. More archers were still out there, but they seemed to have fled far ahead. Scout Orgel did locate four horses though, all with Tlocanian markings, so they knew three more assassins still lurked somewhere. Orgel also found a band of refugees that the archers had attacked further up the road. Wintron insisted on riding ahead to see to their needs, taking along his personal guard and a medic. Bilshor relented in his protests when they heard a horn call from the rear announcing the ceasing of that attack. Even so, the head of his personal guard asked Rolen and Tolara to join them as extra protection.

Up ahead, he found a group of five families huddled over their injured, the children sobbing and the parents looking grim. Apparently, the archers had taken their time and had even retrieved some of their arrows before the men in the party chased them off with pitchforks and rusty blades. Tolara and the medic hurried to offer what aid they could.

Wintron shook his head at the wanton killing. He had already seen too much of it, people killed just to terrify others. Noticing that the archers had also killed the party's draft horse, he gave orders that one of the captured horses be given to them as replacement. The new horse would not be able to pull the overfull wagon as easily, but if they sacrificed some of their heavier belongings, they would still be able to make it up the canyon.

When the cavalry ranks finally caught up Wintron's party, he found that Lord Gordrew had returned. "Councilor! At last! I feared you might have been caught in that attack to our rear."

"No, my prince, though they practically trimmed my horse's tail as I fled up the road."

"Well, was the time you spent lingering at the feet of Old Man worth it? Did you learn anything from the curmudgeonly postmaster?"

"Five messages came through the Old Man post on their way to your uncle: three from your cousin Mordel, one from you, and the last one from one of Mordel' advisors. They were all sealed, so the postmaster knows nothing of their contents."

Wintron frowned upon hearing that his murderous cousin had sent so many letters to his uncle. The messengers must have ridden right past Wintron's men and not been challenged, probably wearing standard Border uniforms of gray instead of Halen-Dabe colors. "Did any messages from my uncle come down from the Highlands?"

"None that the postmaster knew of, but it is easier to avoid changing mounts when heading downhill." Gordrew looked concerned. Wintron could guess that his advice would be full of warnings about what might be up ahead.

He turned to the other of his father's old advisors. "Rolen, what do you advise?"

The Attul had sheathed his blazing sword, but he looked ready for battle nonetheless. "We do not have much choice, my prince. We either shelter among the rocks in this treacherous canyon or we press on to Tor Randis and hope for a warm welcome."

"Does your god offer any guidance on this matter?"

Rolen smiled. "El does offer us direction, but not as a road scout. You should know that, my prince, for you studied at the Elhall during your youth."

The prince smiled back. "Indeed, I remember those times fondly. So then, I must depend on my own wits and not on divine guidance. That settles it. We will go on to Tor Randis. Duke Fors did not write back to his murderous son as far as we know, so I can only assume that he is still loyal to the realm. I think my uncle is too crafty to side with the Tlocanians, even if he has some affinity with their cause. He is a man who loves the Border Realm in his own way, even though he and my father had their disagreements."

"Suddenly you trust him?" asked Gordrew.

"I did not say that. He will let us in because he needs my men. The Tlocanians would as quickly fight him as they have fought me. Mordel's actions have forced his father to our side, whether the Old Fox wants to be there or not. Duke Fors can no longer hide up on the Highlands and stay aloof of the realm's affairs. He fled court over a decade ago, but now the royal court is coming to him. It will be from Tor Randis that we will plan our retaliation and I will expect the realm's last general to be fully involved in planning his son's fall."

* * *

The retreating Border army continued its climb up the canyon towards Tor Randis. Although the great fortress was still out of sight, when Wintron looked behind him he did catch a glimpse of the Old Man monolith, only the top of its head peeking out of a sea of dark fog. The day being almost done, the last of the sunlight gave a red stain on the highest peaks and an orange glow on the western horizon. Already, a few stars twinkled overhead in a sky starting to turn from blue to black.

A coyote began to howl somewhere in the canyon and at first Wintron imagined more dreadhounds, but then recognized the difference. It almost seemed peaceful up here. Almost.

"Old Man seems to be up to his eyes in a cloud soup," said Tolara, noticing where the prince looked. A brief flash of red lit the clouds from underneath. "It is good to be out of that unnatural brew."

"Yes it is," agreed Wintron.

"Scout down!" came a yell from the outriders. Bilshor and his men became even more alert. Everyone scanned the slope above the trail, but so much was already concealed in evening's shadow.

His sense of peace shredded. He hoped the fallen scout was neither Harl nor Orgel. He valued all of his men, but he knew and liked those two especially. "Bilshor, have someone find out which scout died."

The killed man was Bevselt, a quiet man with a poor complexion. A good man who had no family from what the prince could recall. Another life for which the Halen-Dabe brothers would be held accountable.

* * *

They were attacked twice more that evening. One archer became overbold and died of a Border arrow, but the other two vanished into the growing night.

They passed more refugees as they neared the top of the canyon, most of them already camping for the night on the side of the road. Wintron urged each group to keep moving, warning them that Tlocanians could be stalking right behind the army, but he did not force them to join the army's tail. Their lives were their own responsibility.

* * *

Crown Prince Wintron Dabe and his men finally reached the first of Tor Randis' defenses: a lone tower that guarded a gap in a narrow ridge. They encountered no opposition from Duke Fors' men. Instead, they received a personal greeting, when the post's lieutenant rode out. The man wore the usual Border gray and not the blue-and-black of Duke Fors' personal guard. With him came Harl, their missing scout. Wintron signaled for the scout to fall into line. He did as bidden, but first handed the prince a sealed message. Wintron accepted it without comment, but did not open it. He saw the Halen-Dabe seal and that was enough.

"Welcome, Prince Wintron." The officer gave a bow, but he did not come down from his horse. "I am Lieutenant Fontar."

"Fontar, why was Scout Harl delayed in his return to me?"

"That I do not know, my prince." The man now sat straight and stiff in the saddle. "I would think that General Fors is the one to question. The scout came to my post an hour ago with orders to wait there for you."

"How many men are under your command, lieutenant?"

"Twenty-four men," came the terse reply.

"How many horses?"

"We have six mounts. Is there something that displeases you, my prince?"

He gave him a brief smile that did not touch his eyes. "I only want to make sure you have enough men." He turned to Harl. "Scout, ride back for Captain Gish."

Hurl did so quickly, while the others waited in silence. Wintron made no other attempt to relieve the officer's unease. The prince dropped from the saddle and spent some time examining his horse's legs and shoes. As Harl returned with the infantry captain, Wintron climbed back into the saddle. He looked again at Fontar.

"Fontar, do you have enough room to double your command?"

"My prince? I do not think General Fors will send me so many, though he might want to. I have requested more troops in anticipation of the coming trouble, but there are none to spare. I will gladly take any men sent my way."

"You did not answer my question, lieutenant."

The officer grimaced. "The post can handle three times its current number, though we will need more supplies."

Wintron nodded. "Captain Gish, choose a squad with a seasoned sergeant to assign to Lieutenant Fontar's command. Have your chosen sergeant report to me now."

While the captain called for one of his squad leaders, the prince turned to Fontar. "Lieutenant, I will see about getting you even more troops. I will especially want more cavalry and scouts out here. The Tlocanians were pestering our rear line, but seem to have pulled back for now. Expect that to change soon, especially if that evil fog creeps up here. If you see that fog approaching, send warning to the fortress immediately."

A sergeant came running up, a large man with recent scars. Behind him came his squad running in formation.

"This is Sergeant Borton," stated Captain Gish to both his prince and to the lieutenant.

"Borton, we have an important assignment for you," said the crown prince. "You and your men are now with Lieutenant Fontar's command. Your help is needed to secure the watch tower and protect the road for the many refugees that are following."

Fontar thanked the prince for the additional soldiers and then led the squad back to the tower to get them settled. Wintron signaled his men to go on and it was not until they were beyond the tower and well into the gap that he called for Scout Harl.

"Explain your delay, scout." His tone indicated that it had better be a good explanation.

"Yes, my prince. Duke Fors kept me for questioning until just an hour ago. He wanted to know all that he could about the fall of the Borderheart Valley and Regalis."

"I ordered you to return immediately after getting a reply to my message."

"As I did, my prince. Duke Fors insisted that I had to answer his questions before he would write his response to you. He had armed men at the door to reinforce my cooperation. I left as soon as he penned his answer."

"Why did you wait at the tower?"

"The duke's men confiscated my weapons before allowing me into his presence, weapons that they never returned to me. In addition, I was told about assassins on the road that had killed two other messengers. The duke's aide strongly encouraged me to wait at the tower and even gave a veiled threat. He said that some archers in the tower were rather jumpy and might mistake a messenger for an escaping spy. He promised that you would be here within the hour, which you were."

"I will confirm your story shortly. You are dismissed to the ranks, Soldier Harl. Report to Captain Gish for assignment to a squad."

Once the demoted scout left, Wintron's advisors spoke up.

"The duke's behavior is outrageous," protested Gordrew.

"Fors knew about those assassins hiding in the canyon," observed Rolen.

"The duke is crafty," responded Wintron to Gordrew. "You will note that he did not order Harl's disarming, so he can claim it was just an overzealous aide. I can only charge him with being too thorough in his questioning and too slow to write his response."

"Were you not too harsh on Harl?" asked Tolara, having stayed close enough to overhear all.

Wintron gave a wintry smile. "I believe that is what Fors expects of me, though it is hard to know such a wily mind. If Harl still rides among the scouts, Fors will realize that I have serious doubts about the duke's loyalty. Better to demote the man and keep Fors guessing. Also, it could save Harl's neck. They may want to kill him before I can thoroughly inquire about his interview with Fors." The prince paused to look around at the boulder-strewn slopes, now in darkness. "Let us not talk anymore about this particular situation. Fors may have ears among the rocks. Instead, let us light some torches and continue our last leg to the fortress. I want a dinner and I prefer to eat before midnight."

* * *

When the Clear River flowed off the Highlands, it came down Thunder Canyon and then leaped over a sheer rock cliff to plunge into the lower canyon. Tor Randis perched on the edge of that waterfall. The sprawling fortress dominated the rim, with high walls topped by six squat towers. Wintron had never liked the ancestral home of the Dabes, for it was a dreary place full of past horrors.

The fort came into view just past the tower-guarded gap, though it was only a darker shadow looming overhead, concealing some of the stars. Torches could be seen on the ramparts, but they were few.

As soon as they came over the ridge, the roar of the fall became apparent, a steady thunder. The roadway followed the mountainside around to the cliff directly below Tor Randis and then began to snake back and forth up to the rim. The Thunderroll Fall crashed down the cliff side nearby, throwing up a great amount of spray that soaked portions of the road. The moisture added an extra chill to the night.

More than once, Wintron looked straight up to see the ramparts looming overhead and wondered what kind of welcome his uncle would give him. At least the scouts reported the gates open. Although he knew the troops were tired, he did not call for any rest, not this close to their destination.

Finally, they rounded the final switchback and the massive gate tower lurked directly ahead, a set of torches burning to either side. The gate still stood open, though without a welcoming party. The cavalry rode in without challenge, past sentries standing at their posts, through an echoing stone corridor and into the walled bailey beyond. Lampposts lit the courtyard but left the upper reaches of the walls in darkness. Wintron felt very exposed, wondering if archers were taking aim at them from above.

The army moved on, through another corridor and into an even larger courtyard. It was here, in front of the stables, that the Duke waited, alone. The prince broke free of his personal guard and advisors and set his horse to a canter, riding right up to the Old Fox. He did not speak, waiting for the duke to give his greeting.

After a pause, his uncle finally spoke. "Have you come to relieve me of my duty or also of my head?"

"Neither Old Fox, for you are our only general," responded Wintron. "I need you."

The man nodded and then finally gave a welcoming bow to his nephew. "Welcome to Tor Randis, sire."

"I do not wear the crown yet, as you well know." He gave a cool smile, one made fierce in the flickering light of a nearby torch. "Pressing matters kept me from taking time for any ceremony."

"Well then, my prince, shall we go discuss these matters in a more comfortable setting? I have a meal already laid out for you and your top aides. Will you please follow me?"

He nodded, and quickly called Gordrew, Rolen, Captain Jandon of the cavalry, and Captain Gish of the infantry to his side. Wintron did not bother directing Bilshor, for the head of his personal guard always came with him. He left the dismissing of the troops to the squad sergeants, trusting that Fors had set aside enough room in the barracks. Wintron did not want to keep the captains down here to wait as the long line of infantry made their way up the steep climb, for that could take another hour or two, especially for the wagons carrying the supplies, the wounded, and the dead. No, that had to be left to the sergeants to supervise. Wintron also wanted Tolara to join them, but he knew his uncle would frown at a woman in a war council and he also knew that Tolara would want to find her son and see that he was in a proper bed for the night. More for her sake, he did not include her.

Fors led them to a large dining room full of shadows and echoes. At the far end, next to a roaring fire, waited a table laden with a cold meal. Wintron noted the slight but said nothing, for his uncle would merely claim it would have been foolish to serve warm food when their arrival time was so uncertain. He strode across the stone floor, flanked by his two advisors and three captains, and took a seat on one of the wooden benches. There were no single chairs here and Wintron thought that was planned. Fors did not want any seats that could become a makeshift throne. Fors sat across from him, soon joined by

his own advisors. Six of them. In addition, men in the blue-and-black
of Halen-Dabe's personal guard were stationed around the room,
matching up to Wintron's personal guards. It was meant to intimidate.

Wintron decided it was time to make the general a bit
uncomfortable in return. "Lord Rolen, would you pray over the food
for us?"

Rolen gave a surprised look, for the Attul knew that the duke
wanted only the mountain gods worshiped at his table. The prince gave
a slight nod of encouragement, wanting this done before the Old Fox
could object, and Rolen obligingly gave heartfelt thanks to El. Wintron
felt torn between closing his eyes in reverence and watching his uncle's
discomfort, so he chose to pray with one eye slightly ajar. Fors looked
as if he had bitten into something sour.

They ate for a time in silence. Wintron's party ate heartily, having
had little while on the road. Fors' men picked at their food, eating only
because it was custom to do so when playing host. Both prince and
duke seemed hesitant to break the silence, letting it settle over the
room. When finally his hunger was abated, the prince pushed his plate
away.

Taking that as his signal, Fors rose to his feet, as did all of his
party, their bench scrapping on the stone floor. "Let us have our
discussion next to the hearth," he suggested, "for my old bones grow
easily chilled these days. Plouger, fetch us some mugs of cider and
make sure they are properly mulled."

Wintron nodded and also rose to his feet. All of the men moved
closer to the hearth. Two small benches sat next to the fireplace, so the
prince claimed one while Fors took the other. The rest of the men
stood behind them, like a human fence to keep the room's shadows at
bay.

Fors indicated the tall, slightly graying officer at his back. "This is
Major Cilano, my second here at Tor Randis." The others were
Captains Thir, Kovin, and Jordis.

Wintron introduced those with him, since the soldiers had been
under a different general, but he tired of the banter. He decided to be
blunt. "The war goes badly."

"I would agree, if all that you have left are those five hundred
weary soldiers that followed you up here." Fors tossed another log
onto the fire and sparks flew up the chimney. "Where are generals Tesh
and Erileon?"

"Erileon was murdered at the border, while Tesh disappeared at the same time as the king was killed. The dukes of Regalis and Glenford are also dead. The Tlocanians had this all well planned, with help from dragon priests of the Crimson Order."

"Red, blue, why would the color of their order matter? We have already put all the dragon priests under guard, no matter the color that fringes their black robe. I have also stopped them from wandering in the Highlands. It was not hard, since I have had them watched for some time now." Fors shook his head. "I had warned my brother often enough to expel the vermin, but Varen was too nice. He believed their claims of independence from the Dragon Lord, the fool."

The prince gritted his teeth, choosing not to rise to his uncle's baiting. "You have arrested all the dragon priests?"

"There is no room for them in our cells, so they are detained in their temple. Troops keep watch to make sure no one leaves. I am sure that you agree that they need to be controlled."

Wintron nodded, though he would have only done so to those who followed the Red Dragon. "What are your intentions, uncle?'

"Concerning the priests? Well, I plan to send them packing down the road. Tomorrow morning, to be exact. Let them find refuge among their countrymen who squat in the Borderheart."

"No, uncle, this is bigger than a handful of robed zealots. What are your intentions for this war? Where is your allegiance?"

Fors paused to consider, his bushy left eyebrow lifting. The firelight emphasized his weathered and wrinkled face. This warrior had seen many seasons. "I stand for the Border Realm. This invasion cannot be left unchallenged, so I will do my best to defend Tor Randis and then recapture the Borderheart Valley. On this you have my word."

"Do you accept me as your king apparent, as your leader?"

The old man did not speak, but rose to his feet, and stood before Wintron, casting the prince into his shadow. He paused a moment, then pulled out his sword and offered its hilt to Wintron, dropping to his knees before his brother's son and bowing his head.

"I offer my full allegiance," swore Fors, lifting his head to look into his nephew's gray eyes. "We cannot have division or doubt in our ranks, not with the realm under such dire threat. I am yours to command, even if you want me to kill myself as recompense for my sons' betrayal."

Wintron took the offered sword. "I accept your allegiance, Duke Fors." The prince kissed the flat of the blade. "And in return for your service, I offer my protection." The ritual words sounded ironic considering that Fors had far more men under his direct command, but Wintron still said them. He held the sword out for his uncle to kiss it as well, which he did. Wintron then handed the weapon back, choosing not to add any flowery speech. Instead, he rose to his feet and pulled his uncle up as well, giving the man a strong hug. "Thank you for putting the realm first," he whispered into his uncle's ear.

"Of course, Wintron. I would never do anything else."

Eric Lorenzen

CHAPTER TWELVE
Waybridge

MYLANA

The city of Waybridge sat on the eastern bank of the Cleargorn, just below the river's merging with the Swiftgorn. The swirling of the two rivers had made numerous islands and sand bars. A mighty bridge crossed the waters, using two of the islands on its way over. The bridge had stood for nearly a century, replacing what had been a dangerous ferry crossing. It was a heavily used span, by both locals and distant travelers, for the city sat at the meeting of two great highways: the Middle Run that followed the Cleargorn's valley, and the Crossover Road. The Crossover Road stretched from the foggy shores of the Sunset Ocean all the way to the Grandgorn Valley and even past that, to climb up a rocky ravine and onto the Wind Plains.

On the western bank, a town known as West Way had grown around the fort protecting the bridge's approach, but that small town remained dwarfed by the huge city on the eastern bank. The heart of Waybridge city stood behind stone walls on the river's bank, guarding that end of the bridge, but Waybridge had sprawled well past those old city limits. It now had a second wall, this one of wooden piles driven into an earthen bank, which surrounded a far wider area known as the new city. Even that was not big enough to encompass all of Waybridge. Beyond the walls were scattered farms, outlying inns, and a fishing village.

No matter where you were in the area, though, the locals gave directions in reference to "the Bridge". Mylana and her companions learned that quickly enough. And yet there was another feature that dominated the horizon even more than the great stone-and-wood bridge. A beam of pulsing red power shot upwards, splitting into smaller flows as it neared the cloud cover. It looked like some huge crimson tree looming over the city. Its many branches seemed to both cling to and hold up the Dragon Shadow. The locals did their best to ignore this powerful reminder of their overseers, but it dominated the sky.

A Shadow Anchor was not a new sight to the Attuls, but it remained a disturbing sight. The power fed and tied in place the Dragon Shadow. Mylana had seen a similar Shadow Anchor rise over their old homeland of Westbend and she knew it required human sacrifices to sustain its power.

They arrived as evening settled in. Too late to enter the city itself, they chose to stay at one of the outlying inns. The place had a sad look, but it offered shelter and warm food. Their choice was a fortunate one, for the innkeeper had a second trade, making walking sticks. In a corner of the common room sat a large rack displaying his wares, from a richly carved staff to a simple oldster's cane.

When they left the next morning, both Mandor and Coursen carried long, simple staves to discourage anyone who became too interested in their things. Staves would not draw the attention that glowing swords would. They had purchased them at a bargain, since the innkeeper had not completed shaping and shining either one.

The Attuls followed the Middle Run up to the outer wall of Waybridge, an earthen bank topped by a wooden stockade. Two sets of gates guarded a gap in the wall, but both stood open and the black-uniformed local soldiers did nothing except watch the traffic entering and leaving the city. Mylana led the two packhorses this day, with Mandor in front of her and Coursen bringing up the rear. The guards did not even demand any entrance fee for bringing in pack animals, but then Waybridge probably made its money on bridge tolls.

Mylana was not impressed by the city that appeared on the other side of the stockade, though it was twice as large as Westbend. The unpaved road showed ruts from spring rains. The wooden structures stood one or two-stories in height and most needed of a coat of paint. Mylana compared that to the stately, tree-lined avenues of Westbend and decided Waybridge was far more rustic in spite of its greater population. The only greenery she saw peeked over knotty fences, where tiny gardens struggled for sunlight between buildings. Uneven wooden planking served as elevated walkways on either side, yet the boards seemed almost as muddy as the road. The side roads and alleys did not even have walkways. She was glad to be on horseback.

"Step aside!" yelled Coursen, from behind her. Mylana looked back to see him waving off an urchin who had moved too close to one of the packhorses. The boy glared at Coursen but moved away. Mylana pulled the lead line, speeding up the animals, but soon had to slow down again as they were caught behind a man driving goats through the city. Once past the goatherd, their pace did not greatly increase. The people of outer Waybridge showed no care for any road traffic, wandering in front of delivery wagons and merchant trains. In addition, beggars and urchins regularly bothered passersby or scrambled to recover anything of possible value that fell into the mud. It caused bedlam and angry exchanges on every block.

They had decided beforehand to find an inn at the foot of the actual bridge, but it took some time for them to make their way across the outer city. At the massive inner wall, they passed through a cobbled tunnel, dimly lit and echoing the sounds of the crowds. Once again, the city guards only watched to make sure the traffic flowed smoothly, letting all pass without any questions or fees.

Mylana found that Inner Waybridge had paved streets, but they were far narrower and tended to wander. However, at least the streets were far cleaner, due to the cobblestones and gutters, and there seemed to be no urchins or beggars. Many buildings rose five stories in here and trees were non-existent.

The Attuls made their way to where the bridge came down in the city's heart, ending in a large square kept clear of vendors. The clearing bustled with wagons, horsemen, and walkers. A steady flow of traffic flowed onto and off the bridge. The horses and wagons caused a deep rumble from the bridge planking that underscored all the other city noises. A flock of pigeons fluttered about, looking for scraps or dropped seed. Yet, in spite of all the bustling, this seemed the most orderly part of the city. No one wandered aimlessly or lingered to chat; everyone seemed to have a destination and a desire to get there as quickly as possible.

Six inns crouched at the square's edges, announcing their presence with signs and the typical green lanterns of their trade. Though it was daytime, the innkeepers kept their doorway lanterns lit. It was almost midday so Mandor quickly chose an inn called the Traveler's Rest and led them to it.

The inn stood five stories tall, its bottom floor the stables. A wide, wooden stairway led to the front doors on the second story, but they headed towards a dim opening to the right of the stairs, where the stable gates were thrown wide. They rode under the inn, for the ceiling was high enough even though the boys were cautiously when passing under some of the bigger beams. They soon found themselves in a dim gathering yard.

A stablehand stood up from the hay bale he had been sitting on, offered them a smile, and then a greeting. "Welcome to the Traveler's Rest. Have you come for a respite or for a night's stay? Our stable offers safe care for your horses, no matter the length of your visit." His greeting sounded rehearsed and oft repeated.

Mandor looked down at the young fellow, giving him a polite nod. "The length of our stay will depend on the rates."

The groom, who had been staring at Mylana, quickly looked back at Mandor. "Oh, our prices are as good as most on Bridge Square, though I hear it is cheaper if you stay in the outer city." His eyes wandered to Mylana for just a moment and then came back. He began brushing the loose straw from his breeches as he focused on Mandor. "To tell you the truth, business has been a little light the last week or so. For some reason there are not so many traders coming down the Middle Run this month." He paused for a moment, and then gave a shrug. "You might try dickering with Galsot for a lower rate. He pinches his coins like all innkeepers, but he would welcome any boarders, especially if you plan on staying for a while." With the last words, he gave another quick peek at the young woman. It was clear who he hoped would stay, to Mylana's embarrassment.

Mandor dismounted, as did the other two. "I cannot yet say how long our visit shall be, but it will be at least one night. What have you to offer for our horses?"

The stablehand gave the horses an appraising look, no longer awkward as he focused on his duties. "Can they stay together? If so, then I have a fine stall that I mucked and tossed with fresh straw just this morning."

"They can," assured Mandor.

The young groom took the leads for the two spare mounts and then led the newcomers deeper into the stables. He followed a run of hard-packed earth, lit by lanterns. The outside walls of the stable were made of latticework, letting in fresh air and sunshine, though the daylight remained too weak.

The groom brought them to a large paddock that was unoccupied.

"Will this do? Galsot charges two coppers per horse for a night in the shared paddock, but you might as well have your own stall for your little group. Pretty beasties they are... my lord." It suddenly occurred to the fellow that these three might be nobility in spite of their plain clothes.

"No lords us," laughed Coursen as he began to remove the saddle from his mount. "Where should we place our tack?"

"No need to do that sir," protested the groom. "I can settle the horses. Your saddles and gear will be set on the back railing, away from any curious fingers." Suddenly looking abashed, for he knew had put the inn in a bad light. "Not that such incidents happen often here at the Traveler's Rest. This is no peddler's tavern. I keep a keen eye on all who enter the stable and at night the gates are locked."

"Thank you for doing so," said Mylana. "What is your name, young man?"

The youth beamed at her, then blushed. "I am... um... I am Kaden."

"Thank you, Kaden. I am Mylana." She chose to leave off her gifting name, since a surname usually implied a noble, a merchant, or and master craftsman.

"Kaden, I am Coursen. What are those wooden bins at the back of the stall?"

The young man stared blankly at Coursen for a moment, but then understood. "We offer the bins for traders to store their goods. The rent is an extra three coppers for each bin, with use of a lock. I would not lock the family jewels with the thing, but it is secure enough for bulk goods or basic trader stuff." He gave her another quick glance, thinking no one noticed. "I would offer the bins for free to you, but Galsot walks the stable at least once a day." He looked embarrassed that he had to ask for more coins.

"The price is fair," pronounced Mandor. "Our supplies would not entice anyone beyond a beggar. Coursen let us see how tight we can pack our things, while Kaden and Mylana handle the tack."

Mylana suspected that Mandor had put her with the stablehand on purpose. As she noticed Coursen's smile, she was even more certain, but she did not want to protest and hurt the feelings of the awkward groom. Instead, she set about her task, though Kaden insisted on handling the heavy saddles. They were in the middle of their activities when a deep-sounding bell rang. Kaden, having just lifted a saddle, stopped and gave them a look. When he saw that they had not dropped to their knees in worship, he kept working, taking the saddle to sit on the back railing. They all worked quietly through the worship time, pausing when they heard the second sounding that announced the end of noon devotion.

"We filled one bin," noted Mandor calmly. "Could you please provide us a lock?"

"Yes, of course, sir," answered Kale. "Let me go retrieve one for you." He hurried off, down the dim run between the stalls.

"That was awkward," Mylana whispered. "Do you think he will tell others that we did not bow?"

"Not if you flutter your eyelashes at him one more time," guffawed Coursen.

She gave him a sharp look.

"I believe young Kaden will hold his tongue," stated Mandor, and then suddenly smiled. "El's truth, I think even if he did try to tell others he would fumble so much that none would understand. Mylana has his tongue tied in knots."

The young woman set hands to hips and stared at her brother.

"Oh, leave off your glaring, little sister," protested Mandor. "Instead, use his interest to our advantage. Ask him to keep quiet about us."

"I will not mislead the fellow or play with his affections like some cat teasing a captured mouse," she stated. "That would be heartless deception."

Mandor held up his hand to forestall her. "I do not ask that. We all know that El disapproves of falsehood. No, I only want you to intercede for us. Do I ask too much of you?"

She took a deep breath. "You are right; I will do as you ask."

When Kaden returned with the lock and its key, Coursen took it with thanks and secured the bin.

Mylana cleared her throat. "Kaden? Will you please keep quiet about us not kneeling to the dragons? We have no desire to anger the dragonsworn; it is just that we are not of their faith."

He gave her a smile, his heart's desire filling his eyes. "We have many foreigners come through the Traveler's Rest, so I have seen worse. One trader actually spat when the bell sounded." Kaden paused to look around, though he already knew they were the only humans in the stable. "Do not worry about me talking. I will keep your confidences, Lady Mylana. But do be careful. If you are seen in public refusing to bow, they will take you." He did not explain who 'they' were, but his fear for her safety was obvious. "You must kneel if ever you are in public when the bell sounds. You do not need to actually worship; just pretend to pray to the dragons so that no one is suspicious."

"Thank you for your trust and your advice, Kaden," she said, giving him a warm smile, "but I do not worship any dragon and it would be wrong to fake such worship."

"You are so brave," blurted Kaden, "but you do not know how awful they are." He looked towards the two men for help. "Can you not convince her to play along or at least to hide out in private during the calls to worship?"

"We will do our best to keep her safe," assured Mandor. "Now, where do we find Innkeeper Galsot?"

Kaden looked ready to argue longer for Mylana's safety, but then wilted as he realized that he was powerless to do more. "Galsot should be in the common room upstairs. He is a large man who always wears a white apron. If you do not see him immediately, you will probably hear him."

"Thank you," replied Mandor, hefting up his saddlebags and blanket.

Coursen patted Kaden's shoulder. "She is Mandor's sister and is like a sister to me as well. Trust us; we care too much to let Mylana come to harm."

Kaden gave a tentative smile at the assurance.

Mylana did her best to ignore their exchange, turning to follow Mandor towards the indoor stairwell up to the common room.

* * *

Mylana stood at the window, looking down at the Bridge Square from three floors above. She watched as Mandor and Coursen walked out the inn's front door and strode down the stone stairs. They separated, both walking at a quick pace. She lost sight of Mandor when he entered a narrow street off to the right. The young woman looked again for Coursen, but he had also vanished. Frustrated, she let the curtains fall back in place. She was not happy about being left behind and had almost refused when they had argued that it was too dangerous in Waybridge for a woman. It was only when Mandor also pointed out that her knowledge of Warhaven could not be risked, that Mylana relented.

BRODAGAR

Brother Brodagar and Captain Nesron rode through the raised iron gates of the Tlocanian garrison at Waybridge, one hundred men riding behind them, only twenty of them belonging to the priest. They had entered the city a few hours prior, but this was the earliest they could get to the fortress. They had left the rest of the priests and the pack at the Five Dragons Temple that sprawled in the newer section of the city. Brodagar did not like being separated from the hounds, but they would cause too much of a disruption within the tighter confines of the old city.

Nesron's best scout had trailed the Attuls to an inn on the Bridge Square, in the very heart of the walled city. After investigating the location, they decided that the Attuls would not be traveling any further today, so they left a squad of Tlocanian soldiers to keep watch. As soon as that guard was set in place, they led the rest of the troops here to the old stone fortress that had been the home to Waybridge's former ruler.

The fortress loomed not that far from the Bridge Square. Its high walls were decorated with black bunting showing the red dragon in flight. However, the priest felt no pride or awe for the symbol. He served Tlocania because more-powerful demons ordered him to. He did as told, even as he schemed with his Other self on how they could increase their own power. He suspected that Nesron did much the same.

What did catch his eye was the Shadow Anchor. He could feel the power pulsating in that column of red light as it shot up from the keep's greatest tower. Within him, Sahak hummed at the sight, for so much power was a temptation to the demon. It took some effort for Nesron to bring their focus back on the people around him, but it was necessary. He would not be able to relax much until he came to the temple, either the one in the inner city or, even better, the outer city temple where he had left his hounds.

The paved mustering yard echoed loudly as the men filled it. Quickly, Nesron dismounted, handing over his mount to one of his sergeants, with orders to see the men set up in the barracks. Brodagar climbed down with more decorum. He ordered his escorting temple guards to remain mounted and on alert. The army and the priesthood were supposedly united under the emperor, but a rivalry still existed, a rivalry that sometimes turned bloody.

Nesron entered through high wooden doors into the main keep, Brodagar close behind. They came here to see the Colonel Wevro, who commanded the army in this southern area of the empire that was under Lord-Governor Krev Zendron, an area now known as Hasan Province. Wevro was not the Brodagar's superior, but the army colonel did report directly to the lord-governor, giving him great power.

It was not his first visit to the Waybridge fortress, yet the place did not become any more appealing with familiarity. The citadel overflowed with army riff-raff, making it uncomfortable to the dragon priest.

Once inside, a soldier of the colonel's personal guards gave them a formal greeting and then led them to Colonel Wevro's private study.

"So, you two have returned," noted Wevro, looking up from his papers. The only light in the room came from the fireplace, where flames danced sullenly.

"I have come as ordered, Wevro-Skagrosh," replied Nesron with a formal bow. Brodagar noted the other's response. This was not to be some military matter, demanding salutes or titles, apparently. He gave the superior a respectable bow, not too deep since the colonel was not the priest's direct master.

Wevro nodded, which meant that Nesron had judged rightly. He motioned for the two visitors to sit in the plain chairs across the table from him, and then he ignored them while finishing a review of the report in front of him. Brodagar sat calmly and waited, noticing that his companion did not seem as relaxed, sitting on the edge of his chair. Nesron had taken a risk to assume this meeting pertained to demonic business beyond a military role.

Finally, Wevro finished, setting the report aside and focusing on the captain. "Nesron-Swoferosh, Tell me about the Attuls."

The captain gave a succinct yet thorough report, free of any weak human emotions. Brodagar expected as much from an Embraced One who was also an officer. For a moment there was silence, interrupted only by a few crackles from the fire, as the colonel mulled over the report.

Finally, Wevro turned to the priest. "Do you have anything to add, Brother Brodagar?"

He offered a slight smile to show his confidence. "The captain explained our adventures well enough."

Wevro just stared at the priest for a moment. The silence finally made Brodagar nervous and his right hand began to fuss with his robe's folds though his face remained composed. Finally, the colonel spoke, but in a deeper voice, "Sahak, were you here during the

Failure?"

"I was not," responded Brodagar's Other, in a voice raspier than the priest's own.

"Nor I," noted Wevro's Other. "I am not haunted by those memories, yet I have come to understand the fears of our kindred like your companion, Nesron-Swoferosh. Attuls can be powerful tools for the Enemy, though what I have seen of them so far is rather disappointing as an opponent. Are you not worried about our old adversaries?"

Sahak did not respond, leaving it to Brodagar, who felt the Other's contempt for Wevro-Skagrosh. Yet Sahak showed caution, so he had better do the same. "We will be careful with the Attuls. We also understand how important it is to find this Warhaven."

"Indeed," responded Wevro in his normal voice. "Lord-Governor Krev Zendron-Swerkrad wants to be the one to reveal Warhaven to the emperor." He kept his attention on the priest. "I will not tolerate any rivalries or sabotage from the priesthood, Brodagar-Sahak. Is that understood?"

Brodagar gave him a slight nod. "The priesthood will cooperate if it means the exposing of our enemy's redoubt." In his head, Sahak commented: *We will help him so long as it helps us, but no further than that. Never trust Skagrosh, for that demon has no loyalty beyond his own belly.*

Wevro grunted, though the priest was not sure if it was in agreement or doubt. The colonel turned his attention on his captain. "I expect equal cooperation from my own men. Do you understand me, Nesron?"

"Understood, sir."

"Excellent." Wevro stood up and walked to the door in response to a soft knock. Brodagar did not see who stood on the other side, but they said something to the colonel. When Wevro closed the door, he had a slip of paper in his hand. He took a moment to read it, not bothering to hold it up to the firelight. He nodded, and then handed it to Nesron, who quickly read it and then passed it on to Brodagar at the colonel's urging. The note seemed written in haste, lacking any elegance in either style or subtlety:

'The woman holds the key- Free Hawk'.

The priest read it and then looked up questioningly.

"We had advance warning that these Attuls were coming and that one of them knows where the rest of the Attuls are hiding," explained Wevro. "Now we know which one of the three has the secret. The young female."

"Are we to take her and kill the other two?" he asked carefully.

"Oh no, nothing so straightforward." Wevro's tone expressed his frustration with plotting. "The two males are to be spared. We are only to harass the threesome for now. Lord-Governor Krev Zendron-Swerkrad has been very clear about that, if nothing else. I believe the idea is to frighten the woman enough to get her to share her secrets with the others. This Free Hawk person is a pet of the lord's, a traitor close to the Attul Watch Riders. For all I know, he is one of those two males who escort the female."

Wevro shook his head. "It is too convoluted for my simple military mind. Even my Other half cannot fully fathom what Krev-Swerkrad plots. All that I know for certain is that he wants the information the female holds, so I have assigned the two of you to lead this mission. I expect you to get that knowledge for me, doing so without breaking the limits that Lord Krev had set, which includes letting the Watch Riders roamed free until the woman reveals what she knows to her companions. Free Hawk either is one of the men or is close to one of the them. I know the restrictions seem burdensome, but you are resourceful enough to still find a way to get her to talk."

Brodagar nodded, yet he did not need Sahak's hissed warning in his mind. He saw how Wevro-Skagrosh endangered him. The colonel was using him to gain this information and the colonel did not care if it cost Brodagar's life. Maybe Nesron had no problem sacrificing himself for the cause, but Brodagar planned to survive this and even use it to climb higher among the other Embraced Ones.

MYLANA

It was fully dark by the time Mylana let her two companions back into their shared room. No sooner were their cloaks off, then Mylana insisted on hearing what they had learned.

"There is an army marching down the Cleargorn Valley," announced Coursen. "The Reds are on the move."

Mandor nodded that he had learned the same fact. "We will need to decide quickly which way to go, for the frontrunners will be in Waybridge soon. Did you hear where they are headed, Coursen?"

The handsome young man shook his head. "I would not think they are going out onto the plains, for there is nothing worth capturing out among the grasses. I expect they must be heading for the Crossover

Road, to turn either west or east. Whatever is their goal, they certainly prevent us from heading any further north. If the army is anywhere near as large as rumors say, then we will not be able to pass them."

"That narrows our choices," stated Mandor. "Do we turn west into the Lakelands or east to the Grandgorn Valley? Which way would bring us closer to our goal, Mylana?"

She stared at him in reply.

Coursen laughed. "Your sister is no longer that little girl in pigtails so easily tricked by you. She can keep a secret from you now."

Mandor smiled in return. "And now she is angry with me. I only wondered if one of the routes would greatly delay us."

"I do not know, my brother, for I cannot foresee what lies ahead." She walked over to the window and peeked through the curtains at the dark square below. More wagon teams moved on and off the bridge, taking advantage of the lighter night traffic. "It is as dark to me as the city beyond this window."

She thought about how much was uncertain for her people. For generations, they had been watching for the demons' return. Ever the dutiful scouts, they rode their circuits and investigated dark rumors for decades. When they suspected demonic influences, they looked more carefully. When they found some who were demon-possessed, they sent messages northward to the Prayer Warriors, but no reply ever came. When the first of the Dragon Shadow began to fill the southern skies, they sent even more-urgent reports. Still no response came from the Attuls' main army.

Finally, the Guardians had to admit their routes must have become compromised, their chain of riders to Warhaven broken. Apparently, it had been even worse than that, for Mylana's father had spoken of a traitor in their midst. She still could not fathom how one of their own could be so dark.

The two men stepped closer and looked over her shoulder to see what it was that interested her. Maybe it was the darkness outside, but when she noticed her companions reflected by the window, she suddenly wondered if the traitor was one of her companions. Just as quickly, she dismissed the idea. No, not Mandor, always so proper and formal. She looked at Coursen's reflection, but could not imagine him as a wicked man either. He was too light-hearted and caring. She trusted both, yet she was not about to break her word to her father. The two would remain ignorant of Warhaven's location.

Mylana turned away from the window and let the curtain drop

back in place. She recalled what Mandor had specifically asked. "Either route will be fine for our journey," she stated. "The real question is which path will bring us the greatest chance of success."

"Indeed," he replied. "We need to find out where this army is heading, for I do not think that we want it at our heels."

"Well, I do not think we can learn more tonight," said Coursen, stifling a yawn. "I say we turn in for the night and try to learn more in the morning."

So the lamp was extinguished. Coursen and Mandor shared the large bed, while Mylana settled on a creaky cot. She pulled off her boots and then slipped under the blanket still clothed, pulling her own blanket over the top of the inn's bedding. The layers provided warmth against the chilly night. She dosed off wondering if maybe one of the Guardians was the betrayer, instead of just a mere Rider.

* * *

The next morning, after the completion of the sunrise call for worship, the three descended to the common room and ate a breakfast of runny oatmeal flavored with dried apple slices and honey. Mylana had convinced them to let her go along, noting that the city could not be so dangerous during the day. She joined Coursen, because Mandor had other plans. She did not push him for the details, for she did not want to upset Mandor, but she sensed that Coursen did not approve of Mandor's intentions. They ate quietly, with obvious tension between the two men. Upon finishing, they exited the inn on foot, taking the outer stairway down to the bustling Bridge Square. They stopped on the fourth step from the bottom for a final word.

"I will see you back here by sunset," said Mandor, "and do not worry, Coursen. I will be careful."

"We cannot afford a repeat of the Westbend incident, old friend," replied Coursen, raising one eyebrow. "Do not risk our mission, Mandor."

Mandor gave them an assuring smile. "I swear that I will do no such thing. Our mission comes first, Coursen, but I will not pass up on such a reliable source. We need to know where this army is heading." He paused as two men came near, taking the stairs up to the inn. Once they were beyond hearing, Mandor continued. "Keep my sister safe. She is the linchpin to our mission." With that, he took the last few steps and strode off into the crowds.

"What was that about?" asked Mylana.

"He goes to find Hessilyn," answered Coursen simply.

She tried to respond, but no words came. Instead, she stared after her brother, shaking her head in amazement. Only one area had she ever seen her brother act foolishly: when he fell in love with that heathen girl. It took a moment for her to regain her composure enough to respond. "How could that be? What would she be doing all the way up here?"

Coursen frowned. "Her father, Lord-Governor Polis Targan, came north on a diplomatic mission for the Osburg Empire," he explained. "Apparently, he took along Hessilyn as part of his entourage. I do not know why he is here in Waybridge and not on his way to Tlocania proper, but Mandor found out last night that the Gray contingent still lingered here. He is determined to find her again."

She shook her head. "Has Mandor remained in contact with her all of this time?"

He hesitated, and then nodded. "Mandor truly loves her. I think he hopes to rescue her still, for he cannot accept that she stays willingly. Personally, I have my doubts about her wanting to leave the Grays.

"They write to each other regularly, using Riders to carry their letters. I admit having done so a half-dozen times myself. Mandor knew that she was on her way up here, which is why he chose the Middle Run for our ride north."

Suddenly, Mylana wondered if her brother had risked their mission out of foolish affection. "She might turn us over to the enemy, especially since her father is now one of the possessed and a leader with our enemy."

Coursen disagreed. "Hessilyn would not betray your brother, for she cares about him. Additionally, she has no love for her father even though she appreciates the rich life he provides. No, she will keep Mandor's presence a secret. I only fear that he will do something rash, like try to rescue her again. That woman is no damsel in distress, no matter what Mandor thinks."

She sighed. Coursen's judgment about Hessilyn was rather accurate. She and Mylana were almost the same age and grew up together among the wealthy of Westbend. Beautiful and charming, Hessilyn had always attracted the boys but had never settled on any of them. Even as a girl she had eyes only for Mandor, though he had not returned Hessilyn's affection at first. To him, she had been just another of Mylana's little friends. Looking back, Mylana suspected that the only reason Hessilyn had befriended her was to get close to Mandor.

His attitude changed, though, after having gone away for two years of Rider training. During those two years, Hessilyn had gone from girl to woman far more dramatically than Mylana, becoming a tall yet shapely lady of rich dark hair and a fair complexion that was the envy of all the other women in Westbend. Upon his return to their family estate, Mandor had finally noticed her and had been smitten. Only the war had kept them from quick marriage, for their fathers were on opposite sides of the strife.

Mylana sighed again. "I had hoped their romance would have soured with the war, especially since Mandor no longer has any great inheritance to keep her comfortable." They had lost the family horse farm in the fall of Westbend. "What does he still see in her? She is not even Elsworn. Hessilyn is very lovely, but the wrapping does not make the gift."

Coursen shook his head. "Mandor is my good friend, but in this I do not understand him either. I will say, though, that he will be discreet in contacting her. I do not think his actions today will compromise us." Coursen paused to look around, noticing a few of the square's urchins starting to head in their direction. "Yet our chatting on the inn's doorsteps might expose our presence, should we linger here much longer. We will attract a circle of beggars soon if we do not move. Come. Let us be on our way too, for our worrying over Mandor will not help any."

Coursen led Mylana through the streets of Waybridge. They took a few turns and then came out in another square, though one much smaller than the one at the foot of the bridge. It was a crowded opening, full of stands and stalls. They lingered in the market, listening to plenty of gossip but not hearing much that either of them deemed useful. It was becoming common knowledge that a Tlocanian force was marching towards Waybridge. Some spoke hopefully of new business, for soldiers often had nothing else to do with their coins but spend them.

One big man grumbled about higher taxes to feed the extra troopers, glaring as a squad of soldiers rode by. His companion nodded, adding his disdain for the many rules and fees imposed by their new overlords. Tlocania had conquered Waybridge two years ago, but it seemed that not everyone appreciated their presence. Mylana thought them foolish to speak out so, for the demonsworn were not the forgiving sort.

Most of the market gossip was about the weather, especially about the constant overcast of the Dragon Shadow. Produce sellers complained about the weather stunting the crops they offered. A flower seller muttered about the lack of sunshine delaying spring blooms. Similar complaints came from dyers, weavers, and even a potter. All blamed the lack of bright skies for either the shortage of goods or their shoddy quality.

They finally left the market, since it was approaching midday, and sought out a quieter place in that bustling city. They had no desire to be in the middle of a crowd when the worship bells rang. They chose a narrow alley and followed it behind a cobbler's shop. Overhead, lines of laundry ran across the alley at both the second floors and third. A pair of women gossiped across the way as they strung their newly cleaned wash. Coursen and Mylana moved on, hoping to get out of the women's sight. Underfoot, they had to avoid puddles and piles of trash.

They saw a drunk sleeping off his latest binge half inside an empty crate. They stepped around him and kept going. Thankfully, the alley was not a straight way, so that in a half-block they were out of view, though Mylana thought she heard steps behind them.

"Where now?" she asked. "Should we hunker in a doorway?"

Coursen shrugged. "Maybe, though we should keep to this side of the alley, for we are just north of the inner city temple."

Mylana nodded her understanding, for everyone was expected to face towards the nearest temple. She was surprised that he had such a good grasp of their bearings. "I am all turned around in these twisty streets, especially when there is no sun to gauge by." She looked up at the narrow strip of sky exposed between the tall rows of buildings. "Even without the Dragon Shadow, I doubt much sunlight ever fell on the paving stones of this narrow way."

Coursen gave her a mischievous grin, motioning for her to join him in a doorway next to a stack of empty crates. "After as many rides as I have gone on, you learn to gauge such things. Your life could depend on it."

She joined him in pressing against the weathered wood, finding his nearness a bit unsettling in a pleasant way.

Suddenly the worship bells tolled, very near and just to the south.

Coursen looked a bit startled by the volume. He leaned close to her ear and whispered, "Apparently, I am all turned around too. I did not realize that we had snaked our way so close to the Dragon Temple. Did you see anyone near us?"

She kept as still as she could, hoping they were well hidden from anyone looking out on the alley. "I saw no one, but I thought I heard multiple footsteps behind us."

Coursen paused to listen, but heard nothing. "If there are, they stopped to make their prayers."

She thought that maybe this would be their chance to slip away if anyone was tailing them, but then realized it would be too conspicuous for them to be running, or even walking, when everyone else knelt in prayer. No, they had to wait here. The tolling ended and the prayer chanting began. Isolated as they were, the sound was a faint background noise but it still gave her gooseflesh. "So many swearing allegiances to the winged beasts," she whispered, mostly to herself. "How can they be so devoted?"

He almost replied, but then something else caught his attention. She heard two distinct footfalls. Whoever they were, they had no fear of ignoring the worship call. She would have turned to look, but Coursen's light touch urged her not to.

"You were right about us being followed. Make no sudden moves to attract their attention. They are taking their time, snooping in all the corners and shadows as they look for someone or something."

"Will they see us here?" asked Mylana. She wanted to turn and look, but made herself stand still.

"Soon, if they keep up their search," answered Coursen. "They wear no uniforms or robes, so they might be thugs or merchant hires, but we cannot afford any trouble whether from hirelings or soldiers." He gave her shoulder an encouraging squeeze. "If they do not stop, then we will need to run. Just do not draw your sword, for it will draw too much attention."

Mylana nodded, her heart speeding up with sudden anxiety.

Eric Lorenzen

CHAPTER THIRTEEN
Five Dragons Temple

WINTRON

Night's chill still filled Thunder Canyon as Wintron rode out from Tor Randis' upper gate, towards the nearby town of Randisville. At his side rode Councilor Rolen Strongarm and just ahead of him rode Captain Bilshor. The prince knew that he could not have kept Bilshor from accompanying him, but he had insisted that the captain bring only six guards. Wintron had grown tired of his escorts, longing for the freer life of being a mere heir during peacetime. He understood Bilshor's concerns, but he also did not want to intimidate the people of Randisville or seem threatening towards the dragon priests. Even though some helped Mordel kill his father, he understood that they were rogues among the devout. He would leave the threats to his intolerant uncle.

Wintron and his party followed a dozen cavalry soldiers under a lieutenant's command. The soldiers were on a mission to empty out the Five Dragons Temple, for the duke and the prince feared that spies might be hiding inside this temple as they had in Regalis. Even the Old Fox admitted that there could not be any magic welders up here, for no outsider priests had ever journeyed to the Highlands. Fors would know that, since he commanded Tor Randis and there were no other routes up into the high country, besides the White Owl Pass from the far north.

The soldiers were going to oust everyone from the temple, be they priest, servant, or worshiper. The place was to be boarded shut and placed under guard. Wintron and Rolen followed to make sure the troopers did their duty with proper civility.

He had decided to join this excursion out of concern that Fors' men might be overly rough. He had noticed that many of the men emulated their general's devotion to the old mountain gods and his disdain for the lowlander faiths. Too many soldiers under General Fors openly despised the five dragons as foreign gods. Though Wintron was not one of the dragonsworn himself, he still had a respect for those who worshiped the five. The religion had been around long before the Dragon Lord conquered the Seven Kingdoms.

As the king's son, he had been educated at all the various temples in Regalis, including the Five Dragons Temple. High Brother Horris had personally led his instruction so many decades ago and he had found the man to be intelligent and even witty. Wintron had mourned him when he died the year before. For the sake of Horris' memory, he would see to it that the soldiers behaved themselves.

Even though this was another day in the saddle, Wintron enjoyed the ride because it offered a reprieve from all the scheming back in Tor Randis. He did not even bother striking up a conversation with Rolen. Instead, he just enjoyed the peaceful surroundings.

The sky appeared clear overhead, just lightening to blue. To either side, the mountains formed black silhouettes against that sky. A few birds already chirped their morning songs. A woodpecker hammered some tree up the slope. This was the Border Realm he knew, a peaceful land where all seemed right.

They came to Randisville just as the sun rose high enough to shine over the high peaks and into that deep valley. Everything seemed golden in that simple town, from the cottages to the plain shops. At the village center was a public well, the town inn, and four shrines where locals gave thank offerings for bountiful harvests and sent up prayers for sick loved ones. Wintron was very familiar with such places, for they were everywhere in the realm. People gave their simple offerings to the four mountain gods: Winiem, Kila, Cha, and Avoli. He had done so himself countless times, though he did not consider himself very devout. It was just something all Borderfolk did.

The prince nodded a greeting to a trio of women gathered at the well, but he did not stop to converse for he did not want to fall behind. He and Rolen kept on the heels of the soldiers as they turned down another road and headed toward the Five Dragons Temple. He could already see the row of thin spires dedicated to each dragon, their painted turrets catching the early morning sun: red, blue, black, gray, and gold. It suddenly came to him that one of those gods was now an enemy of his. Had others of the flying gods allied with his enemy too? The thought troubled the crown prince. Fighting an army was difficult enough, but knowing that demons and gods stood as your adversaries could cause a man to crumble in despair.

"Have you noticed how much the temple has been enlarged?" asked Rolen suddenly.

Wintron pulled his thoughts out of the darkness and concentrated on his father's councilor. "What do you mean?"

The temple came into full view, so Rolen made a sweeping motion with his hand. "Look how much land is now inside its walls. Within the last five years, they have increased the temple's size threefold. I would not speak badly of other faiths, but I warned your father that it merited further investigation. The dragon temples were suddenly awash in gold. They expanded their temples in Glenford, Regalis, and here. Those extra coins did not come from any Borderfolk who are dragonsworn. That much I know."

"Did my father have someone investigate?"

Rolen shook his head. "He did not want to offend. However, I took it upon myself to talk with the temple High Brother in Regalis. He shared that dragon priests of the Crimson Order now greatly outnumbered the other orders and that many of them had arrived with substantial donations for the local temples. I had the impression that the High Brother was not completely pleased with that aid. I fear that your uncle is right, that Tlocania had been using the temples to bring in spies."

Wintron had not really noticed the expansions of the temples. He was not a particularly pious man nor had he spent much time at his father's court. He found that both settings were too full of matchmakers, people wanting to get their aging prince married and producing heirs, so he avoided both priests and nobles. At least the commoners were too humble to meddle in his affairs; they accepted him as he was, the bachelor prince.

Apparently, Wintron was silent too long, for Rolen looked at him. The councilor asked, "You take offense at the accusation?"

"No, I do not," hastily replied Wintron. "My thoughts wander. I would not have allowed Fors to order the clearing of the temple if I did not agree. I will tell you, though, that I had not noticed the changes, for I had been avoiding the dragon temple in Regalis. I think old Horris showed wisdom in many things, but his attempts at matchmaking were becoming tiresome."

Rolen smiled but refrained from replying, for which Wintron was thankful. Both of them knew that it had been King Varen who had asked everyone to help find his son a wife. The priest had only been diligently obeying the king's wishes. The elderly king had never remarried after Wintron's mother died, but he had no understanding for his son's refusal to marry after Wintron lost the only woman he loved to another man. No matter how beautiful, no woman he ever met matched the loveliness of Zaveeta.

Again, Wintron reined in his wandering thoughts and concentrated on what lay before him. "The temple grounds have indeed grown much. It seems rather overlarge for this hamlet."

Rolen nodded. "The locals say that over a hundred priests and servants lived here at one time, but many fled into the Highlands just a week ago. I worry about what they might be doing out among the farms and dales."

He frowned and stroked his beard. "We will need to chase them down as well, but let us first deal with those still inside." He noticed that Border soldiers were already keeping watch around the temple's perimeter and knew it to be Fors' efficiency. The lieutenant they had been following now spoke with the sergeant in command of the surveillance squad. Once done, they both strode over to the still-mounted prince and councilor.

"Prince Wintron, we are ready to proceed," stated the cavalry officer.

He nodded his approval. "Well then, go ahead and knock on the door. This is your command, Thessen, not mine. The councilor and I are just here as observers. Go about your duty and we will simply watch." It might not be fair to put the lieutenant into such an awkward position, but Wintron had assured Bilshor that he would keep his distance. He dismounted and gave over his reins to one of his personal guards. Councilor Rolen also climbed down, letting the trooper take his horse too.

They entered the temple's courtyard and walked towards the worship hall. The tall doors already stood shut, so apparently no locals were inside for normal worship. Above the doors, on a great stone lintel, was a carved relief showing the great black dragon with its wings outspread. Under its right wing were two more dragons, a red one and a blue one. Under its left wing sheltered the other two, a golden dragon and a gray one. All five dragons showed teeth and long, snake-like tongues. A similar motif was to be found at the temple in Regalis.

As a child, he had sometimes wondered if the beasts ever came alive to strike out at bad people. It had always given him gooseflesh and a smile. Today, however, he had no grin. This was no pleasant outing to burn a bit of incense and dream about flying gods.

The lieutenant, the sergeant, and two more soldiers walked up the stone steps to the front doors. The sergeant knocked hard, and eventually the door cracked open. The sergeant pushed it open completely, forcing the hooded priest behind the door to step back. The officer unrolled his scroll and read it at the top of his voice.

"By proclamation of Crown Prince Wintron Dabe, heir apparent of the Border Realm, and his general Duke Fors Halen-Dabe, all priests and servants of the Randisville Five Dragons Temple are hereby banished from the realm. This temple must be vacated within the hour. You will not be harmed, but you will be escorted out of the Border Realm. Such is the will of Wintron Dabe, rightful ruler of the land."

Wintron noticed that the priest's black robe had red edging on it, identifying him as one from the Crimson Order, those who held the Red Dragon in primacy. That was not a good sign.

The lieutenant stepped forward and held out the scroll to the priest, who pulled back without taking it.

"Have you any questions, priest?"

"No I do not, but we will need two hours, not one. Tell your prince that."

"Be glad that you have any time," responded the officer, never looking in Wintron's direction. "In one hour we expect all of you to be out on the street. The prince will appoint a caretaker for this place so you need not worry about vandalism or theft."

"We need two hours, for our priests are in the middle of a holy rite. It would be sacrilege to interrupt such a ritual."

The prince stepped forward, unable to resist any further. "What rite is this, holy brother? I know of no dragon rituals demanding so much time."

The cowled man turned towards Wintron, but his face remained hidden inside the dark hood. "Then you are an ignorant man as well as being rude. Now leave us to our duties."

"How dare you speak to Prince Wintron that way!" rebuked the lieutenant. The sergeant flexed his sword hand.

The dragon priest seemed unimpressed. He simply sniffed. "We will comply with your request, Border prince, but it will be in two hours." He slammed the door shut. They heard it being barred as well.

The officer turned to his liege, anger evident. "What would you have me do now, my prince?"

"What would you do if I were not here?" asked Wintron, meeting the man's blazing eyes.

"I would break in right now and clear the place out."

The prince nodded, though not happy with the situation. "Then do it. They reject my offer. We must now assume that they are harboring our enemies. I want…"

Rolen interrupted by touching the prince's shoulder. Wintron looked over and saw that the Attul had his blazing sword out. "There is something terribly wrong inside," said Rolen with a troubled frown. "Something evil is happening. I can feel it."

"Break down the door!" ordered Wintron.

The soldiers rushed to comply, but some things cannot be done instantly. It took fifteen minutes of ax work for them to get through. Finally kicked open, they found the hall beyond still empty except for the one priest.

Wintron followed the soldiers, worried that the priests' foolishness might lead to bloodshed, though Bilshor kept him to the rear.

"What is the meaning of this? Where are the others?" demanded the officer.

"As I said before, we will leave but not until the proper time," came the calm response.

"You will leave when ordered to do so," stated the officer. "Sergeant, take four others and search the place."

The priest suddenly hurried to block the doorway that led deeper into the complex. He grasped a long knife in each pale hand. "I cannot allow that. Give us another half-hour and we will leave peacefully."

At that moment they all heard a scream, which came from further within, muffled by intervening walls.

"What now, my prince?" asked the officer, obviously hesitant to kill a priest. "I see no way to remove them without force."

Wintron pulled free his own sword. Next to him stood Rolen, with his shining sword that was almost too bright in that dim place. Something evil seemed to be happening as they were debating with this obstinate man. "Do what you must, but be wary of worse than a priest waving kitchen knives."

The lieutenant ordered two men to subdue the priest. The fellow fought ferociously, even with weapons knocked away. He actually bit one of the men. Soon though, they had him to one side, tied up. The sergeant led four men past the still-struggling priest and entered the room beyond, only to find three armed temple servants in their gray robes. Another battle ensued, but the servants were not trained warriors and so were quickly overcome. One died. The last two ended up bound and bleeding.

"They are desperate to delay us," said Rolen, his tone sounding worried. He pushed to the fore, his sword a blazing light in that shadowy place. Wintron rushed to follow at his heels, ignoring both the officer and Bilshor as they tried to keep him back. He could hear Rolen's whispered prayers to El and it gave him gooseflesh. The councilor was now the prayer warrior, ready for battle. Wintron could see the readiness in Rolen's stride and knew that trouble was nearby.

They entered a long hallway that held no windows, just a few wall lamps behind deep red shades. But for Rolen's bright sword, Wintron would not have been able to see anything. Halfway up the hallway a side door suddenly opened and five temple guards stepped into the hall, shutting the door behind them.

"Allow me to pass, councilor," said the officer, pressing forward with his men. "This is a fight for soldiers. Just keep that sword lit so that we can see what we are hacking." Both Wintron and Rolen stepped to the side and let the troopers rush at the temple guards.

The lieutenant charged forward with the sergeant and eight soldiers. The fight was brutal, for the tight place limited the Border soldiers' ability to overwhelm the others. Slowly the soldiers got the upper hand though, killing one and then a second of the guards. During the middle of that fight, another dragon priest appeared, stepping out of the door at the end of the hallway and then closing the door behind him. The prince did not notice him at first, for the shadows were deep at that end. It was the sudden alertness of Rolen that warned him. The councilor no longer focused on the battle; his eyes kept on the priest.

"What is it Rolen?" he asked.

The Attul warrior answered without looking away. "There is something evil about that one, something wrong clings to him. Are we really so sure that none of Tlocania's magic priests slipped up here?"

As both of them stared at the man, they saw him lift his arms, the wide sleeves of his black robe pulling back to reveal his hands. Red lightning danced across his fingers, coalescing into a red fireball in each hand.

"Beware!" yelled Rolen, charging forward with raised sword. However, before he could do anything else, one deep red fireball flared down the hall, exploding on the temple guards and Border troopers. Rolen stopped just short of where the men burned. The second ball of flame came directly at him, but he raised his sword in defense. The fireball hit hard, cleaving on the blade. Rolen staggered, but kept his sword up. Flames splattered against the walls and ceiling.

Wintron covered his eyes as sparks scattered everywhere. When he could see again, he found that almost all of the men were dead. Rolen pulled the lieutenant, the only survivor, back from the flames. Wintron and Bilshor stepped forward to help, quickly removing their capes and using them to smother the officer's clothes. They then yanked the unconscious man out of the passageway, to the room where the captives lay bound and gagged.

Wintron had to fight his way out of Bilshor's grasp to go back, for the man wanted to keep him safe. When he stepped back into the corridor, he saw that the priest held two more balls of fire. Bilshor stopped him there, near the open door, so that they could quickly flee any more attacks. This time, Wintron did not resist his protective hand. His personal guards crowded in front of him as a human shield, partially blocking his view.

He heard Rolen yell out to his god El and then leap through the dying flames towards the priest, his bright sword muted by the smoke that filled the passage. The prince could only watch, knowing this fight was beyond him.

The fireballs roared up the hallway, suddenly turning everything red except for that sword. Rolen deflected one to the side while the other passed over his head and splashed all over the ceiling. Most of the passageway burned now. Wintron and his guards covered their faces to the shower of sparks. When he looked up again, he saw that Rolen still stood and was now beyond the corpses.

The priest gave up on his fireballs. Instead, he flung red lightning from his hands, trying to strike down the Attul. Between the crackle and explosions, Wintron heard some of the priest's ranting. "You will die Attul! Die for…. I do not care what the Great Lord Silossiak wants….still you will die!"

Rolen fended off each strike as he kept walking towards the dragon priest. He replied with his own shout of defiance. "In the name of El, you shall be slain! Back to the Darklands, you…"

Wintron did not hear the last, for a vicious attack engulfed the

Attul. The prince thought him lost, for everything turned red, but then the whirling blade of white reappeared. Rolen spun it over his head, barely missing the ceiling and the walls, and then brought it down with a slash towards the priest. From the tip of the sword shot a beam of pure light, striking the dragon priest in the chest. The priest slammed against the door behind him, his robes starting to burn.

The dragon priest sank to his knees, but he was not beaten. Screaming with rage, he threw more lightning at the councilor. Rolen whipped his sword around to meet the attacks, leaving a trail of white light through the smoky air. He deflected each strike as he advanced. Wintron did not understand how Rolen could swing his sword fast enough to catch a bolt of lightning, but somehow he did.

Rolen stepped closer, lifted his sword, and plunged it into the priest's heart. A deep voiced roar of anger came from the dragon priest as a white light engulfed him. A surge of power exploded from the priest, toppling everyone still standing and extinguishing most of the fires, and his raging scream cut off.

Wintron struggled to stand. As his eyesight recovered from the glare, he realized that the hallway had become dark. Only a few scattered flames still angrily ate at the floor and walls. He had to step further down the corridor, Bilshor right next to him, so that he could see the end of the passageway. There was nothing left of the priest. Rolen lay nearby, unconscious.

DRASS

After the trip in the giant basket, riding a mountain pony bored Drass. He would have kicked the beast to a run, but he dared not leave his men behind. They were on their way to Halenvale, which he expected to find well-guarded. His father never left the family estate unprotected, even though no other Highland lord would dare attack the Duke's lands. Oddly, though, it was not his father's men that Drass worried about. He was more concerned about his mother, who ruled when the Old Fox was elsewhere. Drass loved her, but he had also grown up fearing the Hen of Halenvale.

He would have to keep a strong hand on his men when they attacked the compound. It would not be good if any harm came to Mother, no matter how much she angered the attackers. He even warned them all to watch out for her, for she would most likely get into the thick of things even though she had no skill with either sword or knife. However, his mother also lacked fear so she might try to attack a soldier with a fireplace poker or a brass candlestick. Growing up, he had experienced her improvised weapons often enough, whenever she felt her hand was not enough.

Drass also needed to watch out for his niece, Zita. Mordel's eldest had been sent to visit her grandmother a month ago. He did not look forward to dealing with that young wildling either. Suddenly, his anticipation of taking over the family estate soured just a little.

* * *

Drass and his men conquered Halenvale with minimal loss, yet he failed to overthrow his mother. No one could rule Duchess Riala Halen-Dabe, except possibly his father. No matter that Drass' men now held the compound, his mother still gave orders and everyone obeyed her as the estate's matron. She had even berated him in front of his men, until he had almost lost control of his anger, and then she had turned on her motherly charm.

Frustrated, Drass considered having her imprisoned but he was not certain that his own men would obey such an order. Such was the strength of her personality. He did end up imprisoning Zita after she tried to flee. There were no prison cells in Halenvale, so he had to make do with a root cellar, having the ladder pulled up. To keep Zita company, he added his youngest brother, Gurash. The youth idolized their father, the dolt, so Drass dared not trust him.

He planned to send both Zita and Gurash down the lifts into Mordel's keeping, but not yet. He did not want to thin his ranks for an escort, at least not until his allies arrived. He had been promised a Tlocanian company and he was just waiting for the news that they were being brought up. Drass looked forward to marching on Tor Randis' back door.

CHAPTER FOURTEEN
Mountain Meetings

AFRAL

"Afral, do you know the story of Tor Randis?" asked his mother. The midday sun touched her brown hair, making it shine. Mother and son stood on the ramparts of the keep, looking over the cliff at the deep canyon below.

"It is the ancestral keep of the Dabes. From here, Prince Wintron's great-great grandfather Lord Ordis Dabe united all of the Border Realm."

"So the scholars taught at the school in Regalis, but your father shared more did he not?"

He nodded to his mother. "Father said that Tor Randis was older than the Dabe family, that Lord Ordis Dabe won it when he defeated a local robber baron. Father also said the uniting of the Border Realm was not as peacefully done as the scholars imply."

"There is even more than that," she stated. Her brown hair was not bound this morning and the valley breeze began to whip it about. She brushed it back behind her ear and then leaned on the cold stone wall to look straight down. Afral followed her gaze, to see the road snaking far below, the very road that he had trudged up just last night.

"The Dabes were only able to conquer this keep because they came at it from the Highlands behind us. The keep only had a handful of defenders too. Even so, Ordis Dabe lost twenty men in the seizing of it. When approached from the south, though, Tor Randis is nearly impenetrable. Look at how it towers over the canyon below us. No one has ever overthrown it from below, so there is a chance it can withstand the coming onslaught from the Tlocanians." She fell silent, staring at the river plunging down the canyon.

He wondered where his mother meant to go with this conversation, but he held his tongue, willing to wait.

She turned her head and caught his eyes. "Tor Randis is very old and it was originally built for evil intentions. Actually, Tor Randis was built to stop our own ancestors. Do you understand what that means?"

Afral's eyes widened. "This was a demon fortification?"

"The demon-led Darshi built Tor Randis, yes. These mountains are called the Border Mountains because they once served as the southern boundary of the Darshi lands. Tor Randis is one of the few remnants of that empire that still stands." She pointed down at the canyon. "Long ago, Belere Anonral stood in that valley we climbed yesterday and looked up at these very walls. With him may have been some of our direct ancestors. In those days, the keep was full of evil men and worse things. The Attuls withdrew, deciding that there had to be an easier route into the Darshi Empire, so Tor Randis never experienced any real battering."

The news shocked Afral, and suddenly the place felt ominous even under a bright sun. "Why have you never told me this before?"

She shrugged, giving him a little smile. "There was no need and we did not want you thinking less of the Borderfolk or the Dabe family. King Varen was a good ruler, no matter that his ancestral home once served as a demon fort."

He nodded, understanding her reason though not fully agreeing with it. "Why do you tell me now?"

"This war may be more than just another bloody fight between cruel men…"

"You think that the demons have returned?" Afral asked in a hushed voice, suddenly fearful.

She sighed. "Your father and I worry that it might be so. The Tlocanians seem to have unnatural powers. Even Prince Wintron noticed that. More than just betrayal and good strategy routed the Border Army. They used fog and lightning, fireballs, and of course the dragon."

Afral frowned, wondering what lay ahead. How could he stand up to a demon, when he faltered before dogs? He was about to express his doubts openly, when a soldier ran up to them.

"Lady Tolara? Come quick. Your husband has been wounded and the prince says you are the only one who can heal him."

They ran through the rambling fortress, his mother urging the messenger to an ever-faster pace, down worn steps and through echoing halls, until they finally came out in the assembly yard. Afral's father lay in the back of a wagon, the prince and a medic kneeling over him.

"What has happened?" His mother asked, climbing onto the wagon.

Prince Wintron told of the battle at the temple and how destroying the priest had brought on Rolen's collapse.

Afral gazed over the wagon's side as his mother began to pray over his father. He looked very pale and suddenly Afral worried for his life. His mother examined the wounds even as she continued her fervent prayers to El. Without a pause in her prayers, she stood up, pulled free her sword, and then knelt again. She set the flat of the glowing blade against his father's chest and the light grew so great that Afral had to squint. The prince and the medic turned away from the blaze of white. His mother continued expending great power for a few minutes more and then, with a shout to El, she pulled away the blade and the light greatly diminished. His mother toppled backwards, against the wagon's slats, the sword falling from her hands and extinguishing.

Frightened for her now, as well, Afral reached out for her. "Mother!" He touched her arm where it rested on the wagon's railing, and she responded by reaching over with her other hand and gave his hand a pat.

"I...I am fine, dear heart."

"Tolara?"

Both of them turned to Rolen's weak call. They saw his eyes open and his head lift a little. Afral's mother push off the wagon's side and knelt beside her beloved, taking his hand in hers. His parents shared a relieved smile.

Afral smiled too, but then he noticed the prince frowning. He turned to see what caught Uncle Win's attention and saw soldiers just entering the fortress, escorting prisoners from the dragon temple: priests and servants bound with ropes. The soldiers prodded them along by sword and spear.

One of the prisoners, a priest in a ragged robe, screamed and cursed repeatedly. Afral shook his head at the behavior and then turned his attention back onto his parents.

Surprisingly, his father recovered quickly. His mother now seemed to be the weaker one as they helped each other out of the wagon. Both of them kept a hand on the wagon's side, using it to remain steady.

His father looked up at Prince Wintron, who was still staring at the prisoners. "My prince, what happened after my fight with the demon?"

Prince Wintron looked at Afral's father with a grim countenance. "That demon still lives. The men drag him and the others into the courtyard as we speak."

Rolen looked over. "That is not the demon; that is its human host. You are right that the demon did not die, for they are immortal, but I forced him out of the man he possessed. The demon had to return to its cruel realm, the Darklands."

Wintron shook his head. "We rode out on a simple task, and instead fought in a magical battle. You did not see the rest of the temple, Lord Rolen, but I did. It was a horrible sight. One blood-soaked room had been used for hundreds of sacrifices." The prince appeared very troubled. "Rolen, they killed more than animals in there. They killed people. We found a dog and a human still tied down on that hidden altar, their blood everywhere…" Prince Wintron's voice trailed off for a moment, and then he looked back at the prisoners. "Duke Fors was right; the dragonsworn cannot be trusted."

Afral's father pushed off the wagon. "With your permission, my prince, I will see if I can learn more from the prisoners." The prince nodded his approval and the two walked over to the captives.

Afral offered his mother an arm for support and they followed. As they came close, the ranting priest noticed. He started shouting at Rolen, but the words were unintelligible. The babble startled Afral and he was glad that the man focused on his father instead of him.

The priest's sunken eyes saw only Rolen. "You! You caused this! I have lost him!" The priest tried to lunge at Rolen, but two quick-thinking soldiers restrained him. The man struggled and tried to bite one of the guards, receiving a hit in the face in return.

"Who are you?" asked Afral's father.

"I am no one, Bright One, and it is your fault. I have lost him!" He tried to kick out at Rolen and then tried again to break free from the soldiers. He threw his head back and yelled to nothing. "Sosrog, come back to me! I will do better this time. I will not let you down. Sosrog, empower me so that I can get revenge on the one who dared challenge us." The mad priest howled like a dog, then doubled his efforts to break free. He threw off one guard and then tackled the other, wrestling for his weapon.

Rolen drew his sword, but could not strike out of fear of hurting the soldier. The priest fought in a mad frenzy, finally wrenching the sword free and then slamming its hilt into the face of the soldier, who went limp. The priest sprang up and glared at Rolen, and then reversed the blade and plunged it into his own belly. Afral's father was there in four steps, but the priest died nonetheless.

GALDON

Finally, Galdon entered the keep at Regalis. He had arrived in the conquered city two days ago, but only today did Lord-General Hraf Kelordok summon him. He strode with confidence, though he did not truly feel it. He was shown into the throne room where Lord Hraf sat alone. Galdon walked forward and offered his best salute.

The general's eyes considered him from helm to boot. Finally, he spoke. "Galdon, where is the princeling?"

The captain heard the Embraced Ones' tone and knew this was beyond being just an army matter. He fell to his knees before his superior and bowed his head. "I do not know, Lord Hraf. I believe he has hid in Tor Randis. I failed to kill him."

"Where are the two priests I told you to guard?"

Galdon kept his head down, his anger towards the priests evaporated as he realized that even there he had failed to follow orders. "I do not know, Lord Hraf. They changed forms and ran off with their pack."

"Where are their belongings?"

He was appalled, worried that his carefully groomed avarice had finally caught up with him. "The horses are back in the army stable, my lord. I...I disposed of the other items."

Lord Kelordok actually chuckled. "I hope you made a decent profit."

Galdon remained silent, not knowing what to say.

"Rise to your feet, captain. I am not going to kill you today. I can tell that you are aware of your failures and that you are remorseful. I expect that you will not fail me again. So, get to your feet."

Galdon stood up and faced his leader. Lord Hraf still held the wisp of a smile.

The commander stood up and beckoned him over to a side table. He obediently followed, to find a map of northern Na Ciria spread out.

"I have a new mission for you, Captain Galdon." His long finger landed on a city far to the north. "You are going to Freetown, where you will continue the hunt for Attuls. I give you two goals: capture a live one and, if possible, expose their hiding place."

This change in circumstances stunned him for a moment, but then he realized that he should respond somehow. He asked the first question that came to mind. "If I may ask, my lord, why this town?"

The general ignored the awkward pause and simply responded, "Emperor Silossiak is now certain that our old enemies hide in the northern wilds. Too many clues have suggested it. For months now, we have chased rumors on the streets and in the halls of Rhendora. Many there claim an Attul ancestry and we have even found many Attul spirit swords, but no one showing any power. The emperor has declared that it is all some elaborate feint of the enemy. Rhendora was given a veneer of Attul ways, with many of its people even claiming to worship the Unspoken One. Yet Rhendora is a decoy; there is no enemy power there. The Attuls designed it all to fool us, but our leader is too wise.

"He believes they are elsewhere in the north, so Freetown should be an excellent starting point for you. There is no direct route north until we win Tor Randis, so you will have to travel around by way of the Triangle Wilds. Ride fast, for you will not have that much time. Our army is coming to the north soon, so you must find these Attuls quickly." Hraf waved his hand over the whole area. "I have promised the emperor that I will find the Attuls. We cannot let them surprise us as they did the Darshi of old. I expect you to locate them for me."

Galdon felt overwhelmed by the order. He had expected execution or at least demotion to mere soldier, not reassignment. Why would Lord Hraf trust him so? Whatever the reason, Galdon was determined not to disappoint his commander again.

"One more thing, Galdon: you are not the only one searching. I do think that you are the one most likely to succeed, but it would be foolish of me to place all of our hope in one man's hands. I am sending you out with three squads and some of our best human scouts. You will not have any dreadhounds or priests to muddle your command, but you will get letters from me to prevent anyone's attempt to appropriate a mere captain. It would be easier to promote you, but both of us know that would not be advantageous."

All those above the rank of captain were Embraced. He suddenly felt the chill of fear. His despising of demons must have been apparent, but the general ignored it.

"You are to report to Colonel Ulen for your supplies and men," continued the lord-general. "Gather those who survived from this last mission; you should have enough to unite them into one squad. The colonel has your remaining two squads already waiting. I know sixty men do not make a full troop, but you will have to accomplish your mission slightly understaffed.

"When you reach Freetown, you are to visit the Five Dragons Temple. If I have any further instructions for you, it will be waiting there. Start your search in that city, but beyond that, it is completely up to you. Do not disappoint your army or your country."

"I will not, my lord," assured Galdon, saluting.

The commander held out a dark red jewel set in silver and hanging on a silver chain. "To help you, wear this medallion." Seeing Galdon hesitate, Lord Hraf smiled. "Do not worry. It is not some dragon priest magic. This is a tool the army uses whenever we need to find items or people. It heightens your sensitivity to certain things, including the magic of Attuls. That is all it will do."

He took the necklace and slipped it on, but could not hide the grimace as the cool metal settled around his neck. He obeyed, but he feared that this might be the end for him. He had always thought an Embraced One came about through some elaborate ritual, but suddenly he worried that this necklace might be a tool to weaken, to prepare him for demonic possession. He struggled to keep his thoughts under control, but they raced away in fear.

"You are still your own man, Galdon," stated Lord Hraf. "The necklace is just a tool, like your sword or dagger." The general suddenly pointed to the dragon priest standing to one side. "Do you know Brother Verdrof?"

Galdon frowned and shook his head. "I do not believe we have met before."

The general motioned the priest over, a thin man in an unadorned robe of an expensive weave. Only the slightest bit of red edging colored the blackness of his clothes.

"Verdrof will also be heading towards Freetown, though I think you will get there before him. Verdrof, tell me your frank impressions about Captain Galdon."

The priest's sharp gaze was like that of a hawk spotting prey. "I wonder that he is not Embraced yet, for I think this one already knows too much."

The general smiled. "Some day, maybe, but right now he is most useful as just a human. What did you sense from him?"

"Loyalty to Tlocania and the army, with a thick coating of greed.

Right now his thoughts are in great turmoil, fearing that you are about to trick him into an Embracing."

Hraf nodded. "Galdon carefully projects his thoughts whenever he is near a known Embraced One. Moments of open vulnerability are rare with this one."

"He can control his thoughts?" The priest showed surprise and concern. "You should kill him or force him into an Embracing."

Galdon's heart began to beat rapidly, fear overwhelming him. The general knew far too much about him.

Hraf smiled briefly, ignoring the captain's sudden panic. "Galdon is a crafty man. Those feelings and thoughts are true to his character, which is why he is so successful in using them to hide his deeper thoughts. I have known Galdon for many years and so I know how to look past that which he works so hard to project. He is a troubled man at times, but I also know that he is loyal to the Tlocanian army."

The wiry priest shook his head. "Yet you still rely on him?" He added hastily, "I say such truths only out of concern, Lord Hraf. I especially do not like talking so freely in front of him. His fears grow with each minute. You are using a weapon that could just as easily wound us."

"You would be right, if Galdon were my weapon, but he is not. That is your role, Verdrof. Consider Galdon to be your scout."

"I do not understand, my lord..."

Hraf beckoned the priest over to the map table. "Verdrof, why do you think we have failed to find the Attuls?"

"But we have captured at least six of them."

That number was a surprise to Galdon. His fear lessened, though he still wanted to rip the necklace off. And yet, he wanted to hear more. Knowledge was a form of treasure, and Galdon really did like collecting what wealth he could.

Hraf waved off the priest's argument. "The ones who call themselves Attul Watch Riders? Yes, I know about their capture, and the numbers seized are closer to one hundred than to just a half-dozen. They serve as isolated spies and scouts; none of them has any worthwhile information. Our methods of persuasion are very effective, but all that we have learned is that the Attul homeland is called Warhaven and that it lies somewhere in the northern third of Na Ciria. Why is this Warhaven still unknown to us, even after we have scoured the north with both priests and hounds?"

Verdrof stared at the map. "I do not know, Lord Hraf. I do not think they have died out, but maybe they are so few that we overlook them..."

"This territory has no real cities left beyond this Freetown, except in Rhendora. None is so large as to hide even a few hundred Attuls. No, I think there is another reason why we have not found them: they can sense those of us who are Embraced and so can avoid us."

The priest raised a bushy eyebrow, curious. "So you leave Galdon untouched and send him out as the advance scout."

"Precisely. If any mere human can find them, it is Galdon. He is a very effective man. You and your hounds will follow at a distance. Let the captain find the Attul Prayer Warriors for you. He will flush them out and you will assist in the final capture."

AFRAL

After the incident with the mad priest, Afral's father insisted that he needed to return to the Five Dragons Temple.

"But I have ordered it destroyed," argued Prince Wintron. "They are going to set it ablaze this evening. What I saw in there is not something you would want to experience."

"This is no pleasure visit," agreed Rolen, "but I must see this atrocity for myself. My wife will also join me."

Wintron nodded his reluctant approval.

"What about me?" asked Afral, unable to keep quiet.

"You will stay here," said his father firmly. "I will not have you exposed to that den of abomination. It is a place perverted by the enemies of El."

Afral knew better than to argue, so he had to remain behind as his parents rode off for Randisville with an escort of twenty soldiers. He lingered in the courtyard well after the prince and his personal guards had gone inside the fort. He watched the soldiers lead away the prisoners, presumably to the keep's dungeon. Yet still he loitered in the area.

He went back to the abandoned wagon, sat down on its open tailgate, and just spent the afternoon watching the various activities of the fortress. He also studied the keep around him, seeing it differently now that he knew its heritage as a Darshi-crafted fortress. It seemed to brood over him. On an upper floor, he could see windows with their wooden shutters nailed shut, rooms where no one ever went anymore. Before, Afral had taken that as a sign of the keep's age and huge size, but now he could not help wondering what dark secrets might be hidden in those abandoned rooms. The thought gave him gooseflesh. He considered fleeing to the rooms set aside for his family, but he decided against it. He wanted to be the first to welcome his parents back to Tor Randis.

* * *

His parents returned as night approached. Relieved to see them ride into the courtyard, Afral ran over. He hungered for a reassuring hug, but his mother warned him away. She indicated her smeared clothing and ash-stained face. "Do not touch us until we have had a chance to bath. I will not have this grime smeared on you."

"I am glad you are here," said his father, dismounting. "Can you take our horses to the stables while your mother and I clean up?"

He took the reins happily, glad for a task that was within his abilities. "I can do that."

"Thank you," his father responded. He tried to smile, but it was a weak attempt. Afral wondered what had him so troubled.

"Do not linger talking with the stablehands," warned his mother, "but please ask them to wash down the horses and our gear, for ashes seemed to have settled on everything. Come straight back to our rooms afterwards, for we will need to see the prince soon."

Afral nodded understanding, and set off with the horses at a brisk walk.

* * *

He saw to the horses' tack and then gave them over to the stablehands for washing and feeding. That done, he ran back to the suite assigned to his family.

He met his mother in the hallway, her hair still wet from the bathing room. "Afral, there is no time to see you bathed too, but you should at least wash after touching our gear."

Afral looked at his hands and saw what his mother meant. His hands were filthy from soot. As soon as they entered their rooms, he went to the wash basin.

His father was already waiting. "Good. You are both here. The prince has already sent word, inviting us to dine with him and we should not leave him waiting. No matter our lack of appetite, we need to meet with him." His parents exchanged one of their cryptic looks that Afral guessed had something to do with what they had seen at the temple. He was not about to ask any questions or else they might decide to leave him behind again.

They came to a small dining room where Prince Wintron already waited. He rose to his feet and welcomed them in, signaling for the food to be brought. "Let us leave off our talking until after you have eaten. That is my royal order, for the two of you still look pale after today's gruesome labor."

They obeyed his wish, and were soon in the middle of a feast. Maybe his parents had no hunger, but Afral did, now that his parents were safely back. He ate heartily, but he was the only one of the four who did. In the midst of their meal, Duke Fors entered the hall and asked for an audience with the prince.

"What do you want, uncle?"

Fors looked at the others in the room. "Can we step out to talk, my prince? I have news about the war."

"No," replied Prince Wintron. "We can talk here."

"Is it appropriate to have a woman and child hear this?" asked the duke.

"Lady Tolara is the second-best sword fighter in the realm," replied Prince Wintron with a bit of amusement, "as you well know, uncle. We have both seen her on the practice field back in Regalis. She is also a wise and practical woman. I have no concern with her presence." He turned to Rolen. "However, maybe we should ask the boy to step out. What do you think Rolen? Is he not too young to be concerned about these troubles?"

Afral was ready to do so, sure that his father would agree, but Rolen motioned for him to remain seated.

"What is happening concerns us all, especially all Attuls," responded Rolen. "I would ask that my son be allowed to stay."

The prince gave his nod of approval.

"Very well," replied Fors, though he frowned at Afral. "I have troubling news from the Highlands. The enemy has somehow gotten behind us and now Drass holds Halenvale."

Afral did not quite understand the direness of the news, but knew it was terrible by how the prince reacted.

Prince Wintron suddenly pounded the stout table. "What? He was behind me when we retreated. How could he have scaled up onto the Highlands?"

Fors shook his head, having no answer. "The two men who made it here are old retainers of mine. They know Drass too well to be mistaken. They say he led the soldiers who overthrew the estate, and those mercenaries had the gall to wear the Halen-Dabe colors, the weasels. We now have enemies on either side of Tor Randis."

His father spoke up. "The situation is even worse than that. Do either of you understand what today's events at the temple signify?"

"That the dragon priests are in cahoots with Tlocania," proclaimed Fors, "which is what I had already said. It also shows that they are slier than we knew, for somehow they smuggled their magic throwers through Tor Randis without my soldiers catching them."

"No, it means more," said Wintron suddenly. "The demons of Darshi have returned, haven't they?"

Rolen nodded. Afral stared at his father, dumbfounded. For two hundred years, the Attuls had kept watch to prevent this day. How could the demons be back? The Attul Prayer Warriors kept vigil just to stop such a return.

"Come now, not those old myths," protested Fors. "Those are stories to scare the little ones, not for grown men to take serious. I can accept that evil men use powerful magic. Magic I have seen." He pointed at Rolen's sword where it hung at his side. "But do not give me fanciful stories about ghosts and demons. I expect better from a king's councilor."

"Doubt as you wish, Duke Fors, but demons have returned to Na Ciria. I am sure of this, for I fought them twice now. And it was not with magic that I withstood it, but in the power of El...."

The duke interrupted. "Do not add religion to this fable. I may not practice magic, but I know it is a skill like any other. One of my own aides has a bit of talent in this area, and I understand that it is through training and practice that he learns what he does. Very few seem to be adept at the art of magic, but please do not try to wrap it in religion. My prince, can you not control your councilor?"

"I speak truth," argued Rolen, his voice still calm even though Afral could tell that he was aggravated.

"Enough, uncle," stated Wintron. "Your badgering gets tiresome." He sat forward and pointed at Rolen. "And you, councilor, need to stay on the subject. Share the rest of your observations, but be quick about it."

Afral saw his father take a deep breath, calming himself before he speaking. "This information is from the records I found in the temple and the few facts we gained from the prisoners. I give you three concerns. As you know, the black dogs that came with the Tlocanians are called dreadhounds, a species bred especially for war and raised to eat only human flesh. One temple servant mentioned that if the dreadhound's eyes glowed red it was far more vicious and cunning. My concern is that the bloody ritual created some kind of link between a hound and a human or made a were-hound. It was an evil yet powerful act.

"My second concern is that the priests plotted sabotage. I found reports mentioning a spy in this very fort but I could not determine whom. It appears to be someone of authority.

"Third, this crisis enfolds more than just the Border Realm. We already know that the Tlocanians have conquered the Seven Kingdoms and all the lands from the Grizzly Mountains to the Grandgorn River. But this is beyond just a human war. No matter your doubts, Duke Fors, there truly are demons involved. Because of this, I must render my resignation as councilor."

"What? What kind of coward are you?" asked the duke. "You are running off in our time of greatest need. Will you allow this, Prince Wintron?"

The prince met Rolen's eyes. Afral knew that they were friends. The prince had been around their home so much that Afral had grown up calling him Uncle Win. Right now, however, there seemed to be doubt in Wintron's eyes. "Why?" he asked.

"I am not running. My own people must be warned..."

"Such is the fickleness of foreigners," interrupted the duke. "My brother was a fool to have trusted you, coward."

Prince Wintron grew angry with both the duke and Afral's father. He hit the table so hard that mugs jostled. "Explain yourself, Rolen!"

"My first duty lies with Na Ciria as a whole. Never before has there been a conflict between this calling and my service to the Border Realm, but now I must choose."

"You would run off to those who once heckled you?" asked Wintron. "I remember the stories you told me of your homeland and they did not show understanding towards you. You pick such arrogant people and would abandon us now? People who hide instead of help? We need your wise counsel and your powerful sword. If the demons have returned, we will need an Attul Prayer Warrior to stand with us."

"You will need more than us three," replied Rolen, "and you are not the only ones in danger. Where else are the Tlocanians advancing? On Rhendora? On the Lakelands? Are they marching southward onto the Midcirian Plains? I must go report to my own people and call them to war. Yes, my family and I are leaving, but I will hopefully return with an Attul army like in the days of old. Surely, this will rouse my people, for they are sworn to stand against evil."

"He seeks only to shelter his family," said the duke with scorn. "The man flees, claiming some grand mission to calm our objections. However, I will not buy his rotten barrel of excuses. I can smell the stench of fear from here."

"That is not so," protested Rolen. "You will need such allies as much as the other lands. The Attuls may not be as numerous as they were in the olden days, but we are still a force to be reckoned with. I am not running away."

"Prove it! Leave your wife and son here as a bond."

Afral's father fell silent, shocked at the demand.

His mother spoke up in protest. "I am no animal to be held as surety. How dare you, Duke Fors! I should challenge you to personal battle for such an insult…" She paused for a moment to let them dwell on that. "But it would not look good for you to lose your head to a mere woman and I do not want to deprive Prince Wintron of his last general, no matter how pompous you are. Rolen and I discussed this thoroughly on our ride back from the temple's burning. All three of us must go, for the message is dire and we do not know how dark the road, nor what obstacles we might encounter. With three of us, we will surely win through to Warhaven and warn our fellow Attuls."

Wintron seemed to realize that it was useless to try to dissuade them. "Should I send along a squad or two in escort?"

Rolen shook his head. "No, for my people carefully guard the secrecy of our homeland. No outsider has been there in over one hundred years. Even if I wanted to, I could not approach the place if your men came along. Ways would be blocked, paths erased. If we persisted, then we would all die. No, the three of us will go alone and we will leave by dawn tomorrow."

Fors shook his head. "I predict that we will never ever see him again."

* * *

At dawn, Afral and his parents were ready. They had tied on their saddlebags and checked the stablehands' work with the tack, finding all in order. Prince Wintron may not have liked their leaving, but he graciously provided for them. They had three fresh mounts and adequate supplies. Even Afral had a horse again.

The prince came out to bid them farewell, along with Lord Gordrew. Prince and councilor came into the stable to bid them farewell, the prince's guards hovering nearby.

Afral's father bowed to the prince, but Wintron stepped forward and embraced him gruffly. "I release you from all your obligations to the Border Realm, except one." He handed him a sealed scroll. "This message is for the Rhendoran king, so please deliver it to his official in Four Corners. Since the White Owl Pass is your only route out off the mountains, I do not think this will cause you any delay. Beyond this missive, I free you from your councilor responsibilities. Know that I will miss you Rolen Strongarm. I admit that my heart feels betrayed by your leaving, but I will trust that you do what is right. Hurry and bring back that army of Attul Prayer Warriors."

His father accepted the scroll.

The prince moved on to Afral's mother, taking her hand and bowing over it. "Lady Tolara Quickblade, I will miss your fair face as well as your healing touch. Please know, I expect Rolen's return but I urge you to seek shelter. It would comfort me to know that you and Afral are safe."

"All must fight this battle, no matter their sex or age," responded Tolara. "El sent the Attuls to Na Ciria to perform this task two hundred years ago and it is still our duty to this day. All Attuls must fight."

"Even young Afral?" The prince reached out and ruffled the youth's brown hair.

She nodded. "We will see to it that his training is completed and then he too will join the cause. I may sound heartless, but service to El is more important than my wishes for Afral's safety."

"You Attuls are a harsh people," stated Lord Gordrew, "or at least the god you serve seems overly demanding."

"No, Gordrew," corrected the prince. "I have found El to be compassionate and patient. He is not the cause of the coming pain. I think that we are entering a time of sorrow and sacrifice, but only because evil men have invited these demons back. And I am thankful that good people, like this family, are willing to fight."

Afral stood taller, reaching a sudden resolve. "I am willing to fight right now. Father, let me stay behind and help Prince Wintron." He clumsily fell to his knees before the prince, right there in the old straw of the stable walk. His awkward attempt to free his sword was hampered by his position. "Will you take me as your servant, my lord? I will do my best for you, even if it is only as a messenger or horse tender."

The prince laid a restraining hand on Afral, stopping the attempt to offer his sword in service. "Not now, young Afral. Go to your people and get your full training. Whenever we meet again, then you can offer your services if you still wish."

The prince helped an embarrassed Afral to his feet.

The youth felt ashamed at being rejected. With hung head, he went back to his horse. He kept his eyes averted, not wanting any to see the tears of frustration that now strained his cheeks.

CHAPTER FIFTEEN

Unexpected Lady

MYLANA

The streets of Waybridge ran narrow and windy near the Five Dragons Temple, each a jumbling flow of people and wagons. The noise echoed loudly off the tall and closely-packed buildings. However, with the mid-day prayers in progress, all that sound suddenly became unified, as traffic stopped and everyone recited praise to the five dragons. Everyone that is, except Mylana, Coursen, and their pursuers. She ran as fast as she could, keeping up with Coursen. Three men chased them.

The Riders tried to keep to the deserted alleys, but failed. Now they were running through a small square where people still knelt in obeisance to the dragons. One man did so while holding onto the reins of his horse. Many gave furtive glances as the two parties ran by, but no one dared to interrupt their worship to interfere, especially not when they saw that the pursuers carried naked swords.

Coursen led her into another alley, jumping over a woman kneeling at its entrance. Mylana dodged around and kept right after him. They had just entered the alley, when the temple bells tolled the end of mid-day prayer. Coursen and Mylana pushed past a man who was just starting to get to his feet. The fellow cursed in surprise and then shouted angrily after them. He cursed again when the three pursuers roughly pushed him out of the way.

Coursen came to a split in the alley and turned to the left but then staggered to a stop almost immediately. The way was blocked at the next twist. Seeing him stop, Mylana yelled for him to follow and chose the other opening. It was a tricky place to run, made slimy by the brackish water meandering down the center. She heard Coursen trying to catch up with her but she dared not slow down for the three others could also be heard. Their pursuers were gaining.

She turned another corner and saw that the alley opened up ahead. She pushed herself, hoping to find a crowd ahead. The alley ended and Mylana found hundreds of people leaving the dragon temple that loomed to the right. She pushed her way across the front edge of the crowd, offering apologies to those who protested but hardly slowing. She ran across the square and into another alley, with Coursen at her heels. The crowd quickly built behind them, slowing the others.

She turned a sharp corner and saw an open door. Deciding it was their best hope to elude their pursuers, she ran inside, finding it to be a weaver's shop. She ignored a woman asking her a question as she held the door for Coursen, and then quickly closed it. The women working at the looms were now all staring, while their supervisor stalked forward and demanded to know who trespassed in his shop. Mylana kept running, ignoring the man.

The shop's front door opened on a different street. She ran out, almost colliding with a customer. With hastily shouted apologies, the two kept going, dodging down another alley and around a delivery wagon being loaded with barrels. Two blocks later, they finally slowed, joining the flow of afternoon traffic on a busier street.

Finally free of their pursuers, they now headed back to the inn.

* * *

"Who were they?" asked Mandor.

Neither Coursen nor Mylana had an answer. The three of them were back in their room at the Traveler's Rest. Beyond the window, the gray day was darkening towards sunset. Soon the bells would toll for evening worship.

Mandor shook his head. "I do not like this. Someone tried to follow me too, but I lost them before I met up with Hessilyn."

"They were not just following us," replied Coursen. "They had weapons out and I think they meant to use them."

Mandor nodded. "Hopefully, just bully boys looking for an easy mark."

She had her doubts about that. "We lost them somewhere near the Five Dragons Temple, but what if they know about this inn? What is to keep them from coming back here and just attacking us the next time we step outside?"

"Do you think they wanted you two in particular?" asked Mandor. "I find it hard to believe that local thugs would do that. It is not as if we are merchants with a bulging money purse. I would guess that by chance you crossed their path somewhere and the thugs decided to have some fun."

Mylana chose not to argue with her brother, but she wondered. Those men seemed far too determined for mere muggers. Why risk being seen flaunting the worship time? Those men either had immunity or wielded enough power to ignore the authorities. Either possibility frightened her. She wondered if their mission was already compromised, still hundreds of miles from their goal.

"But what about you?" asked Coursen, confronting his friend. "Did you meet Hessilyn? Were you followed? Did you learn anything useful beyond the color of her eyes and the taste of her lips?"

Mylana could tell that Mandor was trying to ignore his friend's taunt. "I did see Hessilyn and no one followed me there, for I lost them well before the noon bell..." He tried to stop there, but could not help but defend himself. "Our meeting was discreet and proper, with no more than a brief hug and hand holding. I care for her too much to sully her reputation."

Coursen smiled at the mild rebuke. "I know that, old friend. You are a man of convictions."

"Did she have anything useful to say?" asked Mylana. "I trust that you did not reveal any of our plans."

"Hessilyn knows that I am an Attul Rider, but she would not tell anyone else," replied Mandor. "As for our mission, she knows nothing of it. She thinks I am up here on a normal ride. The risk was minor and I learned much. Hessilyn's father waits in Waybridge to meet one of the Tlocanian generals. Hessilyn would not tell me about his mission, for she would not betray her father, but she revealed much about the Tlocanians. Over twenty thousand soldiers march towards Waybridge. Hessilyn thinks they must have emptied the Seven Kingdoms to send so many. They head this way to skirt the rugged Forest Hills. From here, they will cross the waybridge and head up the Swiftgorn Valley towards the Lakelands. Already, scouts have passed through, searching out the best roads for those that follow."

"Then if we go westward they will take us for spies," noted Coursen, "and I do not want a whole army chasing us."

"Nor I," said Mylana. "That leaves us with the road eastward."

"Not necessarily," replied Mandor. "We can wait out the army here and then continue northward. Once the soldiers are past, the way through the Seven Kingdoms should be clear..."

She shook her head. "You jest. An army that large must have hundreds of demon-possessed. Do you really think Waybridge is large enough to hide us from so many?"

Mandor grimaced. "No, that was foolish of me to suggest. It seems that Hessilyn's presence affects me after all. I want to keep her safe, yet I know her father's entourage is large enough to shelter her. His protection is even better, since he is allied to these Reds. Who would dare harass any of his party?" He met Mylana's eyes. "You are right. We must flee eastward and then go up the Grandgorn Valley. I think the other reason I hesitate is that the way will quickly take us out of the routes committed to my memory." He looked to Coursen. "Not that I do not trust you, dear Coursen. It is just that I am most comfortable leading."

Coursen smiled. "And I am most comfortable following your lead, yet you will need to pass the reins to me just as I will have to pass them to Mylana for the last leg. I am the one who knows the routes through most of the Lakelands or along the upper Grandgorn Valley, so you cannot avoid my becoming the guide. You will have to put your fate into my hands soon, no matter how it galls you, old friend." He gave a winsome smile to take the bite out of his words. "Are we decided then? We will take the Crossover Road eastward?"

The other two nodded.

* * *

The Watch Riders knew enough about their enemy to realize it would be best to flee Waybridge during daylight. They spent the night taking turns as sentry, but no one tried to molest them that night. They ate in their room while it was still dark outside, and then went downstairs as soon as the bells tolled the end of morning worship. They took the stairs to the dim stable, and found shy Kaden. The young man assisted with the saddling of their horses and reloading the pack animals, though most of his focus was on helping Mylana. Soon they were ready to go.

Mandor offered Kaden coins for his extra effort but he shook his head. "I helped because I like you." He could not stop himself from taking a quick glance at Mylana, then reddened and focused on Mandor again. "You seem to be honest and fair people. I can tell it from your treatment of your horses." He looked aside again, this time at the steeds. "They are regal mounts, my lord, that have been lovingly handled."

Mandor nodded and pointed to the spare mount that had just been loaded. "I was there when Fleet took his first wobbly steps five years ago. Our horses are almost like family."

Kaden smiled, put at ease by a topic he loved. "Horses are true and loyal friends." He paused, and then gave another furtive glance at the attractive young woman. "Will you be coming back to Waybridge?"

Mandor answered. "I cannot say, but you have certainly made us feel welcome here." He leaned forward and grabbed Kaden's hand, this time forcing the young man to take the coins. "You have earned this, Kaden."

"Yes, you have," added Mylana with a warm smile. "Thank you for all of your help, Kaden."

The young man lost himself in her smile for a moment, and then looked away shyly.

* * *

Mandor led them out of the inner city by its northern gates. Because the stone wall had only three gates, they had decided it was not worth trying to conceal their passage until they were beyond Waybridge's outer ramparts. Instead, they rode boldly towards the approaching army, or at least seemed to.

They passed through the outer city, still heading north, and exited the wooden palisade that marked the city's limit. They headed up the Middle Run Road for half a day, but did not see anyone following. Traffic on the road remained light, for the merchants did not want to run afoul of the army and have their goods seized. The three saw only local farmers taking goods to the city or coming home with empty wagons.

Satisfied that no one followed, the threesome finally turned eastward at a crossroad in a dreary village called Raven Perch. Mandor assured the others that this road would eventually turn back south, skirting the city, to connect with the Crossover Road. He mentioned that a Rider post was nearby, but they decided it would be best to avoid it.

They rode until dusk, then found a copse in which to hide their camp. They settled in for the night, eating dinner around a small and well-hid fire. As she spooned up her hot stew, Mylana wondered if anyone had noted their departure.

* * *

The next morning, they followed the road as it climbed out of the

Cleargorn Valley, leaving the struggling farmlands behind. Finally, they intersected with the Crossover Road and took its wider path. The road led them into an ever-wilder land of forested hills, where farms seemed to grow in clusters for protection and support. It was a lonely country.

At first, there was some other traffic on the dirt highway, but by late afternoon, no other travelers could be seen. They rode in silence, through dark forests and past still-gray meadows.

Spring growth appeared to be stunted and rare. Where the city fought off the gloom with lanterns, the countryside seemed wrapped in darkness. Mylana had experienced the same during her rides to Westbend after its fall, but the Dragon Shadow still felt oppressive even when familiar. Nothing but gray skies here, leeching the color out of everything. She missed the bright sunshine, colorful spring flowers, and blue skies of the Midcirian Plains.

The gloom had noticeably deepened by the time they finally came upon a tiny village. They had decided to take accommodations this night, hoping to catch some road gossip, but the look of the place made them wonder if many travelers stopped here. A dozen worn cottages clustered beside the road, their roof thatch gray with age and their walls stained by past storms. Smoke wafted from chimneys and chickens still scratched in two yards, but no people were in sight. The largest building in the settlement had a green lantern lit in front of its door, announcing that it was the local inn. It looked to have maybe a half-dozen rooms on its second floor. The Attuls rode around the corner of the inn and into its stable yard, where a boy ran out to take their mounts. Only two other horses stood in the weathered stable that was more of an open shed. Not having enough room inside, he offered them the corral, assuring them it was sound and safe. The corral sat behind the stable, a fenced-in square of bare earth. An old tree towered beyond it, probably a welcomed shade before the Dragon Shadow arrived, but now it just caused more darkness.

"Do not worry about wolves or thieves, for our dogs keep all away from here," the youth said with a gap-toothed smile.

"Will our horses get any hay?" asked Mandor.

The boy nodded. "I will see to it. I can even toss in some oats, for just a bit more money…"

"Hay will be fine," assured Mandor. He agreed to the accommodations for their steeds, but only after the stablehand promised them use of a small stall to store their gear and provisions.

"Don't worry about mice. Our cat keeps the place free of them."

Mandor nodded. "Thank you for that assurance."

They unsaddled the horses and released them in the corral. Once their goods were stored away, the Attuls picked up their saddlebags and blankets and headed around for the inn's front door.

The lad stared after Mylana, probably not used to a woman wearing pants and a sword. Mylana wondered if she should take up wearing skirts, but dismissed the idea as impractical. Besides making it harder to ride, a skirt would not help with the sword and she was not about to go unarmed.

She walked behind Mandor, with Coursen taking up the rear. Mandor opened the front door and a cheery light spilled out on the dirt road. He walked in and there came a shout.

Suddenly, someone seemed to assault her brother.

Mylana grabbed for her sword, but then stopped herself just in time. There was scuffling in front of her, and then laughter. Mylana stepped closer as she recognized the person wrapped around her brother. Hessilyn. It was not an assault but an embrace.

"What is she doing here?" whispered Coursen from behind her.

"I do not know," replied Mylana, "but our route is obviously no secret if she can anticipate it."

"Well, let us not linger here in the doorway. Push your way past those two so we can shut the door behind us."

The common room was lightly occupied, but all eyes turned to Mandor and Hessilyn. The two still hugged, though Mandor whispered something in a stern tone. Mylana went around them and over to the table where Hessilyn had obviously been sitting, the bench knocked over when she sprang at Mandor. She righted the bench and sat down. Coursen took the bench across from her. Finally, Hessilyn let go of Mandor and the two came over.

"Hessilyn is in trouble," explained Mandor, as he sat down next to Coursen. Hessilyn joined Mylana though her dark eyes stayed on Mandor. Her brother gave the woman a stupid smile. "Do not be angry with her for seeking us out. We are her only hope."

Mylana looked at the fair-skinned beauty sitting next to her. Hessilyn's luxurious black hair fell over her shoulders. She wore a richly embroidered dress more appropriate for court than some rough inn. She had once considered her a friend, though not a close one. However, she could not trust her after Westbend's overthrowing. It had been her father who betrayed the king to the Osburg Empire. "Are you alone, Hessilyn?"

Eric Lorenzen

The lovely young woman met Mylana's eyes. "I made certain that none followed me. I would not want to jeopardize your mission." She looked back to Mandor and set her delicate hand on his larger one.

He gave her hand a sympathetic squeeze, but his face showed him to be conflicted.

"How did you know we were coming this way, Lady Hessilyn?" asked Coursen, keeping his voice low. The few other patrons in the common room still watched with the curiosity.

Her eyes never left Mandor as she replied. "I did not know; I only guessed. I had to flee rather suddenly, so I could only hope that I had ridden in the correct direction. I was so worried that I might have picked wrong, that I would never find help."

Mylana had grown up with Hessilyn, though they had never been close. Hessilyn had always been a charming yet determined girl. She doubted that the noblewoman ever felt helpless or doubted her path. Somehow, Hessilyn had known that they would be riding eastward. "Why did you run away?"

Mandor interrupted. "I do not think this is the place to talk about that. Let us wait until we are in a more private setting."

As if to prove his point, a middle-aged woman in a white apron approached. Most likely the wife of the innkeeper. She asked what they would want to eat or drink. They placed their orders and also made arrangements for the night. Mylana would share the room that Hessilyn had already rented, while Coursen and Mandor would take the adjoining one. The four did not speak much over their hasty meal, realizing that they had already said too much in front of the others.

Once their meal was done, they gathered in Hessilyn's room, the women sitting on one bed while the men took the other. They still kept their voices low, for the walls seemed thin.

"Now, why are you here?" demanded Mylana.

Hessilyn took a deep breath, her bosom swelling. "I…I had to run away from my father. It does not matter to him that my affections are for Mandor; he had promised me to a middle-aged Tlocanian general."

Mylana shook her head in sympathy. "I am sorry, Hessilyn, but is that not the way of upper nobility? You grew up knowing that your husband would probably be chosen for you."

Hessilyn met Mylana's eyes and nodded. "That is true, and I was ready to do my duty, but he asks too much of me. This general is an Embraced One, a demon lover. I have seen how being Embraced has changed my father and it is not a pleasant thing. He talks to himself.

His mood changes often, with bouts of great anger. When he is not raging, he is coldly uncaring. As time has passed, the Other has become more powerful and controlling. Some days, it is as if my father is just a shell for that Other to inhabit.

"I have seen the same behavior from other Embraced Ones among Westbend nobility, so I know this Tlocanian general will be just like him. Who will I be married to, the man or the demon? How could anyone submit to such a marriage?"

Mylana had no retort. Hessilyn was right that no one should be forced into such a union.

Coursen took up the conversation. "No matter her dire straits, she cannot join our mission, Mandor." He looked at Hessilyn. "Are you not dragonsworn, Lady Hessilyn?"

She gave him a slight nod. "I am still loyal to the gods of my ancestors, Coursen, but not to these men who try to usurp the Dragons."

"Exactly," replied Coursen. He put an arm over Mandor's shoulders, trying to persuade him. "She cannot go where our mission takes us, Mandor. You know this; no matter how much you care for her."

Mandor looked at Hessilyn, his continence showing his torn heart. "Dear Hessilyn, I am afraid that Coursen is correct. We cannot take you along on this ride." He stood up when he saw her pained face and then knelt before her, pressing her hand to his chest. "I love you deeply, Hessilyn, but I must complete this charge. I will see you safely beyond your father's grasp, but that is all that I can do for now. I hope you will not hold it against me, but duty comes first." He looked at the watching Mylana. "Surely, she can ride with us until we reach the Grandgorn Valley? I will find some refuge for her there, among the river towns."

Mylana did not give him the approval he wanted, though she was tempted. This was about more than just Mandor's happiness since many other lives depended on this ride, so she hesitated to agree with his sudden plan.

The lack of response did not deter Mandor. He looked back into Hessilyn's shining eyes. "We will find a safe place, where your father cannot find you."

"I think it should be up to Mylana to decide if she should ride with us that long," disagreed Coursen, "for Mylana leads on this mission. Maybe it would be best just to take Lady Hessilyn to the next hamlet instead of all the way to Deep Crossing. What do you say, Mylana?"

All turned their attention to her, awaiting her judgment. Mylana saw the hope and love in the eyes of Mandor and Hessilyn. She saw concern on Coursen's face and realized she felt the same. What dangers came with Hessilyn? Would her father chase after her? Would the spurned general also give chase? She had her doubts that Hessilyn would willingly part with Mandor again. She truly seemed to love Mandor, but that did not make the woman any more trustworthy. Hessilyn might want to sabotage their mission, if that meant Mandor would be freed from his duty that much faster. She was a lovely lady, but also a resolute one, used to getting her way. It was too much for Mylana to decide this night. "I think we should turn in for the night. We can talk again in the morning."

The rest agreed and all went to their beds. The men stated that they would take turns as sentry this night so that the women could sleep. In spite of that, Mylana did not have a restful night. Instead, the presence of Hessilyn weighed on her thoughts.

CHAPTER SIXTEEN
Border Highlands

WINTRON

Wintron felt alone, in spite of his ever-present personal guards. The departure of Rolen had bothered him more than he would admit to others. Gordrew was a dependable advisor, but far too cautious. Wintron used to call him 'Councilor No' behind his back, though his father had often chastised him for such impudence. Rolen, on the other hand, could temper Wintron's impulses with sensible advice. Of all of his father's councilors, he had respected Rolen the most. Now he had no one left to confide in, no one to give him wise council.

He moped about this as he walked through the vast keep, his guards walking before and behind him. He headed towards the prisoner cells, for his uncle had learned something about the dragon priests that he wanted to share. As he walked, Wintron had a sudden insight. He realized whom he really missed. He longed for his father. Even though he was in his fourth decade of life, he felt too young to be king.

Wintron and his entourage went down a stairway, to a part of the keep where the walls constantly vibrated and a steady roar came through the thick stone. Here they were close to the powerful Thunderroll Falls. Wintron turned a corner and came to the heavy door that led to the cells. Captain Bilshor, who led his guard, had spied out the way well ahead of him and was already holding the door open. He walked through, to find his uncle talking with the jail warden.

His uncle paused and looked over at him. "Ah, there you are, my prince. Has the coward finally left? Good riddance to him." He gestured towards a side room. "I wanted you to hear what we have learned from our other priestly prisoners. Let us talk with Captain Thessor. He has learned quite a bit."

Wintron followed his uncle through the doorway, motioning for his guard to wait with the warden. The room held a small table. The captain, standing behind it, gave them both a sharp salute. However, Wintron noted that the man still wore the colors of the duke's personal guard. They all sat down around the worn and chipped table that wobbled when Wintron rested his arms on it. He wondered why Fors insisted on doing this all the way down here; the man could have come up to them just as easily.

"Captain, I want you to give the prince a summary of what you have learned."

"Yes, my lord." His face showed no emotion. He was simply doing his duty. "The duke ordered me to learn all that I could about the plots of the dragon priests. I have thoroughly questioned any in Randisville who had dealings with the temple, but most only had gossip of questionable worthiness. I have also interrogated the prisoners that you and Lord Rolen brought back. The priests and servants were not cooperative at all. It took much persuasion and even trickery to get them to reveal as much as they did. What they divulged, though grudgingly, was that the dragon priests approached the duke's sons with their plot of overthrow. The new High Brother of the Regalis temple was the one who initiated all of this, at the behest of the Tlocanian emperor..."

Wintron cut off the captain with a hand motion and turned to stare at Fors, suddenly angry with all of the intrigue. "You brought me all the way down here for this? I already knew that your cursed sons plotted with the Tlocanians and anyone could have guessed that the dragon priests served as intermediaries. Are you trying to claim the boys were duped into treason? I will offer no pardon or mercy for their heinous crimes."

Fors sat very straight, returning a cold look. "My two eldest sons are as if dead to me. I pray that the Goddess Avoli claims them soon and sends them to the frozen lands of the cursed. I only have one son now: Gurash. Do not make such petty accusations towards me, my prince." The duke stood up and motioned for the captain to do likewise. "Thessor, take the crown prince and show him the servant who is finally talking. Maybe Prince Wintron will listen if he hears it from that one's own mouth."

"Yes, my lord. Will you join me, my prince?" asked the captain.

Wintron considered refusing but then nodded, indicating for the captain to lead the way. The captain took him down the prison block to a far door. Wintron and Fors followed, as did Captain Bilshor at Wintron's signal. Thessor unhooked a wall lantern and then unlocked the heavy door.

The room stank of sweat, blood, and urine. A battered temple servant hung there, chained to the wall. A small table sat in center of the room, a whip coiled on its bare slab. Thessor set the lantern on the table and retrieved the whip. His shadow loomed over the prisoner as he turned his back on the light and came at the man sagging at the end of his chains. Thessor lashed out with the weapon, aiming each blow with precision. The prisoner writhed under each blow and soon begged for relief.

Wintron watched with gritted teeth, noting with anger that the captain seemed an expert at this. Questions followed, which the prisoner answered in a harsh, strained voice. Thessor was unemotional and very thorough, getting the prisoner to reveal much. The prisoner told of kidnapping villagers to be used in the priests' bloody rites. He spoke of what they did in those rites. Finally, by the end of the session, the prince heard many of the details of the Tlocanian plot to kill his father. He had also heard of plans to kill himself and his uncle.

It surprised Wintron that the servant was privy to so many secrets. The prince even wondered if some of the information was made up in an attempt to please Thessor, but there was no way to verify the veracity of his tortured confessions. He knew that much of it was true, though, for it matched to information gleaned by others.

When the prisoner finally lost consciousness, Wintron felt relief. He did not want to watch any more torture. He took a quick look at Bilshor and wondered if he looked as disgusted as the captain did. He forced his face to a mask of coldness, aware that his uncle watched him carefully. The three of them stepped out, leaving Thessor behind to clean up from his bloody work.

Fors looked up at his taller nephew, stepping close. "Do not disdain Thessor, for he is merely following my orders. I saw your look of disgust; you need to harden yourself. This war cannot be won unless we grow as hard as the mountains of our Fortress God. Remember your childhood lessons about Cha, for we need his favor to regain our homeland."

"Do not lecture me, Old Fox. I know the mountain gods as well as you." Wintron held his uncle's eyes, barely able to control his anger. "I do not like how adept Thessor is, for it speaks of much practice, but I will not ignore what his work has revealed to us. Do you have anything else you want to show me down here, General Fors? If not, I will return to my study and get to my other tasks."

Wintron strode off without a backward look. His personal guard hurried to surround him. As he climbed back up the stairs, he did his best to ignore Thessor's methods and instead focused on the information harvested. It implied a deep conspiracy planned for almost a year. They had even killed the old High Brother, Horris, to gain control of the Regalis temple. Wintron wondered if Fors particularly wanted him to hear the confession that the duke was also on the assassination list. It implied that the sons considered their father an enemy, but Wintron wondered if the prisoner had been coerced into making that claim just to assuage him. He was still not certain that his uncle was completely ignorant of his sons' schemes. It might be that they merely went further than their father wanted them to go.

* * *

By the time Wintron reached the study set aside for him, he had decided it was time for some bold action. He ignored the breakfast waiting for him, having lost his appetite. Instead, he sent a soldier to fetch Gordrew and started pacing the room, inpatient to set his own plans into motion. When Lord Gordrew finally arrived, Wintron told him of his desire to hunt down Drass.

The councilor nodded. "That will be necessary. Both he and Mordel will need to be brought to justice."

"I mean to set off tomorrow, for he is prowling somewhere in the Highlands."

"Is that wise, my prince? There is an enemy army below us. Who knows when they might try to attack? You will be needed here for your leadership as well as an inspiration to the troops."

Wintron gave a short laugh. "Most of the men here are more loyal to their general, so I may be more likely to incite than inspire. Besides, Tor Randis cannot be taken from the south, especially if the Tlocanians fail to push their Dragon Shadow this high. No, the immediate needs are to clear out the Highlands, gather more recruits, and to see that the refugees are resettled.

"As for you, Gordrew, I need you to carry my call to arms throughout the areas of the Highlands that I will not be able to reach, to Bluevale, Traul's Pass, and High Calton. We need to gather men here to Tor Randis. Will your own men be enough of an escort, or will you need additional troops?" Lord Gordrew's retinue was small, for his lands were poor. Wintron did not want to insult his father's faithful advisor, but he had his doubts over the effectiveness of Gordrew's personal guards.

Gordrew frowned. "I would rather stay here and keep an eye on Duke Fors. Pardon my bluntness, my prince, but I do not trust the general. I remember him to be close to his sons…" Gordrew let his words trail off, implying much.

The prince had similar doubts, but he could not let doubts hinder him. "Fors has sworn his service to me. That should be enough to hold any concerns at bay. Now, will you have need for more men? Please tell me, for I will gladly provide them."

"My men will be sufficient," replied Gordrew. "They know their duty and will protect me on my route, even if it were back to Regalis."

Wintron quirked an eyebrow at Gordrew's boast. Gordrew might be known as Councilor No, but he was no coward. That was a good thing for him to remember. "Do not play the bravado with me, Gordrew. Ride this high country circuit as I ask and then return here. I will not send you with letters to murderous Mordel."

Gordrew gave a slight bow of acceptance. "I have another concern, my prince. Will the duke accept you going in pursuit of Drass?"

"Leave that to me." The prince strode over to the door and opened it. Stepping out, he told Captain Bilshor to send someone after Duke Fors, requesting his presence. When he stepped back into the study, he met Gordrew's watery eyes. "I will use this morning's antics against the Old Fox. He will not like hearing that I go out to hunt his second son but he dare not hinder my efforts, not after we both heard of the assassination plans. Now, while we wait for Duke Fors, we can spend time on other concerns. I want to double our army, but where shall we find the gear for so many?"

The two were still discussing provisions when Duke Fors arrived. The Old Fox listened to Wintron's plans and surprisingly did not object to any of it except Wintron going out himself. "You are no longer a carefree youth, nephew. Frankly, you never were though my brother indulged you all his years. Not only are you middle-aged, you are now our ruler. You must stay safely within Tor Randis' walls and let lesser men take care of this mission. We cannot risk you out there."

"Of what good am I if I hide in this redoubt? I am going out uncle, for the people need to see me, to witness the resolve in my eyes. The lesser lords have not yet sworn fealty to me, so I must show them that I am worthy to follow."

Fors shook his head. "You are a fool. Varen tolerated your whimsies far too much, and now we reap what he allowed to grow. A ruler does not ride at the fore and he most certainly does not go out on scouting excursions. Scouts are expendable; you are not."

"General Erileon did not agree with you. He felt a leader should be within sight to inspire the troops."

"Erileon is dead! Do not put yourself at risk. Instead, send me." The duke glared his challenge at his nephew.

The prince wondered why Fors would want such a duty. They were talking about his rebellious son, after all. He doubted that he could trust his uncle to bring Drass in. However, Wintron did not say that aloud. Instead, he focused on his other reasons for keeping his uncle at the fortress. "Your going is an even more foolish idea. You are our last general. They call you Old Fox for good reason, for there is no better strategist in the Border Realm. You are needed here, for if Tor Randis falls then so will all of the realm. No, you shall stay, as will most of those I brought up from the Borderheart Valley. I dare not thin out the fortress, but I would ask you to assign me one officer and two squads of soldiers familiar with the land around Mount Cha."

Fors scowled and tried arguing some more, but finally yielded when Wintron agreed to take at least a hundred men.

* * *

Dawn touched the mountain peaks, but it was still dark in the main courtyard of Tor Randis. Steam rose from the horses' nostrils. Wintron stamped his feet to try to warm them a little. He held a hot cup of cider in his hand, its steam mixing with his breath. He gulped the last of it and then handed the mug to a servant. The prince slipped on his gloves and then climbed up onto his horse, settling on the cold saddle. His mounting signaled all the others to do likewise. Soon, all one hundred were ready. He motioned for Captain Bilshor to start them off, while he rode over to where Fors and Gordrew waited. "I know you will hold Tor Randis vigilantly. If you need to contact me, send your message to Chashade. I will use that town as my headquarters. With the gods' mercy, I will be back shortly."

"We will do our duty," replied Fors, "for the good of the realm."

"For the good of the realm," echoed Gordrew. He and his men would be leaving in a few hours.

Wintron nodded and then turned his mount, falling in at the back of his troop, just in front of their supply wagon. He did not bother with any long good byes, for he was not particularly fond of either man. Both were useful to him as the future king, but neither was a companion or friend. Instead of lingering with the two, he took a moment to observe his troops, a third of whom came from Fors' ranks. He hoped they proved to be reliable and loyal, but they would have to earn any trust he gave them. Wintron did not like being so suspicious, but his cousins had shown him what came from being too trusting.

The force pressed closer together as they passed through the three sets of massive gates that would let them out Tor Randis. Their passage echoed off the high walls as the troops snaked through the two baileys and under two gatehouses. It was a shadowy route. As they came through the final set of gates, the troops spread out again. Wintron was one of the last through. He nodded at the gate guards but did not stop to talk with them.

His thoughts still gnawed on the troops he had gained from Fors. He would need to get to know the captain who led these new men, this Captain Kevlo. Might as well start now.

Wintron urged his horse faster, to move around the last ranks, swerving to the right to get around their ordered rows. The sudden change saved his life for, just as his horse sped up, two arrows hit the ground just behind him. He recognized the sound and turned his horse with a shout. Others heard it as well and the men reacted by trying to spy the assassins. They were still close to the fort's walls, so all craned their necks to see who was above them.

"Two assassins!" shouted Wintron. He too looked up at the towering ramparts, but no one leaned outward. He saw only stone. They must have ducked back right after shooting. "Did anyone see them?"

No one had.

He motioned for two of the cavalry to come near. "Go quickly and report this to whoever commands the wall this morning. Maybe we will be lucky and catch them."

The two kicked their mounts in their rush to obey.

As the troops milled about, still trying to spot the assassins above them, captains Bilshor and Kevlo rode back to Wintron's side. He told them what had occurred. Bilshor urged him to either shelter back in the gatehouse or get away from the wall quickly. Wintron nodded and urged his horse forward, his personal guard around him again. The two captains got the troops back into order and had them set their horses trotting after their prince.

* * *

That evening, as the men set up camp in a meadow beside the road, Bilshor came to see Wintron in his large tent.

"Come in, Bilshor. Take a seat." The prince placed a second mug on the folding table and then reached for the kettle heating over the small fire. Though he thought that such an extravagant tent was ostentatious, Wintron knew the men expected such lodgings for their leader. He had to admit, at least to himself, that the added comforts were nice.

The captain gave him a bow of thanks and took the offered chair, but he did not relax. Wintron recognized the hesitancy and knew it meant Bilshor had something unpleasant to share.

"What news?"

The captain answered softly. The smooth voice had always seemed a bad fit to the rough man, thought Wintron. "The two men you sent back to the keep have caught up with us. The assassins were not found."

The prince nodded, having expected this. He did not speak, though, for he sensed that Bilshor had more to say.

The captain took a sip of hot tea, frowning slightly in response. Wintron repressed a smile. He knew Bilshor well enough to know he would rather have ale, even ice-cold ale on this chilly night. Wintron continued to wait.

At last Bilshor spoke. "My prince, I cannot continue as head of your guard, not and command this force too. Either give the command over to Captain Kevlo or replace me as head of your security. Having two roles makes me incompetent at both."

He nodded understanding. The attempted killing had upset Bilshor more than it had Wintron. "Kevlo cannot command, for I do not trust him. At least not yet. Whom do you suggest as your temporary replacement? Sergeant Yosif?"

"He would be acceptable," said Bilshor, relief showing on his face.

This time Wintron let his smile show. Apparently, the captain had been expecting a fight from him on this change. Well, he was no fool. He saw the wisdom in Bilshor's assessment. "Old friend, I have learned to heed your counsel. Do you think I am still as stubborn and brash as when we journeyed to the Lakelands two decades ago? No, do not answer that, for I see that twinkle in your eye. The choice of Yosif is a good one. I will leave it for you to inform him of his new role. Now, what news do you have from the scouts?"

Bilshor smiled as well, then settled back on his folding chair and took another sip of tea before speaking. "Orgel came in with their report just as we started setting up camp. They have ranged as far as Tenderfoot Pass and have found no signs of Drass or his men."

They conversed about the routes ahead and which directions to send the scouts until a soldier came in with Wintron's dinner, the same hearty stew that the troops ate. Bilshor declined the offer to eat with his prince, wanting to talk with Yosif as quickly as possible.

* * *

They arrived in Chashade five days later. It was not that the distance was so great but the terrain was very rugged, causing them to travel three times as far with all the switchbacks on the road. When they arrived in the late afternoon, the shadow of Mount Cha was just starting to creep across town, setting half of it in shade while the other half still felt sunshine. The scouts reported no immediate concerns, though they had already heard rumors of past disturbances.

Wintron headed for the town's inn, a large stone-and-wood structure just starting to come under the high mountain's late-day shadow. As he dismounted in the inn's stable yard, he gazed up at the looming peak, named for the Fortress God. He hoped the mountain gods would grant him a quick and complete victory and silently sent a prayer towards the Autumn God's supposed home. Wintron wanted to hurry back to Tor Randis, for he did not trust his uncle without supervision. Even greater, though, was his need for revenge on Drass the Poisoner. He would relish taking off that one's head.

With such bloody thoughts, Wintron wondered if he should be beseeching Avoli, the Crone Goddess and bringer of death. But no, he had never felt any awe for that one, the wrinkled goddess of winter. At least Cha looked strong in his statues, as either a warrior or a face on a mountain. Wintron even wondered if he should be praying to Rolen's El, but thought the better of that. El seemed a jealous god who wanted sole devotion, and Wintron was not ready for such a commitment. He considered visiting Cha's temple here in the village to make a sacrifice. Such a pious act would soothe the locals and might just win that god's favor.

He refocused on the towering mountain looming over the community. Though it was only breezy down here, he could see that high winds whipped snows off the rocky summit, the white streams highlighted in sunlight high overhead. The sight made it seemed far chillier down here among the tall pines. Though Tor Randis was a dank and rambling fortress, it still had many large and blazing hearths. He could have enjoyed such a fire on a cold evening like this.

"Prince Wintron! Welcome to the Galloping Horse Inn."

He turned his attention back to his near surroundings. A middle-aged woman of some girth bowed before him, clenching the hem of her white apron with nervousness.

"Thank you. Are you the innkeeper?"

"Yes, my prince. I am Surinda, at your service."

"I hope you have a cheery fire inside. Is the town council already gathered?" he asked. This was one of the few communities without a lord.

"Yes, my prince. They await you in the common room."

"Thank you. Please let them know I will be with them shortly."

She gave another nervous bow and hurried back inside to do his bidding.

Wintron turned to Bilshor as the captain returned to his side, for he sensed that his old friend had something to share.

"Scout Orgel just reported on some town rumors that you will want to know. A messenger from 'Prince' Drass rode through earlier this week, announcing his rule over the Highlands, as appointed by 'King' Mordel. The city council met with Drass' man. Also, there have been dog attacks in the area. Black dogs."

Wintron gave the news a curt nod. "In that case, have soldiers stand guard *inside* the common room too. The councilmen might need a reminder of who I am. This may be a longer meeting than we discussed, but I want to make sure Chashade is a safe base for us. I want to leave that supply wagon here, for it will just hinder us on our next leg."

DRASS

Drass punched his right fist into his left palm, unable to hide his frustration. He wanted to strike out at the dragon priest in front of him, but he knew better. "Why must I be there to greet them? Cannot the Tlocanians find their own way from the lifts to Halenvale? Can you not guide them? You seem to have found your way easily enough."

His anger did not seem to affect the hooded priest. Even though the priest wore civilian clothes and a borrowed cloak, it did not diminish his aura of authority.

"Do you wish to remain alive?"

Drass blinked at the calmly spoken threat. He suddenly realized that he had once again been too insolent. "My apologies, holy brother. You Tlocanians are our allies and deserve proper hospitality. I will go back to the lifts with you, Brother Prekor."

"You misunderstand, Prince Drass. I have a different mission. Brother Zaphrion and I are just passing through with our pack. We relayed this message only as a courtesy to the army. Now, if you will excuse me, we need to get the dreadhounds out of Halenvale before they decide to eat some of your fine citizens."

He was almost tempted to offer his mother as fodder, but realized that the priests would take his jest seriously. Instead, he just bowed a dismissal. The priest gave a slight nod in return and left. Drass stared after him. Neither Prekor nor Zaphrion had ever explained why they showed up dressed in farmer's garb. It was not for secrecy, for they came in with their growling pack and no one would ever mistake dreadhounds for common dogs. He received reports of two missing field hands of comparable statures and could guess how the priests acquired their shabby attire, but it still did not reveal their motivation. He gave up trying to understand and left his father's assembly hall.

* * *

When Drass departed Halenvale four hours later, he left behind only a small contingent under one of his sergeants. He fully expected to find all coerced to his mother by the time he returned. He only hoped his younger brother would still be locked up. The woman was that forceful in her personality. Doubling the force would only mean twice as many men compromised. She would not release Gurash herself, but she would try to order it or bribe someone else to the task. The Hen of Halenvale gathered all under her wings, unless the person was as strong as Drass. After so many years of her manipulation, he was immune to her cajoling and threats.

He regretted that he was forced to lock up his niece as well, since Mordel would not like hearing that. The little vixen had actually tried to stab him while trying to flee, so he did not trust her not to do something else foolish. Zita was someone who would obey the Hen's orders and let Gurash out. His mother was too fat to make her way down the ladder into the root cellar, so he did not fear that the old lady would do any releasing herself. He just hoped the men would be strong enough to resist the duchess.

Drass wanted to take both prisoners to the lifts, since he had planned to send them down to Regalis anyways, but then the Hen informed him that Zita had taken a cold when she hid in the well during her escape attempt and would certainly die of the coughing sickness if she was forced to travel so far. Some of his men even had the nerve to try arguing for the girl's safety. The Hen of Halenvale had already won over some.

He went down the rickety ladder to see his niece and she certainly coughed with great drama, but he was not totally convinced that it was genuine. However, to stop Mother's incessant nagging, he decided to leave Zita in the cellar, with plenty of blankets and warm food. He also left Gurash, too worn out to fight the Hen over that one too.

He promised himself to send both of them away as soon as he returned with the Tlocanians. His mother would not be able to coerce them.

CHAPTER SEVENTEEN

Crossover Road

MYLANA

Mylana awoke to frantic screams from somewhere in the inn. She threw off the blankets and sprang to her bare feet. Grabbing her nearby sword, she rushed to the door, listening for anything in the hallway. The young woman hastily pulled on her pants and shirt, but did not take the time to pull on her boots. She ignored Hessilyn's questions, but instead yanked the door open. Coursen and a shirtless Mandor were already in the corridor, both with still-sheathed blades in hand. Growls and more screams came from downstairs. No other patron dared to open their doors, so no one took note of their state of undress. The threesome ran down the dark hallway and charged downstairs. The common room's fire had died to angry coals, so the room was very dark. Mylana noticed the front door hanging askew and open, even as she turned to the sound of a growl.

"To arms," ordered Mandor. "El light our way and guide our swords!" He pulled his sword free, the sudden white light illuminating the slaughtering that had occurred.

Three dreadhounds retreated from the glare, hiding among the overturned tables. To one side, Mylana heard the moans of an inn servant. Another two lay quietly on their shredded bedding near the fire, obviously dead. When Mandor charged at the nearest dreadhound, the two other dogs ran out the broken door and into the night.

She was about to join Mandor, when Coursen laid a restraining hand on her. "Keep your blade in its place," he hissed. "It is bad enough that one of us has been exposed as an Attul. We dare not draw such attention to all three of us, when Mandor can handle the remaining beast on his own."

Mylana wanted to protest, but saw Coursen's wisdom. When she finally nodded agreement, Coursen pointed at the wounded servant. They both went over to see if they could help her.

* * *

As another gray dawn lightened the sky, Mylana pulled over a bench and sat down. The injured worker was still unconscious, having lost so much blood to the hound's attack, yet she would live thanks to Mylana's healing work. Coursen had grudgingly allowed her to pull out her sword and do that, but only after he made sure no one was near enough to see. She had healed the woman and then quickly put her sword away. Now the woman rested and, hopefully, she would recover completely. Mylana also needed some rest, for the healing had been difficult.

Mandor had killed the one dog, and now stood guard at the damaged front door. Tired by his fight, he leaned against the doorframe. His sword was sheathed at his side. Just then, Hessilyn appeared at the top of the stairs, softly calling out for him. She was fully dressed and carried a bare knife in her right hand. When she spotted Mandor, she rushed down and gave him a hug.

Coursen watched for a moment and then left the room, going to explore the kitchen and the rooms beyond. Mylana was not certain whether he approved of the affection or not. She was not even sure of her own feelings. Mandor was a good man and deserved to be loved, but his choice was a rather odd one. Mylana wondered what these two had in common, besides their mutual good looks. Even before the betrayal by Hessilyn's father, the young noblewoman had lived a life far apart from Mandor's existence as a messenger and scout.

Coursen came back to report that the innkeeper's family and the cook were both well, having barricaded themselves in their rooms. "Mandor, will you come with me to see about the horses?"

"Of course," said Mandor, pulling free of a clinging Hessilyn. "My dear, could you go upstairs and gather up everyone's belongings? We will need to leave here soon. Mylana will go with you to help and offer protection."

Hessilyn rose to her tiptoes and gave Mandor a chaste kiss on the cheek. "I will do so. Be careful out there."

Mylana followed her to the stairs, not sure whether she should be upset at Mandor for tasking her with guard duty.

* * *

It took some time for the boys to return. By the time they did, both women had bathed and dressed. While Mandor took his turn in the bathing room, Coursen explained what they had found.

"The stable hand is dead, as well as all the horses in the stable. The dogs leaped over the stalls and fell on each horse. We found one dreadhound trampled. I fear your mount is among those slaughtered, Lady Hessilyn. Our own horses survived, amazingly. That poor excuse of a coral was to our benefit, for it collapsed when our mounts pressed against it. The horses galloped off, too fast for the hounds to catch. It took us some time to catch them, without saddle or bridle." Coursen rubbed his tailbone. "Maybe your family is used to riding bareback, Mylana, but it is not an easy trick for me. I am glad that the horses are all from your family's herds though, or else we never would have been able to round them up. They came to us after Mandor's coaxing."

"What about the rest of the village?" asked Hessilyn.

Coursen shook his head. "I fear that we will hear about many more deaths. The dreadhounds attacked the nearby cottages too."

* * *

Midday, when they finally rode out of the tiny settlement, they left behind a village in mourning. Hessilyn came along, riding one of the spare mounts. They had learned nothing of traveler's gossip or road conditions, but they were relieved that no one had noticed the Attuls in their midst.

Beyond the village, the Crossover Road climbed over a forested pass and through a wild country where no one dwelt. As they crossed the wilderness, they became more concerned. Here and there, damp soil showed the recent passing of many horses and dogs.

"What do you make of it?" asked Coursen of his old friend.

Mandor climbed back into the saddle after having examined the tracks. "If we were in Westbend, I would say that a Gray patrol had traveled this way. A large patrol. I do not know if these Reds do similar tours of their lands."

"Do you think last night's attack was planned or was it just some of their dogs gone rabid?" asked Hessilyn, leaning over in her saddle to stare at the hoof prints.

"Oh, that was a planned attack," Mandor responded. "They do not let dreadhounds just run free. I would suspect that their keeper lurked nearby, overseeing their attacks."

"But it makes no sense," argued Mylana. "Why would they send in just the dogs? The tracks show a party large enough to have swept up the whole village."

Mandor began to respond, and then paused. Mylana guessed that he did not want to frighten Hessilyn.

Coursen had no such qualms, though, so he answered her question. "We have seen it before. The dreadhounds like to eat humans, so if their keepers have no prisoners on hand as fodder they will turn them loose on some settlement. That is what happened to Broken Willow."

Hessilyn's eyes narrowed. "That is not what my father told me. Broken Willow's residents were massacred by the king's followers."

Coursen shook his head. "Mandor and I rode into that village just after the Grays left. They had set fire to the place to hide the evidence, but we saw the mauled and half-eaten bodies before the flames could consume everything."

Hessilyn shook her head in disbelief.

"Neither of you ever told me about this," stated Mylana, joining Hessilyn in her saddened surprise.

"I did not want to upset you, little sister," explained Mandor. He looked at Coursen. "The two of us have seen many horrible things while scouting out the Grays. What you saw with us during our last ride into Westbend was bad enough; there was no reason to frighten you with worse."

"Do you think my father was responsible?" asked Hessilyn. She sounded worried.

Mandor ran a hand through his blonde hair. "That I do not know. He is certainly capable of doing such crimes, now that he is demon possessed."

Hessilyn nodded. "I am surprised you endure my presence, if my father is so horrid." She paused. "Maybe I should just ride on alone."

Mandor hastily set his horse in front of hers and grabbed her reins. "No. I would never hold you responsible for your father's misdeeds. I love you, Hessilyn."

She gave him a weak smile. "And I love you, Mandor." She sat up straight in the saddle with new resolve. "I will just have to prove that I am worthy of your affections." She gently yet firmly took her horse's reins back. "Now, are we riding on?"

Mylana smiled at the woman's resolve. "Yes, let us get moving. We have foes ahead of us and behind us, most likely, but we expected that when we accepted this mission. Will you take the lead, Coursen?"

In answer, Coursen set off at a quick pace that forced the others to hurry after. Mandor looked as if he wanted to say more to Hessilyn, but her rush to follow Coursen caused him to follow quietly. Mylana came last, leading their one remaining packhorse.

* * *

Over the next few days, the foursome kept a steady pace eastward but never caught up with the Tlocanians. On the third day, they were alerted to trouble up ahead by circling vultures. Rounding a hill, they came upon the remains of a trader caravan, the wagons burned, animals slaughtered, goods spilled, and the humans partially eaten. The foursome kept their distance from the massacre, but its stench still reached them. The scene took away any desire for banter. Instead, they rode in silence for the rest of that day.

That evening they set up camp near a small stream. After dinner, they bedded down for the night, Mylana taking the first watch. She sat on a log, looking out into the darkness while their little fire crackled behind her. Images of the dead kept entering her thoughts: those she saw with that caravan and those from the inn.

Sighing, the young woman stood up and decided to check on the horses. She walked over with care, for the night's darkness was deep under the Dragon Shadow. She reached the tethered steeds and hugged the first one she found, finding comfort in its thick mane and that horse smell. She was still there when the horses all stirred, their ears perking up at some sound. At first, Mylana heard nothing, but then she made out a faint baying. She shivered. There were dreadhounds somewhere behind them. When the horses settled down, she knew that the hounds were still far off. Nonetheless, it took some time for her heartbeat to slow. She walked back to the log and sat again, still listening carefully. She heard a lone owl, but no other animals.

Finally, her watch ended and she went to wake Mandor for his turn. She found him already awake, staring across the fire's embers at a sleeping Hessilyn. Mylana's nearness broke his stare. He gave her a little nod and stood up, folding his blanket and then buckling on his sword. He put on his cloak and then proceeded to their makeshift sentry post. He was a bit surprised when Mylana followed.

"I heard something rather disturbing," she whispered. "There are dreadhounds behind us, but they sound still far off."

"I was afraid that might happen," he replied softly. "The hounds that attacked the village did not run ahead to join the patrol. They must have lingered near the settlement, sleeping off their feast."

"What are we to do?"

"We go on," he answered simply. "This countryside is not like the Grandgorn Valley around Westbend, where there are many roads and lanes. Nor is it like the Midcirian Plains where we could ride off in any direction. Father's directions indicate only two ways across the Yucai Wilderness and the other road is far to the north. No, we are tied to this path until it drops down towards the Grandgorn Valley."

"I do not like this."

"Would you rather that we turn back? There is a demon-led army just entering Waybridge."

"You are right, but I still do not like it. And this is not the only dangerous road you are taking, Mandor."

He was silent for a moment. "Do you mean Hessilyn?"

"Yes, I do. She could compromise our mission, for she is not an Attul. She is not even Elsworn. You have already revealed too much to her, Mandor, or how else would she have found us?"

"I erred," he admitted, "but Hessilyn will not expose us. I know her to be a trustworthy woman."

Mylana sighed, choosing not to argue that point. "You are walking down a road of heartache, brother."

"Maybe, but it is too late to turn back. She has captured my heart, little sister. We love each other."

"But what of your differing beliefs? She rejects El, in favor of those winged monsters."

"Our beliefs are dissimilar, but we have so much else in common. You have known her for some time. Is she not a sweet and intelligent lady? Have you ever seen her to be mean or rude or ugly?"

Mylana chose not to mention the times when she had seen Hessilyn acting the noble, for her rudeness had been more out of ignorance and habit then from meanness. "She is dragonsworn, Mandor. Even though she is a nice person, how could she remain loyal to gods that allow such awful deeds done in their name?"

"You will need to ask her that. All that I know is that she would never participate in the evils that other dragonsworn are doing." Mandor put a hand on each of Mylana's shoulders and turned her around. "Now, go back to the fire and find your blankets. You need some sleep."

* * *

The next day, they followed the Crossover Road up onto a plateau. The day was darker than usual, with a wind out of the west. The cloud cover seemed deeper, as a natural storm added to the forced clouds. By late morning, a drizzle began falling, chilling everyone.

When a city appeared out of the mist, the soaked foursome was ready to seek out a warm inn. They had come to Gratoro, one of only three cities in the Yucai Wilderness. Mylana took note of the high stone walls and then the dragon temple's high spires within the city. The tips of the five towers were hid by the mist. They gave the city an eerie feeling, as if the towers pulled the Dragon Shadow down lower.

The foursome rode up to the city gates, where local sentries stood guard but did not challenge their entry. They rode through the gateway, the stone passage echoing with their passing, and into a dreary city of dirt roads. As they looked for a promising inn, the drizzle turned into a solid rain. Mylana wondered if that Tlocanian patrol was somewhere in the city as well.

BRODAGAR

Brother Brodagar walked through the kennels at the Gratoro temple, satisfied that the dreadhounds were being cared for properly. This small city saw only visiting packs that sometimes came with the road patrols. They certainly were not used to having three packs at one time, but that was how many Brodagar had brought with him from Waybridge. He had also brought five Embraced priests with him, all of them Houndmasters, so they could take care of the dogs. The High Brother of Waybridge's outer temple had handed over the dogs and men without any fuss after Colonel Wevro had relayed the lord-governor's desire for a well-equipped team.

Only two of the packs were here right now, for the third had not yet caught up. It had been Nesron who had ordered the dogs sent to terrorize the hamlet. Brodagar had agreed, for it made sense to scare the Attuls, but he had not liked that it was Nesron's idea. Apparently, the army officer felt he was in charge of their expedition simply because an army colonel commanded them. The priest needed to consider how to disown him of that fallacy.

He decided to walk around the outside of the temple, going to the public courtyard at its front gates to await Nesron. The courtyard remained empty, due to the rain, but the priest ignored the drizzle. Sometimes he needed fresh air. The temple was a smaller one, the incense from the hourly sacrifices lingering in its low-ceilinged chambers. The fumes had started giving him a headache, which aggravated Sahak too. Wandering out here allowed him to clear his head. So he waited in the rain.

The Tlocanian garrison sat on the same street, so Brodagar's wait was not long. Soon, he could see the captain walking towards the temple, following the servant sent to fetch him. The officer made no effort to avoid the puddles; he strode the straightest route at such a pace that the servant had to scurry at times to stay ahead of him. He entered the courtyard and stopped in front of Brodagar, giving him a nod of recognition. No army salutes for a mere priest.

Brodagar gave the captain a smile as warm as the chilled drizzle dripping off his hood. "Follow me."

They climbed the broad stone steps to the front entrance. Overhead loomed the usual facade, showing the five beasts with their wings spread. It was a very familiar sight to Brodagar and his Other, yet within him Sahak wondered where the two missing dragons hid. The black, the gray, and the red were all tamed now. Only the gold and blue dragons remained uncaught. Brodagar followed Sahak's musing, wondering what it would be like to ride such a beast.

He entered the worship hall and immediately the smell of sweet incense wafted around him, bringing back his headache. Musings about dragons flew immediately from his thoughts. He looked around the hall. Attendance appeared light, probably due to the weather. A priest recited prayers up front, over the bloody remains of some small animal. Brodagar gave it all only a cursory glance, the look of a professional verifying that underlings were doing their duties. He did not stop for Nesron to pay homage, for they had no need to maintain appearances for local rustics. Instead, he marched the captain to a back room where the temple's High Brother awaited them.

Brodagar gave High Brother Torval-Skarga a respectful bow, for this Embraced One stood above him in the order of things. The other priest gave a slight nod in return and then pointed down a hallway. "It is near the appointed hour and I do not want to be late, so let us get to the Listening Room."

Nesron nodded and motioned for the High Brother to lead the way. They weaved their way through the temple complex to an area reserved just for Embraced Ones, and finally came to the Listening Chamber. The temple's Listener had already started the ritual, having just killed the necessary human sacrifice. The three stepped into the room quietly, not wanting to disturb the ritual, and watched as the Listener cut open his victim and removed the heart. He took a ceremonial nibble of the warm organ and then laid it on the altar fire, chanting the whole time. Now the smell of cooking meat joined the aroma of incense. Brodagar could feel the power released from the victim, for there was always power in death, even from the wheezing last gasps of an old hag. This victim had been young and strong, though. That much Brodagar could sense, even without staring at the bloody remains.

The altar sat against a smoke-darkened wall. Above it hung a stone mask of a demon-possessed face. A face depicting harsh beauty and a cruel demeanor, judged his human side. The demon within him made no judgments about beauty or cruelty. As the smoke from the sacrificed heart swirled around the stone face, its eyes began to glow red. The three onlookers moved forward then, knowing that communication had begun.

The Listener finished his empowering chant and then bowed to the mask. "I, Hoslar-Sisgaro, Listener of Temple Gratoro, have opened my ears. Speak and I will listen."

The mask's lips softened and became fleshly. "We see you, Hoslar-Sisgaro. We shall speak the truths you are to hear. Who else stands in the Listening Chamber? Identify yourselves."

The High Brother stepped next to Hoslar and spoke his own name. He then introduced his two guests.

"Ah, we have a message for the two of you, Nesron-Swoferosh and Brodagar-Sahak," the voice from the mask said. In distant Tlocania, in the Speakers Tower, some priest communicated through this stone conduit. As he spoke, the red eyes pulsed with power. A Speaker might proclaim orders directly from the emperor or he might relay the orders from some other superior. This time, he shared words relayed from the Lord-Governor of the Hasan Province. "Lord Krev sends three orders. First, you are not to kill or capture anyone in the party that you are hunting. He states that his Free Hawk is among them and he will not have his spy lost. You may do anything else that is necessary, but no killing or capturing.

"Second, there are others who hunt your prey. A large party left Waybridge in pursuit, with their own dreadhounds. This party serves a different high demon. Lord Krev desires that there be no direct confrontation if it can be avoided, but he will not tolerate these Others gaining the knowledge that should be his. It is his role to hand this information to our great lord, Emperor Silossiak.

"Finally, Lord Krev sends this order. You must accomplish your task before your prey can reach the Grandgorn Valley. He expects soon to learn the answer and he expects this information to come from the two of you. Do not fail him." The demon mask fell silent, but its red eyes continued to pulse.

They both bowed and responded in almost unison. "I hear and obey."

When he left the Listening Room a little later, Brodagar held a private discussion with his Other. Brodagar had to agree with his demon, that the lord-governor was being purposely vague in his missives. Krev did not want anyone in Tlocania to realize that he was close to finding Warhaven.

CHAPTER EIGHTEEN

Four Corners

AFRAL

Afral and his parent traveled northward from Tor Randis, crossing the Border Highlands. The land up here was rough, with high passes and narrow valleys. The trees (mainly pine, fir, and spruce) grew narrow and tall, for heavy snows pruned off any longer branches every winter. The roads that Afral and his parents followed were often narrow and rock-strewn, winding up steep hillsides and down towards rushing streams. Despite the ruggedness, they encountered numerous villages and small estates, each sheltering among the trees or sitting at the edge of some small meadow. At most of them, they stopped long enough for his father to share the news and to urge the local lord to send men to join the fight, but they did not linger.

Days later, they came to a halt at the top of White Owl Pass, the only route across the last line of high mountains that formed the otherwise impenetrable Border Wall. White Owl Pass climbed well above the tree line, across the shoulders of two of the towering summits. When the three stopped their mounts, the only sound they could hear was the wind and a brief neigh from one of the horses. For just a moment, it felt like they were the only people left in the Borders, if not all of Na Ciria. The thought bothered Afral. He whistled loudly, hoping to find some comfort in its echo off the granite cliffs.

His parents merely gave him a surprised look, but no rebuke. His mother pointed ahead, urging him to look down the pass. From here, the trail dropped quickly, snaking back and forth down the steep slope and then entering a ravine that brought it to the Singgorn Plains far below. To either side of the pass, the mountains soared to cold heights, gathering clouds to their peaks. Behind them stood many more peaks, their lower reaches covered in thick evergreen forest but their heights all rock, ice, and snow. Another of their horses neighed, not liking the wind's chill.

Afral's father took this moment to share with him. "My son, this happens earlier than I had planned, but you are finally leaving the Border Realm." He shifted in the saddle to look at his wife. "Your mother and I have always intended on bringing you north to Warhaven for the completion of your training; we just expected it to be another year away.

"You grew up hearing our stories of the Attul homeland, hearing that we are just strangers in this land, yet I know that the Border Realm has been the only home you have ever known. I admire your loyalty to old King Varen and how you dreamt of serving him as a King's Man, but you have a greater destiny, my son. You are an Attul. You belong to a people who have sworn to defend Na Ciria from evil. Even Varen would not have begrudged your following this greater calling."

Afral shook his head at his father's words. "But I do not want this. I am far more a Borderman than an Attul. Why could I not have stayed behind? Even if Prince Wintron did not want my service, I could have helped plant the fields or care for the sick. With practice, I could sharpen my sword skills enough to be accepted into the army. Let me turn around now and I will go back to Tor Randis on my own."

"That is impossible. We cannot leave you behind, for a half-trained Prayer Warrior is far too dangerous. You have a taste of El's power, but not the wisdom required to wield it properly. Your training must be completed and that can only happen in Warhaven." His father sighed. "If only we had taken you back home years ago to live with your grandparents, then you would not have grown so attached to the Borderfolk. I was wrong to ignore your mother's wishes. I thought I could start your instruction on my own, but instead I just gave you more time to become confused."

His mother spoke up, "Dear one, we love you too much to let you do something so foolish. You must go to Warhaven. However, I offer you this promise: upon completion of your Prayer Warrior training, you can return to Tor Randis. Neither of us will stand in your way. Truly, we will more likely be standing right beside you, for we also care deeply about the Border Realm."

Afral did not respond, for it hurt.

Fallen King

"Look below, son," continued Tolara. "Do you know what lies before us?"

At first he did not want to answer, not pleased with her attempt to redirect their conversation. However, his mother patiently waited for his answer. He finally decided to mutter something. "The Singgorn Plains."

His mother nodded. "Two hundred years ago no grasses grew down there, so huge were the armies that churned it up as our ancestors fought the last demonic invasion."

"So why do we not fight this one? Why are we heading in the wrong direction?"

His father responded with a soft-spoken rebuke. "This is not just about satisfying your own bloodlust or sense of adventure. You might feel brave sacrificing yourself in some heroic last stand, but that is not the aim. We want these demons defeated, and that means that we must find allies. We are heading in the right direction, for we need more Prayer Warriors at our side. Do you understand?"

Afral could no longer hold back his fears. "But Father, I do not think the Attuls will let me go to battle either. If I am not even good enough for the Border Army, how will I ever master the ways of an Attul Prayer Warrior? I am afraid that I will never be allowed to complete training, that I will be rejected there as well and just disappoint you and Mother."

"You are no disappointment to us," said Rolen firmly.

"We are very proud of you, Afral," added Tolara.

He just stared at them for a time, his doubts plain on his face. He saw only more rejection up ahead, but felt there was no other choice but to face it, no matter how bitter its taste. He remembered that a soldier must learn obedience, so he might as well start with his parents. He swallowed his fears and arguments. "Where do we go from here?"

His father nodded, accepting Afral's resolve. "Down on the plains we will enter Four Corners, for I have that missive from Prince Wintron to deliver to the Rhendoran garrison there. From there it will be a ride to the northwest, across the grasses. If you look at the distant horizon, you can just glimpse the Pinnacles. We have many days of riding before we reach those mountains, and then we will need to ride around to their northern flanks." His father suddenly smiled. "Do you remember how you used to badger me for opportunities to ride?"

Afral gave weak smile in return and nodded.

"On this trip, you will get all those wishes fulfilled. By trip's end you will be an experienced rider."

* * *

Two days later, Afral and his parents rode into Four Corner. The late afternoon sun sat low, casting long shadows. There were no trees out here on the edge of the grasslands, just this lone city and its surrounding farmlands. No guards stood on the wooden palisades and the gates were not manned. The three rode in, unchallenged but not unnoticed. Shadows stretched across the dirt road to connect the two-story buildings on either side. He followed his parents up the road, staring at the sights. He saw a half-dozen grubby children run by, chasing a skinny dog. There were no street lamps, but light spilled out from some of the shops and all of the taverns they passed. He saw a mule train of five beasts in front of a supply store, with two guards keeping watch to prevent any pilfering. An evening breeze blew through, picking up some litter and tossing it across the street and down an alley. The buildings became more crowded with each block, with some even reaching to three stories. Almost all of them built of wood.

His father took a moment to give some cautious instruction. "Afral, this city is rather lawless, though not as corrupt as infamous Freetown. Do not be surprised if you sense vague evil here. However, if you sense something strongly wrong, you must tell us immediately. Is that understood?"

"Yes Father," responded Afral, suddenly wondering if demons lurked somewhere in Four Corners. He looked at the many people milling around and tried to sense them spiritually. Was that unshaven prospector a demon? How about that painted-up woman? He looked at rich people and poor, but still sensed nothing. Four Corners held quite a hodge-podge of citizens, but all seemed to be simply humans. His suspicions lessened and he started enjoying this adventure again.

A few blocks later, six soldiers rode by, dressed in blue uniforms. "They are going to visit that trader," murmured his father.

"Not much else that will motivate Freetown militia, no matter the color," agreed his mother.

Afral did not quite understand their comments, so he shrugged it off. Instead, he just enjoyed his first sights and sounds of a strange city. The streets bustled with people, going about their business or gathering to chat at the end of the day. He heard the sounds of a lyre and a flute coming from the common room of an inn they passed. He was about to suggest that they stop there for the night when he caught a whiff of some foul smell. Stables? Garbage Pile? Kitchen? Whatever its source, something had spoiled. He was glad that they rode on and the breeze brought fresher air.

By the time they reached the town center, the evening star was visible in the sky and the western horizon blazed red and orange. The four corners at the central intersection held four large buildings of stone, each flying a different flag. Each stood back from the road, behind high walls. Guards kept watch at the four gates, showing four different uniforms. The street crowds were still evident in spite of night's approach, but Afral noticed that people kept a respectful distance from all the guards.

Rolen guided his family across the square and up a street beyond. Finally, he turned in at an inn that he knew from past trips. When they entered the stable yard, a groom sauntered out and gave them a warm greeting.

"Welcome to the Unthar's Inn."

They dismounted, and Afral winced. He had never ridden this much before, so his legs and buttocks were still tender. To think that he used to pester his father for any chance to ride. While his father saw to the horses' stabling, Afral walked about to loosen his tightened muscles. In spite of his soreness, he was in a cheerful mood. Tonight he would finally experience the inside of a strange inn. He imagined that it would be very different from the simple lodgings in the Border Realm.

They led the horses into a large stall that the animals would be sharing for the night. As they pulled off the saddles and bridles, the stable man brought in fresh hay and some grain. Afral heaved his saddle up onto the fence rail where his parents had placed theirs. He hung his saddlebags over his right shoulder and took his blanket roll in the left hand, then followed his parents out of the stable and over to the inn proper.

His first impression of Unthar's Inn was the greasy smoke that stung his eyes and the clatter of pots and pans as they walked down a dimly lit hallway past the kitchen. Next, he heard the chatter and occasional laughter from the common room. The corridor brought them to the large room half-full of men eating, drinking, and talking. A lone musician sat in the far corner, strumming on a guitar without much enthusiasm. Afral counted three women, but two of them worked as servers hustling to take orders or bring food and drink. Rolen motioned for his family to wait along the wall as he went to see the innkeeper standing behind the bar.

Afral noticed a few men turning to stare at his mother and then even more took time to look at her. He knew that his mother was pretty, but their staring did not seem very polite. He was glad when his father came back and led them off to their room. They ate in their shared room, a meal of cold beef, lumpy mashed potatoes, and overcooked carrots.

* * *

Breakfast was not much better than last night's meal, Afral decided, but at least the gruel warmed his belly. He still felt tired, for the bed had been lumpy and creaky. His expectation of excellent facilities had been dashed, but he did not complain. He felt that would be petty of him, especially after his father spent good money for these accommodations. His parents ate stoically, so he did the same. At least the common room was less crowded and the air a bit fresher. There were still some unsavory people lingering here and there, including one fellow wearing a hat indoors, but none of them made comments about his mother.

"How long will you be with the Rhendorans?" she asked Rolen.

He gave a little smile of humored frustration. "It could take all day. I will have to go through numerous officials before I ever get to see the minor lord in charge of their forces here. Lord Gordrew warned me that it would be that way here, for the Rhendorans do not want to make it easy for the locals to bother them with their petty disputes. I pray that no royal runs this place, because their presence increases the hangers-on tenfold, from what I recall from my visit to their realm a few years ago. I have seen it before, while counseling Wintron's father. They are people who pride themselves on ritual and proper place. Even with a sealed document from a king, I will still be seen as just a minor official."

"You certainly have more patience than I," mused Tolara. "While you spend your day meeting with Rhendorans, Afral and I will go replenish our stores. I doubt we will find anyone willing to trade with us between here and Freetown and we will not have time to stop and hunt."

After finishing their meal, they stepped out into a sunny morning. With everything close by, they decided to walk. Rolen gave his wife a hug, his son a friendly slap on the back, and set off for the Rhendoran compound. Tolara and Afral went in the other direction.

Afral enjoyed the fresh, cool air after the stuffy inn. They walked to one side of the dirt road, staying out of the way of passing wagons. He looked curiously around at the city, already busy with deliveries and commerce. The morning shadows stretched long, casting themselves across the dirt road, but the upper floors of the buildings caught the sunlight, showing peeling paint and faded signs. Most of the people walked, well-bundled against the early chill. A dozen mounted soldiers swept by, wearing green overcoats.

"Mother, who rules here in Four Corners?"

Tolara smiled. "That has no simple answer. Four Corners has a council of elders, but they have no militia to support them. Instead, the soldiers are from the three Families of Freetown: Blue, Green, and Purple." Tolara stepped closer to her son and lowered her voice. "To be blunt, Afral, Freetown is run by criminals who band together as these families. Their soldiers are not to be trusted. Here in Four Corners they are mellowed by their few numbers and by the presence of Rhendoran soldiers, but they are still not civilized. Keep your sword in its sheath; I do not want any of the greedy Colors attracted to its glow."

They walked another block to the store that the innkeeper had directed them to. It was a large, disorderly, and dim place. As the proprietor approached Tolara, her son wandered off, fascinated by the clutter stacked everywhere.

Afral was aware of others being in the store, but he did not really pay them much heed. He had wandered to the rear of the store to looked at their leather belts, when saw two gray-robed men approaching. He looked around and caught his mother's eye. She nodded assurance to him, apparently not worried. As they got closer, he itched to grab his sword. Something was not right about these people. Afral fought off the urge, but he stepped back so that the two could easily pass. They did not walk by, but instead stopped in front of him.

"Who are you?" one of them demanded. "You do not work here do you?"

Afral cleared his throat. "I am here shopping with my mother."

The man just stared at him. "But who are you?"

"I am Afral, son of Rolen Strongarm and Tolara Quickblade. Who are you, sir?"

The man ignored the question. "You are not from Four Corners. Where are you from?"

He was confused by the man's rudeness. "I am from the Border

Realm. Where are you from, sir?"

The fellow grunted and turned to his companion. "A refugee. We will need to inform the holy brothers about this one." He walked on, now ignoring the youth. As he passed, he brushed against Afral's side and sword. The man leaped back with a cry of pain, bumping against his companion.

"How dare you try to burn me! What is that at your side?"

Puzzled, Afral touched his sword hilt to resettle it, but he did not pull it out. Its glow was not exposed, but his feeling of wrong intensified. "I did nothing to you, sir."

Tolara noticed the disturbance and called out to her son. "Afral, please come here to help carry our purchases."

He looked over, glad to be called away. "Excuse me, sirs. I am needed by my mother." He quickly walked away.

After he and his mother left with their purchases, he told her about the incident and asked why the man acted as he did.

"The shopkeep said they are servants from the Five Dragons Temple. I think they sensed that you are Elsworn, just as you sensed their association with demon-held men."

"Should we worry about them?"

His mother shrugged. "We should be cautious, yes. Dragon temple servants are not to be feared, but they may work for men that are far more dangerous. Come along, let us get back to the inn and see if your father has finished his final duties for Prince Wintron."

* * *

When they returned to the inn, they found that Rolen was still away. They took their newly-purchased supplies out to the stables and packed it amongst their other gear. This took some time, for they had to unpack and repack quite a bit. His mother would not have their supplies just haphazardly thrown together. She insisted on an order to everything. Once done, they went inside and ate a late lunch. When Rolen still had not returned, his wife and son went upstairs. After another hour, Tolara declared that she would like some quiet time for contemplation and prayer, but she gave Afral permission to return downstairs to the common room, even giving him a few coins to spend on a mug of cider and some cheese. He gladly took the offered coins and hurried downstairs.

He chose a small table in a corner from which he could watch the front door, wanting to greet his father as soon as he arrived. The chair he sat in wobbled just slightly. Afral placed his order and then settled in to observe the people around him. He had been sitting there for some time, sipping on his second mug of cider, and noticed that the inn was getting busier.

As the door opened and closed, he saw that evening had arrived. More locals came in, greeting each other as they walked in the door. He guessed this to be their daily ritual, a drink at the end of the day's work. A boy moved from table to table, lighting the worn lamp sitting on each. Afral thanked the boy when he lit the lamp on his table, which brought a brief smile in return.

Afral's third mug came along with some cheese and bread, so he gave over the last of the coins to the servant woman. As he nibbled at the crumbly cheese and sipped his warm cider, he noticed the evening's entertainer taking his stool near the hearth. He hoped the man played some songs that he would recognize. Afral felt grown-up sitting here, surrounded by working men. He felt mature and even cheerful. It was the kind of adventure he would have relished telling his playmates about. However, that thought took away his enjoyment. He would not be telling the others about this. He probably would never even see them again. His gaze dropped to the battered mug in front of him and he traced a crack down its side, lost in memories of the childhood he had just abandoned.

His daydreams suddenly fled when someone sat down across from him. Startled, Afral looked up and saw a dragon priest in black robes, the cowl pulled low to hide his face. A feeling of wrongness overwhelmed Afral, but before he could bare his sword or flee, the priest spoke to him in a calm voice. "Do not be alarmed young man. I only want a moment of your time so that we can talk. That is all. I mean you no harm. After all, we are in a common room surrounded by people."

Afral looked about and noticed that none of the other patrons showed any concern. He noticed that another dragon priest stood nearby, a reddish haze in the air around him. Afral idly wondered what caused that, but was distracted when the priest at his table shifted in his chair.

"You are Afral of the Border Realm," the priest stated, "but that is not your homeland. I can sense the enemy's presence in you, Attul. Your god has exposed you." The priest leaned forward, but the table's lamp only lit the rim of his cowl; his face remained hidden in shadow. "We will leave you unharmed, Attul, if you answer one simple question. It is a straightforward thing, and no one will know who told us. I make a modest request of you."

"What is your question, sir?" asked Afral, suddenly feeling very young and vulnerable.

The priest leaned back in his chair. "It is of no matter; just something to satisfy my idle curiosity. The question is this, where is your homeland?"

Afral suddenly wanted one of his parents to appear, to have someone offer him protection. He tried to scoot his chair, but something blocked it. He looked over his shoulder and saw a temple servant looming over him, the very same dragon servant who had confronted him at the store earlier in the day. Before Afral could object, the big fellow grabbed his right arm and pinned it to his side, well away from his sword. Panicking, he tried to break free, only to have the other dragon priest step in and grab his left arm, forcing him to turn around and face the first priest.

"We will have none of that," said the priest seated across from him. "We know about Attul swords. Just answer the question and you can go back to enjoying your evening."

The second priest spoke up, in a voice that was very deep. "Tell us where the others are, Attul. Tell and you will live."

Afral shivered at the other's voice, it seemed unnatural. He wanted to look at that priest, but was unable to turn in his seat now. He glared at the one across from him. "I will not talk of such things with your kind."

The seated priest shook his head at Afral's intransigence, the cowl moving but never exposing his face. "Let us take him outside."

Suddenly Afral was yanked to his feet, the chair banging against the wall and onto the floor. The chair's crash seemed to be the only sound in the room, for all the other hubbub became distant to him. The servant held him tight to keep him from his sword. The first priest stepped closer and took over holding Afral's other arm, while the second priest started chanting something nonsensical.

Afral shouted for help, but no one seemed to notice. He looked around at the inn's patrons, but none of them looked his way. There was a reddish haze in the common room, but it was not so thick as to hide anything and yet he seemed invisible to them. He tried yelling directly at the nearest drinker, but the man never reacted.

"They cannot hear you," murmured the first priest into his ear.

Afral ignored him, shouting for help. He even tried to call for his mother. No one heard. He flailed in his captives' hands, yanking in every direction, but no one saw.

The second priest continued his chanting as they escorted Afral across the room and the red haze deepened into a crimson fog.

Afral struggled mightily to get to his sword, but the servant's grip was like an iron fetter. He felt panic rising. If they got him outside, they would surely kill him. He tried kicking them, but they expertly avoided most of his blows. He even tried to bite, but could not reach them.

"We will take him out the back entrance," said the first priest.

Afral continued fighting to break away as they pushed him towards the rear door. He tried desperately to wrench his arm free. The temple servant twisted his right arm back in response to his struggling, causing a sharp pain.

"Help! Mother, Father! Help! Anyone, help!"

"I am tired of you screaming in my ear," growled the priest holding his left arm. The priest loosened his hold for just a moment and hit Afral in the mouth with the back of his hand. "Just tell me what I want to know and I will let you run off to your mother's bosom."

"No! I will not betray others," argued Afral, tasting his own blood from the hit.

"None can hear you, Attul. No one will run to your aid," stated the priest at his side. "You will only have one more chance to spare yourself. When we get outside you will tell us where to find the other Attuls. Refuse me again and you will die a horrible death."

Afral fought harder, but the two full-grown men had iron grips on his arms. "I will tell you nothing."

"Maybe this will loosen your tongue."

Suddenly, it felt like Afral's arm was on fire. He screamed and looked down to see red lightning chasing over his sleeve.

"You will talk, either freely as soon as we are outside or you will do so while begging me to end the pain."

Afral's heart thumped inside his chest. He tried to think of a way to fight back, but the panic rose up and chased off all rational thought. Like an animal caught in a trap, he started pulling and yanking in all directions, desperate to escape.

They were nearly to the back hallway, when suddenly a white light blazed behind them, casting their shadows large against the wall up ahead.

"In the name of El, let him go now!"

Afral rejoiced at that command, for it was from his mother. The chanting priest faltered; the red haze began to disperse. Afral renewed his struggle to break free and did so briefly when the first priest loosened his grip, but then that man pulled out a knife and held it to Afral's throat, swinging the youth around as a shield.

"Leave off witch woman, or we will kill your spawn." The priest was now behind him. Afral saw his mother at the foot of the stairs, her sword blazing.

"You have been warned, demon lovers!" she yelled, charging at them. Her sword swirled in her hand, leaving a trail of light in that gloomy room.

Afral, his panic lessening, recognized her motions as the Diving Eagle and wondered who would be the target of the coming blade. As the power of the red haze weakened, others began to notice the fight. They shouted, pointed, and dove to get away from the two sides.

His mother threw her sword with deadly accuracy. Afral felt the knife prick his throat as the priest twitched in surprise, but the priest could not flee the thrown weapon in time. The blur of light spun as it approached, perfectly aimed. It sliced into the priest's shoulder and then spun on, hitting the wall with a thud. The sword's light faded as it buried its tip into the wall.

Afral broke free as the priest doubled over in pain. The youth ran towards his mother. She did not stop to embrace him, but instead grabbed his weapon and then charged at the priest that had been chanting. That priest threw a red ball of flame at her, but she easily deflected it with a swing of white power. Sparks flew all over the room, causing the remaining spectators to hastily duck for cover.

A serving woman came out of the kitchen just then and the second priest grabbed her. "Get back, Attul! How dare you attack us for no cause, you evil woman. We will report you to the city authorities; this room is full of witnesses who saw your vicious attack on us. Thankfully, the Dragon Gods have spared us, praise to their names."

The temple servant pulled the injured priest to his feet and then all three hurried out the door, using the servant woman as a shield until they got out the door.

Afral was glad that his mother did not chase after them, for he felt very vulnerable. Instead, she handed his sword back and then went to dislodge her own. The inn's proprietor came over, red-faced with anger.

"What is the meaning of this? Why do you attack the dragon priests?" The man tried to intimidate them with his size.

Afral saw her face the man with calmness. "I did nothing except protect my son. They were the ones trying to abduct him."

"I will not have troublemakers in my inn. Get your things and leave!"

"We will go, but you owe us a refund, since my husband paid for two nights of lodging."

"No. That will help pay for the damages you have caused. I should take your horses to pay the bill in full."

Afral tried to protest that it was the priests who caused the ruckus, but his mother laid a hand on his shoulder and said, "Keep the coins, innkeeper, though you are being unfair. But should you try to take our horses, I will be forced to oppose you."

The man was not done with his complaint. "I will call in the authorities..."

"I do not fear the Colors, no matter their shade," remarked Tolara. "Now, will you allow us to leave in peace, innkeeper?"

The man grumbled, but gave a quick nod. He then ignored Afral and his mother, ordering his employees to get the furniture righted and the mugs filled.

* * *

Afral and his mother retrieved their belongings and then went out to the stables. They saddled the horses and then packed the spare mount with its burden of supplies. They were almost done when Afral's father suddenly entered the stable. Tolara looked up and gasped, for the lantern light revealed a man disheveled and bleeding.

"Unthar blocked the door and told me to get away from his place," Rolen said. "Only grudgingly did he admit that you were in the stable. What happened?"

"What happened to you, my dearest?" asked Tolara in return, hurrying to his side. She took a cloth and dabbed at his head. "Surely the innkeeper did not assault you, did he?"

"I am fine, praise to El," responded Rolen, gently removing her hand. He quickly explained his day's adventure. After a wasted day at the Rhendoran compound, waiting for one lowly official after another, he was finally ordered to leave because of the day's end. As he left the compound, a distressed woman called out from a nearby alley, asking for anyone's help. Since the gate guards ignored her pleas, Rolen went to her help. However, it was a trap with her as the lure. Once he entered the alley, a pair of dragon priests attacked him. He killed one and then fled the other. "It took me this long to lose his pursuit. So why are we being expelled from the inn?"

In turn, Tolara told of the attack at the inn. She concluded, "Best that we get away from this lawless place. If we linger any longer, then those demon-possessed men might finally succeed in overwhelming one of us."

Afral's father nodded grimly. "Yes, we need to flee, but first I have a message to deliver."

"Did they not tell you that they were closed for the day?" asked his mother.

His father pulled free his sword, Truth, and let the bright light fill the stable. "I will simply need to get their attention. Let us ride to the Rhendoran compound."

The center of Four Corners was not far from Unthar's Inn. The three Attuls arrived within minutes, but then an unhelpful guard brought them to a halt. The Rhendoran compound's entrance stood shut and barred for the night and the guard who responded when Rolen banged on the wood glared through a peephole. He yelled at them to go away.

"I have a vital message for your prince," replied his father, for he had learned enough earlier to know who was in charge here.

"Come back in the morning when petitioners are allowed," the man replied, slamming the peephole shut.

"Throw Wintron's missive over the walls and let us be gone," suggested his mother, agitated by Rhendoran obstinacy. She held out Rolen's reins to him, urging him to mount.

He ignored her offer, and instead banged on the gate again until the guard returned. The man snarled through his little opening. "Leave or I will have archers feather you from the walls."

"I will see Prince Castel tonight," replied Rolen. "You interfere with a message from one ruler to another. Let us in and then…"

"You are claiming to be a king now, are you?" interrupted the guard with a cruel laugh. "The archers will start shooting in just a moment. You had better flee the plaza." He slammed the peephole shut again.

"We cannot storm the gates," said his mother, "so we had better leave as ordered."

"Or we can teach them about the power of El," replied his father in what Afral guessed must be a jest.

However, his mother took his father seriously. "Here? In full view of the Freetown garrisons? That rabble will rush out and overwhelm us, hungry for a magic sword. Is there no better way to get the

Rhendorans' attention?"

He listened to his parents talk while he gazed nervously up at the walls. He saw a trio of men stringing their bows.

His father finally yielded to his mother. "Very well. Let us retreat for a short time and see if we can catch one of the Rhendoran patrols. We need to find someone with the authority to override that obstinate doorkeeper."

His father mounted and they turned away from the compound, quickly riding around its corner. Afral did not breathe easily until the place was out of view. They rode along a main street and then turned their horses into a dark alley, stopping there. They waited in silence for a time and then rode back to a spot where they could watch the front gates of the compound. The archers were no longer in sight. They had to wait another hour, until the doorkeeper let out a full platoon of sixty men for night patrol. As soon as the gates closed behind them, the Attuls set out to intercept. They caught up with the patrol a block from the central square, just as their officer was splitting them up into six half-squads.

His father spoke up. "Excuse me, lieutenant. May I have a word with you?"

The patrol leader gave a slight nod. "What can I do for you, sir?"

"I am Lord Rolen Strongarm, advisor to the Border Realm's ruler, just recently arrived in Four Corners with a message that must be passed on to your king. We cannot remain until dawn, so can you help us reach Prince Castel this night?"

Afral thought the officer looked amused. "You ask much, Lord Rolen. I have no more access to the prince than a stablehand, maybe less because the prince loves his horses. If you wish, I can take possession of this message." The man held out his hand. "You have my word that I will endure until it gets to the prince."

"Thank you," replied Rolen with sincerity, "but Crown Prince Wintron Dabe wanted me to share more with your prince concerning the Tlocanians. I mean no offense at declining your offer."

The lieutenant nodded. "Well, I can get you through the gates and into the hands of the night commander, but that is as far as I can accomplish." He motioned for his men to turn around. "Juress will have to judge the validity of your claims."

They returned to the Rhendoran compound, and this time made it inside. However, as the gates closed behind them, Afral wondered if they would find it just as easy to leave this fort.

Surprisingly, the night's commander was of high rank, a major if Afral recognized his uniforms braids correctly. The officer took their plea seriously. Afral did not understand why others had delayed his father all day, but this man was one of action. Within minutes, he escorted the three of them into the prince's presence.

They were now on the top floor of the Rhendoran redoubt, the large windows showing only night's blackness, but the many chandeliers made up for the lack of natural lighting. The Rhendoran prince stood next to a large table with two officers.

"My lord, I present to you Rolen Strongarm, messenger from Prince Wintron Dabe of the Border Realm." The major bowed and withdrew.

"Please come forward, Rolen Strongarm," beckoned the prince, a man near the age of Afral's father. "What is this message, that you could not entrust it to my staff earlier today? I assume it is both vital and confidential."

"Yes it is, my lord," answered Rolen, striding forward towards the three. "I bring word from the ruler of the Border Realm to your king."

One of the officers stepped forward and held out his hand.

"I am to place the message in the hands of the king's representative for Four Corners," responded Rolen, attempting to pass by.

The officer put a restraining hand on his shoulder. "No one is allowed near the prince while armed. Four Corners is a lawless place; others have tried to kill him before."

Rolen turned to the officer and gave him a silent nod. He reached into his shirt pocket and brought forth the sealed letter, giving it to the man. However, before he released it he said, "I caution the three of you. This message is from ruler to ruler. Please do not pry."

The prince stiffened in offense. "You lecture me, messenger Rolen?"

Afral's father let go of the message and met the noble's eyes. "I am just trying to emphasize the importance of this note. I mean no offense. If I were not on a more pressing mission, I would be delivering this directly to King Graldeon, for he knows me."

The officer holding the message gave a short laugh. "Why would our king remember you?"

Afral's father gave the man a small smile in return. "I spent many days with him two years ago, when King Varen Dabe and he met. I was King Varen's chief advisor for that meeting." The officer's mirth ended. "Again I emphasize that I mean no offense, but this message must be sent on to your king with haste and it should not be opened or even manhandled."

"Thank you for the warning King's Advisor Rolen," stated the prince with more politeness.

"I have a second message for your king, a personal one. Will you please pass that on to him as well?"

The prince locked eyes with Rolen for a moment and then gave a quick nod. The officer held out his hand for the second message, but Afral's father shook his head. "This one is not written down." He stepped back and pulled out his sword. The two officers grabbed for their own weapons but hesitated as the brilliant light surprised them.

Afral was also surprised. Why would his father reveal their identity so openly?

Sword held high, Afral's father spoke in a loud, firm voice. "Please tell King Graldeon to hold tight to El during these hard times. Tell your king that some Attuls are already aware of his diligent defense of the Grandgorn Valley. Tell him that I go to call the Prayer Warriors to battle." He sheathed his sword Truth and the room seemed gloomy in comparison.

"Truly an Attul?" The prince seemed more amused than alarmed. "Should you appear at Rhendora's court with that flaming sword, you would be proclaimed a legendary hero and many would want to embrace you as a long-lost relative. So many Rhendoran nobles make claims to Attul blood. In truth, even my own family does, revering an ancient sword that is said to have come from the East with Belere's own army. I held that old sword once, but it certainly never shown like yours, Rolen Strongarm."

"King Graldeon showed me a similar blade; it was indeed a spirit sword. Pardon my theatrics, but I felt the need to gain your attention."

"Are there more Attuls in the Border Realm?" asked the prince, looking quizzically at Afral and his mother.

"No longer," answered Afral's father, ignoring the curious stare at his family.

"Will your people join us in our war against the Tlocanians? We have dire need for strong allies."

"I have not the authority to make such a promise, though I wish that I could soothe your king with such news. But do tell your king that I go to find aid and, with El's help, I shall bring back others to these troubled lands."

"I will bring your messages to King Graldeon personally,"

announced the prince suddenly, holding out a hand to his officer for the note from Crown Prince Wintron.

"Thank you, Prince Castel. As you may have surmised, things are not well in the Border Realm. King Varen is dead and the Borderheart Valley taken, but Prince Wintron and Duke Fors hold out at mighty Tor Randis. Rhendora is not the only land in need of allies. Now, I must be going for I have my own mission ahead of me and time is short."

"You ride out of Four Corners at night? May I offer you an escort?"

Afral's father shook his head. "Thank you for the offer, but I shall decline. We have need for stealth more than strength."

* * *

So Afral and his parents fled Four Corners in the middle of the night. His father led them through the city in a roundabout way, but eventually they ended up on a farmer's lane heading northward. When dawn arrived, his father finally called a halt, leading them off the faint path they had followed and over a grassy hillock. They staked the horses down and then Afral and his father went to sleep while his mother took first watch. Afral did not think he would be able to sleep, not after all the excitement and with daylight coming on, but he was wrong.

GALDON

Galdon set an aggressive pace for his soldiers. They rode south, out of the Border Mountains, and into the city of Lepis Fra. He did not linger in that depressing city, for its citizens still cowered from Tlocanian uniforms and their pockets had already been emptied when the city was sacked.

From Lepis Fra, they headed west, following the now-abandoned Halfhill Road. He remembered marching this route not so long ago, as Lord-General Hraf Kelordok led them out to conquer the Ejoti kingdom of Halfhill. That had been Galdon's most bloody and brutal campaign ever, where he had lost all six of his best friends. The Embraced Ones had failed to compromise the locals or to surprise them. Only by the use of brute force and those terrible demonic powers did they achieve victory, a blood-soaked victory that had left Galdon exhausted, injured, and mourning. He remembered and those memories gave him fitful nights.

The land was a wild and unfettered country with few human inhabitants, but with an abundance of wildlife. The Forest Hills were indeed thick-forested, so their way was a gloomy one under both Dragon Shadow and tree shade. At times, they had to light torches even during the day. The gloom did not help his mood.

Finally, days later, they entered the boundaries of now-abandoned Halfhill. The thick forests thinned into more-open country. Halfhill had once been a fair land, full of small farms and quaint villages, but all of that was rubble and weeds now. The ashes were long-cold, but in his mind's eye Galdon could still feel the burn of smoke in his eyes, still smell the stench of death in his nose. Looking back over his three squads, he could see which ones had served here: jaws were set, eyes hardened. Some felt anger; others experienced remorse or sadness. No one felt pride over the Battle of Halfhill.

"Scouts and squad leaders to me!" he yelled, riding a little off the rutted road to the top of a knoll. The two scouts currently with the platoon came over with the three sergeants. Galdon did not dismount. He did not want to touch that soil again.

"We had better not ride all the way into this cursed land." He turned his horse, looked to the southwest, and saw what he expected: the high and distinct summit of Halfhill loomed over the closer hills, its sheared face visible in partial profile. It was on the slopes of that great hill that the Ejoti had built their capitol, the namesake of this now-empty realm. It was there that Galdon had lost his last two friends, Hargel and Fross. "No, it would be best for us to avoid that haunted place. Scouts, find us a route to bypass the worst of this fallen kingdom. I will not have us wasting time meandering along some goat herders' lane but I do not want us too close to the battlegrounds either. See to it."

The scouts hurried off in obedience as the captain turned his attention to his three subordinates. He realized that only one of them had been with him on the Halfhill campaign. Dresh's face reflected what Galdon felt. The other two seemed so young and naive, looking curious and slightly puzzled.

When Galdon left Halfhill the last time, less than half of his men marched out with him. This time, he wanted to slip out of here with all of his men at his back. He was not a superstitious man; he carried no Fate charms like many soldiers. However, if any place held ghosts that attacked men, it would be here.

The three sergeants still waited for his orders and suddenly Galdon realized he had none. What could he say? Watch out for angry spirits? Beware of my nightmares? Finally, he spoke, "Halfhill was one of the Empire's hardest fought campaigns and its costliest victory. We have no time to linger here, even to commemorate our fallen comrades. Duty calls us to the far northern Na Ciria." Suddenly, he remembered holding a dying Fross.

Galdon shook off the memory. "I also do not want anyone wandering off from their squad, for I do not know if any magic still festers in the area. For those of you who were not at this campaign, the Embraced Ones released huge gouts of power, so much that it even tore the Dragon Shadow asunder for a time." Galdon fell quiet as he remembered that as well. He usually relished any time under the bright sun but, on that day, he had felt exposed to the Ejoti. Unable to resist, he looked up at the ever-present cloud cover above them. Again, he forced his memories down. "Warn your men. Stay close to the road and do not pick up any souvenirs or even hunt game here. Anything might be tainted."

Dresh nodded fervent agreement, while the others just acknowledged his orders as good soldiers must.

CHAPTER NINETEEN

Halenvale

WINTRON

The crown prince had five squads of twenty soldiers with him, one of which was strictly there to protect him. When he left Tor Randis, he thought one hundred soldiers would be more than enough to root out his cousin. After all, there was no way Drass could have brought a large force up from the Borderheart Valley, not following goat paths and climbing over cliffs. And yet, he now learned that his cousin had at least as many men, and they were all mounted. Where had Drass found a hundred horses, let alone the tack required? Well, at least he had learned something of worth from Chashade's councilmen.

The prince was frustrated as he left the meeting. The five were full of honeyed words but offered nothing solid. The talking had gone so long that the night was nearly half-gone. Wintron walked out of the inn's light and then gazed up at the stars sparkling overhead, letting the peace of the night calm him. In one direction loomed the high Mount Cha blocked out the sky, but in all other directions could be seen an abundance of heavenly lights. The only sound was that of some dog barking in the town and the footsteps of his two captains as they followed him out.

"Do you want to head to our camp or stay the night at *this inn?*" asked Bilshor.

He heard Bilshor's preference in that short question. Bilshor did not want the men divided in two locations. "We will return to our troops shortly, but first I want to hear your thoughts. What should we do now?"

Though the darkness hid Bilshor's face, Wintron saw him lift a hand and touch his right finger to the tip of his nose. Bilshor did that whenever he weighed his words, but Wintron did not know if the captain was being careful for his sake or because of Kevlo's presence. "The most cautious thing would be for us to return to Tor Randis for more soldiers, but you will not want such a delay. I recommend just the opposite then; we should boldly pursue. We need to stop Drass before he can gather even more supporters."

"Where do you suggest we go?" pressed Wintron. The prince already knew where he needed to start this chase, but he wanted the captains to bring it up.

"Halenvale," said Bilshor without hesitation.

Wintron saw Kevlo nod agreement, so he turned to the other man. "What route would you suggest, Captain Kevlo?"

"Take the mountain paths," he replied without hesitation. "Lord Drass will have the main road watched and he knows the best places to lay an ambush. If we can slip behind him, though, we can surprise his force."

"You are talking about narrow game trails," argued Bilshor. "We will be dangerously spread out, should Drass discover us."

"Kevlo, you think Drass knows we are here?"

"He knows or will soon." Kevlo looked back at the inn. "Those men did not say it, but I think Drass has someone here in Chashade even now, keeping watch. It will be some local whom the councilmen would be hesitant to betray."

The prince nodded agreement. "Bilshor, signal for the guard to gather up; we are heading back to the camp. At dawn we will move out, heading for Halenvale."

"Do we take the main road or Kevlo's back ways?" asked Bilshor.

"I think our best chance will be Kevlo's route, for I want Drass defeated quickly and I want his head in payment for his treason." Wintron looked back towards the dark mountain. "May the mountain gods guide and protect us."

* * *

The next morning, Wintron ordered that the supply wagons to be left at the inn, for there would be no way to drive them over the paths they planned to take. He also left behind the four soldiers who served as drivers, to guard things and to see to the caring of the wagon teams. The innkeeper gladly accepted his coins as a down payment for board and bed.

The force headed out of Chashade, crossing a small bridge and then following the road towards Halenvale. They entered a thickly forested country, full of pine, spruce, and fir, following numerous switchbacks as they made their way out of Chashade's vale. More ever-white mountains loomed ahead, though none as tall as Mount Cha behind them. This was the high country of the Border Realm, a rough and wild area. Though many of the villages and towns were centuries old, still most of the land remained untamed.

Wintron kept his thick cloak close to him, for the sun had not yet warmed the day, especially under the trees. The climb out of the vale was uneventful, and they came to Kevlo's turnoff faster than anticipated. It lay through a sunny meadow, where Wintron and the others could pull back their cloaks and feel some warmth. The troop paused here to let their horses drink from a stream, while Captain Kevlo joined the scouts in spying out their route.

After about an hour, Wintron decided the scouts had enough of a lead and gave a nod to Bilshor. The captain ordered all those still lingering at the stream to mount up. Though he did not yell, his voice still carried in the mountain air. They did not try to hide their trail, for you cannot conceal the passage of a hundred mounts, especially not through the damp, soft ground of a meadow. At the upper end of the clearing a path appeared, meandering beside the stream. They soon rode under the trees again, through a forest of thin and tall evergreens that grew close together.

For the next four days, they followed game trails and herders' paths, without incident or discovery, until they finally came upon Halenvale.

* * *

Wintron stood with scouts Gaddy and Orgel in the shade of a fir tree, looking down on the long valley where Halenvale nestled. It had been years since he had last passed through here, but it did not seem much changed. All of the lands before him belonged to his uncle, from the dark forests that covered these slopes to the series of rich grasslands that ran down its center. The Halenvale compound topped a small hillock overlooking the largest meadow. The rambling manor sheltered behind high stone walls, along with his uncle's stables and other outbuildings. A small village lay outside the walls, at the base of the hill. He could spot workers out in the fields, tending the just-sprouting crops but, within the actual compound, it seemed eerily quiet. Another oddity caught his eye: the many pasturelands were empty except for a small bison herd and a pair of wandering deer.

"Where are the Halen-Dabe pony herds?" he asked, though he could already guess the answer. This is where Drass had found his mounts.

"We have not seen any horses, beyond a pair of drays used by the farmers," replied Gaddy.

"Have you seen anything of Drass' force?"

"We have not seen any warriors outside the compound, but there has been so much coming and going along the main roads that we cannot tell which direction they may have gone," answered Gaddy. "It seems that not all of Drass' force is in the valley."

"We could not spy out the interior of the compound," added Orgel, ever cautious, "so we do not know their numbers in there."

Wintron nodded, understanding what the scout had not said: the enemy might be hiding inside the manor. The place was spacious from what he remembered, but not so large as to swallow five-score of troops without being noticed. He considered the risk, and decided it would be worth it to take the compound from his cousin. "I want you scouts to ride the roads. If Drass is not inside the manor, then he will be back here soon. I do not want to be surprised."

"We understand, my prince," replied Gaddy. Both men slipped away.

Wintron stared at the peaceful valley a moment longer, and then returned to his men. Bilshor and Kevlo were both waiting.

"We will take the compound now," he informed them. Bilshor nodded, though Wintron saw the concern in his eyes.

Kevlo shook his head. "Be wary, Prince Wintron." He looked to Bilshor. "You are my witness, captain, that I am warning the prince. I will not have Duke Fors accuse me of leading you into a trap." He looked back at the prince. "Even if Drass is not there, he will not have left the place undefended. He must know you are hunting for him, so he will expect you to come here."

"I agree, but nonetheless we need to take over Halenvale. It is the closest thing to a keep in this whole area, so we cannot leave it in Drass' hands."

"If you are determined to do this, then you should at least stand aside while the men move in. If something goes horribly wrong, then you can flee."

"I wholeheartedly agree," added Bilshor.

Wintron barely stopped a sharp retort. He was no coward, but these men already knew that. He was forced to admit they gave sound advice. He was no simple soldier, to risk himself so extravagantly. With a disgruntled grumble, he accepted their plan to keep him out of the fray. So Wintron Dabe and his personal guards kept back while four squads of soldiers rode hard on Halenvale.

There was no way to slink up on the compound, since it sat on a hillock above meadows and fields, so Captain Bilshor chose boldness. They found no resistance among the fields or even in the village's streets. The fighting did not start until they came within bowshot of the manor's high walls, then it became intense. Bilshor knew how to fight though, and within an hour had the wall breached and the gates opened, forcing the rebels to retreat to the manor. During that whole time, the prince paced around his overlook, fighting off his eagerness to get in there and confront his murderous cousin.

He waited for Bilshor's signal that Halenvale was subdued. Finally, he saw the waved banner and quickly climbed back up onto his horse, ordering Sergeant Yosif to lead their ride in.

He found the village eerily quiet, for the people had all hid inside, taking their children and chickens and dogs with them. Once, some brave mutt tried to bark out warning from inside a cottage, but its owner somehow silenced it quickly. Wintron kept on riding.

He was glad to see that Halenvale's gates were still sound, so apparently Bilshor had sent men over the wall to open it from within instead of ramming them ajar. That was good, in case the rest of Drass' force suddenly returned. In his eagerness to see if he had caught his cousin, Wintron did not ride around to the stables. He stopped at the front door and called out for the captains. Both Bilshor and Kevlo stepped out of the manor to greet him.

"Is he here?"

Bilshor shook his head. "He left with most of his men, heading southwest. The place fell so easily because he only left one squad of mercenaries to hold it."

Wintron frowned with disappointment. He dismounted and approached the officers. "Did we catch anything worthwhile?"

Kevlo answered this time. "The duchess awaits you just inside. She is not happy that we have her under guard."

Wintron grimaced, remembering his aunt all too well. He gave the men a nod of dismissal and headed inside.

He strode into the disheveled manor and found his aunt being watched by two of his men.

"What is the meaning of this, Wintron Dabe?" she demanded. Her attempt to approach him was stopped by a sword point.

"Aunt Riala, have you no warmer greeting for your nephew? I did liberate you from your treasonous son after all."

"You made a shambles of the manor; that is what you did." She indicated the damaged furniture and a dead soldier heaped in the corner. "You have not freed me from Drass; he will be back and then there will be a repeat of this carnage. Must you always be so impetuous? You are as fickle as the Spring God."

He raised an eyebrow at her sharp tongue. The duchess was known for her tart words, but he had expected at least a smidgen of gratitude. "Drass will not find this place as vulnerable as I did."

"Come now, you cannot be that ignorant, or are you?" The duchess gave the prince a hard stare, and then sighed at whatever she saw. "Call off your men, Wintron Dabe. I see that we need to talk. Let us have a cup of tea in my solarium, shall we?" When he did not instantly obey her wishes, she grew irate. "Be quick about it, Prince Wintron, for you do not have much time to correct your folly. I may not particularly like you, but you are my husband's only ally."

He still paused. "So, you claim to be opposed to your traitorous sons? And yet my men did not find you imprisoned or even under guard."

"Do you not have even a pinch of common sense in you? I am Drass' mother; he knew better than to disrespect me. I raised him to esteem his elders." Her tone implied that he failed to show that appropriate respect. "He did not show such restraint with his younger brother or even his niece."

"Where are Gurash and Zita?"

"Finally, a sensible question." Riala pushed away the bare sword in front of her. Uncertain, the soldier let her, stepping back but keeping his weapon out. "Put these brutes to a more useful task: send them to free Gurash and Zita. They are imprisoned down in the root cellar. You will find the entrance off the kitchen. When your men go fetch them, have one of them tell the servants to bring us refreshments in the solarium, will you?"

Wintron gave a slight nod, realizing that he had better yield to his aunt on this. He motioned a soldier near and whispered some additional instructions. He wanted the prisoners brought to the solarium as well. He also requested that all the refreshments be scrutinized and any potential weapons removed from the flatware. He did not trust his tempestuous aunt to handle even a butter knife. She might not stab a crown prince, but the duchess might try to take a swipe at any soldier within reach.

When the troopers hurried off to find the prisoners, Wintron motioned for his aunt to lead the way. Captain Bilshor had entered the room and quickly appraised the situation. He came over to Sergeant Yosif and gave his successor some whispered advice. Wintron was thankful for Bilshor's interference, though he did not acknowledge the captain's aid in front of his aunt.

As the prince and the duchess headed towards the solarium, Yosif quickly ordered the men into proper ranks, sending six to sprint ahead and make sure their route was secure. Bilshor nodded his approval and then strode off to other duties. Riala looked straight ahead, ignoring the guards around her as well as paying no attention to her nephew. Her long dress swished as she waddled up the hallway.

She acts as if she is the rooster of this coop, thought Wintron.

The solarium of Halenvale had many tall windows looking out onto the formal gardens arranged on this side of the manor. The airy room contained a collection of couches and padded chairs, made to encourage intimate conversation. With so much glass, it was cool in here even though a fire roared in the fireplace already. The duchess went to her favorite chair, near the fire and across from a couch.

Wintron remembered that chair from his childhood visits to Halenvale; it had always reminded him of a miniature throne. The fabric had been renewed, but the rich carvings on its legs and arms were unmistakable. Whenever a youthful Wintron and his cousins Drass and Mordel had been caught misbehaving, as adventurous boys were prone to do, she would have them brought here for punishment. His cousins had called it the Judgment Seat. Today, the duchess sat down like someone getting ready to render a verdict, then motioned imperiously for Wintron to sit on the couch across from her.

He did as she bade. Around him, soldiers positioned themselves at Sergeant Yosif's quick orders. Prince and duchess sat in silence until two servants hustled in with a steaming kettle of tea and an assortment of pastries. One servant poured the duchess her tea, adding a large dollop of honey, while the other servant offered the prince his choice of sweets. He picked two, though he did not share his aunt's fondness for the flaky things, and set them on a small plate. When the tea was presented, he also accepted, though with far less honey. Riala inhaled the steam with a contented look, and then took a careful sip. Satisfied, she carefully set down her cup and turned her attention to her nephew.

"Do you know where my second son is?" she asked, but did not wait for his answer. "Drass has gone to retrieve more of his murderous allies. Somehow, they have found a way up to the Highlands that bypasses Tor Randis. He has ridden off to guide them here and when they arrive, you will find yourself trapped. He will have twice your number, if not triple, and most will be Tlocanian regulars, not the ragtag group he calls his personal guard. Flee now Wintron, and take Gurash and Zita with you."

He considered her claims before answering. His aunt was pompous and intolerant, but not known for imaginary fears; she must think her claims true. "How could they bring men up here, unless they came by way of the White Owl Pass?" His tone indicated that he doubted the Tlocanians would send men all the way around the Border Mountains to come up from the Singgorn Plains.

"He rode off to the southwest," replied Riala. "They have some route up from the Borderheart Valley."

Wintron did not argue with her, but he knew that only mountain sheep could find any path up those steep slopes. However, his face must have shown his doubt.

The duchess pointed a bony and bejeweled finger at him. "Do not become an even bigger fool, Wintron Dabe. Listen to my warning. Drass will soon return with not only his men, but also Tlocanian soldiers. In addition, he has those haughty dragon priests too, the kind with a love for human blood. Have you something to fight off their blood magic?"

He thought of Rolen and his family, but they were probably through the White Owl Pass by now. Just then, Captain Bilshor escorted Gurash and Zita into the room. The two hurried to Riala but did not embrace her. The duchess was not the kind of person to endure hugs. Wintron had not seen either of them for years and was surprised at how they had grown. Gurash appeared to be a young man, his resemblance to his father Fors obvious. Zita, eldest child of his cousin Mordel, was practically a woman. Actually, she was turning into a rather pretty woman, even with her hair disheveled and her clothes ruffled from sleeping in them.

"Well, there you are Gurash, Zita." Riala waved them over to a second couch and then motioned for a nearby servant to offer them refreshments.

The two sat down and accepted the offered tea and treats. He noted that Zita had her grandmother's sweet tooth, taking plenty of honey in her tea. Gurash just nibbled at the food, proving the prisoners had certainly not been starved.

"Son, I have been talking with your cousin, the prince. You do remember Crown Prince Wintron, do you not?"

Gurash hastily swallowed a bite of cookie, then stood up and gave Wintron a proper bow. "Pardon me, my prince. I did not mean to be rude. Welcome to Halenvale."

Gurash played the host, ignoring the fact that Wintron's men had just set him free. It brought a smile to the prince's lips. He wanted to distrust this young man, considering who his brothers were, but Gurash seemed eager to please. "It is good to see you, Lord Gurash. Please be seated."

Zita also stood up and gave him a fine curtsy, followed by a shy smile. "Thank you for freeing us, Crown Prince Wintron. We are in your debt."

"It was my pleasure, Lady Zita."

The young woman's smile turned a bit mischievous. "You remind me of King Brave or Lord Truelove: so brave and right and ..."

"Do not be fooled by her sweet words," interrupted Riala. "Zita was locked up for good reason: she tried to escape and then when cornered, she actually tried to kill her uncle Drass. She did not even have the decency to use a properly feminine method, such as poison. She tried using a dagger, the young fool. Drass overpowered her easily and would have killed her right then if she were not Mordel's child. Instead, he had her locked up."

The young lady gave her grandmother a frown. "There is no reason to bring up such things, Grandmama. I am sure the crown prince would prefer other topics."

"Oh, do sit down, Zita," said Riala, pointing peremptorily at the couch. The duchess turned her attention to Wintron. "What that girl needs is a husband to control her. Her mother is a weakling and Mordel was ever the absent father. Zita has much promise, but needs someone to prune her wildness." She paused for a moment, considering. "You still have not married, have you?"

Wintron choked on his last swallow of tea, not liking what his aunt's implication. Zita was young enough to be his daughter, as well as being too close of a relative. Was Riala being serious or was she just trying to unsettle him? Before he could respond, Zita spoke up.

"Grandmama! How could you suggest such a thing?"

"Can you think of a better match, little bobcat? I mean a real person, not one of your imaginary heroes from those silly tales you admire so." The duchess waved off a servant trying to refill her tea. "However, this does not need to be resolved today. No, the more important thing is to get all of you safely away from Halenvale before Drass returns with his reinforcements."

Wintron felt the beginnings of a headache, which was typical whenever dealing with his irritating aunt. Riala was well aware that he had once tried to woo the girl's mother, before Mordel had won Zaveeta's affection. Zita even looked much like her mother, which just caused Wintron that much more discomfort. "I think I have heard more than enough." He set aside his cup and stood up. "I ask that the three of you remain here for a moment while I converse with my officers. I will be back within an hour." He did not wait for any response, but strode out quickly, asking Yosif to leave four men to keep watch over the solarium.

He convened with his two captains and most of the sergeants in his uncle's study. He did not try out the leather chair that sat before the big table; instead, he paced as the officers stood in a group. For some reason, his aunt's attempt at matchmaking upset him more than the news that Drass had more help on the way. Her words touched an old yet still fresh wound. His father had consistently urged him to find a wife and had even paraded many maidens before him. None interested him since he had lost his true love to another suitor. Lost her to Mordel. The woman he still wanted was Zita's mother, and Riala knew that. That was not something the Hen of Halenvale would forget, so her suggestion had been meant to bite. Why such a cruel barb?

Wintron forced himself to stop pacing and faced his men. Quickly, he shared with them what his aunt had revealed about Drass and then asked for their advice.

"Have we a count of how many men follow Drass or how many more are joining him?" asked Bilshor.

"A sergeant we captured spoke of one hundred riders," stated Captain Kevlo. "I know this man and he is not smart enough to be imaginative. So this confirms what we heard in Chashade, though I do not know where Lord Drass found so many. They cannot all be from the Halen-Dabe guard or the regular army stationed up here."

"Could that include farmers and other recruits?" asked Sergeant Fioler.

Kevlo gave a tentative nod. "It may also include sell-swords.

Though General Fors ignored what his sons had been up to, many of us knew that Mordel and Drass recruited their own guard squads and trained them elsewhere. I know that Major Usro had warned the general more than once of his sons' play soldiers."

"Major Usro?" It was a name unfamiliar to Wintron.

"He commanded the Halen-Dabe personal guard here at Halenvale," explained Kevlo. "The general wanted a strong guard to protect his homestead when he was so often away at the king's beckoning. Usro died four months ago, by an apparent misaimed hunting arrow. Looking back, I wonder if he were not the first victim of the brothers' mad dream to rule."

He did not like learning that Fors commanded such a large independent army that he needed a major, in addition to captains like Kevlo. Apparently, his cousins were just following in their father's footsteps. It would be one more thing over which to confront his uncle. The Halen-Dabes enjoyed scheming too much. "From what you say, Drass' force may match us in numbers but certainly not in skill. That leaves these rumors of some other route up from the Borderheart Valley. Is he truly bringing in Tlocanian reinforcements? Do you know anything about this, Kevlo?"

The young captain shook his head. "No, my prince. I have never heard of any other way up here and I grew up in these woods. There is only the road through Tor Randis, unless they came up from the Singgorn Plains…"

"I cannot believe the Tlocanians would have arranged that," argued Bilshor. "They are at war with the Rhendorans, so the eastern approach is blocked, and it is a very long ride by way of the Triangle Wilds to the west. I cannot imagine them sending a force to circle the Borders just to get behind us."

"Such an action is believable of them, but just not this quickly." Wintron began to pace again, musing as he walked. "Could it be that they have made some path with their magic? Have they blasted some tunnel or stairway into the granite?"

"Might it be that the duchess raves or misleads?" asked Bilshor.

Wintron dismissed the idea of insanity; Riala was too wily yet, though she might be deceiving him. "I think her loyalty lies with her husband, though I am surprised that she is willing to betray her own son to me, no matter his crimes. However, her warning is too dire to ignore, no matter how outrageous the claim." He stopped his pacing, having come to a decision. "I want a full squad sent in the direction she indicated. If they encounter a large force, then half are to gallop back while the rest are to make their way around the enemy and seek out this secret route. Bilshor, appoint those who are to be on this assignment and be sure to add some of Kevlo's locals."

The two captains and their sergeants discussed whom to include and then talked about how to defend the compound. Wintron listened, adding only a few comments. Finally satisfied that their defense was well planned, Wintron returned to his relatives. He did not linger, but gave permission for them to wander the manor, as long as they had a soldier escort. He noticed that Zita no longer smiled at him and was thankful. He had no time for a girl flirting with him, especially not her.

As much as he tried to get away before any more confrontations, his aunt had to give him a final barb. "Have you officially changed the line of succession, Wintron Dabe? Or are you going to leave that to my Fors, since you seem determined to stay here and die."

He gritted his teeth, walking out without a response, but her words stayed lodged in his mind. Who should be his heir? Currently, it was the duke and then the king slayer. It was just another thing he needed to consider, now that he ruled the realm.

* * *

Three days later, Wintron received his first report on the large army heading his direction. He called the gods' curses down on Drass upon hearing its size. His aunt had been right and now he had to decide if there was still time to retreat or would they be forced to make a futile stand at Halenvale.

CHAPTER TWENTY

Sleepless Nights

MYLANA

Mylana stepped into the inn just as the evening worship bell began to ring, a packet of goods slung over her shoulder. She hurried upstairs as the common room's patrons pushed back their seats and knelt. Even the wait staff stopped their tasks and joined in the mandatory prayer. She made it upstairs before the tolling ended, but then had to step lightly to avoid making any noise. From downstairs, she could hear the prayers recited in rough unison. Thankfully, no one was in the hallway upstairs to see that Mylana did not comply. She hurried to her room and used one of the worn keys that the innkeeper had given to each of them. She slipped in and was surprised to find the room empty. She decided that Hessilyn must be in the boys' room but dared not walk down the hall to verify. If Hessilyn were with them, then they would know that Mylana had left the inn. Oh well, they would realize it soon enough by the restored supplies. She dropped her packet on one of the two beds and waited out the worship time.

Finally, the temple bells tolled again, announcing the end of the prayer time. She strode out of her shared room and down the hall to the room shared by the men. She paused a moment to gather her wits, and then knocked. Coursen let her in. Hessilyn, seated on one of the beds, quickly rose to her feet and came over to give her a hug. It seemed genuine and Mylana awkwardly returned it.

"I worried about you," she said softly. "I tried to keep them ignorant of your leaving, but they found out."

Mandor turned from the window. "Do not be angry with Hessilyn, sister. She thrice ignored our knocks on your door. We thought maybe both of you were gone or captured. We nearly broke the door down, when she finally relented and answered."

"Mylana, you are vital to our mission," said Coursen. "That was foolish of you to wander off."

She pulled away from Hessilyn, ready to argue her own defense, but Mandor held up his hand.

"Hessilyn, my dear, could you wait in the other room?" he asked. "This is Attul business that we are sworn to keep private."

Hessilyn startled a moment, as if her thoughts were elsewhere. "Oh, but of course, darling. I will go back to my needlepoint. Please come and get me once you are done with this." She gracefully left, closing the door softly behind her.

Coursen waited for a moment and then peeked out to make sure she was not lingering outside. Mandor scowled at the implied mistrust but he said nothing. Mylana nodded approval at Coursen's prudence.

"Well, sister, what is your excuse?" asked Mandor.

She sighed. "I have none. I tired of waiting around without anything to do. I went to the market to snoop, though I did replenish some of our stores at a good price."

Mandor shook his head. "You cannot take such risks. If something were to happen to you we would never be able to get this message through to Warhaven."

"The Guardians put us in a precarious place," stated Coursen. "Since you are the only one of us who knows our final destination, it was foolish of you to go wandering off alone. That was a childish act unbecoming of a Rider. What if you had stumbled into one of those demon-possessed soldiers or priests?"

She wilted under their condemnation, realizing her selfishness.

"Will you promise not to do anything so headstrong again?" asked Mandor.

She let go of her stubbornness and nodded. "I will do my best to listen to the counsel of my fellow Riders."

Mandor held her eyes for a moment, and then seemed satisfied. "If only we all knew the whole route," he sighed. "Then we would not need to keep you on such short reins, little sister."

"The Guardians had reasons for their caution," stated Coursen, though he too seemed wistful. "They did not know us well and there has been someone betraying Riders. I can see their rationale for picking Mylana; she is too new a Rider to be this long-term betrayer. I only wish they had known us well enough, Mandor, to realize our innocence too."

Mandor nodded agreement. "Well, there is more to be dealt with than Mylana's little trek. We have not even had the chance to compare our observations. What have you found out, Coursen?"

"The worst is that a large Tlocanian patrol entered the city a half-day before us and is still here in Gratoro. People did not mention any dreadhounds, but confided that over a hundred men rode in."

"I heard the same," stated Mandor. "I also heard nothing about the dogs. Maybe they are still out in the surrounding countryside. Then again, they may have slipped into the city at night. Did you learn anything else?"

Coursen frowned. "I heard grumblings about horses being seized for the Rhendoran war front. Apparently, the army will take what they need, handing you a slip of paper as payment. One merchant complained that it took three months for the Tlocanians to redeem the script. It is a warning to us that we need to be careful with our own horses. There are no Rider posts where we can get new mounts. I did not hear much else, except complaints about the weather, prices, and the quality of goods."

Mandor ran a hand through his hair. "I just hope that Tlocanian patrol stays put. I do not want them in front of us again, nor behind."

"Do you think they know that we are here?" asked Mylana.

"I doubt that," replied Coursen, "or else they would be at the inn's door demanding our heads."

Mandor agreed. "We just need to be careful not to reveal our presence. We need to avoid anything that draws attention to us."

"How long do you think they will linger here?" she asked, looking to the boys.

Coursen shrugged. "The Grays were fairly regular in their patrols, but they did not cover as large a territory as the Reds do. We do not even know if they will continue on to Deep Crossing or if they will turn back to Waybridge. What do you think, Mandor?"

Mandor shook his head. "None of us know their patrol patterns, and we dare not ask about it. However, I do not want them near us on the road again, for next time they will surely notice us. Maybe we should linger another day and see if we can observe something of their habits."

The other three saw the wisdom in Mandor's suggestion.

* * *

They stayed two more days in Gratoro, the men spending most of each day spying on the Tlocanian garrison. They found that the locals did the city patrols, though every day they saw the Tlocanian soldiers at arms practice in the garrison's open yard. On the second evening, Coursen came back to the inn excited. He had learned something useful. "I overheard two soldiers at a tavern talking about having to spend another two days in Gratoro, though I never heard if they were returning to Waybridge or pressing on."

Mandor smiled. "It does not matter. Two days will give us a good lead on such a large party, for we can travel faster than a hundred men and their supplies. What say the rest of you? Should we depart at dawn or wait another few days to dawdle behind this force?"

The others agreed with Mandor that it would be best to get ahead of the Tlocanians.

* * *

The next morning they set off just after the sunrise prayer. The city watch gave them no trouble at the gates. One of them was emboldened to wave farewell to Hessilyn, inviting her to return soon and see him at the nearest tavern. She gave him a little smile but also a shake of the head. The other guards laughed at their rejected comrade. Mandor did his best to ignore the soldier's words, though he undoubtedly wanted to challenge the man for even implying such impropriety.

Mandor's struggle showed on his face, bringing another smile to Hessilyn. She leaned towards his horse and whispered loud enough for Mylana to overhear, "Keep calm, my darling. They are only boys playing. They mean it all as a compliment, though their tongues are as rough as tree bark."

The soldiers said no more to them, for their sergeant had stepped out of the guardroom.

Mylana found it all humorous; she doubted Mandor would have been so offended if she had been the soldier's target instead. She gave a quick glance at Coursen and wondered if he would be so quick to defend her honor as Mandor was for Hessilyn. It might be worth baiting him to see.

She shook her head at such a girlish thought; this was not a Westbend gala with all of its romantic intrigue and social scheming. Coursen rode as her companion on this mission and deserved better treatment. She would hold off any flirtation for a more peaceful time, if ever it arrived.

The foursome rode off into a dark and misty morning without any further harassment. In spite of the dreary day, Mylana felt light-hearted, for they no longer had a Tlocanian patrol ahead of them. She hoped that they would soon be in the Grandgorn Valley and turning north towards Warhaven. It felt like they were finally making progress again, instead of waiting and worrying about their enemy's next move. She just hoped the Red patrol would turn back towards Waybridge.

They made good time, for the road was in fair condition and with little traffic. At midday, they decided to take their meal beside a trickling stream. As they rode over, a low hanging branch slapped Hessilyn in the face, spraying her with its collection of droplets. With a sound of disgust, she pushed the branch away and shook off the water. Mylana snickered, and then tried to cover it up with her hand.

"So Lady Hessilyn, you must be missing the finery of court life," observed Coursen with a grin.

Hessilyn gave him a cool look, but could not sustain it and soon grinned in return. "I would enjoy a cheery fire right now, with a mulled cider in my hand and nice lap blanket covering my legs," she admitted, "but I do not miss the flattery of court life. If this were a hunt with the court sycophants, they would not smile or tease. Instead, they would be showing me polite concern and then laugh at me as soon as they rode out of hearing range. I much prefer your honest mockery, Coursen."

He gave her a slight bow. "I will do my best to please you, my lady."

Hessilyn wagged a finger at him. "I am sure you will, you rogue. One thing you can do is stop calling me 'lady'. You do not use a title for Mandor or Mylana, so why for me?"

Coursen gave it a moment's thought. "I had not ever considered that. I see them as fellow Attuls, not as Westbend nobility. Should I be calling you 'lady' too, Mylana?"

She laughed. "If you do, I will start calling you names as well. Our titles are minor, as you well know, Coursen. Westbend's king gave our father his title in thanks for a matching pair of our finest horses, not because of some great and noble deed."

"Coursen, I think you are right," stated Mandor in a serious tone as he dismounted. "From now on call me Lord Mandor as is appropriate from a commoner like you. Come here, servant, and take the horses' reins. You will see to their watering and then set out our lunch..."

Mandor got no further, for Coursen sprang from the saddle with a yell and soon the two were wrestling in the wet grass. Hessilyn demanded that they stop, but a smiling Mylana assured her that this was not their first play bout. Mylana calmly stepped down and urged Hessilyn to do likewise. The two women led the horses down to the stream to drink while the boys continued scuffling. Mylana realized that all of them felt relief at having made it past the Tlocanians.

By the time the women had finished with the horses and tied their leads to branches, the young men completed their wrestling. Breathing heavily and laughing, Mandor and Coursen came over with their arms over each other's shoulders.

Mylana eyed their wet and grass-stained clothing. "I hope you boys have had your fun while we took care of the mounts. However, now it is your turn to work. I expect you to prepare our meal and it had better be more than jerked meat and a shriveled apple."

They still smiled, but nodded to her terms.

BRODAGAR

Brodagar watched the Attuls through the eyes of one of his dreadhounds. There were now four in their party. They traveled carelessly; no one rode ahead to scout the way. He observed them carefully, but learned nothing else, so he ordered the dog to slink away, back to the rest of the pack. He withdrew from the animal after giving the pack orders to follow at a distance. As he became aware of his body's surroundings, he realized that Captain Nesron was there.

Nesron must have noticed the change in Brodagar, that his eyes no longer glowed red, because he spoke, "Well, what knowledge have you gained?"

The priest took a deep breath. It was never easy to come out of a mind link. He was glad that he was not one of the shape shifters who actually turned into a were-dog, for that could drive a human insane. When he felt his mental balance return, he smirked. "They act like their traipsing through some walled garden, with no worry about attack."

Nesron nodded. "Attuls are prideful. For too long they have been the top predator in Na Ciria, with no one to fear. They will soon learn the terror of becoming the prey."

"It will be hard to follow Free Hawk's bold plan," stated Brodagar carefully. "The dogs go into a frenzy at the smell of human blood."

"Are you saying that you cannot do this?" asked Nesron. Free Hawk had left a message in the Gratoro temple's offering box. The spy wanted the group terrorized in a specific way.

"I will follow the plan," said Brodagar, not liking that the other questioned his abilities. "Just realize that some caution is required. I do not want the hounds killing everyone and leaving us without our answer."

MYLANA

The first attack occurred that night, during Coursen's watch. Ten dreadhounds slipped up on their camp and suddenly sprang at the horses where they were tied up for the night. The dogs made no sound, but the horses screamed their terror. That noise awoke the others and brought Coursen running. Mylana was still confused as she struggled to get up. She saw Coursen rushing to the horses. She heard the dreadhounds and then saw them, black beasts moving through a dark night. A horse let out a terrible scream as it fell under the onslaught.

One hound with red shining eyes turned from its original prey and leaped at Coursen, so fast that he did not have time to pull free his sword. He grabbed the beast with his hands, deflecting it from his neck. Instead, it sank its teeth into his arm. He cried out in pain, throwing the dog off him. It regained its footing and started to circle him.

Mylana cried out in fear for him, grappling for her own sword. She rushed over, with her blazing sword, and slashed into the beast's side so hard that it went sprawling. Coursen collapsed from shock and lost blood. She pursued the injured dog, determined to give it a killing blow. She slashed at the beast twice more, then straightened and looked for another hound to kill. However, just as suddenly as the attack came, it ended. The dogs ran off, leaving behind a slaughtered horse.

Mylana looked around for her brother, and saw him next to the fire's ember, Hessilyn clinging to him in panic and sobbing. The remaining horses were still trying to pull free of their ropes, but she did not have the time to calm them. Not with Coursen in such bad shape. She hurried to his side, and in the light of her sword saw that he was unconscious. She raised her sword towards the heavens and began to pray for El's guidance in healing. She knelt and carefully placed the blade's flat side against the worst of his wounds and started the exhausting work of healing him. The worst seemed to be his right arm, with numerous bites already darkening with sudden infection. She set touch the glowing metal to each wound and experienced the drain of healing power, but it did not feel quite right. It was as if the infection twisted the healing away and it seemed to take so much more of her own strength. She tried to examine the wound be the light of her blade, but the sword flickered due to her exhaustion. Still uncertain if the healing had worked, she sheathed her sword out of weariness, bringing darkness back.

She was not finished, however. Coursen's broken arm needed to be reset, so Mylana called her brother to come over since she doubted that she could do it herself. Coursen moaned when Mandor pulled the bone back into place but he did not come to his senses. Mylana took over again, doing her best to bandage Coursen's many wounds. Hessilyn did her best to assist her while Mandor built their fire up.

No more attacks came that night, but the only one who slept was the exhausted Coursen. Mandor moved the surviving horses away from the shredded carcass and then tied them up again, doing his best to soothe them. The humans huddled around their small fire, listening for any strange sounds.

Mylana wrapped a blanket over her shoulders and brooded over the sleeping Coursen. He was laid out close enough to the campfire to get some of its warmth, the flames making a dance of light and shadow across his sleeping face. Had she healed him correctly and fully? She was not certain, for healing was not something she had done often and never on such ugly wounds. She regularly went to feel his brow, worried that a fever might set in, but none did.

* * *

When the land finally lightened with a fitful dawn, she awoke Coursen and told him it was time to leave. Mylana felt relief that his eyes were clear and his response lucid though weak. She tried to look at his wounds, but he shook off her ministrations, saying that he could sense that the infection was now gone. She stood over him, arms crossed, refusing to leave until she could examine him. He finally relented, allowing her to peal back the bandages. She was surprised to find the bites as he had said, clear of and infection. She replaced the bandages, letting him know that he was right.

"See? You should not doubt your healing work. Now, go help the others since I am an invalid still."

At least he admitted that he was still too worn to help pack, so she gave him a bowl of porridge and then went to help Mandor and Hessilyn.

They no longer had any horses to spare, for they had lost their last packhorse last night. They shifted all the supplies deemed essential onto the remaining four horses and then left the rest behind with the carcass. Mandor helped a still-unsteady Coursen up into the saddle, and then they set off. The cheerful mood of the day before was gone.

The lower clouds lifted by mid-morning, but the ever-present Dragon Shadow remained. They headed eastward at a steady pace, making sure not to go too fast for Coursen's sake. Whenever the dark forest crept near the road, they would ride closer together in fear of what might be hidden there, but no dreadhounds attacked.

The whole day passed without another incident, for which Mylana thanked El, since it gave Coursen time to recuperate. By late that day, he looked far better, though still not his boisterous self.

* * *

They had just passed through another dreary wood, when Mandor rode close to his sister and said that they had better find a secure campsite now, before the sky darkened any further. Mylana agreed and the two of them searched both sides of the road for a likely site. It took another hour of riding before they found a promising place: a pond with an irregular shoreline. Mandor led them to a grassy spit that ended in a close-grown stand of young pines leaning over the water.

"Let us set our fire here," he said, pointing to where the spit began, "and tie our horses to the trees. No dogs will be able to sneak up behind us this night."

When the gloom finally darkened into night, they were settled in around a cheery fire, a large pile of branches and deadwood at hand. The light shone out over the water, but tonight they were more concerned about defense than concealment.

As the night deepened, the baying began.

"Where are they?" asked Hessilyn, hugging herself against the night's chill. She looked worriedly out into the dark.

"Not too near," stated Coursen, using his good arm to toss another twig into the fire. "But they are fleet animals. They could be on us within a few hours."

Mandor laid an arm across Hessilyn's shoulders to comfort her. "They will not overwhelm us here, unless their pack has tripled."

"It may have," stated Mylana from where she sat on the other side of the fire. "We saw so many tracks on the road before Gratoro."

"But we have not seen so many since," argued Mandor, frowning. The firelight emphasized his displeasure at his sister's gloomy words.

"I pray that El spares us from having to face all of those beasts at one time," said Mylana thoughtfully, "but we must prepare for what might be out there."

As if in answer, there came a lone howl from across the lake. Hessilyn, unfamiliar with living far from a city, jumped. "What was that? It sounded different."

Mylana nodded. "It was. That is the call of a wolf."

Hessilyn turned to Mandor with wide-eyed concern. The confident city girl was at a loss in these wilds. "Are all the evil beasts converging on us?"

Mandor gave her an encouraging smile. "We have nothing to fear of wolves. They usually do not bother humans, especially not when fire is near."

"But the dreadhounds are a different matter," argued Coursen, "and with the hounds may come their dragon priest keepers. Mylana is right that we should consider what might be stalking us."

They all fell silent for a time, the only sound coming from the crackling fire. Another round of baying came, a bit closer this time. Finally, Coursen stood up. "Well, we had better get some rest. I can take first watch."

Mandor also stood up. "I think not, old friend. Your sword arm is useless. Mylana and I will take turns on watch this night. Instead, I would ask that you keep back with Hessilyn, on the spit's end. We will need the two of you to keep the horses under control, should another attack come."

Coursen stared at Mandor a moment, seemingly ready to protest, but then he gave a nod. "You are right. Come, Hessilyn. Let us see if we can find a pair of soft spots to lay our blankets."

With a worried glance back at Mandor, Hessilyn complied. The two walked towards the horses, out of the fire's light. Soon both were bedded down, though Mylana doubted that either slept yet.

"Go ahead and try to sleep," Mandor told her. "I will take the first watch."

Mylana curled up within her blankets, yet sleep evaded for over an hour. Three hours later, she suddenly awoke to an overpowering sense of evil. Sitting up quickly, she stared off into the dark. "What was that?" she whispered urgently to Mandor.

He stood there, staring off into the night, not responding at first. Finally, he looked over at her. "I know not, but something evil stirs this night."

They heard an owl hoot somewhere off to the right and then the fire crackled, seeming very loud to them. They were just starting to calm down, when they heard dreadhounds off in the distance, baying on the hunt. Mylana listened for a time, but the dogs seemed to be getting further away. She told Mandor as much, but he was hesitant to agree.

BRODAGAR

"Who follows?" Nesron demanded the answer from Brodagar. The two had ridden away from the others for privacy. They had just caught up with the Attuls, but now a new disturbance had occurred. While they had been tracking the Attuls, something else had been stalking them.

"The pack does not respond to me or my men," replied the dragon priest. "They are not from the Tlocanian kennels."

"Feral dreadhounds?"

"There is no such thing. No, they are from another high demon's brood."

Nesron glared to the west. "What game are the high demons playing? Who could have sent them?"

"There was a party from the Osburg Empire in Waybridge," observed Brodagar, wondering why Nesron seemed ignorant of that fact. During their time in Waybridge, he had made sure to collect all the news in the city and the surrounding Hasan Province. He was not about to depend on Colonel Wevro for all of his information. "The Osburgen party had dreadhounds with them."

"Can you tell how many soldiers or priests are with that pack?"

"No. As I said, they do not respond to me," replied Brodagar calmly. "I have ordered Brother Worlon-Shindro to change and lead his pack to investigate."

At that moment, they both felt the surge of power as Worlon-Shindro transformed into a were-hound. Soon thereafter, they heard a pack of hounds baying as they raced back up the road. Some of the dogs in the two remaining packs whined, for they were eager to run as well.

Nesron frowned. "Brodagar-Sahak, I will not have another rob us of our prey. Drive off that pack!"

The priest glared back. "Worlon will do what is needed. Now, what have you planned for the Attuls?"

Nesron stared back for a moment, pausing to show that he would not be ordered around. Finally, he shared his scheme, to which Brodagar grudgingly agreed. They had a few things to prepare for a morning confrontation.

* * *

Dawn. Brodagar could feel its hostile touch even through the comforting blanket of the Dragon Shadow overhead. Out of habit, he touched his robe's hood to make sure it properly shaded his face. He disliked being out during the day, but this seemed the best time to catch the Attuls unaware.

He had to admit Nesron was right to pick this hour, for the Attuls would have expected another night attack. Some of Nesron's soldiers waited on the other side of the pond, hidden among the pines that edged the water. These were practical men, who did not feel uncomfortable missing the morning prayer time. The rest of the troops had been sent further down the road and Nesron had instructed the sergeant to lead them in prayer during his absence, for the men could get superstitious about missing. Brodagar had watched all of this quietly, not offering to send along any of his priests to lead the prayer time, for his entourage held only Embraced priests and they were too important for such trivial matters.

When Nesron finished with his orders, he turned back to Brodagar. "Are the hounds in place?"

"Yes. There are only four of them, for we cannot control more than that." He indicated the three other priests nearby. "The other dogs have been sent away so that the blood lust does not overwhelm them."

The captain grunted, probably not liking the need for the beasts. Most of the army only tolerated the dreadhounds; rarely did any offer thanks for how the priest-bred dogs so efficiently hunted down any enemies. Brodagar sensed the other's feelings of superiority, feelings any experienced Embraced One could easily mask. Nesron's openness was a direct challenge to him, saying that the captain felt that he should lead this expedition, instead of sharing it with a mere dragon priest. Brodagar would have to see about correcting his companion's misunderstandings.

Nesron looked down the shoreline to where the Attuls' fire acted like a beacon. "Then let us start today's torment," he muttered. He signaled the archers across the pond, but they missed his gesture in the darkness. Frowning, he rode closer and repeated his signal with greater gestures. They finally saw it and raised their bows.

MYLANA

The Riders decided to get an early start, since sleep had fled all of them. The horses were already saddled, though still tied to the copse of small pines on the spit. They had decided to eat while riding, hoping to gain some distance on whoever followed them. The women had just thrown dirt on the last of their fire, while the men retrieved the mounts. At that moment, arrows began to rain down upon them. Yelling warning to the women, the men ran to gather the reins. The arrows were not well aimed, flying such a distance at an arc, but one grazed Mylana's horse and sent it into a frenzy.

Another arrow grazed Hessilyn, ripping down her fine cloak and glancing off her thigh. She cried out and stumbled, but did not fall. Mylana gave her a supporting hand as the two ran the remaining distance to the boys. Reins were hastily handed out. Hessilyn was an expert horsewoman, so she was able to mount up in spite of her injury. Mylana struggled some with her aggravated horse, due to its injury, but she soothed Sundancer enough to climb on.

Another round of arrows fell, none hitting them this time.

They rode hard off the spit, fleeing the deadly hail. Coursen had the lead. As the horses thundered back towards the road, dreadhounds suddenly leaped out of the brush. The horses swerved, with Mandor's stallion sending a kick at one dog. Another hound sprang at Mylana and nipped her leg, shredding her pants. The foursome broke free and galloped down the road, trying to get some distance from their attackers.

When at last they seemed to be well away, Mandor called for a halt to look at their injuries. Both Mylana and Hessilyn sagged in the saddle, weak from blood loss. He was not as gifted in curing as Mylana, but no one else could do it so he set the flat of his blade on their various injuries and sought El's help in healing. He attended Hessilyn simple arrow wound with a light touch, for the injury was shallow and clean. Mylana, though, already sweated with fever, her leg swollen. Coursen had done what he could to cleanse the wound, but the infection already raged.

Mandor called on El's power and guidance as he set his blazing sword against the ugly wound. The white light flared and then sparks settled all over Mylana's leg, though concentrating on the bite. Mandor kept his eyes closed in deep prayer, beseeching El for a miracle. Mylana, leaning against Coursen for support, almost fainted from the fever and the blood loss. Finally, Mandor finished, lifting his sword from his sister's leg and then sheathing it with a sigh. He looked haggard and still concerned.

"How is she?" asked Coursen softly, as he lay Mylana down. She heard the question, though they thought her unconscious.

"I am not certain," admitted Mandor, still kneeling at her side. "The infection spread so fast and with such virility. It has stopped spreading, I think, but it may not be all purged as of yet. I do not have the strength to do more. What of you, Coursen?"

"You know very well that I have no gift of healing," his friend remarked. He still lingered at her side. "Should the infection worsen, I will try to help. However, my past efforts in curing have been meager at best. At this moment we have another concern, though."

"What is that?" asked Hessilyn. From the sound of her voice, Mylana guessed her to be standing behind Mandor, but she did not have the strength to open her eyes and turn her head to see.

Coursen's voice became harsher. "Do you not hear it? They are still after us."

Mylana listened and realized what Coursen meant. The dreadhounds barked and bayed on their trail, far too close. She struggled to sit up, receiving aid from Coursen.

Mandor sighed and climbed unsteadily to his feet, with help from Hessilyn. "We need to get Mylana back on her horse. We are not strong enough to face these foes now."

Mylana wanted to protest that she could climb up herself, but realized she could not even get to her feet unaided. Coursen helped her up onto Sundancer. He kept her horse's reins, since her consciousness remained precarious. They rode off with Coursen guiding her horse, forced to a slower pace than before.

* * *

Mylana startled awake when Coursen spoke her name loudly and patted her hand. She realized it was the end of the day. "Mylana. You will need to hug your horse's neck for this last section. The place is rather overgrown."

She looked around and barely noticed the charred and deserted cottage buried under vines and brush. "Where are we?"

"This was once a Watch Rider Post, according to Mandor's knowledge, but has been long-abandoned. It is the only refuge that he could find for us. Now hunker down so that I can lead your horse through to the barn he found."

Mylana obliged, though the ache in her leg intensified. Coursen walked both horses between young trees and around bushes. Even bending low in the saddle, she had to guard herself from numerous low-lying branches. Finally, the underbrush thinned into a grassy area that revealed their night's refuge. The barn was more of a shed, meant only to hold six horses at the most. Mandor's horse stood patiently nearby, tied to a sapling. Coursen led their horses inside, revealing a sad structure nearly reclaimed by the wilds. The roof had collapsed at the far corner. The walls seemed to lean a bit and showed numerous gaps. Mylana did not care much about the details, though. She just hoped to find a soft corner where she could sleep.

"This is our shelter?" asked Coursen, sounding dubious.

Mandor nodded. "A flimsy refuge, I admit, but we have no other. The walls are still solid, even though the wood is weathered gray."

Coursen helped Mylana from the saddle. She made it, but broke into a sweat from the effort. Her leg now throbbed horribly. Hessilyn spread a blanket and then all three helped her to sit down. The jarring caused Mylana to clench her teeth and close her eyes in pain, but it soon subsided back to just throbbing again.

Mandor straightened from settling Mylana on the ground. "Hessilyn, can you see to the horses? Try to keep them to that corner of the barn. I think we should keep them saddled this night." He turned to Coursen. "Can you gather firewood? I will go and do my best at hiding our trail."

Mylana wanted to help, but her weakness betrayed her and instead she dozed a bit while the others did their tasks. When she awoke next, she was offered a warm stew and a mug of water. While she ate, Mandor looked at her wound and declared it to be healing. Mandor turned to Coursen next.

"How is your wound?"

"Do not worry about me," stated Coursen, but Mandor insisted on looking at it. Mylana could see that Coursen's arm was still swollen and aggravated around the slashes. Besides the irritation of a day's hard use, the arm showed a slight return of infection. When Mandor's hand went towards his sword, Coursen pulled away. "Oh no, you will not waste your last strength on me."

"But it is still infected," argued Mandor.

"Perhaps, but not badly," replied Coursen, awkwardly tugging his bandages back into place.

Mylana would have insisted on healing Coursen, but her brother respected his friend's reluctance.

Mandor caught his eyes. "Promise that you will let me know if your wound worsens."

Coursen nodded, but seemed focused on getting his arm positioned comfortably in its sling. He looked up and caught Mylana watching. "What about you? You scared me today. There was a time we wondered if you might be slipping away from us to the eternal lands of Havenel."

"Do not frighten her," urged Hessilyn.

"I am not trying to," said Coursen, "but if she would have died our mission would have turned to ash."

"She would not let herself die without passing on her secret," claimed Hessilyn.

Mylana appreciated Hessilyn's faith in her, but she wondered. What if she had not regained consciousness? Coursen was right; their mission would have failed. If only the Guardians had not sworn her to secrecy, she would readily share it with her fellow Riders, for both were trustworthy.

"Mylana will keep her secret," stated Mandor, "and we will keep her alive. That is our duty."

With Mylana still too exhausted to help, they were down to three. They gave Hessilyn the first watch, since both young men believed any pursuers would not catch up with them during that shift. Before going to sleep, Mandor handed his sword to Hessilyn, since her knife would be of no use against any hound. The blade's fire flickered and then faded as she grasped the weapon, but Mandor assured her that it would keep its keen edge. She did not handle it for long, for it seemed to make her uncomfortable. She sat next to their small fire, laying the bare blade on the ground beside her so that it no longer touched her skin but remained within easy reach. Mylana kept her company, for she no longer felt sleepy, in spite being weak.

Two hours later, the baying started again, drawing ever closer. Again and again, the dogs sounded off as they sniffed out the Attuls' trail. Each time she heard them, Hessilyn would almost grab the sword, but then stop. Mylana tried to assure her that the dogs were still far off, but even her heart sped up every time they howled.

The dogs never attacked that night, but a lone dog came very close to stare at them, its red eyes glowing out of the darkness. Coursen was on watch when it appeared, but Mylana was also awake and saw it. She was surprised that Coursen did not yell for the others. "Are you not afraid of it?" she whispered.

Coursen startled, not aware that she watched. He answered her without taking his eyes off the dreadhound. "It is not here to attack. Maybe it acts as a scout, but it is just watching. If I wake your brother, Mandor will go charging after it and might stumble into the whole pack. I want to let him sleep as long as he can, because he needs it."

"You play a dangerous game, Coursen," warned Mylana, struggling to sit up. The dog gave her a quick look, but then refocused on Coursen again. She wondered how much Coursen knew about these black dogs, for surely he had encountered them during his many Rides. He seemed so calm, as if he could anticipate what they might do.

He seemed to sense her thoughts. "The dreadhounds always hunt in packs. When they attack, it will be at least a pair of them. When there is only one, it will avoid any human who can defend himself."

She was impressed by his confidence. "It is as if you understand those dreadful dogs."

Using his good left arm, Coursen lifted a burning branch from the small fire. "You should always know your enemy well. Know who to fear and who you might be able to turn." He threw the flaming brand at the animal and it ran off.

She wondered what Coursen truly feared, for he seemed such a brave man.

Eric Lorenzen

CHAPTER TWENTY-ONE
Another Retreat

WINTRON

It galled Wintron to be fleeing again. He had not even had the time to gather up all of the scouts that were still out. Upon hearing how many Tlocanians had invaded the Highlands, he had no choice but to order a retreat. He took along his cousin Gurash and had planned to take Zita as well, but the girl had suddenly vanished, to everyone's frustration. She had apparently climbed out her bedroom window during the night and slipped past the guards patrolling the grounds. The duchess grudgingly admitted that Zita had muttered something about going to convince her father about the error of his ways. A resourceful girl, though wrong headed; Wintron hoped nothing bad happened to her, even if she was deserting.

His aunt refused to flee with him, claiming she would come to no harm from Drass. Wintron had to admit to himself that he was glad to be free of the Halen-Dabe women, though his uncle might not appreciate his failing to rescue her. She did not even come out to see his departure, nor thank him for leaving most of the estate's stores untouched. Instead, she had complained of his thievery and ordered him out of her presence. He left gladly, dragging her youngest son with him.

Soon after departing Halenvale, two scouts caught with him with more information about Drass' force. They spoke of an infantry company wearing the black-and-red of Tlocania that marched behind Drass' motley cavalry. The confirmation spurred Wintron and the two captains to speed up their retreat. It soon became apparent that Drass knew about the prince and had turned to pursue.

* * *

For three days, they fled back towards Tor Randis and still they were being followed. Even worse, Drass was catching up due to the weather, though the Tlocanian foot soldiers had fallen behind. A cold spring rain had swept in, weather that favored the sure-footed mountain ponies over the bigger horses of Wintron's men.

At the moment, the prince and his men rode above the tree line, through a rocky pass where the rain turned to sleet. This miserable weather kept them from pressing the horses to any faster pace. He moved his horse closer to Captain Kevlo and raised his voice over the storm's bluster. "What do you think, captain? Will we make it to Tor Randis before they catch up with us?"

"I do not know, my prince." Kevlo looked concerned, but it might just be worry for the general's youngest son. Gurash rode just behind them. "Those garrons are hardy beasts. Our horses could easily outrun them in a sunny meadow, but those small mounts seem to thrive in this weather and landscape, which is why Duke Fors breeds them. Let us hope none of those dragon priests are at our heels, for I have heard how they threw lightning at your forces in the Borderheart."

Wintron nodded, pulling his hood a bit lower against a wicked gust of sleet. "I do not know much of their magic, but I think they need the Dragon Shadow to call down their lightning strikes. Thank the gods; this is but a natural storm."

"Winiem is playing the Trickster again," mused Kevlo. "The storm may be natural but it works in Drass' favor, my prince. Let us hope the other mountain gods talk some sense into the Spring God, or else we may not escape."

He did not answer, but found his thoughts wandering to the many gods of the Borderfolk: the mountain gods, the dragon gods, and some of the local spirits. He even considered Rolen's god El. Quietly, he prayed to each one he recalled, hoping that someone would hear and offer help. Surely, some god somewhere would see the justness of his cause and would send aid.

"Rider coming!" yelled back Bilshor from just ahead of them.

It was Scout Orgel returning from spying out their trail. Wintron and the captains gathered to hear his report.

"There is trouble ahead," stated Orgel. "Some of Drass' men hold the top of the pass. They have piled stones into a low wall across the road and they are hunkered behind a bunker overlooking it. The weather is too foul for their arrows, but it is also too wet for us to try jumping that wall. The ground is too sodden, too unsure. We will need to use the small opening directly beneath their shelter, where they can rain rocks down us instead of arrows."

"Did they see you?" asked Bilshor.

Orgel nodded. "Certainly. They keep a good watch, but they did not bother trying to chase after me in this awful weather."

"Can we send men to sneak behind their redoubt?"

Orgel gave the prince a grim look. "We will have to, though it is not a good place for sneaking. They are up against rocks that only a marmot or a mountain goat could love. Even if they set no traps, those boulders will be a great danger, for they are sheer as well as being wet with sleet. No one who makes it over that rubble will be able to do so in secret. The rebels will hear their approach."

Wintron did not like the sound of that. He looked to the captains for their advice.

"We must press on," stated Kevlo, "even if it will be costly."

Bilshor agreed. "I will ask for volunteers for the rock climbing, for it will be a dangerous job." When he saw that Orgel was ready to be the first, he forestalled him. "Not you, scout. You are needed elsewhere. As soon as we start the battle, I want you to sneak past and explore the downhill slope, for there might be other traps still ahead. We will win our way past this post, but we may be too tired to see any second line. It is your duty to make sure no other surprises are waiting for us, scout."

When they finally arrived at the narrow gap, Wintron could barely see the barrier wall because the storm had turned to hail. The ground quickly turned white and it was sticking to the horse mane in front of him. Due to the weather, they did not send soldiers clambering to get behind the rebel bunker, for the pass wall was too steep and the rocks too slick with hail. Instead, Bilshor ordered the soldiers to attack the bunker straight on, first from horseback, shoving hastily cut poles into the openings, and then followed by an assault on foot. Wintron allowed Bilshor to plan their assault, for he was a competent officer, yet it promised to be an ugly battle.

The prince had reluctantly agreed to keep back during the fighting, as had Gurash even though the youth seemed eager to taste real battle. From where he sat on his horse, the prince could not see the fight very clearly, but he heard the orders, screams, and curses. Many died trying to breach the stonework, but still their overwhelming numbers won out and the rebels were overpowered. Once the Border soldiers gained the bunker, they made quick work of the rebels.

Wintron and Gurash focused on the battle just up the road, so they did not see the small band of rebels closer by. The men rose out of a gully where they had been hiding, and then ran directly at the two nobles. Suddenly, Wintron's personal guards were in a mad fight, as rebels tried to rush the crown prince. Two made it through, forcing Wintron to defend himself. Although on foot, the two knew how to come at a mounted man. They might have succeeded, but Gurash took one from behind, his sword cleaving the man's arm. Wintron killed the other quickly. The rest of the rebel band died just as swiftly.

The battle ended as suddenly as it had started and soon the continuing hail had covered any red stains. Even the dead rebels were quickly blanketed in white.

Bilshor ordered that the wounded be helped back into the saddle and then sent the able-bodied to put the dead Border soldiers into the bunker and then collapsed its walls on top of it to create a cairn. Wintron ordered the rebel corpses thrown onto the roadside, for they were traitors to their homeland undeserving of a burial. When all of that was done, the Border army passed the wall and then he ordered that rocks be pulled down into the gap to obstruct those following. Finally, they moved on, now heading down the far side of the pass.

It was still only late afternoon, but the tiring battle and the horrid weather made it feel much later. They had lost twenty soldiers in that battle just to kill fifteen rebels. A whole squad's worth, dead. Weariness showed on the dripping faces of the remaining men. Nonetheless, Wintron and his captains agreed that they had to press on, needing to get back to the protective forests that waited below. An exhausted army finally set up camp under dripping evergreens two hours later, struggling to find enough dry wood to create sputtering fires. At least the sleet did not follow them to the lower elevation; they had only rain to contend with here.

The prince huddled beside one of those fires, gratefully holding a bowl of hot stew. Next to him squatted Gurash. The young man ate quietly, for which Wintron was thankful for he had no desire to talk. Once done, he handed his bowl to one of those on cooking duty and then headed to his small tent. Under its canvas, he found it merely damp instead of sopping wet. He did his best to get warm beneath the cold blankets, spreading his wet cloak on top of them.

* * *

He was sleeping when the next battle began, waking up when someone fell on his tent and collapsed it. Struggling in the darkness, Wintron found his sword where he had set it beside his blankets and then cut his way out of the tent, pushing whoever it was aside. He finally broke free to a camp in chaos. Rebels had ridden their horses into the camp and were attacking with abandon. Half-dressed men struggled to fight back. The body that had fallen on his tent was one of his guards. Two other guards still fought, keeping the rebels away from their prince. More of his guards came running over, led by Yosif. Wintron pulled away the entangling blankets and canvas, and stood up.

"What is happening, Yosif?"

"Our perimeter sentries are slain; the rebels have caught us unaware. I fear the horse lines have been cut too."

Wintron cursed. How had Drass caught up so quickly? How had the rebels overwhelmed their sentries?

"There must be traitors in our camp," growled Gurash from nearby.

Though Wintron did not necessarily like the young man, he was thankful that Gurash was no ally of his rebellious brothers. "What makes you think there were traitors?"

"How else could the rebels fall on us so effectively? Drass had the same help in taking Halenvale."

Wintron cursed again, seeing the truth of his cousin's logic. He should have taken the time to talk with Gurash to learn what he could of Drass' tactics. "Well, we have no time to sort that out now. We must drive them from our midst first."

He did not let his guards keep him away from the fight, for he realized all were needed to gain the upper hand. The next few minutes passed in a blur of melees around the camp until they finally defeated the rebels. The last handful fled, riding off into the stormy night.

When Wintron finally sheathed his sword, the exhaustion sank in. Someone handed him his cloak, retrieved from the ruins of his tent. Gurash limped over.

"It is only a bruise, Prince Wintron," Gurash said in answer to his query, dismissing any concern. "Where is Captain Kevlo?"

"I am here, Lord Gurash," the captain answered, walking up.

Gurash turned on him. "I hear that some of our own turned on us, helping my brother's men. Did you have anything to do with this?"

Kevlo answered with restraint. "I am loyal to your father, to the crown prince, and to the realm. I did not betray us."

Wintron looked between them. "Do you claim that Kevlo serves your brothers?"

Gurash gave Kevlo a hard look. "Did Kevlo ever tell you about his mentor? Ask him who his constant companion was during his youth."

Kevlo gritted his teeth, but held the eyes of Gurash.

"Well, what are your answers, Captain Kevlo?" asked Wintron.

The captain looked at Wintron, his gaze still steady. "I was once close to both Mordel and Drass. That is true. However, I did not follow them into revolt."

Bilshor interrupted. "I do not think this is the time. We have wounded to tend, dead to bury, and horses to gather. This was not Drass' full force, but if we linger here, they may soon be on us."

Wintron nodded at Bilshor's good judgment. "We will talk more, Captain Kevlo, but right now we must flee. Take a squad of men and capture of our loose horses as well as any of those rebel ponies that might be near."

Traitor or not, Kevlo did well in gathering up stray mounts. There were enough for all the survivors, though three soldiers ended up on mountain ponies. The battle had cost them another fourteen men, including two sergeants. What had begun as a force of one hundred had dwindled to just sixty-one.

Wintron ordered their dead placed in a small hollow and then had them covered with dirt and rocks. It was a poor and unmarked grave, but the best they could provide. One sergeant volunteered to say the proper burial prayers while the diggers stood quietly nearby. Wintron could not even afford to have all the men gather, not when every minute counted. However, he joined the brief ritual himself, for the fallen deserved at least that much respect for their sacrifice.

Soon, the Border soldiers rode onward. They kept moving even as dawn arrived with a break in the weather. Bilshor did not call for a halt until they came to the village of Farfaran Meadow. The troops homed in on the green lantern of the small inn, still lit due to the cloudy day. As Wintron and Gurash went to meet the town leaders, Bilshor and Kevlo arranged for the care of their men. They filled the common room with the wounded. A local healer woman did her best to help, though her skills were limited. The rest of the soldiers sought refuge in the dryness of the barn, filling its hayloft with sleeping men. In all, the Border force was able to rest a half-day in Farfaran Meadow, but Wintron would not allow them any more time than that. He did not want to fight Drass in the middle of the village.

The prince was riding out of the village with his men just as the sun finally broke through the late-afternoon clouds. The brightness did nothing to cheer his mood, for the troop had been reduced to nearly half its strength. They had to leave another four men in the village due to their injuries. Wintron gave the healer woman plenty of coins and she promised to conceal the men from those pursuing.

The rain left but heavy dark clouds still traveled the skies. The sunshine did not last, as another cloud moved overhead and chased the sunlight off to the far side of the valley. Looking back, he spotted movement on the mountain road beyond the settlement. Drass' scouts came riding down the far slope, caught in the sudden ray of brightness.

Gurash saw where he looked. "My brother is stubborn; he will not let up until he catches us or we escape through the gates of Tor Randis."

Wintron grunted.

"He will catch us before we ever see the fortress," assessed Bilshor. "We will need to choose our battleground carefully."

"Can we fight him off and still stay ahead of the Tlocanian infantry marching in his wake?" asked Wintron.

Bilshor shrugged. "We do not know how far behind they are, but I would guess that more than a day's delay and we will be in danger of seeing our enemy reunited."

The prince grimaced. "Well then, see to it that our scouts find us a good battleground where we can finish off Drass quickly."

* * *

They made their first stand on a steep mountainside, where the road snaked along the slope above a mountain lake. Wintron allowed Kevlo to continue as Bilshor's second, for he was still not convinced by Gurash's accusation. However, they kept Kevlo under careful observation. It was Kevlo who suggested sending men above the road to loosen rocks and try to bring an avalanche on the rebels. Six men were sent to do so, clambering up the steep slope and setting to their work. The men and mounts had a chance to rest while they waited for the rebels to catch up. Only when the rebels began their ascent did Bilshor order the Border army to mount up and move on.

Drass' men finally saw their prey near and let out victory shouts. They began to charge their garrons up the road, or they did until the rocks began to cascade upon their heads. Kevlo's plan worked better than any had hoped, sending the rebels into a hasty retreat and fully blocking the road under shifting rubble.

Eric Lorenzen

Wintron was not certain, but he thought the rockslide caught at least five of the pursuers. He thanked the gods for giving them a reprieve. However, as the Border troop turned to go on, a sudden flash came from the enemy's ranks and a sizzling ball of red flame arched over the rubble and fell among Wintron's men. A horse shrieked, and everyone yelled in anger and sudden fear.

They had miscalculated how far a priest could throw his fiery magic, to the rue of their men. Wintron shouted his orders, trying hard to be heard over the sudden confusion. "Ride! We must get distance between us and the dragon priests!"

DRASS

Lord Drass Halen-Dabe eyed the dragon priests with new respect. He had seen their power in the Borderheart Valley, but not from this close. He watched them build those great balls of fire in their hands and then throw them at the enemy. He was close enough to feel the heat and hear the crackle of the flames. It surprised him that they had no device to lob the fire, but then maybe nothing besides their hands could handle such power. They looked almost comical in their robes, pulling back those voluminous sleeves and tossing fireballs as if they were tossing rocks or playing ball. He dared not smile at their undignified actions though, for the two had no sense of humor. He was simply glad to have them as allies and not enemies, in spite of their arrogance.

Drass watched them toss a half-dozen balls of flame each, becoming noticeably weaker with the last few. Those last tosses landed on the rockslide though, blasting some of the rubble. Finally, the two stopped their attack.

The ever-present temple guards helped the priests into the shade where they sat down on a fallen log to rest. Drass gave them some time while his men worked at clearing the road of rubble, but he wanted more help from the priests. After what he felt was a respectful delay, he walked over to the two. The temple guards let him approach, though they still kept him under careful watch. He stopped in front of the leader of the two.

"Brother Cavish, what else can you do to help us?" he asked the lead priest.

The priest, eating a slice of cheese, hesitated in mid-bite, considering, then finished his morsel. "What do you mean, Lord

Drass? Surely you do not expect us to be shoveling gravel?"

Drass frowned. The man's tone sounded mocking, and that was something he could not tolerate. Yet these men were allies, so he chose to assume Cavish was simply tired. "Can you not use your magic to help clear the rubble?"

"You are an ignorant one, Lord Drass," scoffed Cavish.

Drass could not see his face inside his deep hood, but he would not be surprised if the priest had rolled his eyes. The priest did pointedly return to his eating, offering no further explanation. Drass would have grabbed his robes but the nearby guards gave him pause. He was relieved when the other priest finally answered his question.

"Any blast from us would likely cause more damage," explained Brother Hurko. "The land is just too unstable."

He did not like that answer. Drass did not like that these Tlocanians deemed themselves above manual labor, not even sending their dandy guards to help. "So you just sit and wait while my soldiers do all of the work…" Suddenly he caught himself, realizing that he was playing a dangerous game to criticize the dragon priests. "My apologies, holy brothers. I know that you do what you can to assist. Do you have any needs?"

"Well, the hounds often grow hungry…" Hurko suggested. "Maybe you can inspire faster work by telling your men that the slowest five will become dog food."

Drass was not amused. He felt no endearment towards any of the hirelings in his force, but he knew better than to terrorize them with threats of a devouring. Surely, the dragon priests were not already recalling the beasts. The dogs had scampered over the rockslide hours ago. He paused to listen but could not hear any baying indicating their return. "Have you at least kept your hounds on their trail or are have you recalled them?"

"We are not incompetent," remarked Cavish coldly. "The dogs track their assigned prey even now. They did stop for a snack, but it was one of the prince's scouts. The Border force has gained a few hours on us, but they still have quite a distance to their haven. We should be able to overtake them before then."

Swallowing a biting retort, Drass nodded. "Thank you, brothers, for your help." He gave them a small but respectful bow and withdrew. He did not like these men but he was smart enough to realize that he needed them. He would endure their rudeness for now, but he hoped Mordel would consolidate his power soon and then be able to dismiss their aid.

It took another two hours before the men had cleared enough rock to allow the horses to get through. Drass was glad he was not burdened by wagons or they would be at this for another day. As it was, the Tlocanian infantry had almost caught up with them. He ordered his men to mount up and move out, too eager to wait for the captain to give the order.

WINTRON

Wintron considered Captain Kevlo as he rode. The night of the camp attack, some of his troop had betrayed them, of that he was certain. Bilshor reported three men missing and presumably fled with the rebels. If any other sentries had helped the rebels was unknown, for all the others had died in the melee afterward. He pondered whether any squad leader or officer might be involved. The only officer he knew with certainty to be loyal was Bilshor, for they had been together since the days of their youth. The captain rode nearby, so he turned to him. "Do we have any more traitors in our midst, Bilshor?"

"Most likely," answered the captain. "Let us hope we do not give any betrayer a chance to endanger us."

Wintron nodded. "Keep the duty soldiers mixed, when possible. Kevlo seems a sincere man, but he and his squad still belong to Fors and maybe even his son. I would be naive not to realize that the three missing sentries all came from his squad."

"I am already doing that," stated captain. "There is another matter we should discuss. The rear scouts are overdue."

Wintron could not help but look over his shoulder, though there was nothing to see except the soldiers in his troop and the dark forest all around them. "How late are they?"

"Corlo should have reported four hours ago. For Gaddy, it is only a two hour delay."

Wintron looked up, catching a glimpse of the sunlight rays breaking through the trees overhead. It was already dark here in the woods, but the day beyond the forest had been mostly sunny. He considered the length of the shadows he saw among the tree crowns. "We only have another hour or two before dark. Have the forward guards reported back any promising campsite?"

Bilshor nodded. "We will soon reach the place Orgel has found us, a rock-strewn outcropping."

Fallen King

"Good. Once we set up camp, send all the remaining scouts back to investigate. I do not want another band surprising us tonight."

They did come across Scout Orgel shortly thereafter, waiting patiently on his horse in the middle of the dirt road. Upon seeing the first ranks, he nodded and headed off into the woods. The troop followed through the gloom, until the trees thinned to reveal a small, rocky point. The late sunlight still soaked the hilltop, giving the trees and rocks a golden glow. Orgel let his leaders catch up with him. "My prince. Captain. This is the best we can find for tonight. From up there you can see most of the surrounding land and there is a shallow bowl on the far side where we can stake the horses. Water will be a walk, but otherwise it meets our needs."

"Thank you, Orgel," replied Wintron. "I am sure you have already found the best route up, so please lead us further."

The scout smiled at the compliment as he flicked his reins.

The ride up did weave quite a bit, but they were at the top faster than Wintron expected, fast enough to catch the last of the day's sun. He dismounted and climbed one of the larger boulders, looking westward and enjoying the feel of the sunlight on his face.

In the distance, he saw smoke rising from scattered locations, indicating a village or town. Bilshor, Kevlo, and Orgel had followed him up. The scout saw where he gazed and offered an explanation. "There lies Vorsdunville."

"I do not remember seeing any recruits from Lord Percell's lands while at Tor Randis," said Wintron. "Do you know why, Kevlo?"

"I am not one of the duke's advisors, but I heard some excuse about trouble planting the spring crops. The men are promised, only delayed."

Wintron guffawed without joy. "I am sure Baron Percell Vorsdun had some excuse. Let him sit on the margins if he insists, as long as he gives no aid to Mordel. I have seen the sorry state of his armsmen and so I will not really miss them."

"You do not think he sides with our enemy?" wondered Bilshor.

"Percell is the opportunist," replied Wintron. "He delays to see who will be the eventual victor and then he will rush to that person's side. Whenever he came to court, I saw him act that way. He would sit quietly in council while others argued, but once he knew which side the king favored, he would speak up boldly in agreement. Percell has no backbone."

"So you do not think he will give us aid should you demand it of

273

him?" asked Bilshor.

"He might do so, but it would be grudging and miserly. However, we do not have the time to detour to his lands. It seems close from here, but there is no road in that direction and the forest would rob us of our horse's speed. Should we try cutting across land, not only would Drass' men be on us, but the Tlocanian infantry as well."

"You have the right of it," agreed Kevlo. "I have not journeyed through this area that often, but I know it well enough." He pointed westward, about halfway to where Vorsdunville lay. "There are bogs out there somewhere, watery ground at its worst with spring melt. That is why the road into the baron's land only comes from the west, across that pass there." He pointed out a gap in the peaks above the lands, an opening where the sunlight streamed through.

"So confronting Baron Vorsdun will have to wait for another day," stated Wintron, turning now to look north and then east. He saw no signs of settlement in either direction, but folds in the land hid much. Looking south, he wondered where Drass hid. "Have the scouts gone out yet?"

"They ride south," confirmed Bilshor, "except for Orgel here, and he will leave shortly."

The crown prince looked at the remaining scout. "May Cha protect you and may Winiem bring confusion upon our adversaries."

* * *

Orgel made it back before the rebels arrived. He rode up to the hillside recklessly in the dark, shouting for the prince. Wintron and the captains met him at the foot of the boulders.

"Their scouts have found us. We tried to stop them, but the black dogs suddenly charged. For once, those dogs made no sound, attacking us in silence. The dreadhounds brought down Nolis."

"How close is Drass?" asked Wintron.

"He will be here within an hour."

"Thank you again, Orgel," said Wintron calmly. "Go and get some dinner and then see us again afterward."

As soon as the scout had left, the prince turned to the two captains. "It looks like this hill will be our last stand. How can we make this victory very costly for Drass?"

"Such talk is foolishness," argued Bilshor. "You cannot be captured or slain; you are our ruler." The captain turned to Kevlo. "Do you think you could find your way to Vorsdunville with a small party?"

"I could," acknowledged Kevlo cautiously, "but never fast enough to bring help. The bogs will cause many detours."

"You will not be coming back," said Bilshor. "You, Lord Gurash, Yosif, and Orgel will take the prince through to Vorsdunville while the rest of us hold off Drass here. I will buy you enough time to get a fair lead."

Wintron laid a hand on Bilshor's arm. "I cannot allow this…"

"You must," interrupted the captain, "and you must sneak out without anyone realizing, even from our men."

Wintron wanted to refuse, but he saw the logic of Bilshor's plan. It was a desperate move, but it seemed his best chance for getting back to Tor Randis alive. The words of protest died on Wintron's lips, for he saw that Bilshor was right. Instead, he pulled the captain close for a rough embrace. "Do what you must, old friend, but do not simply volunteer to be the altar sacrifice. Promise me that you will try to escape once you have bought us enough time."

"I promise that I will try to escape with any survivors, once we have delayed them long enough," assured Bilshor, though Wintron sensed that he said it only to comfort his prince.

Soon, the five slipped away from the Border camp, avoiding the scattered torches and the men patrolling. Bilshor had made certain to alter the lines just enough to offer them a way to slip off the rocky point unnoticed. As the others waited among the dark trees, Orgel quietly retrieved their horses and soon they were riding off to the west.

Their absence went unnoticed at first, as everyone hustled to get ready for another battle, but Wintron expected that Drass' spies would soon realize that their main prey had fled. He wondered if any of them would try to chase after.

Eric Lorenzen

CHAPTER TWENTY-TWO
Singgorn Plains

AFRAL

Dawn neared, starting to lighten the eastern sky above the grasses of the Singgorn Plains. With the approaching daybreak came a cold wind, blowing from the west. The sweat on Afral's face and arms chilled with the wind's touch but he did not pay it much attention; instead, he focused on his sword work. Facing him on the uneven ground was his father, the finest swordsman in the Border Realm. They had been fighting by the light of their blades for nearly an hour already, keeping their swordplay inside a grassy hollow so that the glow would not broadcast over the grasslands. He knew that his father held back to lengthen the session, but he still found it invigorating to endure this long.

Suddenly his mother stepped forward, sword in hand. "Rolen, go eat your breakfast. I will continue the lesson."

His father smiled. "Work him hard, Tolara. If we exhaust him, we will not have to endure his constant questions during today's ride." His father stepped back and lowered his blade, but Afral did not get any chance to rest. His mother launched into an aggressive series of attacks, causing him to retreat halfway up the bowl's side, then she shifted her attack and he had to retreat back down. He stumbled over a groundhog's burrow and fell, hitting the damp earth with a thump. His mother's blade pricked his neck, telling him that he was now dead. However, his lesson was still not over. She stepped back and motioned him back to his feet and soon the blows were raining down upon him again.

When his mother finally called an end to the session, Afral could do nothing except collapse to the ground, breathing heavily. His father came over with a waterskin and a bowl of porridge. "You are getting far better, my son. Now eat quickly so that we can get to our prayers. We have another long day of riding ahead of us if we intend on reaching the Singgorn's banks this day."

Afral complied as soon as he had his breath back. Once finished, he took his bowl and walked over the hollow's lip and down to a stream where his father was rinsing out the pot that had held the porridge. Afral washed his bowl and then set it aside on the green grass so that he could pull off his shirt. He used the now-clean bowl to scoop icy water over his head and torso, getting rid of the worst of the sweat and dirt. He had not thought to bring a blanket, so he had to scramble back to their camp dripping a watery trail. His father smiled at his folly but said nothing.

After, he was dried and dressed, he joined his family at the hollow's rim and knelt for prayer. Today they faced eastward, into the just-appearing sun. This day's prayers began with a time of remembered thanks to El for bringing the Attuls out of the East to come fight in the Great War. From thanksgiving, they moved into intercession, praying for those they had left behind in the Border Realm and especially for Prince Wintron. Finally, they also petitioned El for their own needs, asking for protection and guidance during this day's travels. The prayers ended with Tolara leading them in a song of adoration towards El.

Afral found comfort in the familiar rituals for, although he thought of himself as more of a Borderman than an Attul, he was still Elsworn. Daily worship had been part of his routine for the earliest days he could remember. Here, out an open country that was so different from the soaring heights of the Border Mountains, it was pleasant to still have something familiar, something consistent.

* * *

They rode across the rolling grasslands under a huge sky for another three days. Rolen guided them to a large stream that they followed northward. This put them in a shallow valley that provided enough shelter for Afral to practice his sword skills as he rode. His parents did not think the glow of his sword would be too noticeable, especially under such bright sunlight. So Afral practiced as they rode northward, aiming for the Singgorn river. Whenever they stopped for a meal or to water the horses, his parents would set him to even more exercises, from running attacks to speedy retreats. He enjoyed these days, for the activities made him feel like a soldier in training. At the end of each day, his whole body would be sore but he had a sense of satisfaction.

As they drew closer to the river, Afral saw many buffalo herds slowly meandering their way westward towards their summer grazing grounds. The great but gentle beasts were known in the Borders but only as domesticated animals, for the mountains were too harsh and its pasturelands too poor. The vastness of these wandering crowds amazed him. Though his mother assured him that the bison were wild, they were so tame that he could ride up close and reach out to touch their shaggy sides.

Finally, they came within sight of the mighty Singgorn, the greatest river Afral had ever encountered. It was late afternoon, and the sun was already sinking towards the horizon. As Afral rode down the last grassy slope, the wide ribbon of water and its surroundings held his eyes. Trees lined each bank, casting long shadows in the late sunlight. However, in one place on the far bank stood a huge jumble of rock mixed in with the trees. He pointed it out to his mother.

Tolara followed his gaze. "Those are Darshi ruins. We will see more of them now that we are at the river. Not many of their keeps are intact like Tor Randis; most were either felled by our ancestors or destroyed by the Darshi themselves."

"Where are the Darshi now?" asked Afral. These ancient foes were as mythical to him as Attuls were to most others.

"That empire is gone," pronounced his father. "You know that, my son."

"Yes Father, but I did not mean the country. I meant the people. Are there any Darshi still alive?"

His mother answered this time. "Their descendants still remain, though few are aware of that ancestry and even fewer would ever boast of it. Only the people of Freetown are open about such a dubious heritage."

"Are they really... do they... look different?"

Tolara laughed. "They are humans, Afral. Nothing else. Some fables may paint their ancestors with red glowing eyes, but most of those tales are fiction. It was just that these humans communed with demons. Their descendants are no different from other humans, though they may be more prone to a life as a rogue or robber."

His father nodded agreement. "Most of the Darshi died in the

Great War or fled its aftermath, which is why far northern Na Ciria is so wild and unsettled now. However, those who remain are just ordinary people."

As they rode further down the slope, he lost sight of the ruins. Instead, his eyes fell on the still-distant Pinnacles.

"Father, is there no way we can reach Warhaven from this side?" he asked, pointing towards the mountain range directly north.

"Warhaven is barred from the south," said Rolen. "Look at the height of those jagged peaks. From this side, we would have to trudge over icefields that do not melt even in high summer. No, our path parallels the river for now, upstream to Freetown. Please remember, our countrymen have for generations kept their gaze on the ruins of Darsheol, watching for any demonic stirrings there. Since the Darshi capitol sat on the shores of Cirian Bay, the Attul stronghold also faces that great northern inlet. On a clear day, you can see those blue waters from some of the mountainside watch towers."

"Will we be riding through Freetown?" asked Afral. Even in sleepy Regalis, people heard tales about the robber families that ruled there. Now that he had seen some of their Color soldiers in Four Corners, those stories about theft and murder and ransom seemed more real.

Rolen nodded, even though his wife frowned. "The Singgorn flows too full with spring melt for either fords or ferries. The only bridges are all the way downstream in Rhendora or those in Freetown."

"We will need to be very cautious when we go through that robber den," said his mother. "Can we take on a disguise while there? We do not look like refugees, woodsmen, or trappers. I fear that too many will notice us and that some might inform the dragon priests."

Rolen smiled. "If only you had a beard, my dear, we could label ourselves a band of men-for-hire."

"If it could guarantee our safety, I would do my best to grow one as full as Prince Wintron's," she smiled back, then gave Rolen's head an appraising look. "Maybe I could shave you a bald pate and use that as my whiskers."

Rolen's eyes widened and his hand pressed on the top of his head. "I would rather go dressed in red."

"Are those stories true too?" Afral remembered tales about the lost fourth color of Freetown.

His mother nodded. "There were once four robber families in Freetown: Blue, Green, Purple, and Red, but the Reds became too honest and were attacked by the other three. Afterward, the others squabbled over who would rule the Red Core and so none do. When your father and I came through the city, almost twenty years ago, the locals warned us to avoid that district even in daylight. I cannot imagine that the area has gotten any better." Tolara now focused on her husband. "Do not even jest about wearing crimson. I saw how they treated any who dared to go in red."

"Do not worry," he assured her. "I do not want any disguise that would put us in even more danger."

That evening, as they set up their camp beneath those riverside trees, Afral asked many more questions about the infamous Freetown. Rolen and Tolara did their best to satisfy his curiosity, but they had only stayed in that city a few days and that was two decades ago.

* * *

The next morning, they turned westward on the Singgorn Road, a dirt way that paralleled the river just beyond the ribbon of trees. Afral's father informed him that this was the main road between Freetown and Paralon, the capitol of Rhendora. Afral thought it was a little-traveled road, for often it faded to barely more than two ruts in grasslands.

At noon, they saw others: three covered wagons and a line of mules also heading towards Freetown. By late afternoon, they had caught up with the trader. They rode past the last two wagons and pulled up beside the lead one. Afral's father greeted the two men on the wagon seat. "Hail wagon!"

"Greetings, riders!" answered the older of the two. The younger man just sat there, wrapped in a voluminous cloak, and scowled at the newcomers. "What brings you on the road to Freetown?" Two dogs ran over to investigate.

"We travel to that city," answered Rolen, avoiding the details. "I wonder if you would be willing to share any news from your travels, good trader."

The man laughed. "Call me Hollin. I say that any conversation to break up the road's monotony is welcome, but first introduce yourself and your companions, rider."

"My name is Rolen Strongarm." The merchant's gray eyebrows rose at that surname, and Afral realized that he probably thought it some fighter's bragging. Rolen motioned to his family. "This is my wife, Tolara Quickblade, and our son Afral. We come from the Border Realm."

Hollin gave a respectful nod and a smile. "I am honored to meet all of you. I am Hollin Yadsett, from the Lakelands. I am pleased to make your acquaintance. The young man sitting next to me is my able assistant, Pad." The big fellow continued to scowl at them, giving them only a grunt in greeting. Pad kept his cloak wrapped tight around him, making Afral wonder if a bare weapon lay hidden underneath. Hollin continued, "Would all three of you ride beside my wagon so that we can exchange gossip of the road?"

"Gladly," answered Afral's father.

For the next few hours they traveled together, with Hollin doing most of the talking. He spoke of brisk business in Rhendora, since the Grandgorn warfront cut it off from any southern trade. He shared about the many squabbles among the Lakeland kingdoms and claimed that he no longer considered any his homeland. "I have trading houses in five of the lands, each house headed by one of my sons. However, I still prefer trading outside of the Lakelands." He paused for a moment. "On second thought, this latest journey may cure me of that itch. We encountered ..."

Pad coughed loudly, interrupting whatever Hollin was about to say. Hollin looked at his worker, paused, and then nodded. "But enough about my adventures. Rolen, tell us of your recent journeys."

His father told of their travels over the White Owl Pass and through the Four Corners. He spoke of war with the Tlocanians but he did not mention the fall of the Borderheart Valley or their mission to Warhaven.

"But why do you travel the wilds with your family?"

"I apologize to you Merchant Hollin, but I cannot answer that," answered Rolen.

The man nodded. "I understand. Let me venture a guess. You were in a position of influence in the Border Realm, maybe nobility or king's advisor. You have been sent to find help for your besieged land, and are taking along your family to get them out of harm's way." Hollin paused to see if any of them would react. Afral fought hard to keep his face impassive, for he felt the trader's eyes on him. Hopefully, he had revealed nothing by his countenance. Hollin continued, "You need not confirm or deny, but I will say that if you are seeking aid in Freetown then you are on a fool's mission. They think only of themselves."

Afral's father nodded. "Thank you for your advice, Merchant Hollin, but what makes you think we are on such an assignment?"

Hollin shrugged. "You seem too honorable of a man to be fleeing and you do not travel with all of your belongings like a refugee. Therefore, that makes this a journey out of duty. Do you seek allies and soldiers to push back the Tlocanians? Well, Freetown is the only settlement of any size along this route. You will find many fighting men there, but none who are trustworthy. Things must be desperate in the Borders, if they send you to Freetown for recruits."

Rolen chose not to respond, but it seemed the merchant took his silence as an affirmation. "Well, if you are set on such a folly mission, then at least consider going on to Newtown, for in that settlement there still are men uncommitted to a Color."

His father frowned. "What is this Newtown?"

"Well, it was only a small village until five years ago. Some called it Bayside or Old Kra's Outpost."

Tolara gave the merchant a keen look. "The place on Cirian Bay where the fishermen and whalers sometimes call?"

Hollin nodded, showing surprise that anyone knew even that much. "It has grown greatly over the last few years as the troubles increased in other parts of Na Ciria. People everywhere are looking for shelter in some corner where the sun still shines and no soldiers march. Even in the Lakelands, there is anxiety about the encroachment of Tlocania's shadow. People have fled into these wilds, although I would think only desperation would drive people to such a weather-beaten place as Newtown. And yet it has grown large enough to attract other traders. These days, trading ships come up the coast to buy furs and ore."

"This is news to us," stated Rolen. "Why would captains risk their ships in such stormy waters?"

Hollin sighed, looking troubled. "The Forest Hills are not the only place where trouble brews. Something is amiss in southern Na Ciria too. So many ships have vanished, that the northern risk seems tame in comparison."

"The Jagged Coast pirates?" asked Tolara.

"There is always that," agreed Hollin, "but I think it worse. The few vessels that have made it back speak of wars in the south too. My son Grovner heads the Yadsett house in far western Pinesdell, so he does more business with the sea traders. Grovner heard whispers of more dragons flying in the southern skies. As if the red brute in Tlocania were not bad enough..."

Apparently, the topic troubled Hollin greatly, for he avoided it from then on. It was obvious enough for even Afral to notice. The merchant turned the conversation to road conditions and weather, both of which he complained about. He also asked about Four

Corners. His questions were sharp, wanting to know if the southern trade route would be worth taking next time.

Towards late afternoon, they encountered a traveler heading in the other direction. He was a lone man sitting on one mule and leading another loaded with a pick, shovels, pans, and other mining equipment. They stopped to ask him of the road conditions ahead, but the fellow was not very social. After ten minutes of one-word answers, the shaggy man claimed the need to get further down the road. They moved on, having gained little new knowledge.

As evening approached, they decided to camp beside each other. Hollin's group set their three wagons in a semi-circle, dropping the mule loads within that protected area. Their horses and mules were picketed close by. Over a shared dinner, the Attuls met the rest of Hollin's people: two drivers, the mule team guide, and two additional big men besides Pad. Afral thought them guards, but he was not certain. Pad still kept his cloak about him all evening, making no effort to help with any of camp chores. He noticed that the other two guards did, but both walked with prominent limps. The heavily armed men carried both sword and cudgel; men whom Afral would be leery of if his parents were not so near.

After the meal, the two parties turned in for the night, with a night watcher from each group. Just as they Attuls returned to their own fire and tent, all three felt a sudden sense of evil to the east. They all looked, but saw nothing among the trees around their camp.

GALDON

Galdon sat near a campfire, lost in thought. Around him, the three squads went about their business: picketing mounts, preparing the evening meal, and setting up their tents. As usual, he had pushed them past sunset now that they were no longer under the Dragon Shadow. Since entering the Triangle Wilds, they had strong sunshine and blue skies. He appreciated the weather for two reasons. First, Embraced Ones could not stand bright light, so it confirmed that none of his bareheaded men were demon possessed because none tried to hide under cowls or shield their eyes. Secondly, he simply enjoyed seeing the sun again after months of thick clouds. Even a clear night was a pleasure to behold. He looked up and appreciated the stars that now twinkling overhead. He wished that his dear Tlocania could once again sparkle in the daylight as the stars sparkled in the night sky.

Galdon left off stargazing, and instead watched his men setting up camp. His heart swelled with pride. At least his beloved Tlocanian army was still as solid as ever. They did their duty without fuss, be it staking tent lines or killing the enemy. Maybe the land around Lake Tlocan no longer seemed so bright, but nothing could dim the shine of the greatest army in all of Na Ciria. Even this small detachment showed the glory of Tlocania's troops.

His ruminating ended as he noticed one of the sergeants coming over with a scout. He sighed, for he sensed that his peaceful evening was about to be disturbed.

"Sir, you will want to hear this report," stated Sergeant Dresh. He stood across the fire from his captain, the scout at his side.

Galdon nodded for the scout to proceed. The wiry man gave his report with alacrity. All five outriders and two of the scouts had been intercepted and detained by a Tlocanian border patrol. Galdon had sent the men out to verify that the pass was clear all the way to center of the Triangle Wilds, where the Cornerstone overlooked the meeting of the three passes. This explained why the men were late in returning.

The captain asked a few questions of the scout and then dismissed him with thanks, telling him to get some dinner and then find a new horse for another ride later.

"What now, sir?" asked Dresh. "You can retrieve them, but you will have to do so personally and that could pose a risk."

"Soldiering is always risky." Galdon stood up. He did not look forward to this confrontation. "Have one squad saddle up as my escort. Not yours, for I am leaving you in charge."

Dresh nodded. "I hear and obey. I will tell Lausher; his men are more disciplined. I will also see to the saddling of your horse."

Galdon soon rode through the pass, twenty men around him. The scout led him to the patrol's camp easily, for the others made no attempt to hide their blazing semi-circle of campfires. The night watch let them pass without much concern, obviously expecting their arrival. Galdon did not stop at the picket lines, but rode right into the camp, passing between two of the fires and trampling someone's blankets. Two bear carcasses were staked out near the fires, recently gutted. He could see they had been fine animals, though he had never found any pleasure in game hunting. At each of the five fires, bear meat was roasting. Not a taste he enjoyed, due to its gaminess, but it would fill the soldiers' bellies.

He saw the men he had lost; they were near one of the fires, lying on the ground and tied up like some more game. Galdon kept his calm, though their mistreatment angered him. He rode towards a large tent that stood back from the fires, its entrance turned away from the light. He recognized by its placement that an Embraced One slept there. As he came around the tent, an officer stepped through the canvas flaps and stood there with crossed arms. He was just a lieutenant but he showed no diffidence to Galdon's superior rank. Galdon sighed. The man had probably just recently Embraced, for he reeked of arrogance and yet his rank was still low.

Galdon stopped his horse in front of the other but said nothing. The lieutenant was a mere shadow in the night gloom, his face well hidden inside the dragon helm, but Galdon did not doubt that the other could see him very clearly.

The man still did not acknowledge the presence of a superior officer, so Galdon finally spoke up. "Lieutenant, you will release my men immediately and return to them their mounts and anything else that was taken from them."

"You are not my commanding officer."

Galdon made no attempt to hide his feelings of anger. In his earlier years, he would have severely beaten any underling who was so blatantly insubordinate, but those were the days before the Dragon Lord brought in his demon allies. Embraced Ones sometimes created their own law now, using their magic to enforce it. His aim was not to discipline a rebellious officer, but to get his men back.

Galdon finally dismounted, though doing everything slowly so as not to provoke the demon-held officer. He carefully pulled out his papers from Lord Hraf and held them out. "At least you recognize that I am an officer. Would you perhaps recognize the written orders of a lord-general?"

The man strode forward and snatched the papers from Galdon. He read them quickly and then held them in one hand while calling forth the red lightning in his other. Galdon did not lunge to rescue the papers from the fire, though he wanted to.

"He is not my commanding officer either." Galdon could hear the smirk on the other's face, though he could see nothing inside the dragon helm.

The captain could barely suppress his sudden rage. "Unless you plan to rebel from the empire, lieutenant, you will obey those orders. Is that understood? You may be able to turn me into ash, but do you plan to kill all of my troops as well? That will not go unnoticed, especially since another party rides after me and it includes a veteran dragon priest. Choose quickly, for I tire of this game. Kill us or release us."

The lieutenant flung the papers at Galdon's feet. "Take your men and go, but their horses stay with us. We lost a hand's worth taking down those bears. Count it your fee for crossing my path."

Galdon retrieved his papers and carefully tucked them in an inside pocket of his shirt. Turning to Sergeant Lausher, he gave a calm order. "Have the others cut free."

Lausher saluted. "I hear and obey, sir!"

Galdon made it out of the camp with all of his men and their weapons, though he lost seven horses. The papers from Lord Hraf had passed their first test, though just barely.

As he rode, he fingered his medallion through his shirt, noting that it seemed to react to something the Embraced One was doing. He pulled out his shirt to peek down at it, and saw that it gave a sullen red glow. The light and the vibrating sensation dissipated, so the lieutenant must have ended whatever magic he had been doing. Galdon grunted. This could prove useful, though he did not like it.

Eric Lorenzen

CHAPTER TWENTY-THREE

Pain in Hightower

MYLANA

Somehow, Mylana and her companions made it to the next city on the Crossover Road without being attacked again. They heard dreadhounds every night, but the dogs were never close. It was four weary riders who approached the gates of Hightower just before evening worship. The gate guard collected a minor entrance tax, but did not bother them any further. The man seemed eager to get back to the warm guardhouse and an interrupted card game with his comrades. The foursome turned down a litter-strewn alley as soon as the gates were out-of-sight, for they did not want to be on any main road when the worship bells tolled. They stopped in the darkness behind some unknown shop and dismounted, using their horses as a shield against anyone who might be looking their way. They had just helped Mylana to dismount when the bell ringing began. Mylana, pressed against Hessilyn for support, gave the woman a curious look.

"I have wondered... why do you not worship with all the others?"

Hessilyn gave her a slight smile. "I worship according to the old ways. Those truly dragonsworn detest the recent perversions of forced obeisance and gruesome rites. We still worship our beautiful gods, the heavenly fliers, in the correct way and we pray for a return of true dragon worship."

Mylana considered, as the bells finished their tolling and the murmur of collective prayer could be heard throughout the city. "I certainly do not pray for any such thing," admitted Mylana in a whisper, "but I respect your sincerity. My prayer is for a Na Ciria free of oppression and deception, where all men can hear of El's justice and mercy. No one should ever be forced into worship of anyone or anything. Worship that is not freely given is not worship at all, but slavery."

"In that we agree," responded Hessilyn, helping Mylana settle onto an abandoned crate.

They stayed in that alley through the worship time, and then remounted and found a way out from behind the buildings. They saw only glimpses of the city's namesake tower, now a Tlocanian outpost, as well as the rivaling five spires of the dragon temple. They rode on until they found the welcoming green glow of an inn's lantern, the Sleeping Bear. A high wooden wall, its gate closed except for a call window, surrounded the stable yard. Coursen shouted through the opening about their need for entrance and a stable worker finally responded.

They soon learned that this was a distrusting city because petty criminals were ignored by both the local troopers and the Tlocanian soldiers. They heard the stories from the two stable boys and from the plump lady innkeeper. Mylana stood there, leaning heavily on Mandor, and did her best to nod in understanding at the woman's grievances. However, all that she wanted was to get to a bed and rest.

The foursome finally made it upstairs to look over the accommodations for the night: a single room with just two beds. They were not as large as the innkeeper had promised, but it would have to do. Hessilyn lit the room's oil lamp, while Coursen latched the window shutters.

Mylana sat down heavily on one bed, her injured leg stretched out before her. Mandor pulled out his sword and laid it on the hardwood floor. He then knelt beside her leg, carefully rolled up her pant leg, and loosened the bandages. Whenever the wrapping caught due to dried blood she winced, but did not cry out. Mandor saw that the wound still had an angry tinge to it. Taking a deep breath, he realized he had more healing to do. While the others watched, he prayed and then set his shining blade against the wound. The act sapped the energy from healer and patient, leaving both tired.

Coursen proclaimed that neither was strong enough to go back downstairs for their supper, so he appointed himself and Hessilyn for the job of retrieving meals for everyone. When they returned, they caught Mylana asleep, but she soon sat up and ate her share of the meal: pork chop, applesauce, and fried potatoes. The greasy food sat heavy in her stomach but at least it was warm and filling.

When they finished the meal, Coursen stood up and started gathering up the plates, holding them in his right hand in spite of the sling ."Hessilyn and I will take first watch, for the two of you still look over-worn. Hessilyn, can you keep watch in the room while they sleep? I will take these plates downstairs and then see who is lingering in the common room. I will also check on the stables. Bolt the door behind me." Coursen slipped out into the hallway with the dirty plates.

Hessilyn bolted the door behind him and then helped Mylana under the covers of one bed while Mandor climbed into the other. Mylana was well aware that when neither of them protested over being sent to bed it showed their exhaustion. Hessilyn gave Mandor's forehead a chaste kiss even as his eyes drooped shut. Turning down the oil lamp to a mere glow, she quietly settled on the edge of Mylana's bed, looking determined to keep a careful vigil. Mylana turned toward the wall and was soon asleep herself.

BRODAGAR

Nesron looked out the tower window at the darkening city. The captain spoke to the city's governor standing behind him without turning his head, showing his contempt for the other Embraced One. "You offer excuses. I will not tolerate such. I will hear no more claims of other duties; you will place this mission as your priority. Send your men to find where the Attuls are staying."

Brodagar stood off to one side, watching the performance. Nesron wanted to be the leader, so the priest decided to let him do so, at least for now.

The city's leader grimaced behind Nesron's back but merely said, "I hear and obey."

The captain looked over his shoulder. "See that you do, Verdan-Shoovisk. Understand that I only want the Attuls watched. Do not try grasping for the glory, for you will only bungle it. Lord-Governor Krev will brook no failure. Now, go and send out your soldiers. Once you have located these Attuls, report back to me"

Once the local commander had left, Nesron returned to gazing at the city.

Brodagar allowed the captain to ponder for a bit, then added a barb. "We are running out of time. The Osburgens may grow bold enough to enter this city and take them... I hope you have a plan."

The officer turned, his face showing his anger. "I do have a plan, priest. We will divide and terrorize the Attuls. If injury was not enough to get that woman to talk, then I will drive the answers out of her by fear."

Brodagar raised one eyebrow but said nothing. The eyebrow was enough to express his doubts.

"You have been to the temple. Any word from Free Hawk?" asked Nesron.

"None yet, but they have not been in the city for very long."

"Any other news from the temple?"

Brodagar decided to tease his companion. "There is nothing new from Tlocania specifically for us."

Nesron caught his careful phrasing. "There has been something else of interest from Tlocania."

He decided to tell the other his news. "Word has been sent that Lord-General Hraf Kelordok-Slurtaler is now ruling as Steward of the Empire. It seems the Dragon Lord is elsewhere..." Brodagar had found the news intriguing and unsettling. What was their ruler planning now? He wondered how he could use this upheaval to increase his own power and position in the empire.

The captain frowned. "The main army heads towards Waybridge, on its way elsewhere. So much is occurring while we dawdle here with these Attuls. I say that we finish this tonight. Either we frighten this woman into talking or we capture her and torture the answers from her. What say you?"

Brodagar was surprised. He had not expected such boldness from Nesron. It spoke of unexpected cunning and also of recklessness. He would have to be careful or else Nesron would snatch all the glory if successful or smear him with the shame if he failed. He decided to answer the captain cautiously. "The sooner we know where this Warhaven is hidden, the better. However, you have not explained your plans to gain this knowledge."

Nesron's frown actually turned up, into an almost-smile. "To understand how we are to get our answers you must first remember your human side, Brodagar-Sahak. We are going to play on her human weaknesses to break the woman's spirit. She must be unnerved through despair and confusion, sleep deprivation and loss of companions. All that she clings to must be removed, until she is so shaken that she cannot help but confess her secrets to Free Hawk."

"I see," mused Brodagar, intrigued. "Share with me the details, so that I will know how best to commit the temple guards and priests."

"Let us talk while we ride over to the temple," suggested Nesron. "Though he is something of a fool, Verdan should be able to locate our prey within a few hours. There cannot be that many inns in this half-wild city. This night we will rouse them out of their beds and give them there most frightening night ever. If the rest do not live through it, so be it. We need only the woman and Free Hawk."

MYLANA

The banging on the door awoke Mylana from a troubled sleep. She rolled over and saw that Hessilyn was still on watch, though it must have been late into the night. The Westbend noble appeared tense, holding her sharp knife ready.

Hessilyn walked over to the door, but did not get too close. "Who is there?"

"It is Hinnia, the innkeeper," came the low reply. "Let me in, for I have a warning for you."

Mandor had also awakened and now got to his feet and went to stand to the side of the door. He motioned for Hessilyn to open it. She quietly pulled back the door's bolt and then cracked it open to expose the hallway. It truly was the fat innkeeper, covered lamp in hand, and she seemed alone. Hessilyn opened the door wider and motioned her in. Hinnia entered, though she almost stepped back out when she saw Mandor looming to one side.

"I have come to warn you," she said. "Your friend sent me. He said his name is Coursen. He said that the robbers who attacked you on the road are here in Hightower and are looking for you." At that, Hinnia frowned greatly and then raised a fat finger to point at Mandor. "I will not have any fighting in my inn. I run a respectable place, do you hear me?"

"Did he tell you anything else, Innkeeper Hinnia?" asked Mandor.

The woman nodded. "Your friend said he would get the horses ready. He said that you are to hurry to the stables. Now, do not disturb my other guests in your haste to leave. I will tell my stable boys to let you out, for the gate is locked during the deep-of-night. But hear me, do not think to abuse me or my men because of your need to flee. You shall handle your own horses." She glared at all three of them. "I do not want troublemakers at my inn. The Sleeping Bear is a respectable place. If you are truly in trouble, then I suggest you seek shelter at the

Eric Lorenzen

Tlocanian barracks. They may be harsh masters, but the army does not tolerate highwaymen bringing their anarchy to the city. Now, out with you."

As soon as the innkeeper left, Mandor rushed to gather their things.

"Do you believe her tale?" asked Mylana, slowly getting to her feet. Hessilyn had to help pull on her boots.

"We dare not ignore the warning," said Mandor, "though we should not assume it totally accurate either."

When all their things were gathered, they left the room, with Mandor assisting Mylana while Hessilyn bore the extra weight of Coursen's belongings. Mandor made sure to keep Mylana on his left side, so that he could pull his sword easily, if needed. They slipped down the hall and down the stairs. Two low-burning lamps and a sleeping fire provided dim lighting to the common room. They noticed the innkeeper watching them from behind her counter, fondling a large cudgel for reassurance, but they ignored her. Hessilyn opened the side door that led to the stable and had stepped out before she realized something terrible was going on.

Tlocanian soldiers filled the stable yard, two of them holding Coursen. Some soldiers looked over at them and gave a shout, running towards them with drawn weapons.

Mandor dropped his belongings and pulled Hessilyn back. Mylana almost fell due to his sudden movement, though she clung to his left arm. He slammed shut the door and dropped its lock bar. Spinning both women with him, he turned to confront the innkeeper. "What other exit do you have?"

"Why should I help you?" asked the woman, lifting the cudgel to show that she would not be intimidated. "It seems your friend lied to me. Those are not highwaymen out there, so most likely you are the actual robbers."

Mandor handed Mylana off to Hessilyn. The two women had to drop all of their belongings. Behind them, they heard shouting and a banging at the door. Mandor sprinted to the front door and made sure the lock bar remained in place there. Next, he pulled out his gleaming sword and advanced on the innkeeper. The woman's eyes grew wide at the sight of a blazing white sword.

"We are Attuls, foolish woman, and not robbers. Our crime is that we stand against the demons and all who serve them. Show us another way out and we will not harm you. Once we have fled, you can go back

294

and let those demon lovers in."

Hinnia must have realized that her shelter behind the bar was also her trap. She would not be able to flee from Mandor. "Do not hurt me and I will tell you. Through the kitchen is another exit, this one to the back alley. There is no way out there from the stables, so the Tlocanians will be delayed."

"Thank you," said Mandor, urging the woman to lead the way to the kitchen. She gave up her refuge behind the bar and led the way into the kitchen. Once the innkeeper started walking to the back room, Mandor put away his sword, for the demon-possessed could sense the power being used. He kept his hand near it, but he doubted the innkeeper would try any tricks. Hessilyn and Mylana followed after him.

The innkeeper pointed to the back door and then suddenly fled to the cook's bedroom, slamming the door behind her. Mandor had no time to chase her. Instead, he pulled open the door and gave a quick glance out into the dark alley. The way was clear, so the three hustled out of the Sleeping Bear and fled down the lane.

Mylana politely but firmly shook off Hessilyn's help; she needed to carry her own weight now. Her leg complained, but she could still hobble at a decent speed. She was not strong enough to run, but she did not want to be a burden on the other two. The three escaped, leaving behind their horses, their belongings, and their captured friend.

* * *

They had been fleeing across Hightower for an hour now. Mylana stumbled often as they fled down one dirt alley after another. She scraped her hand on a rough stone wall as she struggled to keep on her feet, but she was determined to keep up without assistance. She even broke into a hobbling run a few times, though only long enough to sprint across deserted roads and into another dark alley.

Every time they tried to stop for a rest, another group of soldiers would appear around some distant corner and spot them. This deep into the night there was no street traffic to hide them, only the occasional stray dog or feral cat.

"Always they appear on our route, forcing us to turn towards the north," muttered Mandor. He kept his voice low, for the night seemed to amplify any sound. "I think we are being herded toward some trap."

"Why would they do that?" asked Hessilyn in a whisper.

"The demons fear the power of Attuls," replied Mylana, wiping her skinned hand on her cloak, hoping to get the grit out of the scratches.

"They want us at a place where they can overwhelm us."

"Let us try to break free of their snare," declared Mandor, thinking quickly. He slipped between two buildings on the south side of the alley. When he came to a fence, he jumped up and grabbed its edge. Pulling himself up, he balanced at the top, and then instructed Hessilyn to help Mylana to climb. Awkwardly, Mylana scampered up the fence, with a push from Hessilyn and a pull from Mandor. She hung precariously onto its top. "You will need to drop down," urged Mandor. "There is not enough room up here for all three of us to perch."

Mylana nodded understanding, lowering herself down the other side as far as she could, then dropping the last few feet. She landed with wince, as a pain shot up her injured leg, but she kept her balance. She looked back up to see Mandor leaning over for Hessilyn. Suddenly a squad of Tlocanians came on them, with loud shouts and bright torches. Through a chink in the fence, she could see angry men advancing on Hessilyn, their weapons threatening. Her brother jumped down to defend his love, the spirit sword suddenly washing the whole area in a bright light that seemed to dim the torches. Just before he engaged the enemy, her brother shouted one last order to her. "Run Mylana. We will follow as soon as we can fight our way free."

She did not want to flee, but knew she could not get over the fence to be of any help. She wanted to bring her sword out and resist, but she realized that would endanger their mission. Fighting back tears of frustration, she hobbled away.

CHAPTER TWENTY-FOUR

Failed Prince

WINTRON

It took two days to reach the lands of Baron Percell. The prince and his escort finally arrived at the baron's manor tired, muddy, and hungry. The commander of the baron's guard gave them a cool welcome, even though he recognized the two nobles in the party. He informed them that the baron was out reviewing his just-budding vineyards. The officer had enough sense to let them in and offer both Wintron and Gurash decent rooms, but they were at opposite ends of the sprawling place. In addition, he wanted to shove the other three out in the enlisted barrack. Wintron angrily insisted that the officer provide them with one suite to share, and that he bring in beds for the soldiers. The commander grumbled but gave in when Lord Gurash echoed the prince's "request." Once the commander left, Gurash asked Wintron why he insisted such accommodations.

"The man knew his lord too well. Percell would want us separated so that he can flatter or threaten as needed. Do not trust Baron Percell Vorsdun, for he is a friend only to himself."

Gurash smiled. "I finally realize why you and Father butt heads so much; the two of you are too much alike. He would be just as suspicious."

Wintron thought his cousin was wrong, but did not bother to argue the point. Instead, he called out in response to a knock on the door, bidding the person to enter. Servants came in, carrying fresh linens and a tray of food. One stepped up to the prince and gave a bow. At Wintron's acknowledgment, he informed them that two tubs were being filled in the bathing room down the hall. More servants came, carrying three cots and bedding. The staff was efficient, finishing their tasks quickly and then quietly leaving. By the time the newcomers learned of the baron's return, they had all bathed, changed, and eaten a little. The two nobles were invited to join his lordship for a meal, which they accepted, though they brought with them Kevlo and Yosif. Scout Orgel asked to stay behind, admitting that he did not know the first thing about proper table manners. The prince agreed to his request.

The foursome was shown to a formal dining room where the baron already waited, sipping wine. He rose at their entrance and offered a smile as if freshly sewn onto his face. Wintron found no comfort in it, though he still strode confidently over to the little man. Percell gave him a just-deep-enough bow and then a slightly less deep bow to Gurash. He ignored the soldiers. "Welcome to Vorsdun manor. My prince. My lord."

"You should address me as 'sire'," corrected Wintron.

The baron gave a surprised look. "I had not heard of your enthronement. Actually, I heard that your cousin Mordel claims the title."

Wintron considered his answer carefully, choosing true words that implied something far different. "Mordel and I reached an agreement. Why else do you think I travel with his younger brother?"

Percell glanced at Gurash, the many questions apparent on his face. "You seem to have me at a disadvantage. I have heard nothing about any of this. In fact, I did not even get any advance notice of your touring the area, or else I would have prepared a more appropriate reception.

"Oh, leave off the flattery Percell," said Wintron. "You are well aware that we came here across the bogs and not on some silly tour. I can see the curiosity sparkling in your eyes. Behave and I may just give you some answers. Now, have your servants set two more places at the table, for our officers shall be joining us."

Percell raised one combed eyebrow. "Two officers to supervise one soldier? How interesting." He motioned for the two extra settings and then asked all to join him at the table. Wintron sat at his right with Yosif next to him, while Gurash and Kevlo sat across from them.

As soon as everyone was seated, the servants swept in with the first course, chicken soup, well seasoned. None spoke as they ate. Wintron wanted the baron's curiosity and confusion to build. The soup was followed by a plate of spring greens. Then came the main course of roasted pig with potatoes, carrots, and dried apples. The baron restrained his questions only as far as his second bite of pork, then one slipped out.

"How is it, sire, that you arrive at my gates without a proper escort?"

Winton paused in cutting his next bite. "Well, I left Tor Randis with a good hundred soldiers at my side. Have they not arrived yet?"

"Why no, should I be preparing a welcome for them as well?" He did not look pleased at the prospect.

"Oh no, do not bother with that, Baron Percell. My soldiers will not be stopping here. In truth, we cannot linger either." Wintron set down his utensils and leaned forward. "As you have surmised, we are in trouble. The Tlocanians do not want Mordel and I to work things out..."

Percell interrupted. "Frankly, my prince...er... my king, I cannot imagine that you could be so forgiving. Mordel killed your father. How could you ever look past that?"

Wintron frowned. This game of words was becoming tiresome. "Baron, I put the good of the realm above my own desires. I suggest you do the same. Now, we are in need of mounts, for ours are worn out from hard riding. Will you grant us the pick of your stables? I will see that you get properly reimbursed, along with getting our current horses."

Percell did not appreciate being forced to help but he gave a nod of agreement. "You may have your pick, save my carriage teams. They would be too hard to replace."

"You are most generous," replied Wintron with a fake smile.

Percell took a bite of food, giving him a moment to compose himself, and then asked another question. "You still have not explained how you arrived in such a sorry state, my king. Did you encounter trouble?"

Wintron swallowed his food, took a sip of wine, and then replied. "Is it not obvious? Did I not tell you that the Tlocanians are angry with me? We had to detour over the bogs to avoid a confrontation. Yet I do not doubt that my enemy will still follow in this direction. That is another reason why I do not want all of my soldiers encamping here." Wintron noticed the worry that came to the baron's face as he imagined a battle churning up his lovely fields and wrecking both the village and his manor. The prince let those fears build a moment. "No, that would not be fair to you, our gracious host. As I have said, we cannot linger. I do not even want to bring all of my troops within sight of your estates so that our tracks do not lead our pursuers to your door. No, that would certainly be unfair. It is best for you that we leave right after this meal and draw any pursuit away from your gates…"

"Have you brought war down on me?" demanded Percell, truly alarmed.

Wintron reached over and patted the man's hand comfortingly. "We mean to do no such thing, Baron Percell Vorsdun. Indeed, I promise you this: I have already ordered my soldiers away from your estate and I will not change those orders." He paused for a moment. "That is, unless you give me cause to bring them here." He held the baron's eyes with his own. He had spoken the truth, for he had told Bilshor to flee with any survivors to Tor Randis. Let Percell assume that he still spoke of a full troop of over a hundred. He had added that last veiled threat because he did not want Percell scheming to turn them over to the Tlocanians.

"You and your soldiers will move on?"

Wintron sat back and gave him an assuring nod. "Most certainly. Why bring any conflict to this peaceful vale? Now, we should finish our meal. The sooner we are done the quicker I and my companions can ride off to reunite with the rest of my force."

Percell nodded, motioning for the servants to bring in the final course of desserts.

* * *

The five left on decent horses. As soon as they were away from the manor, the baron had the gates closed and barred. They rode in silence through the village. Whenever anyone tried to speak, Wintron would shake his head. The prince would not allow petty Percell to learn how he had been fooled.

Finally, as they rode past the estate's fields, Gurash could hold it in no longer. "Prince Wintron, I am amazed at how you deceived the baron. You could give my eldest brother lessons on honeyed speech."

"Oh no, I could never reach the level of that charmer," argued Wintron, trying to keep the conversation light, though he detested the comparison. Mordel took relish in lying, while for him it left a bad taste in his mouth. "I told Lord Percell only the truth; I merely allowed his scheming mind to fill it in the gaps with wrong assumptions."

Gurash actually chuckled. "I am surprised that he was not more careful in parsing your words."

"It is the advantage of being my father's son. Both of us have always been seen as blunt, simple men. Who would expect duplicity from good old King Varen or his brash son Prince Wintron?"

"Again, you remind me of Father," said Gurash with a smile.

Wintron smiled back, but it was forced. He did not like being compared to the Old Fox either. It was time to focus again on their route. "Kevlo, is the pass our best way out of here?"

"I would say so," answered the captain. "Under General Fors, I came to this vale twice and both times we used that route. Over the hillock saddle we will come upon the road that stretches between Calia Meadows and Goorsol."

It agreed with what the prince had guessed. They would turn towards Goorsol and then on to Tor Randis by a more direct road. "Orgel, I need you to scout ahead. Beware of the hounds, though I think they are still behind us. I plan to ride through the night, no matter how it will tire us out, for we need to get some distance from our pursuers. Now go and find us our fastest way out of this vale."

"Yes, my prince." The scout spurred his horse to a faster pace and was soon hidden by the woods up ahead.

* * *

They rode hard for three days, finally coming upon Goorsol, a small city behind stout walls that overlooked a narrow valley. The lord's keep was a simple, practical fort above the city, attesting to the barony's wartime past and current poverty. Goorsol's lord was absent. In fact, Lord Briv Goorsol was already at Tor Randis with most of his men-at-arms. However, his elderly steward welcomed Wintron and his party, giving them good beds for the night. The rest was much needed, for they had not truly slept for many days. The steward asked no questions but he perceived their needs. In the morning, he offered them fresh mounts and an escort of ten soldiers.

"I apologize that it is not more troopers, but my lord took almost all with him to Tor Randis."

Wintron gladly accepted the horses, but politely refused the men. "Considering the size of the force pursuing us, ten more men will not make that much difference but they may help save Goorsol. Beware, for rebels and Tlocanians pursue us, and they number in the hundreds. I hope that they will not pass this way, for they were on a different road, but bar the city gates as a precaution."

"Thank you for your warning, my prince."

They left Goorsol after breakfast, riding excellent horses. Their saddlebags brimmed over with fresh supplies, and all of it was given to them with good cheer.

DRASS

Drass watched as they brought the informant to him. For two days, he had been trying to dislodge Wintron and his men from the rocky hilltop without success. The fireballs from the priests had little effect when soldiers ducked behind boulders. He wished the priests were willing to press in, but they insisted on keeping a safe distance from the enemy. Drass hoped this man would give him a key on how to take the hill, for his only other hope was the soon arrival of the Tlocanian infantry. The delay in victory gnawed at him.

"Here he is, Lord Drass," stated the captain who led him over. "This is Brevion."

He did not care to know the man's name. "What have you to report?"

"Prince Wintron and Lord Gurash have fled. They are no longer in the camp."

"What?" Drass turned on the captain. "How could this be? I thought we had the hill surrounded."

"We do," assured the captain. The officer confronted the informant. "When did they sneak away? Where did they go?"

"I am not certain of their direction, but they fled right before you engaged us in battle."

Drass stepped forward and struck the man in the face. "They are gone and you took this long to tell us? I have wasted two days fighting against a decoy?" He struck him again, sending the soldier to his knees. He turned to the captain. "Have this man executed for his incompetence and then call the priests to my tent. We must find the prince and my brother."

Suddenly, he remembered the priests telling him that their hounds trailed a small party that that had struck off westward, through the forest. He had assumed they were scouts going for aid, but now he was not so sure. Angry, Drass spat at the soldier who was glowering up at him. What a waste of time, just because this man had been so slow in sneaking off to report. It raised his anger to a greater level.

"On second thought, I will clean up this mess." His sword sang as he whipped it from its sheath and then down on the soldier's neck. The man tried to defend himself, but was too late. Drass quickly stepped back to avoid the spurting blood. He made no effort to finish his execution, letting the man die slowly. "Captain Hewson, go retrieve those priests." He stalked off to his tent.

He restrained his anger when the priests arrived, for it would do no good to strike out at them, not unless he wanted to die or receive a severe burning. He explained what had occurred and sought their advice. Together, they decided their best chance to catch the crown prince would be to get ahead of him. Drass knew that the prince had to be heading for Tor Randis, so he urged taking the roads instead of trying to track Wintron through bogs. The priests agreed, assuring him that the dreadhounds would drive them onward even without oversight.

* * *

Drass left it to the Tlocanian infantry company to clear those on the hilltop redoubt, while he rode off with his soldiers. The dragon priests went with him, even though it would take them out of range for linking with the hounds. He did not like leaving behind unfinished business, but the empire's infantry were quite capable of killing off the last of Wintron's soldiers.

He set a hard but sustainable pace and they chewed up the miles to Tor Randis. Though Drass wanted to intimidate the many villages and keeps they passed, he foreswore trying to bring them under his control for now. There was no time for such pursuits, so it would have to wait for his return trip. However, he took careful note of any nobleman or town leader who slighted him in anyway. The Highlands would soon be his dukedom and then would come his justice.

When they finally entering the vicinity of the keep, Drass slowed their pace and sent out many scouts. They dropped down into the Clear Valley well upstream of Randisville, for he had no desire to tangle with his father yet. Actually, he still held out hope that his father would join their cause, would realize the wisdom of his eldest sons. His father would be incensed if he heard of an enemy force behind him. At the right timing, it might persuade him to join his sons, but if he was alerted too soon, then he could become trouble for Drass. That was why he sent out his scouts and moved his men with caution, for he did not want to alert the Old Fox. So far the reports told of a valley unguarded and rarely patrolled.

They had just started passed some of the valley's more isolated farms, when a temple guard rode up the line and asked Drass to drop back to the priests. He did so, finding one of them lost in a trance. The other, Brother Hurko, provided an explanation. "Brother Cavish is very gifted at linking with the dreadhounds over great distances. He has located the pack following Prince Wintron. They are still behind us."

"Excellent." For once, he had good news. Now it would only be a matter of setting the proper trap. "How many are in his party?"

"Only the five of them. Apparently, they have gained no allies along the way."

Drass nodded, taking a moment to stare at Cavish, the priest in mind link with the dreadhounds. The man seemed completely unaware of his surroundings, just sitting there in his saddle. Drass wondered if the priest would even notice if he were to lean over and knife him right now.

"Do not even play with such thoughts, Lord Drass," rebuked Brother Hurko, his voice suddenly harsh. "Such thinking can lead to a very painful death."

Startled, Drass looked over at Hurko and found him with one hand raised, red lightning playing across his fingers. He swallowed any claims of innocence. Instead, he gave a silent bow towards the dragon priest and then urged his horse forward. He resisted the desire to look back, but he did listen intently for the crackling sound of a fireball aimed his way. Drass was glad to get some distance between him and the priests. He also decided that he must guard his thoughts when near them. Reading his mind! It gave him gooseflesh. What might those two have snooped from his memories? It was just not right. A man's thoughts should be known to no one but himself and the gods.

WINTRON

Wintron and his party encountered no opposition for days, though Orgel did see a dreadhound once. The prince worried about that, even though they heard no howls or baying. Were the beasts still on their trail, but stalking them in silence? He had to assume so, just as he had to presume that Drass waited somewhere ahead of him.

The road crested a rise and Clear Valley came into view, still far upstream from Randisville. The valley was a mixture of wood lots, budding orchards, and newly sprouting fields. There were clusters of homes on the larger farms, but no villages or towns in the area. The nearest thing to a settlement lay where this path ended at the road following the valley. There sat an inn, a general store, and a handful of cottages.

"What shall be our route now?" asked Gurash, catching sight of

Orgel as he rode ahead of them.

"I want to wait for Orgel's report, for now our way grows more perilous. Drass must know we are heading to Tor Randis and I know of no other approach accessible to us besides this valley. We will ride directly into his arms if we are not careful."

"Could we take the river?" asked Yosif.

Wintron sighed. "You must be from the Borderheart, young man. That river might seem mellow from this distance, but it is shallow and rock-strewn, like all Highland waterways. It was a good thought, but no. "

"I do not know this area so well," apologized Kevlo. "Most often when I was stationed at the keep I had either wall duty or was sent down the canyon and into the upper Borderheart Valley. And yet, I do know there are back lanes here. We need not ride brashly down the main road."

He nodded, though Kevlo's statement gave him another thought. Maybe the main road would be their best choice. "Captain, do you have any idea what the general's patrol schedule would be like up here? Maybe we can catch a squad on its return to the keep?"

"You think Drass would not attack a patrol squad?" asked Gurash. "My brother would have no such misgivings."

"I disagree," replied Wintron. "He will at least hesitate, for he will not want to attract your father's attention. That pause may be enough to get us past any trap he has planned. In addition, we would number over twenty instead of just five. I just hope he has only his horsemen and not the Tlocanian infantry." He paused to consider and decided this would be their best option. "We need not stay on the main road, but the addition of a squad with current knowledge of the roads would be a great boon. Let us follow Orgel down there, for this rise is too exposed, and let us search out the nearest Border patrol."

"We must be cautious," stated Kevlo, "for Drass' men could be wearing the same colors as those from Tor Randis."

Yosif nodded his agreement with the captain.

"There is that," granted Wintron, "yet any legitimate patrol squad should have someone in it that one of us recognizes. I doubt the Old Fox would send out a patrol of just new recruits." He urged his horse back into motion.

"No, Father would never do that," agreed Gurash, kicking his horse in pursuit of the prince. Kevlo and Yosif fell in right behind him.

* * *

For once, the gods seemed to be smiling down on them, thought Wintron, for they met a half-squad on patrol only a short time later. The squad's leader was none other than Sergeant Paon, who had recently served as Wintron's banner man. They gathered at the small inn to talk, sitting on the benches around a table in the empty common room.

Paon explained why he was now riding the rounds. "The general assigned me to patrols; he said he had flagpoles to do my job in Tor Randis."

Gurash laughed. "That is Father, blunt as ever." Paon smiled back at him, having already reconciled with his demotion.

Wintron, sitting next to Paon, slapped the sergeant on the back. "You are far better than any flagpole, sergeant. You served honorably throughout our retreat up the Borderheart, and now I need your help again."

Paon nodded, sobering. "We have not yet run into Drass' men, but we are just riding back in after three days on patrol. Actually, we should have already encountered another patrol on its way out. Do you think Drass may have taken them?"

The prince frowned. "He has probably done exactly that, and would have taken you and your squad had you ridden blindly into his path. Where is the other half of your squad?"

"Corporal Shully has them across the river. We did not plan to unite until the bridge at Randisville."

"Ah, there's a thought," exclaimed Gurash. "Should we also cross over?"

Wintron and Kevlo both shook their heads, while Paon answered the young man. "Not at this time of year. The Clear River is too full. There are bridges further upstream, but that would cost us a few days' travel."

"We do not have the time," protested Wintron. "Our only hope is to break through before the Tlocanian infantry arrives, if they have not already. Eighty to a hundred irregulars are more likely to make mistakes or leave us gaps to flee through. Add in another hundred seasoned warriors and there will be no chance for such errors."

Wintron pointed at the table they were at, a wooden trestle of pine boards. "The middle board represents this valley." He stretched to set his mug at the far end of the table. "My cup represents Tor Randis, and Kevlo's mug is our current position. So, what lies between here and Tor Randis? Where would my cousin be waiting? I want to hear everyone's thoughts."

They fell into deep discussion, making plans on how to survive this gauntlet.

Eric Lorenzen

CHAPTER TWENTY-FIVE
Rider Post

MYLANA

After a few hours, Mylana could no longer keep going. She had been dodging through the empty streets of Hightower for hours now. Alone. Coursen was captured and, as far as she knew, so were Hessilyn and Mandor. She had kept hoping that her brother would soon catch up with her, but he never did. Completely exhausted, she hunkered behind some deserted crates and leaned against a cold wall hugging herself for warmth. She meant to rest only for a moment, but instead she fell asleep. When she awoke to the sound of dog fighting, dawn had made its fitful appearance. She startled, thinking it was dreadhounds coming for her, but then realized they were just some common curs.

The Tlocanian soldiers had not found her, but neither had her companions.

For two days, Mylana haunted the alleys of Hightower, wondering what to do. She had seen nothing more of the others. Once she had her bearings, she had returned to the Sleeping Bear and had even slipped into the stable yard, but the Tlocanians had left, taking with them Coursen and the horses. She wondered if the innkeeper had possession of her saddlebags, but dared not inquire. Instead, she slipped away.

A cold rain began to fall, for which she was somewhat thankful. It gave her an excuse for keeping her cloak's hood up. That was important, since the Tlocanians were still looking for her. She may have lost her saddlebags with all of her belongings, but at least she still had a full money purse and her messenger's envelope tucked within her shirt. Mylana bought food from street vendors, avoiding any inns or taverns where she might be recognized in better lighting. She saw many patrols, but none ever spotted her.

Mylana finally decided to approach the actual "high tower", which the Tlocanians had taken over as their headquarters. She came at it circumspectly, not daring to walk up any of the main roads that approached it. She chose to hobble towards this danger because if her companions were to be found, it would be there. She had no definite plan, just a desperate hope. She wanted to rescue them.

Eventually, she came close to it, standing across from the High Tower and watching from the shadows of an alley. It was an ominous building, its gray spire vanishing into the misty sky. Around the tower sprawled a palace nestled behind stone walls. Her hope withered as she saw the wall heights, for even if her leg were fully healed she would have been unable to climb that. She dropped the apple core she had been gnawing and stepped back, not wanting to linger here too long. She needed time to plan something more definite.

As she turned away, a large man stepped into the alley behind her and quickly caught up. He laid a large hand on her shoulder, spinning her around. Desperately, Mylana grabbed for her sword, but he was quicker, stopping her.

"None of that. We do not want any light exposing us," he said. His voice was deep and practically in her ear as he held her from behind.

She looked over her shoulder as she struggled to break free. His features remained hidden under his cloak's hood, but he stood two heads taller than Mylana and that was enough to intimidate her. She saw no uniform or priestly robe, but she had no doubt of her danger.

He pulled her in closer, trying to stop her attempts to break away.

She threw her head back, into his chin. The man gasped and his hold loosened. Mylana pulled free and ran, though her injury made it more of a fast shuffle. He came charging after her, ordering her to stop.

Realizing that she could not outrun him in her condition, she turned and pulled free her sword. It shone brighter than ever, filling that dark alley with light. The man stopped, a huge shadow projected behind him.

"You are being a fool," he hissed. "Put away your sword, woman!"

Mylana held her weapon ready. "Leave me, and I will not harm you."

"I am here to help. Are you not Mylana Farsight?"

She gasped, comprehending now that her enemy knew more about her than she would ever have guessed. "Away from me, demon lover. You will not lure me to drop my guard."

The man sighed, pulling his rain-soaked cloak back to expose his own sword. Mylana advanced, not wanting to give him the chance to draw on her, but he moved faster and yanked out his sword, bringing it between them. His sword also shined white, but Mylana did not grasp the importance of that. She attacked. Their blades crossed with a shower of white sparks. Mylana almost struck again before she understood who this opponent was.

Finally, she stepped back, though she kept her spirit sword out. "Who are you?"

"I am Wordun Gentlehand, Watch Rider of the Hightower circuit. Your brother Mandor sent me to find you." Seeing that she finally understood, he quickly put away his sword. His hood had slid back in their scuffle showing him to be a middle-aged man with a chiseled, weathered face. An older woman would probably call him handsome in his maturity, but she thought that he looked hardened by life. A little blood dripped from the corner of his mouth, probably from a bit lip or cheek caused by her head-butt. "Woman, will you please sheathe your sword? Such a light will call all the demons in Hightower down on us. It is bad enough that you made me speak aloud my name and heritage."

Mylana hastily complied. The alley became dark again. "Where is Mandor?"

"He is safe, along with his companion Hessilyn." Wordun stepped forward and again took hold of her arm. "We must hurry away from here." He looked around the once-more darkened alley, though hardly anything could be seen. "The Tlocanians have many willing eyes and ears." His grip tightened with urgency. "Come woman, or else we will soon be captured or killed." With his other hand, he set his hood back in place. "We need to spend a few hours dodging through the streets to make sure we are not found out. Take the lead for a time, so that I can hide our trail; it does not really matter what route you pick, just move quickly."

She pulled her own hood lower, and then strode resolutely down the alley, trying her best not to limp. Wordun found a piece of scrap wood, too splintered for anyone to salvage, and used it to stir the mud, hiding their passage some. He kept that scrap as Mylana turned between two buildings and then hurried across an empty street and into another alley. Before she could rush across another street, he whispered for her to stop. He stepped onto the road and bent over a horse trough to rinse the mud off, then walked back to her at the alley's mouth. "We need to go up this road for a ways. Let us walk side-by-side like a couple would, but I will be leading."

Wordun did not wait for a response; he took hold of her elbow and led her out onto the street. They walked at a quick pace, but no more than what would be expected from people caught outside in the rain. At times, they hurried along the main roads of the city, other times they slinked through more alleys. Twice they lingered in sheltered doorways to make sure no one was following. Her limp was far more pronounced when they finally reached their destination: a small room off another dark alley. The room held three others, an unknown woman and two people Mylana knew well.

"Mandor! Hessilyn!" She hurried to her companions; they rose from a bench and embraced her in spite of her drenched condition.

Wordun closed the door behind him and then took off his sopping cloak and hung it on a peg near the door. He walked over to the other woman in the room and stood beside her, his arm resting comfortably on her shoulders. Her age was similar to his, and she too showed a beauty edged by wear and hard times. He towered over the woman, yet they fit together.

Mylana finally pulled back, apologizing for getting her companions wet.

"Berala Bloomgatherer, this is my sister Mylana Farsight." Mandor introduced the two women. "Off with that cloak, Mylana, before you soak everything in the room." Mandor took her garment and hung it beside Wordun's. "Wordun and Berala are the last Watch Riders in Hightower."

"It is a pleasure to meet you both," Mylana said. She gave feeble smile, for her leg now throbbed.

"We can wait on the greetings for when we reach a better safe house," stated Berala. "We are stopping here just so that I can see to your injury. Wordun, would you please take Mandor and watch for patrols and priests?"

The men donned their cloaks and went out into the storm. Berala told Mylana to remove her pants and sit down on the bench. She asked Hessilyn to stand to one side. Berala knelt over Mylana's injury, pulling back encrusted bandages, for the wound had reopened during her flight. Berala inhaled sharply upon seeing the angry wound, but then pulled free her shining sword and began a prayer to El for healing. She worked quickly and efficiently, and quickly the wound no longer looked ugly with infection; instead, it had a healthy pink to it. Mylana felt the strain on her own strength, yet sighed as the pain lessened tremendously. Berala stood up and sheathed her sword, obviously drained. The room suddenly darkened as her sword's light extinguished.

"I find that amazing every time I see a healing," said Hessilyn. "Most rulers would give quite a treasure for someone with powers like yours."

Berala frowned at her, disapproving.

Mylana answered, "It is not a power or magic, but the empowering of our god. Each healing is a gift from El, given because we asked for it. Even then, he requires us to add in our skills and strength."

"Stop the chatter and get dressed," said Berala to Mylana, and then turned to Hessilyn. "You are being foolish. Such healing is not a skill like what a doctor or herbalist practices. Each healing is a separate gift from El. Now, you two get into your cloaks. We need to be away from here before the demon-possessed come to investigate. So much power expended will surely draw them."

BRODAGAR

"You felt that?" asked Brodagar, pulling back on his horse's reins. The priest was disgusted with being soaked.

Nesron nodded. "Some Attul has invoked the Enemy's power near here." He turned his horse to look in that direction.

"Do we chase them down?" Brodagar's temple guards noticed that he had stopped and so they turned their horses back.

Nesron frowned when he noticed that his own men responded slower than the temple guards did. "That would be expected, so we will. Lord Krev's pet had better deliver on all of those promises soon, for I do not enjoy these childish games. Maybe we should have held onto Free Hawk for some torture before letting that one fly free. Some pain would have encouraged quicker obedience."

"I will not misuse one of Lord Krev's spies," stated Brodagar flatly.

"Nor would I," replied Nesron, "but when Free Hawk demanded that all of them be allowed to escape, I was almost tempted to."

The two Embraced Ones took the lead now, heading towards that awful disturbance. Brodagar was of a divided mind on this. On one hand, he hoped they could learn the secret of Warhaven soon and report it to the Speakers Tower. On the other hand, he wanted this plot to fail so that Nesron would be humbled. Brodagar wanted all the glory to come to him and not have to share it with another.

MYLANA

Wordun and Berala led Mylana and her companions to another section of Hightower, near its eastern gate. They brought them up a narrow stairway, to a residence above a seamstress shop. When they entered, the two locals quickly set to various tasks. As the visitors hung their dripping cloaks near the entrance, Wordun stirred up the fireplace and Berala lit an oil lamp. The three journeyers sat where indicated, on benches at a large table. Wordun set a kettle to hang above the fire, while Berala faced their guests.

"You must speak softly while here," she explained in a near-whisper. "The walls are thin and sometimes our neighbors try to listen to each other."

"Understood," said Mandor in a low voice. "Can we finally hear more of your story? For two days we have waited patiently, while Wordun searched for my sister. However, all this time you have politely refused to answer my questions. Will you now tell us about yourselves?"

"We are not much of a post," demurred Berala, "but we offer what hospitality that we can. We will provide you shelter until you are ready to go on, unfortunately this post no longer has replacement mounts."

Wordun gave a harsh laugh. "Do not try to sweeten the bitter dregs, my dear wife. We are no post, just Attul refugees. At one time, we rode with the rest of the Riders on the Hightower circuit, from Waybridge to Riverrealm. We watched diligently for the enemy's encroachment, but our generations of effort were for naught. Suddenly, the enemy appeared and caught us unaware. It was as if we were found asleep.

"So many Riders died, including our own son and daughter. The Guardian of our circuit also fell, as the Tlocanian army swept through on their way to conquer Riverrealm. We sent messengers to report what had happened, but never heard back from any. The few of us remaining tried to keep the circuit in place, spying on the demons. However, one-by-one those in our small group were exposed and captured, until the only ones left are the two of us. Since then, Berala and I have hidden here, waiting for a replacement to arrive and take up the watch. None has. You are the first Riders we have seen in nearly three years. We had begun to wonder if any other Attuls still lived."

"Well, take heart, for thousands of Riders still stand," said Mandor. "You have done your duty, Riders. You have served El faithfully."

Mylana felt sudden pride in her brother, for his words sounded like something their father would say.

Wordun gave a brief nod to Mandor, though it appeared that he felt uneasy with the praise. "Have you encountered any other Rider posts intact?"

"We have avoided them since leaving the Midcirian Plains," admitted Mandor, "for it is known that many are compromised."

Wordun pointed at Hessilyn. "If this has become common practice, then I have no doubt that many posts have been exposed. No offense, woman, but you are not Attul. You are not even Elsworn, from what my wife has whispered to me."

"I am dragonsworn," replied Hessilyn with a smile, "but I am no friend or ally of these demons. I follow the faith of my ancestors, from before these others perverted our rituals."

Wordun shook his head, looking at Mandor. "What have you done? You have exposed our last safe house."

"Hessilyn will not reveal your secrets," he assured the couple. "She may not be of our faith, but she is still an honorable woman."

"You treat your mission like some lover's ride in a park," rebuked Berala. "It is bad enough that you swoon for some heathen, Rider Mandor, but why have you brought her on this ride?"

Mylana took up her brother's defense. "Hessilyn was not part of our original party. We encountered her in Waybridge and then she followed us on her own, fleeing from her demon-possessed father."

"There is more to this story," stated Wordun. "They may have crossed paths in Waybridge, but I do not think that was mere accident. I will not rebuke your romance, Rider, for that is the responsibility of your father and your circuit Guardian. However, it is foolhardy to involve a defenseless outsider on a dangerous mission. And do not deny that you are on a perilous ride, for all rides are dangerous these days." The older man stared at Mandor, daring him to deny being a fool.

Mandor met his eyes, but nodded agreement. "I was unwise to ever have contacted Hessilyn in Waybridge, but my heart convinced me that she would be a good source of knowledge about the Tlocanians. Her father is an ambassador to them, after all. And I am glad that I did speak with her, for it emboldened her to flee her father and his wicked schemes. She will not be joining us for our whole ride. We will find her a safe place in Riverrealm."

Wordun shook his head. "That land is also in demonic hands. I begin to think there are no longer any safe places in all of Na Ciria, El help us." He turned back to the now-hot kettle, removing it and then pouring hot tea for everyone.

Berala sat down next to Mylana, accepting a steaming mug from her husband. Mandor and Hessilyn shared the bench across from them. Berala looked at the young couple with pity. "You two obviously love one another, but what of your differences? You two walk opposite roads, one serving El and the other those dragons."

Mandor handled the mug in front of him, but did not drink at first. He seemed to be looking for wisdom in the rising steam. Hessilyn was also quiet.

"Please drink," suggested Wordun. "We may seem poor hosts to confront you so, but we do not know how much time we will have with you." He moved to their pantry and retrieved a bread loaf and some cheese. "Please, all of you, eat as well. This should hold you over until a proper dinner can be made."

"Yes, let me start our meal," said Berala, getting back to her feet. "Our abode may be humble, but at least we have a full pantry. Wordun does well for himself, as a blacksmith's assistant, while I do some embroidery and sewing for the shop below. Hessilyn, would you be willing to help me cook?"

Hessilyn hesitated at the request, but then nodded. "Yes, I would like that." Her answer surprised Mylana and brought a smile to Mandor. They both knew that Hessilyn did not know how to cook, for servants did those tasks in her father's manor. On the road, she usually handled cleaning or tending the horses. She did not shy from work; she was just inexperienced with domestic tasks.

They watched as Berala led her to the pantry, talking about mundane things. "What is that necklace you wear?"

Hessilyn looked down, pulling the slim gold chain from beneath her shirt, to reveal a golden bird in flight. "This? It was a present from my mother, one of the last things she gave me before she died. I used to love looking at the hawks riding the air currents over the Grandgorn as a small child."

"I am sorry for your loss," said Berala sympathetically.

"Thank you, but it was long ago. Mother died when I was only eight." Hessilyn changed the topic as she tucked the necklace back inside her shirt. "What do you want me to do with the potatoes?"

"Could you peel them?"

Hessilyn nodded, but then admitted. "I will do so, if you show me how. I was never taught how to cook."

Their conversation turned to food preparation. Meanwhile, Wordun took Hessilyn's place next to Mandor. He spoke to the siblings in a lowered voice, so that Hessilyn would not hear. "Now Attuls, tell me what brings you through Hightower."

Mylana replied. "We are foresworn by the Guardians not to speak of it."

Wordun nodded, having expected as much. "Do any of the circuits still stand in central Na Ciria?"

"As I told you before, we avoided all posts since leaving the Midcirian Plains," admitted Mandor.

"Well, that is not too far to flee," muttered Wordun. "We can make it to the plains. Could you provide directions to me? I do not think we can linger here any longer. Your presence has disrupted too much."

Mylana looked to her brother, letting him decide how much to reveal. Mandor gave her a slight nod of understanding and then turned his attention back on Wordun. "I would tell you if I could. Truly. However, all of those posts were closing, even as we rode through. The Watch Riders are moving, getting ready for battle."

"The Prayer Warriors are finally on the march?" asked Wordun with sudden hope.

"That I do not know," replied Mandor. "The Guardians held a Meet and have decided to begin this war whether the Prayer Warriors join in or not."

Wordun considered. "So be it. El must be guiding their plans, for it is almost past time to resist this invasion. Could you direct me to where they gather now?"

The siblings were quiet for a moment. Mylana pondered what they could reveal. A journey to the Waterflow Mountains would be a perilous one, where Wordun and his wife might easily be captured by the demon-possessed. They would not want to give forewarning to the enemy. However, this couple had already seen so much and they would have much to share with the Guardians if they won their way through.

Mylana made her decision. "Tell him," she whispered to her

brother.

He nodded, agreeing with her. He leaned closer to Wordun to make sure nothing could be overheard. "As far as we know, they gather in the Waterflow Mountains. We were not told exactly where, out of caution, but we know which towns to approach once we complete our mission. Go to any of these three settlements: Wellen's Ford, Varowteal, or Fair Lupine. Look for the proper signs and ask discretely. You should find someone who will be able to direct you further along."

Wordun repeated the names to make sure he heard correctly and then he thanked them. "You give me new hope. Berala and I cannot keep up this hiding, always fearful to use our El-given talents. It wears on the soul, having to watch while the enemy enslaves all those around us. If it were only me, I would have long ago begun to fight back, but I have Berala to protect." He paused to give Mandor a long look. "That is why I spoke so harshly to you, young Mandor. I know how much love can entangle your sword arm."

Mandor nodded his understanding.

Mylana's thoughts were elsewhere. "Mandor, did you tell them about Coursen? Is there any way we can rescue him?"

"He told me," replied Wordun, "but your friend's state is beyond my ken. I have been unable to learn anything about him, except that he was captured at the Sleeping Bear Inn, beaten, and led away. He is most likely in the high tower itself, either among the slave pens or in some prison cell. Even if I knew exactly where they hold him, I have no way of reaching him unless we storm the gates with swords ablaze..."

"He is my best friend," said Mandor, "but we cannot do something so foolhardy. This mission comes before any Rider; we all knew that before we accepted this charge. We can only trust him to El's hands, for there is nothing we can do."

Mylana nodded sadly. "El save him."

"Maybe El will miraculously deliver him, like he did Mandor and his love," said Wordun.

"What does he mean?"

"After we fought free of those attackers, Hessilyn and I fled in a different direction, wanting to draw them away from you. In the midst of the chase, we became separated too. I thought I had lost all of you. It was in desperation that I sought out the rider post here in Hightower."

"He went to one of our deserted safe houses," said Wordun, picking up the story. "Your brother would have missed us completely, but El had put it in my heart to check on all the old safe houses that day. I had not done that in almost a year, but on the very day that Mandor needed me there, I felt the urge to go. When I found Mandor, he was frantic with fear for all of you. He waited in that place while I went out searching. I found Hessilyn a few hours later, practically on the dragon temple's doorstep. I reunited her with Mandor, retrieved my wife to help, and then went out again to find you."

"El has watched over us," declared Mylana in amazement. "I only pray that he will spare Coursen too."

BRODAGAR

Within the tower that was this city's namesake, the local leader knelt before Nesron and Brodagar in fearful submission. The priest was sorely tempted to blast Verdun-Shoovisk, but he had no desire to take over the ruling of Hightower. The thought of leaving Nesron to do so did tempt him, but he knew the captain would refuse. Brodagar shook his head in response to what the city's ruler had just said. "Verdun-Shoovisk, how could you lose the Attuls?"

"They had unexpected help," muttered Verdun, his face still pressed against the floor. "Apparently, there still was a nest of Attul Watch Riders hidden in the city. Your priests and I tried hard to track this woman, but we lost her…"

"Not only did you lose her, you allowed her to reunite with the other two," snapped Nesron, his tone showing that he was equally frustrated.

"That is not yet certain," argued Verdun, looking up from the floor. "Does your spy know anything about these other Attuls?"

Brodagar ignored the question. "Go, Verdun-Shoovisk, and see to it that you do not lose the one Attul we are still tracking. Hopefully, he will lead us back to the others."

"I hear and obey," replied the city's ruler, bowing his forehead once more to the stone floor and then scampering from the room.

Once Verdun left, Brodagar confronted the captain. "What now, Nesron? We are no closer to learning where Warhaven hides; even worse, we have lost the woman. Your plans have turned to ash."

"All is not lost, even with the one we just let escape. Yes, the Attuls will be reunited when they leave Hightower, but that means Free Hawk is with them too. If only that woman had not found someone to heal her. I am sure that is what we sensed, so we must find another way to pressure her. We are in no worse shape than when we arrived in Hightower."

He did not agree with Nesron, but he saw no point in trying to correct the other.

MYLANA

The next morning, the rain had faded to a drizzle. A pair of horses waited patiently outside of the small home of Wordun and Berala. Mylana sat on the driver's bench, keeping watch, while Mandor, Hessilyn, and Wordun loaded it with some meager supplies. Mylana eyed the wizened horses, wondering how they ever came by their names, Lightning and Courage. They seemed far too timid for such monikers. She stretched her leg, finding it still weak but thankful it was no longer infected.

Mandor slid a small crate under the tarp that covered the wagon's bed. "We are almost done, little sister. With what they have given us and what we purchased, it should be enough food to keep us until Riverrealm."

"Wordun and Berala have been most generous," she answered, "especially since they are planning to leave soon too."

Mandor nodded. "I tried to give them some coins in return, but they refuse. Wordun claims he is simply doing his duty, as a Rider post."

Just then, the others came downstairs. Hessilyn put a clothing bundle under the tarp, while Wordun added another crate of supplies. Berala handed a warm basket to Mylana. "Be sure to eat this bread before it gets soggy."

The women exchanged hugs, while Wordun put a hand on Mandor's shoulder and shared a few last words just for him.

Finally, Mandor and Hessilyn climbed up to join Mylana on the wagon's bench and they set off. Wordun and Berala stood in the mist and watched until the wagon turned a corner.

Mylana drove the wagon towards the eastern city gates, which was not that far from their hideout. However, she had to proceed slowly, and not just because of the age of their team. Too often she had to pull back on the reins to avoid hitting some pedestrian running across the road, head down to avoid the drizzle. They even came upon a squad of Tlocanians patrolling on foot, but were apparently not recognized. She whispered thanks to El, for it seemed that no demon lived in any of them. The troopers marched past, never bothering to question them.

In all, it was a nerve-wracking and slow journey across the wet city. Mylana tensed more when the city gates finally appeared through the mist ahead. Traffic remained light, due to the miserable weather, so the gate guards would have time to look at everyone closely. She focused so hard on the guards ahead that she did not at first see the shadow running through an alley and straight towards their wagon.

"Beware your left," warned Mandor.

Mylana turned and saw a cloaked man running across the wet paving stones. She pulled back her cloak so that her sword was within easy reach, yet she dared not draw it, in fear of being a beacon for their enemy. The man ran closer, definitely aimed at them. Two foot soldiers ran right behind him, in close pursuit. She had no way of knowing if the man was a fleeing thief or some innocent victim, so she kept her sword sheathed. She hoped he would run past and not draw the soldiers to them. They had no need for such attention.

However, as the man came closer, he pulled back his hood to expose his face. It was Coursen! He ran up to the back of the wagon, grabbed the wagon's tailgate, and clambered in. He still favored the one arm.

"Drive those horses!" he yelled as he dropped on top of the wet tarp, "or they will be on us in minutes."

Mylana complied, snapping the reins repeatedly, for the old horses responded slowly. The following soldiers yelled out for them to stop. Already, the gate guards were looking up, having just passed a peddler with a handcart through the opening. The two-horse team was now up to a cantor, the noise of their hooves alerting pedestrians to spring aside. She drove the team towards the opening, where the two guards now had their swords bare and were motioning her to stop. She ignored them, trusting that they would leap out of the way. They did so, with one of them hitting the gate's wall in his haste to avoid being trampled. She drove through the gate opening, the stone tunnel echoing loudly their passing, and suddenly they were out of Hightower.

Eric Lorenzen

CHAPTER TWENTY-SIX

Freetown

AFRAL

Dogs snarled and barked everywhere. Afral sat up in his family's small tent and looked around. Both his parents were gone. Worried, He grasped his sword but left it in its scabbard. He heard his father yell out, "Beware!"

He crawled to the tent flap and carefully looked out. His father was fighting off three of the huge black dogs. Afral hesitated, not certain whether he could be of any help or not, but then a man in black robes stepped out from behind some aspens and raised a hand full of red lightning. "Father! Danger to your right!"

His yell attracted the dragon priest, who threw a fireball at the youth. Afral flung himself away from the tent, desperately pulling at his sword and praying fervently for El's empowering. Thankfully, the entangling canvas ripped and his sword became free, glowing in his grip. Nearby, the grass burned, threatening the tent. Afral was barely to his feet but he raised his sword just in time to intercept a second fireball, knocking it aside as if it were a ball pitched at him. The thing exploded when his sword hit it and fire splattered everywhere, singeing his hair and his clothes. It hurt, but nothing burned. For a moment he was simply stunned at his narrow escape and staggering from the force of the impact.

It might have been his death, for he was too off-balance to counter any more attacks, but suddenly his mother appeared behind the priest. Before the black-robe man could react, she cleaved his neck from behind. One final fireball burst from his dying hand, shooting straight up and setting the trees branches on fire. His mother danced away from the falling flames.

His father had finished off two of the dreadhounds and the third had run off, so both his parents had a momentary respite. Both moved closer to him and his father gestured toward the now-smoking tent. "See if you can rescue some of our things."

Afral nodded and quickly yanked everything out, with his mother carrying them further off. Afral poured out their waterskins on the side that was smoldering, but it only slowed the eventual. Without water buckets there was no way to rescue it and so they just had to let it burn. Rolen lingered for a moment, to make sure his family was safe, but then he ran off to help Merchant Hollin's men, for dreadhounds could still be heard on that side of the camp. Afral was glad that his mother stayed near. He was also glad that all remained quiet near them.

The peace last only a minute, and then a dog charged silently out of the dark, right at them. His mother stepped forward to meet it with her shining sword. Afral had all of his attention on the fight, when suddenly he heard something behind him. Whirling, he saw another hound approaching. Fear filled him as he remembered how he had failed when last he had faced such a beast. He lifted his sword, but it seemed dull and flickering. The dreadhound leaped towards him.

"Oh El, oh El, help me!" he cried, swinging his sword at the charging beast. At the last moment the sword's light steadied, just before he gave the hound a glancing blow. The huge dog howled in pain and ran off.

Afral turned in all directions, terrified that more dreadhounds were after him, but he saw none. The one his mother had faced was now dead. Heart beating hard, Afral ran to her side for he wanted his mother's comfort. His sword, once again, faded and sputtered. Embarrassed, he slid it back into its scabbard.

His father strode back, a look of concern on his face. "Are you two unharmed?"

"We are fine," assured his mother, giving Afral a one-arm hug.

Rolen looked into the darkness around the camp. "Where are they now?"

"I know not," she replied. She still held her bare sword, glowing in the night.

"Do you sense any evil near?"

Tolara shook her head, sliding her sword back into its scabbard. Its light died off as soon as her hand let go. "What I feel is quickly fading to the east, as if the men run off with their dogs. I do think there were more priests than just the one I killed."

"I do not feel anything nearby either. Let us see to the rest of the camp, for some need healing," stated Rolen, sheathing his own sword. He gave both wife and son a quick embrace. The three of them walked together over to Hollin's side to offer their aid. They found the trader and his guard Pad in the back of one of the wagons, weapons ready. Pad's cloak was finally thrown aside, revealing an arm in a sling.

"The attack is over," stated Rolen. "What help do you need?"

"Thank the gods!" exclaimed Hollin. "What an ill-fated trip this journey has become; what god did I anger to be attacked twice? Is anyone else still alive?"

A quick tally showed that two had been ripped apart by the hounds: the driver who had been on watch and one of the guards. Both of Hollin's dogs were also dead and some of the horses and mules were missing. They decided to wait until daylight before searching for the mounts. The dead were placed in a row and covered with blankets to await burial in the morning. The campfires were rekindled, messes cleaned up, and Tolara attended the various wounds. She used her sword three times, including once on Pad's old wound, causing much curiosity.

After the effort, Tolara fell into an exhausted sleep inside a worn tent offered them by the merchant. After Rolen and Afral brought their horses and belongings over to Hollin's camp, Rolen urged his son to get some sleep too, but he refused. Instead, the youth stayed at his father's side. He did not say so aloud, but he was still too frightened to try to sleep. Rather than sleep, Afral followed his father as he went around the camp comforting Hollin's people.

Merchant Hollin came near. "Lord Rolen, may I have a word with you?"

"Please just call me Rolen. I am no nobleman."

Hollin gave a slight nod to Rolen's request, though he did not seem convinced by his denial. "I do not want to be forward, but what is this power in your swords?"

"Our swords are sanctified to our god, El Shaddai, but there is nothing magical about them." Rolen pulled his free and it glowed again. Hollin's men stopped their clean-up work to stare. Rolen held out the blade to the trader. "Take hold of it, Merchant Hollin."

Hollin stepped back. "I have a dislike for such things, be they talismans, necklaces, or a weapon." When Rolen still held the sword out to him, Hollin gave in and took it in hand. As soon as Rolen's hand withdrew, the light faded. Hollin gingerly touched the blade's side and found it cool, not hot. Afral noticed that he checked Truth to see its balance and weight. When he handed it back to Rolen, he gave a slight nod of approval. Truth shone briefly, until Afral's father set it in its scabbard.

Hollin looked around at their audience. "Back to work," he ordered. "The quicker we have things back in order, the faster some of you can go back to your interrupted sleep." They all obeyed.

Hollin lowered his voice. "It may not be magical, but that sword is still worth a Freetown ransom. Do you know its heritage?"

Rolen answered in a soft voice. "I do not know it in full, but Truth came to Na Ciria with an army from the east."

Hollin sharply inhaled, giving Rolen a long, appraising look. "Attul?"

"Yes. The sword came with Belere Anonral's army."

Afral was surprised that his father shared so much, but maybe it was best to sate the trader's curiosity. His father would know, after having been a king's councilor for so many years.

"Was it in old Belere's grip?" asked Hollin.

Rolen shook his head once. "That is doubtful. It is said that Belere Anonral lost his sword at the same time he lost his life, when he defeated the Darshi king."

"So, what are Attuls doing out here on the Singgorn Plains?" pondered Hollin, then lifted his hand. "Please, do not answer that. I do not want to know. However, if legends are walking among us then times must be truly dire. I think that I will finally listen to my sons and retire from the road life."

The merchant paused, looking thoughtfully at the youth. "You have a good son there, Rolen, but I sense that he is hurting inside. I will go and see to my people. Why do you not spend a moment talking to young Afral?"

Father and son watched the trader walk off and then Rolen looked at his son.

Afral looked down, unable to hold his gaze. He feared that his father would ask him about his failures tonight, but instead his father stepped close and gave him a hug.

"I love you, Afral."

The youth looked up at his father, suddenly unable to suppress his pain anymore. "How can you love me? I am a failure. Even El has fled

326

me."

Rolen answered softly, but passionately. "No! He has not! Our god is not so fickle."

"Why then did my spirit sword not light up with his empowering? I tried, Father, I really tried. I could not get it to shine and it was so needed too." He stepped away from his father and then pulled out his sword. It flickered just a little and then went dull, catching only a reflection from the firelight. Afral quickly sheathed it, then lifted his hands to his face and sobbed.

Rolen quickly stepped forward and gave him another strong embrace. "El is not condemning you, but neither does he act as your servant. A Prayer Warrior asks for god's help; he should not just expect it. You have been trying to do this on your own strength. On your own, you will never make any sword shine. Afral, what occurred is something all young Attuls face; doubts will assault you. Unfortunately, it happened to you during battle. This is precisely why we want you to stay in Warhaven for warrior training. Will you do that for me?"

The crying ended. His son looked at him with tear-stained face. "Yes Father," Afral replied, but he was still full of doubt about his own abilities.

* * *

In the morning, they captured the missing horses and mules and buried the dead. Afral helped with both tasks, as did his parents. Afterwards, Afral and his father were down at the riverbank when Merchant Hollin walked over.

"I have a proposition for you, Councilor Rolen. Yes, I know of your former role as aide to King Varen Dabe, though I thought you were just another Rhendoran puff when I heard the rumors of you being an Attul. So many in Rhendora claim Attul heritage, but I have never seen any of them show your powers." Hollin sat down on a boulder, ignoring the chill that must have seeped through his pants. "Are you interested in hearing my proposal?"

"You are no mere trader," noted Afral's father, picking up a twig and tossing it into the river. The branch floated away in the fast current. "What better role for a spy? You swirl with the flow of trade, unnoticed. Who do you work for, Merchant Hollin?"

Hollin smiled. "I work for myself, and have been very successful. Oddly for a Lakelander though, I am also a patriot and a confidant of my king. My apologies, but I cannot reveal which king I name my liege. Alliances are too fragile among the Lakeland kingdoms. If my true loyalties were revealed, it could cause two or more wars.

"But enough about my tangled life. My proposal to you, Lord Rolen, is to take you and your family on as guards for the remainder of my trip to Freetown. It will be good for both sides: I need more guards to protect my goods and you need a disguise for entering that thieves' hold."

To Afral's surprise, his father gave the offer serious consideration. "Before I can make such a decision, I will need to know your color and its hue."

Afral did not fully understand the request, but the trader seemed to.

"I wear the grass green of Darby when in Freetown. Since you know enough to ask, what is your color and hue?"

Rolen smiled. "I have been in Freetown only once, and that was nearly twenty years ago. At that time Tolara and I wore the deep blue of Razon."

Hollin shook his head. "That is a dangerous hue. Please do not wear it in my company." The trader stood up. "At least you did not wear red. I know that the Razon clan was one of the few factions who repudiated the Red Slaughter, but it is a dangerous shade of blue." He shook his head again, saying no more on the topic. Instead, Hollin returned to their original topic. "Well, do you accept my proposal?"

Rolen nodded. "One more thing, though. Last night you mentioned that this was the second attack you have endured. Please explain."

Hollin gave a apologetic smile. "Ah, you noticed my slip of the tongue? Well, just as we left Rhendora, those dogs set on us, killing four men and slaughtering two mounts. I hope you will not part from me now, knowing that the beasts seem attracted to me..."

Rolen actually laughed. "No, Merchant Hollin, for I too have fought them. They are foul mutts who do the bidding of the dragon priests. Their presence in the north is just one more sign that the Tlocanian Emperor has his eyes turned this way."

Hollin frowned. "Another reason for me to retire from the road. Let us go back to the camp, for I want to get my wagons hitched. We need to get far from here."

* * *

By late afternoon, they came to a small settlement beside the river. Clustered behind a thick mud wall were a small group of homesteads and a small inn.

"We will overnight here," stated Hollin to his Attul escorts.

"But it is still early," said Tolara. "Why not gain more miles between us and those hounds?"

"It has been long since you have come this way," responded Hollin. "This is Hopalalo's Place, the first rest on the road into Freetown. The Colors have placed inns along the roads to the city, set a day's journey apart for us merchants. They alternate Colors for each settlement, but are fairly safe no matter your own tint. The proprietors are retired officers, but most are not zealots. To bypass this stop would mean camping in the open again. It is said that a hard-riding messenger can stop at every third stop, avoiding the other colors, but we certainly cannot. Better that we cut our day short today and gain shelter for the night."

Tolara nodded at his wisdom. "How secure are these way stations?"

Hollin shrugged. "There are muggings and pilfering but little else. I tell all my men to stay together and I do not let the night's watchmen have the local fare. Twice in a dozen years have we fallen "ill", but my caution spared us any further mishap."

"What color is this Hopalalo?" asked Rolen.

"Purple, but since he is the last and newest way station, he works hard to make all feel welcome. He is more honest than most. Look at his settlement; it is all mud and thatch. As we go further along, we will see some settlements rich with timber from Rhendoran strays."

Afral could not help himself from asking, "Rhendoran strays?"

Hollin smiled. "When the Singgorn is in its summer calm, lumbermen from the forests above Freetown will float logs down to Rhendora for sale. Every now and then, a log will break free from its ties and wash ashore as a stray. When you see a way station rich in timber, you have to wonder how so many logs wandered loose so conveniently in that area."

* * *

That night they heard dreadhounds again, but suffered no attack. The next morning, they left the compound with great caution, worried about an ambush. However, the dogs left them alone. They traveled the whole day without any harassment.

The next night they stayed in another compound and again the dogs made no attempt to attack. After a few more days of this pattern, it became obvious that the hounds still followed but their masters kept them back from any more assaults. Maybe they had lost too many on that first attack or maybe they had some other scheme in place, but the merchant train remained unmolested.

* * *

Merchant Hollin and his Attul companions made good time to Freetown, reaching the city's outskirts in six days. That morning, as they assembled in the final inn's yard, Hollin and Pad handed out green armbands to all his people. Hollin walked over to Rolen and his family as they were preparing their horses. He had three more armbands in his hand.

"Lord Rolen, I will give each of you the color of the Darby line if you will swear to honor it as long as you wear it. I will not be destroyed by anyone's foolishness. Will you respect the color?"

"I give my word that we will do so," assured Rolen.

Hollin gave each an armband. "Please put them on now, for we will reach the outland wall by midday. I will not be accused of changing Colors upon approach. That is a crime worse than murder to these Freetowners." Hollin went back to oversee the packing of the mules.

Afral looked after him with curiosity. "Father, why must we wear colored armbands?"

"Freetown duties are divided among the three families," Rolen explained. "The three take turns guarding the city-state and collecting its fees. One watches the city bridges and squares, earning the bridge tax and market tax. Another staffs the city walls and collects the entrance tax. The third takes care of the outlands, which includes the road tollhouses and the river fords. Each month the families switch duties, rotating their family soldiers. The soldiers are usually helpful to those of the same color, while heavier-handed on those who are of another tint. Nonetheless, the color provides some protection even with those of a different tint. Should some troop find you without a color, they will know that you have no family, no defender. It means you are easy pickings."

They had no more opportunity to talk, for it was time to get the wagons and mules moving. Once they were well past that night's inn, Afral asked the merchant a question. "Merchant Yadsett, have you always worn this grass-colored shade of green? Why this shade?"

Hollin chuckled, but did not answer Afral directly. "As for the different shades of color, that is a bit harder to explain. I have seen many shades come and go over the years of visiting Freetown. We wear Darby green, which is fairly harmless, and I have worn it for many years now, whenever my travels take me this far north. Father Green himself has been known to wear this shade."

Afral looked up from fingering the fancy stitching on the armband. "Who is this Father Green?"

"The head of each family is called its father," said Hollin. "It is not a real family, though most kin are of the same color. Each color is far larger than any normal family. I have worn the Green for many years but I have never met Father Green personally. I hear he is a large, middle-aged man who has a love for white stallions. I have seen his grand stables before, deep in the heart of the Green Core, and they seem well appointed. It is said that his favorite steeds are better cared for than his own grandchildren are. Or so I've heard."

"They say Father Blue collects swords and knives," said Pad, for once being a bit more talkative, "while Father Purple collects pretty women. He is said to have a particular fondness for..."

"Best not to gossip," interrupted Tolara, "especially not in front of the young man."

"Yes, my lady," replied Pad with a look a chagrin, falling back into his usual silence.

"Tell me, Merchant Hollin, is it true that the rains never cease in the Lakelands?" she asked, changing subjects.

The trader chuckled. "Oh, we do get sunshine, unlike those under the Dragon Shadow, but a person cannot sit too long in one place or moss will start growing on him. Water is so plentiful in the Lakelands that even our lakes have lakes."

Afral's doubtful look made the man laugh.

"That part of my tale is true. Out on huge Monarch Lake there are islands that have their own hills, streams, and lakes." He chuckled a bit more. "It is a wet country, the Lakelands, but bountiful and even beautiful in its sogginess."

The conversation died off, so Afral returned to watching the land around him. The Singgorn widened, forcing the River Road to turn a bit south to avoid a marshy area. They passed through more aspen groves then entered an open field. Ahead they saw a low stone wall, starting in the marsh and crossing over a low hill to the south. Where the wall met the road, there stood a stone tollhouse where a handful of Freetown soldiers kept watch. The soldiers wore Green. It had been decided that Tolara should hide her femininity, wearing a wide-brimmed hat borrowed from one of the drivers and keeping her cloak about her. She took up her disguise now.

"Ah, my luck has turned," said Hollin with satisfaction. "If there is one place where the Color soldiers will waylay a caravan it is at the outland tollhouses, for there are few witnesses to report such abuse. I am glad we will not have that worry, for no Green soldier would dare attack someone of his own color that way. Kill over some woman or card game, yes, but not to rob a trader. Some god must be smiling at us."

They went on and soon Afral could see fields and a small gathering of buildings just beyond the tollhouse. "Is that Freetown?"

Hollin laughed. "That is the village of Easttoll. It is just a small hamlet here in the outlands, but it could be considered a part of Freetown. We have to ride a bit before we will see the actual city, young man."

They came to the tollhouse and Hollin paid the entrance tax for the whole team, grumbling about the high rates. The guards took the money and ignored the complaining, ordering the caravan to get moving.

Hollin's caravan soon entered the nearby village. As they passed through Easttoll, Afral was shocked at the poverty there. The village looked sad, with muddy streets and a few worn shops. He noticed that each place displayed its color loyalty by painting their window shutters blue, green, or purple. The colors were faded and flaking, exposing the gray wood underneath. Most of the homes seemed mere shacks, leaning and patched. A few older women gathered at the hamlet's well, washing clothes as young children played nearby. The children were the only ones who seemed happy in the whole place.

Beyond Easttoll, Afral saw many fields and orchards, most of them very large. Hollin explained that nearly all of the land belonged to the powerful branches in each family. The hirelings who labored in the fields received few coins and gave most of that back to pay for housing and meals. The workers in the field all wore dirty color patches. Even the plow horses wore colors. Each field had a rock tower or wooden platform where a sentry watched over the work. Afral was not certain if the men were there to protect the workers or to make sure they worked diligently. He guessed both.

* * *

Finally, in the late afternoon, they came to Freetown proper, with its high stone walls and well-tended gate. Afral was impressed, for it was far larger than Regalis. The city was really two, explained his mother, divided by the Singgorn River. He could barely see any of the city on the far bank, just a few of the highest spires.

They came up to the gate and he had to crane his neck to take in their massive size. Throughout his childhood, Afral heard tales about the constant bickering of the Freetown families, but they seemed to come together for the city's defense. The guards in blue overcoats and blue pants also seemed very professional. They collected the entrance tax from Hollin without any attempts at extra bribery.

Afral looked around with interest as he rode through the gates and started down a wide road. Immediately, the sounds, sights, and smells swirled about him. Apparently, the street divided two of the city's districts, for the buildings on the right showed green banners and shutters, while those on the left displayed purple highlights. People milled about everywhere, most of them with some color patch or armband to show their allegiance.

"Guard Rolen! Take rear watch!" yelled Hollin. The orders surprised Afral, since Hollin was usually so polite. "And keep an eye on those little brats!" the merchant continued. "They might try to poke the sacks to see what spills out!"

Afral's father nodded and did as told.

"Guards Afral and Tol! You to take the fore. Get us a clear path!"

"Come on, my son," said Tolara, trying to keep her voice deep and husky. "It is time to earn our keep with Merchant Hollin. Keep your eyes on the road in front of us, for we want to spare the trader any troubles or tramplings."

Afral took up his role, following his mother's lead in warning people away from the caravan's path. In spite of their efforts, they could not clear away the traffic with much speed, so the caravan made slow progress through the crowded city. The way was paved but not well kept, so Afral and Tolara had to avoid the worst of the potholes. The buildings to either side were packed close and squeezed tall, towering three floors up. It felt rather closed-in to him.

They came to a large crossroad, where Hollin directed them to turn right, and now only green banners fluttered from the buildings. Hollin directed the caravan down a smaller, quieter way that shot into the heart of a Green neighborhood and then took various turns through the disorderly maze of streets. The crowds thinned some, now that they were away from the market, but the streets were by no means empty. Freetown was a busy, crowded place even on its lesser streets. Finally, they came to an inn called the Green Apple. Hollin guided them to the stables behind the inn.

"Do we start unpacking the mules?" asked Rolen, dismounting and tying his horse's leads to a rail.

"Do not bother, Guard Rolen," said Hollin, nodding for Pad to leave. "Pad will get laborers from my factor. They will have them unloaded quickly. You will need to guard their route once they start the unloading. It is safer here among the Greens, but I would rather not have anyone snooping to see what goods I have brought. I need to turn some profit out of this disaster of a trip."

Soon Pad returned with six men. The workers stripped the first mule of its goods. Pad stayed at the stables with the other guard, while Hollin and the Attuls followed the laborers. They carried the goods through a dark alley, expertly sidestepping the garbage.

"Hey Lona, the Lakelander is back."

Afral looked up at the shout and saw an older woman leaning out a third floor window where she hung laundry on a line stretching over the alley. Across the way, another woman looked down.

"Looks like some expensive stuff."

"How many loads do you guess this time?"

"For the six of them? I say twelve trips."

"I'll say twenty. Hey, Lakelander, will you give a gold coin to whoever guesses closest?"

When Hollin did not respond, the women laughed.

The alley intersected another and the laborers turned to the left. Hollin requested that the Attuls stand guard there where the alleys met. So they did, watching Hollin and his workers go down the way and then vanish through a wide wooden door. Not much happened during their watch, except for chasing off some curious children. Afral puzzled over Hollin's odd behavior and finally asked his father about it. "Why does he not bring the mules directly to his house?"

Rolen shrugged and then spat against one of the walls like a rough guard might, aware that they could be watched. "Freetown is full of odd rules, son. For a bunch of thieves, they like to find as many ways as they can to gather in more coins. You need to buy a license to board animals; you need one even to unload them. Hollin is probably using the inn to get around some of those rules. The innkeeper probably gets a small bribe and conveniently looks the other way."

"Their laws are strange," added Tolara. "While in the Borders they would laugh at anyone proposing such, here it is part of everyone's day. It is not honest men who run Freetown, but criminals. The city is full of laws, but it is also full of bribes to get around those laws. It is their way."

Finally, all the goods were unloaded and carried to Hollin's place. It took eighteen trips for the laborers. As the men passed with their last load, Pad came as well.

"Come," said Pad. "Master Hollin wishes to talk with you one final time."

They followed him to the warehouse, entering a shadowy room where the goods were being sorted into various bins and stacks. They waited on the side while Hollin gave more instructions to his factor, a small gray-haired man, and then Hollin came over and led them into another room. He sat down at a large desk with Pad standing at his back. He unlocked a drawer and took out a coin bag.

"The expected pay for a guard is a copper a day..."

"There is no need for that," argued Rolen. "We rode together for companionship and mutual protection."

Hollin nodded and smiled. "That is true, but I will still pay you. It will provide you with a genuine answer should anyone question how you came to Freetown. You came here as paid guards of Trader Hollin Yadsett and were then dismissed when your services were no longer needed. This story, proved true by the payment of these wages, protects both of us. It is a small price for the continued health of the Yadsett trading house."

Rolen bowed in respect to the older man. "Thank you for your generosity and insight, Merchant Hollin."

The old man's eyes sparkled with mischief as he continued, "And we consider the money paid daily by House Yadsett, being held in safekeeping until arrival in the city, so that the only money actually paid to you while in Freetown was for today's labor. That means only that last copper is taxable as Freetown income. My factor will note your income in our monthly report to the neighborhood's Green tax collector, but it is too little for any withholding."

Hollin held out three small coin bags to them

"You are generous Merchant Hollin," repeated Rolen, taking the coin bags, handing one to Tolara and one to Afral.

"Someday I will savor the telling of this story," stated Hollin, rubbing his hands together. "A lowly merchant guarded by such a prestigious family." He held up one hand. "But do not worry, I will not tell this story anytime soon. Your secret is safe with me and my men."

The Attuls untied the armbands they had been loaned, but Hollin refused to take them back. "Please keep them. Wearing colors will make your time in Freetown much safer. I ask only that you honor the

Green while displaying it. I may not be a native Freetowner, but I do my best to keep their traditions while here."

They parted, with the Attuls walking back to the inn's stable and reclaiming their mounts from Hollin's man there. The three rode out of that Green District, coming out at a market square full of booths. Colors mixed freely, among both the people and the stalls they patronized.

"Look to the west," said Rolen to his wife.

From atop of his horse, Afral looked too. They spotted clouds brewing in the sky, billowing high and dark.

"Can we stay at an inn tonight rather than trying to ride out of here?" she asked. "I would rather not be outside when that overtakes us."

Rolen nodded. "We can turn back to the Green Apple if you wish. It seemed a respectable place."

"I would rather not," replied Tolara, and then lowered her voice to avoid being overheard. "I would rather turn blue."

Afral was not certain that he heard his mother correctly, but his father seemed troubled. Rolen replied, "Are you still determined about that? Darby Green is a far safer color."

Tolara nodded emphatically. "No one else stood up for those killed."

"It happened one hundred and fifty years ago."

"I still do not want to imply approval of their actions," responded Tolara firmly.

His father nodded, though Afral could tell that he had misgivings. His mother was too passionate about the injustice done to the Reds so long ago. She would only wear colors of a family clan who opposed the Red Slaughter. His father knew better than to argue the point. Instead, Rolen pulled his cloak around him, hiding his current armband, and indicated that his wife and son should do likewise. He then led them on a search for a private location to change colors. Afral did not question any of it, for he guessed that if anyone saw them in the act, they would be quickly arrested.

They passed a Purple patrol, but were thankfully ignored. Being on horseback made them more noticeable, but they eventually found an alley where no one was in sight. They dismounted so that they could stand behind a pile of old crates. Rolen handed the new armbands to his family, making sure they kept them hidden in their hands.

"Change armbands under your cloaks," he whispered, "then hand me your old ones."

Afral carefully kept his cloak around him as he untied and pulled off the green armband, then tried to tie on the new one, not even certain of its color. However, as he attempted a knot one-handed, he dropped the old one. It would have caught against his clothes, but he overreacted, trying to grab the cloth. It fell at his feet. Quickly, Afral stooped and hid it again. Ashamed, he handed it to his father, expecting a reprimand. Instead, his father simply asked him to make certain the new armband was secure. He gave it a tug and found his awkward knotting to be adequate.

Afral worried that someone may have seen his blunder. He looked around, but no one could see him. His parents and the horses offered a fair shield against any passerby. They stood against the windowless brick wall of some warehouse, its doors shut tight. Across the alley was another warehouse wall, its nearest doors also shut.

Afral doubted anyone saw his blunder and for that he was thankful. Just as his heart began to slow, though, he noticed a warehouse door move. When no one came out, he decided not to mention it.

"Be careful to keep your new armband hidden as you mount up and ride," ordered Rolen in a whisper. "We have a ways to go and there will soon be winds whipping through the city."

Afral nodded understanding and mounted very carefully, keeping his new colors hidden.

GALDON

Galdon led his troops northward. They came around the Cornerstone, the most western of the Border Mountains, and turned up the gap between the White Mountains and the Borders. They followed a road across a land of grass, spring flowers, and scattered pines. The mountains on either side rose steeply to rocky heights still thickly covered in snow. Galdon now saw the northern face of the Borders and understood why it was called the Wall, for even this far west it formed a snowy picket fence where only high clouds crossed.

The Tlocanians passed through the Triangle Wilds and came upon the open grasslands of the Singgorn Plains. The road split, with one heading east along the Border's foothills toward Four Corners and Rhendora. He ignored that way, picking the road heading straight towards Freetown. There were a few others traveling in the area, but

Galdon chose to molest no one.

CHAPTER TWENTY-SEVEN
Race to Refuge

DRASS

Lord Drass had confiscated a secluded manor, an empty winter house for some baron who was now back home near the White Owl Pass. It was a faded mansion, hidden away among orchards and vineyards. He doubted that anyone would notice his presence, for the servants were too scared to talk. Right now, he stalked down hallways and through rooms, over faded rugs and past old tapestries. He needed to control his frustration, for he could not afford to anger the priests. So he walked. While he walked, he stabbed at random things in the house with his sword. Tumbling a vase, slashing a tapestry, ripping an upholstered sofa. It was better to destroy these things than to lash out at the priests.

Once he felt more composed, he turned his steps towards the mansion wing the priests controlled. He walked up to the door protected by temple guards. The rooms that the priests had commandeered had been the suite belonging to the mansion's owner and so they were sumptuous. A guard gave a brief knock of warning and then opened the door to him, for Lord Drass was expected. He walked into an almost pitch-black room, especially after the door closed behind him, for the windows had been covered by the thickest of drapes.

It took a moment for his eyes to adjust enough to make out the two men sitting quietly on couches at the far end. "Holy brothers, where are my enemies? I need to know where Wintron and his men are hiding."

Cavish turned his head towards him, but Hurko kept still like a statue. Cavish spoke. "The prince and his men are in this valley now, just to the east of us. However, they are lingering at an inn and that is good. The dreadhounds need a respite. The dogs are tired, for it is not easy for them to keep up with horses for such a long distance. Hurko is keeping one of them nearby, but the others have gone to find a temporary den in which to sleep."

Drass did not like that news. He wanted the dreadhounds to flush the enemy out and drive them into his hands and to do so now. However, he understood he was in no position to make such demands. He nodded his thanks to Brother Cavish. "I understand. Is there anything that you are in need of?"

"No, Lord Drass. The manor workers have met our needs sufficiently. We will send you word if we learn anything more about the prince." The dragon priest stood up and came closer. He lifted one hand and red lightning began to play across his fingers. In the darkness it seemed very bright, though it still did not light up the priest's face hidden under the cloak's hood. "I have other news for you. Major Wor will not be coming; Colonel Ulen has recalled the infantry company."

Drass could not help it; he cursed in sudden anger. With that company of soldiers, he would have been able to cut off Tor Randis from the north. He would have been able to teach his father to respect him at last. This could not be happening, not when he was so close. "How do you know this?"

"A messenger arrived just recently, so recently that he is sleeping off his exhaustion in the bedroom." Cavish moved his lightning-filled hand closer to Drass, causing the lord to stand very still. "Control you anger, for there is more. Hurko and I will be leaving as well. We will stay long enough to finish your scheme to kill or capture Prince Wintron, but then we must return to Regalis."

Drass' eyes narrowed with rage, but he said nothing. He dared not. However, he could not control his thoughts. These fickle allies were running away before he and Mordel could consolidate their hold on the realm. Because of them, his task would become far more difficult. Conquering all of the Highlands could take years instead of just months. He wondered what his brother faced down in the Borderheart Valley. Were the Tlocanians withdrawing there too?

Cavish sighed. "Your feelings still seethe, but at least you control your actions. I think it is time for you to leave, Lord Drass. As I have said, we will send you a message when the prince and his men get closer."

The dragon priest pulled his hand back, but then started tossing a small fireball from one hand to the other. Drass did not trust his voice, so he merely gave a small bow and withdrew. He did not start cursing again until he was well away from the priests' wing of the mansion, but then he swore at the top of his lungs and slew his fair share of furnishings.

WINTRON

When the prince came out of the little inn, he found the day almost gone and the light faint. As he walked around the inn to the stable, he looked west towards the red sky and Tor Randis, though the great keep was not in view. He sincerely hoped to greet the next day from the ramparts of his ancestral home, but first he had to live through this night. It promised to be a hard ride before he would again see the sentry torches burning on those stone ramparts. He looked at the others already in the stable yard and noticed that the two sergeants had their heads together. He wondered what they discussed but did not inquire.

Wintron's party had grown to fifteen now. He just hoped that would be enough men to win their way through to the keep. They had decided to move out with nightfall, for though that was optimum hunting time for the dreadhounds, the darkness would make it easier to elude Drass' mercenaries. Wintron, Kevlo, and the sergeants had decided that that was the best bargain the gods had for them this day.

A soldier came over with his horse. Wintron thanked the man and swung up into the saddle. As he settled in place, Yosif strode over with two soldiers.

"My prince, we have assigned Irek and Jolodo to your personal guard. Men, see to it that no harm comes to the prince."

Wintron frowned. "What is this foolishness, Yosif? We have too few soldiers to pull men as my nannies."

"This is not foolish," argued Yosif, who was usually so quiet and diffident. "You are our uncrowned king. Even if all the rest of us win through to the keep, should you die then we have failed. You are not the only one with a personal guard. One soldier has been assigned to Lord Gurash as well, since he is now third in line to the throne."

That last caught Wintron by surprise. He had not considered who his heirs were, in spite of the dig by his Aunt Riala back in Halenvale.

His uncle Fors would be next in line. However, with Fors' two eldest sons in rebellion, Gurash became the heir of both prince and duke. As Wintron considered all this, he was quiet. Yosif took that silence as acceptance. Satisfied, the sergeant walked off to the stable for his own horse.

The prince caught Captain Kevlo's eye and saw him nod with approval. It was as if they were all in a conspiracy to protect him like some newborn babe. He understood their reasoning and even agreed with it, but he did not have to like it. Gruffly, he told the two soldiers to retrieve their mounts.

Wintron and his men left soon after, first taking the main road west and then turning off to catch a back road that offered more shelter. It was a quiet night as they rode past orchards and fields, until a pack of dogs ran out from one farmstead, barking at the strangers. The pack ran across a field and dove through a gap in the gate. When first they charged, Wintron feared they were dreadhounds, but it was soon obvious these were just ordinary canines. They put up quite a ruckus but kept their distance from the horses.

The seven dogs followed the soldiers until they came to the property's limit and then they turned back, satisfied that they had chased off another incursion. The prince hoped there would not be too many more such encounters, for it exposed their presence to any listeners in the area. He was glad to get around a bend and out of sight of that farm. He was considering how they could avoid such noise when he heard the pack start up again.

It startled him.

"Kevlo!" he hissed. "Send Orgel and another back up the road, and make it quick! Someone or something is following us. I want to know if it is a man or a dreadhound."

The captain nodded and detailed the two to head back. The rest of the troops waited, anxiously listening. They heard the dogs barking more fervently and then snarls echoed through the calm night. One of the dogs yelped out in sudden pain, while the rest sounded more desperate in their barks. Another dog yowled, and then came more vicious growls and snapping. Finally, they heard the two soldiers riding back to them, no longer trying to be silent.

"Get ready," whispered Kevlo to the soldiers. "I hear only two riders, but who knows what might be following at their heels."

Orgel and the other came into view, finally slowing. Orgel quickly reported. "It is as you suspected, my prince. A dreadhound tracks us. I did not see its pack mates, but they are likely near."

"There was only one?" asked Wintron.

"Only the one that we saw," replied Orgel, "but the night could be hiding dozens of those black beasts. And yet, none come to its aid against that pack of mutts."

"Turn the men, Kevlo. Let us try to kill the thing before it can call others to our trail."

They raced back to where the pack surrounded the dreadhound. At Kevlo's orders, two men aimed their hunting bows and shot, one of them catching the black animal in its shoulder. It was just enough to give the advantage to the pack, which swiftly moved in and brought the dreadhound down.

"What goes on here?" demanded a new voice. The farmer and his men had come out to investigate the noise. They held pitchforks and shovels. One had a hunting bow with an arrow already drawn. They were three older men and one fellow barely old enough to find a chin whisker.

Wintron guessed their young men already enlisted. He decided to answer carefully to avoid revealing too much. "We are today's patrol, and your dogs have done us a boon. They have brought down a vicious hunter, a dreadhound. Have your men take a careful look at the thing so that they can spot any of its pack mates that might follow." He motioned them over to the carcass. The dogs did not touch the thing once it died. The farmer opened his gate but had only one of his men approach carrying a lantern. The rest kept leery watch.

The man came over and shined his light on the huge, lean body. He used his foot to move its muzzle for a better view. "It is a black dog," the man yelled back to his employer. "Even its teeth look black, as well as the blood pooling beneath it. Never seen anything like it."

"These things are man-eaters," stated Wintron, keeping a soldier between him and the lantern's light. He did not want anyone recognizing him. Although he doubted a farmer would betray him purposely, it was best that all remained ignorant. "They have been known to pull a man from the saddle or crash through a barred door just to get their taste of human flesh. Be careful, for where one roams there will be others."

"Thanks for the warning, soldier," replied the farmer as he motioned for his man to return to his side.

"We ask that you clear the carcass in the morning," continued Wintron. "Now, we need to get on with our patrol. Good night to all of you."

DRASS

Hurko suddenly let out a shout, grabbing his side in remembered pain. He fell back against the couch cushions, moaning. Lord Drass, who was also in the room, startled at the sudden movement and sound. He wished he could see more clearly if the man was truly wounded; he did not like how the priests insisted on keeping their rooms so dark.

"What has happened?" asked Cavish of his fellow priest.

Hurko struggled to sit up, his hand still pressed to his ribs though Drass saw no injury. "They discovered the hound when a pack of dogs attacked her. One of them shot her with an arrow just before I withdrew my mind link."

Cavish nodded understanding, coming over to place a hand on Hurko's forehead. "Show me where your hound was stalking." The two fell silent. Drass wondered if they had some means to communicate without words.

Cavish stepped back, removing his hand. "I will call the other dreadhounds from their sleep."

Drass, who had been listening quietly to all of this, could not keep from interrupting. "Why were not the other hounds already on the trail?"

"Silence," warned Brother Cavish. "You speak in ignorance. We cannot wake the dreadhounds easily, not from a distance. Besides, they needed their rest. Now, be silent or get out of here. I must concentrate on how to break through their dog dreams." The dragon priest chose a chair in the far corner and settled in, breathing deeply and losing his awareness of those around him.

Drass stared angrily at the man, not even trying to hide his thoughts. As powerful as these priests were, he would be glad to see them ride off soon.

"He is right, Lord Drass," said Hurko, rising to his feet carefully. "You are ignorant of our ways, though maybe someday you will be deemed worthy of an Embracing. Would you like that? It would grant you power far beyond anything your brother or father have ever experienced. Would you like to have our powers?"

Hurko left the question dangling in front of Drass. The priest walked over to the door to the bedroom, his pain seeming to lessen with movement. He knocked on the door and someone gave a muffled reply. The door opened to reveal another dragon priest. Drass recognized the billowing robes and realized this was the messenger that had brought the orders to withdraw. He still had not discovered how the priest had slipped into the compound, past his soldiers, and into the manor.

"Brother Frissen, your unique skills are needed again," said Hurko. "Cavish is trying to awake the sleeping pack, but the prey has slipped past them and is somewhere on their way towards us. We need to know exactly where they are."

Frissen nodded, but then gave a quizzical look at Drass.

Drass had the feeling that Hurko smiled, though he could see nothing of his face with his cloak's hood still up. "I think the lord needs to have a taste of our power, though not too much. Maybe you can transform in the other room…"

"Very well," replied Frissen in a whispery voice, turning back.

There was a moment when Drass felt something oppressive against his chest, as if the wind had suddenly struck him even though nothing stirred in the room.

A dreadhound came out of the bedroom, causing him to pull back in fearful surprise. The beast's eyes shone red in the gloom as it gave Drass a hungry look.

"Lord Drass, would you open the door for Brother Frissen?" asked Hurko. "He must get on with his mission."

His mouth fell open. "Are you saying… you mean this beast… he is a were-wolf?"

"A were-hound," clarified Hurko. "Now, open the door please."

Drass backed up to the door, not taking his eyes off the black monster. If not for those glowing eyes, he would have trouble seeing it among all the shadows. He fumbled with the door handle and then pulled it open. The dreadhound rushed out, brushing him as it passed. Drass restrained a shiver, a shiver of both disgust and desire.

"Would you like such power, Lord Drass?" asked Brother Hurko again, tempting him. "It is only the Embraced Ones who can experience such things."

WINTRON

Captain Kevlo, who rode in the lead, called for a halt. They were on the main road again. Directly ahead of them was the village of Fairfruit, deep in slumber. "What do you think, Prince Wintron?

Should we try to sneak around or gallop through?"

"I tire of sneaking like a thief," he replied, urging his horse forward. The others hurried to keep up. The horses gained speed and soon were racing along the wide road. Up ahead, someone yelled and six archers stepped out of an alley and lined up across the road in the green light of the village inn. Wintron did not slow, pulling his sword free and pointing it at one of the archers. Irek and Jolodo whipped their horses to pull ahead of him, as did Yosif. He let them, for they were only doing their duty. As they passed the first cottages, a squad of riders appeared and fell in behind Wintron's men, shouting threats. The archers released a hail of arrows and Jolodo sagged in the saddle, his horse galloping along only because of those around it. The archers released another volley, hitting another soldier behind Wintron as well as a horse. There was no third volley, for they had to dive aside as the horses thundered past.

Suddenly, they were past the settlement. Jolodo fell from the saddle, dead from the arrow in his throat. His horse faltered without a rider. Wintron raced by, saddened but unable not stop to give him any burial, for behind him galloped two dozen of Drass' cavalry.

DRASS

"They just came through Fairfruit," announced Brother Hurko. He was on horseback now, along with Cavish and Lord Drass. Cavish sat in a trance, his horse's reins held by a temple guard. They were east of Randisville.

"How do you know?" asked Drass. "Did you link with Brother Frissen?"

Hurko shook his head. Unspoken was his opinion of Drass' ignorance. "I linked to a dog in his pack. Brother Cavish guides our pack this way, but the horses move too fast to catch. They are galloping down the road."

"That is foolish," pronounced Drass. "The horses cannot run all the way to Tor Randis. They will ride them to death."

"No matter that. They made it through Fairfruit with few losses and now Frissen and his pack are also falling behind. Some of your cavalry are in pursuit, but we will not have a clear idea of where they are."

Drass grimaced in frustration, but then realized how quickly he had become used to this magical communication. No matter. His plans were well laid. They were sure to stop Wintron and Gurash.

WINTRON

"Turn!" yelled Wintron from the lead. The half-squad swerved left, up a side lane between two hedges, for Wintron did not trust staying on the main road any further. The darkness was a hindrance on this route, however, with night shadows hiding ruts and holes. Their pace slowed, for now both horse and rider had to watch for hazards. He immediately realized his error, for they had lost the advantage of a wide, moonlit road and now their pursuers were catching up. And yet it was too late to turn back. They were committed to traveling this lane.

Wintron realized that he would have to find a favorable place to make a stand. He did not know if any of the pursuers carried horse bows, but the twists of the lane might prevent their use for a little time. Their passage arrowed between pines lined up in two rows, whose shallow roots made the road even more treacherous. On the right side, a hedge made a living wall just beyond the pines, while on their left hand a rail fence ran the distance. The dirt lane came to the end of another property line and veered sharply right, forcing them all to slow as they turned.

He decided to take a stand just beyond there, for their pursuers would not be able to charge at them. He yelled out his order. "Turn and halt! To defense!"

With just that simple order, the Border soldiers knew their roles. Swords came out, as they took their places among the pines. His two remaining guards, Irek and Sergeant Yosif, placed themselves between him and the road, forcing him to back his horse up against the tall hedge. Nearby, Gurash's horse also brushed the wall of sharp holly. When their pursuers came around the bend, Wintron's men surprised them, downing eight before they even realized that the Bordermen had stopped to take a stand. It was a quick and vicious struggle that his men won handily.

One of Drass' men fled on horseback, though, while all the others lay dead or dying.

Wintron's half-squad lost only the soldier that had been wounded earlier. There was no time to care for their dead or even help the injured enemy. Kevlo ordered the troopers to continue, having Paon and Orgel take the lead. Kevlo fell in right before the two nobles.

"What route now, my prince?" he asked, looking over his shoulder.

"We can take the side lanes to Turlo's Post," suggested Gurash.

The prince considered but then shook his head. "They will expect that, now that we have swerved up this lane. No, now that we are free of them, let us consider a stealthier path. Find us a way back across the main road, Kevlo. I want us to follow the river into Randisville."

"Is there a lane or path that follows its bank?" asked Kevlo, recalling none.

"Nothing but game trails," replied the prince. "Scout Orgel will have to work through such a maze, but I think it will be worth it. Drass would not expect us along that route."

Kevlo gave a short laugh. "No, I doubt he will."

DRASS

When Drass received word that Wintron had turned up a side lane, he felt a certainty where the man was headed. Asking Brother Hurko to join him, he rode quickly for Turlo's Post, taking along two squads. Drass hungered for a quick victory; he could not wait for the prince to come to him. He left Cavish and the last two squads to guard Randisville.

WINTRON

The darkness deepened under the riverside trees. The damp ground crawled with berry vines and other tangled shrubs. It was slow going, but Orgel found them paths to follow and eventually they came to the outskirts of Randisville, arriving at a watermill.

Someone peeked out from behind curtains, but no one came out. The miller's dog bravely barked at the intruders from the safety of the porch. They regrouped in front of the miller's door, ignoring the yapping canine. They would now have to strike out by road again.

Once regrouped, they set their steeds to a trot, heading into the town. The pre-dawn already lightened the eastern sky. If they did not get through soon, they would lose the advantage of darkness. Kevlo insisted on putting most of the men in front of the nobles, with only Orgel taking up the rear. They all knew this would be their final run to the keep.

DRASS

"What is the delay?" asked Drass, frustrated. The nearby sergeant tried to offer lame explanations, but he waved him to silence.

At that moment, Hurko came out of one of his trances. Drass recognized the sudden return of awareness.

"What news, Brother Hurko?"

"They turned back to the main road and then crossed it and are apparently following the riverbank towards Randisville." Hurko motioned for a temple guard to hand him some nourishment.

Drass cursed. "They try to sneak around Cavish's position." He ordered those with him to abandon their hiding places and to regroup. Archers climbed off roofs, while horsemen came out from behind various buildings around the village. He hoped they would have enough time to race back to Randisville.

"Do not be too upset," said the dragon priest. "Cavish knows as much as I do, for he held the dog that ran next to mine. They will not surprise him."

WINTRON

The road from the watermill was well kept, for many wagons carried grain sacks back into the town along its wide way. It allowed Wintron's half-squad to set a fast pace and they were soon passing the cottages and garden plots on the town's edge. Randisville had no town walls, not with Tor Randis close by, for which he was thankful.

The troop made it as far as the main road's cobbled way before encountering any opposition, but then chaos descended upon them. Drass' men appeared on rooftops and in alleys, raining arrows down or charging their flanks.

Kevlo shouted orders for the men to keep going, not to turn aside or engage anyone unless unavoidable.

Men began to die, mainly Wintron's men. Still they charged on, now at a gallop. He felt some relief when the arrows died off, but enemy soldiers still rode on their tail. Up ahead, Wintron saw the central square. In front of the town's fountain waited a group of horsemen, one of them in black robes.

He saw the fireball arc in the air as it flew towards his squad and then it hit the horsemen in the second row. The fireball exploded all over them, burning some to ash while other men and animals screamed horribly. Globs of red fire splattered over the squad, the cobblestones, and the buildings nearby. Soldiers lost momentum, as they had to swerve around their flaming comrades.

"Keep going!" yelled Captain Kevlo. "We must win past him or we will all die here." The soldiers found it hard to ignore the screams and moans of their fellow troopers, but they obeyed, even as another fireball hissed in their direction.

"Beware the center of the road!" warned Wintron. "Everyone ride close to the buildings."

They were already moving that way, as all sought shelter. The next fireball hit the cobblestones and then shattered in an explosion of red sparks. This time, no one was hit directly but many were splashed with flame.

Wintron hastily smothered his smoking cloak while trying to control a mount upset at being singed. Around him, others also struggled to rein in their panicking steeds. Regaining control, Wintron aimed his horse in the right direction and kept going. He did not at first notice that Irek was gone, another casualty.

Only nine riders made it to the square, charging towards the dragon priest and the temple guards. The priest reacted by setting up a wall of flame as protection.

"Ride past!" yelled Sergeant Yosif to the remaining men. "We must get the prince through to Tor Randis!"

Wintron realized that both Captain Kevlo and Sergeant Paon were no longer at his side, though Gurash remained. The squad raced past the dragon priest and headed down the road towards Tor Randis. Behind them there was still much shouting and screaming. Wintron looked over his shoulder and saw a dozen soldiers in close pursuit.

Suddenly, another fireball came hurling their direction, this one larger and faster than any of the ones before.

"Faster!" yelled Wintron, kicking his horse. The soldiers tried to outrun the magic, but did not succeed. The fireball crashed across the rear line of riders, fully engulfing four of them as well as some of their pursuers.

Wintron's eyes filled with tears of frustration. He could not save any; he had to let them die in his defense. This was not even honorable battle. Instead, the troopers burned like unwanted chaff after the harvest. What evil had Mordel invited into the realm? These dragon priests were inhuman in their killing, burning men on either side of the battle.

He wiped away his tears with the back of one hand and swore to the gods that he would put an end to all of this. Though he did not feel worthy of it, Wintron would accept the Border Realm crown and then he would drive these evil men from the land. He did not yet know how he would do it, but he vowed to the gods that he would. Mordel had not only killed the king, he had brought evil to the Border Mountains.

Wintron, Gurash, and the last of the squad made it to Tor Randis just as the morning sun touched the mountains to either side. It took a few anxious minutes to convince the fortress guards who they were, and then the great gates opened to them. Wintron had ridden out with a hundred men and high hopes of capturing or killing Drass. He returned with just five companions: Gurash, Yosif, Orgel, and one soldier that had not even been in his original company. He wondered if anyone would want to follow his lead now, after such devastating losses.

Eric Lorenzen

CHAPTER TWENTY-EIGHT

Bloody Inn

MYLANA

Mylana guided the horses out of Hightower, around a peddler's cart, and still kept them charging up the dirt road, past mist-hidden orchards and fields. It was almost as dark as twilight, with the drizzle added to the Dragon Shadow, so that her pace was dangerous to the horses. Mandor reached over and encouraged her to rein in. As she slowed, he looked back at Coursen, who still breathed heavily, lying there in the wagon's bed.

"Coursen, are you well?"

The other looked up, revealing a bruised face with dried blood around his nose and mouth. He smiled bravely, though his pain showed. "I am alive, to my own surprise, and I have no injuries that require immediate healing, so keep going."

Apparently, Mandor did not want to take him just at his word, for he climbed over the wagon bench and made his way over to his old friend.

Mylana, still guiding the horses, could not keep herself from looking over her shoulder regularly to watch Mandor minister to their companion. Coursen's clothes were ripped and stained, his sword and its belt now gone. He cradled his right arm, as if it were still injured.

"How did you ever escape?" asked Mandor, looking over his injuries.

Coursen shook his head. "That I do not fully understand. They caught me in the stables and quickly bound me. They threw my sword into the dung heap after it burned the hands of one of the demon-possessed. I was beaten, robbed of my coins, and questioned harshly by that demonic officer. He asked where you others were, so I knew that you had escaped. He seemed very upset about that. When I did not provide an adequate answer, he hit me with that red lightning."

He paused and shuddered, as if reliving the experience. "I do not know what being struck by real lightning feels like, but I would guess it similar. His blow threw me across the stable yard, where I lay helplessly while they searched for you. Later, they took me to their tower for more questioning and then threw me into a dark cell. I lingered there, with little food or water, but no one interrogated me further. It was as if they had forgotten I was there.

"Then one day, a jailer pulled me out of there, and took me outside to their mustering yard just inside the high tower's gates. Supply wagons had arrived and they made the prisoners do the unloading. When two prisoners began to fight, a handful of us used the distraction to run for the gates. Three of us made it out, though I lost track of the others during our escape. I made my way to the eastern gate, hoping to catch you as you left. I dodged patrols all of last night and into this morning, trying to stay near the gates. At times, I despaired that you might have already left the city, but I had no other plan. I kept avoiding the soldiers and lurked near the gate, hoping to find you. They came upon me just when I spotted you. I guess I must have frozen in my surprise at finally finding you."

"I find your tale hard to believe," stated Hessilyn with a frown. "I have never known the demonized to be so inept."

"Do you think they purposely allowed him to escape?" asked Mylana, startled at the thought.

"Yes, so that they could flush us out," replied Hessilyn. "They may have used you as a lure."

"That would mean that you are in greater danger because of me," observed Coursen. "If only I had not found you…"

Mandor interrupted. "Do not say such things. We are all glad that you are safe and back with us. Hessilyn, can you pass back that food basket? We cannot heal Coursen this close to the city, for that will confirm our flight, but we can at least feed him."

The thought of making Coursen suffer any longer grieved Mylana. She grabbed the food basket herself and handed the reins to Hessilyn. "I think our flight is already known," she stated, carefully climbing back into the wagon bed. She crawled across the lumpy tarp, stepping carefully among the covered bundles, until she was next to Coursen. She pulled out her sword and it blazed very bright on the almost-dark day. "I will heal what I can."

Coursen had already removed his stained cloak and tattered shirt for Mandor's examination, so she could readily see the cuts and bruises all over his torso. She did not wait for Coursen's permission, but began the ritual of prayer for healing. Once again, the worst injury seemed to be to Coursen's arm. Mylana laid the flat of her flaming blade on the ugliest of the wounds, causing Coursen to scream in agony.

Shaken, she pulled back. The wound bubbled and darkened, looking worse instead of better.

"What happened?" asked Mandor. Coursen passed out from the pain, going limp against Mandor.

"I...I do not know," answered a confused Mylana, checking to make sure their friend still breathed.

"Do no more healing on him. They have done something to him to make his body reject your ministrations."

She sat back, grasping the wagon's side when it jolted suddenly. "It is as if El's touch is suddenly a poison to him."

Mandor struggled to get the unconscious Coursen dressed. Together with Mylana, they moved the man towards the head of the wagon, making a spot for him under the protective tarp. There seemed little else they could do for him.

* * *

Mandor took over driving, while Mylana stayed at Coursen's side, sheltering his head from the drizzle. He awoke after an hour, but was at first incoherent to her questions. Eventually, though, she was able to understand that they had done things to him in that prison, things he had not wanted to mention.

"They know that we are Watch Riders and they also know about you," he finally confessed, looking up at her. "I told them a tale about us riding a circuit through Waybridge, Deep Crossing, and then downriver to Westbend, but they did not seem to believe me. Instead, they kept asking me questions about you."

"Do you think they know about our mission?" she asked.

Coursen frowned. "I...I am uncertain. They seemed uninterested in our destination, but whether that was because they were ignorant of its significance or because they already knew that it was a secret to me as well..."

Eric Lorenzen

For a moment, all were silent as that truth sank in, then Mandor spoke up. "What did you tell them?"

"Not much, but they already knew too many things about us...far too many things. They knew we came from the south, that we were Riders, and that we had been in Waybridge. They were even aware that Hessilyn was not a Rider."

Again they fell into silence.

Finally, Coursen spoke again. "They knew who I was, but they seemed unconcerned once they took away my sword. They saw me as no threat and that is troublesome. How powerful are these demon-possessed men?"

"They are very powerful," answered Hessilyn. "Once a demon is inside a man, he changes into a different person. He becomes fearless and cunning."

"Could they have planted a demon in me?" Coursen asked.

Mylana quickly protested. "They did no such thing. You are Elsworn. El's presence within you is protection against such. Besides, I would sense any demon this close."

He gave her a timid smile. "Then I do not know what caused my reaction. I thank you for trying to heal me, even though El's touch failed."

She frowned at the slight towards El, but chose to let it pass since the healing had failed for Coursen. "Here, Coursen, eat something. You need to build your strength." She held out a bread loaf heel, which he took and bit. As he chewed, she stared at him.

"What is it? Do you see something else wrong with me?" he asked, pausing in his meal.

She reached out and brushed a wet lock of hair back from his forehead. "Nothing is wrong, Coursen. I am just amazed at your courage. Try to sleep. Apparently, you will need to heal naturally."

He nodded, settling back after finishing the bread and letting his eyes close. Mylana stayed at his side until he fell asleep again, then she carefully rose and climbed up on the driver seat next to Hessilyn.

"He is a handsome man," observed the Westbend noble.

Mylana startled out of her thoughts. "What did you say?"

"I said that Coursen is handsome. Surely you have notice that fact." Hessilyn gave a mysterious smile.

"Coursen is only a friend. A good friend, but only a friend." For some reason, Hessilyn's insinuation nagged at her.

They kept the horses to a fast pace, pushing the team to its limits.

They expected to face an attack soon, but none materialized.

By late afternoon, they relaxed a little in their silent vigilance. Mandor and Hessilyn began to chat quietly, isolating Mylana, though not intentionally. It left her with much time to her own thoughts. She quietly considered her feelings for her brother's friend. He was five years her senior. Growing up, she had always appreciated his humor and wit but he had seemed so old. Her friends had sometimes mooned over Coursen (and Mandor of course), but she had never seen the attraction.

Was Coursen handsome? She had to admit to herself that Hessilyn was correct about that. However, she was not about to swoon over the man. He was a wandering rascal, not at all the established man she longed to find. Apparently satisfied in being only a Watch Rider, he never pursued any other profession. Coursen enjoyed the dangerous life of the messenger and scout too much, choosing that over learning any trade skills. No, he would not be able to support a wife or a family. He was not at all the type of man she wanted.

She then pondered about what kind of man she did want, until Mandor interrupted her.

"We approach a village and just in time. I do not think the horses can pull us much further today."

Mylana looked up to see the grouping of cottages appearing out of the mist, chagrined that her wandering thoughts had distracted her so. She could just make out a green lantern through the mist, identifying the inn. "We will need to take a room so that we can see to Coursen's injuries."

"We should look for a healer," said Hessilyn, "since your powers seem not to have helped Coursen. Leave that task to me."

Mandor gave her a surprised look.

"I may be a noble, beloved, but I am not helpless in the countryside. Besides, that healer could be the local dragon priest. I think I will be more comfortable entering a temple than either of you."

Mandor nodded at her wisdom. "Please see that you are back before dark, even if you cannot locate a healer. I fear that the enemy will be upon us again tonight."

He directed the horses to the back of the inn, where an overhang provided shelter to a pony. In a nearby corral, six mules stood with hanging heads, pressed close together for warmth. A stable boy hailed them from the shelter, telling Mandor the cost for a dry stall as opposed to the corral. "I can't promise that them mules won't bite," he added, trying to sell them on a stall. Mylana wondered if he was trying to make the inn more money or just did not want to step out into the mist. Mandor finally agreed to a shared stall for the horses, if he could pull the wagon under the shelter too. The boy readily agreed, offering help once Mandor drove the horses under the sheltering roof.

As Mandor and Mylana saw to the horses, Hessilyn asked the boy about a local healer. The youth looked at the groggy Coursen who struggled to sit up. "It ain't catching, is it?"

Hessilyn assured him that Coursen was only injured, not sick. The boy did not seem totally convinced, but he told her that the village priest served as healer too. He gave directions to the local temple and Hessilyn strode off to go find the man.

* * *

Hessilyn did not return with the dragon priest until after the evening worship. The priest was an elderly man, short, slim and bald. Unlike his city counterparts, he showed humility and a wry sense of humor. He did what he could for Coursen, placing a poultice on his most horrible wound and smearing a cream on the many minor cuts. Coursen had passed out again, in spite of the priest's attempts to keep the young man talking. "Your friend seems a magnet for injuries. If possible, let him rest for a few days, giving him broth and bread until he is up to eating heartier meals."

"Thank you for your help, Brother Frigard," said Hessilyn, holding out coins to him.

The priest shook his head. "I do not charge for helping those in distress."

Hessilyn still pressed the coins into his hand. "Please take them for the temple," she insisted.

"Thank you, daughter," he replied, slipping the coins into a plain and nearly-empty money purse. He laid a hand on her head and prayed a blessing over her. Hessilyn accepted it reverently. The priest seemed to realize that the others were not dragonsworn, so he only gave them a friendly nod and then withdrew.

BRODAGAR

Brother Brodagar sat in a simple room at the local temple, carefully guarded by his personal temple guards standing just outside. Two of his priestly entourage, both of them gifted at linking with the dreadhounds, joined him inside the room. The place held more shadow than light with but one flickering candle, so it was a soothing dimness. They sat quietly, eyes closed, concentrating on guiding two dog packs through the village. Brodagar chose to lead this time, for they were running out of time. As usual, he found this link to both stimulating and unsettling. Adding a third persona on top of his demon Other seemed to dull his wits a bit, even if the third one was a mere hound. Brodagar felt the animal's eagerness for human flesh; it smelled the nearness of the villagers and was eager to attack. The priest concentrated on the need to reach the inn. He aimed the hound at the place, urging it to keep the rest of the pack in line too. Only the promise of fresh meat kept the hound obedient.

The dreadhounds ran in silence, for they did not always bark or bay when on the hunt. Their black coats blended in with the night, making them almost invisible. They came on the inn just as a patron opened the front door. Brodagar forced his dog to push past the man and into the common room. One of the dogs following had less restraint, knocking the man down and tearing into his throat for a quick kill. The rest of the pack ran in behind Brodagar's hound. Once inside, all control was lost, as the dogs' hunger for human flesh overwhelmed all attempts to guide them.

He sat back, opening his eyes. The glow faded from his eyes as his link to the dog ended. Around the table, the other two priests also stirred. Sometimes Brodagar enjoyed staying through a feeding frenzy, but he chose not to this night. "Did either of you see the Attuls?" he demanded of his underlings. Both replied that they had not. "Well then, let the dogs eat some to get past their yearnings. Yashok-Sekaos, return to your link but merely observe. Let us know if the Attuls barge in." The one priest nodded and then closed his eyes to concentrate on finding his hound.

MYLANA

The foursome ate a late meal in their room. Coursen came awake enough to eat his soup and bread and to take unappreciative sips of warm milk. He sat up against the pillows, while Mandor sat at the foot of the bed eating his dinner. The women sat on the other bed as they quietly chewed the old bread and crumbly cheese. Suddenly, they heard the screams from downstairs.

"What is happening?" asked Coursen.

"Not again," sighed Hessilyn. "Will they not give up on us?"

Mandor and Mylana met eyes and she nodded. "We cannot let others suffer because of us," she said, rising to her feet. "Join me, brother. We are needed."

He seemed ready to argue for her to stay behind, but must have seen the resolve in her eyes. Instead, he simply nodded and followed her out, asking Hessilyn to lock the door behind them and do her best to protect Coursen.

Mylana hurried down the hallway, not yet able to run with her still-tender leg. Just as she came to the head of the stairs, a dreadhound came bounding up. Drawing quickly, she had her sword ready before the dog reached the top raise. With a fierce maneuver, she beheaded the beast, splattering blood all over the stairwell.

Mandor charged past her, stepping over the carcass and then bounding down the rest of the stairs.

She followed, though she could not run as he did. She prayed as she descended, asking El to guide her sword and to use her for his justice.

Mylana found the common room full of dreadhounds, many of them fighting over their victims. Tables and benches were overturned. A small group cowered in the corner, using a table as a shield and benches as weapons. Mandor ran over and attacked one of the lean hounds. She followed, taking on another dog that meant to slink up behind him. She killed her second hound quickly, but then another came at her and she was forced to retreat before its snapping jaws. Whenever the dog seemed to lag in its attack, another hound would bark fierce encouragement to it. It was as if the other dreadhound directed the pack's assault.

With sudden resolve, Mylana dodged past the first hound and went after the one barking orders. The dog's eyes had a red glow about them. That hound tried to flee, but Mylana was able to corner it and keep it there. She was cautious in her strikes, determined to kill this monster while making sure no other dog came up on her from behind. The huge, lean dog barred its great teeth in obvious anger, drool dripping on the dirty wooden floor.

It tried to go on the attack, but she proved too fast with her blazing sword, the light of which made the animal cringe. At times, she sensed the animal hesitating, as if of two minds. The delays allowed her to keep it hemmed in and also keep other dogs away. However, she was unable to get in a killing blow.

Suddenly, the ebony dog tried to flee her, lunging to the right. She noticed that the dog's eyes had darkened and lost their red glow just before she brought her blade down with a two-handed stroke and severed its spine.

Mylana turned quickly, fearing that another dog might come after her. However, the remaining dogs had given up the attack and were now fleeing out the door. Soon, all were gone, leaving the Attuls in a room with moaning and crying people. Seven dog carcasses also littered the room.

"Are you well?" asked Mandor.

"I think a dog clawed my injured leg," she replied. "Can you try to clean it of infection? I will need my strength to assist the wounded."

Mandor walked over to her. His shirt was torn and blood-stained. "I will help you as I can, but my own wound is draining my strength."

Her eyes widened at the sight of his injury. She ignored his attempts to help her; instead, she had him unbutton his shirt and expose the oozing, blackening wound at his side. With fervent prayer, she set her sword against the wound and power surged and fought in Mandor, sending off sparks that charred his garments, until the wound was cleansed of infection. The act drained both of them. When Mandor moved to try healing Mylana in turn, she restrained him.

"My injuries are not so great," she stated, realizing the greater needs around her. "We need what strength we have left for the many wounded." She looked over at the people who had been trembling in the corner. "You who are unharmed, we need your assistance. Help us to gather the wounded."

As the men and women began to stir, Mandor approached one of the men. "Will you go to retrieve the temple priest?"

The man hesitated, looking towards the open door and the deep darkness outside.

"I will go part of the way with you," added Mandor, "to make sure the dreadhounds have truly fled."

The man nodded his agreement then, though he still looked frightened at what might be lurking in the night.

* * *

As dawn arrived, a bonfire blazed next to the inn. They broken furniture had served as the kindling to burn the dog carcasses. An awful stench rose with the acrid smoke.

An exhausted Mylana watched as the remains were consumed. With her stood Coursen, Mandor and the innkeeper. Hessilyn was somewhere inside, tending to the wounded. The dragon priest came outside, carrying rags that had been used to clean up the dogs' gore. He tossed the rags into the flames, for the blood was too corrosive to wash out. He came over to them.

"Thank you for all of your help, Attuls," he said. "Your healing work has kept many from dying or being maimed."

"Your thanks are misplaced," argued Mandor. "The hounds would never have attacked if we had not stopped here."

The priest shook his head. "That is not so. Do you really think this is the first time we have been used as fodder? The Tlocanians have let their hounds loose on us many times before. Sometimes I think that they left our village intact only so that it could serve as a feeding trough." The priest motioned for the innkeeper to step away, which he did by going back inside. Once he was alone with the Attuls, the dragon priest continued. "The masters of the hounds are at the temple right now. These men wear priestly robes and claim to be faithful dragonsworn, but I know better. They serve demons, not my dragon gods."

Mylana looked down the street to where the small temple stood. Though a poor structure, it still had its five spires representing the five dragon gods, so it towered over the tiny settlement. "They are here in the village?"

The priest nodded. "They came in last night, a group of priests with twenty temple guards as protectors. I hear that an even larger group of Tlocanian soldiers rode in with them, though they would have sheltered at the local garrison."

The Attuls shared a look of concern.

"You walk a dangerous path, priest," stated Coursen, rubbing his still-aching arm. "They will not like that you have confessed their secrets to us."

The elderly priest shrugged. "What more could they do to me? I tire of their cruelty and deception. They have kidnapped my once-pure religion and have butchered my countrymen." His eyes blazed with fervent indignation. "Though we are not of the same faith, I can see you as allies. These demon lovers must be stopped."

"Brave words when no one is here to witness them," replied Coursen harshly. "I do not think the villagers would appreciate your candor or rebellion."

Mylana looked at Coursen, surprised at the other's unsympathetic words, but the priest nodded agreement with him. From the response, she guessed her judgment of Coursen was too harsh.

The old man said, "The villagers are all cowed; that is true. They cannot see any way to withstand these cruelties. They only want to protect their families and to keep from starving. However, I still hope to see the sun again some day, to see these invaders pushed back along with their oppressive cloud cover."

Coursen nodded. "You join many others who hope for the same, others who do what they can to fight these oppressors."

"Ah, that reminds me. I have something that you might need," the priest said to Coursen. He strode back to the inn, but soon returned, carrying a sword in a scabbard. "This sword belonged to a local killed last night, one without any heirs. Old Orvis kept this thing from his early years as a soldier, feeling safer by wearing it. He died before he could ever pull the thing out." The priest shook his head at the futility of it, then met Coursen's eyes and held it out to him. "I have noticed that you are unarmed, which is not wise in these dangerous times. I think you could use it, warrior."

Coursen accepted the simple weapon, pulling it free. Mylana could see that the weapon had been well cared for. "My thanks, sir. I will put the sword to good use." He buckled the scabbard around his waist and sheathed the weapon.

The dragon priest nodded and then sighed, looking up at the lightening overcast. "Well, the day is upon us, as much of a day as we ever see anymore. I am worn and must go sleep, even if my quarters have been commandeered by these demon lovers. If you need me, I will be curled up in the back of the worship hall, for that is the only space they did not take over last night." The priest gave each of them a slight bow and then walked off to return to his temple.

"We need to flee again," said Coursen as he watched the man walk away. "We cannot stay here if our enemy is that close."

Mandor nodded. "I will go find Hessilyn. Are you strong enough to help Mylana retrieve our horses and wagon?"

"Yes, I can do that," said Coursen absently, distracted by the approach of the innkeeper.

The middle-aged man came back to the fire, tossing in more rubbish, and then stepped in front of the Attuls. He did not meet their eyes, but looked at the ground. "I...um... I have an offer for you people. Those awful dogs killed some of my customers and now I have to make sure their things are taken care of, you understand? Four of them are known to me. I will see that their belongings are sent on to their families. But...um... one fellow was a stranger, a merchant passing through, along with his two road guards. They came in with a mule train loaded high with goods and winter pelts."

The innkeeper paused as the bonfire sent up a shower of sparks. "Got nowhere to send their belongings, because I know of no kin or business partners. I am going to sell his goods and keep his money purse." He finally looked them in the face. "I am no vulture, though. Understand that, please. I never steal from my customers, especially if one of them dies. The problem with this fellow is that I know of no one to claim his things. Brother Frigard told me to keep the coins. He said to use it to pay for the damages and to help those locals who lost loved ones last night." The innkeeper shook his head at the tragedy. "I will sell what I can sell, at a fair price mind you, and I will keep half of the money in my strong box in case someone comes looking for the poor fellow. Brother Frigard suggested holding it for one year."

"That is all good, sir," said Mandor. "We approve of your actions; however I do not understand how this involves us."

"Oh? Did I not share that? Well, there are six mules in my corral that I now have to get rid of. The Tlocanian ruler at Hightower has ordered that no horse, mule, or donkey can be sold except to the army, and they will pay little to nothing. Brother Frigard suggested that you take the mules. It will not be a sale, so there is nothing to report."

Finally, the Attuls understood what the innkeeper was proposing. They shared a look of surprise and then Mylana responded. "That is generous of you, but we do not want to cause your village more problems."

The innkeeper shook his head in denial. "Taking the mules will alleviate a problem, not create a new one. He left saddles and tack for three of the animals and I think we can find a fourth set of gear. It is small repayment for your fighting and healing work, but please accept our offer." He then held out a crumbled paper. "Take this too. It will prove that they are properly owned beasts, approved by the Tlocanian governor's office in Deep Crossing."

Mandor accepted the paper, folding it up after a quick glance and placing it inside his shirt for safekeeping. "Will you find a place for our wagon and team? The horses are old but can still do a fair day's work."

The innkeeper nodded. "They will be put to good use." He looked over his shoulder at his inn, then back. "Can we use the wagon now? We need to deliver the dead to their loved ones…"

"Please do," said Mandor quickly.

The innkeeper nodded again, gave them each a small bow, and

then retreated to his establishment.

Eric Lorenzen

CHAPTER TWENTY-NINE
Changing Directions

WINTRON

The crown prince looked out from the northernmost tower of Tor Randis. The sun stood high overhead, but smoke hid most of the narrow canyon, smoke billowing from Randisville.

"Your traipsing through the Highlands brought nothing but sorrow," said his uncle from behind him.

Wintron stiffened in reaction but he did not retort. How could he, when the Old Fox spoke only truth? His prideful pursuit of Drass had lost them a hundred men that they desperately needed, while his uncle had stayed in Tor Randis, valiantly defending it against Tlocanian assaults. The duke had even suffered a leg wound in one of the battles, when a spy had tried to breach the gate from inside. No, thought Wintron, he had much to regret. He turned to face his uncle Fors. "I was in error. I apologize for how I wasted good men."

Gurash, standing behind his father, waved off Wintron's words. "You could not have known that Drass had a new way up to the Highlands, my prince. How could any of you have known? Drass accomplished what all considered to be impossible."

Fors gave a scathing look over his shoulder at his son. "A good leader must always consider the impossible, especially when fighting against an army with magic on its side." He turned back to the prince, limping closer. He now used a cane to favor his still-healing leg. "You sacrificed all those men for what? Drass will still cut us off with from the Highlands."

Wintron nodded, frustration and regret warring inside him. "I know my blunder, general; you need not recite it to me. I have said that I am sorry."

"That is not good enough, the gods curse you," spat Fors, striking the floor with his cane. "Your recklessness slaughtered those men just as if you had lined them up for an executioner. If you were one of my officers you would have been stripped of your rank and locked in the cells to await the flogger." He glared at his nephew.

"What do you want from me?" demanded Wintron, now angered. "Do you expect me to relinquish all the leading in this war to you?"

"That would be a fair start," replied the general bluntly. "You are not worthy to command. I have sworn allegiance to you as my future king, but I will still speak truth. You are no general, for you are too reckless. Leave this war to me and I will bring us through it. As long as Tor Randis stands the Border Realm stands, and I will not let this keep fall."

"Do you seek to usurp me as well?" he asked, wondering if Fors was as traitorous as his eldest sons were.

"If that were my plan, then I would have gathered witnesses," stated Fors, motioning to indicate that they were practically alone. "I speak for the good of the realm, Prince Wintron Dabe. You will make a decent king once peace has returned to the Borders, but until then you must let me lead. Will you do this?"

Wintron did not like what Fors said, and he certainly did not fully trust his uncle. Yet, the Old Fox was correct. If anyone could lead the Borderfolk back to freedom, it was the realm's last general. Maybe he had been taking the wrong risks; maybe he ought to risk trusting Fors. Wintron considered, but he could not admit it aloud.

"What? No response?" Fors asked. "Well, if you will not allow me to lead, then I resign my commission. Find yourself some other general, for I will have no part in your slaughtering of more soldiers. I remain your loyal duke, but find someone else to command your army. I will vacate Tor Randis within the week."

Wintron thought quickly. He could not afford to lose the Old Fox and his decades of experience. "If you are loyal, then I order you to stay at Tor Randis to command its defenses. Call yourself duke instead of general if you must, but both of us know that Tor Randis is like a second home to you. Who else could I entrust its defense to?"

His uncle glared. For a moment, Wintron thought he would refuse, but then Fors replied. "I will guard this fortress, but find someone else to run your ill-planned war. I want no part in your inevitable fall."

368

The general turned and limped from the tower room, his last son following in his footsteps.

DRASS

Drass' eyes burned from the smoky air as he walked across the camp set up just outside of Randisville's ruins. There was a bitter taste in his mouth, but not from the fires; it was from failing to kill Wintron. His brother Mordel would not be happy with any failure and Drass felt sure that he would get the sole blame. Mordel wanted his rival eliminated.

The escape of Prince Wintron frustrated him, but surprisingly he did not feel his usual rage. Brother Hurko kept hinting about becoming an "Embraced One" and it was beginning to intrigue him. The priests may have failed in catching Wintron, but they had certainly shown their power. Who else could turn into a dog, hold lightning in his hand, or burn a whole town singlehandedly? These dragon priests were nothing like the doddering old fool who had given Drass his religious instructions on the dragon faith.

He was on his way to visit their tent right now, for they had requested his presence. Actually, it had been more of a command, but he had nothing else to do this evening so he walked to their little camp that sat a bit away from the rundown farmhouse he had confiscated as his headquarters.

Two temple guards stood at the tent opening. One of them held the flap open for him, so Drass stepped through into the dark.

"Lord Drass, welcome," stated Cavish from where he sat on the ground. Drass could only faintly make out his form. "Come, sit with us."

He did so, sitting on some of the cushions and furs piled at the center of the tent. The large tent had been confiscated from a dry goods store before Cavish torched the building. Drass had thought the priests an austere group, yet they seemed comfortable in this setting.

"You are right, that we are more familiar with simple accommodations," said Cavish, once again reading the noble's thoughts. "However, we are not adverse to some comforts on occasion."

He thought wryly that Cavish was not so rude towards him anymore. He said so aloud, for the man would read it in his thoughts anyway.

Cavish did not deny the charge. "Before you were just another pompous lordling, but now you are a candidate for the Embracing. Am I not right? You will take Brother Hurko up on his offer?"

Drass gave a definite nod, knowing the other three could see him clearly. There were three, though at first he had not noticed Brother Frissen sitting further back in the darkness.

"You are fortunate," said Hurko. "You will not have to travel all the way to Tlocania for your testing. You need only go to Regalis. A testing requires Embraced Ones from at least two of the orders, so Regalis will do."

"There are different orders among your kind?" asked Drass, curious but hesitant to press too hard. He guessed that Cavish did not mean priestly orders, but some other type of positions.

"The Embraced serve many roles among the Return," answered Cavish. "You will learn more if you are chosen."

Drass nodded, accepting the restrictions. He was raised in a military home; he knew that new recruits remained ignorant of many things. He did not relish being considered a raw recruit again, but if it would lead to so much power, it would be worth it. That made Drass wonder about something else. When would they want to start this process?

"You are to return with us," answered Hurko to his unspoken question. "We leave tonight."

Drass hesitated. He had duties here: Mordel expected him to seal Tor Randis off from the Highlands and that task was going to be much harder without any Tlocanian help. If he just walked away, his brother would consider him a traitor.

"You will have to make a choice," stated Hurko. "You cannot be your brother's faithful underling and an Embraced One. Choose. Now."

He still hesitated. He had already betrayed his parents, how could he now do the same to his brother?

"Get out," ordered Brother Cavish. "We have no place for timid doubters. I appear to have been mistaken about you, Drass Halen-Dabe."

Drass flung himself on his face before them, afraid that he had ruined his one chance to achieve real power. "I will go with you. I want to become Embraced." He did not fully understand what that term implied. It seemed that he would receive some kind of helper, a companion to indwell him. "I will abide by your commands."

Fallen King

Hurko spoke up. "I say we give him another chance. He may yet learn what obedience means."

Cavish was quiet for a moment, and then gave a slight nod. "Very well. You may join us on our return to Regalis." Cavish looked over to Brother Frissen. "You have witnessed his acceptance; now head off on your assigned task."

Drass looked up from the floor and saw the silent Frissen stepped behind a curtain that hid part of the tent. Drass once again felt an oppressive pressure and then a dreadhound with glowing eyes came out from behind the curtain. The animal gave them all a passing glance, then dove through the tent flaps and ran off.

"Get to your feet," order Hurko. "You have much to do this evening. Set your affairs in order, for you will not be coming back here any time soon. Appoint a new commander and give away your possessions. Candidates for Embracing are not allowed any luxuries."

Drass stood up, his mind full of questions. Who should take over command? Would the priests let him bring coins? A change of clothes? His sword? He had never seen any of the priests wearing swords, but the military officers did.

"You heard him, child," barked Cavish. "Obey!"

He rushed from the tent.

* * *

The dragon priests allowed Drass to ride, for he needed to keep up, but they insisted he abandon his personal tack with all its silvered finery. He was permitted to carry two changes of clothes, a blanket, and plain food, but nothing more. He was not even allowed to keep his coin purse. When he tried to explain to Brother Cavish why the coins might be useful, the priest sent a burst of lightning at him that sent Drass sprawling. All candidates must show unquestioning obedience and they expected him to learn that lesson now. They no longer considered him a noble; he was simply a candidate for Embracing.

When they stopped for the night in a meadow, Drass quickly learned that they expected him to do his share of camp duties right alongside the soldiers. He did all that was assigned to him without complaint, but the scowl never left his face and he took note of how the sergeant and one other guard seemed to enjoy ordering him around.

Not until all his duties were done to the satisfaction of the sergeant, was he allowed to get his plate of food. The bread was hard and the stew cooled, yet he ate all of it with gusto, squatting next to the fire to get some warmth. As he ate, Drass went over the day and the many slights he had received, promising himself to get revenge for each. He guessed that the priests probably monitored his thoughts, but he could not help it. At least he controlled his thoughts towards the two priests. Actually, he was too frightened of them to plot any retribution towards them.

After dinner, he was summoned to the large tent the priests shared. The two priests sat on the bare ground, the only light coming from a sullen fire that filled the tent with smoke. His eyes started burning as soon as the tent flap closed behind him, but he suppressed a cough out of fear that it might offend the two.

"Do not dawdle, candidate," rebuked Cavish. "Place a little wood onto the fire and then sit down in front of us. It is time for your first lesson."

Drass hurried to obey, hoping that the new wood would burn cleaner. The fire did burn brighter for a moment, but then Brother Hurko tossed some incense into the flames. The light dimmed and more smoke filled the air, though now it had a sweet scent.

He sat down and waited. Were they going to teach him some of their magic now?

"No, not now," answered Hurko aloud. "Only the Embraced Ones can work the blood magic. Instead, tonight we will teach you about our beliefs."

Drass nodded. As a child, he had been tutored on the dragon faith but maybe there was a higher mystery to the faith.

"Your ignorance is showing again, child," remarked Cavish, overhearing his thoughts. "We will not be teaching you about the dragon religion; that is what is taught to the masses. Do you really think Hurko or I bow to flying beasts? Do you think dragons endow us with our powers? If so, then you are deceived like so many other fresh candidates. My power comes from my ally, the Other by whom I am Embraced. It is the same for Hurko.

"Tonight, we will teach you the basics of what we believe; what we know to be true. We will share with you just a sliver of the vast knowledge that comes to anyone who is Embraced."

Drass leaned forward, suddenly eager.

WINTRON

After his confrontation with his uncle, Wintron had spent the day walking the ramparts of Tor Randis, thinking. He was cordial to every sentry he encountered, but he did not linger to talk with any of them. As dusk approached, he found himself looking southward from the keep's high wall, peering down the steep canyon to where the Dragon Shadow lurked. The late sun shone on the monolith that stood at the head of the Borderheart Valley, though from the backside the Old Man had no human resemblance. The dark clouds washed against the granite, and Wintron imagined it probably covered the Old Man to his chin. He saw red lightning flashing in the clouds regularly.

"There you are," came a voice from behind him.

Wintron turned to see his cousin Gurash, accompanied by Lord Briv Goorsol. Gurash was still heavily bandaged from their narrow escape but he looked rested. Wintron nodded at the two, but did not go over to them. He looked again southward, but the sun had sunk beyond the far mountains and now the Dragon Shadow was lost in the gloom. Night's coolness touched them in the form of a chill breeze following the canyon. The keep's banners snapped overhead, showing both the royal Dabe white ram on a gray field and the Halen-Dabe eagle on blue.

A murder of crows suddenly rose up and squawked past just as the two newcomers came to stand beside him. Wintron looked straight down, to where the birds had come from, and saw the remains of enemy soldiers on the rocks below. Fors had refused to gather them up, so they rotted where they fell. Only their own had been retrieved. "When did they last attack?"

"They have been quiet," admitted Lord Briv, leaning over the wide wall. "It has been two days since the Tlocanians and Mordel tried to overwhelm us. The assault was brief yet intense. Those dragon priests flung fire up at us ceaselessly while their soldiers slipped close with ladders. They almost breeched the gatehouse."

"Yet they have never come close to taking the keep," observed Wintron. "Even if they had gained the gatehouse top, we could have easily swept them clear."

Lord Briv turned his attention to his prince. "True enough, but now they are behind us too, and Tor Randis is not nearly so formidable towards the north."

He sighed. "That is true. Fors will have his hands full."

"I hear that we have also lost the canyon watchtower," added Gurash. All of them looked toward the tower barely peeking over a ridge in the canyon below. They could see no one on that top walk or any light, but that did not mean it was empty.

Wintron suddenly wondered what had happened to Lieutenant Fontar who had commanded that outpost, as well as the sergeant that Wintron had assigned to join Fontar. Most likely, they had died when the post had fallen. More lives lost. "I wonder how many soldiers crowd in the canyon."

"Fors hesitates to send any more scouts to find out," answered Lord Briv. "We have already lost four."

Wintron looked away from the tower, feeling responsible even for those losses. The crows came back for one last feeding before going to roost for the night. Wintron did not want to watch, so he stepped back from the wall. He was about to ask Briv another question, when all heard a shout from the gatehouse. The crows flew up in a flurry.

Wintron and the others all rushed to the wall to see what caused the commotion. Looking carefully, they finally spotted what the sentry had: two robed men plodding up the road. It seemed the Tlocanians were going to attack again. "Do their priests always walk ahead of the army?"

"No, my prince." Briv frowned. "I have always seen them shelter their dragon priests. Where are the temple guards? Where are the Tlocanian soldiers or even Mordel's ragtag rebels? In addition, the priests approach bareheaded. Something is odd here."

One of the priests held up a pole on which a dirty white cloth hung. They seemed worn out, leaning on each other as they continued to climb the steep grade up to the fortress.

"Is that a parlay flag?" asked Wintron.

"What kind of trick are they trying?" wondered Briv. "I hope the guards do not open the gate for those two. We should leave the wall, my prince, for the dragon priests have quite a range with their fireballs."

"You can leave if you are fearful," stated Wintron, "but I will loiter here. I promise that I will duck behind the stonework if they work any of their magic."

Briv did not seem happy, but he stayed at his leader's side. Gurash had ignored their exchange and kept his eyes on the scene below. He called out to the other two, pointing out more activity. Apparently, someone opened the sally door, for they spotted a half-squad marching along the wall's base. The drawbridge dropped over the dry ravine that ran just beyond the fort's foot and the ten marched across. The drawbridge rose again as soon as they crossed. The two priests stopped to rest, letting the soldiers cover the distance between them. There was a lengthy discussion between the two parties and then one soldier ran back to the walls to report. He yelled his message up to his commander, but Wintron was too high up the ramparts to hear.

"What do you think is occurring?" asked Gurash. "I cannot imagine an offer of peace, not from Mordel or the Tlocanians."

"It is rather peculiar," agreed Wintron. His curiosity rose. Mordel and the Tlocanians would not yet have news of the defeat at Randisville, so what were their intentions? He did not want to remain ignorant any further. "Let us go find the general. I would guess he is near the gate."

Wintron strode off along the wall towards the nearest tower. The other two had to scurry to catch up. They made their way down through Tor Randis and over to the gatehouse. Fors was indeed there, talking with the major in charge.

Wintron walked over and interrupted them, having no desire to show any courtesy to his uncle. The only way he could control his continuing anger towards the old man was to ignore him. Therefore, Wintron turned his attention to the major. "What is happening? Who are those two?"

Fors gave a cold stare for his nephew's rudeness, but Wintron disregarded him, concentrating on the major. The man looked between the two and then gave Wintron a quick explanation. "They claim to be the High Priest of Cha and a dragon priest of the Azure Order, although his black robe is trimmed in red. They say they fled the Tlocanians to bring us a warning. They claim that the Tlocanians plot to sacrifice over two thousand in one of their magical rites."

"I have my doubts over this story," stated Fors, with a frown. "I think it an attempt to lure us out."

Wintron raised an eyebrow at his uncle. "Surely you have someone who knows the High Priest. I would trust the Father Bilchaso's word, for he has been a dependable man."

Fors leaned on his cane harder, as if feeling his age. "What if Cha's high priest has been possessed like so many of the dragon priests? You know the stories reported to your father over a year ago, that the Tlocanians take over priests, nobles, and military officers, changing their personalities and giving them magical powers. I know you heard the reports, Wintron, for we were both in attendance when Varen was told. Who is to say that the Tlocanians cannot do the same to priests of other religions?"

"I will not have these two slain out of fear; we must hear them out." Wintron held the general's eyes until the man finally gave a reluctant nod. Wintron turned to the major. "Have the two brought in and placed in separate rooms, with guards ready to slay them should they show any signs of magic. Keep them in the gatehouse; I do not want them inside the main keep."

"Tie each with stout cords, with his hands turned towards his body," added Fors. "The power seems to flow from their fingertips and palms."

"I would suggest you bring in the Cha priest first," said Gurash. "If he is somehow under the influence of the other, then separating them might break that hold."

The major nodded understanding to all their instructions then strode off to give his orders to his men.

As soon as the officer left, Fors turned to his nephew. "I would suggest that we withdraw from the gatehouse, in case something goes awry. I will have reinforcements sent in, just in case." He paused to give a growling sigh. "I pray that we are not inviting in our own destruction."

Wintron also sighed. "I pray that as well my uncle, but we must take some risks, especially to gain information from the Borderheart Valley. We could have them questioned out there, on the roadside, but that would leave everyone exposed. What if these two are being followed? It is best to bring them inside and then question them thoroughly." Wintron moved towards the door. "But you are right that we should vacate the gatehouse. If I am wrong, then this will become a dangerous place soon."

The four of them took the stairway down and came out in the tunnel underneath the gatehouse. Wintron could not help but look at the great ironbound gates, still closed and properly barred. Four soldiers stood guard on this side. Wintron knew that more men waited in the rooms above the tunnel, behind the dark holes in the ceiling, ready to rain down arrows or pour hot oil on any invaders who made it past the gate.

Wintron and the others turned in the other direction and walked out of the gatehouse, following the cobblestone road through another pair of gates under the keep's main wall and into a large assembly yard. A few stars already shone overhead as night approached. Out of the shadows, Yosif stepped in front of them.

Wintron stopped, surprised to see the sergeant already returned to duty, for he had received a fair amount of wounds during their mad ride through Randisville. Fors, Gurash, and Briv also stopped, curious.

The soldier gave them each a nod, but he focused on Wintron, giving him a smart salute. "My prince, how am I to guard you if you wander off without notice?"

"You were getting your wounds tended. Do not worry Yosif; I did not leave the keep."

"Have you forgotten the assassins who tried to feather you from Tor Randis' walls?" asked Yosif.

In truth, Wintron had forgotten. He would have to ask Fors if the two had ever been caught, but did not want to do so at this moment. "I was as safe as I could be, for I kept mainly to the guard walks and towers."

Yosif looked around to emphasize that they stood in a courtyard exposed to many heights, but he did not argue further. Instead, he returned to another topic. "May I have your permission to recruit men to your personal guard? You will need more protection than just I can provide."

Wintron inwardly winced at the reminder. All of his other guards had perished in the Highlands, with the last ones falling during their fight through Randisville. He wanted to deny Yosif the chance to recruit more, but he knew he could not. Hence, he gave the man a nod. "See to the recruiting."

Yosif gave him another salute then motioned another to come out of the shadows. Apparently, his first recruit was already nearby. Scout Orgel stepped forward, seeming uncomfortable in his new role as bodyguard to a noble, but he took his place next to the prince. Yosif headed off to the barracks to see about additional guards. Wintron, Fors, Gurash, and Briv headed off to find warm drinks to hold off the night's chill. Orgel followed, staying ever vigilant.

* * *

It was nearly midnight when Wintron finally had a chance to question Father Bilchaso. He and Duke Fors went to talk with the elderly man. They found the high priest of the Fortress God sitting against a wall in an empty room. He was just starting to nod off, so when they entered his head snapped up and he forced his eyes open.

"Finally you are here, my prince. I would rise to my feet, but I cannot in these bonds." His hands were still tied behind him so that the palms pressed against his lower back, making his elbows stick out to either side.

Wintron squatted down near the priest so that he was at eye level. "Father Bilchaso, what is this talk about a mass slaughter?"

"It is true, my prince. The Tlocanians must perform some vile ritual to create an anchor for the Dragon Shadow. They plan to sacrifice thousands to work their blood magic."

"How is it that they let you leave Regalis?" asked Fors.

"No one allowed me to leave, Duke Fors. I fled with the help of another priest…"

"That dragon priest? You claim that he is some innocent?" Fors' voice revealed his doubt.

"Do you know nothing of the dragon religion, Fors?" asked Bilchaso. "Brother Werth is of the Azure Order, while the others are of the Crimson Order. Werth is a Borderman who served the dragons long before the others infiltrated. The only reason he wears a red-trimmed robe is as a disguise. He pretended to be one of the Crimson so we could make our escape from the city."

Fors would not back down. "Is he the one who told you these wild stories? How do you know that he has not deceived you? Maybe you have brought one of the enemy into our midst, priest."

"Werth and I grew up together in the streets of Regalis," replied Bilchaso. "I know him well, even though we are of different faiths. He fears those black dogs and the secret rites of sacrifice disgust him. You know me, Fors Halen-Dabe. Do you not trust my ability to judge a man's motives?"

When Fors did not answer, Wintron spoke up. "I trust you, Father Bilchaso." Wintron stood and motioned the guards over. "Untie him and be gentle about it, for the father is not a young man anymore."

He watched as the two men did as ordered and then helped the elderly priest to his feet. "Come with me, Father Bilchaso, and we will find more comfortable accommodations."

The priest rubbed his aching hands together. "What about my companion? It is not right for me to enjoy freedom while he still suffers."

Wintron quickly replied, before his uncle could. "I will have Brother Werth released as well. I want to hear the full story from both of you."

* * *

Wintron stepped outside, hoping the predawn cold would chase off his sleepiness. Sergeant Yosif stepped out with him, carefully scanning the shadows, rooftops, and high walls. The prince wondered at the man's stamina, for he did not seem at all tired. Wintron stretched and suppressed a yawn.

The questioning of Bilchaso and Werth had taken long, and not just because of his uncle's doubts. Honestly, Wintron had many of the same concerns; he just let his uncle express them. What the two old priests told about the Tlocanian plans was truly horrifying. He shivered and it was not because of the cold.

Mordel had broken his promise to protect the citizens who remained behind. Instead, he would let his allies kill thousands of them. Thousands. How could anyone do such a crime? Murdering people for power? Killing on the battlefield could be justified because both sides were armed and ready to kill, but this was simply a slaughter. A butchering of Wintron's people.

"My prince, can you go back inside?" asked Yosif, his eyes still on the many shadows around them. He tried to keep his body between Wintron and the shadows across this small courtyard. "The darkness conceals too much. Those assassins could be taking aim at this very moment."

"I will do so." Another yawn threatened to escape. How could he feel so tired instead of being on fire with rage? Maybe it was just shock from the news. He realized that he was in no condition to make any major decisions. "I want to head back to my rooms and try to get at least a little sleep. I will need to be sharp for what must be done."

He turned back to the door and started turning the handle, when Yosif shouted and pushed him roughly to the side. Wintron fell to the stones, skinning a hand and knee. Yosif yelled again and then fumbled to open the door, a door with an arrow lodged in it. The prince crawled through, with Yosif right behind him. They heard two more arrows thump into the wooden door.

"Are you injured my prince?" asked Yosif, looking him over carefully.

He brushed gravel off his scratched hand. "No, I am fine but for a few new bruises. Did you see where they lurked? Can we send soldiers after them?"

"We can send troopers, but the two will be far gone," replied Yosif. "I saw just the faintest of movement on the wall above the one skirting the courtyard. If they had been closer they would not have missed."

"I am glad Avoli has not demanded my soul tonight," said Wintron, adding a silent prayer to the Winter Goddess, asking that she also spare the many lives threatened down in Regalis. For some reason, he also felt the sudden need to ask the same thing of El, Rolen's god. "Thank you for your diligence, Yosif. Are you hurt at all?"

"I am uninjured," assured the sergeant, "but we should take a different route back to your rooms if we want to remain uninjured. Those two might relocate to try again. May we go back by way of the barracks? Some of the new recruits should be released from their other duties by now."

The prince nodded his permission, willing to admit that more guards were needed. As they headed off towards the barracks, Wintron hoped they would have no more trouble, for he was just too tired to react quickly. They retrieved four others at the barracks and then made it safely to his suite, where Orgel already stood guard. Wearily, the prince went into his bedroom and collapsed on the bed, hoping that sleep would come and chase off some of these waking nightmares.

* * *

Wintron awoke to a persistent knock. Groggily, he told the person to enter. Orgel came in, though he clung to the door handle. "My prince, I apologize for waking you, but the general has asked to see you. There is some kind of trouble to the north."

He sat up and ran a hand through his unruly hair. His clothes were wrinkled from sleeping in them. A bad taste lingered in his mouth. The dark circles under his eyes attested to his failure at catching a good rest. Overall, he knew he was in a foul mood, so he paused to form his answer. "Please tell the general's messenger that I will join him shortly... and find out where I am to locate the Old Fox."

Orgel nodded and quickly withdrew. Wintron forced himself to get up and use the cold water on the nightstand to wash his face. That helped a little. He stripped off his rumbled shirt and washed his upper torso too, then found a clean shirt. The rest of his clothes would have to do.

* * *

When Wintron arrived at the duke's study, he found Gurash also there. The Old Fox looked up from a map that he was studying with a group of officers. He motioned the prince to come over. As Wintron approached, the officers separated and he suddenly recognized the man on the other side of the table.

"Bilshor? Bilshor!" He rushed over and gave the captain a bear hug, and then held him out at arm's length. "How is this possible? I left you on a suicide stand."

"It is good to see you alive, my prince," replied Bilshor. "When the Tlocanians suddenly left, I feared they had captured you. I debated on whether to pursue their withdrawing army or coming here for help. I am glad I chose Tor Randis."

Wintron insisted on hearing his tale right then, no matter what other concerns Fors had. Bilshor complied, telling about his desperate stand on that rocky promontory, enduring one attack after another, with fireballs in between. He lost half of his men, but then one night the attacks stopped. By morning, the Tlocanian infantry could no longer be seen. Scouts found them marching back in the direction of Halenvale. Bilshor knew better than to try pursuing. Instead, he turned his suffering troop towards Tor Randis. He found Drass' motley cavalry when he arrived in Randisville this morning and fought his way through without too much trouble.

"I would have pressed my attack against them to a full rout, but I was desperate to get here and report what had happened. I had no idea that you were already safely here."

"Are Drass' men truly so disorganized?" asked Wintron, surprised at such a change.

"We captured a pair of soldiers who have since talked. They tell of Drass leaving with the dragon priests. The officer left in charge has apparently endured some insurrection among the mercenaries. I think you will find them easy pickings."

"The news keeps getting better," exclaimed Wintron, but then he saw what maps Fors had been studying, maps of the Highlands. He swept them aside. "No! You have it wrong, general. We cannot concentrate on our backyard now, not when thousands are at risk. It is time for boldness. Tomorrow, we will march on Regalis."

For once, his uncle was speechless.

"Bilshor, do you think you can clean out the last of Drass' riffraff if I replace the men you lost?" asked Wintron.

"With a hundred mounted men? Yes. I will do so, my prince, even if it takes until winter."

"Good. You will have your hundred then. Chase down as many of the fleeing as you can. If they hold up in some keep, then set a watch and send word back here so that we can mount a siege. Also, I want you to head for Halenvale and find out how those Tlocanians got up onto the Highlands in the first place." He gave his old friend one more slap on the back, unable to restrain his pleasure at seeing him again. Bilshor's presence meant that he had another trustworthy officer, and those were a scarcity right now. "While you are securing the Highlands, the rest of us will be fighting our way to Regalis."

Fors finally spoke out. "Wintron! Do not do this. You cannot commit all of our remaining army to a blind charge into the fog. No matter how sincere those two priests are, it still might be a trap."

The prince nodded, for he knew that was a possibility. "I will have the scouts range far and wide to prevent any surprises. However, we must try to stop this atrocity. How can I ever claim to be king if I stand aside while the enemy slaughters our people? The risk is great, but the consequences of doing nothing will be far worse. I understand if you want to remain here, uncle, though I would prefer you at my side."

Fors glared at him for a long time, but then finally lowered his eyes with a mutter and a shake of his head. "I will join you, though Gurash will have to stay behind. That way, at least one member of the family will be sheltered."

Gurash protested, claiming he to be healthy enough to ride, but on this Wintron agreed with his uncle. "You must stay here, Gurash, for I am officially declaring you my heir."

That news silenced the room. No one had expected Wintron to make such a declaration. After a moment, Gurash protested. "But my father should be next in line."

"I need your father as general, not heir," replied Wintron, noting out of the corner of his eye his uncle's nod of approval. He had meant to discuss this with Fors in private, but once again his own impetuousness won out. "You will remain my heir unless I should marry and have children." He laughed at the notion. "Even should a woman want my hand in marriage, she would likely be some aged widow past child bearing years, so you are secure Gurash. After me, you shall rule the Border Realm."

"I am glad that is settled," remarked Fors under his breath, but loud enough for the prince to hear.

Wintron ignored the comment, calling instead for a map of the Borderheart Valley. "We have an attack to plan."

DRASS

Drass ran, his breath ragged, sweat soaking his shirt. Brother Cavish had declared this his punishment for being prideful. He struggled to keep up with the riders, his pride the only thing that gave him strength. Drass' thoughts kept coming back to the priests, how he would like to take revenge on them. Yet each time his mind dwelt on that dangerous subject, Drass would force himself to think about something else. It was the priests who would initiate him to these powerful secrets.

He stumbled over a half-buried rock, but kept going. Finally, the road began to descend into a valley and he found it easier to keep up with the horses. When they came to the bottom of the grade, Cavish called them all to a halt, letting Drass take a deep drink from a waterskin.

"I hope you have learned from this lesson, candidate. Now, get up on your horse, for we need to make better time. We are expected in Regalis within a few days and we still need to retrieve your niece."

Drass sincerely thanked the holy brother for his lesson and then gratefully got up on his horse. Not until they were moving again did he consider what else Cavish had said. Someone in Regalis already knew that he was now a candidate and he doubted that was his brother Mordel. Also, they wanted Zita for something. These Tlocanians were deep thinkers, with subtle plots and grand schemes. Drass wondered if he would acquire that skill once he became an Embraced One. He would like that, though not as much as the new powers he would gain.

Eric Lorenzen

CHAPTER THIRTY

Down into the Fog

WINTRON

Dawn colored the mountaintops as five thousand soldiers departed Tor Randis, one third of them on horseback. Wintron and Fors rode side-by-side among the forward cavalry squadron, though neither talked. They traveled past the empty watchtower, its door missing. The prince felt a chill from the stark spire, a feeling like someone watched him. It made his skin crawl. He fought off the urge to go investigate, though, for there was no time. The army needed no more delays or distractions. He also passed scattered bones along the side of the road and knew that dreadhounds had feasted on those killed or captured here. He made a mental note to send someone back here to give those poor victims a proper burial.

The army traveled ever lower, their passage echoing across the otherwise-silent canyon. By the time they came to the Dragon Shadow, the sun was high enough to light the steep ravine. General Fors called for a halt when two of their scouts rode up out of the fog to give their report. Wintron recognized one of them as Orgel, back in his comfortable clothes. The pause was brief, however, for they reported a clear road ahead all the way down to the post house at the foot of Old Man. Upon hearing the horn calls to march, the squad leaders sent their men forward.

Somewhere near the head of the force rode Major Cilano, Fors' second, whom the general insisted on bringing along rather than leaving him behind to assist Gurash at the keep. Wintron had his doubts about Cilano, for the man seemed for more committed to the general than even to his country. This might be Wintron's army, but most had not sworn fealty to him personally. It felt like he rode a half-wild stallion, unsure if it would buck this time or not.

At first the Dragon Shadow was barely noticeable, just a haziness to the air. Yet as they rode lower, the clouds grew thicker and soon the sun was lost to them. The ravine became thicker with trees the lower they rode, making it even darker. At some turns, Wintron could hear the river roaring in its rocky channel, but most of the time he only heard the men and horses moving with him. The forest remained quiet around them. Even the skies were silent, with no red lightning or rolling thunder. He mentioned that to Fors.

The Old Fox nodded. "I noticed that as well, but I do not know if it bodes well or ill for us. Are they saving their energies for this Shadow Anchor rite or are they setting some ambush for us? When we get to the bottom, I want to ask the priests about this anomaly."

Wintron nodded agreement.

DRASS

Drass, his niece Zita, the dragon priests, and four temple guards climbed into one of the large baskets. Zita still sulked about her capture, for she would have rather stayed with her grandmother than return to her parents. The priests would have none of her fits though, and one near blast of their power was enough to silence Zita's tongue. Drass paid her no more heed, for she was Mordel's spawn. He was just glad to be standing, for they had been riding hard for too long. The stop in Halenvale had been just long enough to switch mounts and grab his niece.

The basket creaked and swayed as they climbed in. He concentrated on the marvelous contraption again. It pitched as it swung out over the deep ravine and, for a moment, they just hung there rocking back and forth. Finally, the basket began its descent, a jarring, swirling ride down the mountainside. As the basket spun, he saw first the sheer granite wall and then the open air. He looked down at the quickly approaching sea of clouds. The sun stood high enough to light the top of the Dragon Shadow even in this narrow ravine, but the sun could only brush the dark and sullen cloud billows. Drass appreciated the mood.

As they dropped into the cool mists and lost sight of the rim, he had a sudden fear about the operators not knowing when to slow their descent because they could no longer see the basket. His grip on the basket's lip tightened, but then he just as quickly dismissed the fear. The rope leads were an exact length and the horse team had done this task dozens of times. They would know when to slow and when to stop.

The basket continued to spin lazily, but he mostly saw only clouds around them. A few times, the cliff face came near enough to lurk out of the mist, but the basket never scrapped. Finally, Drass heard the men who manned the landing as they shouted to one another on who would first grab the basket. The lift slowed as it neared the end of the line, but its spinning continued. First one man jumped up and grabbed hold of a dangling guide rope, trying to stop its revolutions. Another man caught a line on the opposite side of the basket. They had the thing stable just as it jerked to a halt, just above the floor of the landing platform. Two other men pushed a wooden stairway over so that the occupants could climb out.

Horses waited nearby. He noticed that someone had anticipated his presence, for the count was just right. The animals were fresh, so they made good time riding out of the steep canyon. The priests wanted to be in Regalis by nightfall and it looked like they would make it. They came to the Valley Road somewhere between Glenford and Regalis and turned north.

As he rode, Drass considered what lay ahead. He realized that the offer of becoming Embraced had not been a spontaneous thing: Cavish and Hurko had been ordered to pursue him. The thought brought him comfort. Someone thought that he was important enough to recruit. They also seemed to be in a hurry to get him initiated. Though they warned that not all candidates were accepted, Drass had no doubts about himself. They would not have taken so much effort if they were not already certain of his suitability. He hoped the process would be quick, for then he could face his brother as an equal... or even as a superior.

The Dragon Shadow hugged the ground once they were in the Borderheart Valley, so there were no vistas. Drass saw only grayness everywhere, which turned to black as the daylight began to wane. It made for a monotonous ride. Finally, they reached Regalis' south gates, which suddenly loomed out of the foggy darkness. Cavish let red lightning dance in one hand as he pounded on the rough wood with the other hand. Upon seeing the display of power, the tower watch yelled for the gates to be opened.

Passing through, they rode quickly onward. Regalis seemed too quiet. Although the night was still young, not many lights flickered in the windows. Drass did not know if this was due to the people having no fuel or because so many houses lay empty. Either way, it did not reflect well on Mordel's reign.

When they came to the Temple District, he was startled at the change. The Five Dragons Temple stood alone now; all the other temples and chapels gone, with only some rubble showing their old outlines. The dragon temple loomed out of the darkness, torches lighting its entrance gate and revealing the squad of temple guards on duty. He had expected this to be their destination, yet they kept riding. He now knew better than to ask any questions, but still he wondered.

They turned towards the King's Keep and when the keep came into view, Drass saw something strange. The clouds seemed thinner around the fortress, allowing him to see more. A faint red light shot skyward from the keep's highest tower. It gave off a hum and a thrumming he could feel in his chest.

They rode through the keep's gates, where he had another surprise. Tlocanians guarded the fortress, instead of Mordel's men. Drass kept quiet, but he could not still his many questioning thoughts. Was his brother still in power? If so, where was Mordel? Surely he was not foolish enough to be attacking Tor Randis from below? That would only be a waste of men. Maybe he was sharing the King's Keep with the invaders. Well, if the Tlocanian command had moved into the keep, he did not blame them for replacing Mordel's riffraff with their own seasoned troops.

They stopped at the stables, surrendering their horses. Zita was sent off with two of the guards without any explanation to Drass. He did not really care, except that if any harm came to her then Mordel would surely blame him. He was just glad she had not attacked him during this trip, for the little bobcat liked trying out her claws. Apparently, the priests had intimidated her enough.

He followed the priests inside the keep, past vigilant soldiers, and up the grand stairway. They climbed almost to the top of the keep, coming out on one of the floors that had been used by King Varen's many officials but now belonged to the dragon priests. Temple guards stood at attention on this floor, instead of empire's army, and the smell of incense lingered.

At the smell, Drass wondered if he would want to be a dragon priest. He already understood that not all Embraced Ones wore black robes, but he had the impression that most did. He wondered if he would be given an option or if they would assign him a place. He would not find much pleasure in doing minor chores or playing the pious role. Drass realized that he did not know very much about how this worked. Was he making the right choice? Should he not demand more answers first?

Hurko must have caught his thoughts, for he looked over his shoulder and posed a question, "Candidate Drass, have you wondered what others are thinking? As an Embraced One, you will have the power to know."

Before he could reply, Cavish interrupted with his own question for Hurko. "Did you notice that the Shadow Anchor is still not complete? Is that why we have been recalled?" The other priest did not respond, at least not aloud.

Cavish turned down another corridor, past two silent guards. The only lights were small lamps set under red shades, giving their route a faint red glow. The way was narrower, so that Cavish had to walk in front of Hurko. Whether purposefully or not, he spoke loud enough for Drass to overhear. "Mark my words: we will be recruited to initiation duties."

"Enough of that, Cavish-Screnvor," replied Hurko. Drass was surprised at how much deeper Hurko's voice had become. It was if another person walked just ahead of him in that dark hallway. "You will do your duty, even if it means standing on the center tower. Your life is worth nothing in comparison to our cause. We are here to bring about the Return. Remember that, Cavish-Screnvor."

"I hear and obey," responded Brother Cavish, sounding intimidated.

Drass reconsidered who was the superior between the two. He had always thought it was Cavish, who was the most outspoken, yet Hurko had just humbled the other. Cavish came to the end of the hall and walked through an open doorway into a small, spare room where another priest stood waiting in the shadows.

"Brothers Hurko and Cavish, welcome back to Regalis." The very tall priest gave each a slight nod. Drass could see nothing of the man's face within the cowl, but the voice sounded older.

"High Brother Zuler-Sostono, your request lacked details," replied Hurko. Once again, he noted the deeper voice. "I was surprised at our recall, for some other plans have been either ruined or compromised by our early return."

"Colonel Ulen-Snargrof is the one who told me to recall you, Hurko-Sporrid. If you have a complaint, take it to him. Events in the larger world change our plans, brother. The lord emperor has turned his eyes elsewhere, so we must also. The lord-general and most of his officers are now marching back to the capitol, leaving us shorthanded among the Embraced." He paused for a moment to let them absorb the information. "The taking of Tor Randis is no longer vital to our cause. As for your other assignment…" He gave a slight nod towards Drass. "He will either accept his new role or die."

"True enough," mulled Hurko. "May I ask what our new duties are?"

Zuler did not reply; instead, he gave a questioning motion towards Drass.

"Oh, out with it," said Cavish peevishly. "He is uninitiated now, but I suspect you plan to change that very soon."

Zuler gave a slight nod. "The two of you must help with the Shadow Anchor. We had some…difficulties while building it and are now short on staff."

Drass' companions did not respond but he sensed a new tenseness. Frankly, his thoughts dwelt more on what Ulen said about his having to accept or die. It no longer sounded like he would be making a choice. They expected him to submit to this secretive rite or else. Though he still hungered for the power, he did not like their methods.

Zuler moved towards another door, pausing as he touched the door's handle. "He is to be tested tonight. The Listening Room is nearly ready, so you might as well take him to the Preparation Chamber."

"Tonight?" asked Hurko, sounding displeased.

"I began the preparations as soon as I heard you were on your way here." Zuler opened the door, but did not turn his back yet. "I set the time as a favor to the two of you, so that you have a chance to rest before the Shadow Anchor dedication rites start in earnest."

Drass wondered how the High Brother could have received word ahead of their arrival. Was it one of those were-dogs or just a galloping messenger?

"Well I, for one, want to get this over with quickly and get on to some sleep," said Cavish. He took hold of Drass' arm. "You are to come with us, candidate."

He pulled free, but then thought better of open rebellion and turned his maneuver into a small bow. "Lead the way, holy brother."

He tried to sound submissive but he knew it lacked sincerity. He expected Cavish to give him another punishment. Apparently the time was pressing, for the priest ignored his behavior and pointed for him to head towards another door. High Brother Zuler was already gone.

The time for his testing had arrived, the test to see if he was worthy to become an Embraced One.

"Move, candidate," repeated Cavish, starting to sound peeved again.

Drass hurriedly obeyed, striding through the door that Hurko opened. He felt his heartbeat quicken, for the priests implied peril in the testing. He tried to swallow, but his mouth became suddenly dry. This was not like facing an opponent in battle, where the enemy was obvious. Danger seemed near, but he did not know its face.

* * *

Leaving the Preparation Chamber, Drass walked barefoot behind the two priests. The stone floor was cold. He walked naked but for his underpants, with blood smeared on his chest in strange patterns. He guessed it to be human blood. The pair had chanted over him in different voices, as if four beings attended him instead of just the two. Other than terse instructions, they did not talk to him and he dared not ask any more questions. Whatever they were chanting, it caused the hair on his body to stand on end. Even now, as he walked down the almost-dark hallway, he felt power pulsing in the air around him.

They entered a red-lit room where the smell of blood almost overpowered him. This must be the Listening Room. Another priest already waited inside, standing behind an altar. In the dim light Drass could not be certain, but the priest's robes seemed wet from something. He wondered if it might be more blood.

As he stepped into the room, Drass almost slipped on the wet floor. He looked down and saw more than just blood smeared on the stones. He retched violently.

WINTRON

Wintron stared at another empty hamlet as the army rode through. Fors sat on a horse beside him while a scout's mount pranced in front of them. "Have you found no one else?" Wintron asked of Orgel.

"Only her people," answered Orgel, pointing towards the woman he had brought back with him, "and they had hidden their settlement well. We only found it because Scout Herdon is from the area and knew there should be a lane heading through the woods." The scout patted his horse's neck, though it seemed he was the one needing comfort. "Every other village and farm we have searched is empty. All the land north of Regalis seems empty. I know many fled to Tor Randis, but not everyone did. I know the king slayer gave you solemn promises, my prince, but this woman claims that the Tlocanians have taken them all. You will want to hear her stories, though they seem far fetched…"

Wintron sighed. "I fear that she is right, that the others have been taken captive."

"But my prince, what about Mordel's promised amnesty?" asked the scout.

Fors answered him before Wintron could. "Who would trust a king slayer to keep his word? Mordel has betrayed these people twice, killing their rightful monarch and then failing to protect them after he claimed the throne for himself. May he be twice cursed by the gods."

"What about dreadhounds or enemy soldiers? Have you seen any lurking about?" asked Wintron.

"They are absent too, my prince. We have not ridden within sight of the city walls yet, but we have found no one, at least no one who is alive. As for the dogs, we heard distant howling, but it must have been from within the city itself."

"Any of the red lightning?" asked Fors.

Orgel looked skyward at the mention of lightning, but shook his head. "None of that either."

"I do not like this," muttered Fors. "Why are they silent? It feels like they are luring us into a deadly trap."

"Maybe it is as Brother Werth guessed," said Wintron. "The creating of this Shadow Anchor is taking all of their focus and strength. It would explain why their army has pulled back, for the priests may be vulnerable while so preoccupied."

The duke frowned. "I pray that it is so, but we must plan for the worst." He turned back to Orgel. "Order the scouts to skirt around the city and see if the land is similarly empty beyond, and then have the most furtive of your group sneak up on the city to find what he can see or overhear."

Orgel saluted. "I will do as you say, my general." He turned his horse and rode off into the fog. Farmer Borgella nervously watched the scout leave. The woman seemed almost tempted to ride after him, thought Wintron.

"I do not like this," repeated Fors.

"I concur," said Wintron. "However, we must press on, for there are thousands of lives at stake." He turned his attention to the farmer woman, the only one brave enough in her community to come out and talk to him. "Please come closer, Borgella, for we have some questions for you."

The woman brought her horse nearer. She was a middle-aged woman, weathered yet still handsome for her age. Her long, gray-streaked hair was pulled back into a ponytail. The animal she rode frisked, reflecting the nervousness of its rider. "How can I help you, sirs?"

"How many people are hiding in Wardem Dell?" asked Wintron softly.

"Counting the little ones, we have about three dozen. About half are from our village and the rest are from the surrounding countryside. We gathered in as many as we could before hiding the roads. I wish it could have been more, but there was no time."

"What happened to all the others?"

"Eaten or taken." Borgella shook her head at the loss. "None of us wanted to evacuate when we were told. I know you wanted us to, Prince Wintron, but we had new crops sprouting and two of our women were close to birthing. As a group, we decided to stay, for no one ever bothers us in Wardem Dell. We are so small a place and tucked away among the trees, even the peddlers forget to drop by. No army would trouble with us. Many of our neighboring settlements felt the same way." She paused to swallow. "They never did find us, but all of our neighbors are now gone."

Wintron was surprised to learn that she had actually seen some of the others being captured. She had gone out to a neighboring hamlet in pursuit of some necessary supplies that those in Wardem Dell did not have and had come on the other settlement just as the people were being led away in a chain line.

"The soldiers did not see you?" asked Wintron. "Were there no dreadhounds on their flanks?"

Borgella shook her head. "No, the black dogs came later. It was just men in your colors, sir." She pointed at Fors' great cloak in Halen-Dabe blue-and-black, "and the Tlocanians in their black-and-red uniforms. I saw them coming and hid my horse in old Hawren's tilting stable, for though it looks ready to fall any minute, it has stood ten years past Hawren's death. I then slipped around Hawren's cottage and into his root cellar. I was able to watch my neighbors pass by through a gap in the outer door."

"Were you not afraid they would find you, woman?" asked Fors, sounding a bit doubtful of her story.

She shook her head. "Hawren died two years ago. His son has a better place down in Gilven Meadow so he gave over Hawren's place to the weeds. No one else wanted the place, for it is weathered and Hawren built it with such a great overhang of the roof that hardly any light could reach the windows. Tilda, may she be forever hugged by the mountain gods, complained about it until her dying day. Nonetheless, Hawren insisted that large eaves gave the best winter shelter. Hawren was a stubborn fellow."

"Orgel said you overheard something?" asked Wintron politely.

"Yes sir. Hawren's cottage sits fairly close to the road. For some reason, one of those dragon priests and a Tlocanian officer got off their mounts to stretch their legs in the darkness of the house's eaves. Why they would want to linger in that gloom I do not know, but it set my heart thumping madly to have them so near."

"What did you hear woman?" demanded Fors, showing his impatience.

Borgella gave him a nervous smile. "The two spoke while they watched my neighbors trudge past. The officer complained about having to do such demeaning work. The priest reminded him that it was essential. The officer asked how many more were needed. The priest mentioned they still needed a few hundred more to reach the four thousand required." The farmer woman glanced at both of them. "What would they want with so many people?"

Wintron ignored her question, for he did not want to tell her. The woman would be devastated if she learned that the Tlocanians planned to sacrifice all those thousands. "Did they take everyone from the town?"

Tears came to Borgella's eyes and she did not bother to hide them. "I went into the village after the soldiers left, hoping to find some people to rescue, but found no one. They took all of the able-bodied. The old, sick, and lame were slaughtered." Her voice caught. "There were too many for me to bury and I am glad that I did not try. As I fled that horrible place, I heard the dogs coming. I think they ate most of the bodies, at least the... the fresh ones."

"Did the dreadhounds ever find your village?" asked Fors.

Borgella nodded, finally wiping away the tears. "They came soon after I arrived, probably following my trail. It was a small pack of only three beasts. Though it cost us nine good men and seven brave women, we succeeded in killing all of the dogs. After that, none of us went out of Wardem Dell again, fearing that we might attract other attacks. At least, we did not until your scouts found us."

They spoke with her a little while longer, but already most of the infantry had passed through the abandoned village. It was time to ride on. They both thanked her for coming and Wintron offered an escort back home.

"Thank you, sir, but I would rather go alone so that I can cover my trail." She looked around. "The dogs are being quiet right now, but it is just a matter of time before they return. I hope to do better at covering my scent this time."

"You and your fellow villagers can still flee to Tor Randis," noted Fors. "The way is clear right now."

Borgella paused to consider, but then shook her head. "I will stay put, but I will let the others know of your offer. Good bye, sirs, and may the gods bless your mission."

The prince and the general rode on, their personal guards gathering around them, while Borgella left in another direction and was soon hidden by the fog.

DRASS

Drass stumbled from the blood-soaked room a changed person. The demon had accepted him as its host, but he did not know if that was a good thing. At least he still lived. He was wearing only his underclothes and they were now filthy, though he avoided inspecting them because his stomach was still queasy. Instead, he looked down the well-lit hall and wondered what he should do now. Was he to wait here until Cavish and Hurko finished whatever else they were doing in the Listening Room, or was he supposed to go somewhere? As he considered, a servant in gray robes turned the corner and came towards him. The elderly man carried a lamp burning so bright that it made Drass squint. By the time the servant was near, Drass had his head turned and eyes almost closed because the glare hurt so much.

"Forgive my harsh light, Embraced One," the servant said apologetically. "I am here to see that you get a bath and a change of clothes. Please follow me."

The man turned back, keeping the lamp close to him. Drass

followed in the man's shadow, careful not to look towards the glare. He came to a bathing chamber where a steaming tub of water awaited his arrival.

"Would you like me to help scrub you, Embraced One?" the servant asked.

"I can bathe myself," stated Drass, waving him off.

The man gave a bow in response and then pointed to a chair a. "Fresh clothes await you beneath that stack of fresh towels on the chair. If you need anything more, please shout for me, for I will be just outside the door. I am called Goval."

The servant gave another deep bow and then withdrew, taking that horrible lamp with him. Drass sighed with relief, finding the bathing room comfortably lit with just one, small wall lamp beneath a deep red shade. He finally looked down at himself and admitted that the servant was right. He did need a good washing, for he was drenched with his own sweat and others' blood. His sweat disgusted Drass, yet he felt an urge to lick up some of the rich blood. Its aroma teased his nose. He grimaced at the strange thought and quickly peeled off his underclothes and climbed into the tub.

He let the hot water ease his tense muscles as he wondered when the changes would start, for he did not feel any different. When would his new powers manifest? He wished they had given him more details, but the priests had rushed him into all of this, wanting to get it done before the start of this Shadow Anchor rite. Drass hoped they did not expect him to help with their ritual, for they had taught him nothing worthwhile yet.

He lingered in the tub until his fingertips wrinkled and the water turned lukewarm. That the water was cloudy from the blood did not bother him and he would have remained there even longer, if a growing hunger had not rumbled in his belly. He dried off and went to retrieve the clothing laid out for him, surprised to find that it was his own, freshly laundered. He had expected they would force him to wear robes from now on.

Dressed, he went to the door and opened it to find Goval waiting. Drass averted his eyes from the bright lamp. "Where to now, Goval? If I am not wanted elsewhere, then a meal would be appreciated. I find my stomach growling."

Goval quickly shielded the lamp with his body and then looked over his shoulder at the young noble. "If you will come with me, Embraced One, then I will see to it that you are provided with nourishment. However, first I must take you to meet with Brother Cavish and Brother Hurko. Right this way please."

Drass complied, surprised that the other two were already cleaned up. They must have finished their work soon after he departed. Goval led him down the same narrow hallway he had taken earlier, though this time the passageway was brightly illuminated. He was brought to a room almost empty of furniture. Upon a bare table pressed against the far wall a lamp shone brightly, casting a red glow over the whole room. The two priests stood in the room's center, awaiting him. For the first time, he could clearly see their faces within the shadow of their hoods. He wondered what kind of odd lighting effect would allow the light to reflect back to reveal their usually-hidden countenances.

Goval entered, motioned Drass in, then bowed and withdrew.

"Drass-Slosoro, how are you feeling?" asked Hurko.

"I am feeling fine, thank you for asking. But why do you call me that?"

"That is you new name, now that your Other has entered, for your Other is known as Slosoro."

Drass frowned. He did not feel like some other being was sharing his head and heart now. Maybe their ceremony had failed. Well, he was not about to tell them that. "Drass-Slosoro. I will remember."

Cavish gave a sharp laugh. "There is no way you will ever forget your Other. You will realize that over the next few days."

"What do you mean?" he asked, wondering if Cavish was mocking him.

Cavish held up his two hands and interlocked his fingers. "The two of you will meld and blend, becoming a greater being. Right now, Slosoro is still absorbing your thoughts and becoming acclimated to his new environment, but soon he will make himself heard and you will become truly acquainted with him."

Just then, High Brother Zuler entered the room, drawing the attention of everyone. He looked briefly at Drass, as if assessing him. "He will be fine on his own for the next few days. I do not think Slosoro will overwhelm him, for I have assigned Goval to work with the new recruits and he is knowledgeable of their needs."

He then turned his attention on the other two. "We begin the Shadow Anchor Ritual in five hours, so I suggest you get your rest while you can. You are to release your dreadhounds to roam outside the city; all the hounds are being sent out to roam."

Cavish gave a slight bow of acknowledgment. "I hear and obey."

Hurko did not bow. "Is it wise to send all of the hounds away?" Drass noted that Hurko's concern was for the animals and not for him.

"It is necessary, for we do not have enough kennel masters to keep them all controlled and fed. We have no Embraced Ones to spare, not with the recall of Lord-General Hraf-Slurtaler to the capitol. We shall all be involved in the Shadow Anchor rite."

Hurko gave a curt nod. "I hear and obey."

Zuler gave a curt nod in return and left them. Drass watched him leave and wondered again if they expected him to help in the upcoming ritual in spite of his ignorance. He turned back to the two in front of him. "Brothers, am I to help as well?"

Cavish scoffed at the thought, his curled lip obvious to Drass. "You would only be a hindrance. No, you are forbidden to even come near the towers where we will be doing this ritual."

Hurko added, "You will be in the care of Goval. He is not Embraced, but he has served the Embraced for many years now. He knows enough to help you until we are free. Now, enough talking. Cavish and I must send our hounds off and then get a little rest. We will see you again in a few days."

Hurko and Cavish left without any further instructions. As they walked out, Goval entered. He brought with him a plate full of food and set it on the bare table. Drass came over and looked at the plate. The meat was very rare, far bloodier than he would normally have liked, yet it smelled wonderful.

"The meat is bison, so you need not worry," stated Goval.

Drass sat down and began eating greedily. "What do you mean by 'not worry'? Are some of the meals here at the King's Keep of questionable quality?"

Goval had just a hint of a smile. "No, Embraced One. As humans have their appetites, be it food or women or gold, the Others also have their hunger. They desire power, especially the power released with blood. I do not fully understand it, but some sacrifices excite the Others more than most. In the first few days of your Embracing, your Other should not be tempted by too much blood, especially that of other humans. Because of that, they will not want you to climb any of the keep's towers during the ritual, for there will be too much blood spilled. However, eating rare meat will give satisfaction to both you and your Other. Go ahead and eat, Embraced One."

After his meal, Goval led Drass to his assigned room, a spare sleeping chamber with a simple cot, dresser, and nightstand. He noticed that his cloak lay on the bed, freshly laundered. He suspected that the rest of his clothes were in the dresser, but he saw nothing of his saddlebags or tack.

He went to the shutters to open them, but Goval restrained him. "Be cautious, Embraced One, for your sight has changed. You are far more sensitive to light now. Maybe you should put on your cloak first and raise its hood to protect your eyes."

Drass ignored the servant, yanking open the shutter to see what lay outside his room. The sudden brightness caused him to avert his gaze. Grimacing, he retrieved his cloak and threw it over his shoulders, letting the hood provide some needed shade. He tried looking outside again and found the day still very bright, even with the cloud cover. His room looked out on an enclosed courtyard. Above the roofline, he could see a large beam of red light shooting up into the clouds. Where the beam disappeared into the Dragon Shadow, the clouds seemed noticeably darker. The light was faint and flickering, but it was something new. Drass wanted to see more of it, maybe even to touch that mysterious light.

Goval saw where he looked and nodded. "Your Other is drawn towards the power, but you must deny it. That is the start of the Shadow Anchor. By the end of the ritual, that beam of light will be solid and firm, like some mighty tree trunk of power. It will tie the Dragon Shadow to this area. As I said, your Other hungers for power, all Others do, but you must help him to control such urgings."

WINTRON

"The fog is lifting," noted Fors as they continued the march towards Regalis. The general and the prince had just come out of another stand of trees.

Wintron looked around and saw that it was true. He could make out farmsteads in the distance to either side, though it was still hazy. "What is happening? Is this just a fluke to this area or is it occurring throughout the Borderheart Valley?" He motioned a messenger over. "Ride up and speak to the fore-riders and any scout who is with them. Ask if they have seen the fog lifting anywhere besides these pasturelands."

Within the hour they had an answer, the Dragon Shadow was indeed lifting everywhere the scouts explored. By afternoon, they could see quite a distance but the skies remained overcast. Wintron and Fors debated the reason for this change. Wintron saw it as a weakening of Tlocanian power and it raised new hope in him. However, Fors suspected a trap of some kind.

When Wintron heard the report of the beam of red light coming up form the King's Keep and how the clouds darkened over the city, his new hope dampened. Fors just nodded at the news, as if it confirmed his suspicions.

* * *

By evening, the two leaders stood under a large spruce on a small ridge to the east of Regalis. They kept to the shelter of the trees, though they were still too far away for any wall sentries to spot them. Night approached and seemed already arrived upon the city because of the black clouds hovering overhead. The mist had lifted enough to show the whole city clearly, from the outer palisade to the gray King's Keep, lights twinkling throughout the capitol. Most noticeable, though, was the red column of light that shot up from the keep's highest tower, straight up into the dark clouds.

The two priests stepped through the trees to join them. Wintron gave them a brief glance, but his gaze returned to the city he had grown up in. His capitol, by all rights. He pointed at that pulsing crimson light. "Father Bilchaso, was this happening when you left the city?"

The old priest rested a hand against a tree trunk to keep his balance on the uneven ground. "No, my prince. When we left, there were red flashes going between those four smaller towers and then out to the center one. This light must be the Shadow Anchor."

"Are we too late then?" asked Fors. "Have they already killed those thousands?"

"I think not," replied Brother Werth, who came to stand next to Bilchaso. "I am ignorant of this abominable rite, for it has no place in true dragon worship, yet I overheard others describing what was planned. Temple servants complained that they would have to climb those towers for three days, bringing the priests food and drink during the ceremony. It has only been two days since we fled so, even if it has begun, the ritual cannot be completed yet. I also heard a temple guard describing a Shadow Anchor to a newer recruit. He told of a solid red light shooting up into the gray clouds, spreading out into the clouds like red trunk and branches. That does not sound like what we see here. This beam is still faint and flickering. No, I do not think the ritual is complete."

Bilchaso spoke up. "But some have already died. Good people

undeserving of this." He looked over at the dragon priest that had been his companion for the last few days. "The mountain gods are not so prone to jealousy and they permitted other gods to be worshiped by the Borderfolk. However, they are grieved by the bloody practices of these Tlocanian worshipers." He looked back at the capitol and the faint red light. "The Tlocanians kill to release power, preferring the killing to be as bloody as possible. They were already sacrificing people before we escaped and I doubt there has been any surcease unless you put a stop to their butchery."

"So the question is, how much time do we still have?" observed Wintron Dabe. "I think we must assume that the ritual is imminent if not already begun. We hope we can breech the walls quickly."

Fors sighed. "I do not like this, but it must be done. I will send the scouts to take a closer look at both the northern gate and the two eastern gates. We should aim our attack at whichever one is most vulnerable."

Suddenly, from the woods closer by, they heard a series of barks and baying. All four of them stared in that new direction. "The dreadhounds are hunting again," said the prince. "Those scouts might need a full squad for protection."

"That is obvious," replied Fors, turning away from the view and heading back towards their waiting horses. He had to walk slowly, using his cane more than ever, to keep from tripping over roots and loose rocks.

Watching him go, Wintron noted his uncle's age. The Old Fox should be back at Tor Randis, he thought, not on the field. However, he was the only field commander left to the Border Army, no matter his years or his uncertain loyalty.

Father Bilchaso seemed to read his thoughts. "Trust him, my prince. Duke Fors loves our realm and hates what has been done to it. If anyone detests Mordel more than you, it is the father whom he betrayed." The elderly priest came nearer, placing a hand on Wintron's shoulder. "I think you both want the same: the freeing of the Border Realm. He may be old and cantankerous, but he is your best ally now."

Wintron wished that were not so, but he realized that the Cha priest had it right. He offered the priest a hand over a pair of gnarly roots. "No one has studied Regalis' defenses as long as he; that truth I will acknowledge." He assisted Brother Werth next. "Let us hope the general remembers his duty even if he sees one of his sons standing across from him."

They would not be able to attack this day, for the dim daylight was quickly fading, but Wintron knew it would be a busy night nonetheless, for they had much to plan.

DRASS

Are you inside of me? Drass asked the question for the fifth time this day, but he still heard no answer. He had been resting since late afternoon and now it must be near midnight, yet it had not been a solid sleep. Repeatedly, he awoke to wonder about the one possessing him. Would he ever be able to communicate with the Other? He sat up in his cot and looked around the small room. Realizing that the lack of lighting no longer hindered his sight, he had to admit that something was different about himself.

Since it was now the middle of the night, Drass stood and went over to the window again, throwing open the shutters and looking out at the red beacon. He did not bother pulling on any of his clothes, for he did not feel chilled even standing there wearing only his underclothes. He had to crane his neck to see where the light shot up from the keep's tallest tower. The red light was still faint and flickering, but it drew his gaze. Once again, he felt that longing to approach it, to absorb some of its power. This was not a normal feeling, so maybe the demon stirring, finally. Is that what you want? The power? Or is it just bloody power you want? Will you ever speak to me Slosoro? Maybe the demon was mute or an imbecile. Drass chuckled bitterly at the thought. All of this work, and he gets possessed by a half-wit demon.

Finally an answer came, though it was not in clear words. Instead, Slosoro expressed himself through action. Drass' right hand moved on its own, reaching over to his left arm and clawing it viciously. Pain seared through him and he tried to make his body stop. As blood welled up, his left arm came up to his mouth and he sucked up the blood. Again, it was not Drass' decision to do this.

He had lost control of his body. Stop! You cannot do this! He began shouting at the Other in his head, then out loud as well. "Stop!"

Now his left hand clawed up his right arm and again he sucked blood. His body kept moving without his guidance. Only his voice was his own.

It took effort to fight an urge to swallow. Instead, Drass spat out the blood. "Stop! I am your host; we are partners, Slosoro. What you do is wrong. To hurt me is to weaken yourself, for I am your host. Stop this!"

A thought blazed through his mind. *Agreed.*

Suddenly, Drass regained control of his body. Breathing heavily, he sat down on his cot. Both arms pulsed with pain, blood dripping off his limbs onto the blankets. He shivered now, but not from the coldness of the night. He shook with sudden fear over what he had done by accepting this thing inside of himself. He did not think the demon was cowed. More likely, this had been a lesson for Drass.

True, came the response inside his mind.

Drass almost howled in response, his sudden fear was so strong.

* * *

He dared not get up again that night nor did he call for a servant to tend his wounds. Instead, he stayed on his cot and let his wounds stop bleeding on their own.

Slosoro said no more that night nor did the Other manipulate his body again, but Drass hovered near hysteria nonetheless, expecting it to happen again any minute. Finally, near dawn, exhaustion claimed him and he slept a few fitful hours.

WINTRON

The darkness fitfully lessened as the sun returned somewhere above the thick clouds. The Border army marched to an area just out-of-sight from the upper east gate. Wintron watched as two straight oaks were chopped down and formed into battering rams. Though green wood and without iron caps, the rams would do, Fors claimed. The general felt that no more than ten blows would be needed to break through.

Prince and general had agreed it would be best to come upon the gate with surprise, for they did not know if Mordel's men had mastered the watchtower drums yet. The idea was to break through quickly and prevent any attempt to beat a warning on the tower drum. It promised to be bloody work, but speed would be the only way to win through and stop this madness.

Wintron looked up at the black clouds over the city and saw that the light beam seemed brighter today as it penetrated the Dragon Shadow. How many had already died for this magic?

"We are ready," said Fors to his nephew. The prince had not even noticed that his uncle had ridden over to him.

He gave his uncle a nod of acknowledgment. "Today is the day,

Fors, when we will liberate Regalis."

The Old Fox returned the nod, his face grim. "Getting through the gates will be the easy part. However, what we will find behind the palisade? They have terrible magic, my prince, and we have nothing but our weapons and our bravery."

"That will have to do. We cannot wait for some Attul army to suddenly appear."

Fors guffawed. "In that we agree; I do not think we will ever see Councilor Rolen again."

"Oh, he will return," argued Wintron, "but it may take some time. Though he never said where the hidden Warhaven lies, he implied it was some distance away. We must free the Border Realm on our own, but we will need their blazing swords to keep it free."

Fors obviously clenched his teeth in disagreement, but he did not argue.

Wintron broached another topic. "Any more word of the dreadhounds?" They had lost almost two dozen men during the night to bold raids.

Fors paused in answering to watch horses drag the first ram towards the city gate. Wintron wondered if he paused simply to aggravate. Finally, the Old Fox looked back to his nephew. "Nothing yet on those black beasts, but I expect them to fall on us once we are distracted with the assault. I have ordered four squads to patrol our rear just to warn us of any imminent attack."

Wintron had to admit that the general knew how to defend his men. However, Wintron had the strong sense that it would be up to him to discover the best way to attack the keep, for it would probably call for something bold and even risky. If only he had the answer.

DRASS

Drass awoke to Goval's movements in his room. Groggy, he sat up and looked at the elderly servant who replaced his bloody wash water. He had rinsed his arms a few hours earlier but had not completely succeeded in cleaning them of the dried blood. Goval said nothing of the pink water or about the rumpled and stained blankets.

The servant merely noted that Drass was awake and gave him a slight bow. "Will you want a bath to refresh yourself this morning?"

Drass wondered how much the man could see in the dark room. Everything seemed bright and clear to him, but maybe Goval could not see his still-weeping wounds. Certainly the man must smell the blood, for Drass certainly did. He sniffed a bit harder and was surprised that he could smell Goval's presence too.

He sighed and rubbed his nose vigorously, wondering if this was all just a bad dream, especially the confrontation with Slosoro. No, that had been real, for he had the wounds to prove it. Drass looked again towards Goval and found the servant waiting patiently for an answer. "I will take that bath, along with some bandages for my arms."

"I hear and obey, Embraced One," replied Goval with another small bow. He hurried from the room with the bloodstained water, though he did not slosh a drop of it.

Drass had his bath and then Goval helped to dry him and wrap those scratches that still wept blood. To do that, the man had to light a clear-glass lamp.

The young noble averted his eyes from the harsh light and let him do his task. Goval asked nothing about how he obtained the injuries and the young noble was too embarrassed to admit anything. He was not about to say that he had been fighting with himself. He felt better once Goval had him bandaged and could extinguish the lamp.

He dressed while Goval drained the tub. The servant had set out fresh clothes for Drass, on top of which he laid a knife in a sheath.

When Drass asked about the blade, the old servant explained, "That is your Sakar. It is used during rituals. You are expected to wear it at all times."

Drass pulled out the knife and saw that it was a sharp blade with a rather simple hilt. "Does it have some magical property?"

"I am not the one to ask, Embraced One," demurred Goval. "I can only say that all Embraced wear a Sakar, whether they are priest, officer, governor, or tower keeper."

He realized he would learn no more from the servant about this, so he dressed and added the knife to his outfit. "Tell me, Goval, am I allowed to leave this floor of the keep?"

The man straightened from pulling the drain plug. "You are not a prisoner here, Embraced One, but they have set a few limits for you. You are not to leave the keep nor climb any of its towers. Have you a certain destination in mind?"

"I thought of visiting my brother the king."

Goval nodded. "I understand that he still resides here, on the first two floors of the fortress. If you seek him out, I would humbly suggest that you also pay a visit to Colonel Ulen, who now leads the Tlocanian

Eric Lorenzen

forces in these mountains. He also resides on the bottom floors and he is Embraced."

* * *

After a quick meal, Drass found his way down through the keep, doing his best to remember the way to the Great Hall. This was not his first time at the King's Keep but he had not been here in many years. In addition, it seemed somehow different with his newly enhanced eyesight. He kept his hood up after encountering an area lit far too much.

He finally found Mordel's mongrels guarding the Great Hall's doors, but they did not seem to be anywhere else in the keep. He refused their request to show his face. Instead, he announced himself and ordered them to open the doors. The men considered, talking amongst themselves, unconcerned about being overheard. Finally, they relented, deciding that Mordel had enough guards inside to protect him, should his brother prove rabid.

He entered the echoing hall, waving off an attempt to announce his presence. As he strode towards the throne where his brother sat, he had to squint against the glare of many lamps. Mordel's advisors stood behind the king's chair. Drass recognized only some of them, for his brother had a knack at gathering flatterers.

A Tlocanian officer was there in his dragon helm; Drass guessed him to be Colonel Ulen. The officer stood alone before the seated Mordel and his crowd, but he seemed to dominate the room. Drass smirked; it would not be hard to surpass Mordel's sycophants. The colonel even dominated over Mordel, for the Border Realm's throne was not some looming seat nor did it rest on a high pedestal. It was just a stately chair. He was surprised Mordel had not replaced it already.

It appeared that the colonel and the king were in the midst of an argument. Ulen's back was to Drass, but he saw the obvious signs of anger on his brother's face. At first, no one noticed him drawing near. Mordel sat straight in his chair and pounding on its arm for emphasis.

"What do you mean, they have withdrawn? My father is attacking and your men have fled the city walls?"

Ulen seemed nonplussed by Mordel's anger. "The outer wall is indefensible. We will hold the King's Keep. Once the ritual is done and the priests have recovered, then we will sweep these fools out of the valley."

Mordel sprang to his feet and stood nose-to-nose with the Tlocanian colonel. "Waiting until the conclusion of this ceremony is pure folly. I demand that you send your men back to the walls. You will obey me on this, for your emperor has signed a treaty with me. I will not allow any cowardly desertions in my realm."

Drass walked to the side, keeping out of the harsh light that bathed the throne area. He could now see Colonel Ulen's crossed arms. The man did not look at all cowed by Mordel. The two were about the same height, yet the Tlocanian officer seemed to loom over Drass' older brother.

"Make no threats towards me, King Mordel. If the Shadow Anchor does not become established then the cloud cover will dissipate…"

"I care nothing for this Dragon Shadow. Actually, I would enjoy the return of sunlight over these dreary skies."

Still appearing calm, the colonel raised a hand between their faces. He held up only two fingers, but red lightning flickered there, in unspoken threat. "Be careful what you wish for, King Mordel. If the cloud cover dissipates, then so will your Tlocanian support. You and your realm are but a flyspeck in comparison to the empire and of no importance. Do not presume otherwise." Colonel Ulen looked away from Mordel and made eye contact with his younger brother. "Lord Drass, it is good to see you. May I have a word in private?"

"No you may not!" yelled Mordel, furious at being ignored. "I am the king here. Show proper respect, soldier."

Slowly, Ulen turned back. Calmly, he flicked his fingers at Mordel and the red lightning sizzled out, striking the king slayer. Mordel flew back, collapsing against his throne, twitching uncontrollably. He screamed in agony. Ulen took no further notice of him. Instead, he motioned for Drass to follow him. The two of them walked halfway down the hall, away from the trembling advisors and gawking guards.

"I see that you are now one of us," Ulen said with approval in his tone. "Once you and your Other have become acclimated, we will need to talk. I remember my first days after being accepted and so I know you are full of questions. However, it is best to wait until your Other has a better grasp of the language and culture of Na Ciria. Do not worry, for the Others are all quick learners. Within a week, the two of you will be having full-length conversations."

Ulen gave the new recruit a wintry smile. Drass found the shadows of the dragon helm no hindrance to his perception. "Now, I ask you to do what you can to talk sense into your brother. He will alienate the only ally he has if he keeps up these childish demands of his."

He gave the officer a slight nod. "I will do what I can, Colonel

Ulen."

"Good. You have my thanks, Lord Drass."

The colonel left the hall without another look towards King Mordel.

Drass sighed as he walked back towards his brother, for he could tell that Mordel was still angry. Mordel no longer twitched, but he was rubbing a sore arm and his normally perfect hair was disheveled. Some of his advisors were trying to talk to him, but Mordel waved them off angrily. Instead, he just glared at his younger brother.

He knew that look; Mordel's charming mask was now askew.

"You were ordered to take the Highlands, little brother. Surely, you could not have succeeded in conquering all of that territory already, so why are you here?"

Drass stopped in the same spot where the colonel had stood. "I was told to come back, but your men are still up there harassing Father's backside. I left the best mercenary officer in charge."

His brother slammed his right hand down on the throne's arm. "Fool! That man is not trustworthy. He is a sellsword. He will now either turn rogue or flee to Freetown as soon as things become difficult. Why have you betrayed me?"

He could not help but laugh. "No, Betrayer is your title my brother. They call me the Poisoner." Mordel obviously saw nothing humorous in it. His brother could be so over-serious sometimes. "Have you not already guessed that I am no longer yours to command? I am now an emperor's man."

"What? You have joined their forces? Has that colonel promised you some high rank or lands? How much did it cost for them to buy you?" Mordel sprang to his feet to stare his little brother down. Mordel tried to throw back Drass' hood, but the younger brother caught his hand and held it tightly.

As Drass held off his brother, he had to fight an inner urge from Slosoro. The demon wanted to crush Mordel's throat. Fighting off both, Drass shoved Mordel towards his throne and then stepped back. Guards sprang to defend their king and the advisors muttered angrily. Drass did not intimidate them, for they did not know what he had become.

He went for his sword, but when he raised it, he saw red lightning chasing up from his hand and along its length. The guards froze when they saw the crackling light.

"So you are one of their possessed men now," spat Mordel. "You have forsaken me to become a demon's slave." His tone implied deep disdain.

Drass ignored the slander, too fascinated by this newfound power. He swung the sword through the air and watched its red trail of power. The guards moved away from the sparkling sword.

"Do you hear me? The Tlocanians deceive you. They play you for a fool, but I will have no part in this jester dance." Mordel stood behind the highly carved throne, his hands clinging to its top edge. He obviously wanted something between him and his possessed brother. "I will not allow you to be their spy in the midst of my people. Do they plan to set you on the throne in my stead? I will not give you the chance. Demon lover, I hereby banish you from the Border Realm. Get out of my kingdom, you traitor."

Drass finally looked at his brother, seeing the anger in his eyes and the spittle at the corner of his mouth. He laughed. "I will gladly leave, Mordel…"

"King Mordel," corrected one of the advisors, finally growing a spine.

Drass ignored the interruption. "…for I finally realize that I have nothing here. I may just be a tool for the Tlocanians, but at least they offer me real power as a reward. What did you offer me for killing General Erileon and defeating the Border army? Nothing but more work, conquering the realm for you. You drink wine, while I must be satisfied with stream water. You hold feasts, while I chew jerky and shriveled apples. You sleep in a featherbed, while I toss and turn on the cold ground. No my brother, I am not deceived. At last, my eyes are truly open to how you used me.

"So keep your blood-stained throne, for I want nothing to do with it. I will leave as quickly as I can, have no fear of that. However, I promised the colonel that I would try to talk some sense into you, Mordel. Can you not see that the Tlocanians are your only allies? Maybe you do not like that they squat in your keep and use it for their magic, but at least they are not retreating completely. The fact that they are willing to place one of their Shadow Anchors here shows that they are committed to this land. Do not be a fool, Mordel. You can at least act humble while they are around, for I know you are good at pretending."

Mordel did not respond to him. Instead, the usurper king turned to the nearest guards. "Escort this Tlocanian puppet out the King's Keep. I do not want to see his face again."

The guards moved hesitantly towards Drass. He smiled at their timidity. "One last thing, brother dear. If you are so fearful for yourself and your family, maybe you should flee to Glenford for the next few days. Father will be too distracted by Tlocanians to notice your retreat. Run south, Mordel, since you fear war so much. As for my leaving, I will go when the Tlocanians tell me. No earlier. For now, I will retire to the upper floors of the keep where the Tlocanians already rule."

Drass was ready to leave, but he did not want to turn his back on Mordel's guards. They just might try to spear him from behind. He wanted to teach them a lesson and suddenly he knew how. Sheathing his sword, he raised an empty hand and let crimson lightning dance in his palm to coalesce into a small fireball. He tossed it at the boldest guard and the man turned into a human torch. Everyone dove out of the way, including his dense brother, giving Drass the opportunity to leave unmolested.

CHAPTER THIRTY-ONE
Fleeing by Mule

BRODAGAR

"You have lost a whole pack of dogs? How could that have happened, Brodagar-Sahak?" Nesron anger was obvious. The two of them had been standing in front of the dragon temple, waiting for their troops to get organized, when the priest reported the loss.

"They are gone and the priest who was linked in guiding them is dead." Brodagar told his news without emotion. He had done his ranting before Nesron's arrival. By now, his anger had cooled into an ice-cold desire for revenge. He motioned for his horse.

"Attuls?"

He waved the suggestion aside. "Not that enemy. This attack came from some of our own. My pack was stalking the other pack that is behind us, the Osburg dogs. Someone powerful must be riding towards us, someone who can grab a linked priest and shatter him."

"Have you tried to reestablish a link with your hounds?"

"I did and I could not find them." Brodagar paused to accept his horse's reins, and then met Nesron's eyes. "The whole pack is gone. Dead."

Nesron cursed. "What has Lord Krev gotten us into? I will not gain the knowledge of the Attul hideaway, just to have it stolen from me by another."

Brodagar climbed into the saddle, and then motioned for a nearby soldier to bring Nesron's horse over. The soldier hesitated to obey a priest, but then did so. Nesron appeared too distracted to notice.

It is time.

Brodagar nodded, for he agreed with Sahak. It might even be too late, for Nesron had already bungled this mission. If left in charge, he would bring certain failure. It was time to put the soldier in his place.

"We need to ride, Nesron-Swoferosh," stated Brodagar. "I agree with you, that we cannot allow some other to steal our glory. However, if we do not get going on the Attuls' trail, they might slip from our grasp anyway."

The captain mounted, not yet aware of the shift in power between them. The captain's thoughts were too jumbled. That much was apparent to Brodagar and he took full advantage of the other's confusion.

Nesron remained silent, probably consulting his Other on how to withstand a stronger demon.

Brodagar and Sahak had already discussed this very thing. It would take at least a trio of lesser demons to overwhelm a stronger one, and that meant Brodagar now led. Nesron was the only military Embraced One; all the others were under Brodagar's priestly command. If Nesron did not yield, then the priests could just step aside and let their pursuer have him.

The captain must have realized his predicament, for he gave the priest a spiteful look, yet Brodagar wanted to make sure there were no doubts.

"You need the priestly Embraced Ones, Nesron, and they belong to me. Maybe Colonel Wevro would have been wiser to send along a few more army Embraced Ones, but he did not. You are cornered, so either submit to my leadership or face a stronger demon alone. What will you choose?"

The army captain grimaced, his face within the shadow of the dragon helm looked as if he had swallowed a dozen sour grapes. However, he yielded. "I hear and obey, Brodagar-Sahak."

He nodded acceptance, choosing not to rub the man's face in the stench of defeat.

Nesron asked if the priest was ready to depart and received a nod, so he barked orders at his men, sending forward outriders. He accepted the new situation rather quickly. That was good, for Brodagar knew the mission required unity for success. He wanted even more than success; he wanted to come out of this still alive. Though the Attuls had already fled the village, he had no doubt that they would find their trail again shortly. Dreadhounds were not so easily thrown off the scent. However, that was also true of the Gray dreadhounds and that was his greater worry.

MYLANA

A mule may get its size from its horse mother but its disposition often came from its donkey father. Mylana could not deny that fact as she struggled to saddle her chosen mount. The animal did not recognize her and so was rather uncooperative at first, yet she eventually had him bridled and saddled. His gait was also different, but she quickly became accustomed to it. She decided to call the fellow Ears, for the mule had those huge ears typical of his donkey sire. By focusing her thoughts on the animal, Mylana tried to avoid the growing desperation within her. She did not want to think about how close the enemy lurked; that their mission seemed close to failing.

The foursome rode out of the village by way of a small path that a local had shown them, hoping to avoid notice. Mylana suspected that their efforts were futile, though she never saw anyone watching them leave. If they could not hide in a larger city like Hightower, then how could they avoid notice here? However, there was nothing else to do except to ride on and hope to elude the demonsworn.

She rode third in line, behind Mandor and Hessilyn. Thankfully, Coursen was now strong enough to stay in the saddle, but all of them felt bone-tired from lack of sleep. Mylana looked back at Coursen and he gave her a smile of encouragement, though he still sagged in the saddle. She returned his smile, suddenly feeling awkward. A tree branch brushed her, making her hurriedly turn forward again. She chastised herself for acting like a fluttery city girl. This was not the time to be falling in love…. Was that what this was? She sighed.

As the day progressed, Mylana grew thankful for her mule Ears, for the beast had stamina to compete with any Westbend horse. She would not be able to win any race on him, but he kept a solid pace that ate up the miles of this winding trail. The other mules seemed equally steadfast, so that the foursome made good time in spite of their wandering route. The path took them past decrepit orchards and struggling fields, and then into a dark forest where the way regularly disappeared under the leaf litter. Finally, their route took them around a hill and back to the Crossover Road.

When they returned to that larger way, they noticed signs of recent travel: horses and dogs. They discussed what to do, but realized turning back would not serve their mission, so they pressed on. At every turn or tree-darkened dell, they worried about an ambush but none came. As evening approached, they chose a campsite beside a rushing stream, hoping the flow might provide some protection to their rear.

After eating, the men bedded down while the women took first watch. The women sat beside the fire as night darkened around them. An owl hooted somewhere in the woods. Wolves howled in the near distance, which Mylana took as a good sign. She doubted they would be hunting in the area if the dreadhounds prowled nearby. How much longer before those awful dogs attacked again? She thought of the messenger satchel stuffed inside her shirt and how much further she had to carry it.

"Your burden must weigh you down," said Hessilyn softly.

Mylana looked over the fire at her, resisting the desire to finger the satchel. "My burden?"

Hessilyn brushed her long, dark hair back from her face. "Yes, your burden. Mandor has not told me what it is, but you carry something that is a secret from the other two, some knowledge. This mission would fail should something happen to you. So why do you not share it with them? Surely they have proven themselves trustworthy by now."

"I promised others to keep the secret. I have sworn an oath."

"Such vows are folly," declared Hessilyn, adding some twigs to the fire. "These others had no way of knowing the dangers you would encounter. They were wrong to demand such a promise from you."

"Nevertheless, I will hold to my word."

Hessilyn frowned. "You have a terrible choice before you, Mylana. What is more important, the success of your mission or the keeping of some vow? Let go of your prideful obstinacy, for your duty requires it of you."

She did not reply, though Hessilyn's words cut her to the bone. Was she risking their mission by keeping Warhaven a secret from the others?

* * *

After midnight, the men took over the watch. The night remained quiet until the early hours of the day, but Mylana had difficulty sleeping. She quietly rested, watching the two men as they sat over the fire. She was awake when the dreadhounds started baying, coming from the west. The dogs became louder, awakening Hessilyn.

Mylana sat up, trying to gauge how close the enemy was.

The mules now stirred, their long ears aimed towards the

approaching danger. The men walked over to soothe the animals and then quickly loaded them, while Hessilyn and Mylana gathered their belongings. The foursome rode out, even though it was still night-dark, deciding that it would be better to flee than make a stand. Once back on the Crossover Road, they set the mules to a canter. They dared not try anything faster, at least not until after dawn. Behind them, the dogs continued their pursuit.

BRODAGAR

"They are early," stated Nesron when a scout reported that the Attuls were approaching the trap he had laid. The Tlocanians stood on a rise further up the Crossover Road.

"They are being chased, captain. We heard dreadhounds in pursuit," continued the scout.

Nesron gave Brodagar a curious look. The priest shook his head slightly to say that they were not his dogs, though only Nesron could see the movement within the darkness of Brodagar's hood. He dismissed the scout and then waited for the priest's instructions. Brodagar whispered to one of his underlings, who hurried off. The priest finally confronted the captain.

"I wish we had completed our mission back in Hightower." His tone said who he thought at fault over that failure. "I do not want to confront this demon out here, away from any other help. Can we pry the knowledge from the Attul woman and still keep away from the Embraced One following?"

Nesron grimaced, obviously not liking his new role as lackey and blame-taker but he had no choice. "We need to keep the Attuls riding hard, which means our next terror cannot injure their mounts." Nesron paused, his frustration growing. "You should end this spy nonsense. So far, Free Hawk has provided us with nothing except haughty orders and empty promises. How much longer can we wait on Lord Krev's mole? I say take the woman and torture the answers from her."

"That is a foolish suggestion. Free Hawk is not just Krev's pet. Our orders came through the Speakers Tower, so Emperor Silossiak must also know. You are overbold in your impatience, Nesron-Swoferosh. Your human side is showing, which is not a flattering trait in an Embraced One." Brodagar motioned for a temple guard to bring him his mount. "No, I am not about to disobey the demons above me. We will coddle this Free Hawk as much as needed in order to coax out

415

the secret of Warhaven."

The priest climbed onto his horse and motioned for Nesron to do likewise. This ridge offered an excellent vantage of the road, but he did not want to be spotted. Soon, the Tlocanians were riding down the other side, to where their next trap lay. He had chosen a particularly dense wood in which to ambush the Attuls. He had given strict instructions to all of the Embraced to refrain from any use of their powers, for he did not want to give the enemy any warning. He would fulfill Free Hawk's latest request, left as a note at that last village. The Attul woman would be wounded to remind her of her frail mortality. Not killed, just gravely injured.

Two hours later, the Attuls cautiously entered the forest, riding mules now. Brodagar noted which one was the Attul woman and pointed her out to the archers waiting nearby. Finally, he signaled for the attack, motioning to the soldiers while giving a silent command to the priests restraining the hounds. What followed seemed quite chaotic, even though it followed Brodagar's plan. They terrorized the foursome. In the midst of the bedlam, a select archer carefully shot the Attul woman.

She received a grievous wound. He was tempted to have Free Hawk feathered as well, since the spy was slow in getting the information, but resisted the temptation. He needed Free Hawk lucid when the woman confessed her secret. Brodagar just hoped that the plan would work, for they were almost beyond Lord-Governor Krev's territory. Riverrealm Province began after the city of Edgevale. It would be best to get this done without involving another high demon.

As soon as the Attul woman was wounded, Brodagar let the foursome get away. The mules ambled at a ridiculously slow speed, but he made sure they escaped. He ordered his forces to follow so that the Attuls would not stop and heal the woman, for he wanted the wound's infection to do its work. As the Attuls fled, the priest heard dreadhounds baying further down the road and it made him pause.

The Osburgen force was almost too close. If he did not time this right, he might lose his prey to whoever followed.

"Captain Nesron, we will need to push the Attuls hard."

Nesron had obviously heard the hounds also, but he made no comment on them. "I hear and obey," was all that he said before ordering his soldiers in pursuit of their prey.

MYLANA

They were attacked just as the road led them under the canopy of a dark forest. Mylana rode at the fore, followed by Hessilyn, Coursen, and then Mandor. They could still hear the pack of dreadhounds following, but the dogs were no closer than they had been this morning. Mylana kept careful watch as they rode into the trees' gloom, but she did not see their attackers until too late. Suddenly, dreadhounds barked all around them, leaping at them from the brush. Arrows flew, though all seemed wildly aimed. The mules screamed in terror, kicking out at the dogs. Mylana and Mandor used their shining swords, while Coursen swung his mundane blade and Hessilyn used her newly acquired stave. In the melee, three dogs died and more were wounded, but the foursome did not come out unscathed.

An arrow struck Mylana.

She bent over in sudden pain. The tip had torn through her clothes and pierced her side, though not deeply. It was already working itself loose as her mule started running down the road. Carefully, she pulled the arrow free and tossed it. She kept one hand pressed against her side, trying to staunch the bleeding, for there was no time to stop and properly bandage it. Behind her, the others also fled.

The foursome rode down the road, letting the mules run, and were soon away. Mylana did her best to hide her wound, for she did not want to worry the others. Once the danger was past, she planned to ask Mandor for his healing aid. But for now, they had nothing to do but flee.

Behind them came snarling hounds and men on horseback. For the first time since Hightower, the Tlocanian soldiers were open about their pursuit. Fighting back a sense of panic and still pressing a hand against her side, she kept the lead. The mules were not stallions, so they had to settle back to a slower pace, but they were long-winded. Their pursuers seemed disorganized at first, missing their chance to quickly seize them, and now followed without catching up. She would have laughed at her enemy's confusion, but her side hurt too much. Already she felt light-headed from the blood loss, but she still kept quiet about her injury. It was not until an hour later that Hessilyn spotted her darkening shirt and brought it to the attention of the others.

Mandor insisted that they stop so that he could look at her wound. Mylana stayed in the saddle while he delicately pulled up her shirt. She winced as pain shot through her side. "It is an ugly wound," her brother said, ever the blunt one. "It should be cleaned before I try any healing…"

Coursen interrupted him. "There is no time, Mandor. I can already see two dreadhounds coming at us quickly. We must ride. Now."

Frustrated, Mandor said a quick prayer and pressed the flat his shining sword against Mylana's side, but he failed to heal it completely. Mylana could tell that from looking at her brother's face.

In spite of her pain, she gave him a brave smile. "Thank you. I am sure that will start the healing process. Now, climb on your mule, for we have to flee."

Mandor just stood there, frowning at her injury. She thought he might try healing it again, but then Hessilyn shouted a warning. Both of them looked over at a charging black dog. The vicious hound would have taken Mandor if it had not been for Hessilyn kicking her mule forward and swinging her staff wildly at the thing. She gave it a solid thump on the head that made the beast scamper back.

Her brother was now on his mule, but the dog had circled around Hessilyn and was getting ready to spring at him again. Coursen interjected himself, swinging his mundane blade, and it seemed enough to make the dog hesitate. However, now the second dog was almost on them. They kicked their mules to a gallop, having to abandon the supplies tied on the dying pack mule, and soon the dogs fell behind. Their mules could only run so far though, and soon fell back to a more steadfast speed.

The Attuls kept to their dogged pace throughout the day, with Coursen now taking the lead. Mylana sat in a haze for most of the ride, as a fever set in to go along with her pain. Her hair became matted with sweat, her clothes soaked, but she kept to her saddle with ragged determination. She sped up when ordered and slowed whenever someone yelled at her to do so, but they had to repeat their orders more and more as the day continued. A few times, she heard dreadhounds baying nearby and even the shouts of Tlocanian soldiers, but she was not sure if it was real or just a figment of her fevered mind. At least twice, Hessilyn forced her to drink from a waterskin and leaned close to check on her condition, but they never stopped. Instead, she had to endure the jarring gait of Ears for hour after hour.

Somehow, they ended up in a city. Mylana could not recall passing through any gates, but they rode on cobblestones now between closely-set rows of buildings. When they finally came to a stop, Mylana just sat there stupidly staring at the green lantern in front of her. Why were they stopping? The dreadhounds would be on them very soon.

"Mylana. Mylana!"

She looked down at her brother, shaking off his helping hands. "We need to keep going," she insisted in a raspy voice. "The hounds will get us if we stop."

"No. We are safe for now. We entered Edgevale just as the city gates closed for the night. We can stop now. Come. I will help you down and into bed, and then we will see to getting you a healer."

She was still unclear, but could not resist his urging. In a daze, she dismounted. Actually, it was more like she fell, but her brother and strong Coursen caught her and helped her inside. After that, she remembered no more.

Eric Lorenzen

CHAPTER THIRTY-TWO
Return to Regalis

WINTRON

By agreement, Wintron and Fors kept apart as the attack on Regalis began. Both of them had seen how devastating Tlocanian magic could be, and they did not want the army losing both leaders in one blow. Wintron sat on his horse, watching as they unhitched the first ram and twenty bulky soldiers carried it towards the gate. They chanted a bawdy love song to keep their steps in rhythm. Each man was paired with a shield bearer who offered some protection.

More rebels appeared in the watchtower, aiming their bows, but it did not cause the ramming crew to pause or slow down. Wintron distinctly heard the lead man order them to a trot. Their coordination impressed him, for they only had a day's practice. Arrows rained down from the guard tower, but since the archers could only line up six across it was not a hard rain.

The ram struck the gate with a loud boom and crack. The impact tore it from the crew's hands, but on an order, they lifted it again.

"Cavalry ready," ordered the prince, for he could already see gaps in the gate. The plan was for the infantry to swarm through once a large enough opening appeared and take over the gatehouse. The cavalry would charge in at their heels, first Fors' squadron and then those under Wintron. "We ride in behind the left flank and then swing southward. Beware the ram and do not trample any of our infantry."

The ramming crew retreated a few steps and then ran forward again. The gate shuddered and then came a loud crack. One more swing and the gates failed completely, one side splintering from top to bottom. Hundreds of soldiers swarmed through, moving quickly to avoid the expected fireballs and lightning, yet nothing came at them besides arrows and swords.

Wintron frowned. Why did they delay their magical attack? Was this a trap like Fors feared? It was too late to slow the attack, though. Already, Fors' cavalry units were picking up speed. It was time for Wintron to signal his men to charge as well.

Just as the horses set in motion, warning cries came from behind them, followed by terrible barking and growls in all directions. As the Border army moved in on the city, dreadhounds struck. It was too late to turn his men around, not with so many of the army already through the broken gate, so Wintron urged his troops to a gallop and hoped they could get inside before the packs hit. As the horses picked up speed, he looked behind them and saw hundreds of dogs burst out of the trees in pursuit. Maybe the Tlocanians did not rain down their lightning and fire, but their dreadhounds were out in full force.

He had never seen so many packs together before, not even when the Tlocanians overran the border forts. He hated to think what would happen to any soldiers that fell behind. Wintron yelled at the banner man riding next to him. "Tell them to ride hard! We must gain the city walls before these hounds catch us."

The fellow waved his flag to signal for speed.

Wintron focused on the wooden wall in front of him. It was surreal to be storming the very city where he had grown up. As his horse brought him closer, the palisade loomed overhead. No arrows flew from the guardhouse, for soldiers were now fighting each other up there. He thanked all the gods who could think of that the gates were falling so easily.

He kept in the center of his personal guard as they thundered up on the shattered gate. They swept past the now-abandoned ram. Suddenly, the gate loomed directly ahead. He and his men swept through the gap, horses jumping debris. Once through, Wintron looked all around but found no one to engage in combat. The only fighting he could hear was up in the gatehouse and even that grew quieter. He motioned his men onward, heading towards the temple district, even as some of Fors' squadron pushed the remains of the gate shut and prepared to fight off the dreadhounds charging at them.

As he rode into the city, Wintron looked around. The skies were now so dark that it seemed like night. He ordered some torches lit, as he eyed the ominous clouds overhead. Red lightning regularly flashed and thunder rumbled, but no bolts struck the earth. Still, the sight made him nervous.

The streets lay empty before them, without even a barricade to hinder their progress. Wintron and his men set a fast pace, riding through a city that seemed nearly deserted. If not for the smattering of lit windows, he would have thought all of the residents had either fled or been rounded up. They encountered no one else until they neared the temple district, and then it was some of their own men. Wintron called a halt at the sight of Orgel and another scout waiting for him. The prince met with them in an alleyway so that they would not be so exposed.

"What do you have to report?" he asked. His guards watched the windows, doorways and rooftops around him.

Orgel was the one who answered. "The temple district is gone, just like the priests said. Only the Five Dragons Temple stands, though it does not seem strongly guarded. The King's Keep is sealed and its walls are teeming with Tlocanian soldiers."

"Did you encounter any Tlocanians patrolling the city?"

"No, my prince. The Tlocanians are only at the fort. The rebels, however, are about the city. So far, they have not tried to hunt down our scouts, but they have not fled from us either."

"Send someone with this information to General Fors, back at the upper east gate. Let him know that I will await his arrival before assaulting the keep. Tell him I expect to see him at the dragon temple." Wintron considered a moment. "Orgel, I want the scouts to capture one of the rebels. We need to find out if these two forces have truly separated, as it seems. I also want to know where the king slayer is hiding."

After Orgel rode off, Wintron sent one of his personal guards to retrieve the squadron's leaders. It was time to plan a quick seizing of the temple and then a far-harder assault on the keep. This would be no easy matter like the city gate.

DRASS

Lord Drass wandered the upper floors of the keep, not really paying attention to where he was going, and soon found himself on the wall walk, right in front of the tower that served as the Shadow Anchor. He realized Slosoro guided his steps and tried to resist. "I cannot allow you to lead me there," he whispered. "Farwatch Tower is forbidden to us."

Can you not feel the power? Slosoro asked inside his mind.

He caught his breath at the clear response.

Look.

Drass suddenly knew how to look and did so. Now the pulsing light was not just a crimson beam. He sensed all the power being used, linking into the Dragon Shadow looming overhead. He felt the power in the clouds as well, though it seemed more dispersed.

Let us go embrace that power.

"No," he whispered, tempted. "That would not be right for either of us. We cannot interrupt the ritual." Drass turned away, taking a small door off the wall walk so that he would not have to see that temptation. Slosoro did not protest.

The young noble chose to go in the opposite direction, heading down through the fort until he came out in a courtyard behind the stables. The open area was now full of cages holding humans. He halted, surprised.

Can you feel the power locked in their blood? Kill them and we will be able to feed on that power.

Drass grimaced at the thought, but he did sense the power of those lives. Unintentionally, he stepped closer to the nearest cage, which held five men. Without conscious thought, he raised his right hand and crimson lightning danced across his fingertips. The men inside the cage huddled on the far side, watching him fearfully but not bothering to plea for mercy. He fought against a strong urge to strike out at them.

"See here, Embraced One. Do not slaughter those, for they are already scheduled for the rite upstairs."

Embarrassed, Drass quickly lowered his hand, letting the lightning dissipate. He looked over his shoulder at the three men approaching from another row of cages. Before Drass could say anything in response, the man in the middle spoke again.

"Have you the need for a personal sacrifice, Holy One? If so please come with us, for there are some already set aside for you, sir."

Drass hesitated. He almost swore at them to leave him alone; that he had no such need. However, the desire came on even stronger and suddenly he gave the man a silent nod. Drass let the three slave masters lead him off to his first victims.

WINTRON

The day turned windy as Wintron and Fors rode into the area that had once been the temple district, an area now empty except for piles of ashen rubble and the lonely Five Dragons Temple. A few temple guards had tried to bar the entrance, but Wintron's men had quickly overwhelmed them. They found the complex practically empty. As the two leaders rode into the cobbled courtyard, they saw a few temple servants lined up to one side. A squad of Border soldiers stood guard over them. The two dismounted and walked up to the temple's five narrow spires, each topped with a different-colored turret. The door to each tower lay open, awaiting their choice.

"I will wait down here," stated Fors, patting his still-sore leg. "See what you can spy of the King's Keep, but please make it quick, my prince. We only have a few hours of daylight left, as weak as it is. While you are hiking the tower, I will question these traitors."

Wintron glanced over at the gathered servants in their gray robes. "It is a shame we have no priest to question. But then, it seems that most of them are demon-possessed these days, and that would have made for a terrible fight. Do what you can to learn something useful from them." He then looked around for the head of his personal guard and spotted him coming out of the temple with his arms full of robes.

Sergeant Yosif strode over to his liege. "My prince, these robes are threadbare but they are freshly laundered. Will they do?"

"Good enough for such a distant perch," replied Wintron, grabbing the topmost garment and pulling it over his head. It hung short and tight across his chest, but it would do. He motioned for the others to take a robe as well. He would now spy out his enemy's nest.

He chose the center spire, going through the black doorway. He found a pair of red-shaded lanterns hanging near the entrance, already lit. He took one and started up the narrow stairs. Accompanying him for the climb were half of his personal guard and some of the army officers. The spiral was so tight inside the thin spire that he had to stop halfway up, his head spinning from going in an upward circle. The others paused too, their heavy breathing the only sound besides the wind whistling through the tower.

He continued to climb and finally came to the narrow landing near its top. He pulled up the robe's hood and stepped out onto the balcony. The wind blew stronger up here, whipping at his cloak and trying to push his hood back. He held it in place with one hand. He followed the balcony around to where he could gaze at the King's Keep. At his side stood Yosif and Major Cilano, Fors' second.

Wintron's eyes caught on the red light shooting skyward from Farwatch Tower, the highest spire within King's Keep. The light pulsed and throbbed like a living thing. The Tlocanians had removed the tower's roof, exposing the top landing to the elements. He could not see over the jagged wall, but he imagined that an altar sat up there where they killed victims to release their life's power. The light beam seemed thicker now and more solid. Looking up, he saw that the column now separated at the top, becoming multiple red branches that clung to and supported the cloud cover.

"El have mercy on us," he whispered. "Look how it has grown."

"The Shadow Anchor is much more solid now," agreed Yosif, "and it also emanates from other towers too."

Wintron had not noticed, but now that the sergeant mentioned it, he could see fainter glows coming from four other keep towers, angling up to Farwatch. The red light came from West Spire, Queen's Tower, Old Tower, and Windcharm Tower, linking each to Farwatch with a blood red stream of light. The sight made his skin crawl. "That is not good. They are spending their power extravagantly. I fear how many lives it costs to bring each escalation in their magic."

Lightning flashed regularly in the clouds, illuminating the fortress in faint red. Whenever there was a pause in that light show, he could see nothing of the keep except the Shadow Anchor and small lights used by soldiers on the various wall walks. Those patrol lights were also red. The prince wondered why the Tlocanians had such a fondness for that particular color.

"I can hardly observe anything," complained Major Cilano. "I have never seen clouds so black as those over the keep. They seem to lap up the light like a kitten laps up the last drops of milk in a saucer."

"How many men would you expect with each lantern?" asked Wintron, ignoring the man's complaint.

"Every sentry walking in that darkness would need a light or else risk tripping off the ramparts," declared the major.

"They might be walking in pairs or even half-squads, for the wall walk is wide enough," said Yosif at almost the same time, then looked apologetically towards the major.

Wintron guessed that Yosif did not want to contradict a superior officer. He agreed with the sergeant's assessment, but did not say that aloud. "We cannot see even half of the wall walks from here, and then there are those guarding the prisoners and those manning the gates. I think the estimate from the two old priests was not far off. The place is crawling with Tlocanians."

"How can we overthrow it in time?" asked the major. "It is no Tor Randis, but veteran warriors hold that keep. It could take days or even weeks to breech any of the gates."

Wintron considered. The major was right. He thought of each of the keep's entrances, but could think of none that would be easily overrun. They would need to find some other entrance into the King's Keep. The defenders were strangers to the fortress, but surely they had spied out all of its side gates and sally ports. He weighed each approach, but none seemed a sure entrance. If only he had men on the inside, to open the river gate or the butcher's door. Baron Gordrew had been one of the last to escape the keep and he had claimed all others suffered imprisonment or death. Even if Wintron knew of someone within those stone walls, how could he ever get a message to them? If he could get a messenger inside, then the messenger could just as well be the one unlocking a side gate. Then suddenly, an old memory came to him and he knew how to get someone inside.

Yosif interrupted his thoughts when he leaned over the stone railing and looked straight down. "The temple burns."

Surprised, Wintron saw that it was true. Smoke wafted up from the rambling wood and stone structure. "What is happening down there?" He pushed through the men crowded on the balcony and made his way back to the stairwell. The others rushed after him, either out of curiosity or out of fear that the fire might spread to their slim perch.

By the time he reached the courtyard far below, the temple was well engulfed. The Old Fox stood with arms crossed, watching it burn.

Wintron feared that the old man's devotion to the mountain gods had driven him to revenge. "What have you done, Uncle? Has not enough of Regalis been destroyed?"

Fors turned his head, the fire revealing the hardness in his eyes. "What? Are you a dragon lover too? I thought it was the Attuls' god you favored, or is it just that you have an over-fondness for Lord Rolen's wife?"

Wintron felt a sudden surge of anger towards his uncle's snide remarks. "Take your little snips at me, old man, but do not impugn Tolara Quickblade. Even worse, how dare you slander all the dragonsworn? Many good Borderfolk worshiped here, but now they have lost their temple, thanks to your actions."

"Your father's killers hid here. This is how Mordel got so many men close to Varen. They slipped in disguised as temple servants and then assembled in this very courtyard. I burn a traitor's nest. Besides, your dragon priest agrees with me."

Only then did Wintron notice old Werth standing nearby. The priest stepped closer once the prince looked his way. "The duke speaks truth, my prince. This was no longer a true place of dragon worship. It had been desecrated with human sacrifice. Too many abominations happened here, so let the fires cleanse this site. We can always rebuild when the time is right."

"May that time never arrive," replied Fors. "This is the land of our mountain gods. You can worship your winged beasts elsewhere. All the dragonsworn should be driven off to the lowlands."

Father Bilchaso interceded for the dragon priest. "No one can question your faith, Child Fors. However, the mountain gods are not as jealous as you believe. Brother Werth is a Borderman, same as you and I. I think he has already proven his loyalty to the realm."

"It was the dragonsworn who aided my treacherous offspring, who spied for the Tlocanians, who…"

"Enough of this," ordered Wintron, speaking over him. "We must gain the keep quickly, uncle, and I think I know how. Did you ever explore Engro's Ways as a youth?"

Fors stopped his argument in mid-sentence. There was a pause and then he actually grinned. "The tunnel! Certainly, I explored the Ways with Varen during our childhood. All Dabe children have crawled through Engro's narrow passages and peeked out his spy holes."

The Old Fox considered a moment. "I never told my sons about the hidden ways. Did you ever take Mordel or Drass exploring when they came to visit as children?"

The prince chuckled. "Oh no, I guarded that secret well. Engro's Ways helped greatly whenever I play hide-and-hunt with them." He turned to the two old priests. "Brother Werth, Father Bilchaso, can I leave the temple servants in your charge? We must go and make our plans and I do not want any of them sneaking off."

"We will keep them busy," promised Brother Werth. "There will be much to clean up after the temple burns down. And I am sure there are people who need aid and comfort in this terrorized city."

"Thank you," replied Wintron, pulling off the gray garment he had been wearing. "We will keep these robes though. They might prove useful once we gain the keep." He beckoned Yosif closer, holding up the red-shaded light he had used while climbing the tower. "Have someone search each tower for more of these lanterns. We will need all we can find." He motioned Fors and the officers to follow him back to their horses. As he strode, he continued his conversation with his uncle. "How many do you think I can lead through the Rabbit Hole?"

"You? Really, my prince, you should not take such a risk. You are the future of the Border Realm. Let me lead the troops through the tunnel."

"Uncle, you are over twenty years my senior. Memory of all those twists will have faded with the decades. The Rabbit Hole is simple enough, but we will need to take Engro's Ways as high up as we can. It will be hard enough for me to remember."

Fors grumbled in frustration. "You have it right. It has been too long since either of us crept through those hidden passages. You will need to lead, but I must go as well. With the two of us recalling our youthful explorations and with the gods' help, we should remember enough."

Wintron did not want his uncle along, for he still wondered how trustworthy Fors would be when faced with either son in-person. It was one thing to be furious with absent children, but quite another to sustain such wrath when they are close enough to embrace. There would be need for a false assault on the keep's main gate and that was where Wintron would prefer his uncle. As they mounted, he carefully proposed that assignment.

"No, I must go along on this mission. My son overthrew the King's Keep, so it is only fitting that I take part in righting the wrong. Besides, there are probably routes I found as a child that you never did. You cannot claim to have discovered all of Engro's secrets. Our ancestor honeycombed the keep with so many."

Wintron sighed. His uncle was right. King Engro must have been a very suspicious man, for there were spy holes all over the older portions of King's Keep. "Did you ever take any route up Farwatch Tower?"

Fors had to admit he never had. "That spire was added after Engro, so it may have no hidden stairs. Nevertheless, we should be able to get our force to its base. If you mean to interrupt their Shadow Anchor ritual and stop the slaughter, then we both must guide our troops inside. Time is pressing, nephew."

"What about your injured leg? There will be much climbing and walking."

Fors raised an eyebrow. "Do you think I will risk our mission with my limp or the tapping of my cane? I will leave my cane at the Rabbit

Hole's door and just have one of my personal guards give aid when climbing. Should I fall behind, leave me. I know the risk, but I also know that my knowledge could prove essential. I will not be able to run fast, but I can still hike and I can certainly swing a sword. Now, as I said, time is pressing."

Wintron yielded to his uncle's arguments.

DRASS

Drass was surprised when Goval told him of the summons. The priests had warned him to stay far away from all of the towers, but now Colonel Ulen requested his presence inside the highest one: Farwatch Tower. Drass dared not ignore the request, though it went against the orders of Cavish and Hurko. He found his way to its base with only two wrong turns. A guard at the foot of the stairs directed him to a room halfway up the great tower. He hiked his way up, past the guarded doors behind which they kept the ones waiting sacrifice. The stairway was lit by red lanterns, a bit too bright for him yet necessary for the weaker-eyed commoners.

Finally, he came to a landing where a door sat open, an awful smell coming from the rooms beyond. He put a hand to his nose as he walked inside. This had once been a guest suite, but now the furniture was soiled and the once-rich carpets stained. He avoided looking into one corner that had been turned into a makeshift privy, but its reek made itself known. Colonel Ulen stepped out from one of the bedrooms with two Tlocanian soldiers.

"There you are, Lord Drass. Pardon the stench, but we have just sent another fifty for sacrifice. One hundred more are already coming up and to take their place, so there will be no time to clean the room. We just check to make sure all victims have been removed before refilling the place."

"You could not use the dungeon or the gardens?" asked Drass, disgusted by the state of the rooms.

Ulen shrugged. "The priests insist that their victims must be close, in case they need more fuel for their fires. I make sure there are enough close by, yet those other places you suggested are also full. The coming ritual will be costly, but it is necessary for the empire. Killing people is one of the ugly parts of being an Embraced One. However, the benefits far outweigh these undesirable tasks. I hear that you have already discovered that truth." The colonel moved towards the door.

"Come; let us step out onto the landing for fresher air.

The soldiers stayed behind but the smells followed Ulen and Drass out the door. Drass took his hand away from his nose but still dared not breathe deeply. The two of them walked over to the far side of the landing, near the stairs leading further up into the tower.

Drass was not about to admit that he had found pleasure in killing a prisoner earlier in the day, for Ulen might use that fact against him. However, he had to admit to himself that the power released by killing was a delicious thing. Slosoro had taken over, expertly sucking the life energy from his victim. He had been a mere observer in his own body. At first, he had been scared at losing control, but then the power sensation overwhelmed his fears. He also sensed Slosoro's feelings too, heightening it all.

"Have you decided what path you will take?" asked Ulen.

The question confused Drass. "I do not understand…"

Ulen smiled. "Not all Embraced Ones are dragon priests, obviously." He pointed to himself as an example. "There are four roads you can choose from, though how far you travel on a road depends on your strength and perseverance. But no matter, you will learn all of this soon enough. I did not call you up here to instruct you." Ulen looked down at his spotted boots and frowned. "It has been decided that you shall have a duty during the ceremony after all. At midnight, they will start the heart of the ritual. You are to be at the top of this tower at that time. Another new Embraced One will join you; both of you will take your orders from the priests up there. Is that understood?"

Drass had heard the expected response often enough to know it. "I hear and obey."

Ulen nodded, though he still looked at his sullied boots. "You might want to borrow a priest's robe for the night; unless you have a set of clothes you will not mind getting blood-soaked." He finally looked up at Drass. "Go and get some rest and a hardy meal, for it is a long ritual."

WINTRON

No matter how much King Engro had desired otherwise, the King's Keep was never a rival to Tor Randis. Though more graceful in appearance, with its tall towers, grand halls, and lovely gardens, it could not compare to the demon-wrought fortress in the strength of its ramparts. Wintron wondered if it had galled his ancestor to admit that inferiority. Nevertheless, Engro must have faced the truth, for he had the Rabbit Hole dug. The secret way was meant as an escape route, should the keep ever be threatened. The tunnel led north, of course, to speed any refugees on their way towards Tor Randis. It surfaced within the city, near a long-unused sally door in the north wall. The Rabbit Hole actually came out inside the constable's prison, in a storage room within the cellar.

Wintron now stood in that constabulary's courtyard as hundreds upon hundreds of men crowded in around him. He was taking two thousand men under the city. Only a few dozen robes had been taken from the Five Dragons Temple, so Yosif handed them out to those men who would be in the vanguard. The others would have to go in without any disguise.

The men waited patiently as the last of their numbers pressed in from the street, impressing Wintron with their calm and serious demeanor. They understood that the realm's survival rested in their hands.

The wind had grown stronger, swaying the lantern Wintron held. Even though many were expecting him to speak, he waited as Fors pressed through the soldiers. Finally, the Old Fox joined him in front of the empty building.

"Have you any final words for the men?" he asked his uncle.

Fors grimaced. "Nothing more than stay alive and kill our enemies. It is time for action and not pretty words, my prince." He walked past his nephew and into the jailhouse.

Wintron dampened a sudden irritation with his uncle. It was time for encouragement and exhortation, he thought. He turned to the gathered troops. "Men, we are about to enter a place even darker than this." He pointed at the black sky. "Not the tunnel, though it will be dark enough, but the keep at its end. You will see things to turn your stomach, fill your eyes with tears, and set your heart afire for revenge. However, I ask three things of you now. First, move silently, for we will be creeping behind walls and past spy holes. Do not betray us all with noise.

"Second, remember our goal. We are here to stop the killing and destroy that evil beacon." Without looking, Wintron pointed over his shoulder to where the huge light seared skyward. "Do not become distracted by any hunger for vengeance or overwhelmed by sudden despair. We must press on all the way up Farwatch Tower to stop this.

"Finally, know that righteousness is on our side. Show no pity or forbearance towards our enemies. We may pass over killing some because it would expose us or stop us from our goal, but eventually we will hunt them all down. Hold your empathy for the Borderfolk who suffer under their cruel hands. Know this; we might spare some of our enemies for a short time, but it will only be justice slightly delayed. They will all face vengeance once that beacon is shattered and the captives are freed. Know this and be heartened. Now, follow me to our victory!"

Some cheered, while others shouted defiance towards the King's Keep. They all surged forward to follow Wintron down to Engro's Rabbit Hole.

He strode into the austere jail, past empty cells, and into a back room. He could hear Fors and his cane on the wooden stairway even with all the noise behind him. The prince passed through another doorway and descended after his uncle. The cellar was well lit and the hidden doorway lay open already, for a handful of scouts had gone ahead to make sure the tunnel was still passable. Wintron stepped off the stairs and crossed the stone floor to where Fors now waited. He had already leaned his cane against the wall.

"Sensible words," remarked Fors. "I hope they obey all three commands."

Wintron was surprised that his uncle had bothered to listen. He stepped aside as those assigned to the vanguard hurried past them, all of them in temple robes. The secret doorway exposed a wooden ladder leading to a deeper level. Even though the men tried to move quietly, still an echo came up the shaft: sounds of breathing, swords bumping the ladder, and boots scraping on rungs. Once the vanguard was down, Fors took his turn, followed by the prince and then Yosif.

Wintron stepped off the ladder onto an unfinished stone floor. King Engro's escape tunnel ran through rock most of the way, deep enough to avoid discovery from any new cellar diggers. The prince walked up to the duke. In the red light of the various lanterns, Fors appeared ill. He hoped the Old Fox had the strength for this night's task. "Let us get going, uncle. We have a far way to march just to get under the fortress walls. Only then can we start our sword work."

The general gave up leaning against and wall and pushed off. "It looks like we have already begun our bloody work, what with everything bathed in red."

Fors strode into the tunnel, one of his personal guards walking right behind him. Though the Old Fox limped, he kept up with the vanguard. Wintron entered at his heels, with Yosif and the rest of the prince's personal guard at his back. Behind them came a long line of soldiers, stretched out by the narrow passage.

DRASS

Drass could not sleep. He had given up on trying and was sitting on his bed in his underclothes, when someone knocked at his door. "Enter."

His older brother stepped in. "Drass? Are you in here?"

"I am right here," he replied, almost directly in front of the usurper king.

"I can see nothing in this pitch darkness," complained Mordel, feeling his way across the small room until he bumped into the small bed and Drass' shoulder. Mordel sat down next to him. "Are you alone?"

"Of course," replied Drass. "What do you desire, brother of mine? You said that you did not want to see my face again, but I guess you cannot see it now."

Mordel gave a wary look in his brother's direction, which Drass saw clearly. "I need your help. You are one of them now, but you are also a Borderman. You need to explain to them that they need to find some other place for these rituals. Anywhere but the King's Keep, for they defile it with all of this killing."

He found that humorous, coming from a man who butchered the last king. "It is too late, Mordel. The Shadow Anchor must be placed soon or else they will lose the Dragon Shadow and with it a major reservoir of power. They cannot just stop all of this after so much preparation. Leave off this folly, Mordel. Let your allies do what they must."

"They have taken over most of my keep," argued Mordel. "How will anyone see me as king when others have free rein around my residence?"

"You are no free king; you are the Tlocanian emperor's vassal. You rule by his suffrage and it is best that you remember that."

Mordel stood up, the anger obvious on his face. "You are no help!"

Drass held up one hand and let lighting play across his fingers. "As you said, I am one of them now. Go now, my brother, and I will not mention any of this to the colonel. See, I still have some compassion for my sibling."

"Compassion? You spout threats and call it compassion? You have some nerve, little brother."

He had no desire to continue this tiresome discussion. If only he could leave Mordel to Slosoro. Suddenly, Drass felt his voice being taken over by the demon. He tried to resist, resulting in a series of deep coughs, but then he let Slosoro do whatever he wanted. "Be gone, Mordel," ordered Slosoro in a far deeper voice than Drass ever used.

"Who is that?" demanded Mordel. "You said we were alone. Who is in this room with us, Drass?"

"There is only one other person in this room," said Slosoro through Drass' mouth, "but your brother is now far greater than you, Mordel the Betrayer."

Clearly frightened, Mordel backed out of the room without another word. When he was gone, Drass chuckled. "I do not know when last I saw Mordel so terrorized."

He was that frightened on the day you pushed him off the wall at Tor Randis, replied Slosoro in his thoughts.

Drass remembered that day, from over twenty years ago. They had been playing a game of siege and he had been defending the keep against Mordel's invasion. He had pushed off Mordel's ladder, sending him sprawling on the stony ground far below. Mordel broke his arm and bruised his ribs.

Suddenly, his smile faded. "You can look at my memories?"

We are one now, Drass Halen-Dabe. Our brethren will now call us Drass-Slosoro. I know all about you and you must learn more about me.

"How will I do that?" wondered Drass aloud. Suddenly the 'how' came to him, and he began reliving some of Slosoro's memories. They were not memories of the Darklands but of Slosoro's last time in Na Ciria, two hundred years ago. Drass began to learn about the Darshi Empire from one who had been a powerful leader in that ancient realm. He gained a better understanding of what the demons wanted and caught enticing glimpses of the demonic powers used during the last invasion.

Eric Lorenzen

CHAPTER THIRTY-THREE
Father Blue

AFRAL

His father's prediction of blustery weather proved accurate. As the clouds began to overtake the city, it brought gusts of wind. Afral and his parents passed through another market where many of the sellers were packing up their goods early. The three followed a wider avenue northward, where each block showed a riot of colors, the flags and bunting now snapping in the wind. Behind them, the clouds started to fill the sky. It reminded Afral of the Dragon Shadow and he shivered, even though he knew it was just a natural springtime storm. People on the streets walked faster, now aware of the imminent storm, but the crowd did not thin forcing the Attuls to keep their horses to slow walk.

As a scattering of fat drops began to splash down, they came upon one of the city's bridges. Going around a slow-moving wagon, they rode up onto the stone span. At the center stood two tollbooths, one against either rail, where taxes were collected from those heading in either direction. A soldier in purple overcoat and pants stepped out to collect the fee from them. He did not ask to see their colors. Rolen paid, and the man hurried back into his shelter to await the wagon behind them. As they rode past, Rolen drew near to the railing and tossed three pieces of cloth into the swirling waters below.

The city on this side of the Singgorn did not seem any different to Afral. Most of the buildings still stood close together and three stories tall, though some now rose to four levels. The area was predominantly Purple here, so they kept riding. Finally, they came upon a city block where both blue and green were displayed, neither dominant. An inn called the Blue Pelican came into view, its stable taking the ground floor of the four-story hostelry. His father declared that they had better end their search for night's lodging here and led his family into the stable yard. They boarded their mounts and then climbed the broad steps to the common room. The innkeeper demanded to see their colors before he would rent them a room. Rolen showed his dark blue armband and the man suddenly became much more cordial. They received a key to a room on the third floor and hiked up to drop off their things. Once they were settled in, Afral's father went down and retrieved three meals, for his parents had decided it would be best to avoid the common room. Afral felt a little disappointed, for he would have liked the chance to see more of the locals while in the safe company of his parents.

* * *

At dawn, someone began to pound on the door to the Attuls' room. Afral, in the middle of buttoning on his shirt, looked to his father with concern. Rolen quickly finished fastening on his scabbard and then called out to know who was there.

"This is Sergeant Fauleon of the Blue home patrol. Open in the name of Father Blue."

His parents shared a look of concern. His mother quickly put on the large hat and wrapped her cloak around her to hide her figure. She stationed herself as far from the door as possible, yet still in a position to come to his aid quickly. She quietly beckoned Afral to her side. When Rolen open the door, he found a squad of six men crowded in the hallway. They were all wet, causing puddles on the wooden floor.

Afral's father spoke up. "What can I help you with?"

The sergeant took a moment, as if comparing their faces to ones described to him. "I am here to invite you to see Father Blue. Will you come along peacefully?"

"May we keep our weapons?" asked Rolen.

The sergeant laughed. "Bring every weapon you have, for he expects it. You should actually bring along all of your belongings, just in case Father Blue offers you lodging for the night"

He said the last without any threat in his voice, but Afral wondered if he was suggesting staying as a guest or as a prisoner.

His father ignored the implied threat. "Please give us a moment to gather our things. We have also not had our morning meal. Will there be time enough on our journey for us to eat a little?"

Fauleon nodded. "Enough time. You can grab some of the

Pelican's notorious biscuits. The rain might soften them enough to make them edible."

An escort brought them back over to the western half of the city, unchallenged by the bridge patrol. Sergeant Fauleon led them into an area where all the street banners and shutters were blue. Even the street puddles seemed blue, as they reflected the limp blue flags and blue-painted doors. They turned a few corners, but everything remained Blue territory. Street traffic was light due to the weather and early hour. They came to a street of tall houses, each behind its own wall. The way ended at a cobblestone square with a large fountain at its center. Water sprayed out from stone dolphins, to join the rain falling in the basin. Beyond the fountain stood a huge house, well-guarded by sharply dressed Blues. Fauleon brought them up to the gate.

"I will take you in to see Father Blue's doorkeeper," announced Fauleon. He turned to his troops. "Jallis, you and Ren fall in. Trog, take the rest back out on patrol." He turned back to Rolen. "We will take you to Uncle Jander now."

Afral's father smiled, but only nodded agreement. The sergeant gained them quick access, for they were expected. They rode through the iron gate and past a well-kept garden of neatly trimmed trees. Early flowers hung over in their flowerbeds, heavy with rain. They came to a large stable bustling with activity. Grooms rushed forward to take their horses. Fauleon assured them that their personal items would be laid to one side, out of the rain, and their steeds taken care of properly. "You do not have to worry about thievery here."

The sergeant led them back into the rain and around to the front of the mansion. They climbed a flight of stairs to a pair of oversized doors painted a deep blue with golden highlights. Two Blues stood there, statue-still. Only when the sergeant's boot touched the top step, did one of them move, turning sharply and opening the right-hand door. An attendant stood just inside. He took their soaked cloaks and offered towels. They wiped their boots on thick mats. Fauleon stared at their deep blue armbands for a moment, for it was the first time he had seen them, but he did not mention them.

"This way," he said when all were drier, leading them past more guards and into a huge anteroom. Afral looked up at the gigantic chandelier that hung overhead, amazed at the sight. The opulence of the place overwhelmed him. This was a robber baron's lair, yet it seemed more regal than the King's Keep in Regalis.

They followed the sergeant down a side hall where tapestries hung on the walls and carpets muffled their footsteps. They came to a large room well lit by rain-soaked windows and a roaring fire.

An old man stood up from behind a desk and came over with a sudden smile. "Thank you Sergeant Fauleon. You and your men are dismissed back to your normal duties." He turned to the two guards already in the room. "Men, please wait outside." Doorkeeper Jander then closed the door on the soldiers, before turning to greet his guests.

"Welcome Rolen," he stated, offering a slight bow. "Please introduce me to these others. Your family?"

"Jander, it has been a long time since we last saw each other," replied Rolen. "This is my wife Tolara Quickblade and my son Afral."

As the elderly man offered them each a slight bow, Rolen explained. "I met Jander over ten years ago, when he and Father Blue's eldest son came through Regalis. In those days, he was the boy's mentor. By now, Eagan is fully grown and his great-uncle Jander appears to have a new role in the Blue family."

"Eagan will be disappointed to have missed you, but he is traveling. You made quite an impression on him, to the rue of his father." Jander chuckled. "I was nearly killed when Eagan came home spouting words like justice and nobility and fairness, Dalton's anger did not let up for days, and it took years to repair how you corrupted Eagan in just those few short days."

"Only in Freetown would honorable traits be seen as corruption," responded Afral's father. He shook his head, yet still smiled.

Jander motioned them to sit on the padded couches. "What brings you here, Rolen?"

"We are just passing through. How did you know that I was in town?"

Jander chuckled again. "I did not. It was reported to me that three newcomers entered the city as Greens working for a trader and then turned into Blue assassins. Those in Razon blue are rarely seen in public these days, and especially not three together. I wanted to make sure that this was not the start of some Blue clan war."

Rolen looked at his armband. "Obviously, we have blundered. The Razon family has changed since last we came to Freetown."

Jander nodded. "For generations they have lived with their legacy of being Red lovers. They tired of being looked down upon as too soft, too nice. Their leaders decided to earn a different reputation, so they have trained their young men to be skilled assassins. The Razon are still despised by others, but now they are also feared."

Tolara tore off her armband. "I will not associate with murderers, either of the past or of the present." Rolen and Afral followed her lead, placing all three strips of dark blue cloth on a table nearby.

Jander gave a slight nod of approval. "I am glad to have that corrected. You scared that innkeeper greatly. He feared that this morning he would find corpses in half his rooms."

"May we leave now?" asked Rolen. "I would enjoy lingering to talk about our lives, but we need to get going."

Jander gave a small shake of denial. "Not yet. My nephew, the Father Blue, will want to see you and I am not one to disappoint him. Be warned, he has a long memory so do not expect a warm welcome for the man who confused his eldest son. He almost disinherited Eagan for expressing such radical ideas..."

"I understand," replied Rolen, rising to his feet. "Could you please take us to see him now?"

Jander shrugged, also standing up. "I might as well, for Dalton's attitude will not improve from delay." At the door, he called over a servant and whispered to him. The fellow hurried off, probably to alert Father Blue. Jander led them out of the reception room and down the hall to a wide stairway. They climbed two flights and then went down another hallway, coming to a room with hard wooden benches along two walls. Double doors stood shut to one side, with two guards at attention. Jander ignored the stiff men, went up to the doors, and knocked. He opened the right door when he heard a muffled acknowledgment.

"Father Blue, here are your visitors," he said, motioning them in.

It was a plush room, full of cushions and carpets. At the far end, large windows overlooked a garden. In front of the window sat a large desk. Behind the desk stood a gray-haired man with a bare sword in his hand. "Come in. Uncle, please stay but close the doors."

Afral heard the door shut behind him, but his eyes were elsewhere. Along the side wall hung weapon after weapon: swords, bows, crossbows, and staves. Some looked wickedly efficient while others seemed too pretty for actual use. In the corner stood a rack full of staves and lances. As Afral moved forward with his parents, he saw that a side table had a glass top. Under the glass was displayed a large collection of knives.

"Greetings, Father Blue," announced Rolen with a slight bow.

"Well, at last we meet, Attul Rolen Strongarm."

Rolen paused from his bow, surprised. "Why do you call me an

Attul?"

"Are there any listeners on duty, Dalton?" asked Jander, looking around the room.

Dalton shook his head. "They were all sent away. Now please, everyone take a seat." He looked over at Jander. "Uncle, could you bring that pitcher of mulled cider and mugs over? I am sure our guests would enjoy a warm beverage on this wet day and it is a bit too early for any hot wine."

Rolen and his family took chairs before Father Blue's desk. Jander passed out the drinks and then sat to the other side of Afral.

Dalton sat down, laying the naked sword on his desk, and leaned forward. "In spite of our reputation, we Freetowners do believe in honesty at times. I named you an Attul because you are one. Do you deny it?"

Afral's father chose not to respond.

Dalton nodded, taking his silence as confirmation. "Do you like my weapon collection?" He lifted the naked sword in front of him, extending its hilt towards Rolen. "Try the heft of this ancient blade."

Rolen almost took hold of it, but then hesitated.

"Go ahead," stated Father Blue. "I insist."

Rolen smiled, said a quiet prayer to El, and took hold of the offered sword. It began to glow. "As you have deduced, we are Attuls."

Dalton nodded, fascinated by the blade's white glow. Jander sat forward, enthralled.

Rolen set the sword on the desk and its glow faded.

Dalton sighed, still gazing at the now-dull blade. "I have owned that sword for almost five years, but it has never shone like that before." He looked up at Rolen. "How do you perform such magic?"

"No magic," replied Rolen. "My god infuses the metal with power. The sword has been consecrated to his service, though this one has seen many other hands since. As a Prayer Warrior, I seek my god's help in battle. When a Prayer Warrior and a consecrated sword come together, power for good is the result. The power is all from our god."

Dalton nodded. "That would be the god El. I have heard the old tales from the Great War." He paused for a moment, and then continued. "Do you realize that I could make a tidy profit on the three of you? For months now there have been people hunting for Attuls. We have seen Tlocanian spies, dragon priests, and bounty hunters all looking for you legends. Can you give me a good reason why I should not march you down to the Five Dragons Temple today and get my reward?"

Afral could not hide the concern he felt at the thought of their mission failing now. He looked to his parents and saw that his mother was now upset. He saw his father touch her arm, to restrain her obvious anger, and then he answered Father Blue calmly. "No matter how big the reward, I doubt you have need for it. If you would do this to gain favor with the Tlocanians then you do not understand the ways of demons."

"Demons? Are you telling me that those legends are true too?" Dalton sat back in his chair. "Do you claim that those hairy midnight monsters are about to ravage Freetown, howling for blood and carrying off our young? What other nursery tales will come to life? Ejoti midgets? Rock eating Ogres? Alluring Mermaids?"

"The enemy is real," stated Rolen. "They ruled the Darshi in the Great War and they now rule the Tlocanians. The demons are not those hairy beasts from bedtime stories; they are clever beings who come to live inside willing humans, taking them over."

Father Blue looked incredulous. His Doorkeeper, Jander, seemed puzzled. Before either could interrupt, Rolen continued. "Even if you refuse to believe such stories, surely you have heard about the treachery of the Tlocanians. Their army is huge, but their quick victories came more from betrayal and intrigue than just brute strength. Surely, you do not trust them to uphold any promises made to you."

"Are you offering Freetown an Attul treaty?" asked Dalton.

Rolen shook his head regrettably. "I do not have such authority. Even if I had such powers, Freetown is a divided city."

"The three fathers are not as divided as you believe," answered Father Blue. "We see the danger on the horizon, but for now we are protected at either end of the Singgorn Plains. Rhendora battles the Tlocanians to a standstill and with the Lakelands they have an uneasy peace. Besides, I doubt they will continue their aggressions much longer, for it is much be too costly. They already rule everything from the Border Mountains to the Midcirian Plains, from the Grandgorn Valley to the Grizzly Mountains. I think they will tire of war before winning through to us. What profit would come from conquering these wilds?"

"Spoken like a merchant, Father Blue, but the demon followers are not driven by profit. Please heed my warning: you have at most two years before Freetown falls, whether you give in to their delegates or not." Rolen turned to the doorkeeper. "Speak to him, Jander. You know that I am a man of my word; I speak no deception."

"There is no need for me to convince Father Blue," said Jander.

Afral looked at the leader of the Blues and saw Dalton nod.

"Your assessment is fairly accurate, though we might be able to buy a bit more time by pretending to capitulate. They try to play off Father Purple against Father Green and myself. We let them think they are making progress. Maybe, if we hand them three Attuls they will be further appeased."

Rolen frowned, but did not respond. Tolara opened her mouth to protest, and then thought better of it. Their son just listened with a fast-beating heart.

"However, I do not yet know if that would truly benefit me," continued Father Blue. "I require some time to discuss this with my fellow fathers, so you are now my honored guests until tomorrow. Uncle Jander, please see to their needs." With that, he dismissed them from his study.

Afral's father must have seen no value in protesting, for he just stood up and motioned for his family to do likewise. They followed Jander away from Dalton's private suite. The Doorkeeper brought them to a guest suite that was one floor down and around to a far wing of the mansion. It was a set of well-appointed rooms, but the presence of guards made it obvious that they were expected to remain here.

"Please do not use your powers here in the Blue Residence," stated Jander. "No matter your might, I do not think you can win free through hundreds of Blues. Instead, be patient. I believe Dalton has seen the wisdom in not only letting you go, but also helping you on whatever is your path." He paused to make sure they had no protestations. "For now, please refresh yourselves and enjoy the comforts you have been denied while on the road. I also extend you an invitation to join me for dinner this evening. Good bye for now." He gave them a slight bow and withdrew.

* * *

Afral explored their rooms thoroughly, but then became bored and sat down. His mother paced the living room still. His father gazed out the window at the Blue barracks that sat across a courtyard from their upper-floor suite. Afral watched both his parents and wondered why they remained in this resplendent prison. He finally spoke. "Can we not just fight our way free of this manor?"

Both parents turned to look at him. Tolara responded. "How do you mean, Afral? Should we just attack these Blues?"

He nodded. "Are they not forcing us to do so? They keep us from our mission. Should we not just overpower them and break free?"

"Listen to what you are saying, my dear. You know that El would withdraw his power if we used it to kill innocents or even the questionable ones. The spirit swords are not for our convenience; they are weapons for righteousness. So far, the Blues have not tried to kill us or even seize our weapons. We would have no cause to attack them." But then his mother looked pointedly at the walls and Afral remembered that there might be spies listening in. "However, if they try to sell us to the Tlocanians, then your father and I will have to resist. It would be a shame to destroy their pretty blue palace."

Afral never knew if anyone overheard that warning from his mother, for no one ever mentioned it. That evening, they had a quiet dinner with Doorkeeper Jander. Afral liked the variety and richness of the food, as well as the softly playing quartet that gave them music to eat by. Not much was said, which seemed to be what Jander preferred. He seemed distracted by other thoughts. After the desserts, Afral and his parents walked back to their suite under the careful watch of eight Blues.

* * *

The Attuls awoke at dawn. Afral pulled back the drapes and looked out at the still-wet courtyard. Blues were already mustering down there, heading out for morning patrols of the neighborhood. The three had taken turns on night watch, not letting the plush suite relax their vigilance, but nothing had happened. His mother had taken the last watch, so she was already fully dressed and ready to be gone. She returned to pacing as her husband and son began their morning routines. When a servant politely knocked on the door to offer Jander's invitation to breakfast, they were all ready.

The servant led them to a small, sun-filled room where food already waited. The ten guards that had stood outside their door marched behind them and took stations outside this doorway too.

Just after they arrived, Jander came in and motioned towards the cushioned chairs. "Please sit and join me for a final meal. I have the pleasure of informing you that the three fathers had their meeting and have decided that it would be best for Freetown to release the three of you."

"We are free to go?" asked Rolen.

"Indeed. After our meal, I will pass you over to one of our captains. He and his soldiers will escort you out whichever city gate you choose. The fathers wish you well on your travels, but do not want you here. It is nothing personal; any Attul would be a lightning rod attracting unwanted Tlocanian attention. Now, please sit and enjoy the wonderful food. Maybe we can talk about our past travels, Rolen."

GALDON

Galdon and his sixty men made it within sight of Freetown without encountering any Color patrols. It had been a simple task; he had merely avoided the roads up here. The Colors acted more like merchant guards than as an army, so their focus was on the traveled routes and getting their share of bribes and road fees. The recent rains also helped, for the Color dandies seemed to have a disliking for mud.

He came up on Freetown from the southwest, at some distance from the nearest road. From a grassy rise, Galdon could see the towers and rooftops of the distant city and was surprised to find it fairly large. For some reason, he had expected a settlement of sod-covered huts and not an actual city. Apparently, some civilization existed on this sea of grass. However, he nearly laughed when he looked at the city's outer protection- a wall so short that any good horse could jump it. Apparently, the leaders considered the outlying farms dispensable.

Galdon had considered trying to sneak his men into Freetown. He even had colored armbands from Lord-General Hraf to help him get past the gate guards. However, the idea did not sit well with him, for no Tlocanian soldier should have to hide his uniform. The empire was officially at peace with this city, so he decided to ride boldly into Freetown. Besides, Galdon thought it less likely that his force would be waylaid if they stayed together.

He led his men back to the dirt road that ran from the Triangle Wild to the city, letting his banner man finally unfurl the empire's black-and-red banner. He had no great love for the red dragon, but the beast did look intimidating on the snapping flag. He also knew that his damnable dragon helm would cause many to pause, for it too looked intimidating even if he still found it impractical after all these years.

The Greens manning the outer wall's tollbooth came out as they approached, staring at the uniforms and the banner. One of them leaped on a horse and galloped for the city. Galdon smiled. The city leaders would soon know of their arrival. Coming to the city openly had another advantage.

Because he came as a delegate from another land, the Colors did not enforce their entrance fees. Galdon appreciated that, for he did not have unlimited coins for his troops. He hoped to replenish some of the platoon's funds from the dragon priests, since there was no Tlocanian garrison or embassy here. The lord-general had provided a contact name.

They made it past the tollbooth without much questioning. Galdon guessed that the size of his force had a part in that. They made good time across Freetown's surrounding countryside; people paused in their work to watch them, but no one tried to hinder their progress. Squalor was evident everywhere. Apparently, the failed thieves had to work the fields. Galdon did not even see any country manors out here, only simple cottages and dilapidated barns. Maybe they kept all their fabled wealth within the city's high walls.

When they rode up to the city gates, he noticed a crowd of officials waiting. Not only were all three ruling Colors represented, Galdon also saw some of the detested Reds lingering in the background. The Blues had control of the city walls this day, so the first person to approach him was an officer from that force. A short fellow wearing the insignia of a major stepped beyond the shadow of the gate, being sure to avoid the larger puddles from the last storm. Behind him was a full squad of blues at the ready, though more to keep the others away than to withstand any attack from Galdon.

"Welcome to Freetown, Captain…"

Galdon dismounted so that he did not loom over the officer, for it seemed the polite thing to do. However, even down from his horse, he was still a head taller than the slim major. "I am called Galdon. Captain Galdon."

The man nodded. "What brings you this far north, Captain Galdon?"

He had given much thought on what he should answer to such an inquiry, and had already decided bluntness would be best. Go right for the attack. "I am searching for Attuls."

"Well then, today the sun shines brightly on your search. Someone will be meeting you at the Five Dragons Temple this day. He will set you on the right path."

Galdon frowned, not knowing what to make of the major's speech. Was he trying to play the prophet? "Sir, I do not know if you are trying to warn me or assure me."

A slight smile touched the man's thin lips. "I am doing both, Captain Galdon, for the man you will meet should be heeded as well as feared."

He raised an eyebrow. "Tlocania fears no one, sir. We embrace our allies and slay our enemies, but we fear no one."

The smaller man nodded again. "Well then, Fearless Galdon, enter our city with my welcome. I know that you will receive numerous invitations as soon as you pass through the gate, but I would suggest that you first go to the temple."

The major turned on his heels and marched back toward his men, once again careful to avoid the worst of the puddles and mud. Galdon was thoughtful as he remounted.

They were let in without any further delay and, once clear of the gates, people pressed in on the helmed officer. The major had been correct about the invitations. They came from multiple people and from all Colors. Galdon politely declined, doing his best to get past these odd people. None were important officials or high officers. They were just their lackeys and servants, trying to arrange a luncheon or dinner for their betters. He felt like the season's first minstrel after a long winter, everyone clamoring for the latest news and the newest song. Finally, he just ignored the persistent invitees and ordered his men forward, having decided that anyone too stupid to get out of his way deserved the trampling.

He found the Five Dragons Temple easily enough, a vast complex on the edge of an unruly market. The temple was built in the old style, with a separate spire gate dedicated to each of the Five. Galdon chose to enter by the red gate, of course, though that color had a different significance in this city. This was the gate preferred by the poor, who still associated the color with the long-gone Reds of Freetown. He noticed that temple guards at this gate wore red touches to their uniform for the Crimson Order, so there was some of the new order of things here.

He rode through the tall gate without challenge, his men following. They emerged in a paved courtyard where many milled about, coming and going to worship. More temple guards strode here or there, but they all wore blue edging on their dark uniforms, indicating a loyalty to the Azure Order. Apparently, this temple was not yet under the full control of those loyal to Tlocania. He wondered if the Azure dragon priests showed as much loyalty to the Lakelands as the Crimson Order did towards Tlocania.

Galdon told his men to wait, while he dismounted and entered the high-ceilinged worship hall, to sounds of prayer and the smell of incense. He caught a gray-robed servant and sent him scurrying for Brother Lanzo, then positioned himself at the back of the hall to wait.

* * *

Galdon still waited. Around him, worshipers came and went, making their offerings and prayers to the five dragons. He had already stepped out once to check on his men. After an hour of waiting, he had cornered a priest and made a second request for Brother Lanzo, but he still had no answer. Finally, after two hours, he confronted another priest and asked to know where Lanzo lurked. He did not bother to hide his irritated thoughts.

Apparently, this priest was Embraced, for he showed none of the humility the first one displayed. Instead, the priest answered in a cold voice, "You are an impertinent one, soldier. I am sure the brother will see you once he is done with his more-important duties."

The captain immediately bridled his thoughts. "That is fine, holy brother, but I wish he had the decency to send me a note saying as much. I am here at the direction of a lord-general, not on some personal mission. Tell him that I will return in the afternoon."

Galdon sensed the priest glaring at him, though his face remained hidden under the priest's cowl.

"I am no errand boy. Leave a message with one of the servants." The priest stalked off.

Galdon dared not try to restrain him, though his answer was less than satisfactory.

It was as Galdon began to leave that another priest came near, a priest with a blue-trimmed robe with the hood thrown back. "Excuse me, my child, but do you have a moment to talk with the temple's High Brother?"

Galdon met the elderly man's eyes, curious. It was dim enough in here for an Embraced One to go uncovered, but they usually remained hooded even on the darkest night. He guessed this priest to be one of those truly dedicated to the dragon gods. The type was rather rare in the empire these days. "Please lead the way, holy brother."

The priest brought him through a series of halls and across one sunny courtyard, until they came to a small chapel where another bareheaded priest awaited. "Here he is, High Brother," announced his escort, quickly withdrawing.

"Captain Galdon, am I correct?" asked the white haired man, approaching with a warm smile and an extended hand.

He grasped it in welcome. "Yes, I am Captain Galdon of Tlocania.

You wanted to speak with me, most holy brother?"

An easy chuckle escaped the priest. "The gods are holy; I am not. I am but a mere man, so I prefer that people do not give me such a title. I am definitely not the 'most' of anything, except maybe in temple mischief. Call me Brother Brannon or simply Brannon. I am glad you were willing to meet me, but I want to include one other in our conversation. Follow me, Captain Galdon."

Brother Brannon passed through a sun-drenched room without a flinch, further surprising Galdon. Here was a temple leader who was not demon-possessed. Eventually, they came to a bright garden tucked in a far corner of the temple compound. He noticed that temple guards kept watch on the garden, as did some Blues. Brannon led him down a winding stone path amongst the foliage until they came to a pair of benches next to a small pond.

A tall man waited for them there, seated on the left-hand bench with his long legs stretched across the paving stones. Upon seeing Brannon and Galdon, the man quickly stood up, though he stayed there and let them approach. Galdon judged him to be an officer, for he had the air of a commander about him.

The man held out his hand in greeting. "I am called Dalton and I have news for you, Tlocanian. However, before I tell you anything worthwhile, I must insist that you remove that dragon helm."

Galdon stopped halfway to clenching the fellow's hand. A Tlocanian officer never removed his helmet, except to bath or to sleep. Embraced Ones probably did not even take it off for such activities. The black-and-red helm with its fierce dragon profile was the epitome of the empire's army. To ask this of him was a major insult by the empire's standards. He did not feel offended, though, only curious. "Is it the red color that offends you or does the dragon's visage make you quake?"

"Neither, captain. We know about your demon-held officers and their fear of daylight. I only ask that you prove that you are not one of them."

Galdon was further surprised at the man's knowledge. Apparently, Freetown was not so isolated after all. By the army's rules, he should refuse this request. However, he had a gut feeling that he needed whatever information this man had. If any of his soldiers had been with him he would have still refused, but they would not see him bareheaded. Galdon complied, pulling off the great helmet and revealing his unruly dark hair. He had to squint against the bright day, but he kept his gaze steadily on this Dalton.

The Blue nodded. "Thank you. It is good to know that you are a human like us."

Dalton slowly pulled free an ancient sword belted at his side. Galdon noted that it was not meant to be a threatening move, so he let him proceed.

Dalton presented the blade for Galdon to look at. "Do you recognize this sword?"

"Should I?"

"It once belonged to the sworn enemies of your demon lovers. It is an Attul spirit sword."

Galdon raised an eyebrow at the news. The sword did not look magical. Where was the white glow mentioned in the old tales? He noted that his medallion did not have any reaction to the thing. He was starting to become peeved, for this seemed just more of a delay. "I am no treasure hunter, Dalton. I am after living Attuls, not their artifacts, real or fake."

Dalton gave a wisp of a smile that did not touch his eyes. "Oh, this is no fake. A living Attul set this sword ablaze only a day ago. I still do not know how they cause it to come alive, but it certainly did when that Attul touched it."

That news caught Galdon's attention. "There is an Attul here in Freetown?"

"There are three of them and they have just left our city. I will set you on their trail, captain, if you will offer me something in return."

Galdon became suddenly cautious. Dalton had said "me", not "us" or "my superiors". The distinction was clear to a man who grew up under the rigid authority of the Tlocanian army. Dalton was either a rogue or the head of the Blues, and Galdon doubted a rogue could convince the temple's High Brother to go along with his plots. He faced one of Freetown's robber barons. "What is it that you want from me? Realize that I am a mere captain; I am no lord-general or lord-governor."

"Understood. I ask only two things of you, and neither would be a betrayal of your empire. Obviously, someone of authority sent you here. When you report back to that person, let them know how Freetown cooperated with your search. We in Freetown have no quarrel with Tlocania. Instead, we seek an alliance."

Galdon knew that the empire rarely made alliances but he merely nodded that he would convey the message. "What is your second requirement?"

Dalton pulled out a leather pouch from his shirt and then unbound its ties to show a sealed letter within. "I ask that you hand this letter to the person who sent you on this mission."

He considered and then held out his hand for the missive. "I will do so. You have my word as a Tlocanian officer."

Dalton handed over the leather pouch and then he told the tale of Rolen, Tolara and their son. He told his tale briefly, but left out nothing important.

Galdon was amazed, suddenly realizing that these were the same Attuls that he had chased through the fogs of the Borderheart Valley months ago. He was not a religious man, but he wondered if the red dragon god was favoring him.

When Dalton finished his tale, Brother Brannon spoke up. "I did not realize this was your scheme, Dalton. The gods do not love betrayers. Why did you involve me in this?"

The Blue leader shrugged. "I meant no offense, holy brother, but I had to catch the captain somewhere away from the priestly spies that swarm the city. This seemed the best place to avoid unwelcome spies, since it is right beneath the nose of the Crimson order. I do not like betraying the Attuls, but it is necessary for the good of Freetown."

Galdon realized that the Freetowners suspected more intrigue among the Embraced Ones than there really was. He doubted that the Embraced priests would keep anything from the Embraced officers, but he had no desire to enlighten the other two. "Is that why you reveal all of this to me instead of to the Crimson priests?"

Dalton nodded. "The red dragon priests have nothing but contempt for our land. I hope we will find a more welcoming ear by using this route, for I have found soldiers to be a more practical lot."

"Well, I will do as I promised but I cannot keep this information from the priests forever. I will need to use them to help capture the Attuls."

Dalton frowned. "Can you not call on some of the demon-held officers up in Newtown?"

Galdon had not heard of any Tlocanian garrison this far north. He did not even know where this Newtown lay, but he was not about to admit his ignorance to the others. All officers understood that Tlocania must appear all-knowing and all-powerful. "If the opportunity presents itself I will seek other help, but it is the priests who are the closest. Keeping them ignorant was not part of our bargain."

Dalton sighed. "It is a bad day when a stranger out bargains a Freetowner. Do what you must, Captain Galdon, but remember to speak well of us to your superiors."

"I will tell them of your aid. Should I praise only the Blues or should it be for all of Freetown?"

"In this, the Colors are united," Dalton replied.

The confidence with which Dalton spoke told Galdon even more about whom he faced. He was now sure that this was Father Blue himself, the leader of that Color.

The High Brother spoke up again. "In this, even the temple is in reluctant agreement. The saving of a city by sacrificing the three is sensible. I do not like it, but I understand the need."

Galdon raised an eyebrow. Dragon priests seemed always so quick to sacrifice others. Apparently, even those who were not Embraced shared the sentiment. Well, he needed to catch an Attul and there could be no better lead than this. "I had better start the chase. Brother Brannon, may I leave a note for Brother Lanzo? I can no longer await his pleasure but I will not have him claiming that I did not report in. I will also have a note for a Brother Verdrof who will be reaching Freetown in a day or two."

The high brother did not seem pleased that he wanted to communicate with Crimson priests, but he still agreed. "I will see to it that your notes are delivered."

"Thank you, holy brother." Galdon turned his attention back to Dalton. "Will you provide a guide to set me on the trail of these Attuls?"

"That is my intention. A Blue squad will meet you at the temple gate in one hour to escort you and your men."

Galdon nodded, wondering at the intrigues of the robber barons. He had a feeling that they would be just as quick to betray him, for the right price. It made Galdon feel dirty to even deal with the man. He had no desire to touch him in another handshake, so he turned and strode back out of the garden without any fake farewell. As he walked away, he looked skyward and noticed clouds quickly building. It would probably start raining again by this afternoon.

Eric Lorenzen

CHAPTER THIRTY-FOUR

Telling Others

BRODAGAR

Free Hawk's plan just might work, thought Brodagar, as he watched the Attuls through the eyes of a hidden dreadhound. The woman barely clung to her saddle as they entered Edgevale. Surely, she would realize the need to share her secret with the others now. He planned for this to be their final stop, for this was the last city in Hasan Province. Brodagar wanted the secret of Warhaven now. He would not allow them to leave Edgevale without that information.

The city gates closed right behind the Attuls, but that did not concern Brodagar. The locals would be quick to open them, once they saw dragon priests and Tlocanian soldiers outside. He had already decided to order the gates barred to an Osburgens or Shade Order dragon priests. That way, he could leisurely play this out with Free Hawk, all within the safe confines of Edgevale's high walls.

Brodagar released the mind link to the dreadhound and swayed in the saddle a bit, as he tried to reorient to his true surroundings, which were a distance behind the Attuls.

Nesron must have noticed the change in him, for he spoke up. "What now, Brother Brodagar? How many more times must we injure someone to get this woman to confess her secret?"

"She will not leave Edgevale without telling the others where Warhaven hides." He stared at Nesron, making sure the other saw the look of contempt on his face. "Where you failed at Hightower, I will succeed here. The woman will talk."

Nesron frowned. Brodagar could not read his thoughts but he

sensed the anger. And yet, Nesron knew better than to try defending his mistakes, for he kept his mouth shut.

"I am glad we have an understanding," said the priest.

Watch that one, advised Sahak. *Swoferosh is probably plotting inside of him at this very instant. We cannot be deceived by his seeming submission.*

Brodagar agreed, but he needed Nesron's troops. "I want you to send in two squads to oversee the securing of the city gates. We must make sure that the Osburgens do not gain entrance."

"I will order it now," said Nesron, calling over two squad leaders. He gave them their orders and sent them galloping off for the city. That done, Nesron confronted him again. "What about your dogs? Are you going to shelter them in the city too?"

"With so many southern ships porting in Deep Crossing, I want to make sure no more of our 'allies' are coming up from Riverrealm. I have already sent one pack to circle the city and spy out the road heading down into the Grandgorn Valley. The rest of the dogs will come into the city with us."

Nesron nodded understanding. "So that is why we linger out here among the cold hills. You wait for a later hour so that the dogs can enter mostly unseen."

He wants to go in ahead of us, warned Sahak. *Do not let him or we will rue it.*

Brodagar was not about to let Nesron roam the city unleashed. He was explaining that to his demon, when his inner conversation was interrupted.

"Ware the dogs!" yelled out his underling priest suddenly.

Brodagar shifted in his saddle to stare at the other Houndmaster, but the priest's eyes were unfocused again as he returned in his mind link.

Unexpectedly, Brodagar heard dreadhounds growling all around them. He reached out with his mind to one of the nearer dogs. As his conscience slipped into the animal's mind, Brodagar caught the dog's thoughts: enemies approach. The thought smelled of a competing pack and not of wolves or coyotes. He broke the link with a curse, fighting off the dizziness that came with such a wrenching of the mind.

"Prepare for an attack!" he yelled out to the soldiers and temple guards. "Nesron, to me! Rival dreadhounds stalk us. To arms!"

All around them, dogs raced out of the woods, dreadhounds that did not obey him.

MYLANA

Mylana awoke to an older woman cleaning her wound. Though the cleaning caused her some pain, she kept still as she watched the woman, trying to recognize her. However, she must have made some sound, for the woman looked up.

"Good. You are awake. I am Mother Marda, a healer here in Edgevale. Please do not be alarmed, my lady. Your companion is right next to you, though she has fallen asleep." She indicated the other bed.

Mylana saw the rich dark hair of Hessilyn spread over the pillow, her back turned towards her. Marda finished cleaning the wound and then applied a poultice and a bandage.

Mylana sighed at the coolness of the paste touched her hot skin. She tried to get up, but was too weak. Marda helped her to a sitting position, but told her she could not get out of bed yet. She was not about to admit she was too weak to even try.

Marda gave an encouraging smile as she looked down at her patient. She handed Mylana a mug of cold water, which she gratefully drank. "I have a soup ready for you and I expect you to eat it, for your body needs to be replenished. Do not worry; it is not from the inn's kitchen. Their cook is notorious for thinning her soup and then trying to disguise the watery broth with a strong dash of pepper. Mine is a hearty chicken soup that will feed your belly and help to heal your wound." She ladled a steaming bowl from an urn sitting on the side table, bringing the soup over to her.

Mylana thanked her and hesitantly tasted the first spoonful, not certain if she could eat. The soup tasted wonderful and her hunger roared its sudden desire. She was nearly finished with the large bowl when Hessilyn.

The young woman got up quickly and came to Mylana's bedside, giving her a gentle hug. "You are awake! How are you feeling?"

"I am weak and a bit sore, but both will pass soon enough." She grabbed Hessilyn's hand and gave it a squeeze in appreciation. "Where are we? What has happened while I have slept? Please tell me, Hessilyn."

Marda spoke up. "I need to go brew some tea now that your companion is awake to care for you." She gave Hessilyn a stern look. "Make sure she does not talk too long, for it is sleep that will restore her with the most haste."

"I will see to it, Mother Marda."

The elderly lady raised a doubtful eyebrow but still left. As soon as she was gone, Mylana looked to Hessilyn for answers.

"We are in the city of Edgevale, nearly at the lip of the Grandgorn Valley, and we have been here for three days. We arrived in the evening and were the last ones through the city gates, so our pursuers were at least delayed if not shut out. The boys have been scouting the city each day, but they have seen no sign of anyone looking for us. There are Tlocanians here, of course, but no dreadhounds. We have not been harmed or even threatened, yet Mandor still insists on taking watch every night. He worries about another massacre like occurred at that village. Coursen thinks those that were following us are still outside the city for some reason, waiting for us to leave."

"How will we ever get away from this place?"

"You will regain your strength quickly, now that your fever has broken, and then we will ride hard. We will soon be in Deep Crossing."

Mylana frowned. "Please do not try to shelter me because of my condition. Hessilyn, you are too shrewd to be so blithe."

The other woman gave a sad smile. "What would you have of me?"

"The truth, as you see it. You are a very perceptive woman."

Hessilyn shrugged. "So be it. We are in a dire situation, for we do not know where our foes hide. Every day the boys go scouting in the city, asking travelers if they have seen any sign of the dreadhound pack or of a squad of soldiers. They seem to have disappeared and it worries all of us. Coursen may have it right. Maybe they do not want to attack in this city due to some disagreement among their own factions. The gods know that I witnessed enough of that in Westbend after my father took over. But I worry that such an explanation is too convenient. Maybe the Embraced Ones are playing at some deeper game with us. Maybe they just want to terrorize us before they kill or capture us. I really do not know…"

Hessilyn paused, staring at Mylana. When she spoke again, it was in a whisper. "Does that satisfy you? Now you can worry with the rest of us."

Mylana reclined against her pillows. The Tlocanians were probably watching every city gate, just waiting for them to leave. The next time, that archer might not miss and that thought worried her. It was more than a fear of dying; it was that the mission would die with her. She suddenly came to a decision. "Where are the boys now?"

"They are both out prowling the streets, or else I would have already retrieved them to your side. Both have been very concerned about you. I am not sure which one was more worried."

"Could you see if they have returned? I would like to speak with all of you and I would rather not have to repeat myself."

"I will look," promised Hessilyn. "Usually, one of them stays close, in case a Tlocanian patrol comes this way."

Soon after Hessilyn left, Marda returned with a tea kettle. She poured a steaming mug and then set the kettle on the table next to the soup urn. Mylana gladly accepted the beverage, blowing on it to bring the temperature down. The older woman settled onto a stool in the corner. When Mylana protested that she did not need to be watched, the healer simply replied that she had promised Lady Hessilyn that she would stay. Not having the strength to protest, Mylana finished her tea and then rest more.

Finally, Hessilyn returned with the boys. As soon as they entered, Marda stood up and announced that it was time for her to get home. Coursen saw her out.

Hessilyn sat down next to Mylana, while the two young men perched on the second bed.

"What is it that you wanted to share with us?" asked Coursen. "Hessilyn would give us no details."

Mylana gave him a warm smile, recalling Hessilyn's comments about him worrying over her. "I wanted to say this just once, for I have much to share and little strength yet. My injuries prove the folly of the Guardians' over-caution. What if I had died of my wounds? It would have meant failure for all of us. This mission is too important to depend on only me. I must share with you the knowledge of Warhaven, so that even if I die in the next attack, the rest of you will be able to carry on."

Hessilyn rose to her feet. "I will wait in the common room."

Mylana caught the edge of her cloak to restrain her. "No, please stay. I trust you, Hessilyn. You are now a part of our mission, so you should know our destination too."

Hessilyn smiled warmly, sat back down, and gave her a careful hug to avoid straining her wound. Mylana returned the hug.

"Are you certain about this, little sister?" asked Mandor. "You will break a vow made before El."

"My vow of secrecy conflicts with my vow to see this mission completed. If I do not violate the first, the second is at terrible risk. I have decided, Mandor; I need to tell all of you where the Prayer Warriors have hidden Warhaven." Mylana paused, to look at the three.

Hessilyn smiled encouragement. Mandor looked worried, conflicted. Coursen seemed curious, almost anxious, to hear Warhaven's location.

"As you two know, and Hessilyn has probably already guessed, Warhaven lies in northern Na Ciria," said Mylana. Hessilyn nodded that she had indeed figured out that much. "The city is hidden among the Pinnacles; its entrance is through a valley called the Ambassador's Gate. It lies in the northwest corner of the mountain range, with a high peak at its mouth that is called Beartooth. The Prayer Warriors chose that location to keep watch over the ruins of Darsheol. I will share the route details as we ride, but that should already be enough in case we are separated or I am killed."

"You will not be killed," argued Coursen. "I swore to protect you and I shall."

She gave him another warm smile for his statement.

"You have given us a great burden," stated Mandor. "I swear before El that I will keep this secret you have shared, telling no one of Warhaven's locale."

"Of course we will keep her secret safe," agreed Coursen. "Who would want such knowledge to fall into the wrong hands?"

Hessilyn met her eyes. "I am of a different faith, but I swear by my gods to keep your secret. I have a deep respect for Attuls, and it is not only because Mandor has my heart. I can see that all of you are Na Ciria's last hope. Also, I would not betray your trust."

Mylana felt a relief now that the others knew her secret. It had felt wrong to keep such information from the others, since they all took the same risks. Having finally told, she felt suddenly very tired. She drank the last of her tea and then told the boys it was time for them to leave. As Hessilyn helped her to settle under the covers, Mylana thanked El for her faithful companions, three people who were so loyal and good-hearted.

BRODAGAR

The priest looked down from the saddle at his two dead companions, shocked. Two Embraced Ones lost, their demons forced back to the Darklands and their hosts destroyed. The Osburgens had killed them from a distance, killed them while they were linked to a pair of dreadhounds. Brodagar did not even know that such a thing could be done.

"What now?" asked Nesron. "They are retreating. Should we chase them and get revenge?"

He looked up with a glare. "They are not fleeing us, you fool. They go after the Attuls, now that they have driven us away."

"It could have been worse," replied the captain. "At least my soldiers came though this largely unscathed."

"They killed all the dogs that were with us and two Embraced Ones. Do you really think they fear mere soldiers?" Brodagar turned his horse away from the corpses. "We must race back to Edgevale and hope that the Attuls are still safely inside the city walls. Order your men to form up and send out your scouts. We have a long ride back and we have no dreadhounds to run ahead of us."

Nesron might be dense, but he was efficient in his duties. Soon they were heading north again, back towards the Crossover Road they had been forced to flee two days ago.

Brodagar seethed at this turn of events. He had been so close to repairing the damage of Nesron's bungling, only to see his careful planning ruined.

At least you are still alive, remarked Sahak, *and the Attul woman may have finally told her secret to our spy. Maybe our plan came to fruition even without our presence.*

I hope so, thought Brodagar. We need luck to finally turn our way.

Eric Lorenzen

CHAPTER THIRTY-FIVE

Betraying a Secret

MYLANA

When Mylana finally shared her secret, it created quite a stir among the group. It took awhile before the others even remembered what else they had to discuss, but then Hessilyn finally urged the young men to share their news.

"Mandor, you said that something odd had occurred. Tell us about it."

He nodded. "Yes, I should... well, Coursen and I were in a tavern when we overheard some of the local soldiers talking. The night we entered Edgevale, there was quite a lightshow outside of the walls. The guards saw red lightning and fireballs among the trees to the west of the city and then moving southward."

"Do you think our pursuers had some kind of falling out among their party?" asked Mylana.

"Possibly, but who can tell?" Mandor looked at his friend for support. "I do not think we should assume that our troubles have lessened any."

"I agree with you there," added Coursen. "The lights may have moved off to the south, but that does not mean all our enemies had done likewise. We do not know what was going on out there. Besides, we have also heard about new dreadhound attacks on the road ahead of us."

"Maybe we should just stay here in Edgevale for a time," suggested Hessilyn, "for they have not attacked us since we arrived. The road might be safer in a few more days."

"Or far more dangerous," replied Mylana.

"Hessilyn may have a point there," said Coursen. "We have no idea what awaits us outside of the city walls."

"We cannot allow ourselves to become trapped here," argued Mylana. "Instead, let us flee the city in an unexpected direction. We should go north from here."

"But there are no roads," protested Mandor. "Father made it clear that we should not wander the Yucai Wilderness. The hills are steep, the valleys are often filled with bogs, and he hinted at other dangers as well."

"We are nearly at the edge of the Grandgorn's valley. Let us flee northward for just a bit and then turn east."

"Do you have the strength?" asked Hessilyn.

"I will not be wearing the saddle," replied Mylana with a smile, trying to lighten the mood. "Ears has a lurching pace, whether on a road or going cross-country. I will manage."

She succeeded in swaying them to her chosen path, but then raised another round of objections when she declared that they should leave today. However, she prevailed there too and they began to pack.

* * *

The foursome left Edgevale, heading briefly east. Though there were now Tlocanian regulars added to the gate guards, they were focused on those who were trying to enter instead of those leaving. They were able to leave without even being questioned and rode their mules down the road until they were out-of-sight. Once hidden, they circled the city and joined up with a smaller road heading out towards the farms north of the city.

Mylana held out well, in spite of her lingering weakness. She was determined not to hinder the others.

Their chosen road lasted only for a half-day, and then they were forced to pick their own route. They kept going generally northward for the rest of that day and then turned eastward and traveled for another two days. It was not until late afternoon of that third day away from Edgevale that the trees thinned and they found themselves on the lip of the Grandgorn Valley. The land dropped in forested steps towards the great river.

From this height, they could spot areas in the distance where lumberjacks had cleared out the trees. Coursen pointed to the lumber lots. "I say we head that way to find a road. We need to head back towards Deep Crossing."

"Why backtrack?" asked Mandor. "Why not keep moving northward?"

Coursen shook his head. "We are now entering an area where I must guide. There is a Rider route on this side of the river, but our best hope is to cross to the far bank and so avoid the Tlocanian army camped further upstream. I was told very strongly to avoid this side of the river, for there is a warfront north of us. Your father also told me that the only place offering transport to horses in Riverrealm will be the Deep Crossing ferries, where the Crossover Road ends." Coursen smiled. "You can try to swim across the Grandgorn, Mandor, but I prefer the ferries."

The others agreed to Coursen's proposal and they rode onward, starting down the rolling slopes towards the distant river.

BRODAGAR

By the time they came back to Edgevale, the Attuls were gone. When Brodagar learned that Nesron's soldiers had let them exit without setting a tail on them, he became livid. His anger was only partially cooled when a sergeant recited a message hastily given by his one-remaining underling. The priest had taken their last pack northward in pursuit of the Attuls.

"Northward? Into the wilds? Why would they flee that way?"

"I do not know those answers, holy brother," replied the sergeant before him. "The priest showed up naked at the north gate, proved who he was by throwing a fireball at the city wall, and then ordered me to tell you what I just did. He did not stay long, for he claimed that he had to get back to his pack."

Brodagar ignored the obvious questions brimming in the man's mind. His last priest was not just a Houndmaster, but also a Shapeshifter. Obviously, he had decided that the best way to keep up with his hounds was to take on that form.

He pushes his host, observed Sahak. *He has gone as a were-dog many times now.*

Sahak was speaking of the demon, not the man. Taking on a third persona too often could drive a human to instability or even insanity, so a demon would usually urge his host to be cautious. The priest was taking a risk, so he must have seen no other way to keep up with the Attuls.

"Should I send my scouts out to find their path?" asked Nesron.

465

"That would be useless. We cannot catch up with them out there." He pointed at the higher hills that could be seen over the city's walls. Without any dreadhounds of his own, he could not hope to chase them effectively. "But at least we know that the Osburgens do not have them."

The southerners had come upon the city earlier that day and had forced their way in through its southern gate, as evidenced by a gapping hole and forty dead soldiers. They had quickly learned about the Attuls escape too and had then left the city, heading eastward. Apparently, they did not know about the Attuls fleeing northward.

"What do you plan to do now?" Nesron did not bother to hide his satisfaction at the other's difficulties.

Brodagar came to a quick decision. "We go on to Deep Crossing. I believe they will want to cross over the Grandgorn and that is the best place for them to do so."

"What about the others? We do not have the strength to face them again."

"We must be cautious, but that is our direction." He had no reason to explain himself to Nesron.

* * *

They approached Deep Crossing carefully, sending scouts ahead to make sure no more ambushes awaited them. However, they arrived at the city unmolested and entered its teeming streets with only a cursory stop at the city gates. Tlocanian soldiers held the gate, which assured Brodagar. However, as they rode towards the Tlocanian garrison that sat on the river's bank, they encountered many Osburg soldiers roaming the city. They did not seem on patrol, Tlocanian soldiers were still at that task, but the Osburgens were nearly as numerous. It obviously bothered Nesron as much as it did Brodagar and finally he stopped a Tlocanian foot patrol to ask.

The sergeant, a mere human whose hair was mostly gone, gave a quick and respectful reply to his superior. "The Grays have been sailing up the river to join the war. I, for one, am glad they came to help. We have been sitting at Rhendora's front door too long and it is past time to overthrow those horse lovers. When have we ever taken so long to conquer any land? I just hope the Grays march on soon, because those boys show no respect towards our authority. They don't drink more than ours do, I'll admit, but when our patrol shows up they don't scurry away like our boys. They just keep on swilling their beers, challenging us to stop them. If you ask me..."

"Thank you, my child," said Brodagar, interrupting the man. He did not want to linger here, sharing army complaints.

The sergeant was no fool; he knew a dismissal when it came. He gave a friendly nod of understanding and then a respectful bow to the priest. He turned to the captain and gave a sharp salute. With that, the sergeant turned back toward his men and ordered them to move on.

"Should we divide our forces?" asked Nesron, for they had planned to go to their respective barracks.

Brodagar sighed. "I see no other option, since we entered the city so openly. You will go to the garrison and I will go the temple, but we will need to keep in communication. Those who assaulted us are most likely at the Osburg encampment near the docks, but they could be watching for us even now."

Nesron raised an eyebrow. "Do you think they will try to attack us here, in front of so many others?"

Brodagar doubted that, but chose not to answer Nesron's question. "I expect that we will need to move quickly as soon as the Attuls enter the city. Just remember, Nesron, that we are no longer in Hasan Province so our authority is weaker here. However, we are still in the empire, no matter how many of these southerners swarm the place."

* * *

Brodagar paused when he came upon the huge temple complex. Behind him rode twenty-three temple guards, who were the last of his personal force. He looked up at the temple. Its architecture caught his eye. Few of the grand temples still existed from the time before the rise of the Dragon Lord. He noted that it was built according to the old style, with a tower gate for each dragon. Newer temples tended to cluster the five spires in a row, but the old grand temples gave each dragon god his own entrance, carved and painted to glorify that god. A high stone wall, setting aside the holy grounds from the outside, surrounded the complex. On this side of the compound stood two of the tower gates: red and blue. Both towered high, richly carved and brightly painted. Beyond them, and to the right, he could see the gray and black towers, muted by the dreary weather. To the left stood the gold tower. Without even approaching it, Brodagar knew that gate would be narrow and rarely used. That was how it was done, just like there were never any dragon priests of the Gold Order. Tradition demanded such things.

Brodagar realized his delay came more out of uncertainty than any desire to enjoy holy architecture. Maybe the nearness of the blue gate brought it to recall, but he remembered that this was not a temple controlled by the Crimson Order. The High Brother came from the older Azure Order, those who held the blue dragon as supreme. It had been the elite order before the rise of the Dragon Lords and it still governed most of the older temples.

All of this meant that Brodagar had to be more circumspect in his actions, but that was not his greatest concern. Upon entering the city, he had noticed Osburgens, including a priest of the Shade Order. What if the Shade Order had infiltrated the temple and overthrown his own Crimson brethren as the hidden rulers of the place? Brodagar worried that he might be riding into another trap, but he had little choice.

MYLANA

The next day, the foursome kept moving east. At midday, they topped a ridgeline and finally saw the lumber lots just ahead. They also had a more distant view, catching a glimpse of the Grandgorn, a dark ribbon under the cloudy skies.

"Is that what I think it is?" asked Hessilyn, pointing further eastward. "There is an end to these oppressive skies." Beyond the wide river rose the High Wall, the cliffs that formed the eastern edge of the valley. Above the High Wall lay the Wind Plains. A narrow band of bright skies shone that way.

"The demonsworn do not bother shading lands they do not want to possess," said Mandor. "I hear that no one lives up on those windblown grasses except transient hunters."

"Do your instructions include any route across the Wind Plains?" asked Mylana of Coursen.

"Well… yes, but such a path would add months to our journey. The way back down, in eastern Rhendora, is treacherous at best, and not to be taken in winter or storm according to your father's warning. We would have to abandon our mounts at the top because the route's steepness. I would rather stay nearer our true route."

"Can we take the river?" asked Hessilyn.

Coursen shook his head. "There are rapids upstream of Deep Crossing, so most ships do not go beyond its river docks. It is said that smaller boats ply the upper river, in Rhendora, but we have to ride some distance before we can seek any passage there."

"Well then, let us get off this ridge before we are spotted," advised Mandor. "I think I see a road over that way."

468

They did find a lumbermen's road and followed it to settled lands. It took them two more days to reach Deep Crossing, crossing a gentle land where forests and fields intermingled. They stayed both nights in small villages where the dragon temples were just tiny clapboard chapels, the five spires merely colored poles planted nearby. No one bothered them, though some stared in curiosity at the strangers that were neither lumberjacks nor trappers.

The last few miles to Deep Crossing they traveled on fair country roads, making good time. They realized that the city was near when they spotted the temple's five spires soaring on the horizon. The spires stood further apart than usual and each had a different appearance, yet all five towers dominated the skyline almost as much as the Shadow Anchor that beamed up into the clouds and seemed to hold the Dragon Shadow in place. As they drew closer, they could see that the Shadow Anchor originated on an island citadel that was probably the Tlocanian's garrison as well. Lying between the city and the island were docks choked with ships, creating a veritable forest of masts.

They approached the nearest entrance, just behind a shepherd and his small flock, and followed by a farmer pulling a handcart full of early potatoes. Local guards manned the gate, crisp in their Riverrealm uniforms of navy blue with bright yellow trim. The guards let the shepherd enter but they halted the foursome.

"Do you have papers for your mounts?" asked one guard, holding out a hand.

Mandor took out the paper that the innkeeper had given him and held it out to the man.

The guard snatched the paper and looked it over. "Says here that you are a trader, but I don't see any goods." He turned to his companion. "Go get Sarge."

"You get him," the other replied. "I'm not about to wake him from his midday snooze. Not for mules. Even if we confiscate those grimy animals, we won't get any money from it. The Reds or the Grays will just grab them from us."

The two stared at each other for a moment, and then the first guard gave a reluctant nod and tossed the paper back at Mandor. "Get those beasts out of my gateway."

Deep Crossing bustled with people to the point of crowding. Besides all of the locals and visiting farmers, the foursome passed merchant trains and patrolling troops. They saw both local soldiers and black-and-red Tlocanians. On one street they even saw a group in the black-and-gray of the Osburg Empire, though they quickly disappeared into a tavern. Thankfully, they did not encounter any demon-possessed officers or priests.

Though it was still a few hours before the evening worship, they decided to find an inn quickly. The first green lantern they found hung over the front door of the Drunken Skunk, a tired looking inn whose only advantage was its proximity to the city gate they had entered.

They found satisfactory boarding for their mounts and then went in to see if they could get anything comfortable for themselves. They ended up with two tiny rooms. Mylana looked into her and Hessilyn's room to find a sagging bed that seemed ready to fold.

"I think the mules have the better accommodations," stated Mylana with a shake of her head.

Hessilyn shrugged. "That seems fitting, since they did most of the work today."

Mylana smiled at the jest and realized she felt a bit lighthearted too. Somehow, the telling of her secret had relieved much of gloom she had felt. No longer did she feel the need to be suspicious of her companions. Not even of Hessilyn. They had proven themselves trustworthy many times over already. From here on, their ride would be a shared mission.

The two women stepped in and Mylana closed the door behind them, using the key to secure the door. "Well, at least the door's lock seems adequate."

Hessilyn gave a little laugh. "You are too trusting, Mylana. Who knows how many spare copies there are of that key you hold? The lock will keep out vagrants, lost guests, and the mildly curious, but anyone who is determined can easily break in here."

"What do you know of such nefarious ways?" asked Mylana, surprised. "You led a far more privileged life than I."

Hessilyn pulled back the covers to check for bugs or worse, and seemed mildly surprised to find the bed relatively clean. She looked up at her companion. "My father helped rule Westbend even before he brought in the Grays of Osburg as allies. As a child, I would sometimes spy on his meetings with his officers and learned all sorts of interesting and scandalous things. I once heard an agent list the fifty ways to win past any lock. I was but twelve at the time, but I still remember a good twenty of his explanations."

"Your childhood differed greatly from mine, in spite the fact that we both grew up motherless," remarked Mylana.

Hessilyn nodded. "My father may have loved me, at least before his demonic possession, but he was devious and often cruel when it came to ruling. He made certain to teach me those skills too. Now, I need to master trust and dependence on others, while you must learn to be more cautious. Such is life, always learning new lessons."

Mylana did not know how to respond, so she chose to unpack her things instead.

After the evening worship hour, the foursome decided that it would be best to learn more about their enemies. At first, Mandor and Coursen wanted to go out into the city by themselves, but the women insisted on their inclusion.

"Two couples strolling the streets will be good enough cover," stated Hessilyn. "Besides, I want to find a street vendor for my evening meal. I do not trust the kitchen downstairs after getting a whiff of a passing plate in that common room. It smelled like the Drunken Skunk was also the name of today's special."

"We should all go out," agreed Mylana, "and we should all stay together. I would lament any repeat of Hightower."

The men gave in.

The foursome left the inn, leaving behind their mules. From their experience at the city gate, they judged that mounts would be too conspicuous. They found the streets well populated, though the streetlights struggled to illuminate against the black blanket of a Dragon Shadow night. They walked further into the city and found a market where some of the vendors still lingered in hopes of late customers. Following the smell of sizzling meat, they found an acceptable food vendor. They bought small wooden skewers of roasted chicken and peppers, and found it delicious.

Moving on from there, they explored that end of ancient Deep Crossing, being careful not to wander too far from their humble lodging.

Mylana and Coursen walked just behind the other couple. Mylana held Coursen's hand for appearance's sake and found that it caused her heart to flutter. She chided herself, for this was no romantic stroll. Coursen's tenseness proved that. Surreptitiously, Coursen and Mandor studied the city as they had been trained to do. Mylana tried to follow their example, though she had not yet received full training in those Rider skills. She wondered if she should be gazing more at Coursen as part of her role, but could not bring herself to do so. Instead, she walked quietly next to him, trying to watch the dark city that they passed through. Hessilyn, though, seemed oblivious as she told Mandor what she knew of Deep Crossing's history.

After a few hours, they returned to one of their rooms to share their observations. Coursen lit the oil lamp and then sat down on one of the beds, next to Mandor. The women sat on the other bed. The single lamp caused them to cast large shadows on the faded walls.

"So little sister, what is your first observation about Deep Crossing?" asked Mandor, letting Mylana share first.

Surprised, Mylana hastily gathered her thoughts. "There are Grays in the city, even though this is well inside the Tlocanian Empire."

Mandor nodded. "They are in transit to somewhere; I would guess the Rhendoran war front. The ones we saw were off duty yet still in uniform, so they are not stationed here. They kept together and kept relatively sober, so they know they might be ordered to march at any time. What next?"

"There are more strangers in the city than usual; at least that is the case in this neighborhood."

"True," said Mandor. "A trade city like Deep Crossing always draws its share of newcomers, but an army will serve like a magnet, attracting those who hope to win some of the soldiers' coins or earn an army contract."

"Also, many of the locals have fled," added Hessilyn. "We passed many dark windows and this is not a poor city where people cannot afford lamp oil."

"You surprise me, Lady Hessilyn," said Coursen with a smile. "With all your babbling as we walked, I did not think you noticed anything beyond Mandor's form."

"Some day you may learn to do one thing while appearing to do something else, Rider Coursen," replied Hessilyn with a light tone. "If ever you want to spy while at court, you will need to do more than scowl as you look around. Light conversation provides good cover. Besides that, my words were meant to be information and not idle chatter, if only you had listened."

Mandor laughed heartily. "She has you there, Coursen. But you malign him, Hessilyn. He did more than scowl and stare. He also spent time gazing at my sister."

Coursen chuckled, not denying his friend's observation.

Mylana actually blushed, and then leaned back to hide her reddened face in Hessilyn's shadow. Were they just teasing her, or was Coursen interested in her? Mylana embarrassment turned to self-anger;

in everything else she was the bold one, so why did she allow this man to fluster her? She decided to retrieve control of the conversation. "I think that some of those missing locals have fled to the Wind Plains. The food vendor mentioned that the peppers came from 'my cousin's own farm among the sunny grasses' and that is the closest sunshine to these parts."

Mandor gave a little frown at her last point. "Possibly. However, the Midcirian Plains still have blue skies and they are not that far from here. It is said that the Wind Plains have poor soil and severe winters, so I would think only the desperate would flee in that direction."

"I have been up there," said Coursen, "and Mandor has it right. It was just the fall season when I went, but the cold winds howled so hard that I thought it was a toss-up whether I would blow off my saddle or freeze to it."

"What business has an Attul Rider on the Wind Plains?" asked Hessilyn, but then quickly added. "Pardon me. That is none of my business; it is just hard to break the habits my father hammered into me."

"It is no longer any secret, Lady Hessilyn," answered Coursen. "We had a small Rider Post up there, on the rim of the High Wall where we could keep watch over the whole area of the Grandgorn Valley upstream of Westbend. I rode there with a warning from Guardian Harwin about a possible compromise of their position. The attempt to protect the Post's secrecy failed, for not that long after they were overrun by the demonsworn."

"We ride off course," protested Mandor. "Let us keep to Deep Crossing and what is happening here and now."

"There is nothing left to share," stated Coursen. "The women caught the most of it. I think we will have to do more spying tomorrow, though. We need to verify whether our pursuers are already here and we also need to investigate passage across the river."

"Agreed," said Mandor.

"But we will need to go our separate ways tomorrow," added Coursen. "There is too much to cover otherwise. We will want to spy out the citadel, the temple, the docks, and the markets."

Mylana saw the wisdom in Coursen's suggestion, but was surprised when her brother did not object to it. She gave him a puzzled look.

"Do not stare at me like that, little sister. I know when advice is sound. I want to protect you and Hessilyn, but I realize I cannot do so all the time."

* * *

Just after morning worship, Mylana walked to the great market, located in the heart of the city. She was glad to be doing her part, instead of just waiting back at the inn, and her pleasure showed in her quick pace. In one hand she carried an empty sack, ready for any decent supplies she might also find. Around her, Deep Crossing carried on its morning business.

The others had different destinations, with Mandor setting off to spy on the citadel and Coursen the docks. Hessilyn chose the temple, for she had not qualms with bowing to the dragon-gods.

When Mylana arrived at the market, she found it overflowing with vendors and customers. She strolled among the carts and stalls, listening in on hundreds of conversations but learning nothing useful. It seemed all the gossip was about personal lives or the weather or the poor quality of food grown under the Dragon Shadow. She had just resolved to move on, when a commotion started at the far end of the square, the end kept free of vendors so that the city traffic would not be hindered.

Mounted soldiers in black-and-gray roughly pushed aside people. Mylana watched as a large contingent rode into the square, complete with snarling dreadhounds on long leashes. She felt the presence of the demon-possessed as she hunkered behind a stall, though she felt compelled to peek out nonetheless. If they sensed her, she did not want them to be able to pick her out by sight. Thankfully, most of the market crowd was staring in the same direction, for dreadhounds rarely were seen, especially leashed and during daytime hours. At the head of the main force, just behind the dog handlers, rode three dragon priests with their hoods up and a southern lord. Just behind the lord rode two banner men, one flying the Gray Dragon and the other bearing the family flag of this particular lord. Mylana knew that banner, for it belonged to Hessilyn's father.

Mylana's heart sped up.

House Targan. What was Hessilyn's father doing here? He must have trailed them from Waybridge. Mylana watched as the large expedition swept through the square and down the road towards the city's temple. On a whim, Mylana straightened up and hurried after them.

BRODAGAR

A knock interrupted Brodagar's writing. He looked up from his work and gave permission for the person to enter. A gray robed servant stepped in and bowed.

"Excuse me, Brother Brodagar, but I have a message for you." The interrupting servant kept his head down in proper respect.

"What is it?" he asked, leaving off the report that he had been trying to compose for an hour. It was never easy to report on delays or failure, even if he shifted the bulk of the blame onto Nesron-Swoferosh's shoulders.

"You have been asked for by a petitioner. I was told that you would recognize the name Free Hawk. I was also told that your presence is needed posthaste."

Surprised, Brodagar set the pen back onto its stand and then made sure no ink stained his hands or blotched on his report. As usual, none did, yet still he wiped his hands on a cleaning cloth as he considered. In the past, Lord Krev's spy had shied off from direct contact, though each knew the other's face by now. "Where is this Free Hawk?"

"I left the petitioner in the worship hall, holy brother." The servant bowed lower, suddenly worried that he had been in error for not bringing the person to a side room.

"That is fine. You may go and return to your duties."

After the servant withdrew, Brodagar took a moment to collect his thoughts. What would he say to Free Hawk? He reminded himself that his main goal was to win the secret of Warhaven. For that nugget, he would be willing to pay almost any coin, be it humility or actual booty. He decided to start with non-committal silence; let Lord Krev's pet set the tone. He pulled up his hood, for though his room was dark, other parts of the temple would be painfully lit. Satisfied that his eyes were sheltered, he left his room, carefully locking the door and then heading towards the worship hall.

Deep Crossing's temple was old and well appointed, but it also rambled in its construction. There was no easy or quick route for him to take, and he was further delayed by a slow gaggle of sisters, most of them prunes so thin that he doubted his hounds would find a decent morsel on their ancient bones and loose skin. He finally made it past the meandering women and hurried his step towards the worship hall. As Brodagar rounded another corner, he nearly ran into the temple's leader, a mere human of the Azure order. This place was rife with brothers and sisters from all the orders, and very few of them were Embraced.

"High Brother Idras. Pardon my clumsiness." He gave the stout man a slight bow.

"Oh, it is you, Brother Brodagar. That is good, for I have been wanting to talk with you about your travels. Come, walk with me and share about the road conditions and what is happening out west."

Brodagar had no choice but to humor the man. He gave as short a report as he dared, and then asked permission to return to his duties. The High Brother released him with a smile. Brodagar took a moment to regain his bearings and realized that Idra's wanderings had led him further away from the worship hall. With a whispered curse, he hurried to get to Free Hawk. When he finally entered the cavernous worship hall that echoed with sounds of prayer, Brodagar looked to the back of the hall for the person he sought. He found no one waiting for him. He scanned the people who knelt in worship and then he saw her: Lady Hessilyn of Westbend's Targan House. He considered approaching her while she worshiped, but knew too well that would be a breach of worship protocol. Nonetheless, he was curious at her presence.

"Over here, holy brother," someone whispered. Brodagar turned and spotted a man in the shadows just outside the hall's open doors. Free Hawk. Obviously, he hid because of Hessilyn.

Brodagar walked out into the wide courtyard, not stopping or even looking again at the fellow. The priest heard Free Hawk fall in behind him as he led the way to an outdoor grotto dedicated to some heroic priest of the Azure Order. The grotto purposely resembled a natural stone cave. He entered and walked its twisting path until he came to the small altar at its rear. He sent a burst of power to extinguish the hurtful candles that blazed above the alcove. In the sudden darkness, Brodagar turned to the man.

"I am here as you asked, Free Hawk."

"You delayed too long. One of the others almost found me."

"I saw her kneeling at worship," he replied, offering no apology or explanation for his tardiness. "What do you want of me?"

"Can we not have a little light? I can barely see your outline in this gloom."

Brodagar smiled. "I would not want to expose you, Free Hawk." It seemed this would be another list of demands and threats from Krev's spy, this time delivered in person. Brodagar considered how to motivate the traitor to focus on his task better. He lifted his right hand in front of the man and let the red lightning spark across his fingers. "Here is your light."

Free Hawk sprang back at the sudden light. His face showed surprise. His feelings spoke of resentment and envy. The man quickly recovered though, and a cunning look came to his face. "Well priest, I finally have your answer."

The words took a moment to sink in. Brodagar paused, to calm his sudden excitement, and then he asked. "So then, where is this Warhaven?"

The other man ran fingers through his hair and Brodagar could see that he savored the power of knowing. The priest resisted the urge to hit the arrogant man, but instead waited for his answer.

Finally, the betrayer spoke. "Warhaven is in far northern Na Ciria, hidden among the Pinnacles."

Free Hawk told all, sharing every detail of the secret that Mylana had entrusted to him, and Brodagar committed it to memory. By the time Free Hawk was done, the spy leaned against the grotto's rough wall, worn out by his recital and the priest's digging for more details.

"Is that all of it?" asked Brodagar.

"Yes, that is all that I know about the Prayer Warriors' redoubt. I have heard and obeyed my instructions from Lord-Governor Krev Zendron."

Brodagar nodded and then struck the man hard across the face with his left hand, so hard that Free Hawk's skull cracked against the wall.

The betrayer cried out in protest, and then spat out the blood that filled his mouth. Brodagar felt the man's rage, his desire to strike back, but the spy did nothing. So many humans were cowards.

"You had no call to do that! I have done my duty. I am deserving of my promised reward and not mistreatment."

"I have shown you mercy, Coursen Highjumper. Your arrogance should have been repaid with a beheading."

Suddenly fearful, Coursen dropped to the rough ground and pressed his face to the floor of the grotto in humility, muttering an apology.

Brodagar felt disdain. The fool should have already learned that there was no forgiveness among the Great Lord's forces. He wondered if Lord Krev had promised this dupe an Embracing for his efforts. If so, Brodagar hoped the promise would not be kept. Some humans were just not worthy to be Embraced.

He turned his back on the pathetic spy, adjusted his hood to keep his face hidden, and then walked out.

As he exited, he saw Lady Hessilyn hurrying away through the blue gate. No matter, for she was no longer important to him. Brodagar smiled as he strode across the wide courtyard. Finally, he knew the Attuls' deep secret, the information that Lord Emperor Silossiak so eagerly sought. As he walked, he considered how he could best use this information to his own advantage. Brodagar was so distracted that he took little notice of the Shade Order priests just arriving in the company of some southern lord-governor.

CHAPTER THIRTY-SIX

Engro's Ways

WINTRON

"Your grandfather called this chamber Weeping Hall," stated Fors as he and Wintron looked around a large, stone-lined hollow under the King's Keep. Fors ran a finger along the wet wall. "It wicks moisture from the river."

"My father called it the same name," replied Wintron, looking over his shoulder at the men descending a narrow stairway to join them. They were now inside the keep and still not detected, but it was the next leg where danger waited. Three passages led away from the Weeping Hall; he tried to remember where each went but could not. He point to the one of the right. "That way goes toward the dungeon and lower store rooms."

"You remember rightly," replied Fors, motioning for his helper, a Sergeant Brem, to give him support as he headed towards another opening. He did not bother to consult his nephew; he just chose their next route. "This passage will take us to the stairs leading up into the keep."

Wintron frowned at his uncle's presumption but did not protest aloud. Instead, he followed. The scouts scurried to get ahead of all of them. The passage ran long and straight, taking them under the keep proper. Fors remembered correctly, bringing them to a narrow stairway. The old man did not yield the lead, but instead limped his way up, slowing down everyone else.

He wanted to press past his uncle, but the way was too narrow. At times, the prince had to turn sidewise to avoid scrapping his shoulders on the rough stone walls. The stairs brought them to a narrow way, somewhere within the walls of the fortress, between a plaster wall and the great stones of the outer wall.

All stepped carefully now, making sure no sword or spear or armor banged against the sides, for noise might expose them far too early. Wintron knew what lay beyond the plaster: the keep's upper storerooms. He was tempted to use one of Engro's peepholes, but the faint lanterns did not reveal any and there was no time to search. The narrow passage ended in an odd shaped room that had a wooden ladder to one side.

Two other passages continued on, heading to the right or to the left, but it seemed that his uncle favored the upward choice, for the Old Fox waited with his hand on a rung. The three scouts waited to one side, for the general had ordered them to keep near for instructions.

He motioned Wintron close so that he could whisper. "We will surface right behind the great hall, if I remember correctly. I want to take Sergeant Brem up to use one of Engro's spy holes. Have the men wait here, for we cannot have them crowd in behind the Great Hall's paneling like some nest of mice in a granary wall."

"The men will stay down here," agreed Wintron, "but I will go for a look too."

Fors frowned, but gave a curt nod. Without another whisper, he started up the dusty rungs, Brem right behind him.

Wintron turned to Yosif. "You and one other guard join us. Have the rest of the guard keep those following from trying to climb. The general is right; we will be vulnerable on the next floor, with just wood paneling between us and discovery."

He climbed after his uncle, followed by Yosif and another guard. Yosif and Brem each held one of the red lanterns, so they had enough lighting. The ladder came out in a small room from which two passages left, along with another ladder heading higher still. Wintron stepped off and to join his uncle and Brem. He noted their own footprints on the dusty floor, but no others. That was good, for it meant no one else had found Engro's Ways.

Brem's faint red light gave the rough walls a bloodstained look. From below, the lantern Yosif carried preceded him up the rungs, held high. Soon, Yosif and the other guard were up. Fors turned towards the door on the right and started towards it, just as they all heard the sounds of an argument in the hall behind the wooden wall. Impatient,

Wintron passed his slow uncle and slipped through the doorway, having to angle his shoulders to pass.

The passage beyond was narrow yet straight, its ceiling lost in the gloom. They were now behind the paneling on the Great Hall's eastern wall. Wintron strode to the far end of the hall, making sure not to bump into the walls or the support beams that held the hall's paneling in place. Reaching the far wall, he searched out an opening he had used often enough as a youngster. It took a moment to find the spy hole, for it was lower on the wall than he remembered, but then he found it. He paused, considering if he should order the lanterns extinguished, but instead just motioned for the two sergeants to keep back. Winton opened the spy hole and looked out through the eyes of a bear carved into the richly fashioned wall panel. Duke Fors bent over another opening, having to set his hand on the wall for support.

DRASS

Drass Halen-Dabe tried not to smile, but it was hard not to find humor at his brother's outrage. He had come down here at Mordel's bidding. For some reason, his brother thought Drass would defend his right to the King's Keep. Not likely, thought Drass. The Tlocanians demanded the fortress for their own, so Mordel should have quietly withdrawn to save his own dignity. Instead, his foolish brother had stubbornly resisted, resulting in this comical scene. Mordel still sat on the Border throne, refusing to give it up.

"How dare you try to throw me out of my own keep! I have been courteous enough to allow you and those priests to take over the towers and ramparts, but I will not surrender the Great Hall to you as well. No matter that you are our ally; no guest has the right to demand that a host yield his place. This is the traditional seat of power for the whole Border Realm." Mordel pounded on the richly carved arm rests. "This is where the Border King must sit."

"I do not care where you place your rump," replied Colonel Ulen. "However, the King's Keep is now ours, as partial payment for our assistance. You want to keep that termite-nibbled piece of wood? Fine." He motioned six burly soldiers forward and they lifted the throne with Mordel still in its seat. "You may keep your throne; just place it in some other hall."

Mordel yelled as the men started carrying him and the throne up the hall. Some of Mordel's men moved to aid their leader, but were quickly and viciously cut down by more Tlocanian soldiers.

Drass walked over to his brother's wife and the children, for they were in the hall as well. He had no love for Mordel, but Zaveeta had always treated him well. The young boys buried their faces in their mother's skirts, terrified by the bloodshed and yelling. However, young Zita looked ready to jump out in defense of her father. Drass put a restraining hand on her shoulder, shaking his head. Zita gave him an angry look, but was unable to pull free. Her mother did not notice; Zaveeta watched her husband with the wide eyes of shock.

Mordel tried to beat the men carrying the chair on their shoulders, but could not reach them with his fists. He kicked at the two at the front, but it made no difference. He ordered his mercenaries to attack, but they now balked. Thoroughly angry, Mordel started wrestling with his sword, having to climb to his feet to pull it free. He looked ridiculous, standing on top of his precious throne, one hand holding its back and the other waving his bejeweled blade.

The six soldiers kept on, walking methodically towards the doors with their heavy burden.

"Dump him from his perch!" shouted Colonel Ulen, sounding thoroughly disgusted.

The soldiers quickly complied, upending the throne and sending Mordel sprawling. Drass had to admit that his brother was athletic. Instead of falling to a heap on the tiles, Mordel rolled and came to his feet with his sword at the ready.

Ulen held up a hand. "Stop right there, King Mordel. Control yourself. Presently, we are still allies, but should you slash at my men once more I will declare you a traitor to the Empire. I think we can find someone else to sit on that silly chair if we must." He motioned for the soldiers to keep going with the throne.

Mordel was wise enough to lower his blade. He glared towards his younger brother, probably thinking the colonel was suggesting Drass as a replacement, though Drass had no interest in the Border Realm any more.

"You can take over any other building in Regalis as the new king's residence, or move to Glenford and take over that airy keep. However, this fortress now belongs to Tlocania. I can no longer endure your petty interfering or the little attempts at sabotage. You will vacate this place."

Mordel replied in a calmer tone. Drass thought that his brother finally realized the danger for himself and his family. "Surely, you do not mean to heave us out into the arms of the enemy? I hear they have already overrun the city walls and are just outside the keep."

"I am tempted to, in response to your churlish behavior," replied Ulen, "but Emperor Silossiak is a big-hearted man and would be grieved to hear that an ally had been ripped apart. Instead, you will be allowed to leave by way of a ferry from the keep's river gate. The ferrymen await you even now. I expect you on the west bank of the Cleargorn within the hour, along with your family and your men. You can either wait on the far bank until the fighting is done, or you can flee to Glenford. It is your choice, King Mordel. Either way, I will not have you and yours underfoot as we start our rituals come midnight." The Tlocanian officer turned his head towards Mordel's family. "I still do not know who tried to free the prisoners, but it was not one of my soldiers nor was it a dragon priest."

To the mere humans the colonel's face remained hidden in the shadows of his great helm, yet still Zita squirmed under Drass' hand. He saw that the man was indeed looking at the young lady. He wondered if his niece was the guilty one. She had enough fire in her to try such a bold thing.

"If I make Glenford my new capitol, will you withdraw all your troops from there?" asked Mordel.

Ulen shrugged. "We will maintain a small garrison, as needed, and we will expect unhindered passage through the city. However, you will keep your throne, Mordel. I have no desire to rule this backwards land of rocks and pines."

Drass caught the colonel's subtle conditions, but Mordel was too upset to notice. "Come Zaveeta. Children. Let us leave this place." He turned his back and walked out with as much dignity as he could manage. Drass let go of Zita so that she could hurry after, along with her mother and two brothers. Mordel's sellswords quietly slinked off too.

Ulen turned to a messenger. "Tell the men to make sure that throne is dumped on the river's far bank. After all, I promised Mordel that he could keep his throne."

The messenger bowed and said, "I hear and obey." He then hurried after the fellows carrying the wooden chair.

Ulen turned back towards Drass, but then paused, for a noise had come from behind the wall. It came again, a muffled sneeze.

WINTRON

The sneezes were far louder inside the passage. Wintron looked around and saw Brem trying to restrain a third sneeze. He failed, and this one exploded with even greater noise. The prince took one more look through the spy hole and saw the Tlocanians rushing towards the wall. He backed away. Quietly, yet quickly, he turned and urged his uncle to head back. Fors tried to move quickly as well, but his wounded leg betrayed him. As he hurriedly stepped around one of the wall's braces, he stumbled and his sword's sheath smacked the brace soundly. Wintron caught his uncle's elbow and kept him from falling to the floor, but the damage was already done. The Tlocanians realized someone or something was within the walls. He heard the officer calling out for axes.

Wintron helped Fors back to the room where the ladders led upward and downward. Fors pulled free and stepped over to the down ladder. "Start climbing men and be fast about it! We are found out!" Brem came to his side to offer his commander an arm to lean on. Fors glared at the sergeant, but took the offered support. The general pointed a bony finger at Yosif. "Tell the men to keep climbing, up that other ladder too. I want as many as possible up to the next level." He then turned to Wintron. "I told you I would remain behind if I became a hindrance, so I guess this is where I will make my stand."

"Ridiculous. Brem, help the general to climb that ladder to the next floor, and if you sneeze again I will cut off your nose with my own knife."

Wintron watched to make sure they both joined the flow of men climbing. His eyes then went towards the other passage leaving the landing, a dark way that headed deeper into the keep. He was tempted to run off in that direction, for it would bring him past the kitchen and the soldiers' mess hall, to a hidden door that came out in the master cook's bedroom. Mordel was leaving the keep by way of the river gate, which was in the same direction. If Wintron hurried, he could catch his father's murderer and get revenge now.

He struggled against the thought, for he knew that if he chased after Mordel then he would be unable to interrupt the Shadow Anchor rite and thousands would die. It was a grievous choice, but he had to place the realm and its people first. "El, deliver Mordel into my hands some day," he whispered. "Do not deny me the chance to avenge my father the king."

He hesitated a moment longer, then turned to the first soldiers coming up from below. The next one off the rungs was Captain Jardon. "Captain, they have found us. You will be responsible for holding this door." Behind them, Yosif ordered the soldiers to keep climbing, following the general upstairs. "Do what you can to buy us some time, and then you can retreat." Wintron motioned to the other doorway out of the odd-shaped room. "That passage heads towards the kitchens and then the soldiers mess hall. Break out somewhere and cause as much havoc as you can."

The captain was about to respond, when an explosion rocked the passageway beyond, shattering part of the panel wall and setting more of it on fire. Whatever the captain intended to say, his focus was now on getting his ruler to safety. "Climb, my prince, and take loyal Yosif with you. We will do what we can to stop them from following." He pulled out two passing soldiers and ordered them to hack free the ladder as soon as the prince came up.

Wintron hurriedly climbed, with Yosif at his back. They were the last two to make it up to the second floor.

He had lost so many men because one man could not stifle a sneeze.

DRASS

Drass heard the sneezes, though at first he did not realize what they signified. He thought it came from some other room, echoing off the stone and tile. Only when Colonel Ulen blasted to the wall to expose the hidden passage, did Drass realize that there were spies within the keep. Tlocanian soldiers fearlessly leaped through the still-burning wreckage and charged up the passageway that ran behind the wall paneling. Drass could hear swords clashing and men shouting. He hurried after the men, wanting to get his chance to throw some fireballs too. Stepping over a smoldering chunk of wood, he looked up the passage and saw Tlocanians and Border soldiers fighting. This gave him another surprise, for he had expected some of Mordel's sellswords, not Wintron's men. Drass held up his hand and let a fireball form in his palm. It felt good, the power throbbing in his grasp. It did not burn him at all.

"How do I throw a fireball?" he whispered to Slosoro, suddenly unsure how to get rid of the thing.

The demon revealed more knowledge and suddenly Drass understood how to toss it past the Tlocanians. He lobbed it over their heads, the high ceiling giving him plenty of clearance. His aim was not perfect though and it glanced off the stone wall, splashing fire all over the Bordermen that held the doorway at the end of the secret hallway. Fire scattered everywhere, killing a few and injuring far more.

He was about to create another fireball, when Colonel Ulen grabbed his wrist. "Stop that, Lord Drass. Too much fire may cause the way to collapse and prevent us from chasing after them. Besides, you could dangerously deplete yourself. Has not your Other warned you?"

"What do you mean?" he asked, posing the same question silently to Slosoro.

You were in no danger, replied Slosoro within his head. *I would not allow my new host to take such a foolish risk.*

"Our magic requires power," responded Ulen as he motioned soldiers to press their attack. "We mainly draw power from life energies, either our own or another's. You have no store of power from others, so the power for lightning and fire comes from yourself. Take too much and you will collapse in exhaustion or even die."

A deep voice took over Drass' mouth. "Do you try to scare him? I have been here long enough to sense his limits Ulen-Snargrof." Drass clenched his teeth, not wanting Slosoro to use him like a puppet.

Colonel Ulen replied, also in a different voice. "So, you are finally willing to talk, Slosoro. It is past time for you to tell us something worthwhile. You are to head to the Listening Room and make your report from the Darklands. Now."

Drass failed in keeping his mouth closed; Slosoro spoke again using his tongue. "I will go, Snargrof, but you and I are not yet finished."

The colonel stood straighter, still speaking in that other voice. "Two hundred years ago you had more power, Slosoro, but this is a new time. Do not presume that you still have the same authority as you did under the Darshi Empire. The Failed must prove their worth all over, so proclaims Silossiak and the other two Great Ones."

"The Failed?" asked Slosoro, using Drass' tongue.

The colonel nodded. "If all of you had succeeded, we would not be conquering Na Ciria for a second time. You were once powerful, Slosoro, and you may be so again, but you must prove your worth first. Now go to the Listening Room and make your report from the Supreme One. Our reporting window will be closing soon, so you should hurry."

Slosoro let go of Drass' voice. He could tell that the demon was angry. It was left to Drass to respond. He gave a slight bow. "I hear and obey."

Ulen-Snargrof smirked. "See that both of you do. Must I direct you to where you must go, or do you know the way?"

Drass remembered the room where they had bound him to the Other. It was a small room on the top floor of the main keep. A room that had once been a guest room before the Tlocanians stripped it bare to remake it for their bloody rites. "I know where I am expected."

"Then go there quickly." The colonel turned his back on him, focusing again on the assault inside the hidden passages.

CHAPTER THIRTY-SEVEN
Embracing Death

WINTRON

The crown prince was yanked back from the opening when the red fire exploded below. He would have fallen if Yosif had not steadied him. Two soldiers stepped up in his place and started kicking and yanking on the wooden ladder, straining to snap it free. Once loose, they pulled it up on Fors' orders.

"The men below will have to find another route to safety," the general explained when some looked ready to protest. "We cannot afford to have the Tlocanians follow us up here."

Wintron saw the wisdom in Fors' decision, but was keenly aware that their squadron had been cut to a third of its size. Not only that, but they had only one high officer left besides the general, Captain Jardon. Wintron now had more reason to hope that old Fors could keep up. "Follow me, men. We have our mission still."

The second floor of the keep had been where his family lived. Wintron's own rooms were off to the left, along with some other bedrooms, while his father's royal suite lay to the right. He chose neither direction. Instead, the prince headed down a long and arrow-straight passage. Old King Engro had designed this floor so that no one could lurk in any niche to spy on him. In addition, the passageways within the walls of the king's apartment lay behind a second hidden doorway that could not be opened from this side, at least not without using axes to hack through the stout wood.

Wintron led the way down the long hall, feeling very exposed even with hundreds of men behind him. His goal was a stairway leading to the next floor. He just hoped to reach it without being discovered, for there was nowhere to hide. He felt a little bit of relief when they finally rounded a corner, for now they were no longer in direct sight of the stairwell down to the Great Hall. The corridor ended at a wooden flight of stairs that spun in a tight circle up a hole in the ceiling. Wintron motioned for the men to step carefully, not wanting the sound of their passage to be heard in the rooms beyond the Ways.

They made it up to the third floor without mishap, though it took some time for all the men to climb up single-file. Fors came up just before the rear guard, appearing a bit worn but obviously determined not to fall behind.

* * *

The third level of the keep was a honeycomb of small rooms that had been used by the many officials of the realm. Each had a study and a sleeping chamber, though none the same size. Engro's Ways snaked between the many walls, for apparently the old king had wanted to spy on all of his underlings.

Wintron and Fors had agreed that they needed to find the Hidden Half Stairs, which led up to the top floor. However, finding it took some time, with numerous missed turns. Finally, they realized that they could not get to it without a dash out of the hidden passages to reach another section of Engro's Ways.

The crown prince ran with the first group of soldiers, across an empty sitting room, down a hallway, and into another room. The area was barely lit and seemed deserted, causing him to wonder if Mordel's flunkies had been purged along with the king slayer, leaving this area now unoccupied. As they ran through the rooms, Wintron was very aware of the noise they created. Thankfully, they did not encounter anyone during their dash, but once in the second room they had to pause while Wintron looked for a hidden opening.

The walls were wood paneled, like most in the King's Keep. Wintron walked to the far wall and began searching for the trigger to the hidden door. He knew it was behind one of the five paintings along that wall, but not which one and he did not have much light for searching. Lifting the first two and running his fingers along the wall revealed nothing, but behind the third one he found the small depression in the wood paneling that seemed promising. He pushed and probed until he heard the faint click. To his right, a doorway appeared, tall and narrow, its edges following seams in the wood paneling.

Yosif motioned two men to hurry inside to secure the passageway and sent another soldier back to inform those waiting in the other room. Soon, the rest of their party hurried down the corridor to join them. They went unnoticed until the last party of five trotted up the carpeted hall.

It was then that a squad of Tlocanian soldiers came around a far corner and saw them. The enemy ran after them, not realizing how many more were in the room beyond, and ran into a trap. A quick yet fierce fight ensued. The Tlocanians were skilled but far outnumbered, so they fell quickly. However, one of them ran off, rather than face certain death.

Fors cursed. "Do you think they will be able to find the entrance?"

Wintron looked down at the carpet. "In this weak light, I cannot see any sign of our passage, yet I fear the demon lovers will find our tracks. Even if they do not, I doubt they will have any hesitancy in taking an ax to all the walls. Take the lead again, general. We need to get the men up those stairs and to the next floor."

Fors nodded and then motioned for the ever-present Brem to precede him inside. After all of the soldiers passed through, Wintron followed. Yosif and five men serving as the rear guard came last, pushing the hidden door shut behind them.

They found the Hidden Half Stairway easily enough now. The wide stone steps were the far left edge of a stairway used by the keep's occupants. Fors stood at the top of the flight, watching the men carefully to make sure no one bumped into the wall separating the two sets of stairs. It was just as the last few reached the top floor of the main keep, that all heard a commotion behind them. The smashing of wood. Everyone knew that pursuers would soon be on their tail.

General Fors doubled their rear guard to ten, ordering them to hold the stairway as long as they could against any soldiers. However, he told them to flee immediately if anyone started throwing magic at them. The men took their orders bravely, though knowing this would likely be their final duty.

* * *

They were now on the top floor of the main keep. Engro's Ways could take them no higher.

They hurried through the Ways to a spot that both leaders felt was the closest they could get to Farwatch Tower. They tasked everyone to search out spy holes and possible openings.

Behind them, all could hear the start of a battle.

"My prince, I have something here," called out one man in a loud whisper. "Is this a doorway?"

Wintron hurried over and examined the place. "Well done. It is not easy finding anything in this dim lighting." He took a quick look through a nearby spy hole, but saw only a dark room beyond. As he ran his fingers across the rough wood in search of the catch, the Tlocanians came around a corner of the Engro's Ways. Wintron and the soldier had to push hard to get the doorway open, for something stood against it on the other side. They had the door only half ajar when the rear guard started dying.

DRASS

Drass Halen-Dabe came to the Listening Room just as Lord Gordrew arrived. Shocked, Drass at first thought him to be one of the invaders, but then Slosoro informed him that this man had also been Embraced by a demon.

"Baron Gordrew? When did you join the other side?"

The middle-aged man gave him a cool smile. "Long before you, Drass. Who do you think talked your brother into his alliance? Who do you think gave safe passage to all of those soldiers that helped him overthrow the throne? I served as the emperor's agent, for I found Lord Silossiak to be the greater ruler." The baron gave him a second look and frowned. "I see that they have allowed you to become Embraced. I hope you realize the greatness of such an honor."

Drass considered making a snide reply, but the servant Goval appeared and asked them to enter the room, so Drass let the other's words pass unchallenged.

Goval had them bare their heads as a sign of humility and then led them inside, where a priest chanted over his latest victim. The listening ceremony was already in progress. Hanging on the wall, a huge stone mask seemed almost alive, its eyes glowing and its chiseled lines seeming fluid at times, as it spoke to the Listener priest.

Goval brought them to one side, and then gave them whispered instructions. "Wait here until the priest calls you forward. Your Others will be giving reports directly from the Darklands, reports that neither of you are allowed to hear, so you must be drugged for a little while." Goval picked up metal cups from a side table and handed them to each convert.

Drass looked at the contents. The liquid seemed as dark as

midnight, giving off a foul smell like some rotted meal. He held it at arm's length to keep the stench from overpowering him.

"Drink," ordered Goval. "That is what the Great One commands."

Drink, echoed Slosoro.

He took a deep breath and then forced the beverage down, nearly gagging on its horrid taste. He heard Gordrew choke some, but he was struggling too much to pay him any attention. As soon as the liquid hit his stomach, he began to feel light-headed. He felt Slosoro take control over far more than his tongue. The demon seized his whole body and Drass had no way to stop him. Soon Drass was as if asleep, leaving just Slosoro aware of their surroundings.

* * *

Drass awoke lying on a cold stone floor. He turned his head to see where he was and recognized the Listening Room, though the huge mask on the wall no longer showed any life to it. A soft moan escaped him as he sat up, his head spinning. He saw the priest who had conducted the rite leaning over Gordrew, giving the older man a hand up. Drass had been about to complain, but he decided not to. Let Gordrew show weakness; he would not. Suppressing any more groans, he got to his feet carefully, placing one hand against the wall to steady himself. Gordrew also stood, though he leaned heavily on the priest.

"Is it always so…so difficult to make a report?" asked Gordrew.

The priest chuckled. "Of course not Gordrew-Shovress. You should know better, simply by consulting your Other. It is only at the beginning that you must drink the Grasienda Dolo. You are not yet fully merged with your Other, so learning too much about the Darklands would drive you insane. We cannot allow that. The need for the stupor potion will lessen the longer you are Embraced. I, for one, never use the vile stuff anymore." The priest looked over at Drass to make sure he was awake too. He nodded approval at his condition. "Your awakening is none too early, for we must leave here at once. There are intruders nearby."

Drass pushed away from the wall, forcing his feet to carry his full weight. His mind was still fogged by the potion's residue. He knew that the priest's words should upset him, but he did not know why. "Intruders?"

"Apparently, the Bordermen used some secret passageways to get inside the keep. Already, some of them have been found on the floor below us." The priest started leading Gordrew towards the door.

Drass stumbled after them, not liking that Gordrew received all the help, though feeling satisfaction that he was the stronger one. When they came out of the Listening Room, three servants met them.

"Embraced Ones, you will need to flee this way," said Goval, pointing the direction to go. "The invaders are now on this floor. We will do what we can to delay any who pursue."

"Why should we run away?" demanded Drass. "We are more powerful than any mere humans…"

"You are drained," stated the dragon priest. "You are defenseless until you recover. Now, take Lord Gordrew and see that the two of you head up Farwatch Tower. You are still expected there at midnight. I will deal with these intruders."

"But Embraced One, you are also worn out," protested Goval.

"Enough. I have spoken."

Goval gave a bow, as did the other two. "We hear and obey."

The priest turned back to the newly Embraced. "Why are you two still here? I ordered you to go."

Drass had no strength to argue, so he took hold of Gordrew, who leaned against a wall, and set off in the direction they wanted him to go. Both were so depleted that they forgot to raise their hoods again.

As Drass came to the hallway's end, he heard shouting behind him. He looked back and saw soldiers rushing at the priest. He thought he might have recognized his father and his cousin in the group, but a huge fireball roared down the hall, blocking his view before he was certain about his relatives.

The priest collapsed, exhausted.

Go, urged Slosoro. *He has no power left to defend your rear.*

Drass shifted his hold on Gordrew and kept going, uncertain how many of the invaders had survived and wondering if he had really seen his father and Wintron behind him. Slosoro was insistent that he not pause to look back, so he struggled around a corner and on towards the Farwatch Tower.

WINTRON

Yosif rushed ahead of his prince, along with three others, hurrying to make sure the dark room was secure. Wintron allowed them to do their duty. As the lanterns were brought in, all could see it was unoccupied. The room was also almost empty, with only a row of neat cots with clothes chests at the foot of each bed. One bed had been pushed aside to free the secret opening. The richly paneled wall had effectively concealed the door from its occupants, apparently.

Wintron stepped into the room, wondering who used the accommodations. He threw open the chests to reveal black robes and underclothes, so apparently some of the dragon priests bedded here. Fors and Brem entered too, while Captain Jardon stayed back with most of the others to fight off those attacking from the rear.

"Brem, go back in there and tell Jardon that I want him to keep moving," ordered Fors. "We cannot let them pour molasses over our feet by forcing us to defend some stupid passageway; we must keep moving."

Brem nodded and went back for the captain.

Fors turned to Wintron. "Do you know where we are? I thought this floor was set aside for the troops, to give them quick access to the towers and wall-walks. Why would they give these rooms over to those damnable priests? There are far better quarters in the tower itself."

"I hope they do not have so many priests that they overflow to this floor too," said Wintron, heading towards the door out. "We will know better once we see what is beyond this bare room."

Yosif stepped in his path. "Allow me, my prince. We do not know what might await us beyond the door."

Wintron frowned but nodded approval. It frustrated him to be so cautious, but he understood the captain's concerns. Yosif motioned his three companions to join him. He carefully cracked the door open, but found the hallway beyond empty. He yanked the door wide and sent his men out to scout in both directions, joining them in reconnoitering.

Finally, Brem came back with the captain and the rest of the men. The last one out carefully closed the hidden door behind them. The captain was cradling his sword arm. He came over to the general and the prince to give his report.

"We killed them all, but they were fierce fighters. We lost a third of our men. Some of our men are pulling the bodies into the bedroom and then we will close the hidden door. However, one of theirs ran off before the fighting started, so I do not think we can truly hide our exit."

"How is your arm?" asked Wintron.

Jardon shook his head in disgust. "It is useless now, but I will live. An unlucky blow; the fellow was already dying on my sword when with his last gasp he struck me." He shook his head again. "I survived the fall of the boundary forts and the retreat up to Tor Randis without a wound and now some young pup renders me useless in his death throes."

"You are more than just a sword, captain," rebuked the Old Fox. "You are a leader of men, so get to it. I expect trouble ahead of us now, for we spent too much time in that maze of hidden ways. Sergeant Yosif is already out there checking our route."

Jardon gave him a curt salute and started shouting out orders, sending men scampering after Yosif's squad. Wintron and Fors strode after the forward squads, out into the corridor. Doors to either side had already been opened and the rooms cleared. Wintron was surprised to find the area stripped of all ornamentation. The rugs, tapestries, and paintings were gone, making this floor appear as spare as a barrack or an acolyte's chamber.

The two leaders and their men walked toward where Yosif waited at a turn in the hallway. He looked chastened.

"I apologize, my prince," he said. "The captain berated me for leaving your side."

"I was in no danger," replied Wintron, waving off the apology. "Have you found any more of the enemy?"

Yosif shook his head. "No one yet."

They all looked up the hall to where Captain Jardon stood directing the advanced guards in checking the many rooms to either side. The soldier furthest forward was just about to open one door, when a half-dozen gray-robed servants came out. He paused, not certain what to do, and that cost him his life, for the servants rushed him brandishing long knives.

Captain Jardon saw it happen but was too far away to come to the man's aid. In anger, he yelled out to the rest of the forward soldiers and they all charged the servants.

"I do not like this," muttered Fors. "The workers stand their ground, even though our men have swords. Brem, call more men forward. I fear that Jardon is charging into an ambush of some sort."

"Yes, sir." Brem hurried back around the corner and started yelling for the soldiers behind them to run forward.

"There is your trap!" hissed Yosif, pointing to a black-robed priest that had just stepped out of another room.

Fors ignored his words, for his eyes locked on one of the men that came out after the priest. "That is Drass behind him!" The general began to hurry that way.

Wintron saw the priest raise both hands, lightning playing across his fingers. "Fors! Stop!" He hurried after his uncle.

Yosif was more forceful. With his three companions, he shoved the two leaders through an open doorway, despite their protests. Just then, a huge fireball came sizzling down the corridor.

Wintron stumbled when the men shoved him into the side room. He saw Fors fall onto one of the cots. Behind him, he heard the roar of fire and then felt the sudden heat. The two men who had pushed him cried out in pain as the flames brushed against them. Wintron caught his balance and turned. One of the men was on fire, so he helped the other soldier in extinguishing him with a blanket yanked from a cot.

That done, he looked around. He saw Yosif helping Fors off the floor.

Wintron stepped over to the doorway, finding the door now gone. He looked out, careful not to touch the smoldering doorframe.

Smoke filled the corridor beyond, its stone walls and ceiling charred. The blown-off door burned angrily where it lay, adding to the smoke. Those soldiers further up the hall were all dead, but back at the corner some still lived, groaning on the floor. Wintron was about to step out, when Yosif put a hand on his shoulder.

"No, my prince. That priest may send another fireball."

"I doubt that," he argued, staring through the smoke. "He appears to have collapsed."

"Still, please stay in here while we go to make sure no others lurk ahead of us."

Wintron frowned, but once again yielded to his protector. He and Fors stayed behind with the burnt man, while Yosif took the other two guards and sprinted up the hallway. He did peek out long enough to see Yosif bend over the priest and slit his throat.

"That was Drass, was it not?" asked Fors. Wintron turned and found the old general sitting on one of the cots and rubbing his sore leg.

He nodded. "Yes, it was Poisoner Drass. Did you recognize the man he held onto? For some reason, he reminded me of Lord Gordrew."

Fors gave a startled look. "You sent Gordrew to the White Owl Pass. How could he be down here?"

"That I do not know. Maybe they captured him and brought him down here by their secret path."

Fors grunted as he got back to his feet. "I think you are mistaken. Gordrew either is at the pass or safely back in Tor Randis. As for Drass, I wish that priest had not come between us."

Before Wintron could ask what his uncle meant by that, a group of soldiers came in led by Brem.

"Are the two of you unharmed, my prince and my general?"

Wintron nodded while Fors grunted and pointed to the wounded soldier. "Have someone see to his burns, Brem. How does it look out there?"

Brem sent a soldier to care for his comrade while he went over to the Old Fox and offered his arm for support. "We lost some who rushed around the corner in spite of hearing that oncoming fireball. I see that Yosif is securing the way ahead. He is waving us to come on."

"We will go," replied Fors, "but I want you to make sure that all the wounded are moved to one of these bedrooms. Leave them some weapons, Brem, and some food. However, no able-bodied man can be spared as medic or guard. They will be on their own to hide until we can come back for them."

"I will see to it, my general," said Brem.

"Then let us get going," said Wintron, eager to get away from the stench though he did not like that they would have to leave their wounded behind. The prince walked out among the soldiers waiting in the still-smoky hallway. The flames were dying out due to lack of fuel. He strode quickly down the hall, avoiding the charred bodies, though he did glance at the slain priest.

Yosif waited for the prince just past the burnt area, in front of a closed door. "My prince, this room is like the one Councilor Rolen found at the Five Dragons Temple in Randisville. Their last victims are still in there, dumped in the corner. I would suggest avoiding the grizzly sight."

"I think not," disagreed Wintron. He opened the door and looked at the murder room. The sight and smell struck him as far worse than the burned corridor. After a careful look, he turned to Yosif. "See that every soldier stops to look into this room, because this is what we are fighting to stop. The Tlocanians plan to murder many more tonight. If we do not win our way through to the tower's top and disrupt their scheme, then thousands more will end up like that. Make sure every soldier looks."

Yosif gave a curt nod. As Wintron stepped away, the captain sent the nearest soldiers to look within the murder room. Even Fors looked inside.

The prince continued on, looking around the next corner, but found only some of his own men holding the far end.

Fors came up beside him, Brem still at his side. "Our ancestor surely loved crooked ways," the duke complained, "but if I remember rightly, the opening to the wall walk should be just around that bend."

Wintron nodded. "We are finally near." He frowned as he looked back at their remaining men. "Maybe we erred by trying to keep to Engro's Ways though. It has slowed us down too much. By now, that Tlocanian officer has sent word up from the Great Hall to the tower. We no longer have surprise on our side."

"Now is not the time to wallow in regrets," stated Fors dismissively. "We have a tower to storm, so you had better focus on that, nephew."

Wintron did not reply to his uncle's baiting. Nor did he interject when Fors began to scheme with Brem on how best to charge the tower and ignored his nephew as if he were merely a figurehead. The Old Fox knew battle tactics, no matter how caustic his tone, so Wintron listened and considered. When Yosif came over, Fors included him in the discussion, acknowledging the young man's skills. Nonetheless, the duke continued to slight his prince, though careful not to bring any public insult. Clearly, Fors saw him as a failed commander, and Wintron could not argue otherwise after losing the boundary forts, Glenford, and then Regalis.

Soon, all the men were done gazing inside the blood-soaked room and it was time to press on. At the end of the hallway, the door into Farwatch Tower lay open, probably from when Drass fled through it. They could see the fourth floor landing and the stairs going both up and down.

Yosif sent six men running to secure that landing, ordering them to avoid any noise that might echo up the spiral stairway. The rest of them followed soon after. Wintron kept to the middle of the troops, as did Fors and his aide. When Wintron entered the tower, he immediately noticed that the two doors that led out onto the ramparts were not barred.

"Yosif, find something to block those doors," he ordered in a whisper, before Fors could. "Use spears if you must."

"And send a few men down the stairwell," added Fors in a louder voice. "The Tlocanians may be lurking just around the turn and I do not want them surprising us as we make our ascent."

The captain did as directed. In less than a minute, those who had descended came rushing back to report that a large force climbed the stairs from the lower levels of the keep.

"Well, thank the gods we do not need to go anywhere but up," said Fors. He quickly called out certain soldiers to take the fore, announcing that they were to advance at a steady pace. Wintron noted that he had called out all the left-handed men, which made sense because the tower's stairway spiraled to the right. Fors also ordered Brem to join the fore. The sergeant protested, but Fors insisted, saying that he would not tie up any officer to serve as his crutch. Brem nodded, though obviously displeased.

Wintron spoke up. He did not want the general falling behind now, for some of the soldiers would not stand for it. "Horg, you are to assist the general as we climb the stairs." He motioned to one of the larger soldiers.

The man hurried to take Brem's place. Fors frowned, probably not happy to have his weakness stated aloud. However, it apparently soothed Brem's concerns, for the sergeant made no more protests and hurried to catch up with those already advancing up the stairway.

DRASS

Drass was glad that Gordrew regained some strength, for it was hard helping the older man up the steep stairs. He made Gordrew take the lead so that he could keep an eye on him, putting a supportive hand on his back whenever he wobbled. They kept to the tightest part of the spiral, even though the steps were narrower there, so that they could brace against the wall if needed. They came to the next landing and found Colonel Ulen waiting for them.

The commander stood in their way. Too weak to go around, the two stopped in front of him. "Where is Brother Groomger?"

"He stayed behind to challenge the invaders," replied Drass.

Ulen sighed. "The fool. He is probably dead, for the listening rites are draining. Well, if he still lives, he will have to take care of his own needs." Ulen motioned toward a closed door where a pair of guards stood at attention. "That means each of you can have an extra victim. Go on in and do what you must."

"Good," grunted Gordrew, shambling towards the door.

Drass, however, gave the colonel a puzzled look. "What are we to do?"

Ulen shook his head in disappointment. "Are you still fighting your Other? Listen to him, for he will take care of the two of you." When he still did not act, Ulen pointed at the door again. "Go in and take the life power that you need. All the other prisoners on this level are already on their way up the tower; just six wait inside to give their strength to the cause. Be quick about it, for I will not linger here to protect you; my greater duty is to make sure the Anchor Ritual is successful."

You heard him, remarked Slosoro inside Drass' head, *get in there and renew our powers.*

Drass gave in, pulling out his ritual blade and following Gordrew inside for the slaughter.

Eric Lorenzen

CHAPTER THIRTY-EIGHT

Separation

AFRAL

They left Freetown by one of its northern gates. Most of their Blue escort turned back at the city wall, but four continued with them all the way to Freetown's outer boundary. The Blues' presence helped get them past the tollbooth without paying, but Afral was glad to see the soldiers stop at the boundary wall. He found them cold, refusing to answer any questions that his father asked of them. The Green guards showed some curiosity, but Afral guessed that had more to do with them exiting by a little-used road. Both sets of soldiers watched as they rode off, apparently curious about their destination.

They passed a handful of farms beyond the boundary wall, but most of the countryside seemed deserted. The land north of Freetown opened up into a rolling countryside of meadows dotted with pine, spruce, and fir. Overhead, the sky was still a patchwork of blue sky and dark clouds, the sun teasing the Attuls as it occasionally appeared and then hid again. The road the three followed was old but not often traveled anymore except by locals, so it faded into the landscape at certain spots.

Afral could see the Pinnacles to the east and the White Mountains further away to the west. Considering their current path, he made a sudden guess on their destination, a guess that made him shiver in spite of the partially sunny day. "Does this road lead to Darsheol?"

"Yes, it does," responded his father, "but we will not go all the way to the burned-over lands. We head north long enough to confuse the Freetowners, and then we will make our way overland to the Pinnacles.

503

Warhaven is less than a week away."

Afral found no comfort in that thought, for he had nothing to look forward to in Warhaven. He expected only rejection from the Attuls, for he would be an outsider to them. He could not help but express his doubts aloud. "Must I stay there? I do not think they will want me, for I am a stranger."

"You are an Attul," corrected his mother. "A pine is no less a pine for having grown among oaks. Your heritage is what it is and you must embrace it. Afral, you have given us your word that you will complete your training at Lorekeep, so do not speak of shirking your commitment. You will keep your word, will you not?"

He nodded, but still felt doubt. His parents wanted him to become a Prayer Warrior, but he did not have the bent for it. Already he had struggled and even failed to bring light to his sword too often. His faith was too week and these strangers in Warhaven would not be as forgiving as his parents were. He wondered what they did to those who failed their training. Certainly not banishment, for they wanted their refuge kept secret. Would it be prison or even a death sentence? Afral feared it might be something like that, and yet he said nothing about those fears, out of shame. He would go through with this as he had promised, but his future seemed as dark as the Dragon Shadow.

Rain returned by midday, the clouds building up over the distant White Mountains and then crowding out the patches of blue sky. By late afternoon, the rain began to fall steadily. Afral's father thanked El for this wet blessing, for it would help hide their scent if any dreadhounds hunted the area. They turned off the road and took the horses into a stream, carefully riding them up the waterway. The splashes from the hooves were ice cold and the riverbed was treacherous with rocks and slippery mud, but his father kept them to that course until they came to a gravel-covered bank. Only then did they exit the stream. They rode into the forest for a time, and then stopped to rub down the chilled horses. After a few more hours of riding, the day's fitful light faded into night.

They stopped in a wooded hollow, where their fire would not be seen. His mother coxed a fire from damp wood and they had a warm meal. The rain lessened to just a drizzle. Later, when his parents thought he had fallen asleep, Afral overheard them talking next to the sputtering fire.

"Should we make our report at First Post?" asked Tolara. "Our delay at Wayfarer's Chapel might be overlong, for our purification rite must cover nearly two decades. The delay could cost the Prayer Warriors valuable time for strategizing."

"I think we must head all the way in before we tell our story," responded Rolen. "We need to confront the Elders in person. Surely, there have been some reports from the Watch Riders about what is happening, yet they seem to have ignored the warnings. We cannot let our dire news become just another message to lay aside. We must force them to at least hear about the demons' return."

Afral peeked out from beneath his blanket to see his mother silhouetted against the fire. She fed another stick into the flames before replying to Rolen. "Somehow, we must get their attention. For too long, the warriors have focused on Darsheol only, ignoring all the rest of Na Ciria. I still think we need to raise the banner that is folded up in my saddlebag."

"Leave it there for now," argued Afral's father. "Waving the Blood Drop banner will cause too much antipathy."

"Probably, but it would get everyone's attention."

His father actually laughed. "Tolara, at times like this you remind me of your father, so passionate and so unafraid to offend when you are right. Hold off on the banner, my dear. We will have enough opposition without implying that the Great War is upon us again."

"But it is, Rolen. Na Ciria needs our aid once again. Let us hope our people are as faithful as they were two hundred years ago, when Belere Anonral led us westward over the Wind Plains. If only we had such an inspiring leader again..."

Afral waited, but his father had no response. Suddenly, he felt very chilled and needed to burrow under his blankets. The drizzly night did not cause the cold to seep into his bones; fear did that. Would the Great War start anew? As he hunkered under his blankets, he worried that the Attuls would not win this time. For comfort, Afral pulled out his sword and let its light shine for a brief moment inside his blanket cocoon. He said a warrior's night prayer by that light and then reluctantly sheathed the blade. Darkness returned instantly, of course, but it felt somehow oppressive. He curled tight under his damp blankets and tried his best to fall asleep.

Sometime during the night, Afral awoke to the howls of dreadhounds. Grabbing his sword, he sat up quickly and then pulled it free, its light for once bright and steady.

"Put that away," ordered his mother in a whisper. "The power and light will attract them."

Afral quickly obeyed. The sudden return of darkness made him feel even more vulnerable. He could no longer see anything. "Mother? Are they close?"

"No dear, they are still far away. Let us hope that they do not find our trail." As his eyes adjusted to the night, he could see his mother's outline against the low-burning campfire.

"But Mother, I thought we would lose them by going through the city. How could they have gotten onto this side of the river?"

"They may not have found us yet. As for how they crossed the Singgorn, that I do not know. Maybe they swim far better than we realize or maybe their handlers smuggled them through the city. Then again, this may be a different pack."

Suddenly, Afral realized that someone was missing. "Where is Father?"

"He has gone to check on the horses, to make sure the baying does not upset them."

Afral heard more howling, coming from another direction and much closer. "They are all around us!"

His mother stepped closer to where he sat and put a hand on his head. "No, that last call was no dreadhound. It was a wolf, which is a good sign. If the dreadhounds were too close, the wolves would not be calling out. Now lie back down and get some more sleep. We are safe for now."

Afral obeyed, but it took some time for sleep to overtake him.

GALDON

Galdon and his men left Freetown just as the next storm broke. Once out of the city, he pulled out the magic medallion. He had been avoiding using it, for he disliked all things magical. Fingering the red gem in its metal setting, he wondered how it worked. He sincerely hoped it did not operate by taking from his strength or soul.

He held it in the palm of his hand, letting it show the direction of power like a ship's compass showed the direction of north. Light appeared in the medallion's stone, but it came from behind him. Turning back toward the city, the thing showed a red glow. He guessed it a response to the blood magic of the dragon priests, not any Attul power. Since the medallion offered no help, he would have to rely on his scouts for now.

They followed the wet road for a time, until the scouts lost the trail at a stream. It was up to Galdon to choose a direction now. He decided to send the scouts following the waterway upstream, towards the Pinnacles. They lost a couple of hours relocating the Attuls' trail, but his men knew their job and did eventually find where they had left the water. They rode on through the storm, finding just enough of a trail to keep after them.

The gloom from the rain felt reassuring to Galdon, though he did not like admitting that to himself. He had spent so many years under the Dragon Shadow that bright day seemed overly harsh after awhile. He still dreamed about the return of the sun to his fair Tlocania, but it was more the soft light of a foggy dawn or a reddish sunset tinting the city's highest spires as evening settled on the streets. Galdon realized he was slowly becoming more like the Embraced Ones, the very ones he disliked.

"Sir, we have a complication."

He left off his introspection and focused on the scout directly in front of him. "What is it?"

"Fresh dreadhound tracks. It looks to be a full pack. They seem to have turned after the Attuls."

Sergeant Lausher was close enough to have overheard. "Sir, did you know of them?"

Galdon suddenly pictured Brother Verdrof who was supposed to be following him. "I did not know of any dreadhounds ahead of us, no. Have you seen any sign of their handlers? Any hoof prints?"

The scout shook his head. "Only the dogs."

He grimaced. Most likely then an Embraced One ran with the pack in were-hound form. He detested such priests, for they seemed more feral than most of their kind. Almost rabid. "The dragon priests who guide them will be somewhere in the area." Galdon knew better than to reveal the priests' ability to change into hounds, for that was a secret that few humans knew about. "If the scouts encounter a priest, offer any aid that is needed."

Night rushed to arrive, due to the drizzly weather, forcing Galdon to call them to a halt earlier than he would have wanted. The men quickly set up the camp and soon numerous fires struggled to burn in the wet weather. He retreated into the tent that had been pitched close by, leaving the assigning of duties to his sergeants. He wanted some time to think, for if an Embraced One arrived he would have to guard his thoughts again.

Galdon considered many things that night, reveling in the freedom he still had. He reminisced about old Tlocania, he plotted ways to catch an Attul, and he wondered what life would be like without demons trying to eavesdrop on his mind.

At one point, he took out his medallion to see if it showed where the dragon priests were, but the jewel showed a different color. It was reacting to an Attul using his power.

Excited, he strode out of his tent and stood out in the drizzle. Moving this way and that, he felt fairly certain the medallion showed one of the Attuls. He was tempted to order his men to strike camp and go in pursuit, but he did not know how great the distance might be. With a bit of frustration, he hung the medallion around his neck again and stepped back inside. At least he knew that he was on the right trail. Now it was just a matter of hunting them down and hoping the dragon priests did not muck this one up.

* * *

The sun had not yet cleared the mountains to the east when Galdon climbed back onto his horse. The mountain range dominated the horizon, its jagged peaks dark against the lightening sky. Yesterday's storm had swept past, though scattered clouds still floated by. With the storm's passing came a noticeable cooling. The breath of both the horses and the riders could be seen in the early morning chill.

He nodded at Dresh, the senior-most sergeant who served as his second, and the man bellowed out the order to move out. Soon, his sixty men headed up the trail that the scouts had already marked.

Galdon had been in the saddle only about an hour when he felt a sudden warmth in the medallion. He pulled it out and found it bright red, but then it faded again. This was no Attul magic he detected, but blood magic. What were the dragon priests up to? He found out about two hours later, when word came to him that three outriders were dead, their horses missing. Galdon confronted the scout who brought the news. "What killed them? The Attuls?"

The scout swallowed, visibly nervous. "All three were mauled and half-eaten, sir. I would say it was the work of wild animals or..." He could not bring himself to say it, but Galdon could guess.

"Dreadhounds." It was a statement, not a question, and it left a sour taste in Galdon's mouth. His stomach churned, suddenly unhappy with his breakfast. The dragon priests were feeding their beasts on his men. He had seen it done often enough on his many campaigns, whenever the priests ran out of prisoners or traveled in an area absent of locals to prey upon. Oh, how he hated the Houndmasters and their black curs. At least they had not been stupid enough to loose the dreadhounds on his scouts. He suddenly wondered if the priests had a second motive for killing some of his men. "Were the bodies still dressed?"

"Sir?" The scout seemed puzzled.

"You saw the bodies. Did the dogs simply tear through the clothes or were the bodies undressed before being consumed?"

The scout swallowed again. He paled as he recalled the butchery, but he kept it together enough to give an answer. "Two were nude. The third was not."

Galdon grimaced. This pack had two dragon priests with it, priests who could change into hound form. Was it Verdrof suddenly turned impatient or was it some other priests? He dismissed the scout and then called his sergeants to his side. He gave them the news without any emotion. Already, he started guarding his thoughts and feelings.

* * *

Galdon did not catch up with the Attuls that day. He would have ordered the troops to keep going even after dark, but the terrain was too rough for night riding. However, his six scouts were still out there, marking as much of the trail as they could. Those in the camp had eaten and many already slept. He sat beside a small fire laid before his tent, consulting with his sergeants about how they might corner an Attul. They were interrupted by a disturbance at the perimeter of the camp. When Galdon heard the familiar growl of dreadhounds, he cursed and sprang to his feet.

"Pay attention, men. I think we are about to find the answer to what happened to those three outriders."

Two dragon priests rode into camp, their hoods up to avoid the firelight. They wore Tlocanian uniforms, but they were no soldiers. The four hounds at their side was a testament of their powers. Galdon noted the heaviness of one rider, made obvious by his ill-fitting clothes, and it caused him to curse a second time. Could it really be the priests who had deserted him below Tor Randis? What were their names? Prendor... no, Prekor... and Zaphrion.

The priests made no effort to avoid the men still sleeping on the ground. They would have trampled some, had not Galdon's sergeants yelled out warnings. Two men rolled out of the way just in time. The priests stopped before him, their greeting confirming his suspicion.

"We meet again, Captain Galdon," said Prekor.

"Brothers Prekor and Zaphrion. I see that you did not lose the scent of the three Attuls after all. What do you want of me, besides fodder for your pets?"

"You are impertinent, soldier," remarked Zaphrion. He raised his right hand and red lightning jumped from fingertip to fingertip.

Galdon nodded. "That I am, but our situation has changed, holy brothers. I have papers from Lord-General Hraf Kelordok stating that no priests can commandeer me, or my men. We are here to do what you have failed at these many weeks, to capture an Attul. Anyone who thwarts me will have to answer to Lord Hraf. Do either of you want to face his wrath? I certainly do not, which is why I am determined to complete this mission soon. I will welcome your aid, but I cannot allow you to interfere or try to take over."

Prekor motioned for Zaphrion to extinguish his power display. "We know of your mission, for we passed through Freetown and heard the news from the temple. Did not Brother Lanzo tell you that we are in the area?"

Galdon smiled coldly. "I did not see Brother Lanzo. He was too occupied to meet with me; instead, the temple's High Brother gave me an audience and told me of these three that I now chase. Will you join my forces, understanding that you cannot order us around?"

"We shall," answered Prekor. Zaphrion hesitated, and then nodded agreement.

"Thank you, holy brothers. How many hounds do you bring with you?"

"The pack numbers fourteen," said Prekor.

Somewhere the priests had gained more dogs. Galdon had never liked the vicious animals, but he knew their effectiveness. "Are any of them close to the Attuls?"

Prekor became silent for a moment, apparently linking to some hound. He finally responded. "None will catch them this night, but we will run the dogs through the day as well. By tomorrow evening they will nip at the Attuls' heels."

"Good. With your hounds and my men, we should be able to surround them and maybe even catch all three." Galdon was not happy to have mind-reading Embraced Ones at his side again, but their power could make the difference between success and failure. It would be worth enduring their presence if it meant finally catching an Attul. He made no effort to hide these thoughts, for he wanted the priests to realize that he was not easily intimidated.

Fallen King

AFRAL

The dreadhounds were definitely in pursuit. Though his parents said nothing about it, Afral could tell that they worried. They had just finished another hard day of riding and now gathered around a well-hid fire to eat their first hot meal of the day. Afral clutched the warm bowl and shoveled stew into his mouth even though it still steamed. He ate quickly, a bit worried that his father might order them back onto the horses before he could finish. Once his belly was full, he began to relax, but that feeling did not last.

A sudden sense of wrongness came at them from the southwest, a feeling that made all three of the Attuls stop and stare in that direction.

His mother pulled out her sword, its light a beacon in the evening. "They are up to some kind of evil. I wish we could take a stand against them now."

His father moved towards her. "Beloved, please sheathe your weapon, for its power announces our location as surely as their foul rites proclaim their presence."

Tolara reluctantly did so, extinguishing her spirit sword by returning it to its scabbard. "If only we could find one of the Attul patrols, then we could fight back against these demon lovers."

"That would be good," agreed Rolen, "but right now we are only three against an unknown force. We dare not try to confront them." He squatted near the fire and checked the rest of their meal. "Besides, we will not find any patrols this far south. It is too far from Ambassador's Gate."

"Ambassador's Gate? What is that?" asked Afral.

Tolara responded. "There are a handful of paths into the Pinnacles, but the widest is Ambassador's Gate. That was the route used by Outsiders when they come to visit; at least it was back in the days when Outsiders could approach Warhaven. We have decided that it would be our best route in."

"What path do the Watch Riders take?" asked Afral.

"The same," answered Rolen, "which is another reason for us to use that valley. Those guarding the Ambassador's Gate expect to encounter others."

"How often do Watch Riders report to Warhaven?"

"They do not go all the way to Warhaven," answered Rolen. "They stop at the First Post. Twenty years ago, they came about twice a year. I do not know how often they ride all the way up here these days."

"Did you ever encounter Watch Riders in the Border Realm?"

Rolen shook his head. "Not that I am aware of, but it is said they do not announce their presence to anyone. Also, they must be spread thin, having to cover all of Na Ciria. I sometimes wonder if your mother and I should have joined their ranks…"

"I doubt that they would have welcomed us in," stated Tolara. "They are a secretive bunch. For good reason, considering their dangerous duty."

Afral knew that Watch Riders were the eyes of the Prayer Warriors, responsible for patrolling the lands while most kept guard over Darsheol, but he had rarely thought of them. Maybe he could find refuge among their ranks if Warhaven rejected him. The thought gave a bit of comfort, but only a bit.

What Afral really wanted was to return to the only home he had ever known, to the childhood he suddenly missed. Instead, he was hundred of miles away, being chased by those who wanted to kill him and running towards an uncertain welcome. It was enough to bring a tear of frustration to his eye, but he quickly wiped it away. Where was El in all of this? Did he not care?

Afral was so focused on his own fears that he did not at first hear his father.

"Afral? Afral?"

He turned quickly to him, holding out his bowl for the offered second helping. "Thank you," he replied more out of habit than actual appreciation. He did not feel so hungry, now that fear chewed at his belly.

"What disturbs you?" asked his mother.

Afral met her gaze, though he felt like looking away. "I do not understand why El does not help us more. Why does he allow us to be hounded by these demons?"

His mother set down her bowl to focus fully on him. "We are not in Havenel, the eternal land. Only there will you find everyone in submission to El's wisdom. Here you will find that most follow their own desires. Even good people are prone to such selfishness, while the bad will constantly seek to use others for their own gain. They do not care if they wrong others; they care only if they get what they want. Some will even destroy society just so that they can loot the ruins. That is why the demons are here, because our fellow humans have invited them."

"But that does not explain why we are oppressed by them. We did not invite the demons to Na Ciria. We are Elsworn, not demonsworn."

His father replied this time. "Yes, we are Elsworn, but El does not promise to protect us from all harm. Instead, he promises to carry us through the terrible times. In Havenel we will find peace, but not here. Not in a land at war."

The night's stillness was pierced by baying somewhere to the southwest. It caused all three of them to look that direction again.

"They get closer," noted Tolara.

Afral had to fight an urge to jump to his feet and pull out his sword. The sound reminded him too much of when the dogs chased him through the fog.

"We will set off again before dawn," replied his father. "It will be hard on the horses, but we must get some distance between us and those dogs. Afral, I want you to take the first watch."

"Me?" His father had never given him such a task.

"Indeed. Keep within this hollow and do not pull out your sword unless something dire happens. Wake me at midnight."

They finished their meal and then his parents went to sleep. Afral began his watch by checking on the horses. For the next few hours, he kept hearing dreadhounds, each time a little louder. Twice he had to stop himself from waking his father too early. It seemed to take forever, but finally midnight had arrived, so he awoke his father.

Rolen stretched. "Did you hear more from the dreadhounds?"

"Yes, Father. They are getting closer." Just then, another hound bayed.

"They are nearer," agreed his father, "but we can still rest awhile longer. Try to get some sleep, Afral. I will wake you when it is time to leave."

* * *

Afral lay on his blankets, doubtful that he would be able to sleep. However, the next thing he was aware of was his father shaking him awake. "It is time, my son. Roll up your blankets and gather your saddlebags. I already have your horse ready."

His father moved on to wake his mother.

"What time is it?" asked Tolara, yawning.

"I judge it to be about three hours before dawn, my dearest," replied Rolen.

"It will be dangerous riding in the dark."

"I know, but if we wait for dawn those hounds might reach us before we can even break camp."

Eric Lorenzen

Afral did not like hearing that. His hand strayed to his sword for comfort. He said nothing though, for he wanted to remain strong for his parents. He tried seeking El's peace, but El seemed so far away.

Soon they were riding again, still heading northeast.

The dogs continued baying, seeming always closer. When dawn arrived, the dreadhounds did not stop. That worried Afral even more, for he thought the sunshine would discourage the night-loving monsters.

His father picked up the pace now that more of the terrain could be seen, but the land became more rugged as they neared the Pinnacles so they were not able to speed up that much. They land favored the hounds.

By midday, Afral was tired, sore, and still frightened. His father allowed for a brief pause so that the horses could drink from a stream and eat some oats, but they ate their own meal while back in the saddle. As they rode on, his parents spoke candidly.

"I hope the rain returns," his father said. "I am no huntsman or tracker, but those following probably have expert woodsmen in addition to those dogs. May El bring us a good, solid rain."

"I am doing what I can to hide our trail," said his mother from the rear. A few times, Afral had noticed her gone from behind him, though each time she had returned within the hour. "However, I join you in that petition to El. It will take quite a downpour to hide our scent from those dreadhounds."

* * *

The hoped-for rain began falling two hours before sunset. Unfortunately, by this time the horses were too exhausted to do more than slog onward. The storm darkened their way so much that His father had to kindle his sword again to light their path. When he lifted high the white-shining sword, there came a sudden burst of barking from behind them. More dogs answered, to either side of them.

"The dreadhounds!" yelled Afral, his heart pounding. He would have kicked his horse to a gallop but for the restraining move of his mother.

"They are not here yet," she told him, putting her steed in front of his. "Calm yourself. Racing off in this storm will do nothing except get us separated and maybe lame a horse." She looked to her husband. "Rolen, what shall we do now? They are behind us still, but seem spread out enough to keep us from trying to ride around them."

Rolen put away his sword, causing everything to seem far darker

514

than before he raised it just a minute before. "Although I had hoped it was only their demon-possessed leaders that could sense our use of El's power, it seems even their dogs sense it. That is not good. For now, we should keep our swords in their scabbards. Stay close behind me as we ride on, for I cannot light our path this night."

The rain turned into a downpour after sunset, yet the Attuls kept moving in the storm. Afral's father worked hard to find a decent route, but the darkness caused them numerous delays. Rolen was scratched and bruised from encountering unseen branches. They heard the dreadhounds around them, ever closer. Trying to avoid them, Rolen turned eastward into the Pinnacles' foothills, but their route became too steep at times, forced them to walk those stretches. All three of them were soaked, muddy, and cold. In addition, Afral's father bled from a cheek wound. They came to the lip of a narrow canyon and Rolen led them down into it. Instead of climbing up the far slope, he turned up the canyon.

"Is this route a wise choice?" asked Tolara, raising her voice to be heard over the storm.

"Trust me, my dear," responded Rolen. He did not look back, but kept his focus on the route he was picking out. The stream running through the canyon grew louder with the new rainwater. He led them up the canyon, following a faint game path. At times, he drew his sword to light the more treacherous spots, in spite of how El's power might attract their pursuers. The canyon walls became steeper and the valley floor rockier as they moved further up into the foothills. Before the sides became too steep to climb, Rolen stopped his steed and turned to his family. He held up his sword to light that section of the canyon. "I want the two of you to lead your horses up over the rim. Do it here, for the next stretch seems too steep for such a climb."

"You want us to leave you?" asked Afral, horrified.

"Rolen, this is foolhardy," said Tolara. "We need to keep together."

"What good is it for all of us to die?" he asked. "I want the two of you to live, and even more important than that, you need to reach Warhaven with our warning. If the demons continue their swallowing of Na Ciria, there will soon be nothing left except Warhaven. This is our best hope, so head north while I draw them up this canyon. If possible, I will make my own escape and seek you out in Warhaven. Go now, while the rain washes away your passage."

"I don't want to leave you," protested Afral.

He could see that his mother wanted to argue, but she said nothing. Instead, she rode close to his father's horse and leaned over to share a final kiss. "Go with El, my beloved. I pray that he protects you from this evil."

"No!" yelled Afral, horrified. "Father, do not leave us."

"I must. Be a fearless warrior and protect your mother for me." Rolen bravely smiled back at his wife. "I love you so much, Tolara. May El direct you swiftly to safety." He turned to back to his son. "Afral, I love you and I am so proud of you. Go with your mother. The two of you need to get word to Warhaven, and you need to finish your Prayer Warrior training."

"But Father..."

"Go, Afral. You must."

The youth gave in under his father's steady gaze and his mother's urging. Tears filled his eyes as the two of them began their ascent of the canyon wall. His father kept his sword held high so that the light might aid them. They rode until it became too steep, and then dismounted. Afral looked back at that moment. His father seemed so alone, a single light surrounded by darkness.

"Come on, Afral," urged his mother, her voice tight with suppressed emotion. "I will not have your father's sacrifice be in vain. We need to get far from here, before the hounds and the hunters close in."

They struggled up the slope, the ground made more hazardous by the rain, guiding their horses behind them. When at last they crested the canyon rim, they paused to look at Rolen far below. He waved at them and then urged his horse to continue up the canyon. He kept his sword raised, lighting the canyon around him. Tolara and Afral mounted up and rode northward on their tired steeds.

CHAPTER THIRTY-NINE
Attul Hunt

GALDON

Galdon sensed that the hunt neared its end. The Attuls were running their horses and becoming desperate, for good reason. With the addition of the dreadhounds, Galdon now had the upper hand on them. He eyed the two priests riding nearby, both lost in their mind-link trances. He disliked both of them, but he had to admit their usefulness. They guided their dogs expertly, even while two of his men guided their mounts. No matter their personal motives, Zaphrion and Prekor would help him capture at least one Attul.

He still did not know where Brother Verdrof and his party hid, but he had a feeling they would catch up with him soon too. He only hoped that the three Embraced Ones would be willing to cooperate with each other, for they could be sticklers about ranking.

They had been riding all day, following the hounds. Whenever the priests were distracted in a mind-link, Galdon would surreptitiously check his medallion. It did not always show something, but he saw enough to verify that the dogs were on the right track. He did not tell the priests about his talisman, for he wanted to keep any advantage that he could. He might have to rely on it should the rains return, for the dreadhounds might lose the scent in a heavy downpour. Galdon looked up at the gathering clouds that threatened a wet evening. The thought of the priests and their beasties having to depend on him and his scouts gave him satisfying feeling.

"Stop your smirking, captain."

Galdon quickly looked over at Prekor and carefully restrained his thoughts. "What do you have to report, holy brother?"

"We have seen the Attuls from a distance and should catch up with them tonight, if the weather holds up. And if it rains, we will still catch them. Do not underestimate our hounds nor overestimate your frail human scouts. As for any magical necklace you have, I doubt it is anything more than a cheap trinket that reacts to your own feelings."

He said nothing in reply but allowed a rude thought to flicker across his mind. Prekor paid him no heed. Instead, the priest demanded food from the soldier guiding his mount. Galdon decided it would be best to get away from the priest before his thoughts caused real trouble, so he rode up to Sergeant Dresh, at the head of the troops.

"Dresh, what do the scouts report?"

"Sir, the tracks grow fresher, though the dreadhounds muck them up. We are certainly catching up with them."

The old sergeant fell quiet, but Galdon could tell there was more. "What else is on your thoughts, Dresh?"

Dresh stared off into the distance, as if he could see their prey himself. "What will we do when we catch up with the Attuls? I have heard enough whispers about these legendary warriors and I would not mind crossing blades with one. However, capturing someone is much harder than simply cleaving their head off. If they are anything like the Embraced Ones, then I worry that most of the men will be slaughtered."

Galdon frowned. He had been worrying about the same thing for some time and still had no solution. "Let us hope that the dragon priests can help us with the capture."

* * *

It began to rain a few hours before sunset. An hour after that, Galdon felt his medallion warming up, but he resisted looking at it because Brother Zaphrion sulked nearby. However, the dragon priest react too, first staring off into the distance, and then letting his head droop as his eyes glazed over in a mind-link trance.

Only when Galdon was sure that Zaphrion was distracted, did he pull out the chained jewel. It showed a strong reaction in the same direction as the Attuls. He wondered if they had blasted the dreadhounds. The medallion also reacted to the dragon priests' power, though it glowed a deep red in response to their blood magic while it showed a paler light for the Attuls. Galdon was beginning to understand the subtleties of the gem.

However, he dared not gaze at it too long, for the Embraced Ones might break their link without notice. In addition, he feared that one of his men might notice the jewel and then obsess over it, which would reveal its presence to the eavesdropping priests. He hid the medallion and schooled his thoughts just in time, for suddenly Prekor looked around.

"Captain, can we move faster than this? It appears that the Attuls are planning to ride through the night. One of them uses his sword to light their path. He is an ignorant one, for such blatant power use makes him easier to follow."

"The men and their horses cannot see as well in the dark as an Embraced One and this rain causes our torches to sputter." Galdon dared not ask for aid, but it would greatly help if the dragon priest lit their path.

Prekor harrumphed. "I hear your thoughts, captain. It is beneath me to act as torchbearer, but I will do so."

"Thank you, Brother Prekor," replied Galdon with genuine appreciation.

They pressed on, into the rainy night. His medallion began reacting strongly to something, vibrating in an irritating way. He wanted to pull the thing out, if only to get it off his chest, but he dared not. Thankfully, Prekor was too distracted to notice any of Galdon's thoughts.

The dreadhound baying grew louder, which told him that the Attuls could not be too far off. Finally, he could no longer keep quiet. He rode up to where Prekor lit their path. "Holy Brother, what is happening? Are the Attuls close?"

"I am not certain, for it is Zaphrion who is linked with the lead hound, but I would say that we will catch up with them within a few hours." The priest paused a moment, as if listening to the hounds. "The dogs are close enough to smell Attul blood now, so at least one of them is wounded. We will have to work hard to restrain the hounds' hunger after such a hard run, or else our prey will be consumed."

Galdon grimaced. He could guess what that meant: some more soldiers slaughtered for dog fodder just to keep the monsters from ravaging the Attuls. He would do his best to let the dogs take the brunt of the attack for once and he hoped the Attuls killed most of them.

"You are being rather ungrateful," noted Prekor with a cold, calm voice. "It is because of the dreadhounds that we have been able to run down these three."

Galdon caught his breath, suddenly concerned. He answered

carefully. "I am no Hound Master. My first concern is for my men. What else would you expect from an army captain?"

Before Prekor could respond, he was interrupted by curses from Zaphrion. The fat priest sat back in his saddle and looked off in the direction that the Attuls were.

Galdon's necklace reacted to something too.

"Their leader makes his sword blaze fiercely and it causes the dogs to cower. The sight of it hurt my eyes." The priest pointed off into the rainy night. "Look, Prekor. Can you see his beacon?"

Galdon followed his gesture and could faintly see the white beacon aimed skyward.

"What damnable thing is that?" asked Prekor. "I do not recall such powers from the Darshi times."

"Nor I," replied Zaphrion.

Galdon said nothing but he felt a chill up his spine that had nothing to do with the rain. Sometimes he forgot about the great age of the demonic Others. These two were no longer just humans.

AFRAL

His mother dropped to the mud, realizing that her horse could no longer carry her. Afral did likewise. They pressed on, leading their mounts through the night. As they walked around the edge of a meadow, they suddenly felt the release of great power. Both looked back and clearly saw a beam of white light shoot into the sky and touch the low-hanging clouds.

"What is Father doing?" asked Afral.

"He is making sure that they only follow him," replied his mother grimly. "Let us not waste his sacrifice. We must press on, no matter how worn out we are. We need to reach Warhaven."

"Will he have enough strength to fight them?" asked Afral, worried at how much power his father was using.

"El has no limits, nor does your father's love for us. He will do all that he must."

"Will he survive?"

His mother came close and hugged him. "That I do not know, but we will see him again either in Warhaven or in the eternal lands of Havenel. Now hurry along, for we must get some distance from our pursuers."

Mother and son trudged onward through a wet forest, leading two tired horses and leaving behind a man who loved them dearly.

GALDON

Galdon and most of his men rode down the slope, into the canyon. His scouts indicated that it was too steep to enter further upstream, but apparently the Attuls did not care or were unaware of that fact. Galdon sent a half squad on top either canyon wall to ride along the rim. He led the bulk of the force along the canyon floor. At the rear of the main force came the two priests still caught up in their trances. The dogs ran somewhere ahead of the army, charging up the canyon. He did not need his talisman to guide him, for he could see the Attul's beacon of white light clearly now as the rain lightened to just a mere drizzle.

As far as he could tell, they were now heading straight towards the Pinnacles as the canyon narrowed. The stream at its center rushed and roared with rainwater but kept within its banks. Trees and boulders crowded the wash and provided many places to hide, especially on such a drizzly night, but he was not about to call his men to a halt. Their prey was so close. He kept his troops to the game path and trusted that his scouts and the dreadhounds would notice if any of the Attuls tried to slip around them and set a trap.

The beacon suddenly ceased.

Galdon touched his chest at the sudden ending of the necklace's vibrating. He doubted that the hounds had brought an Attul down, so it probably meant that his prey tired of being chased and planned to fight back. "Lausher, Kraiken, and Dresh! Prepare your men. I think battle will come upon us soon."

As he rounded a bend in the canyon, the trees thinned enough for him to see that the canyon widened here. A side ravine dropped in, but it looked too steep and narrow to serve as an escape route. Might the Attuls abandon their horses to try scaling up that narrow defile? He was about to order Lausher to send some men to investigate that route when a bright light flashed across a meadow up ahead, like a scythe going through a ripe field. He heard the hounds howl in pain.

That cry was echoed by Prekor and Zaphrion as the two sagged in their saddles. Galdon guessed that at least some of the dogs had just died. He rode over to make sure neither priest was seriously injured, but they seemed only dazed. Most likely, they had remained linked to their dreadhounds too long and had felt their sudden death. He doubted the dragon priests would be of any use for a while, so now it was up to him.

He yelled his order, "Charge! For Tlocania!"

Galdon motioned for the two soldiers escorting the priests to stay behind and then spurred his mount to follow his men.

They charged out into the clearing where one Attul had stopped to confront them. The remaining dreadhounds were trying to bring down the man's horse. It was the older male; the other two were not in sight. The man defended himself admirably, his sword leaving glowing streaks in the night air as he kept the dogs at bay. The squad sergeants knew their business, dividing the troops into three and coming at their foe from different directions. It seemed foolish to send so many after a lone warrior, at least it did until his sword's tip shot out a great white beam of light that seared through anything in its path: dog, horse or man.

Spears and arrows flew, too many for the Attuls to strike from the air, and his horse went down screaming. The man jumped free and ran towards a clump of boulders. Two dogs tried to nip at his heels and gained a mouthful of white power for their effort, dying instantly.

Galdon rode hard after the fellow, admiring the man's swordsmanship even while cursing the Attul for the damage the he inflicted. The Attul took his stand in a crevice between huge rocks, finding a place that would keep the Tlocanians from surrounding him. It suddenly turned from a rout into a dangerous standoff.

Galdon pulled his horse to a halt, signaling for his men to do likewise, but some were already charging in. The first soldiers to reach the Attul's shelter died instantly, thrown from their saddles by a burst of power. Galdon could see by how the burnt bodies lay, that none lived. Their horses survived but ran off wild-eyed. It was an awful slaughter. He called for a retreat, not wanting more of his men butchered. The remaining dreadhounds had also retreated.

"Where are the priests?" Galdon demanded. Let them take the brunt of this attack since they were the magic welders.

He saw them riding out of the woods, apparently recovered from earlier. The two ignored him as they rode to either side of the Attul's redoubt and dismounted just out of sight of the cornered man. The Embraced Ones seemed calm as they kindled their red fire and soon red fireballs rained down on the Attul.

Galdon worried that the priests might misjudge and kill the man instead of draining his powers, but he could only watch. At times, he could see nothing of the Attul, so blinding was the power clash of red fire and white light. Small fires burned all around the boulders and they already showed scorch marks, and yet the Attul endured. Galdon did not think this could go on much longer. If the man failed to stop just one of those fireballs, he would go up like a torch.

Acting boldly, Galdon motioned for his troops to stay back and then rode ahead alone, directly at the Attul. He kept his hands up, obviously away from his weapons. When closer, he shouted at the priests to stop their barrage. It took a few moments, but they finally did.

"Attul Rolen Strongarm, hear my offer. If you surrender, we will not chase after your family. What say you? Is not your capture worth the lives of your wife and son?"

There was silence as the man considered the offer. The captain could see that he was breathing heavily.

Finally, the Attul shouted an answer. "Who are you that I should trust you? You are a comrade to these demon possessed men."

"I am Captain Galdon of the Tlocanian Army. You have my word on this, as an officer. I will let your wife and son ride off unharmed."

The pause was much longer this time, but then the Attul must have realized that Galdon's proposal was the best he could get for his loved ones. "I accept your offer, Captain Galdon. I surrender on your word that my family will be allowed to escape."

Rolen lowered his sword and set it in its scabbard. Sudden darkness enveloped the canyon.

The captain rode closer. "I will have your sword, sir, and my men will have to bind you."

Up close, Galdon noticed the man's exhaustion even in the darkness.

The Attul gave a weary nod, unbuckled his sword belt, and held it out.

Galdon took it, careful not to touch the actual blade. He motioned for his some of his men to approach with ropes. "I cannot guarantee your fair treatment, Lord Rolen, but I will do what I can. If you tell the priests what they want to know, they will not have to resort to torture."

"I will not betray my people," replied the proud warrior. "I expect much pain and sorrow, but it will be worth it for my family's safety."

Galdon was not so sure of that, for the priests were always cruel in their methods, but he said nothing of it to his prisoner. Instead, he turned away as his soldiers expertly bound the man.

The priests had come out and were now conversing with one

another. Galdon aimed his horse towards them, not bothering to hide his feelings of pride at having talked the Attul into surrendering. When he neared, the two stopped talking and turned towards him.

"Zaphrion will be leaving with what remains of the pack," announced Prekor. "The other two seemed to have broken away some time ago, but he thinks he can sniff out their trail still."

Galdon felt outrage. "But I gave my word that they would be able to leave unmolested."

"You do not command us, captain. You overstepped your authority. Zaphrion will either capture them or kill them."

"Do you really think Lord Rolen will cooperate with your questioning when he learns of this betrayal?"

"See that he hears nothing of it," commanded Zaphrion. "You are too soft, human. We are in a war and we are determined to win this time. You must learn that truth, soldier."

CHAPTER FORTY
Capture and Release

BRODAGAR

Brother Brodagar waited impatiently in his room, for a temple's Listening Room was only active at a certain hour each day. For Deep Crossing temple, that came during the third hour, deep in the night. He was anxious to get his revelation to the Speakers Tower, having decided that any delay would not be wise. His Other concurred.

Finally, the hour arrived. He left his room and headed deeper into the Crimson wing of the temple, in that section where no outsiders ever entered. The hallways were empty and barely lit, which comforted the Embraced One, helping him to relax as he walked. He was surprised when he rounded a corner and found three priests blocking the way. All wore robes edged in Crimson order's red.

"Brother Brodagar-Sahak! I have been waiting to talk with you," one of them said cheerily. "Please join me inside."

The three quickly urged him into a side room. He was surprised but not concerned, trying to place these three priests. He could sense that they were Embraced, but their thoughts remained guarded. They were of his order, though, and so he had no great fear of them. They might report to another lord-governor, but all of them submitted to Emperor Silossiak. They would dare not interfere once they understood whose orders he obeyed.

We have never met them before, stated his Other, *at least not in this form. I sense more of my kind near, so expect at least one more Embraced One inside.*

Brodagar still went, for what did he have to fear from his own brethren? He walked into a room with a half dozen priests, but these did not wear crimson stoles. They wore gray edging to their black robes. The door slammed behind Brodagar and they all struck with their powers. Red lightning lashed at him from all sides, before he could defend himself. The power sizzled over him, causing his body to jolt uncontrollably and then he collapsed, unconscious. His last thought before passing out was actually Sahak's: *The Shade Order has us.*

MYLANA

The Drunken Skunk seemed no more welcoming in the waning daylight, but Mylana was still glad to get back to the inn safely. She had followed Hessilyn's father to the Five Dragons Temple and then to the causeway that led to the Citadel's island. She dared not follow them further for there were neither crowds along that road nor any escape routes, but she watched from the shoreline. The Gray contingent rode onto the small island but did not go to fortress. Instead, they stopped at one of three inns that sat just outside of the stone keep. Mylana asked a dockworker if any of those inns would be a suitable place to stay.

"Not unless you are espoused to some military officer. The Triplets of Privilege they call them, for only the rich or powerful stay over there. Nor would I suggest any inn along the riverbank, my lady. Those along here would be too rowdy for your kind. Better for you to head into the city and find yourself some quiet inn near the main square, or better still seek out any kin who can shelter you, for even a respectable inn can turn ugly."

Mylana thanked the man and then set off in the direction he had pointed, though only because it had been towards her own distant boarding. Now that she was within sight of the Drunken Skunk, she was eager to get inside and off her weary feet. With the day nearly done, the darkening gloom reminded that the sunset prayers to the dragon gods would start soon. She hurried to get inside before that bells sounded.

Mylana was the last one to return. She found the others gathered in the women's room, with Coursen tending a swollen lip and bruised cheek. With sudden concern, she asked what had happened.

"It is nothing," assured Coursen with a crooked smile. "I foolishly walked between two brawlers down at the docks." He motioned at her. "Close the door. We need not be a show for those passing in the hallway."

She gave an apologetic grin to the others and complied, and then locked the door for good measure. She sat down next to Hessilyn, fighting off the desire to go to Coursen and tend him. "What have all of you learned?"

Mandor, squatting against the wall, shook his head. "Our pursuers are in the city and have been asking about us. It is only a matter of time before they search here. I learned that their soldiers are at the Citadel while Hessilyn found out that their priests are staying at the Five Dragons Temple."

"It is worse than that," added Mylana. "I saw Hessilyn's father ride in with a large Gray force and I do not think it mere coincidence."

Hessilyn nodded, showing that she already knew about her father's presence. "He must be after me. It might be best if I fled in a different direction."

"I think not," protested Mandor, standing up in his aggravation. "If he captures you, beloved, then he will learn of our mission. There is no need to sacrifice yourself so."

"Lord Polis Targan pursues more than just his daughter," stated Coursen. "I do not think a demon lover would go to such lengths just for sentimentality. Surely, he has learned somehow that we Attuls are with her."

"I agree with Coursen," said Mylana. "We will stay together for this whole ride… that is if you are willing to join us in what will be a tough journey."

Hessilyn smiled at their support. "I will gladly go along. Thank you for trusting me."

Coursen cleared his throat to get everyone's attention. "We had better flee this city quickly. I think the ferries are our best route. The docks are teeming with troopers, both Red and Gray, but we should be able to pass through them unnoticed. Hundreds cross the river every day, using nearly a dozen ferries. We should be able to slip through."

Their conversation shifted to practical plans.

* * *

Right after the evening worship time, the four hurried out to purchase all the supplies they lacked. The plan was to leave just after the morning worship. They would have fled now, but the ferries did not usually ply the Grandgorn's strong current after dark. Coursen regrettably shared that news. They did not sleep much that night and not just because they took turns at watch. All four of them worried about those hunting them, both Tlocanians and now Osburgens.

With morning near, they ate a hasty breakfast prepared by the still-sleepy cook, and then were out in the stable to saddle their mules by lantern-light. The stablehand was glad to go back to his haystack when they told him he was not needed. They remained in the stable through the morning worship time, the three Watch Riders quietly finishing the packing while Hessilyn gave homage to her gods along with thousands of others throughout the city, though she did so because dragonsworn had always offered up prayers in the morning.

As soon as the murmur of prayer died down, they moved out.

* * *

It was a chilly morning, so they held their cloaks close as they rode, each leading a pack mule. The street traffic remained light, but there were more delivery wagons to maneuver around. As they approached the river, the street became crowded mainly with men walking in their same direction. Mylana assumed them to be dockworkers and sailors, but she should have looked more closely. She did not realize her error until too late.

Suddenly, most of the crowd turned on them. A man grabbed her sword arm and yanked her from the saddle. Startled, she did not have the time to wield her sword. Another stopped her from hitting the cobblestones, but they had her tightly held. She yelled out to the others for help, but then realized that they were also taken. A gag was shoved in her mouth and a sack pulled over her head.

The ruffians shoved her along. In all of the bustle, she lost her sense of direction, but Mylana realized that they had left the streets and now traveled inside somewhere. Her sword belt and sword had been taken, her hands bound. She sensed that they entered a large yet crowded opening, maybe a warehouse, where she was pushed through a maze of crates and sacks. She could hear others around her, soldiers grumbling and possibly more prisoners. She feared that her companions had also been captured.

They threw her into some room and she heard a door slam behind her. For a moment she just lay there on a rough and gritty wood floor, listening. She heard nothing nearby, though there were muted sounds from elsewhere in the place. Mylana struggled up onto her knees, unable to use her hands to support her weight. She was just standing up when she heard a chair creak as someone shifted his weight. There was someone else in the room.

"I remember you from Westbend," a man said. "It was at one of Lady Hessilyn's dances. You were a budding youngster back then, but now you have blossomed into quite a beauty."

Mylana stepped away from the voice, feeling very vulnerable.

The man laughed. The chair scraped as he stood up. "Do not worry, little lady. I will not harm you, though you tempt me with your prettiness."

His footfalls were loud as he came toward her. Mylana decided to stand her ground. Let him think her docile like some Westbend lady. She could still kick or head butt to fight off any attack. He stopped in front of her; a heavy hand stroked her shoulder once and then withdrew. "Very pretty," he repeated, his voice thick with desire. She was about to throw herself at him, when he suddenly stepped back and cleared his throat. He seemed not to have noticed her ready stance. "My pardons, lady. It has been a long and lonely road for us guards. We do not get the privileges of our officers. But as I said, I will not harm you."

She muttered into her gag, telling him to remove her hood and gag, but the man ignored her. Instead, he kept up his monologue.

"It is not easy being up here in the Red lands, for they are a fierce and rude people. One of their generals gave grave insult to Lord Polis when the governor failed to present his daughter for a promised marriage. They say he did this all on purpose, tempting the man with Lady Hessilyn and then telling her to flee." The man guffawed. "As if Lord Polis would do such a lowly thing."

The man moved away, back toward his chair. Mylana followed the sound with her head, trying to pick up clues through the scratchy burlap that hooded her. He sat down and the chair protested with creaks. He was a big and heavy man, she guessed, taking no comfort at the thought. It would have been easier if her jailer were closer to her weight and height.

"I can understand why that Red general was tempted by Lady Hessilyn. She is another sweet flower. What I would not give to ..." The man stopped his musings as he remembered that he was in the presence of another woman. He cleared his throat again and changed topics. "I hope her father does not punish her too severely, for youth are prone to do foolish things. I had my own fair share of stupidity in my younger days, I did."

The guard fell silent, for which Mylana was grateful. The silence allowed her to time to consider her dilemma. This had been a planned attack, that seemed obvious, but why? Was Hessilyn's father just trying to get her back, or was there more involved here? The questions swirled through her mind, but no answers surfaced out of that uncertain murk of doubt. A half-hour later she still stood there, but now she felt light-headed from her burlap hood, though its weave should have been loose enough to let in fresher air. The door to the room opened suddenly and she heard the guard's chair thud to wood floor, so he had probably been leaning back in it.

"The lord-governor wants to see her now. Bring her and be quick about it."

She expected her guard to respond surly or flippantly, but instead he answered respectfully with "As you command, I follow." The response told her that she was a captive of Osburgens. All Gray soldiers replied that way to an officer.

The guard came over quickly and gave her a shove towards the door. Mylana decided it was not worth resisting, so she starting walking. The fellow placed one hand over her tied-up hands, pressing them against the small of her back. His other hand cupped her right shoulder and guided her through the doorway and down a hallway. The officer who had given the orders had apparently already left, because she heard no other footsteps besides their own. They climbed some steps, turned corners, and followed more hallways, until another guard challenged them. She knew it was just a guard because her escort replied roughly.

"Let us through, Guish. His lordship wants to see this pretty flower. Major Tullis told me so in person."

"They gave you watch over such a lovely? What were they thinking?"

"Mind your thoughts, Guish! I know my duty. Now stop gawking at the prisoner and let us in, or do I have to report you to the officers?"

"You are one to talk, Morfo. You almost stumbled three times, just in this hallway, because you could not keep your eyes off her."

Mylana felt her cheeks redden as she realized the men had both been examining her like a prime cut hanging in a butcher's stall. At least the sack hid her embarrassment, but she had had enough of this. "I will talk to Major Tullis myself if you two do not immediately stop. Do your duty, Soldier Morfo, or have you forgotten how to follow an officer's command?"

Guish laughed. "This one has bite to her, she does. No wonder you behaved yourself."

Morfo grumbled, but said nothing. Mylana heard a door open and then her escort gave her a shove forward. It was not a violent shove, but still forceful.

* * *

"Here is your last companion," said someone with a deep and melodious voice, a voice that nagged at Mylana's memories. "Men, free her now."

Suddenly Mylana was grabbed by multiple hands, as they undid her binding and pulled off her hood. Finally, she could see her surroundings. The place was dimly lit in a reddish hue. Looking around, she saw Mandor, Hessilyn, and Coursen. The men who had freed her stepped back and she saw the man who had spoken; she recognized Polis Targan, Lord-Governor of Westbend. She looked back to her companions when Hessilyn asked her if she was unharmed. Mylana tried to answer, but it came out too garbled. She spat out the gag and tried again. "I am well… considering the circumstances."

"I am glad," said Hessilyn.

Lord Polis turned to his daughter. "You must help me, dearest Hessilyn, for I do not know the names of your friends. I remember Mandor, for who could forget those eyes shining with adoration for you, but these others…"

"They are Coursen, Mandor's close friend, and Mylana, who is Mandor's younger sister."

He smiled at Mylana, but the grin did not touch his cold eyes. "Ah, now I remember you, though you seemed much younger when you came to our estate for Hessilyn's famous dances. My apologies for having you bound, but it was necessary."

She nodded, though she did not really believe him.

The governor looked over at his underlings. "Men, leave us. I will question these captives in privacy." The six men in the room obeyed without question, leaving without another word. Once he was alone with his prisoners, the governor of Westbend walked over to his daughter and stroked her hair.

Hessilyn stepped back, obviously upset. "What are your intentions, Father? Do you mean to drag me off for the wedding you arranged? You are cruel to marry me off to that soulless man, for he has no desires except for power. Do you really think that I could ever be happy in such a marriage?"

Polis Targan pressed his fingers against her lips to urge her silence. "I will not send you back to that man, so lay off your haranguing. Even if that were my desire, the Tlocanian would never accept you. Lord-General Grosard is too proud for that. If I sent you back to Waybridge, he would either kill you or assign you to some brothel. You successfully sabotaged my plans there, my daughter." The governor sighed and stepped back from her. He turned his attention on the two men. "Did you know that we Embraced Ones can sense the presence of Attuls?"

His comment seemed to unsettle both young men. Mylana wondered how specific his senses were, for he had not looked in her direction.

"He can also read thoughts," added Hessilyn with some heat.

Governor Polis chuckled. "That is true. Especially strong feelings like those seething in my daughter. However, it seems that the thoughts from you Attuls are somehow shielded from me. I find that interesting."

"Father, if you will release my friends, I will submit to your plans no matter what they may be."

The governor let out a hearty laugh. "You submit? Hessilyn, you were stubborn even as a child and you have grown no more compliant or sheepish over the years. You mean well, but you cannot change your very nature, my little jewel. Oh, and leave off trying to avoid thoughts of Warhaven, for you are making a mess of it, Hessilyn. I already know where the Attul redoubt lies hidden among the Pinnacles, and I already have sent the information on to my superiors in Osburg. The Attul secret is revealed, so please stop your desperate attempts to *not* think of Warhaven."

Mylana hung her head at the news. She had failed. The demons now knew where the Prayer Warriors hid. Surely, they would soon be on their way to destroy them all. Coursen saw her distress and came over to hug her. She began to cry into his shoulder and missed some of the conversation because of it. When her quiet sobs finally ended, she looked up and saw Hessilyn standing in front of her father.

Hessilyn looked crestfallen, desperate. "Did someone pull the truth from my thoughts?"

Her father shrugged, again stroking her fine hair with a father's affection. When she stepped back again, he frowned with disappointment, his hand slowly lowering. "I am not certain, my dear, for the Red priest who told me the information was not the most cooperative."

Mylana spoke up, still leaning against Coursen. "Can we question this priest? I would like to know how he learned our secret." She felt Coursen grow tense, apparently anxious to learn the truth too.

Lord Polis shook his head. "Unfortunately, Brother Brodagar died and his Other half is now back in the Darklands. None of us will ever learn how he gained his knowledge of your precious Warhaven."

"Do you plan to kill us?" asked Mandor, stepping up to Hessilyn's side. The two took each other's hand.

"My Other half claims that would be the wisest thing to do," he admitted, "but I am still partially a man and I can still resist the demon's voice when I must. I will not kill you. Instead, I will help you for my daughter's sake."

The man with the demon inside of him seemed calm to Mylana. Almost too calm. Was he really in disagreement? Could a possessed man resist when a demon wanted something? She did not know and that frightened her. Maybe Lord Polis Targan simply toyed with them, like a cat with its prey. She wondered about his true plans, and so she asked, "How will you help us?"

"I will get you across the river, which you could not accomplish otherwise."

"It is not that hard to secure a ferry," argued Coursen. "I saw hundreds ride across in both directions just today."

Their captor nodded. "I know about your watching the ferries. I know where all of you were today."

Mylana felt Coursen stiffen again and sensed the she knew why. They had been followed and had not even realized it.

Lord Polis sighed. "To be frank, if I had not seized you, then others would have. The Tlocanians have been playing with you for some reason, but now those in Osburg are aware of you and so I would expect your capture as soon as you tried to leave Deep Crossing."

She frowned. "But you told us that they already know where Warhaven lies. What reason would they still be interested in us?"

"Ah, you are still far too innocent, young Mylana. Your father sheltered you too much on that horse ranch of his. The Osburgens might not want you for your knowledge of the Attul refuge, but you know so many other things. I, for one, would want to know where the rest of the Attul Watch Riders are hiding. I am certain that my comrades would have many more such questions and they are very persuasive in getting answers. No, you will need my help to escape the trap that is Deep Crossing."

That answer did not assure her. "Why should we trust an enemy?" Coursen tried to put an arm around her, but she pulled away. She stood there defiantly, staring at the man who had betrayed Westbend's king, who now governed the city for his Gray overlords. She did not want

Coursen trying to shelter her; she wanted to confront this mad man. "You betrayed a whole city, so why should we trust you?"

Polis Targan laughed and it sounded genuine. "I never told you to trust me. If you are tallying my crimes, add on to it the exposing of Warhaven, for I am the one who had that Red dragon priest captured and tortured for his information. I am the one who sent the information on to Osburg. I hope that you can soon blame me for the deaths of thousands of Attuls. No, do not trust me, Mylana, for I am no ally of yours." He raised one hand and they all saw red lightning leap across his fingers. Mylana felt very helpless without her spirit sword. "I help you out of remembered affection for my daughter and for my own purposes."

"If you mean to help us, then return our weapons," stated Mandor.

He shook his head. "Hessilyn, I know you love this boy, but I find him tiresome. Young Mandor, do you really think I am that foolish? You might get your shiny blade once you are well away from me, but not now. Be glad that I let you live, even if it grates you to know that you are receiving mercy from an enemy." Polis Targan sighed again. "I had hoped for a warmer reception from you, my wayward daughter, especially after I told you that the imminent betrothal was canceled. I see now that my hope was misplaced. You will never love me again as you did when you were a small child. So be it."

He suddenly sent small bolts of lightning flying, causing the four to dodge away from him. The lightning effectively herded them all together into one corner of the large room. He nodded with satisfaction and ceased his attack, though red power still danced among his fingers. "You live only because a demon has mercy on you. I see your teeth clenched, Mandor. Does that irk you? I know my daughter well enough to know it angers her. Maybe the two of you are right for each other after all. If nothing else, you share your hatred of me. Though you may doubt it, I was only trying to marry Hessilyn off for her own safety. That general held good lands up in the Forest Hills, well away from any troubles. He would have left her there, largely unmolested and safe. But instead, she swoons for a man whose destiny is suffering and an early death. Well, that is her choice.

"I have some advice for the four of you, though I doubt you will heed it. Give up this useless mission of yours. You have failed. By the time you reach Warhaven, there will be nothing left of it. Instead, flee up onto the Wind Plains or better still ride south on the Grandgorn's eastern bank. The area is still free of the Dragon's Shadow and is too insignificant for us to bother taking. Settle down in one of those isolated villages and let these hard times pass you by.

"Why strive for a lost cause? The demons have already won; they are merely sweeping up the last of the fools that resists. Do you really think that you four can bring us down?" Their captor shook his head with a frown. "I am still human enough to want happiness for my daughter. Mandor, take her to that little village, marry her, and start a family. Leave off this folly."

Hessilyn started to protest, but her father Polis raised his voice, "No, I do not want any more of your passionate claims. We are now enemies, my daughter. It is good that your mother did not live to see our family shattered so. I see that you will not hear me, for love has dulled your hearing of all others who are not this rash young man. So be it. We will part ways then and most likely never see each other again.

"I would invite you and your friends to join me for a meal, but I do not think it would be an enjoyable experience for either of us. No, let us part ways now, as polite enemies." He let the lightning die in his palm as he strode back to the door and knocked on it. Soon his henchmen were back inside, holding hoods and ropes. "I insist that your eyes be covered as you leave this place, so you will all wear these hoods. If you give me your word not to remove them until given permission, then I will not insist on the bindings. Your choice: will you walk with or without being tied?"

* * *

They submitted to being hooded and were led back out onto some back street of Deep Crossing, in an area that Mylana guessed to be a few blocks away from where they had been captured. Three squads of Gray regulars joined the governor's personal guards, creating an escort large enough to discourage any Tlocanian patrols in the area. The four were not given back their weapons or their mules, but were marched down to the harbor. At the river's edge, the soldiers herded them onto one of the larger ferries. Only then did they get back their weapons, along with small coin purses. Mandor tried to reject their enemy's money, but the officer insisted.

"Lord Polis ordered it. He wants you to take the money and find a quiet place to settle, away from the troubles." The man paused, his face hidden under the gray-and-black dragon helm. "Not many get such an opportunity; listen to his counsel. In addition, the lord-governor had horses put on this ferry for each of you. See the ship's captain for your horses' tack, for it was also placed on board. Lord Polis has been most generous."

The officer then left without another word, taking all the soldiers with him.

Mylana looked over the ferry's wide deck and saw a corral holding four steeds. "Look! I see Sundancer!"

She hurried over and had a heartfelt reunion with the horse that had carried her so far. The others followed her, all amazed that the demon-possessed governor had retrieved their original mounts for them. Whatever his motive, he had done them a great service.

Apparently, the ferry had been waiting specifically for them, for it was soon on its way across the wide and swift-flowing Grandgorn.

Once the foursome had greeted their horses and checked their condition, they made their way to the railing. They had to stay close together though, to avoid interfering with the ferrymen who manned the oars against a brisk current wanting to carry them southward. Overhead, a sail angled to catch the morning breeze and help them across.

Mylana gazed eastward and saw again the hint of lighter skies, of lands beyond the reach of the Dragon's Shadow. Lord Polis Targan's insidious words wormed to the surface of her thoughts. It would be good to leave these darkened lands, to flee towards light and peace. Out of the corner of her eye, she could see handsome Coursen and wondered what it would be like to run away with him, to become his wife in some peaceful land, and to raise a family of their own. It was an alluring thought. Especially now, that her mission had failed so utterly.

They had been sent to warn Warhaven that enemies were hunting for them and had instead revealed the Attul Prayer Warriors to that very enemy. She looked away from the distant sunshine and from Coursen, and looked northwestward, into the depth of the Dragon's Shadow.

Mandor seemed to catch her thoughts and spoke them aloud. "It will be a dark road for us, but now our mission is even more pressing. Warhaven must be warned that their secret is now known, that the Attul haven will soon become a battlefield. However, we will win our way through to them. We must."

"You still want to finish the Ride, after what we heard? We might arrive to a place already destroyed."

"We must try. Coursen, Hessilyn, and I will ride with you, if you will still have us. Hessilyn is distraught that your secret may have been plundered from her unprotected thoughts. I hope you will not hold that unintended betrayal against her."

Mylana gave a quick glance at Hessilyn, who huddled at the railing, gazing down at the swirling waters with a worried frown.

"I do not blame her, Mandor. She would not have known anything had I not failed to keep the secret as I had sworn. The betrayal of Warhaven is my crime. You three are innocent, while I am guilty. When we reach Warhaven, it will be up to the Attul Elders to determine my punishment. Until that day, I will be honored with the escort of you three."

Brother and sister hugged.

Eric Lorenzen

CHAPTER FORTY-ONE

Blood Soaked Tower

WINTRON

They rounded the stairway to the next landing and found four abandoned rooms, all of them filthy from having been packed with people. They also found the six bodies. Wintron noted that the blood was still fresh. "The killer must have just left this room."

"Six more innocents for us to avenge," said Fors, pulling the door shut behind him. "That old dragon priest told us the ritual would occur on the tower's top. What else did he lie about?"

"Maybe this was not part of their Anchor Rite," stated Wintron.

Fors lifted a graying eyebrow. "This is the second blood-soaked room we have found, nephew. I have a feeling they are doing this all over the King's Keep while we chase up this tower. We are neatly trapping ourselves."

"You cannot deny that the light emanates from the tower's crown. You can linger here if you want to, uncle, or chase off in some other direction but I insist that the men come with me. I am going to the top and I will find a way to extinguish that horrid light."

His uncle gave him a cold stare. "I never disputed our goal. I only want to make certain that you realize that if we do not succeed, there will be no second chance." He motioned for Yosif to continue onward.

The captain gave a quick glance towards his prince and then ordered the men to climb onward. Wintron had a slight twinge of pity for the young officer; it could not be easy having squabbling superiors.

At Wintron's urging, soldiers grabbed the two lanterns on the landing, leaving the area in darkness as they moved on. He came near the end of the ranks, so it felt like the dark pressed against his back, urging him to move even faster. As he ascended the steps, he heard a muffled roar up ahead and a red flash reflecting off the stones. Wintron and the soldiers around him surged forward, swords at the ready. As he hurried up the stairs, he caught up with the slower Fors just before reaching the next landing. The place was full of smoke and the smell of burnt flesh. Their advance squad lay dead on the charred stone floor.

Soldiers milled about, poking into each of the four rooms and even the privy. Wintron was surprised to see Brem still alive, talking with Yosif near the remains of their advance squad. The two nobles approached.

"What happened, Brem?" demanded Fors.

"They ambushed us," explained the sergeant. He looked over at the charred bodies and shivered. "I am alive only because I stepped into one of the rooms just before the enemy charged down the stairs and threw a fireball at us."

"And we linger here for a second attack?" demanded Fors, glaring at Yosif.

"I have sent another half-squad up, sir," explained Yosif respectfully. "We will have warning if they come for us again."

"I should be up there," stated Brem, looking away from his fallen companions and glanced at the three gathered around him. Wintron felt a sudden chill, as if the man tried to look inside him, but then the feeling left.

"You are too shaken up," stated Fors, putting a hand on his aide's arm.

Brem shook his head, pulling away from the old general. "No, I have my duty, sir. An officer should be up there with the advance squad." He hurried off to catch up with them.

"He is a dedicated soldier," remarked Fors.

Wintron gave another glance down at the ten bodies and wished they could somehow tell him how they had died and why Brem survived. Was it sheer luck, or had their killer spared Brem for some other purpose? The prince did not have the answers. He only knew that his squadron now had just three hundred, with another ten of them under the command of a sergeant whom ill luck seemed to stalk.

The rest of the force headed up, with their two leaders in their midst.

DRASS

"This is as far as I will go with you," stated Colonel Ulen to the two newly Embraced. Behind him, soldiers herded people out of rooms and up the stairs. "Sergeant Florit will escort you the rest of the way to the top."

"I think we can find the way," replied Drass.

Ulen gave a chilly smile. "There are over a thousand of your countrymen on that stairway, climbing to their deaths. Do you want to face them without guards? Do you really want to try pushing your way through their midst?"

Drass hesitated. Within him, Slosoro growled about Ulen-Snargrof flexing his power. He did his best to ignore Slosoro's complaints. "I stand corrected. We will want an escort up to the tower's crown. Of course, I do not want to leave you understaffed, colonel. The invaders will surely be on you soon."

Ulen's smile broadened. "They are approaching, that is true. However, they have already taken losses and I have yet to raise a hand against them."

Drass was puzzled, but Gordrew understood. "You have another spy in their midst," Gordrew stated. "I always suspected there were others, though no one told me. Who is it?"

Ulen shrugged. "Even I am not certain. I do know there are three more Embraced Ones among the Borderfolk, along with an assortment of other spies, but their aliases are secret. I do not know who is sabotaging our enemy; I only know that is happening." Ulen looked at both men in front of him. "You two are new to our cause, yet you are also ancient warriors for it. You will need to be quick in fully accepting your Other half, for I still sense some tension in each of you. Not until you fully yield to your Other will you discover your full powers. Now go. I have no more time to waste on new recruits."

Before Drass could reply, Gordrew spoke up. He leaned closer to the colonel and lowered his voice. "Gloat while you can, Ulen-Snargrof, but I remember your lowly position in the Darklands. A wiser demon would show more finesse in guiding his betters."

He scowled. "At last you remember, Baron Gordrew? It is a shame that I had to use insults to force this on you. However, do not presume that my tactics are anything personal. I treat you as I have been ordered to treat you. Now go." He turned his back on them, showing even more contempt.

Gordrew raised one hand, lightning playing between his fingers, but then lowered it. With a grunt, he went to their assigned guards. Drass followed him, silently asking Slosoro to explain what had just happened.

Ulen-Snargrof lets this newfound power go to his head. Gordrew-Shovress simply reminds him that his current position is only temporary. He will need to relearn humility, if not from us then from the greater demons who will soon arrive in Na Ciria. They will not put up with such insolence, even if we must. I think the human's brashness is affecting Snargrof.

Drass smirked, as he finally understood Ulen's error. It was good to know that he was not the only one fumbling through this experience of being Embraced.

The sergeant who would be leading them up the rest of the way introduced himself to the two nobles. Drass did not bother to remember his name; he just nodded at the fellow.

Gordrew gave him a curt order to get going.

The sergeant saluted them both, apparently used to being treated rudely. With quick orders, he positioned his squad around them and then motioned for all to advance.

Drass had half-expected that they would have to push and shove their way through the prisoners, but that was not the case. The Tlocanians kept all in order, forcing them to press against the inside wall of the stairwell, keeping the area near the outer wall free for anyone needing to go up or down. Every few yards stood a soldier, prodding the people to keep moving.

The soldiers ignored any pleas for mercy or angry shouts with equal aplomb. What they did not tolerate was anyone moving even slightly out of line, even if merely stumbling on the steep stairs. As Drass made his way up, he saw one elderly man receive a hard blow for stumbling. The beaten man did not try to retaliate or even fend off the blow. Instead, he struggled to his feet and kept going. The prisoners seemed all in a daze, having lost their will to fight. Most did not even seem to notice Drass and Gordrew climbing past them.

They passed three more landings, the whole route jammed with people lined up for death. As Drass climbed, he started sensing warmth in the stones. From Slosoro, he learned it was a reaction to the power being used overhead. He let his fingers brush the rough granite and felt a tingle up his arms. With his senses heightened, he looked at the wall behind the prisoners and felt the energy there as well. However, when his eyes fell to the ragged people shuffling up to their murders, he suddenly sensed the power contained in them too. A great reservoir of power when you considered how many lined up to be sacrificed. He had to fight off the sudden urge to pull out his Sakar and plunge into the nearest victim.

Drass was shocked at his thoughts. Slosoro's thoughts. He could not let Slosoro overpower his sensibilities. Drass forced his gaze away from the people and kept his eyes on the steps in front of him. He was determined to be the master in this relationship.

WINTRON

Before Wintron Dabe even stepped up to the next landing, he knew what he would find. The air was still smoky, the stench strong. Men ran forward, ready for battle, but found no one. He saw men rushing to look behind each door. Someone shouted out, for a Border soldier hid in the privy. Two men pulled him out and towards Yosif. The fellow ranted about the killing of his comrades.

Just then, another shout came from one of the rooms, and a man came out dragging an unconscious Brem by his arms. The man from the privy became more aggravated, pointing at Brem and shouting. Wintron hurried over, Fors trying hard to keep up with him.

Wintron happened to look at Brem just as the sergeant opened his eyes, fully aware. Brem extended a hand to the man pulling him and Wintron saw a brief red flash. The soldier shouted in pain, trying to pull free. Brem gained his feet and then shoved the soldier away.

That surge of power caused Wintron's stomach to roil; it felt evil.

He pulled out his sword, shouting for those nearby to get Brem, but most did not hear him in all of the commotion. Wintron ran towards him, while Brem got to his feet and turned to face the prince. He raised both hands and red fireballs formed in each palm. Brem threw both at Wintron, who leaped to the right to try to avoid the blast. The prince lost his sword as he fell. A soldier sprang in front of him and took the brunt of the blasts, screaming in sudden agony as the fire splattered all over him. Wintron kept moving, rolling across the stone floor and then pushing off the wall to regain his feet. There was no time to search for his sword, because Brem sent another fireball in his direction. This time, two more men sprang in its path to save their prince. Both died.

Wintron charged straight at Brem, but the distance was still too great. Brem had already raised his hands to throw more fire, when Fors suddenly appeared and shoved his aide aside. The fireball roared in the wrong direction, splashing off the wall.

In anger, Brem backhanded Fors with a sizzling hand, sending the old general flying.

The distraction gave Wintron enough time to reach the man. Having no weapon, the prince tackled him, being careful that Brem fell on his hands so that he could not retaliate. Three soldiers were there right after Wintron and helped subdue Brem.

One was ready to stab him, but Wintron stayed his hand with a shout. "No! Do not kill him. I want him bound with his arms against his chest. Strike him unconscious if you must, but I want him alive. I will use this traitor against his own people."

As the burly soldiers wrestled to tie up Brem, Wintron moved away. He went over to his uncle and found him surrounded by concerned troopers. The Old Fox moaned as one soldier checked his injuries.

"Enough poking! I know where it hurts." Fors tried to sit up but the pain seemed too much, causing him to fall back onto the soldier behind him.

After the moment of agony passed, he opened his eyes and looked at Wintron. "I have broken ribs, my prince. In addition, the fall re-injured my leg. I will not be climbing any further today." He motioned with his head toward one of the landing's four rooms. "Leave me here and go on. You must bring an end to the massacres."

"Thank you for saving my life," replied Wintron, ignoring his uncle's plea for now. He bent over and gently grasped the older man's shoulder. "You are a true Borderman."

He wanted to say more, but the words seemed to catch in his throat. Instead, he straightened up and motioned for the other captive from the privy. When the man was near, Wintron gave him a cold stare. "Remind me. What is your name?"

"I am Ovarto from Holly Meadow."

"Are you Brem's accomplice?"

The man's eyes became wide and his shook his head emphatically. "No, sir! I am loyal…"

"How is it that you are alive, Ovarto, when all your companions are dead?"

"I… I had to relieve myself, sir. I know the general tells us to take care of personal needs before going to battle, but I could not help it." He looked guiltily at the Old Fox but the suffering man did not notice. Ovarto looked back at the prince. "When we found the landing empty,

I snuck into the privy to …to do my business. I was in there when Sergeant Brem caught up with the squad. I heard the sergeant confront our corporal, then the shouting and the roar of fire."

The man looked over at the still-struggling Brem. "It happened so fast. There I was, with my pants down to my ankles, and the rest of the squad was being murdered. He offered no honorable battle; he just set them on fire. I can still hear their screams in my ears…" The man began sobbing.

Wintron turned to one of the other soldiers still holding Ovarto. "Lead him over towards the far wall, away from the charred bodies, and give him some time to recover. He is right; he could not have prevented what Brem did."

He turned back to Fors. "Uncle Fors, I will see that you are hidden in one of the rooms with guards to protect you."

Fors opened his eyes, the pain obvious on his face. "No guards. You will need everyone to retake the tower. Just have them set me in a corner and you can retrieve me when you come back down. Also, no lantern. I want no beacon to attract the flies that swarm behind us."

He did not like the idea of abandoning Fors, but he knew that his uncle was right. Wintron could not spare even a half-dozen men to guard him, and such would only attract more attention from the Tlocanians who were pursuing them. One lone man in the darkness would have a greater chance of going unnoticed. "I will come back for you, Uncle Fors."

Fors grunted. "You had better. Taking this keep will not be the end of this war. You will need my strategic skills." Fors gave a pained smile, which turned to a grimace as he tried to get to his feet. Two soldiers helped him up. The pain was so intense that Fors could not breathe. It took a moment for him to recover enough to speak again. When he did, he ordered the men holding him. "Help me to my hideaway, men. Find me some corner where no one defecated and set me there."

Wintron wanted to countermand the orders but he knew that he could not. Instead, he just watched as they led his uncle away. He did motion over the nearest corporal. "Assign one of those men to stay with the general. One man cannot offer much protection, but it is better than being all alone in the dark."

He turned from the corporal to find an upset Yosif.

"What are you planning to do with Brem? My prince, is it not better to kill a rattlesnake then to play with it?"

Wintron nodded. "Usually that is so, but we need him. I have wondered how to fight against the magic of these Tlocanians. We have no talismans or magicians. However, maybe we can turn one of their own against them."

Yosif crossed his arms in frustration. "My prince, do you really think Brem will help us?"

Wintron saw that Brem had finally stopped fighting, at least for now. He lay on his stomach, his hands pressed against the cold floor. "I hope that he will try to stay alive. That should be enough for us to exploit." He walked towards the betrayer; Yosif came with him. "I will use him as a shield. We will march him at our fore and let him take any blasts meant for us. Either Brem will fight back or they will kill him. Whichever way, it will give us more opportunity to get at them."

Yosif gave him a worried look. "That may work, my prince, but what if he breaks free and turns on us. The risk is great."

The prince patted Yosif on the back. "Well then, Yosif, I will ease your fears. I shall stay right behind Brem so that if he succeeds in throwing a stray fireball, it will not strike me. Now, I want to get up this tower quickly and get this done. People are dying as we talk."

Wintron Dabe ordered everyone to get away from the stairway and then ordered the two burly men holding down Brem to lift him to his feet, careful that his exposed hands were not aimed at any of them. As they yanked him up, Brem tried to break free. His hands glowed with power, but he had no one in front of him. In frustration, he threw his power against the keep. The fire splattered harmlessly on unadorned stone.

"Hold him tight!" he ordered, coming up right behind the killer. He leaned forward and spoke softly into his ear. "Now you will truly work for me, Traitor Brem. You will have the lead and, if anyone sends red lightning or fire in our direction, it will be you who will die first. I think that is appropriate. Your own will kill you, just like you killed those who trusted you as a Border officer."

Brem replied in a deep snarling voice. "You fool. No one can kill me."

"We can kill your host, demon," replied Wintron. "What would you do then?"

Brem spat and cursed.

"Gag him; I do not want to hear his foul mouth anymore."

A dirty rag was passed over Brem's head and jammed into his mouth. Once it was secure, Wintron motioned to the men restraining him and they shoved Brem forward, forcing him to climb the stairs.

Wintron followed right behind him. The rest of the soldiers came close behind, soon leaving that landing in darkness again. Somewhere in those shadows hid the injured general and his lone protector.

DRASS

Drass finally climbed the last stairway to Farwatch Tower's exposed crown. As he came around the last spiral of the stairwell, he saw the Shadow Anchor shimmering red in the night sky. The power of it sang to him, like a temptress luring a naive man. He stepped onto the landing and looked straight up at the pulsing power that shot into the Dragon Shadow's clouds. Drass barely noticed the wind tugging at his cloak, so enthralled was he by the power streaming towards the heavens.

He did not notice his surroundings until an equally enrapt Gordrew bumped into him, and then he finally looked around. It seemed crowded here, with prisoners, soldiers, temple guards, and priests. It was also loud, with people pleading, weeping, and screaming. But even with all the racket, he could hear the Anchor crackle and hum with power.

The priests were sacrificing on two altars right beneath the Anchor.

"It draws the eye does it not?" said Gordrew huskily. "What would it be like to feel so much power?"

Drass wondered for just a moment, and that was when he lost to Slosoro. The demon grabbed for control of his host's mind and succeeded.

I am the master; you are the servant. To emphasize his point, Slosoro made him dance a silly jig that made a few guards look at him curiously. *If you cooperate, you will taste powers like that overhead. If you fight me, you will simply go insane and I will continue to use your body. It is your choice, Drass. Yield or be forced into submission.*

He tried to fight back, but his body continued to dance, unresponsive to his wishes. "Why are you doing this?" he yelled aloud, not caring who heard.

Yield.

Drass could think of no way to fight this invader. There was no one to hurt but himself. He considered jumping off the tower, but his body would not move towards the tower's lip. He could not even choose to die.

Yield.

He still had his voice, but it was the only thing the demon left in his control. He cursed Slosoro, but the demon merely laughed inside his head. He would have yelled out warnings, but who was there to warn? His countrymen were about to die and the Tlocanians were all far too familiar with Embraced Ones.

You cannot think your way out of my web. You are caught. Yield and I will reward you.

In desperation, Drass grabbed for that ethereal promise of something better, a reward of some sort. He gave in. "I yield to you, Slosoro. You are the master and I am just your host."

Slosoro kept laughing in his head, but suddenly Drass felt a rush of pleasure all over his body, a pleasure so intense that he would have collapsed if he had been in control of his muscles.

You finally learn, Drass. Taste a little of the rewards I can offer.

The feeling grew even stronger.

Drass moaned with ecstasy even while a part of his brain still screamed with rage and horror. Slosoro turned his head to enjoy the latest sacrifice. He could not even close his eyes to prevent seeing it.

Two blood-soaked priests were killing a man. With so many sacrifices to make, the priests had abandoned all fancy ritual. They said no demonic invocations nor tasted the victim's still-beating heart. There was no time for any of that. Instead, one priest held the victim down while the other plunged a Sakar blade into his chest. The two then grabbed hold of the man and lifted him off the stone slab. The man screamed in agony, but they paid him no heed. They also ignored his blood, which poured out to join all the rest splattered everywhere.

They swung the victim and threw him into a pyre of lightless fire at the heart of the Shadow Anchor. The black fire licked the night air, its movement noticeable only for its utter darkness. The magic instantly consumed the man, hungrily swallowing his life's energy. From a second altar, on the far side of the Anchor, another victim was tossed in and also consumed.

The priests turned to the next victim in line, ready to kill another. The sight sickened Drass even as it excited Slosoro. The demon sent Drass another sensation of pleasure and that feeling mixed oddly with Drass' fear, roiling his stomach and causing him to retch again. At least Slosoro did not stop him from turning aside so that the vomit missed his boots.

WINTRON

Wintron took the tower stairs carefully, staying just two steps below Brem and the pair of men holding him. Saugor and Wert. The spy walked willingly now, no longer struggling, though Wintron expected him to try something when they came upon the Tlocanians.

Wintron kept his sword drawn, in case he needed to act swiftly against Brem. Just behind him came the rest of the soldiers, including those carrying the lanterns. The dim, red lighting did not illuminate the stairs well, especially with the confusion of shadows. No light came through any of the tower's narrow windows that they occasionally passed, for the night sky outside seemed as dark as the deepest cave. Even worse, there were no more lanterns hanging in the stairwell; all was dark up ahead.

As the prince climbed, he tried to listen for anything up ahead, but he could hear nothing beyond the footfalls of his own men. Where were the Tlocanians? The stairs came around to another landing, unlit and apparently empty. Rags and refuse littered the landing, probably from when they herded the prisoners off this floor. Wintron did not like the silence.

"Saugor and Wert, point Brem at the wall," ordered Wintron. "Yosif, send men to look into those rooms."

Five soldiers scurried ahead to check inside the rooms and the privy, each carrying a red lantern. Cautiously, they passed Brem, but the traitor stood passively facing the wall. Wintron kept close to Brem, his attention divided between the captive and the scouts.

A soldier opened the nearest door and stepped in with his lantern. The prince could see him looking among the ruins of furniture and then he stepped back out to report the room empty. The second room and the privy also were unoccupied. The third and fourth room also came up empty. As the five scouts came back, a lone person suddenly came down the stairs from above, his head covered by a dragon helm. He calmly raised both of his hands and red lightning sprang between his spread fingers.

"Do you think I am frightened by you?" the newcomer asked in a deep voice, the contempt obvious. He stopped at the foot of the stairs. "I have no need of an ambush or even for my soldiers. You Borderfolk are so feeble that I can withstand you alone."

The five scouts hesitated, not certain if they should attack or flee. Wintron firmly pointed for them to run through the nearest doorway. As they fled, he had Brem turned to face the Tlocanian officer. The officer tossed a lazy fireball after the five, catching the last two and creating screaming human torches. Brem did nothing but stare.

"Who is this?" asked the officer, finally noticing Brem. He also saw that Brem was bound and gagged.

"He is my shield," replied Wintron, urging Brem's handlers to lead him onward. He wanted to get as close to this opponent as possible. "Surrender, demon lover, and I will show mercy on your troops."

The man chuckled. "Maybe you have poor eyesight, but I do not. You are obviously not King Mordel Halen-Dabe, pretender. Why would I want to let a mere human truss me up like you have that fool?"

"Do you think I am a mere human?" asked Wintron, wanting to cause some confusion. "Have you never heard of Attuls?"

"Attul? Is that how you captured him? I had been told that the old king's councilor had fled." The officer stepped closer, trying to get a better view of Wintron behind Brem.

The prince was disgusted at how much his enemy knew, but then Brem was well placed. "El, give me strength," he muttered, urging Brem forward. The traitor resisted, pulling at the grasp of Wert and Saugor.

"You do not seem to have your captive under control, Attul," mocked the officer.

Wintron pressed his sword tip into Brem's back. "He is only reluctant because he knows that he must kill you."

That silenced the Tlocanian. He raised his hands higher, the lightning playing over his fingers more intensely. Suddenly a ball of fire shot out, catching Saugor in the chest. The soldier flew backward, while Wert struggled to keep a hold on Brem. Wintron stepped closer, helping to keep the prisoner from turning on them. Saugor screamed behind them somewhere but he dared not turn to look. Instead, he pushed Brem forward, straight at the Tlocanian officer. Another fireball came at them, but this time Brem responded. The powers collided with an explosion, as fire splashed everywhere.

Brem did not press the attack; instead, he struggled with his bindings. Wert held him tight, as did the prince. Together, they urged him even closer to the Tlocanian.

The officer sent more fire roaring towards them, which Brem met with his own power. This time the Tlocanian pressed his attack, pointing all ten fingers at Brem, sending a constant stream of red fire at them. Brem responded with a similar flow of fire. The hiss and roar filled Wintron's ears as the heat reddened his face. Where the two streams of crimson fire collided, they sent off crazy branches all over the landing, splashing against the stone ceiling, walls, and floor. Wintron and Wert were somewhat protected by being close to Brem, but all the other Borderfolk rushed for shelter.

The red light painted everything in a lurid tint so brightly that Wintron had to squint. He wondered if the two demon-possessed men could see anything at all. What he could see, was frightening. The Tlocanian officer was wearing down Brem. The clash point drew closer and closer. He could see the strain on Brem's profile, including a trickle of sweat.

Wintron decided that he needed to act before Brem failed. Stepping to one side, he pulled out his belt knife and took aim. With a strong overhand throw, he sent the blade spinning at the Tlocanian officer, but misjudged the distance. The knife's handle struck the man's shoulder and bounced off, failing to distract him. However, the scouts who had fled into the side room saw what he attempted and suddenly one of them came running out, right at the Tlocanian. Before the man could react, the scout sank his sword into the officer's side.

The officer sagged, his assault crumbling. Wintron saw the scout smile in satisfaction, right before the lightning from Brem crashed down and turned both to ash. Brem staggered. Wert worked hard to keep Brem from turning his deadly hands toward the prince, but it unfortunately brought the rest of the scouts into his view. Spitefully, Brem flung one more burst of power, killing two of them before Wert flung him to the floor and threw himself on top.

The prince just stood there, his eyes adjusting to the sudden darkness. The door nearest the scouts smoldered angrily, offering the only light. Apparently, Yosif had pulled the others further back to avoid the firestorm. Wintron could hear the still-living scouts moaning in pain beyond the burning door. He could also hear Brem cursing through his gag, though the words were unrecognizable. Wintron went over to help Wert subdue the traitor. He was about to shout for Yosif, when the remaining troops came charging up the stairs, bringing their faint lights with them.

DRASS

Drass still existed, yet he knew he controlled his body only at the whim of Slosoro. He wanted to both sob and celebrate, for he finally had the power he always wanted, power far greater than anything his brother or his father would ever attain, and yet it was not really his power. It was Slosoro's power channeled through his mind and body. Drass stood there, the wind whipping through his hair, trying to find peace with the harsh truth.

Slosoro interrupted his thoughts. *I will show you the wisdom of your decision. I will teach your body how to perform magic that no one else knows how to accomplish.* Drass' mind filled with a sudden vision of great might: controlling others' thoughts, destroying whole armies, causing the very earth to shake. *Together, we will rule many.*

Drass nodded his approval.

"I see that you two have finally merged."

Drass turned to face the High Brother of Regalis, Zuler-Sostono.

"We are one," agreed Drass. He became aware of Baron Gordrew nearby. It seemed that the old councilor had gone through a similar trial with his Other, for Gordrew was sweat-soaked and disheveled. Drass wondered about his own appearance.

The High Brother motioned for Drass to walk with him over to Gordrew. "It is good that you have merged, for both you and Gordrew have duties to perform. We begin the Anchor Ritual in minutes, a rite that you never learned in ancient Darshi, Slosoro. This is not like the old Blood Pool Rituals; it is far more versatile." Zuler pointed overhead, where the Shadow Anchor pulsed and surged. "Once the Dragon Shadow is affixed to this valley, no one will be able to drive us out. Unlike the old Blood Pools, the Dragon Shadow can travel with our armies. You will find this magic worthwhile, Slosoro."

Drass suddenly knew what Blood Pools were. Slosoro chose not to speak through him, but wanted him informed. His Other had great admiration for the old magic that created reservoirs of immense power. Drass added to that knowledge what little he knew of the Dragon Shadow, mainly his memories from the taking of the Borderheart Valley. Their individual knowledge merged into something greater.

"We can see how the Dragon Shadow might be useful," replied Drass carefully. "What is expected of us now?"

"You will take your turn at the altar in an hour, so watch the priests carefully."

He gave a slight nod. "I hear and obey."

"One more thing, Drass-Slosoro. Should any trouble arises with the prisoners, do not try stopping them with any fireballs. Such things act as a lightning rod for the storm overhead, when done this close to an Anchor. Instead, draw power from the Dragon Shadow. I am sure

Slosoro can puzzle out how."

We will fling lightning if we must, Slosoro assured him.

WINTRON

A new soldier had replaced Saugor, helping Wert to lead Brem up the next flight of stairs. Blood ran down Brem's cheek, from Wert throwing him to the ground, but no one had any pity for his injury. Four other burly men marched directly behind them, ready to assist if Brem tried resisting again. As the Bordermen climbed, Yosif consulted Wintron.

"My prince, we almost lost control of him. If he had pulled free, he would have turned on all of us. I would advise slitting his throat now."

Wintron touched his recovered belt knife as he considered, but he decided against it. "No, we need him as a weapon. I know it is like directing a snake's bite, but what other means do we have? Brem will live, for now."

Just at that moment, Brem tried to break free again. He threw himself backward, off the steps. Wert slipped and fell beneath him, but the others rushed to keep Brem turned in the right direction. Fire shot from Brem's hand, but it only hit the stairwell ceiling. Sparks and rock chips peppered the guards, but no one suffered any great injury and soon they had Brem climbing again.

Wintron sighed. "I can see that he is dangerous, Yosif, but we do not know what opposition lurks around the next bend of the stairs. Without him, I know we would have made it past that demon-possessed officer."

Yosif did not argue any further, but Wintron saw enough of his face to realize that the sergeant was still not convinced. So be it. The decision was his. "Has the rear guard seen or heard anything of those behind us?"

"Nothing, my prince. There is only darkness behind us."

"And ever-less light with us," noted Wintron. They had lost half their lanterns and there were no more on the last landing. He paused to look out a narrow window at the oppressive night, but there was nothing to see outside except the dim lights on the wall walk and a few faint lights in the city beyond. Darkness out there appeared almost as deep as it was inside the tower. "Midnight is nearly upon us. We must get up there and stop the atrocity, Yosif. I will get Brem to a quicker pace, even if we must carry him."

He climbed faster to catch up with the traitor's guards. However, before he could reach them, a trio of Tlocanian soldiers appeared with swords drawn. Brem did nothing. The men escorting Brem dared not step in front of him. They simply stopped, uncertain, and pulled Brem to a stop too.

"Keep moving," ordered Wintron. "They will either flee us or die."

The guards pushed Brem onward, upward. The Tlocanians paused a moment longer, assessing how many came up the stairs, and then turned and ran. Brem did not try to stop them and Wintron dared not send anyone in pursuit. Their adversaries would now be warned.

The enemy awaited them just before the next landing, taking their stand on the stairs so that Wintron's men would have to fight at a disadvantage. The stairwell lanterns still hung here, casting a red glow on everything. The Tlocanians stood at the ready, calm and assured. They stood four across, which was the most that could line up in the stairwell and still leave a little room to maneuver. Another line stood four steps higher, and these held bows so that they could shoot over their comrades. Beyond them waited more soldiers, ready to rush forward should any gap appear in their ranks. None of them surged forward when they spotted their foes; they kept rank as ordered.

The prince had to admire their discipline even while worrying about how he would get past them. Brem and his guards were only six steps below them and still the Tlocanians waited. Wintron quickly considered how to attack them, but he could think of no strategy.

"Fire arrows!" came the command from the Tlocanian ranks and suddenly feathered shafts filled the air. Some glanced off the walls or ceiling, for it was a tight area to shoot in, but at least two were aimed true. One guard went down, an arrow in his face. One arrow came flying at Brem, who quickly burned it midair.

Brem tried yelling at them, probably wanting the Tlocanians to kill his captors, but his gag prevented any understanding.

Though Brem had only acted to save himself, his display of power acted as a lodestone for the archers. The next volley was aimed only at him. Again, he seared the arrows in mid-flight without retaliating. However, when a third volley came at him, the demon-possessed man lost his temper, striking down the arrows and then sending more fire searing up the stairwell. Everyone in the first three rows died, burning away under the fierce attack. The troops further up quickly pulled back, onto the next landing.

"Press him forward!" ordered Wintron, coming up to the guards.

They pushed Brem onward, through shifting ashes. The Tlocanians tried to make another stand on the landing, but Brem was still angry. As much as he was able to move, he sent fire everywhere. Wintron could hardly see, for the air was so full of red fire. When Brem finally let off, there were no more soldiers to oppose them. Some still lived, but all suffered terrible burns.

"How many did he just kill?" whispered one guard.

"I think he exhausted himself," said Wert, looking carefully at Brem. The traitor turned his head towards the guard as much as he could and gave a curt nod. It was obvious that he wanted his gag removed so that he could speak.

Wintron considered, then stepped up and undid the gag from behind. Brem spat out the cloth and cursed.

"I did not untie your gag so that you could spout foul complaints. What do you want, Brem?"

"I want them," he said, motioning towards the Tlocanians who still lived. "I need to restore my potency if I am to help you take this tower. Let me sink my Sakar into their hearts and take their strength."

Wintron let out a harsh laugh. "I am not about to unbind you, traitor."

Brem's anger was obvious, but he restrained it. "If it must be so, I can do my rites with my hands bound across my chest. Just place the knife into my hands and let me at these soldiers before it is too late. There is no power in a corpse."

Wintron reached around the man and pulled out the belt knife, holding it above Brem's shoulder so that the other could see it. "Is this the knife you call a Sakar?"

"Yes. Place it in my hands and have these thugs lead me over to each wounded soldier. It will be a simple thrust into the heart for each one. The rites are quick and I will soon be at full strength again."

"I will not aid you in your evil rituals," replied Wintron, filled with sudden anger at all the crimes that Brem had already done. He raised the knife and thrust it into Brem's neck, slashing across the front. Blood spurted out as Brem struggled frantically. It was a killing cut.

"Hold him down! He might still try to strike out in vengeance."

The guards threw Brem to the ground and lay on him as he fought. Even with four on him, still he was able to thrash and flail. With the last of his strength, he struck the stone floor with all of his power. The explosion tossed soldiers everywhere. Wintron slammed into a wall and crumbled to the floor. The center of the landing collapsed, crashing down onto the level below and taking Brem's body with it.

It took a moment for Wintron to catch his breath, especially with so much dust now added to the smoke. He struggled to his feet and looked around at the devastation. The few Tlocanians that had still been alive were no longer, judging from the destruction. He could not see any of the men who have been guarding Brem. Border soldiers staggered to their feet on the far side of the hole, but it was too dark to recognize any of them. "Yosif! Where is Sergeant Yosif? We need light in here."

"Here I am, my prince," called the captain as he rose to his knees near the edge of the steps. Bracing off the wall to get to his feet, Yosif looked back to the soldiers still on the stairway. "Bring forward any lanterns we have left. We need to find a way past this wreckage."

Lanterns were recovered and soon the soldiers carefully made their way around the gaping hole. More of the floor broke off and fell, warning them that it was not yet stable. The first two across helped their prince to safety as well.

Once he stood on the next flight of stairs, Wintron waited until all his remaining men were across. One of the last over was Yosif.

"I sent two men to check on the landing below," he said. "They found no one alive. They say the rubble is everywhere, making it very difficult to cross the area. If nothing else, it should slow any pursuers."

As if to give emphasis to Yosif's point, more of the landing crumbled off.

"We should hear shortly from the five I sent ahead," replied Wintron, gazing up the darkened stairwell. "Have the men keep going, but slowly. I want to know what other surprises are up ahead."

Wintron found out soon enough, when three of the five returned. They reported that some soldiers held the next floor, but they were busy herding prisoners to the stairway. Two of the scouts had remained just out of sight from the landing, to listen in on their conversation. He urged his troops to quicken their pace, heartened to hear that some of the prisoners were near.

The Border soldiers rushed up the stairs, finding new strength in knowing their goal was nearly at hand. They fell on the rear guard of the Tlocanians. The battle was quick, with Wintron's men killed all except one, who fled up the stairs past the shocked prisoners. The captives started cheering and weeping as they rushed to embrace their rescuers. As those further up the stairway realized what was happening, they also broke from the line and came scampering down the stairs.

Soon, the landing was crowded with filthy and weakened prisoners desperately clinging to each other and to the soldiers.

He fought his way through the crowd until he found Yosif. He had to yell in the other's ear to be heard over the celebration and crying. "We need to keep going! There are still three more stories to climb and hundreds more to free!"

Yosif nodded. "I have already sent a dozen men towards the stairs! I told them to grab as many others as they could! When enough start moving, it should dampen this celebrating!"

Wintron saw the wisdom in the sergeant's orders and gave an approving nod. He headed towards the stairs too, grabbing as many soldiers as he could get free from the grasping civilians. Finally, the noise lessened as the Borderfolk realized that the soldiers meant to go on.

Wintron took advantage of the lull to shout out some instructions. "People, we must keep climbing, for there are others still to be rescued. Do what you can to secure this landing and hopefully we will be back soon with the rest of the captives."

Some gave a ragged shout, but others began shouting questions at the prince, terrified that the soldiers were leaving. Wintron wanted to stay and soothe them all, but there was no time. Midnight was surely past by now and the Shadow Anchor Rite happened above them. He gave the crowd an encouraging wave and then headed up the stairs, surrounded by soldiers who were now even more determined to free all the others.

Eric Lorenzen

CHAPTER FORTY-TWO
Shadow Anchor

DRASS

Drass felt the tower shake and wondered if it was a reaction to the Shadow Anchor, but he had no one to ask. There were only five dragon priests up here and all of them busy with the rites except for High Brother Zuler-Sostono, who directed the sorting of the sacrifices. Drass was surprised at how few were here, but it explained why they needed Gordrew and him. It also explained some of the grumbling he heard concerning Lord Hraf and the many who left with him.

Look at the other streams of power coming to the Focal Stone, Slosoro told him. *They do this rite in more than one place.*

Drass looked where his demonic half indicated and saw a fainter stream. He stepped to the ragged edge of the tower and looked over. The light came from one of the shorter towers at the keep's corner. A similar red light streamed from each of the four Little Sisters. "So they are sacrificing at the top of each tower?" he asked his Other.

It appears so. With six altars, they could kill over one hundred an hour. Not as efficient as some of our rites in the Darshi Empire, but it is still impressive. I look forward to participating in it.

Slosoro's comment reminded Drass of his duty, so he hurried back to a place next to the altar that stood on the far side of the Anchor Focal. He was to observe the ritual so that he could take over and allow one of the priests a rest. Drass watched another two killed, their still-alive bodies flung into the Black Fire, but then his eyes drifted upward again. The Shadow Anchor's power called to both of them.

From Slosoro, he understood the need to gather and direct the magic. For the Shadow Anchor, the focus was a pattern of rubies set in a large circlet of gold. Each glowing gem hummed with power. The ruby-and-gold circlet hung suspended above the tower on a thick chain strung between two iron posts three times a man's height. From the circlet, the Shadow Anchor beamed up to the clouds.

Below the circlet pooled the other area of power, though it did not shine. Instead, blackness lurked there. From Slosoro's memory, he knew this to be Black Fire. Even with his enhanced vision, Drass could not see through the lightless area that danced beneath the circlet. The Black Fire came from another, far larger circlet of iron encrusted with black gems from the Darklands. That circlet sat on the tower's stone. Drass could only see the nearer edge of the iron ring; the lightless flames hid the rest.

He turned his attention back to the Shadow Anchor rite. This close to the humming gems, he had to strain to hear the words the priests recited as they did their sacrifices. He was observing Brother Cavish. Soon, Drass would be taking his turn, just as Gordrew would be at the altar on the other side of the Anchor. Drass-Slosoro looked forward to slipping his Sakar into warm bodies again, to feel the life-rich blood between his fingers, to savor releasing the power.

WINTRON

As Wintron and Yosif led the men up another level, they found more prisoners still lined up. A foursome of Tlocanians prodded them from behind. Yosif ordered a squad to attack and they gladly complied, quickly overwhelming the enemy troopers. Once the fighting ended, Wintron told the prisoners to flee downstairs but to keep to one side of the stairwell so that the Border soldiers could continue climbing. Most complied in an orderly fashion, though some at first just stared while a few fled downward with abandon, not caring who they pushed out of the way in their panic.

As the Bordermen continued up the stairs, they found the Tlocanian guards had already fled, leaving the prisoners to mill about in confusion. Wintron's soldiers pressed their way through and reached the next landing. On that level, the rooms were already emptied, though prisoners still lingered on the landing. Both Yosif and Wintron told these people to flee downward also, ordering them to help the weaker ones.

"Two more landings," noted Wintron as he watched the people

heading down the stairs.

"There are certainly more of the demon-possessed above us," said Yosif, looking at his ruler. "How will we face them?"

He turned and met Yosif's eyes. "I do not know. We have nothing that can counter their magic, but they are still mortal. At least the humans they indwell are mortal. If nothing else, we must rush at them with everyone we have and hope someone wins through to land a deadly blow." He shook his head at his own foolish plan. "El help us. We will need to kill every dragon priest we find, assuming all are demon-held. The same goes for any Tlocanian officer. We cannot accept surrender from any of them."

"I understand, my prince. I will instruct the squad leaders of your orders to make sure all know." Yosif looked upward and it seemed he gazed through the layers of stone. "How can we destroy the Shadow Anchor itself?"

Wintron looked up too, remembering the eerie sight of red power shooting skyward. "I hope that simply cutting off the human fodder will cause it to falter."

Yosif looked back towards the prince. "How many... how many do you think have already been killed? I had family, neighbors, friends..."

Wintron was surprised to see Yosif finally showing some emotion, for the man had already endured so much with a composed demeanor. He put an arm across his shoulders, as much to comfort himself as to comfort the young man. "These Tlocanians have a terrible lust for blood, but we will end it now." A hardness came to Wintron's eyes. "Let us charge up these last floors and storm the tower's crown. Give the orders, Yosif."

Only two hundred soldiers responded to Yosif's call to charge upward. As Wintron ran with the others, he realized how few men he had left from the two thousand that had entered the Rabbit Hole. Well, there was no reserve force to call forward. Two hundred would have to do.

On the next landing, they encountered the last of the Tlocanian army soldiers, who were determined to stop them. The fighting was intense, but the Bordermen won. It cost them, however. Only one hundred and fifty continued onward. It was halfway to the top floor that they encountered their first temple guards, fierce men who drove the last of the prisoners upward. The Bordermen made quick work of them.

On the top floor, they encountered more temple guards mixed among hundreds of prisoners. The two sides fought, as civilians scampered to get out of the way. The Bordermen prevailed, but half the guards fled up the stairs to the tower's open crown. Wintron urged his citizens to flee downstairs quickly, for they would only be an obstruction here. A few of the more-hale captives, both men and women, grabbed weapons off the killed temple guards and volunteered to help fight. He appointed them the task of protecting the former prisoners, for he still worried that more Tlocanians might be coming up the tower behind them.

Yosif had sent soldiers to inspect the rooms on this landing and found them to be well furnished and clean. Apparently, they had kept this floor reserved for the priests and not for the prisoners. Wintron asked if they had found any more lanterns, but the soldiers had not.

"They seem to like the dark," noted Yosif. "A reflection of their blackened souls."

The words struck Wintron with sudden insight. He recalled Councilor Rolen mentioning that the demon-possessed disliked bright light. "Yosif, we need to make torches. The demons detest bright light!" He pointed at the lantern in Yosif's hands. "These dim lights only aid our enemies. They can tolerate the reddish glow, but I think anything brighter will pain them. Let us see what we can salvage from their apartments. I want a torch for each soldier, if we can find enough kindling."

Wintron and Yosif had just entered one of the apartments, when a dragon priest appeared on the stairs, tossing two red fireballs onto the landing. Wintron heard the men yelling and screaming behind him. Desperate, he ran to the nearest bed and ripped off its blanket. "Yosif, shred this while I make us some torches." He grabbed a straight-back chair and smashed it against the wall. Soon they each had a cloth wrapped around the end of a chair leg. They lit them off the lantern Yosif had carried. Each caught fast and burned bright.

"Let me go first," said Yosif when his liege seemed ready to charge out onto the landing.

Wintron hesitated, and then nodded. "If you can, thrust the light at his face. I will let you go first, but I will not stay out of this, Yosif. I may be the realm's ruler, but I am also kin or friend to many who have been killed. I cannot stand aside just for my safety."

"Count to ten before you follow," said Yosif, running out the door.

The prince did pause, though not quite so long, and then ran after the sergeant. Out on the landing, chaos dominated. Prisoners and soldiers were trying to get away. Some brushed past Wintron wanting to hide in the room he had just exited. Angry red flames still flickered down the paths blazed by each fireball, burning clothing and bodies. The priest walked among the cowering captives now, red lightning dancing across his fingers.

His attention had been on Yosif, but now he turned to the prince. Wintron ran further out onto the landing, keeping some distance from Yosif. Maybe one of them could make it to the priest.

The priest turned back towards Yosif, his robe swirling. He raised his right hand and lightning shot out, striking Yosif and tossing him backward. Yosif tried to throw his torch before the impact, but the lightning hit the torch too and it exploded in a bright fireball. The priest seemed to wince away from the sudden light, turning his head away.

Wintron used the opportunity to run directly at him. He was not close enough, though, when the priest recovered and raised his left hand. Just before the lightning was released, Wintron tossed his torch to a nearby soldier. "Throw this into his face!" he yelled, and then the lightning hit the prince, throwing him backwards.

He fell hard, his whole body in spasms as the lightning played across it. It took a long moment for him to recover enough to even hear the shrieking or notice the bright light. He sat up, his body still shaking some. The dragon priest was on fire. People kept their distance as the man danced about trying to extinguish the flames. One soldier was brave enough to sneak up on the priest and crash a red lantern over his head, adding more flames to the blaze. The priest fell down, still shrieking. It took a few more minutes for the man to die.

Wintron struggled to his feet, helped by some of those nearby. Once he stood, he cleared his throat and then shouted out orders. "Bordermen, we now have a weapon to use against these evil men. Clean and bright fire. Go and raid the rooms for anything that can be a torch. Any who still have arrows, I want them turned into flaming arrows. We will use fire to confuse and defeat these lovers of darkness. Hurry to your task, before another comes down here to attack us."

He quietly thanked El when he saw Yosif standing up. Why the priest had used lightning instead of fire he did not know, but he was glad that he had not been set on fire.

They quickly made torches and then the squadron reassembled on the landing. By this time, all of the prisoners still able to walk had fled down the stairs. There were a dozen too injured to make the descent. The prince could not spare men to carry them so he had the twelve quickly moved to one of the rooms and made as comfortable as possible.

"So how many archers do we have?" asked Wintron of Yosif.

"Only ten," replied the captain. "I have assigned a personal guard to each, so that they can concentrate on shooting the dragon priests and military officers."

"Send two men up the stairs to see if anyone lurks there, but tell them not to go all the way to the top. That would be sure death."

Yosif sent two scurrying up the stairs. As they waited, Yosif, Wintron, and the remaining squad leaders formulated as much of a plan as they could. Wintron had his doubts about whether they would succeed, but he did not say anything aloud. Even if they failed, they had still interrupted the march of victims to the blood altar. It might be enough for now, but what was to prevent the Tlocanians from just starting the ritual again?

The two men soon returned to report the way clear, though the stairs were covered with bloody footprints, going both up and down. Wintron guessed that the footprints came from the soldiers as they retrieved more prisoners. He warned everyone to expect slippery, treacherous footing up top, without explaining what he feared they might find: a human slaughterhouse.

DRASS

Drass served as the assistant, bringing the victims to the altar, holding them in place, and then helping to heave the person into the Black Fire. The work was strenuous, especially when the victims tried to fight back, but he labored diligently.

He did not notice the commotion at first, not with the noisy hum of the Shadow Anchor, but then he saw the temple guards gathering around the opening where the stairs came up. He looked around for High Brother Zuler-Sostono, but he saw no sign of him. Drass moved to the side, so that he could see around the Black Fire, but still could not find Zuler. He did spot Gordrew standing next to the other altar, resting from his last turn at altar duty. The man looked drained, both to Drass' eyes and to his new magical senses. Gordrew would probably have to take a prisoner for his own renewal before he could continue.

"To work," ordered the priest that rested nearby, speaking loud enough to be heard over the humming.

Drass glared at him, but returned to his duty, grabbing the next victim offered by a temple guard. The brother doing the killing was just turning for the next victim, when Drass brought one forward, being careful how he stepped on the blood-wet floor.

As Drass bound the man to the altar, he wondered if their leader had gone downstairs.

WINTRON

Wintron climbed with the last squad of twenty soldiers, a squad containing most of the archers. Yosif and the squad leaders had insisted he be here, for they not only wanted to end this atrocity but they wanted their ruler to live through it. There were five squads left: only one hundred men.

Yosif led them all to the very last bend in the stairwell at a quick stride, and then the first two squads began to run the rest of the way, torches held high and swords out. It was awkward to run with your hands full, especially running up a flight of stairs, but the forty men did so with enthusiasm, charging out into the night air with swords and torches swinging. After a slight pause, the next two squads also charged up. And finally, Wintron and the last squad dashed out.

Wintron ran out to chaos. Men shouted and screamed, swords clashed, and the Shadow Anchor filled the air with a loud hum of power.

He almost fell on the blood-soaked stones, slipping until he bumped one of the archers.

Looking towards the Shadow Anchor, he saw two priests still doing their bloody work. "Shoot them!" he yelled to the archers, pointing. The archers lit their arrows and took aim. They took their time, ignoring the ruckus. Two of them fell before they could release, but the others shot true. Both priests staggered when hit. Neither died from the arrows, but suddenly their robes began to smolder and then burn. One threw off his robe but the other was too late and soon staggered about as a human torch.

The archers took aim again, but before they could fire the disrobed priest sent lightning in their direction, destroying four more archers. The others shot, but only one hit the priest. He danced about, trying to pull out the burning shaft. The archers shot a third time and the man finally died.

Wintron looked about for more priests, but the only black robe he saw was on the far side of the Shadow Anchor, half-hidden by a black void that flickered like flames though it had no light. He did spot one more hidden beneath a cloak's hood, but this one sat on the ground. Might he be a Tlocanian officer?

"Squad, follow me!" he ordered, leading them towards the altar and the man sitting next to it. He still was not certain if the man was one of the demon lovers or just one of the prisoners, for his clothes were filthy and he seemed so worn. The other prisoners stirred, for their guards had left to fight. The sitting man looked over at him and lifted his hands. Wintron almost ordered the archers to shoot, but the man showed no power. Instead, he removed his hood and revealed who he was.

"Gordrew!" shouted the prince, delighted yet confused. So he had not been mistaken earlier. He had seen Drass pulling Gordrew away from that bloody room downstairs. "Do not shoot, for it is Councilor Gordrew."

Gordrew struggled to get to his feet.

Wintron wanted to go over and embrace his father's old advisor, but now was not the time. They still had more priests to kill. He turned away from Gordrew and motioned for the archers and their guards to follow him. They needed to get a clear view of those on the far side of the tower. "We need to get to the priests that are hiding behind the Shadow Anchor."

One minute Wintron was running across the tower and the next red lightning suddenly flashed all around him. The explosion threw him almost off the tower top. He crashed hard against the uneven lip, his body twitching uncontrollably. If there had been another attack he surely would have died, but none came. Struggling to gain control of his body, Wintron pulled himself to a sitting position, leaning against the tower's lip. Looking about, he tried to see who had attacked.

He finally spotted Gordrew, hands glowing, and it shook him in a different way. His father's trusted advisor was a spy. Wintron had trusted him too, only to be betrayed. He wanted to sink his sword into the man, but he could not get to his feet. His legs still shook like a palsied crone's. Instead, he could only watch as brave soldiers tried to get at Gordrew with their swords and torches.

Gordrew threw lightning again, but the flashes were brief and faint. Men fell, their torches lost, but the lightning was too weak to actually kill. Many got to their feet again and pressed in, and then one determined trooper sprang at Gordrew, sending both of them tumbling over. They fell into the black flames and were engulfed.

As Wintron struggled to get control of his body, he saw another priest walk from behind the Shadow Anchor. The man glanced his way, but must have deemed him to be harmless. The priest stepped clear of the Shadow Anchor and then raised both hands, the lightning coalescing into crimson balls of fire. In horror, Wintron saw him throw fire everywhere, killing both Borderfolk and Tlocanian, soldier and prisoner. In addition to the fireballs, now lightning came crashing down out of the sky, striking the tower indiscriminately.

Wintron pulled himself up the torn sidewall of the tower, until he was on his feet. He took a clumsy step and another. "El, help me," he cried in desperation, lifting his sword with both hands because his right hand shook too much. "Give me your strength El, for I have none left." Tears of frustration fell down his cheeks as he tried to reach the dragon priest. Unexpectedly, a white glow came upon the sword. He did not comprehend its meaning at first, wondering what light reflected off the metal. Then he realized it was the metal that glowed, like an Attul's sword. He did not understand how this could be, but it gave him sudden hope.

The dragon priest had walked past the prince, so he did not notice his approach. Wintron stumbled near, raising the blade high. With a shout to El for help, he slashed down at the priest, who turned suddenly and tried to defend himself. He put up both glowing hands to ward off the blow. White sword met red hands and an explosion threw the men apart. Wintron landed heavily again, though this time he had not been shocked.

Someone pulled Wintron to his feet and he was surprised to see that it was Yosif, bleeding yet alive. The sergeant stared at the glowing sword. "You killed him, my prince. I did not know you had such powers."

"It is no power of mine," averred Wintron. "This is El's doing."

"Whoever or whatever empowers your sword, it killed that priest."

DRASS

Drass was about to tie another prisoner to the altar when Brother Cavish stopped him. "I must take this one for myself," he said. "You should renew your powers as well, for the enemy is upon us."

He had been aware that fighting occurred on the other side of the Shadow Anchor, but Slosoro had warned him about interrupting a blood ritual as great as this one.

"The ritual will falter," Drass protested.

"We cannot complete it now," stated the priest. "We have lost too many of our captives. Let us hope that our brothers on the other towers will be able to do enough to at least stabilize the work."

Cavish sank his blade into the victim and drank of the person's power greedily. When sated, he cast aside the body. "We must do what we can to defend the Anchor's focal. That duty falls to the two of us." The men lunged for the captives that a squad of temple guards still kept under control.

Drass had no such need, so he strode to the side for a better view of what was happening. He came around the Black Fire in time to see Wintron's glowing sword. He was shocked to see his cousin here.

An Attul, observed Slosoro with humor. *I remember how we fought their kind.* Before Drass knew what happened, his own sword came out and glowing with a deep red power. Slosoro let him have control again, though he revealed new knowledge to Drass.

"He cannot be Attul," argued Drass. "That is the crown prince, my cousin. He is a Borderman just as I am. He is no Attul."

You are Borderman and Embraced One. Perhaps he is Borderman and Attul. Name him what you will, I know that power for I faced it often enough in Darshi.

Drass chose not to argue further. Instead, he advanced on Wintron. A smile came to his lips, for his cousin looked worn out. It would be good to kill him at last, to finish what he had intended to do at the start of this war.

WINTRON

Wintron was still staring at his glowing sword when Yosif yelled out a warning. Turning, he found his cousin at last, charging at him with a sword whose length sparked and crackled with red lightning. Drass yelled defiantly as he bore down on him.

Almost too slowly, Wintron brought up his own sword to deflect the blow and the two empowered swords met with a metallic ring, a hiss, and a shower of sparks. Wintron's knees almost buckled from the power of the blow, yet he held.

He blocked a second blow and a third, but each drove him backwards across a slippery and littered floor. He dared not let Drass push him any further or his next step might be on some corpse or fallen brand, so Wintron did his best to go on the offensive. His efforts were weak though and his cousin parried them easily. Soon he was on the defensive again, once more retreating under the onslaught. He sensed that Drass played with him, though he could not see the other's face within his deep hood.

Yosif was suddenly there again, thrusting a bright torch at Drass. Wintron had a brief glimpse of his cousin's face, a face filled with rage, but then Drass looked away, swinging his fiery sword towards Yosif. The officer dove out of its path, letting the torch drop.

Drass suffered no harm, but the break allowed Wintron to catch his breath. "El, I need your help more than ever," he muttered as he took his stand, sword at the ready. Maybe it was just the excitement, but he felt suddenly stronger.

When Drass came at him this time, he responded with greater skill and energy. The two fell into a true sword fight, with thrusts and parries. He held up, though he could not press any attack. He was almost disemboweled when Drass thrust with his sword and light shot out of its tip. Somehow, Wintron was able to deflect the lightning, though he did not know how he did it. They continued to battle.

Out of the corner of his eye, Wintron saw Yosif in a melee of his own, so there would be no more aid from him. He would have to defeat Drass on his own. Wintron sprang to the right as his cousin took another aggressive swing at him. The prince stumbled over a fallen sword, straining his ankle.

Drass laughed. "You will die now, cousin. I am finally the better man."

Wintron chose not to reply, concentrating on regaining his balance.

"Are you afraid? You should be, because I am about to kill you." Drass pressed his attack harder, forcing the prince to retreat again. His blade grazed Winton's left arm.

The prince stumbled as the searing pain shot through him.

Drass gloated. "You were always weak, just like your father. You are only good as a sacrifice to increase our power. I look forward to grabbing your heart with my hands."

Wintron made a desperate attack, but his cousin fought him off easily. He tried to press in close, but that crimson sword kept him at bay. Instead, he only ended up switching places with Drass and retreating under the other's expert blows. With each new series of attacks that battered him, the crown prince retreated further. The constant shower of sparks had already singed his hair and clothing and given him painful burns to add to his throbbing arm. Wintron was quickly weakening and he realized that he had to make an end of this very soon.

Drass drove him backwards with a purpose. Wintron could not see what was behind him, but he noticed that his boots slipped in ever-more blood. The Shadow Anchor had to be near. Wintron tried to hold his ground, but his cousin merely laughed and countered every move. Wintron was forced to retreat more. Suddenly, he noticed they had already passed the altar, for he saw its oozing surface in the corner of eye. He could hear the Shadow Anchor humming directly overhead. Drass was driving him back towards the black flames at its base.

"Death is so near for you," mocked Drass. "Can you taste it? I certainly can smell it on you, the smell of fearful death."

"You are befuddled, demon lover," replied Wintron with ragged voice. "That is the scent of your own death. In El's name, I curse you."

"Your words are feeble and your god impotent," laughed Drass, his voice suddenly deeper. He came at the prince with a series of vicious blows, powerful yet suddenly awkward.

Wintron countered each, but barely. Had the demon just spoken through his cousin? "El curse you, demon. You are not of this world and you cannot reign here. Go back to being worm food. You were defeated in the Great War and now you shall again fall."

Drass snarled. "You are nothing, Attul. Nothing. You humans will either be our slaves or fodder for our powers. That is all that you are good for."

"Do you hear him, Drass?" asked Wintron, appealing to whatever was left of his cousin. "This demon that you have welcomed inside of you considers you to be a slave. You are its plaything, Drass. You mock me for my weakness, but at least I still have my free will. Try to assert your will, but I doubt that the demon will let you. You are its puppet now."

The attack faltered for just a moment, as maybe demon and host argued, but it was long enough for Wintron's desperate counter attack. He slashed at Drass' sword hand and connected, severing the wrist and sending the flaming sword airborne. In his rage, Drass raised his other hand, lightning filling his grasp. However, before Drass could strike, Wintron reversed his swing and buried his sword into his cousin's gut.

Drass' hood fell back, showing the horror on his face. His belly began to shine, and then the light spread throughout his body. He let out a silent scream, collapsing, pulling the sword from Wintron's weakened grasp.

The prince stood over his cousin and watched him disintegrate in the light. After a moment, nothing remained except Wintron's sword lying on the ground, no longer shining. Exhausted, Wintron sank to his knees in the blood and gore, and hung his head.

He mourned for Drass Halen-Dabe, a man lost to evil. His death was right, but still Wintron mourned. He also shed tears for his own father, whom he still had not avenged.

At first, he did not see the last dragon priest coming toward him, but someone yelled a warning. Wintron looked up in surprise, to see the priest stalking in his direction with hands already glowing with power. Desperate, the prince grappled for his sword and raised it, but the blade remained dull and dark. He began muttering prayers, hoping that El would empower the metal again. A faint glimmer came to the sword, but it seemed too late and too weak. He tried to get to his feet and stumbled in his weakness. He straightened up, expecting to be incinerated at any moment.

Instead, the priest burned. From somewhere, an archer shot a flaming arrow and struck the priest in the cheek. The priest screamed in agony, clawing at the thing. Fire was even inside his mouth. He pulled the arrow out, but his hair and robe were now on fire too. Two more flaming arrows struck him and soon he collapsed to burn to his death.

Wintron watched the priest die, but he felt no emotion. He was just too drained.

Yosif limped over to him and offered a hand up. "That is the last of the demon-possessed. We have also killed all of the temple guards. It is over, my prince, and we have won."

Wintron nodded, but he felt no satisfaction or joy. How could he, when so many had died up here? He looked up at the Shadow Anchor and was surprised to see that it still pulsed and shone with power. "Why has it not faded or gone out? We have cut off its fuel."

Prince and soldier gazed up at the Anchor's Focal and finally saw the four weaker beams of light coming from elsewhere. They limped to the tower's rim and realized that a light came from each of the keep's corner towers.

"There are more altars," declared Wintron. "They are still killing people over on each of the Little Sisters."

"We do not have the strength to storm four more towers," replied

Yosif. "We have lost so many already."

Wintron gazed back at the Shadow Anchor. "What if we destroy that talisman where their power meets?"

"There are ropes near the altars," observed Yosif. "Let us pull it down."

They gathered all the Bordermen who still lived, a mere forty of the hundred who stormed the tower top. Yosif had the ropes collected and tied together, and then two soldiers climbed up one of the stone bases and then shimmied up its iron supports to reach the chain spanning across. They tied the rope to that end of the chain, not daring to move any closer to the powerful beam of light.

Once the rope was secure, all the men took hold of its end and began heaving. It took seven mighty pulls and then the Shadow Anchor's focal point shifted. The lights coming from the other towers no longer struck the huge ruby-and-gold circlet. Instead, some of that power caught the support chain and it exploded. The whole contraption suddenly failed and came crashing down, into the black fire and its base.

As the men cheered, Wintron watched the Shadow Anchor flicker. Abruptly, the black flames surged up the beam of light, turning it from red to a black darker than the night. The clouds overhead reacted with a gale of red lightning. The Shadow Anchor vanished, as did the black flames. He was about to walk over to the iron circlet that was all that was left of the talisman, when lightning struck it. Another bolt hit and a third, all centered on the black ring. Winds began to roar.

"We must flee, my prince!" yelled Yosif to be heard above the sudden storm. "The Dragon Shadow is collapsing down upon us."

Wintron saw that it was so. Like a tent with its center pole removed, the clouds were dropping down, now alight with a severe lightning storm. "You are right. We need to get inside."

They fled the tower's top, chased by more lightning strikes. They sheltered on the landing below. Overhead, the lightning continued to crash into the tower. They had a few lanterns to light the area, but it still seemed too dark to Wintron.

They gathered in one of the bedrooms, bandaging wounds, debating whether to go back up and look for more survivors even though it was doubtful any more existed. The tower shook, causing all of them to look up at the ceiling.

"I would feel better if we kept on moving," stated Yosif as he finish binding Wintron's wounded arm. "That ceiling is taking quite a pounding."

The prince agreed, so they continued downward. As they went, they found wounded prisoners and offered their aid. When they finally came to the level where the prisoners had been gathering they found it empty except for one soldier, the soldier that Wintron had assigned to his uncle Fors.

"What are you doing here?" he demanded. "Where is the general?"

"He is below, along with the many you have freed, my prince," replied the soldier. "I am here to escort people around the damaged floors. I have been doing so for the last hour."

"Then escort us soldier," ordered Yosif. "We are the last from the tower."

They made it the rest of the way down, to where the tower intersected the wall walk. Fors sat on the final steps, waiting for them. The doors to the wall walk stood wide open. Wintron could see the lightning hitting the towers to either side. "How are you, uncle?"

"I will live," the old man stated. "You accomplished the task?"

Wintron nodded. "The Shadow Anchor is no more."

A piece of stone came crashing down outside, hitting the wall and bouncing outward. "I do not think much of the tower will be left either," observed Fors.

"Where are the Tlocanian soldiers? You seem rather relaxed, considering the keep is crawling with them."

Fors gave him a wistful smile. "They are no threat any longer."

Wintron frowned. "Do you think the fall of their Shadow Anchor will cause them all to surrender? I doubt that."

Fors struggled to his feet, using a crutch that he had gained somewhere. "Sergeant Yosif, keep your men and those civilians moving down the tower. You will find Major Cilano in the Great Hall with all of the other former prisoners."

"Yes, sir," replied Yosif, ordering his men.

"What has happened down here?" asked Wintron, realizing that he was ignorant of some things.

Fors limped over to the wall walk door and looked out, noticing that the corner tower had started to smoke. "After we were separated in Engro's Ways, the men caught below made their way to the entrance gate. They surprised the Tlocanians from behind and overpowered them. From there, they bravely charged across the bailey and assaulted the main gate from behind. Many were lost, but they were able to open the gate, letting in the rest of our force."

"What about the dragon priests who were in the other towers?"

"We did not get most of them," admitted Fors. "When the lightning storm began, they used it to flee the keep. We had no choice but to let them flee, for they were tossing their magic everywhere. With them went numerous squads of temple guards and whatever army soldiers they could gather. I would estimate they fled with just less than a hundred troopers."

"So the keep is ours." Wintron sat down on the stairs where Fors had been sitting, relieved yet exhausted.

"Let us hope we still have a keep by morning," replied Fors.

"What do you mean?"

"King's Keep is on fire and this awful lightning storm is not ending even though the clouds are dropping towards us." Fors moved away from the door. "Come along, nephew. We need to find Major Cilano too. Bucket lines need to be organized."

* * *

They battled fires all night, but thankfully the lightning stopped after the Dragon Shadow fell all the way to the ground, turning into a fog again and mixing with the smoke. It was a miserable and exhausting night, but the fires were out by sunrise. Most of Farwatch Tower was gone, its rubble all over the bailey. The four corner towers were all scorched but mainly intact. Wintron had just finished thanking those who had been on his bucket line and sending them off to sleep in rooms set aside for them. In some ways, he was glad for the fires, for they had burnt off the places of atrocity.

"There you are, my prince."

Wintron looked up to see Yosif coming down the stairway. "How are things, Yosif?"

"Come and see for yourself," replied the sergeant, leading him over to the nearest arrowslit window.

Sunlight steamed through, causing Wintron to squint. It took a moment for him to realize what it signified, but suddenly he gave a start. "The sun? Has the Dragon Shadow broken up?"

Yosif smiled warmly. "Indeed, my prince. The fog is in tatters. We can still hear rumbles of thunder from further down the valley, but it is clearing over Regalis."

Wintron sighed, letting a bit of joy into his heart. "We have won, haven't we?"

"We have won," confirmed the sergeant, smiling.

CHAPTER FORTY-THREE

Regalis Delivered

WINTRON

Wintron Dabe gazed out the large windows of his father's old study. The room had survived the war almost undisturbed, to his surprise. The study was on the keep's second floor, its southern exposure letting in ample sunlight. The newly crowned king stood there for some time, simply enjoying the sunshine that spilled in. He seemed to need the light to cleanse him of his horrid memories. He stood there so long that the day came to its end as the lowering sun left, though the sky was still blue high above the deep valley.

Wintron found the city peaceful as the shadows of evening deepened in the Borderheart Valley. Sunlight still touched the highest mountain peaks, giving them a reddish tint. The majestic scene inspired him to a brief whispered prayer: "El, thank you for delivering this land. May all of Na Ciria find such freedom soon." A single tear trailed down his right cheek and into his grizzled beard.

Suddenly embarrassed, even though no one was around to see him, Wintron cleared his throat and wiped away the errant moisture. With the discipline of a King's Man, he turned his thoughts to more pressing matters. It had been a month since the destruction of the Shadow Anchor, but there still was so much to restore and repair.

Fors had gone on to Glenford, supervising the cleanup of that city. The Old Fox was a tough one, refusing to let his injuries keep him from his duties. The boundary forts also needed repair. The Tlocanians had withdrawn all the way back to the lowlands, abandoning the Border Realm, but they had left the place in shambles.

Mordel and his family were never found, but Wintron did not doubt that his enemy still lived. He suspected that Mordel had fled to Lepis Fra or possibly all the way to the Seven Kingdoms. Someday, Wintron would mete out justice to that king slayer; he swore such when he buried his father's crow-eaten remains.

Mordel and the Tlocanians had shown the old king no respect, from mutilating his body to treating his throne like scrap timber. However, the Border throne had been retrieved from the west bank of the Cleargorn, mud wiped off its legs, and set back in its place in the Great Hall. It was a bit scratched from its trip but repairable. Wintron had used the throne for his coronation, even though its upholstery was still stained. He felt that using it showed some respect for King Varen Dabe, the last true king who had sat on it. The coronation had been a simple affair with only a handful of Border nobles in attendance.

* * *

Wintron left the window and returned to the map he had been studying. He lit a lamp, setting it close to illuminate the crabbed writing and faded lines. The drawing centered on the Border Mountains but it also showed much of the lands surrounding the mountain range. From what he understood, the Tlocanians held all the lands south of the mountains that were pictured here: from the Triangle Wilds all the way across to the Grandgorn Valley. There were no more free lands to the south, not even Halfhill. Wintron shook his head at that sad thought. The Ejoti would have been fierce allies. Too many had fallen while alone, just like his father.

He thought it only a matter of time before the Tlocanian Empire surged around both ends of the Borders and then the Border Realm would be thoroughly isolated again. He needed allies and he needed them soon. Should he commit forces to Rhendora, though that land seemed doomed? Could any emissaries get through to the Lakelands?

Wintron's thoughts wandered to the Attuls that had served his father so well. Rolen, Tolara, and even their son Afral. He wondered where they were. His finger traced the lands north of the Border Mountains as he wondered where their mysterious Warhaven hid.

The new king hoped they would return soon with their promised aid, for he knew that he had defeated only a small portion of Tlocania's vast army. Wintron would need others if he wanted to keep the Border Realm free and he wanted to do more than that now. Not only did the Borderfolk deserve freedom, but so did all others in Na Ciria.

Wintron silently vowed to El that he would do his part to drive all the demons out of the land.

TRUTH MOCKER
Book 2 of the Cirian War Saga

Coming in early 2014

In the land of Na Ciria, an ancient enemy seeks to conquer everyone. Will the forgotten protectors of the land learn of the invasion in time to stop it?

RIDE OF THE WATCH RIDERS
As the Tlocanian Empire advances into northern Na Ciria, Mylana and her companions must get ahead of them and reach Warhaven first. They bring a warning from the south and a call to war.

DESPERATION OF A WIFE
Her husband has been captured and is facing certain torture. Denied any help, Tolara must try to rescue him alone. Her only possible allies are a city full of thieves and an enemy soldier.

TRAINING OF A WARRIOR
Separated from his family, Afral must now train in a strange homeland. Determined to succeed, he endures ridicule, rejection, and attempted murder. Even if he can prove his worth, they may still banish him.

TRUTH MOCKER, book 2 of the Cirian War Saga, is the enthralling sequel to **FALLEN KING**.

Learn more at Author Eric Lorenzen's website:
http://ericlorenzen.com

About the Author **Eric Lorenzen**

Eric is a science fiction and fantasy author. His writings include the Cirian War Saga, the Unlucky Alien series, and the Ways of Camelot series.

The son of immigrants, he can speak his parents' tongue, though with a decidedly American accent. He studied our collective past and our present (holding a degree in both History and Religious Studies), and still enjoys learning about the world's diverse cultures and beliefs.

Eric currently lives in California, enjoying the sunshine and natural wonders of that unique state. He is married to his beloved Amy and has two wonderful sons.

Learn more about Eric at his website:
http://ericlorenzen.com